# No Regrets

## THE LIFE
## OF MARIETTA TREE

*Caroline Seebohm*

*Simon & Schuster*

SIMON & SCHUSTER
Rockefeller Center
1230 Avenue of the Americas
New York, NY 10020

10  9  8  7  6  5  4  3  2  1


Library of Congress Cataloging-in-Publication Data

Seebohm, Caroline.
   No regrets: the life of Marietta Tree/Caroline
Seebohm.
      p.   cm.
   Includes bibliographical references and index.
   1. Tree, Marietta, 1917–91.   2. Women political
activists—United States—Biography.   3. Women
human rights workers—United States—
Biography.   4. United Nations. Commission on
Human Rights—Biography.   5. Journalists—
United States—Biography.   I. Title.
E748.T75 S43    1997         97–23370     CIP
973.91'092—dc21
[B]
ISBN 0-684-81008-5

FRONTISPIECE: Stopover at the American Embassy in
Manila, where Marietta's friend William
McCormick Blair was ambassador, during her UN
tour of Asia, 1966. (USIS)

All photos are from the personal collection of Marietta
Tree unless otherwise indicated. Effort has been made
to trace the ownership of all copyrighted picture
material; in the event of any questions arising as to
the use of any material, the author and publisher will
be happy to make the necessary corrections in future
printings.

# Contents

| | | |
|---|---|---|
| | *Introduction* | *11* |
| 1 | "A Peabody or a Nobody" | *15* |
| 2 | "As good as gold" | *27* |
| 3 | "I think I'm going to be a senator" | *39* |
| 4 | "Thine adorable Marietta" | *47* |
| 5 | "Maria Endicotti Peabodelli" | *59* |
| 6 | "She was a caged lion" | *69* |
| 7 | "College changed my life" | *76* |
| 8 | "It's really worthwhile to get engaged" | *88* |
| 9 | "The greatest stage in my life" | *96* |
| 10 | "A little inferiority complex" | *106* |
| 11 | "In a kind of fever of happiness" | *118* |
| 12 | From "Miss Boston" to "Miss World" | *129* |
| 13 | Anglo-American Relations | *139* |
| 14 | "A happy married life" | *148* |
| 15 | "You have let down your family and your society and your God" | *156* |
| 16 | "Whose Puss is in My Boots?" | *167* |
| 17 | "I could hardly believe such beauty existed in the modern world" | *177* |
| 18 | "On weekends we have a heavenly, cozy time together" | *187* |

19  "Adlai knew all the right questions"                      196
20  "The great spectacle of our lives"                        207
21  "We'll use Marietta's house"                              214
22  "I hope you miss me just a little"                        222
23  ". . . In gratitude, respect, and love for Mr. J."        231
24  "Who are these blighters?"                                241
25  "Give my love to Mummy"                                   250
26  "The greatest honor ever accorded me"                     261
27  "Keep your head high"                                     273
28  "In you I have so much to be grateful for"                285
29  "Hysterical amiability settling on me"                    295
30  "Astral company"                                          306
31  "Where was Marietta?"                                     315
32  "Ronnie full estate to me"                                328
33  "I love LLD more than ever"                               338
34  "Well, there'll be nothing"                               349
35  "The ultimate WASP"                                       360
36  "I am going to try to keep a journal"                     370
37  "I don't think she wanted to be alone"                    377
38  "I'm just trying to sort things out"                      393
39  "Terribly sorry, I have the flu"                          403
40  "Always look as if you're having a wonderful time!"       412
    Epilogue                                                  418

    Acknowledgments                                           421
    Source Notes                                              425
    Index                                                     435

FOR TOM

*—who was with me every step of the way*

# Introduction

"I find in you a grace, a discretion, humour and intelligence which amounts to a character that fills one with joy." Thus wrote the English author Nigel Nicolson to Marietta Tree after a visit to her in Italy in 1984. He was not alone in his assessment. Some of the most brilliant and prominent people of her time madly admired this woman, whose life traced a path through three-quarters of a century of history, politics, and people. The prewar world she entered was not yet ready for a woman of beauty and ambition who wanted a rich and interesting life. Approaching the millennium, our world has become so bereft of values that her social conscience seems like a rare echo of a bygone age. Marietta said she always wanted to be a combination of Eleanor Roosevelt and Carole Lombard. It is a tribute to her spirit and spunk that she largely succeeded.

Marietta Tree was a participant in the last years of Roosevelt, the rise and fall of Adlai Stevenson, the growing authority of the United Nations, and the development of social policies to cope with the economically beleaguered cities of the United States. She rubbed shoulders with Winston Churchill and Marilyn Monroe, lived in an English stately home, mixed with British royalty and inner-city blacks, advised ambassadors, threw legendary parties, and, blessed by striking beauty, inspired romantic dreams in countless suitors throughout her life.

This richness of experience was wrested from austere beginnings. Mary Endicott Peabody was born in 1917 into a family of clergymen and educators known mainly for their dedication to public service and personal rectitude. She was the eldest and only daughter. While her four younger brothers loved and admired their headstrong sister, in that resolutely male environment they gained the attentions and privileges she was denied, and lacking encouragement from her parents, she was cast out into life without ballast. Yet she was determined to make her mark, following the family tradition of contributing to the world's good, and she applied her Protestant work ethic to the unflagging pursuit of both social and charitable causes.

It is almost impossible for us today to realize what a struggle that was. With little or no support, she had to carve a career path through a thicket of prejudice. As a college student, she was told she could not enter the Foreign Service except by marrying into it. Later, editors insisted on referring to her as a "socialite" in spite of her tireless work for grass-roots politics and civil rights. In her sixties, she unflinchingly assumed the role as the only woman on company boards entirely male-run for generations. However tough the resistance, she never wavered from her goal to be taken seriously as an advocate of democratic ideals—and as a woman.

Marietta had learned early the hard lesson that, for her generation of women, an independent career was a distant dream. So she shrewdly used her considerable charms to reach the men she hoped would help her escape her constricted background and provide her with opportunities to further her ambitions. Although both her marriages disappointed, she found supporters who respected her talents and energies and encouraged her to gain prominence. By the last decade of the century, as a single woman in her seventies, she refused the security of another marriage and achieved her final triumphs on her own.

If men were her compass, it was the grandmothers, mothers, and daughters who set the parameters within which she found the courage to fight for recognition. Both Marietta's grandmothers were strong women, and her mother, a bishop's wife, became famous for being arrested in a civil rights demonstration at the age of seventy-two. Marietta's two daughters also developed successful careers at an early age. Lacking confidence both in her intelligence and in her appearance, Marietta had to measure herself constantly against these high-achieving women so close to her.

Her story is about sex. Not the liberated post-1960s sex, but the sort of sex experienced by people who wrestle with it in the unforgiving shadow of a Puritan God. George Kennan described sex as "the little demon companion," who had to be kept in the background and steadfastly controlled. Emotional excess was despised and despicable. Marietta's family was committed to this view. A *New Yorker* cartoon from the 1930s shows a man talking to his son in a grand living room filled with family heirlooms. "I never knew your mother very well, son," the father says. "You see, she was a Peabody." Although Marietta lived through the sexual revolution in America and was loved by many famous and powerful men, she could not break these restraints. Unlike her more notorious contemporary Pamela Harriman, she was never a courtesan. She achieved her prominence through connections and hard work, not seduction. Marietta's life, therefore, is also about control.

Her story is about class, that dangerous word which rings so falsely in American ears, and yet which affects so subtly the society within which it operates. Marietta's generation witnessed the shift of the American upper class from influential power base in the first part of the twentieth century to amorphous presence at the end of it. Shuttling between the United States, England, and the Caribbean, Marietta was part of that transformation. On the one hand she could say, "Life is so hectic. I've just been to two graduations, my daughter's at Foxcroft and my chauffeur's son's at Groton!" On the other hand, as the old-money families dispersed, and with them the commitment to public service, Marietta's unswerving support of civil rights, her friendships with people of every class and nationality, and her work with the urban poor led her to be recognized as one of the genuinely democratic spirits of her time.

Finally, Marietta's story is about death. For those who believe that what defines a life is not the living but the dying, Marietta's death must be seen as the most precise expression of her character. She was afraid of death, avoided talking about it, and would be furious at her biographer for dwelling on it. She was to all who knew her the personification of health and vitality. Yet when death came, swiftly and prematurely, she faced it with a gallantry and stoicism worthy of her ancestors.

Her eagerness to learn and her belief in self-improvement make her uniquely American. Like Isabel Archer in Henry James's *The Portrait of a Lady,* Marietta Tree was destined by her naïveté and enthusiasm to suffer humiliation at times. Like Isabel, her recourse was redemption through duty. (When Marietta's cousin Francis Parkman sent her a family history, which extolled the strong moral character and public spirit of her ancestors, she thanked him, adding, "But are we satisfied? Is it enough?")

Marietta Tree remade herself as the century aged, moving from wife to working mother to self-supporting professional. But in spite of her achievements, throughout her life she found herself wanting. That is the humanity at the core of this woman's story. What the world saw was a tall, fair goddess, dressed in frisky clothes, radiating a kind of youthful joie de vivre and optimism. The pleasure people derived from her sparkling presence, her infectious high spirits, her encouragement of their work, and her unselfishness enriched their lives. She kept her conflicts hidden, the legacy of self-containment, and paid the inevitable psychic price.

On April 4, 1936, when Marietta was nineteen years old, she went to stay with two friends at her old schoolmate Edith Derby's house in Oyster Bay. That weekend, Edith's mother asked the girls to write down on a piece of paper what sort of lives they saw for themselves. While the others described the familiar path of marriage and children, Marietta was already charting a very different course. "Parties, People and Politics," the young woman wrote. She got her wish.

# CHAPTER *I*

# *"A Peabody or a Nobody"*

O to be born a Peabody! To have two towns in Massachusetts named after your ancestors; a famous school founded by a relative; your name synonymous with the moral conscience of the country! "Peabody" may not resonate with the metallic clang of railroad fortunes, nor with the pungent hiss of industry, as is the case with so many American dynasties. But it has its own unique music that has permeated the complex air of this country for three centuries. The sound is not particularly mellifluous. It has a minimalist tone, with echoes of austerity, of grayness. It is specifically located in and around Boston, the heart of New England. What melody exists has a religious tinge, of hymns perhaps, or of a boys' choir. But there is a firm, regular beat to the music, not Thoreau's beat exactly, but determined, strong, unyielding.

A Colonel Everett Peabody was killed at Shiloh, and there are those who say that he saved the Union Army.[1] There were, of course, earlier Peabodys. There was Francis Peabody (1614–1697), who landed in Ipswich, Massachusetts, in 1635 with the first English settlers and started the Peabody tradition of hard work, profitable trade, and family values. Isaac Peabody (1648–1727), a mill owner, had twelve children, one of whom was another Francis, who beat out his father at least in the reproductive stakes by producing thirteen. One of these was Nathaniel, a teacher at Phillips Andover Academy, whose distinction paled beside that of his three daughters, the famous Peabody sisters of Salem.[2] Sophia married Nathaniel Hawthorne; Mary became the wife of Horace Mann, anti-slavery activist and educator; and Elizabeth, who perhaps was the most well known of the three, while never marrying, started the first settlement house in Boston, later named the Elizabeth Peabody House. She also founded the first public kindergarten in the United States.

The male Peabodys, not to be outdone by the females of the line, chose strong Boston women to marry and produce vast numbers of heirs throughout the eighteenth and nineteenth centuries. Notable among them was Joseph Peabody (1757–1844), who became a highly successful shipping merchant in Salem, plying the China Trade with a fleet of clipper ships, establishing a sailing record between Salem and Canton. The two brothers of Everett, the Civil War hero, formed the investment banking firm of Kidder, Peabody & Co., in 1865.

But perhaps the most significant of all Peabodys prior to the twentieth century was George Peabody (1795–1869), who made a fortune in banking and peppered the family name far and wide in the context of good works. He lived much of his life in London, where he founded the Peabody Trust, which built housing for the poor. Called the Peabody Estates, so impressive were they that Queen Victoria wished to give their creator a peerage, but as an American, he had to refuse the honor. On returning late in his life to the United States, he donated $2 million to support the cause of education in the South— without distinction of race or color—a gesture of quite exceptional political liberalism for the period. George Peabody never married (there were stories of an unrequited love), and when he died (leaving an astonishing $12 million), he was given a hero's funeral in Westminster Abbey. He was buried in South Danvers, Massachusetts, his birthplace, a town that today is known in his memory as Peabody.

The Peabody women competed energetically with their male counterparts in good works and longevity. They also married selectively, and the family tree began to sprout names like Gardner, Lawrence, Whitney, Crowninshield, Sedgwick, Davison—a litany of New England aristocracy. The Peabodys were spreading like a benign virus, multiplying every generation (as European royalty tended to do, to secure the inheritance) in an almost unstoppable procession of rectors, justices, pastors, bankers, and philanthropists. Indeed, a family saying passed down to today's generation went, "A Peabody or a Nobody." A *New Yorker* cartoon of more recent date showed an old dowager seated in a wing chair in front of a large fire above which an ancestral portrait loomed. "Now that they've cracked the genetic code," she says to her portly old-guard husband, "I suppose everyone will want to be Peabodys."

Endicott Peabody, Marietta Tree's grandfather, was in the opinion of many the culmination of the species. The family bloodline by this time was rapturously pure. Endicott's maternal grandmother, Martha Endicott Peabody, was a descendant of John Endicott, the colorful contemporary of the first American Peabody, who became governor of the Massachusetts Bay Colony in 1649, and promptly embarked on a program of religious persecution not dissimilar to that his subjects had left behind. Though it may have seemed to the shocked immigrants that no land was free from bigotry, at the same time John Endicott's high Puritan standards and belief in duty created an indelible imprint on the philosophical and ethical map of the New World.

Heir to this impressive figure, Endicott's father was Samuel Endicott Peabody, a businessman who had inherited Joseph Peabody's shipping line, and his mother was Marianne Cabot Lee, daughter of John C. Lee of Salem, founder of the brokerage firm, Lee, Higginson & Co. Endicott was born in 1857 and grew up in Salem, rocked comfortably in classic Peabody fashion between the twin reefs of financial prosperity and the Unitarian Church.

When Endicott (Cotty to his friends) was thirteen, his father became a partner in the London banking business started by his relative, George Peabody, with Junius S. Morgan (ultimately becoming known as Morgan & Company), and the family (now consisting of five children, three of whom married Lawrences) moved to England. They lived in London for seven years, during which time Endicott was sent to Cheltenham, one of the country's middle-level (behind Eton, Harrow, and Winchester) boarding schools. This experience inspired in him the ideals that the British so efficiently inculcated in their future leaders, that discipline and the most stringent codes of Christian morality would make boys into models of adult rectitude and leaders of men.

After graduating from Trinity College, Cambridge, having acquired a degree in law and a group of devout Anglican Church friends, Endicott Peabody returned to the United States. He attempted a brief stint at his mother's family firm, Lee Higginson, but the work did not satisfy, and he decided to consult the distinguished preacher and minister Phillips Brooks, rector of Trinity Church in Boston. Should he enter the ministry?

"If," Reverend Brooks said, "it appeals to you as the most interesting and desirable thing in the world to tell people about Christ, you had better come in. Does it appeal to you?"

"Well," Peabody later remembered thinking, "that was pretty satisfactory. It was perfectly simple and true, so much better than arousing your feelings."[3]

The feelings of his family, however, were aroused considerably. His mother in particular was disappointed, not only that her talented son was becoming a clergyman but that he had chosen to reject the family tradition of Unitarianism to take orders in the Episcopal Church. Ultimately, however, he was sent, with their blessing, to the Episcopal Theological School in Cambridge, Massachusetts.

In January 1882, he was assigned to the troublesome parish of Tombstone, Arizona, an unlikely destination, perhaps, but one the young minister handled with panache. Six months later he left his gun-toting flock with a new sense of Christian charity and also a new Episcopal church—the first to be built in Arizona.

Back east, the eager seminary student decided that what he really wanted to do was to found a school based on the principles he had learned at Cheltenham. After enlisting family and friends, he bought land, built a building, hired teachers, and at the age of twenty-seven became the first headmaster of Groton School, dedicated, as described in the preface to the Records of the School, to the development of "a type of manly Christian character."

Groton School's motto was *Cui servare est regnare,* which can be freely translated as "Whose service is perfect freedom." Countless manly Christian characters have since graduated from Groton to take up public service, including Franklin D. Roosevelt, B. Sumner Welles, Dean G. Acheson, Douglas Dillon, and Averell Harriman, making the Rector and headmaster, Endicott Peabody, an institutional legend.

By this time, the immense proliferation of Peabodys, most of them living in or around Boston, meant that one ran into family members at almost any social gathering or Sunday service. Owing to their enthusiasm for mating, this led to the serious possibility that at some point one Peabody would fall in love with another Peabody. So it came to pass in 1882 that Endicott Peabody fell in love with his first cousin, Fannie.

Today, marriage between first cousins would be regarded with the greatest suspicion. In the late nineteenth century, however, such marriages were considered merely inadvisable. After much private soul-searching and discouragement from his father, Peabody consulted his old mentor, Phillips Brooks, who urged him to marry the woman he loved.

The ceremony took place in 1884, and by all accounts it was a marriage made in Episcopal heaven. Fannie had a warm and loving personality, and her role at Groton, with the boys, the parents, and the teachers, was indispensable. The letters husband and wife exchanged throughout their lives reflect a certainty of love and gratitude in each other that is distinctly exclusionary. "Good night, my darling. Our lives together are better every day, aren't they?" was the kind of sentiment each wrote the other. Indeed, it was said that the Rector's life-long lack of sympathy to the breakdown of other people's marriages resided in the unclouded perfection of his own.

"Endicott Peabody was one of the most fortunate people I have ever known," said his grandson, Sam Peabody. "As a young boy, he was admired and cherished by all his contemporaries. He was always in good health. He had a vocation which he clung to very early in life. He was at home with the world. He was totally complemented by his wife. He achieved what he wanted to achieve. There was never any question of how the rent was going to be paid. He lived a long and full life, with an easy death. If he had wished for another blessing, I do not know what it could have been."

Endicott and Fannie Peabody had six children. The eldest, their only son, was Malcolm, Marietta's father, born on June 12, 1888. Five daughters followed: Helen, Rose, Elizabeth, Margery, and Dorothy. Elizabeth (Betsey) and Margery never married, but remained wedded to Groton and their brother, living and working on the campus for the rest of their lives. Helen married a Sedgwick, Rose married a Parsons, Dorothy married a Davison, and Malcolm married a Parkman. But while three out of five gave their vows to other men, none of them ever really cut the tie to Groton. When Rose Peabody Parsons was old and sick, she always talked of "going home to Groton."

Malcolm was twenty-seven years old when he married, the same age as his father had been when he became headmaster of Groton. The contrast was striking. Malcolm's development was a long, slow struggle against his formidable Peabody patriarch. To be an only son with five sisters would be considered testing under any circumstances. To be the only son, with five sisters, of the Rector of Groton was to tip the balance unfairly against him. Malcolm was born when the school had been open only three years. There were still under fifty boys enrolled, but traditions were firmly in place, cubicles, schoolrooms, athletics programs well established. Malcolm's parents presided over Hundred House (the largest dormitory), and Chapel was the central event of the daily calendar. Every night, each boy shook hands with the Rector and Mrs. Peabody (known always as "the Madam") before going to bed. Every Christmas, the Rector would gather the boys around him and read, in his sonorous, English-accented voice, *A Christmas Carol*.

This nurturing of so many other people's children was at some cost, ultimately, to their own. In a memoir he wrote for the benefit of his children and grandchildren in 1970, Malcolm summoned up with vividness and affection the large colonial mansions of his Peabody grandparents (on both sides) where he spent summers with his family. But references to Groton were pointedly brief. It was hardly surprising. At Groton, for ten months of the year, he was surrounded by a lot of older boys, and nine girls (his sisters plus four Lawrence girl cousins who also lived on campus), "which left me in the middle without any real buddies." This isolation was aggravated by the loss of the only buddy he did make, Jack MacDonald, who was the local farmer's son. Malcolm's father overheard young Jack tell a "rather shady story," and Malcolm was never allowed to see his friend again. But Malcolm did not forget, and his loss was expressed in uncharacteristically bitter terms seventy years later when he observed, "It takes more than one shady story to blacken a character."[4]

The Rector acknowledged his lack of attention to his own family. "For the last six weeks I have only had occasional glimpses of my wife and children," he confessed to his friend Julius Atwood (later Bishop Atwood) in December 1899. A telling example of the Rector's attitude toward his son is shown in a letter he wrote in January 1897 to Atwood, who had suggested buying a gift to Malcolm on the occasion of the boy's admittance to Groton: "I did not get either prayer book, knife or anything else for Malcolm. Possibly I forgot. . . . Someday I shall be going to Boston and I will try to purchase some tribute for the boy."

Malcolm's early education, by his own admission, was inadequate. He had difficulty learning, and his parents decided to ship him off to a boarding school in Newport at the age of eleven, "to try life out on my own for a year before entering Groton." He was homesick, but his grades improved, and Groton prepared to open its august doors to the only son of its founder. Malcolm immediately found his position almost untenable. He made the mistake of going to his father about a hazing ritual, which made him instantly a pariah amongst his classmates. The Rector, in return, while trying to be fair, in fact demanded more of him than the other boys. The weight of his parents' expectations can be measured from this little note Mrs. Peabody sent to her son:

> Be my best boy—and keep the Groton flag at your masthead—
> you embody more, remember, than any other boy.
> Mama.

Many people, particularly boys who were educated in the old British public school system, feel that their school days, in the intense all-male atmosphere of ritual, discipline, and overwhelming intimacy, were the most important and memorable years of their lives. For Malcolm, his life of loneliness and separateness at Groton was to haunt him, not only at Harvard, where he drifted through his years without much commitment, but for many years afterwards.

He was extremely handsome, which made him attractive to women, and he had the admiration of his five sisters, which helped boost his fragile self-esteem. But Harvard did not make much difference. He did not have any roommates until his junior year. His academic work continued to be a struggle. But thanks to a legacy from his uncle George Peabody, he became a club man, and his social life improved.

In an interesting replication of his one childhood friendship, he chose as a close friend at Harvard a lively and hard-drinking character called Robert Lee, who later became an alcoholic. Malcolm loved this convivial man and felt a freedom with him that he never recaptured once he embarked on his career in the Church.[5]

Malcolm claimed that it was when he went to Trinity College, Cambridge, for his senior year, that he began for the first time to feel flickers of self-confidence. Not that he had escaped very far: the Rector's presence was of course as powerful as ever, casting his weighty shadow up and down the ancient staircases of his old alma mater. But at least Malcolm managed to excel in rowing, and went "Head of the River" in the May Races in 1911. He also joined the distinguished Leander Club, a rowing club, which was very important to him. That summer, feeling much better, he returned to Harvard and managed successfully to graduate.

The Rector took command of his son's immediate future by arranging for Malcolm to be a junior master at the Baguio School in the Philippines, even offering to pay his son's salary. So, in September 1911, Malcolm Peabody sailed across the Pacific. "I had a talk with him shortly before he left," the Rector confided to his friend Bishop Atwood, "and made it quite clear to him that the thing I desired more than anything for him was that he should enter the ministry. I think that he has understood this right along and that he would be glad to give me the pleasure; but he is conscientious and would therefore not contemplate taking up the work unless he felt a pretty definite call to it."

It will not surprise students of psychology to learn that toward the end of his first year in the Philippines, Malcolm had a miraculous vision in which a voice—no doubt suspiciously like the Rector's—told him, "The ministry, my boy, is the job for you."

The year, to that point, had not been easy. The boys at the Baguio School made mincemeat out of the inexperienced and insecure young master. The conditions were spartan. The headmaster, Remsen Ogilby (who later became president of Trinity College, Hartford), gave him only guarded support. The high point was when his friend Pat Barton visited. During a discussion of their plans for the following year, Malcolm allowed as how he thought his father would give him a job at Groton. Pat, a friend indeed, expressed horror at the idea, telling him that he could not possibly undertake such an assignment and maintain his own individuality. Malcolm was devastated by this advice. The very next day he got his call to the ministry.[6]

The Rector was delighted at his son's decision. He wrote about the good news in glowing terms to Atwood. "Every day I give thanks that he has decided to enter the ministry. It is the greatest blessing that has come to us in our married life and we have had a multitude of blessings. This afternoon I beat one of our graduates at squash."

One other significant visitation occurred during Malcolm's two years abroad. After a spring and summer cruising in the islands and working with missions throughout the Philippines, China, and Japan, he returned for a second year's stint at the school. That Easter of 1913, three young women from Boston showed up, on a leg of a rather unconventional, barely chaperoned Grand Tour. One of them was Mary Elizabeth Parkman. Three years later, he married her.

If Marietta's paternal Peabody genes hummed with rectitude, they hummed along with a rather different set of influences on her mother's side. The first Parkmans arrived on American shores in the early 1600s, at about the same time as the Peabodys, with the same dissenting zeal, turning their skills to shipping, farming, producing large families, and of course the ministry. Like the Peabodys, they seem mostly to have been named George, Francis, and Fanny, to have gone to Harvard, to have married local Boston gentry, and to have paid attention in a similarly successful fashion to material and spiritual matters. But there is one very significant deviation in the Parkman line that distinguishes it from the peerless Peabodys. It is as though the stitcher of the Parkman quilt forsook her usual fabrics and suddenly inserted a startling scarlet into the muted color scheme of the design.

He was known to the family as Naughty Sam.

"We have to face the fact that this Samuel (II), three generations back of me, is not an ancestor to be proud of," wrote Francis Parkman (1898–1990), in a privately circulated genealogical account of the Parkman family. What could Sam have done to arouse the wrath of his disapproving descendant? Naughty Sam was born in 1792 to the first Samuel Parkman, a cultivated philanthropist generally regarded as the richest man in Boston. But his son Sam failed to support this comfortable patrimony. After graduating from Harvard and marrying quite suitably a lawyer's daughter, young Sam went entirely to the bad. He divorced his wife, quit town leaving huge debts behind him, and finally settled in Paris, where he died in 1849. Thanks to the help of a nephew, Quincy A. Shaw, Sam Parkman was buried in Père Lachaise Cemetery, where his grave still exists.[7]

The waters mercifully closed over this Parkman's head. But one renegade often sires another. Naughty Sam's son, Samuel III, while not remotely as bad as his father, joined a rebellion at Harvard caused by the firing of a student for misbehavior. The whole of the sophomore class of 1834 was dismissed, and degrees were withheld from eight seniors.

Samuel III went on to become a doctor, but died in his twenties. His son was Harry Parkman, Marietta's grandfather. Harry did not inherit the bright flame of Parkman unorthodoxy enjoyed by his two ancestors. Since his father had died so young, Harry was left with very little money and had to work hard as a lawyer to provide for himself and his family. Yet perhaps some flicker of the family trait stirred in him, for he fell in love with Marietta's grandmother, Mary Frances Parker, and waited some eleven years until this unconventional woman agreed to become his wife.

Frances Parker, daughter of Cortlandt and Elisabeth Stites Parker, came from New Jersey, one of the Parkers who, like the Peabodys, reproduced energetically (Frances was one of nine children) and committed themselves in outstanding measure to the service of their country. Born in 1855, Marietta's maternal grandmother was beautiful, headstrong, highly intelligent, accomplished in the arts, and resisted marriage until she was thirty-five, almost unheard of in those days for a woman, and particularly one so eligible. The target of many ardent suitors, she succumbed finally to the patient siege of Harry Parkman, who by that time was himself forty years old.

Frances Parker married Harry Parkman in 1890 and promptly got the obligatory child rearing over with, producing between the ages of thirty-eight and forty-three, three daughters and two sons—another socially and physically unorthodox feat, particularly in those days. Harry was by then chairman of a savings bank in Boston, an unassuming career for an unassuming man. His grandchildren retained little memory of him after his early death in 1924, except as a loving, gentle, reliable sort of fellow—no doubt precisely the attributes that caused his wife finally to consent to his suit.

Long before she married Harry, Frances Parker had been in love with Robert Weeks de Forest, a New York lawyer almost twenty years her senior. Involved in charities and the arts—in 1913 he became chairman of the board of trustees of the Metropolitan Museum of Art—de Forest was already married when he met Frances, but this did not deter him from continuing a long relationship with his young friend in New Jersey. It came to an end only when Frances decided she could not ultimately fulfill her life as the "other woman" and chose to accept faithful Harry.

But Frances's marital bonds, although of Bostonian manufacture, seem not to have supplanted the bonds that tied her and her New Yorker to each other. Many years later, she took all five children to Europe (on the small but adequate family budget), and as they were going through the cathedral at Reims they came upon Mr. de Forest doing exactly the same thing with his children. Whether this was arranged or a coincidence is not documented, but what is certain is that after this meeting, they never met again.

Their connection to each other, however, remained unbroken. Each wrote letters to the other every day, letters that Mrs. Parkman kept in bound volumes in her house at 30 Commonwealth Avenue in Boston. After Robert de Forest's death in 1931, communications between them became easier. Mrs. Parkman consulted a medium, who came up from New York to carry out séances to communicate with the other side. During these sessions, contact with Robert was made most satisfactorily. While their devotion triumphed gloriously beyond the grave, Mrs. Parkman's behavior seemed exceedingly inglorious to the rest of her family, particularly to her children, who were as unsympathetic to her spiritualism as they were to her unsuitable correspondence. When Mary Frances Parkman died, the letters were hastily disposed of, like dirty laundry.

By this time, she was an almost mythical figure to her grandchildren. She was a social and literary paragon, a fluent linguist, an accomplished cello player, a trustee of Radcliffe College, and a magnet to men. In the summertime, she presided over the vacation community in exile from Boston and Philadelphia in Northeast Harbor, Maine, in a house called Windward on Smallidge Point, which she built with money left her by her father when he died. Northeast Harbor had been discovered by President Charles Eliot of Harvard in the 1880s; following his lead, many clergy and educators built summer homes in this rugged corner of Maine, enjoying the simple life with no telephones, no electricity, chopping their own wood, and generally reflecting the plain Christian values that were so easily mislaid in the lavish resorts farther south.

The Parkmans were longtime devotees of this beautiful and remote part of Mount Desert Island, and later Frances Parkman's own daughter Mary would spend every summer there throughout her life. However, scandal followed Mrs. Parkman even to that enclave of brisk New England morality. It was thought that she had an unusually close relationship with the strikingly handsome local American Indian who lived farther down the point, and from whom the summer residents bought sweetgrass baskets every year.

In the winter, Mrs. Parkman created in Boston a stimulating salon of artists, writers, and thinkers, just like her older friend and kindred spirit, Isabella Stewart Gardner. "Mrs. Jack," as Mrs. Gardner was known, married a very rich man and spent much of her marriage as a chronic invalid. On her husband's death, she, like Frances Parkman, was transformed into a woman of fierce independence and creativity. In the twenty-six years she was a widow, Mrs. Gardner built an Italianate mansion in Boston to house her art collection, and surrounded herself with a cultural mix of people, including John Singer Sargent (who painted her portrait, as he had painted those of the Rector and Mrs. Peabody of Groton), Henry James, Bernard Berenson, and Nellie Melba.[8]

Mrs. Parkman's eldest daughter, Mary, recalled with muted enthusiasm her mother's lively social life, which so flagrantly flouted the stuffy Boston conventions of the time. "My sister and I were always trying to keep her in order," she observed drily. Admittedly, Mrs. Parkman lacked the maternal instincts children like to see in their mothers. This maternal failure placed a particular burden on Mary, the oldest child and first daughter, who felt it behooved her to fill the gap, so to speak, by looking after her sisters and brothers with special care and attention. She felt the burden keenly.

Yet Mary intensely admired her colorful mother, and felt, as daughters of strong mothers often do, that she could not compete. When a young woman, Mary composed a "dirge" to her mother, detailing how her mother's charm and intellect outshone her own.

> *When you and I are seated here,*
> *And beaux on me come calling,*
> *They much prefer to talk to you,*
> *All interest in me falling . . .*

The sad last four lines read: "So now that I have said my say, / And touched on every defect, / May you endeavour day by day, / To be not quite so perfect."

In later years, this conflict surfaced more openly. On one occasion, when Mary returned from a visit to her mother, with face flushed she said to her own children, "If I ever treat you the way my mother treats me, you can take me out and have me shot."

Mrs. Parkman hated growing old, and became depressed and demanding, fighting her physical disintegration and resenting its limitations. Railing until the end, she died in 1942 at the age of eighty-seven. The Peabody grandparents, in contrast, made a far more discreet exit. The Rector of Groton died two years after Mrs. Parkman, in November 1944, in the impressive no-frills style in which he had lived. He was driving a woman friend to the railroad station after a luncheon with him and his wife at Groton, when he felt a pain in his chest. He drove the car to the side of the road, parked it, turned off the engine, and died. His companion telephoned Mrs. Peabody, said to her, "Dr. Peabody has just died," then called a taxi and caught her train as planned. The Rector's beloved wife died peacefully two years later, in 1946.

Marietta's mother, Mary, would surely have preferred the Peabody way. (She always said how much she loved her Peabody in-laws.) But the sense of familial responsibility remained with her throughout her life, to the detriment of her children, in whose eyes she seemed more devoted to her siblings than to her own offspring. Just as the Rector of Groton put his inimitable mark upon his eldest (and only) son, so did Mary Frances Parkman affect in fundamental ways the attitudes and responses of her eldest daughter. Thus, when this son meets this daughter, many complex psychological patterns begin their implacable journey through the generations.

# CHAPTER *2*

# *"As good as gold"*

By 1916, Mary Parkman was finally ready for marriage. She was almost twenty-five, and had spent more than enough time with her mother on Commonwealth Avenue. Mary, like her mother, was educated at Miss Porter's School in Farmington, and also like her mother, did not go to college. Instead, at the age of seventeen, she went to Paris and then decided that since she wanted to do social work she did not need further education. She returned to Boston and worked with Associated Charities and local neighborhood houses, declaring that she did not want a career. "I just wanted to do something useful," she told interviewer Michael Teague much later.

Although a young woman with a conscience, Mary Parkman was no wallflower. In Boston there were coming-out parties, plays, operas, concerts (she was highly musical), football games at Princeton and Harvard, and young men calling on her. She took French, German, Italian, singing, and piano lessons. She traveled to Europe with her parents. Every summer in Northeast Harbor, she played tennis, went on picnics, sailed, danced, and performed in the annual amateur theatricals.

In 1913, she decided to go around the world with two friends, Katherine Putnam and Anna Gardiner. Not many well-bred young ladies of Boston went around the world on their own when they were twenty-one years old, but Mary Parkman arranged the whole thing, paying her way with a legacy her uncle, George Parkman, had left her of $5,000. They decided to aim for the Far East—India, Burma, Ceylon, China, Japan, and the Philippines. Katherine Putnam recalled how efficient her friend had been, writing ahead to missionaries and clerics in the foreign parts they were to visit. Mary Parkman declared quite openly the reason for taking this adventurous trip: "None of us wanted to get married so we concocted this thing."[1]

Some mothers might have been alarmed at this unconventional dismissal of what was, after all, every girl's expected calling, but Mrs. Parkman, given her own history, was hardly in a position to complain. At least she found them the obligatory chaperone, one Miss Hoppin, a seventy-year-old lady who seemed to be entirely in Mary's thrall. According to Katherine Putnam, "We think Miss Hoppin had a slight stroke in the Red Sea, because she never appeared again on the deck, which was convenient."

They were the only Americans on the boat and none of the other women on board spoke to them. "I remember once when Mary was leaning over the railing and talking to a most innocent and nice-looking man, concern was expressed that she was trying to pick him up, whereas she was just exchanging pleasantries. Mary was just not the type of person to pick people up." The young women often used to dance with each other on board. Mary loved to dance, and was good at it. She was also a graceful skater and tennis player. (Her children would inherit these athletic skills.)

In the Philippines, Mary Parkman met Malcolm Peabody. The two already knew each other, from both Boston and Northeast Harbor. Mary was a friend of Malcolm's sister, Helen, and a great admirer of the Rector. There is no evidence, however, that the encounter between Malcolm and Mary that spring was in any way momentous. In fact, when Malcolm reported on the girls' visit, he confessed that "my continued duties here has [sic] made my time with them only occasional and then the pedagogical mask can only be partly pushed aside. . . ." Mary was equally cool. "It wasn't love at first sight in the Philippines," she later declared.

When Malcolm came back to the United States he started courses at the Episcopal Theological School in Boston, and was able to meet Mary frequently. Miss Parkman was happy to see him, even going so far as to have "milk and crackers in the kitchen" with him, but that was all.

In March 1914, Malcolm began pressing his suit. Mary was evasive and continued to go out with others, including Harvey Bundy, a frequent visitor. By the end of the summer it was clear she greatly preferred Bundy to the seminary student. But in October, to Mary's intense surprise and shock, Harvey Bundy announced his engagement to her best friend, Katherine Putnam. That same year, her other best friend, Anna Gardiner, got married. These were the two women who had sworn with her to postpone marital bondage for as long as possible, and now both (most painfully in the case of Katherine Putnam) had betrayed her.

She went on seeing Malcolm, who treated her quite coldly (not surprisingly, after her rejections). As is usual in these matters, the more he withdrew, the more attractive he became to her. Early in 1915, he was so unapproachable that she confided to her diary that he made her miserable. She began waiting for his calls.

In fact, Malcolm had fallen for another—someone his family thought very unsuitable, even flighty, and who went on to marry elsewhere. Mary had once more been betrayed.

By the end of 1915, chastened by his unlikely infatuation, Malcolm returned to the Parkman fold, and one night he and Mary sat comfortably in the Chilton Club "and he talked about his future." In January 1916, Mary heard Malcolm preach at the seminary. She did not think much of it, but thought he had a fine spirit. That spring she spent more time with him, horseback riding, at sporting events, on trips to New York. On April 5, they walked out along the embankment in Boston and he asked her to marry him. "But I couldn't contemplate it," she wrote. "I was quite sure I didn't care for him enough for that." This time, however, Malcolm was adamant. He visited her the following evening, while the family was out, and "overrode all my objections and I finally said I would."[2]

Relieved that she had consented, though recognizing that she had reservations, Malcolm wrote to her encouragingly, "I think that . . . beginning now and here, we have such a basis of mutual sympathy and understanding that if we *start* with 70 percent, there's no reason why we shouldn't eventually attain 100 percent." Thus there was a sense of compromise on both sides.

Having made the decision, Mary did not wish to have time to reflect. They became engaged that same April. Malcolm had just graduated cum laude from Episcopal Theological School. He was ordained on June 1, 1916, Ascension Day, and the couple was married fifteen days later in Immanuel Church, with Dr. Peabody, Bishop Atwood, and Bishop Brent from the Philippines officiating, and Mary's sister Edith as maid of honor.

They spent their honeymoon night at Groton, and then went on to Northeast Harbor. There Malcolm wrote a letter to his father that reveals the emotional temperature of the young husband. After extolling the glories of the wedding, he returned to the theme of unworthiness that was to dog him throughout his life. "Your influence in my whole career (and mother's) has been the almost exclusive one in producing anything you may find in me to rejoice over. That may seem to damn with faint praise. I quite realize that I have not given much account of myself, as Mary has . . . but let me promise you that no stone will be left unturned to make ample returns on so prodigal an investment as is mine."

The Rector and Mrs. Peabody were delighted and relieved by their new daughter-in-law, whose strength of character was already evident. As the indulgent parents watched the young couple gambol on the lawn at Groton, they noticed how Mary seemed always to win the wrestling games as Malcolm "relapsed into weakness." The roles were becoming clear.

In marrying Malcolm, Mary was of course marrying the Peabodys, a family that she had loved for years. It was so stable and decent, compared to the eccentric and unconventional life offered by her mother. She spent many happy hours during the school holidays with the Rector and Mrs. Peabody at Groton, finding their values and attitudes refreshingly similar to her own. Malcolm was once again in the position of accepting the Rector's role in his life. Acknowledging it, he quoted to Mary one of his favorite Old Testament texts: "Let me die, for I am no better than my fathers."

Malcolm's first post was as curate at Grace Church, in Lawrence, Massachusetts. The couple found a second-story apartment at 283 Prospect Street, where they set up house in a manner befitting their modest church stipend. Luckily, the legacy from Malcolm's uncle George continued to help them out, plus the gift of a Dodge car from his aunt Lizzie. Wedding presents also came in useful, with one rather unusual exception. This was a gift from Isabella Stewart Gardner, who gave Mary a picture by Degas. It was painted from the perspective of a box at the theater, looking down on the curtain. From this angle, the women in the box revealed a generous expanse of bosom. Mary disapproved of Isabella Stewart Gardner, and she disapproved of the painting. The little Degas masterpiece was never displayed in Lawrence. Mary gave it to a rummage sale.

Lawrence was a blue-collar mill town, populated largely by Irish immigrant workers, a big change from the protected world of Groton and the seminary. Grace Episcopal Church was a simple, austere stone building in the center of town, looking out onto one of the few open spaces, a pleasant square with grass, maple trees, and walks. Other church spires and towers were visible over the tops of the huge textile factories, mingling with brick and steel chimneys, a far cry from the emerald green of Ireland most of the factory workers came from.

The retiring rector of Grace Church, the Reverend Arthur W. Moulton, went on vacation almost immediately after the new parson arrived, leaving Malcolm in charge of about two thousand parishioners and all the Sunday services, a terrifying thought for someone who had never officiated alone and whose confidence in himself was shaky at best. Moreover, the young reverend recognized that his Roman Catholic rival, Father James T. O'Reilly, "was really the uncrowned king of the place."

Mary, on the other hand, entered into the spirit of the work with enthusiasm. It was fortunate, she said later, that Malcolm had decided to become a clergyman, because she had determined to marry one. It was the only way, as she saw it, to have an independent career within the confines of marriage. At Lawrence, she began to prove her point. "Mary is finer than fine—always ready to sacrifice herself—and me!— for the work at which she hurls us both," Malcolm wrote with exhausted awe to his parents. "It is a pretty wonderful thing to get a backer who pushes all the time. . . ."

A year after their marriage, on April 12, 1917, Malcolm and Mary's first child, a daughter, was born. During the time she was pregnant, Mary said to a friend that she thought that if the baby was a girl, she would name her Grace, after Grace Church, Her friend was appalled at the idea, and the baby's name became the more properly traditional Mary Endicott Peabody—with Mary Endicott soon ellipsed to Marietta.[3]

The time of her birth was inauspicious, for the United States had recently entered the war that had broken out in Europe three years earlier, and Malcolm had accepted the chaplaincy of U.S. Army Base Hospital Number 5, consisting of staff from Boston's Peter Bent Brigham Hospital. Unexpectedly, the hospital was ordered to France; as chaplain, Malcolm was telephoned by the head of the hospital, Dr. Harvey Cushing, and asked to go. As Malcolm himself told it, "I naturally hesitated for a moment, but I need not have done so, because a shrill cry from my wife, who was still in bed after the arrival of Marietta into this world, said, 'Of course you will go. Tell him so *now*.'"

So Malcolm went, and within a fortnight was installed at a British hospital in Dannes Camiers in northern France, where his job was to act as spiritual guide to several hundred wounded men, and over two hundred U.S. and British medical personnel. As would happen so often in his life, Peabody felt deeply inadequate to the task, and found little or no support from colleagues who were all of the attitude of the army organist who said, "We are too busy to go to Church; we are at war!"

He struggled along, enduring the bombing and other horrors of trench warfare. He was moved to other posts, ending up near Verdun, scene of one of the most disastrous battles of the war. In September 1918 he received a full chaplain's commission, which gave him more confidence and authority. He finished the war as chaplain to the 102nd Field Artillery of the Yankee 26th Division, and returned home in April 1919.

Meanwhile, his wife had assumed many of the duties belonging to the curate, visiting the parish, running the church, fund-raising for the war effort, becoming a major figure in the community. She was also a single parent, singularly blessed with an enormous number of gifts for the baby; blankets, bonnets, crib pads, jackets, poured in from Peabodys, Parkmans, Lowells, Hunnewells, Lawrences, Parkers, Welds, Crockers, and on and on. Thus Marietta, this fair-haired, green-eyed child of two great New England dynasties, lay in her crib in the shadow of her ancestors, watched over by those demanding representatives of her Puritan heritage.

The child's first responses were carefully recorded by her mother in *The Mother's Record,* a prettily printed volume originally published in 1882, whose rather Freudian introduction exhorted mothers to study "the traits of character exhibited by her child." Mary Peabody proved to be a diligent observer of her baby's progress. We learn that Marietta weighed nine pounds at birth. Her mother breast-fed her for a year, starting the first bottle (one a day) at three months old. The baby slept well, had her first tooth at eight months, began to walk at sixteen months, and sucked her fingers, "but got over it." Almost the last time the baby saw her father before he went off to the war was at three weeks old, when she was taken to his ordination in Grace Church, through which she slept. Her christening took place immediately after, at which she was "as good as gold to the very end when she gave one little cry." She would not see her father again for two years.

With her husband gone, Mary Peabody started the family routines that were to govern her children's lives. Each spring, at Easter, Marietta—and later her siblings—would go to Groton to stay with their Peabody grandparents. There the visits to Chapel, the work in the school community, the extended hospitality in Hundred House, seemed to Mary Peabody the model of life well lived.

Every summer, they would stay with their maternal grandmother, Mrs. Parkman, in Northeast Harbor, Maine. *The Mother's Record* shows that Marietta's first summer there was a great success. "She used to sit up at tea time on mother's lap and entertain people at tea, a very knowing little person."

During Marietta's first two years, the images accumulate with overwhelming vividness:

> *Jan. 13.* Very sensitive, objects to being laughed at, even at note of laughter in voice, almost weeps. . . . *March.* She reacts in a lovely way to punishment. Bears no ill will and cuddles up to you afterwards. . . . *July 12.* Smells flowers with rapture. Long drawn-in breath and cooes of delight. . . . *July 28.* Found her trying on hat before the looking glass. [The latter was entered under a special category in *The Mother's Record* entitled "Mischievous Acts."] *August 22.* She toddles up the path every morn-

Marietta, aged two, with her mother in Lawrence, Massachusetts.

ing after breakfast, falling down continually but undaunted. Loves to dance, and when mother plays for her, takes hold of her skirts or overalls and dances a wonderful jig, turning round at intervals.

The picture continues to take shape. Dr. Drown (Malcolm's friend from the seminary) used to come to lunch almost every Sunday and developed a great affection for Marietta, calling her his "little female friend." (Mary observed that Marietta carried on "a very serious flirtation" with Dr. Drown.) "The Cushman boys spent a week with us in the summer. Marietta was tremendously taken with them and used to make the most absurd sheep's eyes at them."

Malcolm Peabody arrived home from the war just before his daughter's second birthday. Like most war babies who had never known their fathers, Marietta did not like this stranger usurping her position, particularly with her mother. When Malcolm touched his wife, Marietta resented it strongly, hitting him and crying.

The Peabodys faced more serious problems than infantile jealousy, however. Malcolm's reentry into civilian life was traumatic. The war had shattered him; like many other front-line veterans, he was physically exhausted and emotionally drained. He described greeting his family on the dock in Boston after his homecoming: "My heart did not accelerate one beat even when I saw them down there on the dock, for I had been so torn to pieces emotionally for two years that I had no further capacity for feeling. The family thought that this was odd, and I confess that I acted oddly for almost two years to come."[4]

Moreover, he had come back to find a wife who had managed very well indeed without him. Just as many children had to make room for a rival when the war was over, many wives also had to move over when their husbands returned. For somebody like Mary Peabody, who had married in order to be independent, this change was particularly irksome. The imbalance between them had surfaced and could no longer be ignored. When finally the waters settled, the new configuration confirmed Mary's dominance in the marriage, a dominance that from then on she never relinquished.

Their youngest son, Mike, told a story that illustrates how things worked between his parents. "I went to my father and said, 'Dad, what does it take to get along with a wife? How do you make decisions?' And he said, 'Well, in a marriage you do things together, and if you want to make a decision about something, you say, 'Well, Mary, do you think we should do such and such?' And then I asked Mother the same question. 'It's perfectly simple,' she said, 'I just say, Malcolm this is what we are going to do. . . .' "

Mrs. Peabody, who found any weakness unacceptable, later denied that her husband had been depressed during this period. She preferred to point to the positive side of his life at Lawrence after his return. He was promoted to rector of Grace Church in 1920, when Arthur Moulton was elected bishop of Utah, and plunged enthusiastically into work, his chief triumph being the building of a new parish house. Malcolm himself raised $25,000 from family and friends; his friend Bishop William Lawrence gave him $75,000, the parish pledged $25,000, and the new house got built. (Called the Peabody Building, it bears a plaque to Malcolm Peabody's memory.) Although Lawrence was not yet suffering from the decline that was to overtake the textile industry, to have raised this kind of money was remarkable. Indeed, some who knew Malcolm well often felt that the Church did not come easily to him, and that he would have been happier and more successful as a businessman.

On February 15, 1920, Endicott Peabody was born, two months before Marietta was three. She only saw her baby brother for a few minutes before she was sent away to stay with her grandmother Parkman in Boston. Nowadays, that banishment would be considered a psychological mistake, but Marietta had already begun to form the relationship with her grandmother that was to prove so important to her in later life.

When Marietta came back, she confronted a new world, one that all eldest children have to face. The new baby had seized the fragile crown she had worn for almost three years. Endicott was doubly blessed since he was the Peabodys' first son. Marietta's fate was not only that she was the first born but she was the only girl.

"After the baby came it was hard to keep track of Marietta when I was busy with him," her mother wrote. "At first I made a rule she could not go out. One day she got away, and I found her at the door of the drugstore. I asked her what she was doing and she said she wanted an icecream cone. I told her how naughty it was to have crossed that street. . . . I gave up soon after trying to keep her in, but made a rule she could not go on the street. I punished her for doing so a couple of times and after a while I could trust her."

But Marietta was not satisfied with these small sops to her identity crisis. She became willful and undisciplined, howling if she were corrected. "Malcolm took her in hand, and insisted on immediate obedience, punishment being closet or spanking. She reacted pretty well to it, always ending up the scene with an embrace." Marietta was continuing to act in a "lovely way" to punishment. Her mother got very irritated with her one day. "She asked me if I was mad and when I said I was, she made me kiss her till I forgave her."

Marietta's interest in people was increasingly noticeable. Entries often described her good memory for names and faces. Her mother thought her sometimes patronizing to other children, "talking to them in the most motherly way." But there was one child who did not follow this lead. "On July 4th, we spent the day with the Bundys. Little Harvey kissed her. Marietta stood perfectly still, did not say a word, but blushed and blushed." This cute moment became an item of family lore, and Harvey relived it seventy years later just as poignantly as Mary Peabody had felt impelled to record it for posterity.

Marietta's second brother, George Lee, was born on January 15, 1922. Again, Marietta was sent to her grandmother's, which, as she put it later, was some compensation for being faced with another competitor in the family. Her mother had told her that children were sent from Heaven, so when she first saw baby George, she said to her mother, "He doesn't know anybody, does he, not me, or you, only God?" Another time, she asked whether her mother had come from Heaven too; when her mother said yes, Marietta, desperate for reassurance from her increasingly distant parent, said, "Well, then, we were in Heaven together, you and I, weren't we, Mudie?"

Mrs. Peabody saw nothing significant in this exchange, which was one of the last entries in *The Mother's Record*. After that, there is a lull, doubtless because she had more important things to do than write down conversations with her daughter. Mrs. Peabody was continuing to be active in a major way in the challenging, poor parish of Lawrence; taking Sunday School, visiting the sick, caring for troubled teenagers, raising money for church-related programs, helping her husband in the way she had always intended to, as a fully involved minister's wife.

Marietta was probably too young to have understood her mother's many activities, but her earliest memories were connected with her mother's good works in the community, in particular going with her to social work committee meetings in the parish house, which seemed to go on forever, "although I was made much of by the other committee members."

At the age of four, Marietta was sent to kindergarten. She showed promise at things that required her head but was very clumsy with her hands. She went on to the Hood School, a public grade school in Lawrence. An extreme tendency to "nervousness," as Mrs. Peabody interpreted it, surfaced at this point. It expressed itself in a deep anxiety about getting to school on time, Marietta dressing and rushing through breakfast long before she had to leave. Scenes invariably took place with her father over this, and on at least one occasion Marietta made herself sick.

Clearly Marietta was deeply anxious about this new school. She was set apart immediately by being the daughter of the rector of the Episcopal church, while most of her schoolmates were working-class Catholics. Marietta took swimming lessons, and went to mysterious places like Groton and Northeast Harbor. She was dressed differently, decked out in wonderful sailor suits and outfits from England, fondly bought for her by her Parkman grandmother.

But with her by-now natural ability to make friends, she soon learned to love school, running wild in the neighborhood with all her schoolmates. Questions of moral character were continually raised. Marietta's grandfather, the Rector, was a constant presence, in spirit if not in fact, keeping an eye on his son's family, writing letters with instructions as to their upbringing. Malcolm obeyed him in everything. When the children grew older, to disagree with or criticize the Rector was forbidden. Their father always sided with his father. You had to fit the mold, or be damned.

But discipline was a permanent problem. Both her father and mother administered corporal punishment to their daughter, putting her over their laps, pulling down her underpants, and smacking her with their hands. When there had been some particular scene over her disobedience, Marietta, like many children who feel they suffer injustices at the hands of their parents, imagined that she was adopted and that she was really a princess, waiting to be rescued by a prince.

Any interest the child showed in religious matters was gratefully recorded. "I think she is fundamentally religious," wrote Mrs. Peabody. "She was reading [the Bible] very assiduously soon after her 7th birthday and I heard her exclaim 'Oh,' in a very troubled voice. I asked her what was the matter and she said, 'The children of Israel have sinned *again* against the Lord.' "

In the summer of 1924 Marietta went with her parents and the Rector and Mrs. Peabody to England. (While they were away, her paternal grandfather, Harry Parkman, died. His daughter Mary did not return for the funeral.) It was a very grand visit. The Rector was fêted in England where he still had friends from Winchester and Cambridge. They were invited to many glamorous dinners, meeting Neville Chamberlain, Sir Robert and Lady Baden-Powell, and other distinguished people. They went to Henley (where they watched Groton row) and Wimbledon. Rabid Anglophiles, as were so many scions of Boston and Philadelphia, the Peabodys were enraptured by their exposure to English upper-class society, the high point of which was a visit to Lady Astor at Cliveden, which Mary described in proud detail in her journal.

The following February, Marietta's third brother, Samuel Parkman, was born. Marietta was working on a play at the time, and decided she wanted to perform it on February 21, 1925, the day Sam was due to be born. Mrs. Peabody seems to have seen no psychological implications in this very obvious maneuver on Marietta's part, but merely records that the play was moved to a neighbor's house. The play was *Cinderella,* and Endicott and George were allowed roles in it. No guesses as to which part Marietta played. "She loves to dance and get dressed up and her ambition at present is to be an actress," her mother commented. Almost immediately thereafter Marietta was sent to stay for a week with Mr. Sherman, the senior warden of Grace Church, and his wife.

After Sam's birth there was another major change in the Peabody family's affairs. Malcolm had been rector of Grace Church for five years, and the parish had successfully expanded. The Reverend Malcolm Peabody was making a modest name for himself, and the clerical headhunters were on the prowl. That spring of 1925, Malcolm was offered the post of rector of St. Paul's Church, Chestnut Hill, in Philadelphia. Mary had taken her five-year-old son, Endicott, out for a walk when the representatives of St. Paul's Church arrived to make their offer. When she returned, Malcolm recalls, "she strenuously voted against the invitation on the grounds that my job at Grace Church had not yet been accomplished." On this occasion, however,

Malcolm stood firm, and after Easter, 1925, the family left Lawrence forever and set off for Philadelphia.

At this point *The Mother's Record* ends. (Mrs. Peabody never kept one for her other children.) The last entry is a summary of Marietta's development so far. It is a good report on the whole. "During the year Marietta has improved in personal charm and character. She has a straight, graceful figure, a beautifully modelled face and a good deal of charm of manner. She gets on with everybody, especially with older men." The traits that worried her parents included a lack of perfect truthfulness, "a tendency to get by or around a proposition, especially a command she did not want to obey, and a lack of concentration." Though there are no further entries, Mrs. Peabody later pasted in school reports that pleased her, and saved a few letters sent in Marietta's infancy that praised the child's personality or behavior.

*The Mother's Record* is an extraordinary document. It prefigures much of Marietta's later personality with uncanny accuracy. One wonders if Mrs. Peabody ever looked back and realized the prescience of her observations. But, of course, the writing also reveals the writer. When a woman becomes a mother for the first time, she is often drawn back to thoughts of her own mother. It is noticeable in *The Mother's Record* how proud Mary Peabody was of her daughter's social success, particularly with men. Wasn't Mary sending out a message to her daughter that her flirtatiousness was to be encouraged?

And wasn't she also sending out mixed signals with regard to her daughter's physical beauty? Scarred by her plainness in comparison to her own mother's magnetism, Mary seemed not surprisingly both fascinated by and mistrustful of female attractiveness. In her English journal, she described sending Malcolm off to Cambridge in the company of one Corinne Smith, "who had a good chance to tell him all about herself. She is very attractive but you don't feel you can quite depend upon her." Yet, as we see in *The Mother's Record*, Mary was often encouraging her own little fair-haired charmer to use her attractiveness to advantage. This ambivalence was to prey upon Mary Peabody's psyche and affect her daughter in a way that would give both pleasure and grief as Marietta, blessed with increasing beauty, grew to adulthood.

# CHAPTER 3

# "I think
# I'm going to be a senator"

The Peabodys' move from Lawrence, Massachusetts, to suburban Philadelphia was a migration worthy of their dissenting ancestors. The dark satanic mills of the factory town were displaced by leafy, open avenues, lined with gracious stone and stucco mansions with long driveways and elegant gardens, hushed except for the sound of pruning shears and the occasional bluejay. The mixed working-class population of a northern industrial town was succeeded by a privileged, wealthy society, whose members had played together for a hundred years, many of them listed in a book little read in Lawrence called the *Social Register*. A number were bankers and lawyers, creators of private fortunes, the fabric of the eastern establishment. Boston met Philadelphia when the Peabodys arrived in Chestnut Hill, causing the traditional squaring off between the residents of these two great cities—the former seeing themselves as intellectually and morally superior, the latter believing their history and manners offered a better way of life.

While Mary Peabody objected to Malcolm's taking up a post that seemed so elitist compared to needy Lawrence, she also knew many Philadelphians, some of whom spent their summers in Northeast Harbor just as she did. (In fact, one of the reasons Malcolm was invited to St. Paul's was because so many of the parishioners had heard him preach at St. Jude's, in Seal Harbor, or St. Mary's-by-the-Sea in Northeast.) For Mary, the move was palliated by these old friends. Moreover, their new home was far more comfortable for her growing family than the one in Lawrence. (Her fourth son, Malcolm Junior, known as

Mike, was born in 1928.) Donated as a rectory by a rich parishioner, the house dated from 1867, and was built of fieldstone, with six bedrooms, generous servants' quarters with their own staircase, and a copper elm in the garden. A French nurse, two maids, and a cook were installed. For the Peabodys, this was luxury indeed.

Malcolm also took to the place. He inherited a vestry with a large staff, good church attendance, and a salary of $6,000 a year (with the rectory thrown in). Chestnut Hill was one of the richest parishes in Pennsylvania, with grand houses, parks, and an arboretum. The roster of old Philadelphia names—Pepper, Willing, Cheston, Lister, and Newbold—attended St. Paul's Episcopal Church, secure in the knowledge that they could afford not only the Sunday offertory plate but the very ground upon which their knees were bent in worship.

Malcolm was quick to take advantage of this blessing. The church had for many years been in dilapidated shape, and the vestry had been collecting funds for building repairs. With the new rector's encouragement, they voted to build a completely new church. Malcolm again exhibited one of his greatest skills as a clergyman—fund-raising. The affluent parishioners responded handsomely, and in no time they raised upwards of $300,000.[1] (This was accomplished between 1928 and 1929, propitiously timed to beat the stock market crash.) The building went forward, an ornate Gothic cathedral, with pews to hold over seven hundred worshippers, stained-glass windows, and a nave 116 feet long. As Malcolm proudly said, "The new Church turned out to be beautiful, and a great religious stimulus to the community."

For his daughter, the adjustment to Chestnut Hill had few spiritual benefits. Marietta was eight years old when the family moved, and those eight years had been spent in a world where people spoke in many accents, where neighbors had opened their doors to the rector's little daughter without shame or condescension. After initial difficulties in her public school in Lawrence, she had learned to love it and had made close friends.

Her first encounters in Chestnut Hill epitomized the nightmares of every new kid on the block. The school her parents chose for her was a so-called progressive school, Shady Hill Country Day School. It was coeducational, and promoted arts and crafts, the playing of musical instruments, and the study of Greek and Roman culture. The school did not give examinations, and there were no marks. Marietta did not respond well to this unstructured education. She got bored making clay houses simulating Roman villas (hers always collapsed), measuring the garden as an arithmetic exercise, and learning such useful French phrases as "Does your uncle like candied oranges?" Many parents also felt the same way and had their children transferred. Marietta stayed until the end, graduating in the ninth grade in 1931. The school has since closed down.

Worse than the curriculum, however, was the ferocious teasing she encountered because of her accent and her clothes. "I remember the first time I saw Marietta at Shady Hill," recalled Mary Isabel ("Mezzy") Voorhees (later Hickok). "She arrived a few days after school had started, which was not pleasant for her. She had on horn-rimmed glasses, her hair scraped back, and a skirt that didn't fit at all, hanging down at the back. 'Who is that?' I thought, relieved she was in a class below me." Many of the other girls felt the same way. "Oh, you Yankee!" they would shout at her, pointing fingers at her as though she were crazy.

These were children whose parents and grandparents had grown up together. They ate the same food, swam in the same pools, laughed at the same jokes, felt the same confidence in their Philadelphia background. Marietta was pretty, but she was tall for her age, she didn't look right, she was shy, she didn't speak the correct language, and she was a parson's daughter. So Marietta was mocked. "Hello, goody-goody," they would call out to her. "She's the minister's daughter, she's got to be good."

Shady Hill was particularly cliquish. Louise ("Weasel") McIlhenny (later Roberts) was a student there in Marietta's time, and remembers it as "a hideous experience. My father died suddenly while I was there and everyone began calling me an orphan. I had to run away and hide." Marietta, subjected daily to the jeers of her classmates, would turn purple with misery, the flush spreading from her neck up to her cheeks. She had blushed when Harvey Bundy kissed her, but this was different. This blushing, a habit that would remain with her throughout her life, stemmed from acute self-consciousness.

There was no sympathy from her brothers, even if she had considered asking for it. Endicott, George, and Sam had been too young to put down roots in Lawrence. They went to private elementary schools in Philadelphia and adjusted without difficulty. The fact that a fourth boy had been added to the sibling list only emphasized Marietta's sense of alienation. She suffered alone. She would go home from school every day in tears—tears that she hid from her family, of course, tears that were the inconsolable expression of the outsider.

Much later, musing on the statistic that American families move something like every four years, Marietta recalled the pain of her own uprooting and wondered how many American children felt deprived and discriminated against because of these relocations. "When I ask parents, 'How did your children take the move?' they always say, 'Fine, fine, they loved it,' " she said. "But I wonder if their children haven't masked their feelings from their parents, just as I did."

At home, the routine was familiar. Prayers were held every morning before breakfast in the living room. Malcolm would read the lesson, and the children would kneel and listen to the prayers, ending with the Lord's Prayer. Grace was said before every meal. Meals were spartan, Mrs. Peabody being of the school that promoted good nutrition rather than good eating. Orange juice and cod liver oil every morning before school, and few desserts. Since pocket money was equally spare, there was little opportunity to enjoy candy. Thanks to this deprivation, Marietta never outgrew a craving for chocolates.

Every Sunday was a hurdle. There was Sunday School, of course, and afterwards church, where their father would preach. He looked the part—tall, handsome, with chiseled features, an athletic figure, every inch the charismatic pastor. His appearance, however, belied his anxiety about "his big day," as Marietta remembered it later. "At lunch, he was so tense our mother implored us not to speak to him. One could feel his nerves twanging as he carved the roast beef." During Prohibition, when there was no liquor in the house, her father would drink several small glasses of a legal "sherry" containing alcohol, before leaving for church.

Despite these intimations of faiblesse, his daughter, like all ministers' children, saw Sunday as her father's finest hour. Just as Malcolm had watched his father, the Rector of Groton, proceed with heavy step and solemn visage through the rows of awed schoolboys in Groton Chapel, so Marietta in her turn watched as the Rector's son, now in his father's place, slowly paced down the aisle every Sunday. She saw Daddy, "in his white surplice and glittering raiment, singing Alleluia or something triumphant," bringing up the rear of the procession of choir, vergers, and celebrants, the congregation standing respectfully in front of their velvet-upholstered pews and lustily singing in praise of their Lord and Holy Father. Whose Father? God the Father? The Rector? Marietta's father? The image merged for an eight-year-old in a golden glow of worship.

Just as in Lawrence, every spring the family would go to Groton and stay with the Peabodys. Every summer they would go for two months to Northeast Harbor, where Malcolm and Mary Peabody (allowed, like most Episcopal ministers, two months off for summer vacation) built a house next to the Parkman cottage on Smallidge Point. Summers in Maine were fun for Marietta. Her parents were more relaxed in this small, unpretentious community, and discipline was muted. Malcolm in particular enjoyed these months. He would give his annual sermon at St. Jude's Episcopal in Seal Harbor (as did his father), and spend his days with his boat *Daffydill*. He was a passionate sailor, and would take part in the races every year with a competitiveness that shocked the members of the summer colony who expected the Episcopal minister to show at least some decorum behind the tiller. ("The worst word I ever heard him say was 'damn,' " said his son Endicott, "but he was such a fierce competitor people probably imagined worse.")

The Thanksgiving holidays were generally spent with Marietta's grandmother Parkman at 30 Commonwealth Avenue. Thirty-five or more family members would attend these rituals, with old Mrs. Parkman in stately splendor at the head of the table. White damask tablecloths, sparkling glass, gleaming silver, carved black walnut chairs, and horsehair sofas defined the children's memories of these awesome occasions, which were frequently tinged with tensions between Marietta's mother and the still beautiful, vivacious, and demanding matriarch of the Parkman family.[2]

Marietta had already spent a lot of time with her grandparents, who were a useful baby-sitting service for her excessively busy mother. As the oldest grandchild on both sides of the family, and as a girl, she was given special treatment, and her charm and liveliness beguiled the older set. On one occasion, when Marietta was staying with her Peabody grandparents, Bishop William Lawrence visited. In the presence of all the dinner guests, the bishop asked little Marietta, as adults so often ask children, what she wanted to be when she grew up. Marietta promptly replied, "I think I'm going to be a senator." "A senator of the United States?" "Yes." "And how are you going to become a senator?" "I'm going to be elected like everyone else." "And how are you going to manage all by yourself to be a senator?" "Well, I'll get the other boys to help me."

Marietta's mother recorded this exchange approvingly; Marietta's maternal grandmother, Mrs. Parkman, for her part recognized in this energetic, independent little person a reflection of herself. She showered attention on her pretty granddaughter, including those English clothes so poorly received at school. Much later, when Marietta wanted to go to a party instead of some boring event, Grandmother Parkman whispered to her, "Go ahead, I never did it and I regretted it." Like a permission slip from God, this support was one of the most powerfully enabling forces in Marietta's later life.

In 1984 there was a reunion of the Parker family in New Jersey attended by one hundred and thirty family members, including Marietta. During the after-dinner speeches, Marietta spoke about her grandmother with an exuberance and warmth that recaptured vividly the young girl's admiration for this extraordinary woman. "My grandmother was all charm, and genius, and delight, and spoildom, and she was the greatest grandmother anybody could possibly have!"

The Peabodys would spend most Easters with the Davisons in Locust Valley. By this time Marietta was collecting a lot of first cousins, who usually turned up at these affairs. Trubee and Dorothy Davison had four children, Minturn and Helen Sedgwick had three, and William and Rose Parsons had three. Her Parkman cousins were also multiplying at a rapid rate. She reckoned she had over one hundred second cousins by the time she was grown up.

At the Peabody gatherings, the Rector remained the dominant figure. "My father was a surgeon but he was never allowed to carve the Christmas turkey. It had to be a Peabody," remembers Rosie Parsons Lynch. All the grandchildren stood in fear of the Rector, although Marietta was much less afraid of the awesome patriarch of the family than were her little cousins. On one occasion, she was sent to the Rector by her parents to be "talked to" after some particularly wicked infraction of the rules. She went into his study and remained there for an unconscionably long time, so long in fact that her mother began to be worried. Finally, the door opened and there was Marietta in gales of laughter while the Rector of Groton, on all fours, roared like a lion.

But Groton represented one of the defining controls in Marietta's life. How furious she must have been so often on those hallowed grounds! Born a girl, she was forever disqualified from the privileges and pleasures accruing to the Groton males she saw all around her, and in particular the two older of her brothers, who were admired and awarded all the prizes that she, with her skills and energy, was rightfully owed. Like Vita Sackville-West, who was denied by her sex the inheritance of her beloved family home, Marietta was born to endure the injustice of a predominantly male world.

Her fearlessness and ambition separated her from her cousins at these annual family gatherings. Her first sin was that she was older than most of them, and thus frequently disqualified by age from much of the fun. While her cousins were playing goofy games in the garden, the *princesse lointaine* stared moodily out of the window. Occasionally she would join in (for instance, she taught her young cousin Penelope Griswold how to bleach her hair),[3] but these moments were rare. Marietta was too busy building an interior life that would protect her from criticism and give her freedom.

She read avidly. Her grandmother Parkman took her to movies, played music to her, pressed on her all sorts of books. Her grandmother Peabody taught her social graces, the pleasures to be found in people. Marietta learned social rules from the Peabodys, such as never to use the three "D" words in conversation: Death, Disease, or Domestics.

As Malcolm's family grew, the children's sense of parental deprivation increased. Both the Reverend and Mrs. Peabody spent their days in the parish, ministering, visiting, and generally looking after their large flock. Their children spent more and more time in the kitchen with the cook and maids. It was there they found the warmth and affection lacking in other parts of the rectory. "Endicott was the most thoughtful," Hannah Stapleton, the housemaid, recalled. "He wanted to make sure we got our nights off. Georgie was the playboy, always coming in with the latest jokes he had heard at school. Sam was quiet, serious. Marietta had such airs! She'd tell us wild stories about her rich friends and we used to tease her and tell her she'd never be like them.''

Sometimes parishioners came home to dinner, and Hannah would be the waitress in the rectory dining room. "Very plain, it was," she remembered. "Mrs. Peabody never cared about how the table looked, or if there were sprigs of parsley on the serving platter, like other Main Line hostesses." Marietta hated these penny-pinching affairs. "I can't bear the way my mother lives," she once burst out to Hannah. "When I get married, I'm going to have loads of servants and even if we only have spinach for dinner it will be served on a silver dish!"

This restiveness did not play well in Shady Hill Country Day School. While her early reports were good, cooperation from the first was "very poor." She was persistently careless in handing in work, untidy and undisciplined. How else was she to prove to her peers she was not a "goody-goody"? "Mary is a contradiction of courtesy and playful, childish willfulness," one year-end report read. "She has a weakness for pranks some years too young for her, and she is slow to obey; yet she is in the main a good sportsman about punishment. She doesn't yet meet issues squarely, but her direct word can be depended upon completely." (The Rector was no doubt gratified by this last reference.)

In the belief that bad behavior implied lack of challenge, the school attempted to control this wayward student by advancing her a grade at the end of her first year. Thus she joined Mezzy Voorhees's class, and in spite of Mezzy's initial doubt, they became close friends. Mezzy recognized Marietta's fierce intelligence. "She loved to argue with the teachers. I remember she used the word 'tremense' in an essay. 'There isn't such a word,' the teacher told her. 'I don't care, it's exactly the word I want, a combination of tremendous and immense. It's a wonderful word and one day it will be in the dictionary!' Well, the teacher was stunned!"

Skipping a grade did not improve Marietta's character in the eyes of the school. It merely allowed her to miss learning basic elements of mathematics such as fractions and decimals, as well as key Latin verbs, lacunae that would cost her dearly later. Meanwhile, she continued in her renegade ways, startling her teachers and delighting her friends.

Marietta's conflict with her background was aggravated by her father's intense focus on her school career. She felt very powerfully the burden of his expectations, which manifested themselves in the countless hours she spent in his study, bearing the brunt of his displeasure for what he saw as her inadequate scholastic performance. "He convinced me from the beginning of my school career that I was never trying hard enough," she recalled later. These talks would almost invariably end with Marietta in tears, promising to do better.

The Reverend Peabody was not concerned solely with her school work. The shadow of the Rector of Groton was never far from his side as he performed his paternal duties. Questions of Marietta's moral development received the most stringent scrutiny. On one occasion, when she was about twelve and starting to make friends in Philadelphia, her father discovered she had told a lie and said in retaliation she could not go away to stay with a new friend for the weekend.

"How am I going to explain this to my friend?" Marietta asked desperately.

"You must say that you have told a lie and therefore your father has prevented you from going away as a punishment."

This story, needless to say, was soon the talk of Chestnut Hill, and Marietta felt even more humiliated than ever.

Shady Hill's last report in the summer of 1931 conceded with regret, "Much of the time Mary has been uncooperative. . . . She has done things asked of her, but often so ungraciously as to lose most of the effect; even when they have been done rather well. In preparations she leans upon other members of the class and loses, through laziness, much of the value of the work she does."

There were compensations, however. She was given the leading part of Yum-Yum in the school production of *The Mikado,* to rave reviews, thereby encouraging her love of theater. Two other themes filter through the Shady Hill years. One is the obbligato note of Marietta's dependence on other people to help her do her work effectively. In other words, she never hesitated to ask for advice from teachers or peers. The other reflects Marietta's interest in the world outside the walls of Shady Hill. In the fall of 1930, after the usual comments about her mistakes in punctuation, her English teacher wrote: "She did a nice piece of work on Roosevelt."

In 1931 Roosevelt began his journey toward the presidency of the United States, and Marietta, aged fourteen, went away to boarding school.

# CHAPTER *4*

# *"Thine adorable Marietta"*

For some fourteen-year-olds, leaving home is a painful transition. For Marietta, boarding school was the signal to hurtle out of the starting gate and never look back. What, after all, was she leaving behind?

Philadelphia, historic city though it was, taught her less about democratic principles than about their erosion by the accumulation of wealth. She had seen a certain amount of luxury in the life of her Parkman grandmother, who had a fine house and maids and big cars and took trips to Europe. But her friends in Chestnut Hill came from some of the richest families in America. They arrived at school in Rolls-Royces, with chauffeurs to drive them and French Mademoiselles to chaperone them. Their houses were filled with antiques and Old Master paintings, their tennis courts were rolled daily, and their swimming pools were large and well heated. Marietta's life in the rectory paled before such lavishness.

Her father was an Episcopal minister, therefore excluded from complete acceptance among Philadelphia male society. Mrs. Trollope, mother of the English novelist, once described the strange position the clergy held in society, as being neither aristocratic nor common, but not quite "belonging."[1] While the Reverend Peabody might be among the male company offered port and cigars after the ladies had retired from the dinner table, we may be sure the conversation was more dignified than if the minister had not been present, leaving the faintest residue of resentment.

If Marietta's father was "different," so was her mother. Mrs. Peabody toiled like an unpaid social worker, tirelessly agitating on behalf of the poorer members of the parish. She didn't wear lipstick and designer clothes, or smoke or drink martinis or play golf like everyone else's mother. People felt sorry for the rector's wife. As Marietta later became more popular in Chestnut Hill, particularly with the boys, her friends invited her to their houses for tennis or swimming or dinner parties. The invitations were rarely, if ever, reciprocated.

Life with her siblings was equally unsatisfactory. She was closest to her oldest brother Endicott, who after a slow start became a football hero at Groton and Harvard. Yet her brothers were not only younger in age than their precocious sister but, more important, younger in social development as well, and she found it difficult to endure their silly boyish pranks, many of which she felt were maliciously directed against her. (She was not always wrong. Marietta's friends later recalled what beasts her little brothers could be.) As the eldest, she believed she was always on the line in matters of behavior. Like many firstborns, she experienced the burden of being the icebreaker, and was convinced that her parents' disciplinary measures became more and more relaxed with each child. Or was it that she was really morally weaker than they were? Deep down, she could never be sure.

Moral weakness, for Marietta, to a very large extent meant boys. She had been a magnet for the opposite sex from the very beginning. She had watched her grandmother Parkman's seductive ways at 30 Commonwealth Avenue, learning at the feet of a master. Marietta had always looked older than her age, and since she had skipped a grade at Shady Hill, was accustomed to having friends older than herself. In Philadelphia, she attended parties and dances where she was frequently the youngest girl present, though few would have known it.

Incidents of rebellion accumulated as Marietta grew older. She was given strict injunctions about dress and behavior when she went out to visit friends' houses, and uninfringeable curfew hours. But as soon as she left the rectory she put on lipstick and silk stockings and kicked up her heels. On one occasion, when she was at a party at a neighbor's house and did not come home at the allotted time, her father put on his raincoat over his pajamas, went over to the house, took her by the hand, and led her home.

Temptation was strongest when she was away from Chestnut Hill, in particular during the visits to her Peabody grandparents. For the Peabody grandparents meant Groton, and Groton meant boys—hundreds of them. Visiting Groton for Marietta was an exercise in attraction bordering on a new biological science. Here is Mrs. James Lawrence (wife of one of the founding Groton trustees) reporting to Mrs. Parkman in June 1931: "The great excitement at Groton is Marietta. The whole 6th form tags after her wherever she goes, and somebody gave her a present of some money with which she has got a permanent wave!"

Of course her grandparents were extremely strict. Not only was she not supposed to talk to the students, but the Rector instructed her that she was not to *touch* any of them. However, she appeared every day for meals, to be harvested mentally by one hundred and eighty pairs of admiring eyes, and those lucky enough to be invited to the headmaster's table on the dais might exchange a blushing, mumbling word or two. Boys would attempt to waylay her on campus, walking to Chapel, anything. "She was the honeypot of the whole school," recalled her early admirer, Groton alumnus Harvey Bundy. Marietta responded whenever she could. "I knew the name, including the middle name, of all the boys in the school," she said later. "I knew about their marks, their general character, and I was in love with every one of them at the same time."

Thus Marietta, like a fledgling bird, hovered at the edge of the nest. Going away to boarding school released those straining wings, pinioned so securely to her sides by her parents.

Marietta's four Peabody aunts had all attended St. Timothy's, a small, exclusive girl's educational establishment in Catonsville, Maryland, founded by two Virginia spinsters in 1882. Considered by many to be the female Groton, the school motto was *Verité sans peur,* a saying that the Rector himself might have invented. During Marietta's time, the school consisted of eighty-four girls, drawn from all over the United States, placed under the iron rule of their southern headmistress, Miss Louisa Fowler.

From the first, Marietta loved St. Tim's. Her first letters home explode with energy and excitement. "Here I am and none of the hazing has begun yet. I'm scared to death!! As a matter of fact all the older girls know boys at Groton, so they are very nice to me and ask me questions about Tom, Dick and Harry. . . ."

The fact that Groton is mentioned so early reflects how powerful this weapon was in Marietta's social arsenal. She was merely following a family tradition, as she found out later when she came upon an old issue of the school yearbook *Tit Bits*. In it, Dorothy Peabody, Marietta's aunt, was listed as being admired for her pigtail, and under the heading, "Ambition," her niece read, "to be at Groton with the boys." Word had reached St. Timothy's almost immediately of Marietta's Groton connection. Indeed, one of her roommates announced that she had been told to beware of Marietta, that she was "terribly, terribly wild!!" The hazing or initiation procedure that Marietta refers to with such trepidation required her to dress up in a costume consisting of pajamas, garters, towels, mittens, and high-heeled shoes, and write a 500-word essay on "Rhubarb, or why I am popular with the boys at Groton."

This was all very well for Marietta's popularity stakes. What is less certain is how her parents received these snippets of information that their daughter so enthusiastically relayed to them. "It sounds as if I were talking of Groton all the time but I've mentioned it about three times!" she assured them. Meanwhile, she reported on friendships, trials for the hockey and basketball teams, and the continual struggle over discipline with a lighthearted tone that did not admit remorse.

"Last night, Lydia Sherwood and I had to go to bed right after supper because we had seven black marks apiece. We were the worst in the school! At least we were honest, loads of new girls didn't report on their misdoings."

In fact, Marietta's black marks were not unexpected in a school run on very strict lines, even by the standards of the day. (To her credit, Mrs. Peabody thought St. Timothy's "horribly old-fashioned, and their persnickety little ideas on behavior are most irritating.") The girls had to speak French all day except for meals and recreation time. They could not talk in the halls or classrooms. They could only walk in certain parts of the school grounds. They were not allowed to kiss each other. If a girl kissed another girl, she had to report it in a ceremony called "Kissing Cross." Any letters the girls sent to boys had to be placed, unsealed, in a drawer where Miss Fowler might read them first. (One of Marietta's friends, Alice Spaulding [later Paolozzi], devised the ruse of writing a letter to a boy and forwarding it to her mother to send. She was found out and suspended.)

In the beginning these rules did not bother Marietta. Unlike many of her rich, spoiled friends, she had been brought up with a clear understanding of humility and obedience. Indeed, her work habits and self-discipline were a cause of astonishment and admiration to her classmates. She was happy to wear a uniform, recognizing it as a great boon for someone "poor," as she saw herself in comparison with her friends. She understood the practical purpose of speaking French, albeit with an atrocious St. Timothy's accent. And the restrictions on correspondence relieved her of what she saw as a burdensome duty. Boys wrote to her in an endless stream during her boarding school years, and as she was not confident about her letter-writing skills, Miss Fowler's censorship gave her a perfect excuse not to respond.

Marietta plunged into her work with energy, and her first term reports show marks in the 70s, 80s, and 90s for all subjects except Latin and French (thanks to Shady Hill's erratic coaching). But her greatest success, apart from her reputation as "Groton's girlfriend," came on the playing field. She had been brought up to be athletic. Her Peabody grandfather and both her parents believed in sports of all kinds for both sexes. Her mother also provided a striking example of physical fitness, maintaining a strenuous regime throughout her life,

Captain of the Brownie Basketball team, St. Timothy's
School, Catonsville, Maryland, 1934.

leading her children and grandchildren up the mountains and into the
freezing water of Northeast Harbor long after they begged for respite.

In Philadelphia, Marietta played hockey, tennis, and basketball,
rode horses, and was a strong swimmer, while many of her more
pampered schoolmates had had little exposure to any kind of athleti-
cism. Her height only added to her prowess. The arrival of this young
Amazon at St. Timothy's galvanized the school's sporting program,
which was divided into two teams, "Brownies" and "Spiders." In her
first year, she made all the athletic teams as a Brownie, an astonishing
feat for a freshman, and a confidence builder that was worth more
than all the money on the Main Line at this time in her life.

By her second year at St. Tim's, she was a lead player on the hockey and basketball teams, and had made wonderful friends, in particular Edith Derby (later Williams); her cousin Mary Brewster ("Bootsie") Derby (later Morris); and Alice Spaulding. At the end of the summer term in 1932, Miss Fowler wrote to Marietta's grandmother at Groton that she felt "no young girl in the school improved more in thoughtfulness and consideration than did your own granddaughter." Showing characteristic caution, the headmistress added: "I hope the summer will not undo what I feel the school year has done. That is so very apt to be the case with children who have the kind of summer life that Marietta has at Northeast."

Northeast Harbor as a corrupting influence? Its residents would laugh at such an idea. Yet in truth, as far as Marietta went, Miss Fowler was not far wrong. Marietta's summers were filled with sailing, swimming, and twice-a-week dances, each year encountering the same boys who were, like her, growing older and more sophisticated by the minute. At these dances, socially correct parents would beg their sons to dance with the less popular girls. No boy ever had to be asked to dance with Marietta. Like most of her friends, she appeared in the annual summer vaudeville show at the Neighborhood House in Northeast Harbor, performing in some amusing musical skit such as "The Floradora Sextet." Another regular summer friend, Patricia ("Trishy") Grant (later Scull), remembered Marietta giving the first party Patricia had ever been to with boys present. "She wore black silk narrow pants (none of us wore pants at that time), and a white satin top. And there were *boys!* We can't have been more than fourteen."

While Marietta tried out coeducation in Northeast Harbor, it was Bar Harbor that beckoned. Most of the best parties were in Bar Harbor, where many of the richest families in the United States had built their vacation houses. Bar Harbor, a twenty-minute drive from Northeast, was considered a den of iniquity to the more austere folks summering in the smaller town to the west, and Marietta's parents were not pleased by her constant nighttime visits there. On one occasion, having promised to be back by curfew time ("Like Cinderella, she'd look at her watch and gasp that she had to be home," her friend Susan Mary Jay [later Alsop] remembered), she dashed back with her beau in his car to Northeast Harbor, only to find both her parents silhouetted in the door, waiting for her. "Never again," they told her in furious tones, as the poor young man tried to make himself invisible.

Besides Susan Mary Jay, whose parents summered there, two other friends opened doors to unimaginable material delights. One was Pauline Palmer, her St. Tim's classmate, who belonged to a wealthy and distinguished family from Chicago. Pauline's father, Potter Palmer II, was president of the Art Institute of Chicago, and their

Bar Harbor "cottage," Hare Forest, was one of the great summer mansions of the Gilded Age. (It burned down in the Bar Harbor fire of 1947.) Marietta's other favorite playmate was Peggy Dorrance, whose family fortune came from Campbell Soup. The Dorrance "cottage," called Kenarden Lodge, was so big that it had its own electric generator. (Kenarden was demolished in 1960.) No other house in Northeast Harbor came close to these palaces in size and luxury. The lavish entertaining and seductive leisure life of these families made the austere habits of the Peabodys' summer circle look drab and dull by comparison, and Marietta was drawn to the livelier resort like a sunflower finding the light. Somewhere in Baltimore, Miss Fowler read the tea leaves, shook her head, and sighed.

In 1932, when Marietta turned fifteen, she began to chafe at the restrictions of boarding school, especially after those long, freedom-filled summers. Remarks about the amount of time spent going to church abound. "School gets so ghastly on the Sabbath," she reported blithely. "I nearly pass out with all the church." She began using the tone of ironic resignation in her letters home. The school was referred to as "St. Timothy's the Chaste" or "the hen-coop." She described her team going off to a basketball game against Bryn Mawr: "We all donned our little blue uniforms and looked very s.s. and g. [sweet, simple and girlish]." Another letter explains, "Nothing very exciting happened this week except on Tuesday I got twelve beautiful red roses from some dumbell [sic] at Groton. . . ."

The younger girls at St. Tim's adored her. "She would *defy* Miss Fowler," remembered Minnette Hunsiker (later Cummings), who was two years Marietta's junior. The younger student still had awe in her voice as she spoke of the St. Tim's legend. "She didn't walk, she strode," Mrs. Cummings said.

It probably did not surprise the Reverend and Mrs. Peabody to receive a long letter from Miss Fowler in November 1932, ostensibly to explain a large bill from the school for books, the hairdresser, laundry service, and the infirmary. But after justifying these charges, Miss Fowler took the opportunity to tell Marietta's parents that while their daughter had made progress, "she continues to express herself very often in an irresponsible and exaggerated way. It is a serious fault that I am endeavoring to help her to realize and break, and she is responding." In less optimistic vein than her earlier letter to Fannie Peabody, Miss Fowler went on, "There is excellent material there to develop, and I trust that I am going to be able to do my part towards developing Marietta into the strong, true woman that I feel sure she can be."

By 1933, Miss Fowler's trust in her material began to unravel. There was the surprise arrival at St. Timothy's in the spring of 1933 of two Groton boys, Harvey Bundy and John ("Satan") Drayton, who had driven over in an open car to Catonsville on the off chance of getting to see Marietta—something simply not allowed within the hallowed halls of St. Tim's.[2]

When Marietta was invited to dances both at Groton and St. Paul's over Easter, Miss Fowler remained "stony" and refused to let her headstrong charge leave the school, even after one Groton boy wrote begging for mercy. However, Miss Fowler caved in when it was a question of the Groton Reunion on June 1. "It is a duty as a member of the Peabody family to go," she said self-righteously.

Then there were all the invitations from schoolmates such as Edith, Alice, and Bootsie, girls high up in the social swim, with whom Marietta had become very popular. (Edith Derby's mother was Theodore Roosevelt's daughter, Ethel, and Marietta, a Groton child like Ethel's brothers and cousins, was taken to tea with Mrs. Roosevelt, getting along with her wonderfully.) Marietta was known as "Peapod," or "Peabo." She was fun, she was lively, she loved playing pranks, and they thought of her far more urbane and sophisticated than they were. "When we had our photographs taken, she wore a black velvet dress with a V-neck. I was so impressed." Bootsie remembered. "She was our leader," agreed another roommate. Leslie ("Coupie") Hadden (later Kernan).

Although Marietta's career at St. Timothy's seemed to have been dominated by academic woes, athletic success, and boys, the young girl who had declared her intention to be a U.S. senator had lost none of her interest in politics. Every week she rushed to the faculty room where the one copy of *Time* magazine was kept (no newspapers were allowed), and devoured it, cover to cover. She was one of the only girls in the school who did this, and she never missed an issue. She followed her uncle Henry Parkman's political career with the keenest interest, pasting news of his campaigns in her scrapbook.

"I'm getting so het up about politics and economics, etc., that everybody is very amused," she wrote. In her last term, when Class Five performed their Groton skit about her, they also predicted her future, which they saw as no less than First Lady of the land, making speeches and, as they put it, "defending the Roosevelts."

Marietta a Democrat? Not yet, however, to the Peabodys' relief. During the 1932 election, Marietta had supported Herbert Hoover over Franklin D. Roosevelt, like the rest of the family. She was an energetic supporter, and spoke with fervor on Hoover's behalf at a school debate during the presidential campaign. Groton in general was horrified that Roosevelt won the election, and none more so than the Rector, in spite of the fact that Roosevelt was an alumnus. Nobody even expected the Rector to invite Frank (as FDR was called) to the

Groton fiftieth anniversary in 1934, but he did. Nor did the Rector's political convictions prevent him from accepting the invitation of the new president to officiate at the inauguration in January 1933. (The Rector later supported FDR and the New Deal.) The whole family went to Washington for the event. Marietta was allowed to take her friend Bootsie Derby to attend the ceremony. They stayed in the Lewis Douglas house in Georgetown, and went to a reception at the White House the evening before, the high point of which, for the two girls, was the fact that the entire sixth form of Groton was present.

Social life intensified. By Christmas 1933, her letters home are filled with requests to go to dances, theater, parties, dinners, lunches, coming-out parties, dances at the White House for President Roosevelt's sons. "He is going to come down and pour a bottle of brandy in the punch, and it will all be very ceremonial and funny." Her excitement is infectious, as she writes of her wonderful plans, signing herself "thine adorable Marietta." "Oh, by the way, I just wanted to give you full warning—Harvey Bundy might come and stay with us . . . I don't think the McIlhennys will mind an extra man do you?"

She began to flunk exams. Intermingled with the descriptions of parties are apologies about forthcoming school reports, and warnings to prepare for ever more dire exam results. Mostly, the tone of her letters is a mixture of abjectness and defiance. In one, she assumes that she will be disowned and forcibly ejected from house and home. "Please don't!" When she flunks English, she blames a teacher. "She thinks she's pretty hot but is only an overgrown child! And that's that!" A note of desperate irony creeps in. "I am getting worse by the hour in my studies which is another joyful little item I have to confront you with. I probably will fail every exam, so don't be at all surprised if I appear in the old hometown some sunny day."

By early 1934, her spirits sank to the lowest ebb in all her years at school. Gone was the effervescence of "adorable" Marietta. "Dear Mother and Daddy, I just failed another exam—and I want to give up graduating. I'm so depressed, because all I do is work and work and work, and where does it get me? I'm so mad I can't see. I never have any time to do anything else but study and I still get the same marks."

While these self-flagellating moods are characteristic of most adolescent girls of sixteen or so, the ongoing disapproval emanating from the rectory and from the school authorities compounded Marietta's constant sense of insecurity. Even her social successes left her doubtful. One summer night in Northeast Harbor, Susan Mary Jay was with Marietta, "combing our frizzy hair side by side before the mirror preparatory to stepping out on the ballroom floor of the Bar Harbor Club, when she said, 'The smell of stale face powder in this ladies' room is the smell of fear.' " Marietta knew she attracted boys of Groton, but part of her felt that this was because they felt obliged to be friendly to her because she was the headmaster's granddaughter.

Her height, which proved so invaluable on the basketball court, began to be embarrassing in a social context. Thirty years later, when she was being interviewed for an anthology entitled *When I Was Sixteen,* Marietta used the word "despair" to describe her state of mind as a teenager. "I was five foot ten by the time I was fourteen," she recalled. "That's very painful. I remember my father used to imitate me on the dance floor. He would waltz around—to the laughter of my mother and my four younger brothers—with his shoulders all tucked in and his head at an odd angle."[3] She dreaded dancing "cheek to cheek," which for her meant hunching down with her bottom sticking out in hopes of diminishing her height. The attempt failed, of course. She simply looked absurd, and she knew it. Her father's cruel mimicking only accentuated her shame and frustration.

In addition to this disadvantage, as she saw it then, she developed skin trouble that disfigured her complexion, a problem about which one's mother might be expected to show concern, or at least sympathy. However, it fell to Miss Fowler to bring Mrs. Peabody's unworldly attention to her daughter's plight. The headmistress called Marietta into her office and told her rather tactlessly that several people had remarked on the girl's terrible skin and that Marietta must see a dermatologist. Marietta pleaded with her parents to let her go to the doctor. "I will pay for it myself after telling him that you are a minister—as that will bring down prices. But please just give me permission." The skin doctor recommended twelve X-ray treatments. Somehow the money was found, and Marietta saw at least some improvement.

As her concern over the payment to the dermatologist indicated, Marietta was increasingly confronted with a limitation made apparent after the move to Chestnut Hill. Her letters home are peppered with frantic requests for cash to pay for supplies, clothes, parties, food, and theater—sums that seem pitifully small today, but that evidently made severe inroads on the rector's family budget. Careful accounts were kept by her father, his letters frequently enclosing phone bills and queries about money unanswered for. "It is a good plan early in life to get the hang of how to keep expenses down," he told his irresponsible daughter. As she grew older and her invitations to parties and weekends multiplied, the money issue became enormous. There was to be no respite from this quarter.

During her senior year, Marietta landed the part of Tony Lumpkin in a production of Goldsmith's *She Stoops to Conquer.* Owing to her sinking school reports, however, Miss Fowler told her she must withdraw and concentrate on her studies. Marietta's bitter disappointment was alleviated by the news that she had been elected Brownie captain

of the basketball team, the most prestigious title a student at St. Timothy's could achieve. This pleased her parents greatly, but for her even
this triumph was tainted and she urged them not to tell anyone. Ever
conscious of her effect on the world, she was terrified of being typecast
as "the great athletic type."

After the Easter holidays, an incident occurred that put Marietta
in even more trouble than usual. Traveling in the same train returning
to Baltimore with Marietta and her school friends was Jimmy Durante,
the comedian and film star famous for his large nose. He took a shine
to the young ladies, and regaled them with songs and jokes in their
private car, to the agony of the chaperoning teachers, who were
"frothing at the mouth," as Marietta put it. At Wilmington, when
Durante alighted, Marietta jumped off too for a last-minute exchange
with the famous star, knowing full well that to leave the girls' special
car under such circumstances was strictly forbidden.

A month later, in spite of her bad conduct, the power of the
Peabody name again prevailed and she was allowed to go to the Groton Reunion (again with Grannie Peabody's financial aid). This time
she was more than ever aware of disapproval over her reputation.
"Grannie doesn't think it would be bad to go Friday and Saturday to
Groton," she tells her parents carefully. "I know darn well it would
invoke a *lot* of criticism among many who criticize—but I will be brave
and go Saturday too—*but* I will stay at Ma's [her Boston grand-
mother] as this might lessen the talk above."

Some hope. During her last term, St. Timothy's held its traditional theatrical skit night, at which Class Five took off Class Six. "All
the girl did who took me off was to wiggle around when she walked
and laugh in this atrocious manner and do the hula-hula and sing
torch-songs . . . and everybody in the audience shrieked, 'Marietta!'—
whereupon the girl said, 'Groton is my middle name. And I do drive
those boys insane.' She was really terribly good, though," Marietta
added contentedly.

The St. Timothy's yearbook for 1934 shows a glamorous photograph of Marietta looking soulful in an off-the-shoulder dress. Her list
of accomplishments runs to twenty-five entries, including students'
and attendance prizes as well as the many athletic awards. The two
quotations chosen to run alongside the parting description of "Merry
Marietta" are "tameless, swift and proud" (Shelley), and "That way
madness lies" (Shakespeare). Amid the schoolgirlish prose teasing
Marietta for her enormous number of relations and her tendency to
sing in a "squeaky and melodramatic soprano voice," there is a revealing reference to her only weak point: "Our heroine has really a most
genial sense of humor—but when it comes to getting jokes, alas! She
sits in our midst, and, as an unsteady smile wavers on the distinguished

Peabody mouth, we get the distress signal. Poor girl, the point is lost to her for ever." Marietta's own contribution to the yearbook, as, like all the girls, she states her ambition, is "to travel abroad."

"Tameless, swift and proud," Marietta was now seventeen years old and about to be launched on society. Most of her friends were "coming out," which meant an endless round of debutante parties laid on at great expense by their rich and doting parents. Marietta, like the thousands of young girls who tumbled out of the pens of boarding school into the fenceless fields of freedom, saw a future bathed in an aura of invitations, red roses, dancing, and champagne. She kept firmly at bay the question of whether this was appropriate for the daughter of a minister, a granddaughter of the Rector of Groton, or, most important of all, a Peabody.

# CHAPTER 5

# *"Maria Endicotti Peabodelli"*

In 1934, when she graduated from boarding school, Marietta was seventeen, a year younger than many of her class. Most of her friends were revving up for a year of debutante parties, in preparation for their assured future of romance, love, and marriage. College was not part of the picture. These were women of a class and generation where higher education was not a requirement. Like the hoard of gold that protected Wotan's sister-in-law, Freia, from the two greedy giants, family money shielded these girls from the grim realities of a country deep in the Great Depression, and preserved them from the necessity of working for a living.

Although Marietta readily attracted admirers, she lacked the inbred assurance of these children of Old Philadelphia, Boston, and New York. In spite of her success with boys, the negative signals she received at home canceled out much of her hard-won confidence. Her parents and brothers made sure that the spotlight lingered only sparingly on her fair curls. Family finances limited her. Her panic about becoming an old maid was overshadowed by her anxiety about her ability to cope with a "season." Friends had told her that the girls who came out when they were older had a much better time. "I was too insecure," she said later, "to float myself on an uneager world."

Edith Derby was going with her parents to Italy for the school year after graduation. Marietta's Boston friend Margaret ("Marnie") Hallowell was going to a French traveling school. Others were also doing modest versions of the Grand Tour abroad. Why didn't Marietta do the same? Of course the Peabodys could not afford the kind of travel enjoyed by her richer friends, but there was a well-known finishing school in Florence where she might study—and be well chaperoned in the process. Marietta was enthusiastic. Marked by her modest exposure to politics, she was consumed by curiosity about the world outside the Main Line. Italy was the promise of another country, another horizon.

"Will you have printed in the social news of the *Ledger-Bulletin* and *Inquirer* the fact that I'm going to school abroad next year and coming out the next?" she asked her parents, "because I'm receiving one invite after another to people's dances this spring whom I don't know. . . . Also, people will think I'm coming out this year and won't invite me next year."

Her parents were delighted to comply, all the more so since after much groaning about the cost, Marietta's aunt Dorothy Davison paid for the major portion of the trip, helped as usual by her two grandmothers. The idea of their incorrigible daughter being removed from the dangers of a debutante season for even a year represented a welcome reprieve for Malcolm and Mary Peabody. La Petite Ecole Florentine was a well-recommended institution, run by a Mademoiselle de Jevenois, a Belgian version of Miss Fowler. Marietta would be in splendid hands.

"This is the time when the Brook and River meet," Marietta's Peabody grandmother wrote to her when she graduated from St. Timothy's in June 1934. ". . . So up and at it, dearie. Use your willpower, and forge good habits. They stand one in good stead."

After the Groton Fiftieth Reunion, and a summer in Northeast Harbor where she saw many of her old friends and embarked on several new romances, Marietta set sail for Italy on the SS *Saturnia*. On the dock to say good-bye were her parents and brothers, and a group of stricken male admirers, including one from Northeast Harbor, Minot Milliken, who said later, "Marietta was my first best girl." Mrs. Peabody was uncharacteristically overcome with emotion at the departure of her only daughter. Marietta found this display so unexpected that she may have doubted its sincerity, for she later mimicked to her friends the tears trickling down her mother's cheeks.

Marietta was accompanied on board by Winifred (known as Peggy) Seyburn from Detroit and Louise Stevens from Boston, who were also going to La Petite Ecole Florentine. After much partying and sad farewells in New York, the ship sailed north to Boston, where Marietta's grandmother, Mrs. Parkman, and her uncle Harry greeted her with gifts and candies for the trip. More boys were on the dock to wish her good-bye, and her friend Bootsie Derby joined the ship for the journey to Europe. The ensuing party in Marietta and Bootsie's

stateroom, enhanced by champagne and Mrs. Parkman's marrons gla-
cés, went on until two in the morning.

The ship was a lot of fun. The girls had breakfast in bed, played
games, swam, and stayed up late, to the annoyance of their chaperone.
Marietta worked her famous charms on the captain of the ship, who
sent champagne to their cabin. Walter Lippmann and his wife were on
board. Malcolm Peabody, a Harvard friend of Lippmann's, had asked
the distinguished journalist if he would keep an eye on his daughter
during the voyage, so the Lippmanns occasionally invited her to their
table for meals with their traveling companions, the Hamilton Fish
Armstrongs. Even innocent Marietta sensed the tension seething between these two couples over the dinner table. Not long after, Mr.
Lippmann and Mrs. Armstrong left their spouses for each other in a
scandalous double divorce.

When the ship landed at Lisbon, the girls disembarked, and when
they returned, they found a new group of passengers. Only Marietta's
own words could do them justice: "On our return to the boat we
found about 12 Portuguese boys had got on board who were sent to
Italy to study Fascism by the government. Well, they were very attractive and terribly nice, but they only spoke French or Portuguese so you
can imagine my amazement to find myself speaking French because I
wanted to!" Marietta and her friends saw a great deal of these boys,
who taught them the principles of Fascism. "Made us ardent converts
—gave us Portuguese Fascist pins—a picture of their 'chef' and now
we give the Fascist salute gravely and freely to all." She adds with a
typical flourish: "they are coming to see us in Florence as we hadn't
quite finished explaining the N.R.A. [National Recovery Act] to
them!"

After stops in Gibraltar and Algiers, on Friday, October 5, 1934,
they arrived in Naples, the boat's final destination. Bootsie had a champagne birthday party the night before, which meant they all felt rather
fragile on landing, and even worse slogging through customs with
fifty-six pieces of hand luggage before boarding the train for Florence.

The shock on arrival at the school was immediate. La Petite Ecole
Florentine might as well have been a prison. The windows were barred;
the garden was the size of a postage stamp, surrounded by a high wall.
But worst of all, for the duration of her time there Marietta would be
attended day and night by women who were ostensibly chaperones,
but who seemed more like jailers. She was hit by a wave of homesickness, and wept openly upon saying good-bye to their chaperone. "I
can't stick it out for eight months!" she cried.

The family in Chestnut Hill apparently missed her almost as much
as she missed them. Both parents sent her letters with news of the
Groton and Harvard football seasons, and they relayed the successes

of her brothers, particularly on the playing field. Grandmother Parkman wrote to her about her son Harry's latest troubles on the political front (nearly losing his seat when the "unspeakable Curley" was elected governor of Massachusetts).

More painful still for Marietta were the letters from her friends, describing the wonderful dances and parties going on that autumn in New York, Philadelphia, and Boston: "Last week after six straight nights of 4 a.m. I folded" . . . "The Roosevelts are giving Babe [Barbara] Cushing a dance December 29th in the White House—A special train is going to take everyone down to Washington" . . . "God this debutante racket is the most wonderful thing. . . . Pea, we all look like wrecks. . . . There are 3 parties every weekend. . . ."

They urged her to come home and make everything more fun, they made jokes about Mussolini falling for girls with green eyes, they said if she were going to be at a party, "everyone would flock to be there." The picture these letters paint of what Marietta was missing would have horrified Mrs. Peabody—the champagne, the cigarettes, the pranks, the news of engagements made and broken, the analysis of New York versus Boston debs—the judgment coming down hard on the New Yorkers, who didn't understand the art of "a little good clean fun" nearly as much as the Boston ones, perhaps because of "our proximity to those wonderfully crazy Cambridge youths. . . ."

The "crazy Cambridge youths" were mostly Groton graduates now at Harvard, with others at Yale and Princeton, who squired these young women to the various dinners and dances, and who wrote to Marietta in Italy expressing various forms of devotion in the clumsy language of undergraduate yearnings.

These breathless reports contrasted cruelly with the routine of La Petite Ecole. Weekdays were filled with French and Italian lessons, history of art and French civilization courses, with art walks through the city of Florence and surrounding areas. Though Marietta genuinely loved visiting the churches and museums, she felt deeply depressed by the lack of freedom imposed upon her by the school authorities. She was not allowed to receive telephone calls from anyone, nor speak to anyone without first obtaining permission from Mademoiselle.[1] She could not go out alone or visit friends without permission. The chaperones were her only outside contacts, their constant presence making her tongue-tied and self-conscious in public. ("I thought the point of this school . . . was to give you a certain amount of poise, not to take away the small amount you have got.")

In those early weeks, the only respite came unexpectedly in the form of a visit from the Portuguese Fascists the girls had met on board ship. It turned out that these boys came from aristocratic families with ancient Portuguese titles, and had been invited by Mussolini himself to come to Italy. Impressed, Mademoiselle relaxed her rules and allowed the young counts to pay a call on the American girls. Marietta was much cheered by this occasion, finding it particularly amusing that she had thought the boys' constant respectful references to their "chef" meant their cook rather than the dictator. "They were our last link with our former life," she wrote sadly after they departed. "And now they're gone—all hope is lost."

Marietta was becalmed as the time dragged on at La Petite Ecole. Much of her free time was spent in composing long and detailed letters home, which, as her parents pointed out, served instead of a diary. They express most vividly Marietta's inquiring, ironic, outspoken personality.

> In the evening, this very nice man [the mayor of Florence] came to explain Italy and Fascism to us. He said how terrible the Great War was and all his friends killed etc.etc.etc., and how Italy hated war. So I (in my worst French) asked him why there were pictures in all the streets of the glories of the battlefield (where there are) to spur on romantic ideas in the minds of youth and everybody else; and why did a man's military training begin at 8 and last until 33—and why was it you saw about 2 men in civilian dress as you walked the streets—and why at the slightest murmur did Mussolini order troops up to the Austrian border? He said that this was just to encourage people to defend their country. Then I said that it seemed unnecessary to encourage the first instinct of man—self-preservation—to such a great extent. He then began to quibble and talked about our relations with the Japanese; and became quite mad with me. . . . The teachers were quite horrified by me and one of them said to me afterwards, "Of course nobody really likes war—but men have to fight—and there's nothing we can do about it." This woman is a very intelligent specimen of the upper class too!!! At that I began foaming at the mouth and such French as there was that issued was most incoherent. . . .

Marietta was learning a lesson that she never forgot. "You have no idea how a knowledge of politics and personalities helps you," she told her parents. "You realize this more and more when you want to talk to people with whom you've got nothing in common. Of course all Europeans are so much more 'up' on politics than the average American that it is really fascinating to get all their different ideas . . ." These words could be Marietta's fifty years later, explaining the magic of her famous dinner parties.

One afternoon she saw Mussolini at a ceremony celebrating the Fascist dead. As she watched ten thousand Italians giving the Fascist salute and Mussolini smiling and waving, Marietta admitted that she herself was carried away. "You could *feel* his personality without him speaking. It's the most tremendous experience, seeing a *strong* character like that!"

(Although in 1934 Mussolini was still to commit his worst crimes, her mother with remarkable prescience quickly squelched this girlish fascination: "He certainly is a strong character but he is a dictator, and I don't care any more for Fascism than I do for Socialism," she wrote back briskly. "Anyone who arrogates to himself the power of the Almighty is doomed to have a pretty big fall.")

In Italy, Marietta was beginning to cast a critical eye not only on local politics but on her own situation back in the United States. She and Louise Stevens refused to attend an Armistice Day parade because it was entirely devoted to the military. "We hear *so* much about war and the 'meilleures familles' over here, that you would never know me. I'm a pacifist, democratic and fanatically so. Of course I admire old family traditions, if they're fine ones—but why are we to consider ourselves better than anybody else, simply because we happen to be born in the 'right' circles? It makes me so *mad!* I thank heaven for being an American—where the divisions aren't so iron bound and divided!"

The happiest moment during her first month was a visit to Vallombroso, a town roughly twenty miles east of Florence, where the girls walked up a mountain and for a few minutes she felt free. "I ran away ahead of the others, and you have no idea how marvelous it was being alone, without a cloying chaperone, and being able to kick the leaves and sing at the top of your lungs and look at the shadows of the valley without being told why." The underlying themes in all her letters home, however, were homesickness and frustration. Peggy and she were caught smoking, and had a shrieking match with Mademoiselle over this disobedience "until I began to hate her. . . ." Mr. and Mrs. Peabody became so worried that they contacted Walter Lippmann at the *New York Herald Tribune* to see if he might help by visiting Marietta at the school. He and his wife went to La Petite Ecole and Marietta burst out immediately, "Please, you must get me out of here. I cannot stand it. I don't care about Michelangelo. The school is so strict. When I get home there will be nobody left for me to marry, and I shall be condemned to live in the rectory all my life, a dried-up spinster." Lippmann listened to her complaints, and then told her of the sacrifice her parents were making to send her to Florence, and that if she stayed, she would learn a great many interesting things about art and politics. This argument touched Marietta, and she returned in more cheerful mood. Walter Lippmann later wrote to Malcolm reassuring him that the homesickness was wearing off, and that Marietta was a charming girl.

Marietta now tried various methods to improve her situation, the most ingenious being a little lecture to herself:

> Even though 10 of the 17 girls in your school are meatballs, 7 nice ones in a school of this size is a good average. Also—if Mademoiselle must scream and scratch—let her—at an impartial distance; again, if the chaperones are grim, laugh long and loud, and think how exactly you are like the heroine of countless books you have read in this respect. And since you really are interested in learning French and Italian and seeing everything worthwhile . . . why not be completely relaxed and indifferent about things that irk—and save concentration for the rest? Then another comforting thought is that this happens once in a lifetime, that home is always there, and that my share in the frothy "debutante" life will certainly come.

Few therapists could have done better.

In November, Edith Derby arrived in Florence with her mother, and Marietta was allowed to visit her, chaperoned of course. ("I practically smoked myself under the table but it was *so* marvelous seeing real friends and hearing about everything again!") Her friend Louise McIlhenny had also now arrived in Florence, staying at a much less strict finishing school just outside the city, she too helped to alleviate Marietta's misery.

Another outlet was provided by the concerts she and her classmates were allowed to attend every Sunday. Finding rather unlikely solace in music, Marietta learned to love these outings, where one evening she heard Horowitz perform. She also recognized Toscanini in the audience. ("People think he's a bum patriot because he won't play one of the Fascist songs before a concert and I am in accord with the maestro," she declared.)

There were, perhaps, other attractions at the concerts besides Brahms and Schubert. On one occasion Marietta was seated at the end of the row, farthest away from the chaperone. By chance, before the concert began a young American man she had met at the Derbys sat down right behind her, and they began to talk. Much frowning ensued from the school jailer with messages sent down the row to cease and desist. But shortly afterwards, four friends of this young man sat down next to him. "Their subsequent remarks were so pungent with unaccustomed American wit that I perforce smiled and consequently had to change places with the chaperone."

The chaperone may have thought that would be the end of the story, but no sooner had Marietta changed her seat than a wild-looking Russian she had also managed to meet came over to greet her. After this incident, two chaperones attended the concerts, one stationed at either end of the row.[2]

The best outing of all came at Christmas. The idea of spending her first Christmas away from home sent shivers of panic down Marietta's spine, but La Petite Ecole offered to send to Rome and Naples all those girls who had nowhere else to go. The Peabodys' friends the Sennis (Countess Senni was an American whose sister had married a Milliken) lived in Rome, and they invited Marietta to visit them and their children, Maria Giulia and Piero. Four of her friends from the school were also going to Rome, and then on to Naples. Marietta begged her parents that she might go too, but they said they could not afford to let her go to both places, so she chose Rome.

She spent Christmas Day in Florence. She received Christmas boxes and gifts of money from her loving grandmothers and aunts, and seventeen Christmas letters from friends wishing her well. Only her parents somehow missed the post. Their Christmas box did not arrive in time.

The day after Christmas, she set off with Peggy Seyburn and other friends by train for Rome, staying at the Hotel Elysée on the Via Veneto. Girls she knew from Philadelphia and St. Timothy's had also arrived in Rome, and New Year's Eve was celebrated with the help of champagne smuggled into her room. Three days later was the biggest event of all—a ball at the British Embassy, thanks to an invitation from Maria Giulia Senni. After rushing around to find a chaperone, Marietta found herself the only American girl at the dance, and the evening passed very merrily.

She was invited back with the Sennis (Piero had taken a fancy to the lively American girl), where she met other Europeans her age. "I confess you feel that they are all united in the thought that Americans are beautiful, dumb, amusing, uncultured and unbroadminded and essentially not one of them. You could see that the shock was tremendous when I displayed some slight knowledge of some subject . . ."

Rome was an unending feast. As well as cavorting around as though in an Evelyn Waugh novel, Marietta was a diligent sightseer, writing lyrical descriptions of the Colosseum, the Forum, and all the other glories of the Italian capital, signing one letter exultantly: "Maria Endicotti Peabodelli."

Before she left Rome, Marietta achieved what most tourists only dream of: she had an audience with the pope, arranged through the school. The girls put on black veils and were marched through the Vatican and swept into an immense waiting room. "To my horror, I found, on looking down, that my nails were painted a brilliant scarlet." When Pope Pius XI finally arrived, Marietta found him small, unassuming, and rather fat. He went around the room offering to the twenty people in the audience a quick hand to kiss. "I cagily fumbled my hand behind his so he wouldn't see the red terrors—and then after saying something in some unknown language he blessed us and our families and left as suddenly as he had come—leaving a pompous row of rather paunchy cardinals in his wake." (Although irreverent, this particular letter pleased her parents somewhat more than most of them did, since both Peabodys were thoroughly anti-Catholic.)

While some of the school went on to Naples, Marietta stayed on in Rome, finally returning to Florence on January 19, 1935. The realities of her cloistered life there soon depressed those Roman high spirits. She found she had spent more money than she realized. Her skin trouble had flared up again (her mother thought it was because of the smoking for which she had reluctantly given permission), and the doctors in Florence recommended ultraviolet-ray treatment, which, with the taxi fare there and back, cost a great deal more than her regular allowance.

Although her parents' Christmas box finally arrived, she continued to feel waves of neglect, again urging her mother and father to come and visit her. "Everybody's family are making plans to take their children out in April and May and there are about four sets of parents on the ocean now!" she wrote wistfully. (Her own never did make the trip.)

By the end of February, Marietta was thinking about going home. She hoped to be back in time for the St. Timothy's reunion, to which she planned to drive down with Edith Derby. As the weather warmed, so did her mood. "Spring has most definitely come, bringing with it its own peculiar fever and a desire to dance in the streets." Suddenly, she loved Florence, and no longer wanted to leave. The tone of the letters becomes more immoderate. She talks excitedly about returning to Philadelphia with Louise McIlhenny, "and we plan to collapse in the same car next year after each party." During the Easter break, Marietta went with the school by car to Milan, Stresa (heavily guarded since Mussolini was to meet the British and French leaders there), Lake Como, and St. Moritz, ending up on her birthday in Venice, a wonderful trip that confirmed forever her love of Italy.

One of her last letters home describes Italy's invasion of Abyssinia. Throughout her year in Florence, the specter of war had loomed increasingly large. Although this was only 1935, Mussolini's militaristic appearances, the conversations Marietta picked up with her friends about Hitler's territorial aggression, and the rising tension between Germany and France made the situation in Europe seem to her extremely dangerous. "Florence is swarming with Germans fleeing Hitler," she reported, "and it's accepted by all that there will be war in two years, if not before." Her friend Piero Senni was waiting to be drafted. The schoolgirl who had so avidly read *Time* magazine in the peace and quiet of the Maryland countryside was getting a lesson from the political front lines, and the frivolous tone of her first descriptions of Fascist fun gave way to a sense of horror at the failure of world leaders and the League of Nations to avert disaster.

One of her last memories of Florence in May 1935 was of seeing the king of Italy. Having climbed a statue of Garibaldi in the park to get a better view, she thought the king "infinitesimal" and "probably sits on a cushion so he can see the people in the streets." He received an enormous ovation from the uniformed Fascists who lined the streets. The night before, Mussolini had been in the city to confer with Kurt von Schuschnigg, chancellor of Austria, over the German threat. In early June Marietta left Italy and sailed home. Four years later, the infinitesimal king was gone and the country she had come to love so much was engulfed in World War II.

# CHAPTER *6*

## *"She was a caged lion"*

When Marietta sailed for Europe in September 1934, Harvey Bundy, now at Yale, wrote about her in his journal, "Europe can do a great deal to improve her attitude toward life. She cannot find the pleasure in spending a quiet evening at home. She's always on the go every night . . . Marietta Peabody is too boy-crazy and wants to do something wild."

This perceptive assessment from a young man who had studied her closely over the years expresses what her parents were also coming to recognize. Before her departure, the Reverend Peabody wrote a list of basic rules of behavior that Marietta should follow when away from home for the first time. They read as follows:

1. Try to help.
2. Don't let other girls bother you.
3. Don't be self-conscious.
4. Never be moody, always be peppy—*but* sometimes give looks and get atmosphere.
5. Don't be sarcastic or laugh too much.
6. Don't be direct.
7. When at a dance or public place—think you're as good as anybody else if not *better*.
8. Be glad to see everybody and be nice to everybody.

These instructions were written in pencil in haste, and scrawled so illegibly that Mary Peabody rewrote them in ink so her daughter could read them more easily. In their awkwardness they are emblematic of what might be called "the Peabody philosophy," an attitude of superiority combined with self-effacement that is as offensive as it is admirable; the Puritan ethic written in stone.

Along with her letters to Florence, Mrs. Peabody sometimes enclosed a card on which she had written quotations from the Bible, most of them excerpts from St. Paul's letters to his far-flung converts on the subjects of strength, unselfishness, long-suffering, and temperance. When Marietta came back, she was to realize how far her own spirit strayed from her parents' inflexible dogmas.

She arrived home in June 1935, to the large, sparsely furnished, chilly rectory, where her four brothers, in her absence, had become even more adept at challenging borders and conducting hit-and-run raids on the psychic territory of their nearest and dearest.

Endicott (nicknamed "Chub") was now fifteen, George, thirteen, Sam, ten, and Mike seven. (All four boys were born in February and March, thus conceived at Easter, perhaps a response in the Peabody bedroom to the most carefree festival of the Episcopal calendar.) Four younger brothers were not exactly the most desirable family members for a blushing, insecure, eighteen-year-old girl. She later wrote an essay about them called "Quadruple Trouble," which drew a vivid portrait of her sibling life. "I have four younger brothers," she wrote.

> People come to our house and remark on their sweet young faces, and all four dare to smile back blandly out of innocent blue eyes. They shake hands with those people without being whispered to or prodded from the rear. They generally are on football teams, and sometimes bring home prizes for excellence in history or mathematics. People are always saying, "Aren't you proud of these four?" We say, "Oh, yes," and most of the time through gritted teeth, for they are extraordinary boys and supreme in the art of bringing confusion to the unwary, and hot blushes to the careless who tantalize their imagination.

Marietta warmed to her theme.

> Take for example, the afternoon a few years ago, when a rather timorous young gentleman came to see me pour tea. I had a rather shy nature myself at the time, and in addition to having known the boy for only twenty-four hours, relations were strained enough without Sam, the third blue-eyed innocent, having to clatter in on all fours executing ghoulish facial maneuvers at the same time. He listened to our gay, nervous chatter for fifteen minutes in stolid silence, and then his face fairly lighting up with an Idea, he pointed triumphantly to the shrinking

gentleman. "You know, you're the boy Marietta likes the best!" and departed. Obviously I could not vehemently deny or agree with Sam's statement without further confusion. Finding this impasse insurmountable, the gentleman left, not to return for a couple of years.[1]

She described all this with a light touch, but it was no fun at the time. They fought each other constantly, Endicott with George, George with Mike, Mike with Sam, all of them with Marietta.

The boys' psychological warfare was equally damaging. George would read Marietta's letters from boyfriends and tease her about them, "which killed her," he remembered. "Teddy Roosevelt particularly, very nice letters. She kept them in her desk in her room." Only with Sam did she have moments of truce. In her letters home, Marietta would often single out Sammy for a message of affection, and this affinity remained between them throughout her life.

These conflicts between sister and brothers reflected the boys' problems quite as much as Marietta's. Endicott went early to Groton. Like his father before him, he found the burden of the Rector's presence almost unbearable. The boy made a slow start and was kept back a year. This meant that George, already precocious, went into a class only a year behind his brother when he arrived at Groton, provoking yet another classic situation of sibling rivalry. Endicott became a football star, ultimately becoming captain of the football team and a prefect of the school. George, determined to outdo his brother on the athletic field as well as everywhere else, suffered a serious back injury that deprived him both of the football fame and the prefect's title he craved. The rest of his years at Groton were thus rendered useless in his eyes and deeply hateful to the frustrated, angry boy.[2]

Sam, while implicated in the battling coalitions of the rectory, pursued a different course. For him, as for the others, the family was too disjointed and emotionally distant to give the support he needed. As a little boy he had "rages" and broke things, and was locked up in the bathroom until he calmed down. Like Marietta, he was uncomfortable having a clergyman for a father. Perhaps fortunately for him, Sam had reading problems, which would now be diagnosed as dyslexia, thus disqualifying him from the glories of Groton. He was sent at fourteen instead to the Brooks School in Litchfield, Connecticut.

While Sam was the most sympathetic to his big sister's victimization, Endicott was in some ways at this time the closest to her, not only in age but in spirit. He saw how his Groton friends admired her and enjoyed the reflected glory he received as her brother. He shared the pressures put upon them by their parents. Marietta savored his successes on the football field, and when he later achieved his triumphs at Harvard, she pasted in a scrapbook the many newspaper stories of the "brilliant Harvard Guard" and his All-America crown. As he too began to go to the debutante parties that so preoccupied her, they shared stories and she liked to tease him for being a "parlor snake." They planned to buy a car together when she returned from Italy. He wrote funny, affectionate letters to his "dearest sistah" when she was abroad, signing one of them: "with much love or words to that effect to his most darling, dearest, best sistah from her big, beautiful, adorable brother, Endicott."

All four brothers later attributed the "sib riv," as Marietta called it, to the lack of emotional support from their parents. "When approval is doled out with coffee spoons, then the victims fight for it," George said tellingly. Marietta's deprivation was perhaps made more devastating by the fact that she was the eldest, she was the only female and therefore felt singled out for punishment. The boys often witnessed the rows she had with her parents over smoking, staying out late, wearing too much makeup, generally not behaving like a rector's daughter. But like a Greek chorus they were commentators rather than participants.

They did not understand why their beautiful, brave sister aroused such a violent kind of anxiety in their parents, nor that Marietta's defiance of the rules was of a different order of magnitude than that of her four brothers. They did not understand that spirited, outrageous behavior was somehow more acceptable in a male than in a female. They did not understand that she felt isolated by age and sex from her parents and brothers, that when the boys went to Groton or sailed in the races each summer in Northeast Harbor with their father, she felt excluded. "They had a life with my father which I would not or could not share." They loved her but they could not tell her so. All they knew was that when Marietta came home, the place was filled with excitement. "She brought the world back with her into this very tight, enclosed family," Sam said. "She brought the sunshine in."

But that brightness and fresh air also brought with it turmoil and rage. The year in Italy had transformed Marietta in many ways. She had discovered the excitement of international politics, the glamour and stimulus of travel, and the complex disadvantages of being an American in Europe. She saw how useful a proper education could be to her. She had encountered the European aristocracy, its grandeur, its frivolity, and its money. She was exposed for the first time to the significance of class distinctions. She also began to perceive her own Peabody background in this context, and to reject its implications of superiority.

As for herself, she saw how much she required freedom from restraint, freedom to express herself openly. ("She was a caged lion in

Italy," her friend Louise McIlhenny said later. "All she wanted was to be out of there.") She also learned how to control this wildness when absolutely necessary, and how to distance herself from pain. She was beginning to flex her Peabody muscles of gritted-teeth endurance, muscles that had already had some practice at school, and that would become as hard as iron by the time she died. She also realized how much men liked her, everywhere she went.

She learned all these heady lessons that year in Italy, but she still was not ready to venture out on her own or to separate herself from her family. Her frequent letters home indicate her desire to retain a close connection.

Both her father and her mother wrote regularly to her while she was in Italy. Her father was much more affectionate in correspondence than face-to-face, as he was with all his children, and with Marietta he showed his strong feelings openly in writing. He saw the movie *One Night of Love* "with Grace Moore doing the singing and reminding me of thee!" He always told her how much pleasure her letters gave him. "Pure joy," he would tell her, signing off, "thine as ever, M.E.P." On one occasion, at her request, he sent her a rather glamorous photograph of himself, wearing his dog collar. She loved the picture, teasing him, however, that she wished that "he'd forgotten his clericals that morning."

Her mother related the activities of the parish and her relations, and said how much the family was missing Marietta. More often the tone was wary, if not outright forbidding. Exhortations to behave were ever present. Tensions ran particularly high over the smoking issue. Her father, always more sympathetic, understood to some extent her request to smoke. "No one likes to be 'held down,' at the same time . . . if the rule is there it would be 'cricket' to observe it." Although in the end they reluctantly acquiesced, her mother was unreconciled: "It is bad for you as you know and I think you would be much more sensible to give it up entirely for the present. Haven't you got that much strength of mind?"

Where her parents still most effectively cracked the whip was, as in most families, over money. Malcolm Peabody never wished to withhold money from Marietta, and almost always sent a supplement to her allowance when she asked for it. His position as cautious banker went with the job. Much of his priestly calling depended on the most carefully calibrated fund-raising from his faithful flock, and he had never expected otherwise.

For Mary Peabody, the situation was less simple. The wives of clergymen are taken on an involuntary journey into financial hardship. Knowing that their husbands cannot make a salary commensurate with their peers, they take the high road, expressing pride in the sacrifices their husbands are making, while proclaiming their poverty. This road leads inevitably to charity. Thus they become traders in a barter culture, engendered by community guilt and fueled by a subtle resentment that is never identified.

Mrs. Peabody's parsimoniousness was legendary. When she drove in her mother's grand car, she always made sure everyone knew it wasn't hers. When she was taken out to a meal, she always chose the cheapest items on the menu. As she invariably forgot to give her sons traveling money on their return to Groton, kind parents of friends would bail them out. When Malcolm was promoted to bishop of central New York and they moved to Utica, the new bishop tentatively suggested that the house might be painted. "Why bother, you'll be retiring in ten years," was the sharp reply.

As for the clothes the family wore, her economies achieved a refinement that might have been described as "found" art. The acquiring of Endicott's first tuxedo, for instance, was a particular triumph. "I borrowed from every point of the compass," his mother boasted, "so that he wore the shirt and collar of one, the trousers from another, coat and vest from another. Daddy provided the shirt buttons and tie and Endicott really looked very well."

The theme of proud penury seeped like acid rain into Marietta's relations with her mother. Marietta's hope of meeting her parents in Rome the summer after her Italian school ended, for instance, was received by her mother with typical censoriousness. "Rome in May would be wonderful," Mrs. Peabody said, "but in the first place your school is not over until June, is it? And in the second place, to take you to Rome in the season in order to crash Roman society seems to me a bit odd. If you want any pennies left with which to crash American society you had better not urge me." Marietta tried a light response to this message: "Peabodys never have to crash—I would have thought you had realized before this, they are received with outstretched arms!"

But her mother's harsh remarks were not so easy to brush off. Poised at the starting gate, there was no escaping her mother's reservations about the race ahead. While Marietta was in Italy, invitations poured in for her to attend debutante parties when she returned. Her mother went through them with distaste. "I never heard of any of them but perhaps you know the girls," she wrote to her daughter. "If you don't perhaps you had better ask around a little before you accept."

It is possible that Mrs. Peabody felt a twinge of something other than simple disapproval of her daughter's exciting life. Mary Parkman Peabody had herself been a not inconsiderable explorer, going around the world when only a little older than Marietta, with far less efficient chaperonage. Did perhaps Marietta's descriptions of her trips to Rome and Venice arouse a spark of envy in her mother's heart? Responding to Marietta's story about going to a party with Maria Giulia and Piero Senni where all the other guests were Italian, thus exposing her to an alien culture, "I am so glad you had it," wrote Mary Peabody, adding, "I'm sure I never did."

But the consistently critical tone of the mother's correspondence with Marietta during this crucial year is evidence of a complexity that goes deeper than that of lost or unavailable opportunities. From her earliest observations in *The Mother's Record* to the snappish comments in her letters to Italy, Mrs. Peabody was expressing a feeling about her only daughter's sexuality and energy that went further than pride or jealously or even moral disapproval. It led right back to Mary Peabody's own mother, Frances Parkman, whose wild charms were so damaging to her eldest daughter, and which now that eldest daughter saw surfacing again so compellingly in her own child.

In a postscript to one of her letters to Marietta in Italy, Mrs. Peabody wrote that Mademoiselle had written from La Petite Ecole saying (like Walter Lippmann) that Marietta was "charmante." Her mother then adds smoothly: "So do keep up the illusion till the end."

Marietta was at this time seventeen years old.

# CHAPTER 7

## "College changed my life"

The season, necessary evil as it might have seemed to Mrs. Peabody, played an essential role for women of that era. The enforced coupling of young men and women of a certain class at traditionally specified events and venues was copied from the English system, which ensured the right sort of liaisons and excluded unsuitable intruders into hereditary patterns the system wished to perpetuate. If observers like Edith Wharton, earlier in the century, saw fissures beneath the surface, it was to take another thirty years for any major adjustment to be made to this smooth-running production line of maidens-to-matrons.

Although Mary Peabody had declared a time-out for herself from marriage by going around the world, she never doubted that it was ultimately her fate. Neither did she doubt it for her daughter. The idea of a career, or even of university courses, was not discussed at that time, and in spite of her free-spirited attitudes, Marietta was also committed to this goal.

When she celebrated her eighteenth birthday in April 1935, marriage pressure was increasing, both from home and from friends. Much of her diligent letter writing undertaken in Italy was symptomatic of this anxiety. Although her brother Endicott had told her not to elope over there because the guys in America wanted her and that the whole of the sixth form of Groton would be waiting at the pier when she returned home, she was beginning to wonder if any of them would still be free. Harvey Bundy unwittingly touched a nerve when he mentioned overhearing a debutante remark that if she were not engaged by Bootsie Derby's dance, she would have to resign to a far corner of the "shelf."[1] When Marietta's friend Louisa Wood married William Foulke in November 1934, Mrs. Peabody wrote, "It seems very queer to have two of the girls with whom you were quite intimate for a time, married. I hope Anne and Bootsie won't pop off this winter." "Am I going to be the only spinster left in Chestnut Hill?" Marietta wailed.

During her eight months in Italy, she wrote regularly to all the boys she knew back home, keeping them on the boil with her stories of Portuguese Fascists and Italian counts. So provocative were her letters that gossip about them reached her parents' ears. Her father cautioned her for making "unwise" remarks, and gentle though it was, the criticism made Marietta furious. "Are you merely giving me advice or have you heard something peculiar?" she wrote back. "I can't think of anything I've written I could be sorry for. Are you feeling apprehensive over the fact that I might get 'sloppy' to boys, having nothing else to do? If so, let your fears be assuaged. . . ."

What exactly was "sloppiness" to boys? Could the unthinkable, even for a moment, have flitted across her parents' Puritan consciousness? It is difficult to imagine Marietta Peabody being sexually free in those days. Very few girls of her class were, and those who jumped over the line and into the sheets were immediately branded as "fast."

Marietta's particular upbringing was an even more powerful check than that of most of her Philadelphia and Boston friends. Quite apart from the religious pressure imparted daily to a minister's family, Marietta's father was an unemotional man, and Marietta's mother openly despised any physical expression of affection, even between those who might naturally be expected to display it. "They are frightfully demonstrative with each other all the time in front of everybody which bores me terribly," she said of a young engaged couple who had come to visit the Peabodys in Chestnut Hill. When Endicott became engaged to Barbara Gibbons, Mrs. Peabody told them to stop holding hands in the back of the car.

Marietta was a true child of the Puritan ascendancy, and for her, as for her parents, the act of sex was undiscussed and undiscussable. She never wanted to be considered "easy."[2] Her children, even as grown-ups, could not imagine discussing the subject with her. In an interview with *Vogue* magazine in 1979, Marietta said, "I would never dream of bringing it up with my children or my mother; I should think everybody would be intensely embarrassed and inhibited." She ascribed this distaste to her roots, explaining how for the Puritans, lust was by far the most significant sin, and that women must be "tremendously disciplined" and not "dally sexually."

Yet Marietta, as Harvey Bundy noted, was "wild." While still at

St. Timothy's she had spent many weekends in her grandmother's house in Boston when her grandmother was away, entertaining boys quite freely. Her summers in Northeast Harbor were filled with unsupervised romantic encounters. She enjoyed the admiration she excited in the Italian men she met during her year abroad. She was blond, pretty, vivacious, with a body that was as spectacular as a pinup poster and which she knew how to use. (Mezzy Voorhees remembered watching her dance at Shady Hill: "I saw how she carried herself and moved her body, and I learned more from that than all the dancing classes we ever went to!")

At Groton's Fiftieth Reunion in 1934, when Marietta was seventeen, for the celebratory dinner at which President and Mrs. Roosevelt were present, Marietta was seated next to their son, Franklin Junior. During the meal, Franklin and Marietta flirted with each other until one or the other of them became annoyed. At this point, a friend of Franklin's sent down the table to him a plate of ice with a note written on it. When Marietta asked to see it, Franklin teasingly asked her how old she was. Marietta was so upset she left the table and went into the nearest study to regain her poise.

Harvey Bundy, seated at another table, saw this incident and thought it meant Marietta had been accused—only in more vulgar language—of "iciness." In other words, she was a tease. He thought the accusation fair. "You couldn't even get to bat with her," he wrote in his journal. "She played the field but she didn't play anyone heavy."

In those pre-liberation, pre-pill years, such behavior was acceptable, if maddening, to the opposite sex, who knew the standards of correct behavior toward women of their own class. The dinners and dances were arranged to allow as much innocent social intercourse as possible, the season being like an elongated foreplay session before the triumphal moment of engagement.

Between 1935 and 1936, over two hundred engraved invitation cards arrived in the mail for Marietta at Chestnut Hill. Nearly a third of these Marietta had to refuse, owing to conflicts, for she had cast her net wide and invitations came from the party centers of Boston, New York, and Philadelphia, and as far afield as Chicago and Detroit. There were buffet lunches, teas, theater parties, dinner dances, and balls, as well as the occasional bridge evening (which Marietta found easy to turn down). "Miss Mary Endicott Peabody regrets that owing to a previous engagement she is unable to accept the kind invitation . . ." she would write carefully by hand as she sorted through the delightful pile. She accepted all she could, racing from the Copley Plaza in Boston to the St. Regis Roof Garden in New York or the Bellevue Stratford in Philadelphia.

The pace was hectic, the names of party givers accumulating like the railway stations that rattled past in the dark as she slept her way to the next champagne-filled destination—Whitney, Marvin, Bacon, Biddle, Ingersoll, Weld, Brewster, Strawbridge, Frelinghuysen, Taylor, Morris, Clark, Hallowell—the names of America's old money, the WASP aristocracy, still lashed to the mast before the storms of World War II and its aftermath dispersed their fleet forever.

Travel was easy then. The trains were comfortable, cheap, and safe. The debutantes traveled in packs, with parents conferring and making arrangements as each invitation was brought to the breakfast table. Marietta's friends usually had a chauffeur meet them at their destination, whisking them off to guest quarters on the estates where the parties were to be held.

The grand mansions of Long Island, Brookline, and Baltimore celebrated their children's future with striped marquees, long drive-ways lit with Japanese lanterns, several bands, and unlimited food and drink. At the Wideners' dance, the family racehorses were brought up specially for the party, and in the ballroom a fountain supplied a cas-cade of champagne. Sometimes these fantasies went too far. At a Dor-rance ball, hundreds of tiny birds were held in a net above the dance floor, waiting to be let out and fly charmingly away. But when the net was removed, they tumbled down on the revelers like little stones. The heat in the room had killed them all.

The economic depression of the 1930s be damned. The girls wore chiffon dresses and long white gloves, the boys cutaway evening clothes; they supped on expensive delicacies and two-stepped from public ballroom to private terrace while the orchestras of Eddie Duchin, Guy Lombardo, and Paul Whiteman moved the night along to their seductive rhythms. After one New York party, Mezzy recalls going to Childs for breakfast as the dawn was breaking, and then riding on a double-decker bus all the way down Fifth Avenue to the end of Manhattan and back again.[3] What a way to end a party.

"Naturally, these parties weren't for me," Marietta said later. They were for her rich friends. Her own party was not something she wished to remember. Her parents had suggested a dinner dance in Philadelphia in September, an offer that was hastily rescinded when Mrs. Peabody realized, first, that owing to her husband's position in the community, the invitation list would have to include everybody and thus become much too large; and second, if the party were a success, "immediately rumors would circulate about the amount there was to drink etc. etc." Instead, they decided to have a tea and invite the whole parish. "You may not enjoy this," her mother conceded, "but you can see that it would be a nice thing to do . . . it will probably cost more than a dinner dance and be much less fun, but it would make much better feeling in the community, and that would be satisfying."

A parish tea for her coming out in Philadelphia? Marietta was scarlet with shame.

Mrs. Peabody also had enlisted her mother to give Marietta a dance in Boston in the early spring of 1936, which the loving grandmother was delighted to do. The dance, officially given by Marietta's cousins Mr. and Mrs. Ronald Lyman, was held at 10:30 P.M. on February 14, 1936, at the Women's Republican Club, the least glamorous place possible. Mrs. Parkman would have given her granddaughter anything she wanted for the party, including the best champagne, but Marietta's aunt Penelope Griswold had decided to take on the organization. Mrs. Griswold was not altogether supportive of her niece, thinking her unruly and selfish, and persuaded Mrs. Parkman to serve a punch instead of champagne. "It was the only party I had been to in two years that did not have champagne all night long," Marietta said later. "I was humiliated."

Still, most of her friends were there, and three hundred fifty suppers were served. The *Boston Herald* reported the event in full, announcing that although scheduled as a small dance, it was "one of the most important to take place in Boston recently." Marietta's aunt Betsey Peabody and the Lymans gave dinners before the party, with all the major male players in Marietta's life as their guests—Gordon Palmer, Antelo Devereux, Lincoln Godfrey, Theodore Roosevelt, Jr., Franklin D. Roosevelt, Jr., Huntington Thom, Robert Whitney, Arthur Newbold, and others.

It was quite a week. On the Wednesday before her dance, she was given a dinner and theater party at the Chilton Club by Mrs. Thomas Brattle Gannett, after which she went on with Artie Newbold to a dance. On Thursday she went to the movies and met up with her out-of-town friends, including Anne Scull, Coupie Hadden, Marnie Hallowell, Edith Derby, and Marina Torlonia, who all stayed at 30 Commonwealth Avenue with Mrs. Parkman for the party. Friday was the dance. Saturday she spent all day in the Ritz Bar with her guests. A friend from her Italy days, Louise Stevens, gave her a cocktail party that evening, after which she went to an ice hockey game with Marshall Field III, and then on to three nightclubs. Sunday she went to the movies and the Ritz for dinner with Antelo and Artie, then on to the Ritz Bar afterwards with Gordy, Artie, "and everybody." On Monday, all left, except the usual suspects with whom she spent the week in Boston. Friday she went to Groton, Saturday to Princeton, and Sunday to New York, where she partied for the next two days with among others, Babe Cushing and her old school friend Pauline Palmer who had come in from Chicago. Finally, on February 26, she took the train back to Philadelphia and "general clean up," as the diary entry put it. The next week promised to be just as much fun.

The rich friends held all the cards, but Marietta played on. She had no money for a wardrobe of new evening clothes, so she made do. Forced to wear the same dress over and over, she cut slits in the back of one—a plain black gown with a scoop neckline—then threaded pink ribbons through the slits and tied them with a bow. She would go to downtown Philadelphia with Mezzy to the wholesale fabric houses and buy material for a dressmaker to use. Her skin continued to be troublesome, with recurring acne. Her hair was never right, with permanent waves permanently unsatisfactory. But when she wrinkled up her nose and laughed, the boys melted.

While the days were spent lunching, visiting, shopping, and gossiping with her circle of young women friends accumulated since boarding school—Bootsie, Weasel, Mezzy, Coupie, Marnie, the nicknames of a social class whose confidence transcended even those dizzy diminutives—the nights were a modest masterpiece of male choreography. She would go to a dance in the company of one, and leave with another or several more. Like the custom of cutting in on a girl dancing, which allowed the hunting males the fullest range of sampling, the rules of escorting were open to interpretation, and Marietta was not about to get stuck with any of those "meatballs" she had encountered in her eighteen years of social engagements.

In Maine, while Bishop Lawrence gave his invitational sermon at St. Jude's "on the possibility of uniting rugged individuality and firmness of character with entire courtesy" (so many people wished to hear the bishop that more chairs were brought in), Marietta was unveiling her spectacular figure in all its glory at the Northeast Harbor swimming pool as, from time to time, she put in an appearance, walking down the steps to the pool in an outrageously revealing black two-piece. ("I always wondered why I paid so much to belong to this club," one old member murmured to another. "Now I know.")[4]

Marietta kept a record of this year, which describes the whirling circus of activities she packed into the lengthening summer days: "Saturday, May 16th. Golf in a.m., and to Princeton to see Boat Race in p.m. with Nick Wainwright. Dinner with crowd at Peacock inn and Geneva for dancing. Motored back with Scully," . . . "Friday, May 29th. Winston came in p.m. and to Ritz for cocktails, Spauldings for dinner and with him to train to Phila . . ." Much time was spent at the Ritz Bar and "theatrical clubs," and occasionally an entry reads, "Shopping all day, Collapse all night."

Many of the group drank and smoked to excess. Snapshots of the period show young men with loosened ties, jackets off, and girls with satin dresses sliding off their shoulders, waving champagne glasses, their heads wreathed in smoke. A photograph of Marietta holding a cigarette once appeared in a Philadelphia newspaper, provoking yet another scene at the rectory. Though she smoked too much, at least in her parents' eyes, drinking for Marietta and for most of her female friends was not a problem. They were scared and cautious. Mothers weighed in with stories of the dire consequences of alcohol abuse. (Many of their husbands were examples.) Mezzy Voorhees remembered a party at the Barclay in Philadelphia when a female friend got drunk. After consultation, Mezzy and Marietta decided the only solution was to rent a room where their friend might recover in private. "Of course none of us had any money to pay for the room," Mezzy recalled, "but Marietta sweet-talked [the manager] into giving us one for a couple of hours. She was the only person who could have done it."

There were casualties. The alcoholism rate among these young privileged people was high, especially among the males. Mrs. Peabody once remarked that the stories she had heard of drinking at Harvard almost persuaded her to send her sons somewhere else. Meanwhile Marietta went to parties, watched, and waited.

Finally, one day at noon, while she was sitting at the rectory breakfast table looking terrible in her frowsy old dressing gown, her father came in and told her that he could not stand seeing her like that any more and that she was going to go to college. Marietta was horrified. "I screamed bloody murder and said, 'I'm not going to college. Girls who go to college are bluestockings and they never get married.'"[5] But Reverend Peabody stood firm, and told her that she was going to the University of Pennsylvania in the fall. In fact, the decision to send her to college had been made before Marietta's coming-out party. Malcolm had contacted Penn perhaps as early as December 1935, and had applied officially on her behalf in January 1936.

Marietta was shocked. Her recurring nightmare about being condemned to remain a spinster at the rectory for the rest of her life seemed suddenly all too possible. Not only would she miss the coming year's parties, but her reputation as being brainy would probably make her as popular with the boys as a leper. She exaggerated this fear, of course; several of her friends were taking college courses: Patricia Grant was going to Bennington, Alice Spaulding was at school in Switzerland, and Marnie Hallowell was at Barnard. It was no longer unusual for young women to choose higher education.

But the notion that being a bluestocking carried a dreadful stigma lingered from the nineteenth century, when higher education for women was first bruited abroad along with the early stirrings of female emancipation. In 1836 Mrs. Trollope, although herself a successful authoress, was forced to admit that "the terror of being called learned is in general much more powerful than that of being classed as ignorant." [6] Having found that she could not dissuade her father from his decision, Marietta cast about for a compromise. Ever practical, she came up with a bargain. She would go to the University of Pennsylvania if she could continue going to parties during the week and at weekends. Her father had to agree to this. He could not afford to have her live at Penn, and had already decided that she should live at home and commute every day to the campus.

Despite her overt reaction, Marietta had always considered a university education as a serious possibility. At St. Timothy's she had chosen, with only a few others, to take the College Boards. And so Marietta Peabody entered the University of Pennsylvania on October 5, 1936, enrolling as a liberal arts student. Her freshman subjects were English, history, Italian, French, and physical education. Forever afterwards, she gave thanks for Malcolm's unbudging stance over the issue: "I'll never stop being grateful to my father for forcing me to go to college. It changed my life."

The change, however, was not immediate. She continued to have lunch with her debutante friends, to go to dress fittings, hockey games, hair appointments, and weekend parties. Louise McIlhenny saw a lot of her friend during this time, and used to tease her, saying, "I know exactly who you went out with last night because today you want to be a lawyer." Along with several of her friends, including Louise, Marietta modeled clothes for John Wanamaker's store in Philadelphia that fall. She enjoyed this brief foray into modeling, invariably mentioning it in interviews later in her life. It satisfied her theatrical bent. (She also claimed that it helped pay for her college education—although the wages hardly paid for her travel expenses.)

But for the first time Marietta was leading a daytime life, and typically she gave it her best shot. Most days, she would be given a lift into town by her old friend Antelo Devereux, now a premed student at the University of Pennsylvania, who admired her ability to work hard and play hard without seeming to pay a price. He also recognized her intelligence. "Mentally she was way over my head," he observed later. (How furious Marietta would have been at this assessment.)

In late 1936 and early 1937, Marietta began seeing more of one of the circle of young men who surrounded her. He was R. Stewart Rauch, a handsome young Philadelphian, one of those who entertained her on football weekends at Princeton. Her favorite movie stars at the time were Leslie Howard and Robert Donat, and Stewart Rauch possessed something of these British matinée idol looks.

In the summer of 1936 he came to stay with her in Maine, and then drove with her to his parents' camp in the Adirondacks, where they had a lively weekend with Pauline Palmer and Teddy Roosevelt. That fall when she started her college life, he started working in Washington as a political intern for the senior Democratic senator from Virginia, Carter Glass. There were weekend trips to Washington. Rauch's roommate, William Clark, was very keen on Marietta's friend, Mezzy, and he would urge Stewart to invite Marietta down and bring Mezzy with her. They did not need much encouragement. In Washington, Marietta saw "Soozle" (Susan Mary Jay) and many other friends, and they went to cocktails and balls. "Washington was a small town in those days," Mezzy explained. "You went to the White House and left a calling card and Mrs. Roosevelt would respond with an invitation." (Of course it did not hurt that Marietta knew Franklin Junior well, along with other members of the Roosevelt family.)

Marietta and Stewart also saw each other in Philadelphia when he came home for weekends. These times together meant late nights talking and drinking. On Monday morning, before leaving for Washington, Stewart would try to call her, only to have the Peabody maid discourage him by explaining it would be a case of rousing the dead. Scribbling affectionate notes on the train, he would recommend Alka-Seltzer and icepacks before she returned to getting As on her term papers.

By the spring of 1937, when Marietta turned twenty, they were unofficially engaged. No parents were informed (Stewart's mother did not approve of Marietta, regarding her as "too wild"), and very few friends knew about it, although some suspected. No ring was purchased. Both were uncertain about the commitment. One of Marietta's worries was that they had not been together long enough to really know each other. Stewart had his own worries, largely about his future. Family money was scarce, and he was earning so little as an intern that he took on a night job with the Campbell Soup Company.[7]

In the summer of 1937 Marietta's grandmother Parkman took the Peabody family (except for Mike, who was too young) to Europe. Originally, Marietta had hoped Stewart would be able to get over to Europe too, and they could meet in some romantic place in England. But Stewart's financial and career problems prevented this, which perhaps was for the best. They agreed that while she was away, they should think over the whole idea of their marrying each other, and somewhere over the English Channel, the engagement foundered. "I didn't have enough money for her," Stewart Rauch said wryly half a century later. "Anyway, she wanted to see the world."

Europe was, as it always would be, a deeply satisfying experience for Marietta. The family went to new places—first to Munich, where Hitler was staying, and then to Heidelberg. In England, they rented a car and drove around the countryside, looking at cathedrals, and arrived finally in Inverness, Scotland, where they were to stay for several days.

At this point, George, aged fifteen, ran away.

"I was homesick, left a note, and disappeared," he explained later. He had five pounds in his pocket. He took the Flying Scotsman to London, found a cheap bed for the night, and then went by train to Southampton where he planned to take a ship back to the United States. Somehow he managed to get aboard the *Berengaria,* which was about to sail, stayed in hiding on board for two hours, realized that at the other end he might be sent back, and got off again. He hitchhiked all the way from Southampton back to Scotland, a journey of about twenty rides. Two and a half days later he arrived back in Inverness, where he was finally reunited with his grandmother, parents, sister, and brothers at the Highland Games.

In a family starved of affection, this attention seeking was not likely to garner much sympathy, particularly from the firstborn. As George sat down next to his big sister, Marietta said coolly, "Oh, look, here's George," and went on watching the games. He never forgot this slight.

Marietta started her sophomore year of college in October 1937. Her academic record at St. Timothy's may not have been exceptional, but she did very well indeed at Penn. In spite of her evening and weekend distractions, her work habits remained unimpaired. She shone especially in English. "How splendid that Marietta is doing so well," exclaimed Mrs. Parkman. "Of course we all realized that she is a born writer, having the imagination and power of expression. . . ."

She wrote up a splendid essay on her Italian experiences for her class at Penn, culminating with the audience with the pope. She told the story even better now, embellishing it amusingly as she described trying to scrape off the "pagan nail polish" from her "worldly fingers" before kissing the papal ring. Her professor, W. S. Child, gave her an A.[8]

In another essay, Marietta drew on an event closer to home. While she was in Europe that summer, she had met Bootsie Derby in London. Her old friend had become deeply committed to the Oxford Group, a Christian revivalist movement founded in the early thirties by an American former Lutheran minister and evangelist, Frank Buchman. Renamed Moral Rearmament (MRA) in 1938 (emerging as a crypto-Fascist, pro-Hitler group), it had lured many rich, well-educated members of the American and British upper classes to the cause, including a strong Oxford contingent (hence the original name) and a large following at Harvard. Over tea at Brown's Hotel in London, Bootsie expounded to her friend the movement's mixture of spiritual fanaticism, personal surrender to God, and ritualistic purification by means of public confessions. Marietta was fascinated, and when Bootsie came back to the United States, Marietta persuaded her to take her to an Oxford Group meeting in Philadelphia.

Marietta pounced on this experience to write for Professor Child an essay entitled "Alice's Adventures in Wonderland." She describes an attractive crowd of young people sitting around an expensive Main Line drawing room, listening to an "ex-college boy" address them: " 'When I was at Harvard, I always thought that religion was pretty stuffy, and for those who wanted it, but not for me. Well, I saw these Oxford Groupers around Plympton Street a lot, and they always seemed so happy—getting such a darn lot out of life, that I figured I'd miss the bus unless I joined up with them. So I did—and gee, I certainly am getting a kick out of things now.' "

The narrator, Alice, listens to a volunteer who stands up and "shares" the following; "Well, my trouble was the weather." He explains that he always used to look out of the window, worrying whether it would rain or not. "Since I have surrendered, and listen in to God every morning, I no longer worry about the weather."

At the end of the meeting, an English boy comes up to Alice and asks her what she thinks of them all. "I think you're all a pack of cards," says Alice, laughing.[9]

The essay (which scored another A) is witty, shrewd, well written, and manages to cover many of the essential MRA tenets with remarkable fidelity. It also shows how alert Marietta was, against the weight of opinion of many acquaintances, to what she regarded as a deeply suspect ideology. When Bootsie Derby married DuBois S. Morris, himself an ardent MRA supporter, in 1938, Marietta was a bridesmaid. After that the Morrises disappeared into the intensely separatist and secretive MRA world, and Bootsie lost touch for many years with her old school friend.

There were several more friends' weddings in 1938, including Louise McIlhenny's to Bayard Roberts, at which Marietta was also a bridesmaid. In the summer of 1938, she went on a cruise in Northeast Harbor with a Boston friend, Curtis Prout, and Susan Mary Jay. Also on the cruise were Jimmy Byrne and William Breese, classmates at the Foreign Service School in Washington. Marietta instantly took a liking to Bill Breese, who was extremely good-looking. Curtis Prout could not help noticing how splendid Marietta looked that day, with her long blond hair (unusual in those days of bobs, and perhaps aided by peroxide, if her brother Endicott's teasing remarks on the subject were to be believed), and her gorgeous figure displayed to advantage in shorts and a tight-fitting knit top with its deceptively demure Peter Pan collar. "They sat together all day on the bowsprit of the boat," Curtis Prout remembered later, "Marietta with her hair flowing and her body leaning out against the wind. It was very distracting, particularly since I was doing my best to sail the boat!"[10]

When they dropped anchor in Castine Harbor for cocktails, the conversation turned to people's ambitions for the future. While the two diplomats in training named the Foreign Service, and Curtis Prout professed his interest in the medical profession (he later became a distinguished physician and teacher at Harvard Medical School), Marietta declared that although her background was respectable and well-connected, she wanted more: she wanted power and money. She told her friends that evening that she knew women could not acquire these in their own right. "I intend to get power," she announced, "through connection with a man."

Her words stayed in the memory of at least one of those present. "We were amused at the time," recalled Dr. Prout. "But later I thought it displayed lack of heart."

Marietta's escorts to the parties were getting older, now graduated from their ivy-covered colleges and entering law firms, businesses, medical schools, brokerage houses, politics, comfortably assuming the responsibilities for which their background and upbringing had prepared them. Many had their moments of grace during these warm spring and summer months, when they took Marietta Peabody in their arms and danced the night away. If no engagement was announced, there was no lack of opportunity, and the enthusiasm of her beaux showed no sign of abating. There was still time.

## CHAPTER 8

# *"It's really worthwhile to get engaged"*

Two events in 1938 conspired to put in motion Marietta's final separation from her childhood. In the summer of 1938, Malcolm Peabody was elected bishop coadjutor of central New York. And some time toward the end of that year, Marietta began being seriously courted by Desmond FitzGerald, the man she was to marry.

Marietta said a final good-bye to her family's home life in September 1938, when the newly appointed bishop moved to 1629 Genesee Street in Utica, New York. The Peabody family was beginning to disband. Endicott was making himself nationally famous as a football player for Harvard. George, maverick as always, had chosen to strike out for the unfamiliar territory of the University of North Carolina at Chapel Hill. Sam was at boarding school, and only Mike, just eleven, went with his parents to Utica.

Marietta no longer held any sentimental feelings for the rectory, and she certainly had no intention of moving to Utica. Her father had been nominated for a bishopric in Ohio a year earlier, and Marietta panicked at the idea of having to be cut off from her northeastern social life and exiled to some midwestern desert. Fortunately for her, Malcolm was not elected. (The loss was a blow for him, however, and as opportunities for promotion grew slimmer there was no question he should take the Utica position when it came up.) The Peabodys found a friend in Chestnut Hill, Frances Finletter, who would have Marietta as a lodger while she continued her studies at Penn. Although Mrs. Finletter complained about Marietta's chronic untidiness, much later, Marietta wrote to her in gratitude for those hectic times. "I often think of those happy years that I spent with you in Chestnut Hill, and looking back on them I realize that they were very important years for me. In spite of myself, my brain and curiosity expanded at college and I think I matured a certain amount in those years, anyway enough to feel confident about the man I would marry and the kind of person I wanted to be."

Now, for the first time, Marietta was truly independent, and she made the most of it. In November 1938, the current beau, southern charmer Winston Frost, took her to one of his law classes in Charlottesville, where she stayed with Franklin Roosevelt, Jr., his wife Ethel (formerly du Pont, whose wedding Marietta had attended a year earlier), and their baby. While there she attended sporting events, parties, a wedding, and more parties.

Thanksgiving and Christmas were spent with family in Utica. "How can you do so much for us," she wrote on her return to Philadelphia. "Like the Pharisee in front of the temple, I thank God every night for what I have. I'm so proud to belong to such a family." Then she added with that familiar pleading note, "Is that a wrong attitude?"

Thus the pattern persisted. Just as the letters from Italy swung from provocation to humility, so these letters, two years later, reflect the continuing tensions within Marietta's soul. At times, her writing is simply a catalogue of parties, bars, and nightclubs, with the author signing off "Dorothy Lamour." At other times, she begs for money, justifies expenses, worries about thrift. Academic work remains a torment, and as at St. Timothy's, she warns her parents ahead of time in abject terms about the likelihood of poor marks. Always there are loving messages to the family. Always she seems to be asking for that one expression of approval that they cannot give.

In February 1939, she went skiing in New Hampshire with a group of friends, including a new acquaintance, Desmond FitzGerald. He was a friend of Potter Palmer III, oldest brother of Marietta's boarding school friend, Pauline. The two boys had been at St. Mark's School together, and FitzGerald used to visit Potter at the Palmers' vast "cottage," Hare Forest, in Bar Harbor, Maine.

The usual problems arose about how to pay for this trip. Mrs. Peabody managed to obtain for her a pair of ski boots. "It was very kind of you to go to all that trouble over the boots," Marietta wrote back, "but you ought to know me better than think I would be seen dead in them." On the trip Coupie Hadden got sick; Marietta, always a loyal friend, stayed behind to nurse her, and accompanied her back to New York, carrying all the luggage and skis without a word of complaint.

On April 14, 1939, Anne Scull got married to Chester Ingersoll

Warren, and at the reception Marietta, as was her wont, sang very badly (she had sung at Louise Roberts's wedding too) and was later ashamed "at the lack of poise I have on these occasions." Winston Frost motored her back to Washington, where she had a meal with another new beau, Charles Thayer.

Washington held the greatest allure for Marietta. It was, after all, the center of the political power she had long been drawn to. During her sophomore year at Penn, as well as writing her wonderful English essays, she was taking courses in political science, economics, and sociology. "I soaked them up," she said later. She told her grandmother Parkman about the diplomatic receptions and people in cabinet and government positions she met when she visited the capital. "I think I'll trick some politician into marrying me so I can live there, as the perpetual stimulation of ideas political . . . is my idea of an exciting life."

The new friend in Washington, Charlie Thayer, was a Foreign Service officer who had recently returned on leave to Philadelphia from Germany after a posting under Ambassador William Bullitt in Moscow.[1] Thayer was a fun-loving character, and the story goes that while he was on leave, his friends thought it would be a good idea to try to settle him down by marrying him off. So they put together a group of young women for him to meet, one of whom was Marietta Peabody. It was she, needless to say, for whom he fell.[2]

For her part, while she found Charlie outrageous and witty, Marietta thought his approach to politics altogether too unserious. During dinners together she would harangue him with her newfound knowledge of political theory, her tone becoming ever more zealous. (This was becoming a habit: even her fond father had advised her not to get too "frank and earnest" in her political arguments.) Charlie would twit her out of her solemnity by regaling her with indiscreet stories about the diplomatic corps.

Marietta seemed to be attracted to politics as a child to a shiny golden ball. As she began to see more of Desmond FitzGerald, and thus to meet his older friends, who were mostly staunch Republicans, she remained undaunted. Part of her enthusiasm was fueled by the wish to learn. No burning issue of the day satiated her political hunger. She wrote an essay at Penn on the difficulty of achieving world peace, arguing that in some situations while a dictator (such as in Italy) might be beneficial to a people, democracy is clearly the better alternative.

She decided that like her friends Jimmy Byrne and Charlie Thayer, whose careers she so envied, she too would work toward admittance into the Foreign Service. Studying hard at Penn, she took a trial examination for the Foreign Service a year before she would be expected to take the real one—and passed. She even made plans to go to Washington to sit the written exams. But one of her teachers at Penn, a former ambassador, said to her, "Tell me, Marietta, why are you taking all these courses for the Foreign Service?" Marietta replied that she wished to enter the service. The ambassador laughed. "Don't you realize," he said, "that Roosevelt does not accept women in the Foreign Service?" Stunned, she listened with increasing agitation as he went on: "If you're attractive and brainy, you'll be trained by the U.S. government to be a Foreign Service officer, and the amount of money that is put into your training will be all lost because you'll get married to the first Swedish secretary in your first post and it will all be a waste of time, as far as the U.S. government is concerned. If you're not attractive enough to marry him, we don't want you."

Seeing her look of shock and disappointment, he tried to console her. "Tell you what, you go down to the Foreign Service School in Georgetown where they're all taking the exams and you find a likely man to marry. You marry him and then you can have a career in the foreign service."[3]

Today, for those remarks the ex-ambassador would probably be drawn and quartered, but in those days such condescension passed without comment. The advice was what women of her class and generation expected. In fact, when Charlie Thayer at some point asked her to marry him, remembering her professor's cynical recommendation, she considered accepting the offer. "But I was too sentimental," she said much later. "I felt that I had to be passionately in love with the man I married. So that opportunity was lost."

In the spring of 1939 her friend Susan Mary Jay took a position in New York as an assistant on *Vogue* magazine, joining two other of Marietta's friends, Marnie Hallowell and Edith Derby, in securing jobs in New York. This news further heightened Marietta's frustration at being sidelined from the real world by her seemingly endless academic studies. Her father had recently had a conversation with her about how expensive it was to keep her at Penn. Marietta used his complaint to bring up the possibility of getting a job. "I know a job would be better for me," she pleaded, "as it would require all my attention and effort and give me experience."

She wrote to her uncle Trubee Davison, a colonel in the U.S. Air Corps in Washington, asking if he could help her. She also wrote to David Hulburd of *Time* magazine. Nothing came of these efforts. She went back to her books at Penn.

It was a critical moment for Marietta. She was by now filled with a turbulent mixture of party-girl joie de vivre and serious intellectual aspirations. She was excited by politics and power, and the rigors of social and economic theory. She wanted to work, but what could girls like her actually offer, other than charity work or low-level office skills?

She gravitated both to hard-drinking, fun-loving parlor snakes, from whom she concealed her brains, and to career diplomats with whom she aired her new political savvy. Which way would she finally swing?

Her parents were far away from her now. Marietta was on her own, living as a lodger in another town, surrounded by friends who were getting married, having babies, and putting down mortgages on little estates near their parents and grandparents, while the old money of the WASP fraternity nourished its heirs with career sinecures and family trusts. The dance bands were beginning to sound dated, the champagne was losing its fizz, and the air abroad was splintered by the chill of war. In April 1939, when Marietta celebrated her twenty-second birthday, she had been going to parties for over three years. The season was surely over.

Desmond FitzGerald began seeing Marietta on a regular basis in early 1939, coming down to Philadelphia to take her out to dinner and returning to New York on the late train. FitzGerald was seven years older than Marietta, and as a young teenager she had watched him with the older girls, with at least one of whom he was said to have had a romantic affair. In the eyes of the younger set, he seemed to belong to a different generation, exuding mystery and glamour.

FitzGerald's family was Anglo-Irish in origin. His paternal grandfather was a civil engineer in Boston who moved in the same circles as the Parkmans and Gardners. He had two sons, Steven and Harold. Harold was Desmond's father. Unlike Steven, who spent his days at the Brookline Country Club, Harold had ambitions, and announced to his brother he was going to New York to make money. "Then I doubt we shall ever see each other again," said Steven. They never did.

Harold became a wine merchant with Wildman's in New York. He married Nora Fitzgerald (with a small g) and they had two children, Eleanor and Desmond. Nora died of cancer very young, when her son was only three years old. At a later date, his father married Helen ("Bird") Johnson from Chicago, whose best friend was Marjorie Merriweather Post. Bird was not a maternal type and never became involved with her two stepchildren. The couple spent most of their time in Palm Beach, where Bird had a house, and at Piping Rock, Long Island. Harold left the wine business and became a successful stockbroker.

After St. Mark's, Desmond went to Harvard, where he was very popular both as an athlete and as a prince of the social circuit. A member of the Fly Club, he was very handsome like his father, and he was bright and good company. After graduating from Harvard Law School in 1935, he went to work for Spence, Windels, Walser, Hotchkiss & Angell, a medium-sized law firm in New York.

Marietta enjoyed the attentions of this older man, who had

seemed such a distant figure from her summer holidays. He had a gloss her other suitors lacked. They discovered pleasing similarities in their natures. Like Marietta, Desmond was energetic and intellectually curious. During his years at Harvard, he traveled abroad with his friend Charles F. Adams, driving through Europe and visiting the major artistic centers in Italy, Germany, and France. "If I was indolent I was tweaked by the nose," Adams remembered. "He wanted to get something out of all the places we visited." Desmond read widely, and worked and played hard. His friends, such as Alfred Harrison, William Patten and Charles Stockton, were men in their late twenties and early thirties, whom Marietta found more sophisticated and amusing than her own set. FitzGerald began to feature more regularly in her letters home. "I wonder if you spell Dezzy with 2 zs or 2 s's?" she mused coyly to her parents.

They knew so many people that the social merry-go-round never slowed. Marietta was the first on each ride, eager to savor every whirling encounter. At one dinner party, she sat next to DeWitt Sage, who was secretary to the Republican Party leader, John Hamilton, "and nearly went crazy with argument." She became a proseletyzer for *Union Now,* an influential book published in March 1939 by a *New York Times* foreign correspondent, Clarence Streit, which proposed a federation of democratic nations that would control matters of foreign policy and prevent future wars. Marietta took up the idea with characteristic enthusiasm, urging her father to read it. "Dezzy thinks it's all wrong economically and can't possibly work out, but I would give up all my time working for it, if I had the backing of a few others."

That the couple disagreed on the idea of a union of nations did not at the time seem problematic. After all, Marietta loved to argue with anyone about politics. She refused to recognize the fact that she was opposed to many of Desmond's and his friends' political positions. They went on going to parties together, and as the situation in Europe continued to disintegrate, an alliance was gradually formed between the two that looked as though it would hold.

Marietta Peabody became engaged to Desmond FitzGerald in May 1939, although it was not announced until late June. Plans for an early wedding were discussed, but Marietta stalled. Doubts surfaced. They had hardly ever been alone together. "We ought to make haste slowly," she wrote to her parents. "One step at a time stuff." But Desmond forged ahead, making the rounds of Marietta's huge family, meeting parents, grandparents, and cousins. In June, Marietta's grandmother Parkman gave her a lace veil for her wedding dress, and they shopped for a ring. These rituals, with their message of eternal optimism, reassured Marietta. "It's really worthwhile to get engaged," she declared, as though giving herself encouragement.

Marietta and Desmond share a private moment at their wedding reception.
*(Photo courtesy of Nora Cammann)*

The FitzGeralds took a house in Northeast Harbor for July, and Marietta and Desmond were married there just two months later. It had been a short engagement, to be sure, just like her mother's. But having made the decision, why linger? This, after all, was her ticket out, the ticket to horizons she had so often yearned for. Moreover, by this time everybody was in a hurry. The world was about to fall to pieces, and the air was heavy with uncertainty. Susan Mary had set a date for her marriage to Desmond's friend Bill Patten in October. Better marry now, everyone said, before the situation became any more precarious, or who knew how long they might be able to enjoy their new husbands? Later, Marietta bitterly regretted leaving the University of Pennsylvania before completing her degree. (Her cousin May Sedgwick was the first woman in the Peabody family to graduate from college.) But at the time, marriage, not education, spelled freedom.

So good-bye, Artie, Gordie, Hunty, and all the sad young men who swooned at the sight of Marietta and wrote poems of hopelessness to her as she strode the northeastern shores in search of glory. She was on her way to New York, making a timely bid for freedom from the rectory, suburban convention, and the judgment of the Peabodys.

# CHAPTER *9*

# *"The greatest stage in my life"*

Marietta married Desmond FitzGerald on September 2, 1939, the day after Hitler's troops marched into Poland.

A few days before the wedding, Marietta asked an old friend, Louisa Foulke, to climb a mountain with her. Louisa had known Marietta since their days at Shady Hill School, and summered every year, like the Peabodys, in Northeast Harbor. Marietta arrived for the walk looking very disheveled, with dirty shoes, unwashed hair, and worn-out clothes. When Louisa remarked on her friend's uncharacteristically scruffy appearance, Marietta said, "This is the last time in my life I can be messy." The strange note of misgiving in Marietta's voice haunted Louisa long after they had climbed the trail.

The wedding took place at St. Mary's-by-the-Sea in Northeast Harbor, the church where Marietta's father and grandfather Peabody had so often addressed, blessed, married, and baptized their friends. Her father was assisted by his old comrade, William Lawrence, bishop of western Massachusetts, and the Reverend Endicott Peabody, indestructible headmaster of Groton School.

The bride wore a gown of cream grosgrain silk with her grandmother Parkman's lace veil and she carried a bouquet of gardenias. She was given away by her eldest brother, Endicott. Her nine bridesmaids were dressed in frocks of aquamarine draped chiffon jersey with wide tulle skirts, carried nasturtium bouquets, and wore nasturtium wreaths in their hair.

Desmond's best man was Charles F. Adams. Ushers included Potter Palmer III, A. Holmes Cummins, Alfred C. Harrison, Charles Stockton, Ephron Catlin, Thomas Whiteside, William Patten, Amos Eno, and Marietta's brother, George Peabody.

As they walked down the aisle, Marietta, with her blond curls, green eyes, and splendid figure, and Desmond with his dark, slicked-back hair and chiseled profile, looked as though they had stepped out of *One Night of Love,* the movie in which Marietta's father once compared his daughter to Grace Moore.

There was a pea-soup fog that day in Northeast, and it poured with rain, just as it had twenty-three years earlier for Marietta's parents' wedding. The reception was supposed to been held in Mrs. Parkman's garden, but despite the predictable vagaries of down east weather, Marietta's parents had not had the foresight (or funds) to hire a tent. Needless to say, in the incorrigible way of Mary Peabody's life, help (or God) was close at hand. Sympathetic neighbors, the Symingtons, offered their huge house for the reception, which of course was the perfect solution.

Marietta refused to be downcast by the weather, declaring that it made the party more cohesive and therefore more successful. But the mood was muted. People huddled around radios listening to the increasingly frightening news from Europe. Rather than exclaiming at the beauty of the bride, they asked each other, "Are you in the reserve?" Instead of wishing the couple long life and happiness, they were preoccupied with their own future and that of their fiancés, husbands, fathers, friends.

Some of them also were muted in their feelings about the bridegroom. According to several of her closest friends, he had rescued Marietta, like a white knight, from a doubtful future. But while some found him charming, lively and loads of fun, to others he seemed remote, handsome indeed but intense, rigid, lacking warmth.

Within the family, feelings were also mixed. Endicott and Sam both felt guarded about their new brother-in-law, while George and Mike thought he was wonderful. As for Marietta's parents, they weren't entirely comfortable with Desie (his spelling). He was of Irish, not New England descent. His world was New York and Palm Beach, not Boston and Maine. His father and stepmother were not the sort of people with whom Bishop and Mrs. Peabody felt at home.[1]

But perhaps most troubling for the Peabodys was that Desmond's religious commitment seemed questionable, a trait his new wife must have found titillating. In order to please her parents before the marriage, Marietta said that Desie had been groping for religious understanding for a long time, and needed the bishop's help. "I don't think I'm capable of the job," she conceded. But if he was indeed groping, understanding remained elusive. The Easter after they were married,

Desie and Marietta stayed with her parents at the Davisons' estate in Locust Valley. On Easter Sunday, while everyone was getting ready to go to church to hear Bishop Peabody preach, Mrs. Peabody asked, "Where's Desie?" Marietta said airily, "Oh, he doesn't go to church. He's not coming." It was surprising the sky did not fall right then and there on top of her insouciant head. According to Sam, the bishop's sermon was going to be specifically addressed to his worldly son-in-law.

The night of the wedding the FitzGeralds stayed at the Edwin Cornings' camp on Abrams Pond behind Ellsworth, a fishing hideaway designed for sport rather than romance. After that first night among the fishing rods, they drove south to spend the rest of their honeymoon at The Homestead, in Hot Springs, Virginia, a huge hotel popular with upper-class Philadelphians and Bostonians (and conventions of dentists), who played golf and tennis in the beautifully manicured grounds. Marietta and Desmond met friends there, including golfers for Desie (Marietta studiously avoided playing), and for her, Ambassador Joseph Grew and William Castle, with whom she talked politics to her heart's content.

In her first letter home after her marriage, she wrote ecstatically about her new life:

> Most of the time we have kept to ourselves and the cup runneth over. D. has so many facets and is the most entertaining, most inspiring, most sweet character that you'll ever hear about or know. This is the beginning of the greatest stage in my life, I know, and I hope that I can grow mentally and spiritually so that I can help him especially, *and* others. I want my life to be vigorously dedicated to this, and if you ever see me resting or deviating from this purpose, it is your duty to impress it upon me.

Along with this ringing declaration of conjugal dedication, Marietta made a remark that marriage counseling professionals would not have recommended. After discussing the fun she had with the two members of the State Department, she added: "I tried to persuade D. to go into the Foreign Service for about half an hour afterwards." (Not surprisingly D. was not persuaded.)

In October 1939, Susan Mary Jay married FitzGerald's friend William Patten, on Long Island, and Marietta was a matron of honor. (Shortly after, Patten became a Foreign Service reserve officer, placing Susan Mary at the center of the world her friend so idealized.) That same month, the FitzGeralds moved into 30 Sutton Place in New York, with a cook/housekeeper and unlimited prospects. The young couple began at once to plunge into New York's social life, which was even more frenzied than the years of Marietta's debutante season. There was an air of urgency in the great city, as though time were running out. They were at the opening of a new decade, but people could hear doors closing all around them.

They were often out to dinner three times a week. The group included Desmond's sister, Eleanor, and her husband Albert Francke; Babe Cushing; Stanley Mortimer (whom Babe married); Joe Alsop; the Charles F. Adamses; the Alfred Harrisons; along with FitzGerald's law partners. Desmond was a wonderful dancer, as was his wife, so often in those early winter months of 1939 they would spend long nights at La Rue. They went to Princeton football games, plays, operas, the latest art shows, the Museum of Natural History (Desmond was interested in paleontology), Boston (the Fly Club, more football), and once to Philadelphia for a ball.

Desmond liked fine things. He wore well-tailored clothes, he drank good wine, he traveled with elegant luggage, he knew about art and music. Marietta read the literature he recommended to her, listened to the music he exposed her to, looked at the paintings he pointed out to her, with a keen eye and ear, eager, as always, to learn. Astonishingly, at the time of her marriage she had never read Hemingway or listened to classical music. Desmond FitzGerald was giving his wife an education, and she was grateful.

She was also terrified. Like many young women thrust into a world of her husband's friends, she felt permanently on trial as the new appendage to Desie, and self-conscious about her immaturity and ignorance. She realized how culturally unsophisticated she was, and while she loved to engage in political discussions, she discovered that in a society of Republicans, her liberal inclinations were not well received. In short, Marietta felt out of her depth much of the time. She still blushed when she was nervous, and feeling those telltale red blotches suffuse her face in front of Desie and his friends mortified her.

Desie worked hard and late hours at his law firm. When he came home, he did not want to talk to her about his work; he thought it would bore her. But Marietta had assumed she and Desie would share everything in their lives, and just as during those summers as a young girl she had felt left out from the sailing pleasures enjoyed by her father and brothers in Northeast Harbor, now she found her husband's exclusion of her hurtful and unexpected.[2]

The new Mrs. FitzGerald was even more unprepared for what was to be her major role at 30 Sutton Place—that of a New York City hostess. She was thrilled by the new apartment, and took a great interest in its decoration, learning all the while from Desie what rooms should look like. She went shopping with Susan Mary Patten, showing off to her friend her newfound knowledge of antiques. After a visit to her grandmother, Mrs. Parkman wrote to Mary, "It was delightful to see her trying with all her might to turn into the housewife." At Christmas, she asked her parents for presents that must have caused Mrs. Peabody to glance Heavenwards—"cooking spices or dried rose leaves for a china bowl, or a mirror tissue box."

But while the apartment was beautiful, she had to struggle to keep it tidy. Desie, like most controlling personalities, required order. No more "messy" Marietta. Arranging the expensive furniture, flowers, and objects in a way that would please him filled her with apprehension. What had she to go on, after all, except the rectory at Chestnut Hill, whose interiors were triumphs of the "less is more" school of decorating?

A more serious problem was her inexperience in running a household. She had never told a maid how to make a bed, had never learned how to talk to a cook, or formally entertain. All the details of a conventional dinner party were utterly alien to her. Had her mother ever taught her the orders of cutlery, how finger bowls worked, what the rules of seating were? The idea was laughable. Marietta, raw, energetic, enthusiastic, scared, began almost immediately to drown in etiquette.

When her in-laws came to dinner for the first time, she was beside herself with nerves. That the only interference Mrs. FitzGerald ran was to rearrange all the bric-à-brac Marietta considered a triumph. But not all the evenings were so easy. One night Desie told her that he had invited people to dinner, and suggested she serve sole *au vin blanc*. Marietta's French was good enough to know what that meant, but beyond that she was clueless. She rushed out, bought a cookbook, and read the recipe. She explained to the cook how the dish was made, and went to her husband's wine cellar to find a white wine to use in poaching the fish as the recipe instructed.

The night of the dinner party, when the rather inferior sole was served, Desie asked her in front of the guests where she had found the wine. "From your cellar, of course," she replied. "You don't mean to say you used my best white wine for cooking?" he exploded. Such "hideous mistakes," as Marietta later called them, were a painful part of her early married life, so painful that during dinner parties at 30 Sutton Place she would sometimes have to excuse herself from the table to throw up.[3]

In spite of these humiliations, Marietta never deviated from her determination to make herself useful in the world. Having left the University of Pennsylvania early, she decided to pursue her studies after Christmas at Barnard College, where her friend Marnie Hallowell was still studying. She went back to Penn briefly to see about credits, and in so doing bade a ceremonial farewell to the city she had grown up in. "I suddenly realized I have developed a N.Y.C. attitude. Philadelphia has become one of the delightful provinces and I love to go there but wouldn't think of living there. Ha!"

Desie and Marietta spent their first Christmas with the Peabodys in Utica, and in February 1940, Marietta picked up her education as a government major at Barnard. It turned out to be more of an ordeal than she had anticipated. She had to drive to the college every day, take her classes, play on the Barnard hockey team (a required sport), drive home to face a cocktail party, a dinner—either laid on at home or with friends—and quite possibly dance till the small hours. Then she had to study. She began to feel a fatigue she had never known before.

What compounded the strain was that by February, when she started going to Barnard, she was pregnant.

Later, Marietta said it was unplanned, but having seen so many of her friends in the same state, it is unlikely she was surprised. In those days, birth control was a fledgling science. But for this particular couple the news of a baby so soon created an issue that, in their still exploratory marriage, became the severest test yet of the relationship. For there was no question it was a test. In spite of Marietta's determination to endure the soufflés that turned into pancakes, or the criticisms of her father-in-law, or the exposure to a whole new group of older, sophisticated New Yorkers, she was nervous most of the time, insecure all of the time, and overtired every hour of the day.

If Desmond did not completely understand her desperation, it was not entirely his fault. After all, Marietta was a past master at concealing her feelings. She was not likely to break down now before the man she so eagerly wanted to please. So the pace of their lives continued unabated during the pregnancy. Marietta often drove to Barnard with June Bingham, whose husband, Jonathan, was to become an important figure in the Democratic Party and later a colleague of Marietta's. June was also pregnant, and the two young women sat through classes together in the same state of discomfort. June Bingham sensed something of Marietta's unhappiness at that time. She was shapeless, her complexion had broken out badly and looked blotchy, and she seemed to have no confidence. But every night Marietta pulled herself together once more, and her courage was rewarded by an admiring press.[4] Even under these unfavorable conditions, Mrs. Desmond FitzGerald was beginning to make a small splash in the New York society columns as a delectable new addition to the social scene.

Frances FitzGerald (named after both her grandmothers) was born on October 21, 1940. It was a difficult birth. The labor lasted for three days, and Marietta was not allowed any anesthetics because of high blood pressure and kidney trouble. The baby was finally delivered with forceps, and, like many new fathers, Desie was dismayed at seeing his little girl for the first time so bruised and misshapen.

Mrs. Peabody came down from Utica (she and Desie slept on chairs in the hospital corridor during the two nights of waiting, this

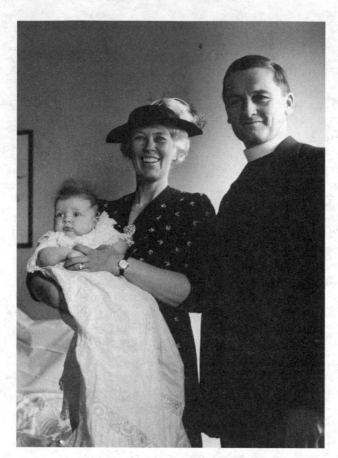

Frances FitzGerald with her Peabody grandparents at her christening, November 1940.

bond causing Mrs. Peabody to become "very fond" of her son-in-law), and Marietta had visits from Aunt Betsey and Grandmother Peabody from Groton, along with many other friends and relations. In spite of Marietta's preoccupation with the baby, she was, characteristically, equally focused on the upcoming election. Her first letter home written from the hospital was just as full of enthusiasm for Wendell Willkie as for Frankie's milk consumption. "We go home on Sunday so I can vote on Tuesday," she announced triumphantly. (Marietta still adhered to the voting patterns of her family and Desie at this time, and Willkie was a particularly sympathetic Republican, being less equivocal on support for the Allies than Roosevelt.)

Bringing Frankie home, Marietta found a new element to deal with in her relationship with Desie. Many first-time parents experience difficulties at such a time, and the FitzGeralds were no different. Like most men of his class and generation, Desie was not comfortable with babies. Fathers had not yet been invited to engage in child rearing, and the idea of Desie picking up, changing, or feeding Frankie was inconceivable. He simply wasn't interested. He was happy to have a daughter, of course (and later, the two became deeply attached), but he had no experience of the joys of fatherhood, and found the nursery unworthy of his attention. Many men today still think the subject deeply boring, and complain about women babbling on about their children at dinner parties. Desmond wasted no time in telling Marietta the same thing. Marietta felt protective of her little girl, but she deferred as always to Desie, succeeding so well that people thought there was something wrong with Frankie because neither Desie nor Marietta ever mentioned her.

Marietta breast-fed the baby in the hospital, but when she came home little Frankie was handed over to a nanny, as was the custom with well-to-do families. In these pre–World War II days, nannies were regarded as the ideal custodians of children, leaving the parents free to continue their lives without the responsibilities of child rearing. Even if some mothers felt "pushed away" from maternal bonding, they obeyed convention, sadly depriving themselves (and their children) of a vital emotional and physical connection.

So life at 30 Sutton Place picked up as though it had never been interrupted. Dinners, new and old friends, parties, concerts, outings with the Fly Club, attendance at Endicott's increasingly brilliant football games, kept the phone ringing and the engagement book full. German-born Peter Kaminer, an associate in Desmond FitzGerald's law firm, said later that they were the only couple in New York who had what could be called, in the European sense, a "salon." Marietta was learning fast. She invited interesting people to her table. People loved their parties.

With both a nanny and cook/housekeeper installed, Marietta found time for charity work. She got herself elected first vice president and then chairman of the Volunteers Committee of the Welfare Hospital board. The hospital (on Welfare Island) was entirely supported by the city and took in the chronically sick. Marietta visited one day a week, going around the wards, helping the nurses, talking to the patients, and offering books and games.

Throughout 1941, the terrible news from Europe dominated headlines and conversation. France had fallen, Britain was under almost daily siege from German bombs, and the German-Italian axis was presenting a new and even greater threat to Winston Churchill's lonely defenses. Desie had signed up in the army reserve, and spent nights drilling. More and more friends did the same, and some were even going over to England to join the fighting. The boys of Groton School started a knitting program to send socks to the brave sons of Eton and

Harrow. Meanwhile, the wives too began to mobilize, assuming their traditional role of providing relief to the troops. Marietta was no exception, becoming a member of the British War Relief Society and the Women's Auxiliary of the Church of the Epiphany, as well as maintaining her hospital duties. She also raised funds with a team from Henry Street for the Visiting Nurses Service.

Such busy, busy lives. Barnard, Welfare Hospital, war relief work, dinner parties, pleasing Desie—such pressure on a young woman who still did not know who she was. When in early 1941 she was forced to bed with a suspected inflamed gallbladder, she still fitted in a visit to volunteer agencies for Welfare Hospital, a dinner for the Fly Club wives and another for visiting cousins. The whirlwind of her social and charitable calendar begins to look suspiciously like a cover-up.

"One of Gotham's most ardent adopted daughters," Marietta was saluted in an article in the New York *Daily News* in mid-1941. This "fascinating lady" is described as having a "fragile, almost medieval beauty . . . and a completely masculine purposefulness. . . . Although married a year and a half, [she] hopes to receive her B.A. degree next February from Barnard, intending to make use of a government major in politics. . . ." We learn that she loves onions, corned beef hash, and champagne, very dry. She likes vivid toenail polish, and for day-time "little" black frocks and admittedly "mad" hats. "Her sense of humor and ready smile make her an asset in any group. . . . Her name: Mrs. Desmond FitzGerald."

A year earlier, driving back from Barnard, fascinating, ready-smiling Mrs. Desmond FitzGerald had stopped at a light and begun bawling uncontrollably. People looked at her from the other cars and stared in embarrassed curiosity. Why was this smartly dressed young woman sobbing at the wheel of her car?

She could not have told them then, but Marietta was weeping for a lost dream. She had married Desmond FitzGerald to escape from a world she saw as limiting and claustrophobic. She had married Desmond FitzGerald because she was running into overtime, with most of her friends making new lives for themselves and their families. She had married Desmond FitzGerald because he made by far the best offer out of the many she had had from all those charming but dull beaux who had pursued her during her debutante years. He offered her education, interesting friends, money, and a way out of Philadelphia and into the heady atmosphere of New York. He offered love too, in his way, but it was a particular kind of well-bred, authoritative, controlled and controlling love that did not reach deeply into Marietta's soul. When she married him, that did not seem to matter. Her upbringing had taught her little about any other kind of love, or indeed, if any other kind existed. And God's love, after all, was always a little on the remote side. As she had written so gallantly to her parents on her honeymoon, she welcomed other responsibilities in her wifely role.

Marietta only completed one semester at Barnard. Exhausted, rattled, frustrated, she quit as she had quit Penn, in the summer of 1940, and lost the chance to complete her degree. For Marietta, failing to get a degree a second time was deeply humiliating. That the newspaper article profiling Mrs. FitzGerald still mentioned her hopes of achieving a B.A. though she had in fact quit a year earlier suggests how hard it was for Marietta to admit defeat. But by that time she was beginning to learn how ingeniously her expectations had outwitted her.

In the summer of 1941, the FitzGeralds went up to Northeast Harbor, where there was a Parkman-Peabody family reunion. The oldest member present was Marietta's godfather Julius Atwood, retired bishop of Arizona, Endicott Peabody's dearest friend, and originator of the remark, "Peabody is the last of the Puritans." The youngest was Frances FitzGerald, aged one and a half, whose pronouncements on Dr. Peabody were not yet available. Eighteen members of the family were present, including Mrs. Parkman (who died a year later), and the Rector himself, who had finally retired as headmaster of Groton. (A cartoon of the period shows two Upper East Side matrons leaning over a baby's crib. "Are you sure you aren't making a mistake?" the older woman asks. "Groton may change with Dr. Peabody gone.")

On December 7, 1941, Desmond and Marietta went to see the movie *The Long Voyage Home,* and as they were watching, it was announced that the Japanese had attacked Pearl Harbor. Three months later, Desmond FitzGerald left for the war.

# CHAPTER *10*

# *"A little inferiority complex"*

"Goodness," Marietta wrote to her parents, "I never thought the war would come this way! There's still an unreality about it which is not dispelled by 'air raids' (false alarms) and black-outs (last night when we had eight for dinner). Nobody could take it seriously. Desie has a grim enlisting look in his eye and says nothing."

The FitzGeralds took one last vacation together in Mont Tremblant, Canada, in February 1942, and on the 23rd of that month Desmond enlisted. As Marietta had feared, he signed up as a private. Charles Adams saw this as characteristic of his friend: "Desie was a man who did not wish to take the easy way through life."[1] After news of Desie's decision became known, friends threw party after party for the departing soldier, "in a wave of hysterical popularity," as Marietta put it. On March 2, wearing an old tweed coat and carrying a simple canvas bag, Desie left for Camp Upton, Long Island, a distribution center, prior to leaving for his first station, Camp Blanding in Florida. Not only were Marietta and Frankie distraught, but the cook, Nellie, was so upset at his departure that she drank three bottles of cooking sherry and passed out before lunch. Having noticed alcoholic fumes emanating from Nellie for some time prior to this last collapse, Marietta felt compelled to fire her. That left Frankie's nanny, Isabel, to hold the fort at 30 Sutton Place alone, a daunting responsibility.

For by this time Marietta's days and nights had begun to take the shape they were to follow for the rest of her life: action-packed. In early 1942 she was invited to become a member of Nelson Rockefeller's

Hospitality Committee for New York City's Office of Inter-American Affairs, a job that came about thanks to a new and very important friendship with Mary Warburg, a friendship that would last all her life. Marietta had met Mary and her husband Eddie through Desie (they all went on the Mont Tremblant vacation together). Marietta was impressed by Eddie Warburg, scion of the wealthy banking family, who had a fine modern art collection and was very sophisticated and amusing. But more significantly, he was Jewish, and Marietta, with her insulated WASP background, had not been much exposed to the kind of cultivated and dynamic Jew that Warburg represented. She was immediately attracted to this exotic personality, and sympathized deeply with the work he was doing for the Jewish refugees as head of the American Jewish Joint Distribution Committee.

His wife, Mary, was equally magnetic. A Texas divorcée, and mother, with Eddie, of an adopted son a year younger than Frankie, Mary was beautiful, witty, and highly intelligent. Nelson Rockefeller had asked her to chair the Welfare Committee for the Office of Inter-American Affairs, and Mary asked Marietta to join her as co-chairman. While it was a volunteer position, the job came with interesting responsibilities, requiring them to meet all visiting Latin American dignitaries who were guests of the State Department, from builders to brain surgeons, and show them New York. (This was part of Nelson Rockefeller's role to encourage inter-American relations for military purposes.) For this assignment, they naturally had to speak Spanish, so both women took a crash course in the language.

Marietta started work on May 12, 1942, at the office at 444 Madison Avenue. IBM was housed in the same building, and the president, Thomas J. Watson, was a friend of Marietta's parents. Watson took a great interest in their sparkling, lively daughter, and showed her around his own offices, discussing business and giving her advice. She had mixed impressions of this man. "He showed a remarkable grasp of what was in hand and made extremely creative suggestions but it was all interspersed with a series of the most naive remarks it's been my curiosity to hear from a supposedly mature man. Is it this naivete that makes him successful or is it a pose—or isn't it naivete?" (Marietta would ask this question again in her encounters with top executives of American corporations in her later career.)

The work was, well, varied. A Uruguayan poet insisted on Marietta accompanying him to see the dawn from the Brooklyn Bridge. She dutifully got up at 4:30 A.M., picked him up from his hotel, and walked across the bridge as he rhapsodized about her—and, of course, the dawn. A professor wanted to take back a certain kind of brassiere for his wife that she had to scour the stores to find. (It was Maidenform's "Spring Time" model, apparently all the rage in Latin America.) Many of the visitors were taken to the Rockefellers' home near Tarrytown, New York, where luncheon and diversions would take place.

Frankie meanwhile was growing fast, and reports of her progress were sent regularly to her father and grandparents. Her father responded from Camp Blanding with carefully written character sketches about the mixed group of people in his training squad, from black Irishmen to Texas farm boys. (His handwriting was small and neat, schoolboyish in style, very different from Marietta's big, breathless scrawl.)

Marietta visited Desie at Camp Blanding that April. Her FitzGerald in-laws had invited the couple to stay with them in Palm Beach, but Marietta, who despised the place, was delighted to be able to refuse, thanks to an offer from Mezzy Voorhees, whose family had taken a house on Sea Island, Georgia. They spent a wonderful weekend there, and hoped for another, but Desie's basic training was suddenly cut short and he was "tossed into the regiment proper," as he explained it to his parents-in-law, and denied further leave.

During the weekend at Sea Island, Marietta celebrated her twenty-fifth birthday. "Celebrate" is perhaps the wrong word, as she declared it was "ghastly" to be twenty-five, because she was already a quarter of a century old, and what on earth had she got to show for it? "Well," she sighed, summoning up the old Peabody spirit, "with the help of my family showing me the way to improvement and a steam shovel behind me pushing—I might get somewhere."

In June, Desie was sent to Fort Benning, Georgia, for officer training. He ranked first of the new class, but got no furlough, so would not see his family for three months. Marietta suggested that she and Frankie move down with him and live nearby, just as other families were doing, but Desie would not let her. "I don't want you to come," he told her, "because I've had a very pampered childhood and I want to see if I can compete on an equal basis with everyone else." If Marietta was hurt by this unexpected new rejection, she did not show it. "I will probably stay here [in New York]," she announced to her parents, "as you cannot follow a private around like Marlene Dietrich with high heels in the sand." (Ironically, some of Marietta's women friends were shocked by what they regarded as her disloyalty in not following her husband.)

Marietta instead threw herself into work—and play. "I have been feverishly gay," she confessed to her parents. "I decided I much better go out than sit at home and mope—although I probably will be criticized for it."

She kept her word. If life with Desie had seemed madly exciting, with the Warburgs she was shifting into an even higher gear. In the daytime she was acting as receptionist to foreign dignitaries and fulfilling their sometimes unusual requests. At night she was meeting Chinese diplomats, English pilots, Argentine polo players, and Basque revolutionists. "Don't you think your proposed 5-room apartment is a bit small for the United Nations?" Desie wrote to her plaintively during a discussion about moving from Sutton Place, whose owner wished to sell it.

Marietta's social skills at that time had not attained the refinement they were to achieve later. "She was very tall, with high color. She blushed easily and often, which she hated," Mary Warburg remembered. "Her figure was wonderful, but she also hated her large breasts. She was very poorly dressed at the beginning. I remember a white dress with fringe hanging down that made us all laugh about it later. She was awkward in many ways during those first years in New York. She was not a beauty, but more like a lovely, overgrown schoolgirl."

Marietta saw that Mary was far more chic and sophisticated, and, with her characteristic willingness to learn, was determined to improve herself. She told Mary she was provincial, "just a parson's daughter." Mary admired her friend's ambition and drive, and took her in hand, taking her to her dressmaker, introducing her to new places and people. Gradually, Marietta became less gawky and more confident.

Although Marietta continued to express enthusiasm for the Office of Inter-American Affairs, she longed to make the transition from volunteer to paid work. She wanted—always—to be taken seriously and earn her own money. Desie gave her a generous allowance of $1,000 a month (roughly $9,500 in 1997 dollars), but her new and glamorous lifestyle reduced her sometimes to borrowing money from her father-in-law, which she found deeply humiliating, as he was always needling her about her Puritan unbringing. By good fortune, that summer she was invited by the head of the Inter-American Commercial Arbitration Association, Frances Kellor, to become a researcher in Latin American matters for the association, a non-profit organization that arbitrated commercial conflicts both at home and abroad. This invitation came about indirectly through Tom Watson. Watson gave a generous donation to the association every year, and the sharp-eyed Miss Kellor, having observed his friendship with Marietta, thought she might be useful in raising money for the organization.

So Marietta started her first paid job in October 1942, to the great surprise and shock of her friend, Mary Warburg, who quickly had to scramble to find a replacement for her committee. Marietta's salary was $40 a week, which she thought wonderful, with a half day on Thursdays to take care of Frankie, and weekends free. She was one of three women in an organization of nine thousand people, and her duties involved keeping the staff abreast of Inter-American business affairs in New York City, in addition to helping with fund-raising.

That October, Marietta spent a weekend with Minnie and Vincent Astor on Long Island. The Astors took her to dinner at neighboring Kiluna Farm, the luxurious eighty-five-acre estate built by William and Dorothy Paley. (Minnie's sister Babe Cushing Mortimer was later to be the second Mrs. Paley.) Marietta was meeting the Paleys for the first time that night, and she was immediately transfixed by their charm and wit. Although she felt that the dinner conversation was brilliant and far above her most of the time, it turned out that only two guests present had been to college, Bill Paley and Marietta, both at the University of Pennsylvania.[2] "Well, it's fun seeing what these people are like," she concluded, "although it gives me a little inferiority complex. I wish they could see Desie and see what a fully developed man is like."

The friendship with the Paleys was another important step in Marietta's social ascent. Bill Paley, by that time head of CBS, and his wife, Dorothy, were "well on the way to being the most glamorous couple in New York," as Irene Selznick said. (Bill Paley and David Selznick were good friends.) The Paleys immediately took to Marietta, and began to invite her to many of their parties in Long Island and New York. Dorothy Paley, like Mary Warburg, was a highly sophisticated, elegant young woman, who invariably made the best-dressed lists and was photographed in *Vogue* and *Harper's Bazaar*. "The Paleys were innovative and stimulating and self-willed," wrote Irene Selznick. "They had advanced ideas on everything from paintings to politics."

Dorothy, only daughter of a well-off California family called Hart, and ex-wife of John Randolph Hearst, had married Paley in 1932. She immediately began to educate the already rich but uncultivated broadcasting czar, introducing him to art, literature, good food and wine, and the other prerequisites of taste to which he keenly aspired. She was a confident woman, who liked to speak her mind, as Marietta did, regardless of the company, and her vivacity and intelligence found an admiring response in the less experienced younger woman.

Dorothy and Marietta were also similar in their passion for politics. Dorothy was independent-spirited, a Roosevelt liberal, and, like Marietta, deeply interested in social issues. The two women often discussed the possibility of their going to England to help in the war effort and even asked the famed CBS broadcaster Edward R. Murrow, whose reports from London were electrifying Americans, if he could find a way to help them get there. "He made light of it," Dorothy Paley (later Hirshon) remembered. "This is when women were not taken seriously."

One of the most significant gifts Dorothy Paley bestowed on Marietta was exposure to the issue of civil rights. A pioneer in race relations, Mrs. Paley was on the board of the National Urban League and helped found a nursery school in Harlem, working with black supporters to raise money. Marietta immediately responded to this cause, and helped paint cubicles for the new, ground-breaking school. Later, the two helped found the first multiracial hospital in the United States, called Sydenham, in the Bronx. As with her sudden love affair with Jews (which was so all-encompassing that she once laughingly remarked to her parents, "When did I last see a gentile?"), Marietta's experiences of racial inequality at this time created a lasting commitment to the cause of civil rights. In the summer of 1943, when Bill Paley courageously ran a CBS radio program entitled *Open Letter on Race Hatred* ("balling [*sic*] out the whites on the negro situation," as Marietta put it), she and Dorothy were at his side, cheering him on.

Coincidentally, Desmond had been transferred to Fort McClellan, Alabama, to train black troops. This was a tough assignment for someone as inexperienced as Desie with southern blacks, who had no sympathy with what they regarded as a white man's war, and his discomfort is clear from his references in letters to "dinges" and "dusky dopes" and their Uncle Tom mannerisms.[3] As time went on, he began to understand their attitudes and the training went better.

While Desie struggled to make sense of this segregated society in the South, in New York Marietta was embarking on a campaign with Dorothy Paley to create the country's first desegregated hospital. War forces social progress at a faster rate than in peacetime, disrupting the gradual routine of evolution and speeding up the processes of change. Thus women's rights, economic equality, and in particular civil rights all took major steps forward during these war years. In their way, both Desie and Marietta contributed to this rallying point of social change.

The speeding-up process also affected people's private lives. Marietta met members of the Greek government-in-exile, refugee playwrights like Henri Bernstein, British army and navy officers on leave, war correspondents Ed Murrow and Charles Collingwood, and *Time* writer John Hersey, who had just published the first of his distinguished war books, *Men on Bataan*. Many of these men threw themselves with a passion into the brief moments of distraction from the horrors of war, giving the encounters a heightened tension and electricity.

Marietta also found herself mixing with a colorful palette of socialites, including the doyenne of them all, Elsa Maxwell. She dined frequently with Minnie and Vincent Astor, and Babe and Stanley Mortimer, both of the latter friends from her debutante years.

This was the major league for Mrs. Desmond FitzGerald. She had come a long way from the rectory in Chestnut Hill, and she knew it. "I still have a wide-eyed, backstairs attitude about meeting people I've read about," she confessed to her parents. Thanks to the influence of her two closest women friends, Mary Warburg and Dorothy Paley, she was learning to carry herself better, to blush less frequently, and to dress more fashionably. She was enormously popular with the new social set, and often went dancing, sometimes with new admirers, more often with favorites such as Henri Bernstein, who was old enough to be her grandfather, but could flirt like a boy (he called her "my spiritual guide and lovely chaperone") and with whom she could have the kind of abandoned yet "safe" fun she craved.

Her Peabody genes, however, retained their critical grip on her psyche. She was well aware that while she amused herself nightly in New York, Rome was burning, "and what a useless, jaded feeling have I as a result," she sighed in one of her self-denigrating moods. As she fired off letters to Desie, she grew more and more guilty about the comparison between his life and hers. "How I wish I could take his burden and have him have my soft life for a while! Each letter that I write emphasizes this difference more strongly and I have about as much self-respect as a plugged nickel."

Her work was equally frustrating. The excitement about getting a paid job had disintegrated into a depression that was making her already look elsewhere for employment. The work at the Arbitration Association—providing research information for lawyers and labor officials—lacked interest. Dorothy Paley's involvement in local and international issues made the arbitration problems seem irrelevant in comparison. Often Marietta did not have enough to do. The only challenge in the job was her occasional duty to make speeches to trade organizations to sell the organization or ask for funds, which terrified her but was good experience.

By late fall of 1942 she knew she wanted to leave and find work connected with political research. As she wrote to her parents,

> The more I learn about government and the better I am trained during this war, the chances are that I might be able to make a small contribution in this field later on. I feel so strongly that the people of our generation must take an active interest in the government, as the world has gotten so small now that whatever we do has a direct and immediate effect on the rest of the world, and we, as the richest and strongest nation, must rise to our responsibilities and help other nations in order to help ourselves. My, how badly put that is! [4]

Badly put or not, the sentiment was quintessentially Peabody, and in particular the Rector of Groton. However, transforming the wish into action came more easily to his Groton boys than to his granddaughter. Marietta sent in trial articles for "News of the Week" sections of *The New York Times,* the *Sunday Times,* and the *Sunday*

*Tribune,* without success. "I have no training or background for it," she admitted sadly. Meanwhile, she continued to keep occupied with new and old friends. Thanksgiving was spent in New York at the Plaza, with the Astors, socialite Doc Holden, and Stanley and Babe Mortimer. "I know this traditionless day will shock you," she wrote her parents. "But I must say it was fun."

Christmas was only a little more traditional. She arranged for Frankie and Isabel to travel to her parents' house in Syracuse (where the Peabodys had moved) on December 16, with Marietta arriving on December 24. Desie was unable to obtain leave, but told everyone he would be home in the new year. So Marietta spent a truncated Christmas in Syracuse, and left immediately afterward, while Frankie and Isabel stayed on. In spite of the brevity of her visit, the Peabodys aroused the usual feelings of inadequacy in her. "Being a part of the unit of our family is the greatest thing in my life," she declared, ". . . but if I go farther, and heed its influence and try to stand for what the family stands for and develop it for my own case and for my own time, then I have the greatest goal I could ever reach for. Let's hope I can at least stay on the road to this goal—but it certainly will require your continued help."

This passionate apostrophe to the family appears strange in light of the fact that Marietta was in fact moving further and further away from it, but her excessively emphatic credo came at a time when she was under extraordinary pressure in her new life. She was singing three songs at once: dutiful daughter, working girl, and model wife. None was satisfactory.

But there was a fourth song, one that Marietta could barely sing at all. It was the song of motherhood. Marietta had had only one experience of motherhood. With Mrs. Peabody as her model, how could Marietta express maternal passion for her baby daughter? This dislocation was exaggerated by the early separation from her child by nannies, and by Desie's distance. Thus, while celebrating the idea of family, it meant nothing to her to leave her three-year-old daughter alone with her nanny and grandparents for almost three weeks over the Christmas holidays. She could reasonably have argued that this was no different from her own experience of being sent off alone to her grandmother for extended periods as a child. But while some women, however they themselves were mothered, bond immediately with the warm bundle at their breast, Marietta suppressed whatever maternal predisposition lay within her in a frantic output of external activity.

The results were, of course, what any psychologist might have predicted. Frankie was a very bright child, but she was difficult and introverted. She chose not to talk until she was three, to everyone's great concern. (When she finally spoke, she stunned everyone by saying a perfect sentence: "I see the horse.") She was willful at times, and her teasing ways could quickly lose their charm, as when Marietta took her shopping and Frankie kept darting in and out of the crowd and yelling at the top of her lungs, "I'm running away from Mummy!"

Frankie's own recollections of those early years are not happy. She thinks she was angry much of the time. "The memories I have before the age of three are not of my mother, although she was there, I suppose." What Frankie remembered was on frequent occasions going to her mother's dressing table where Marietta was preparing to go out for the evening, and demanding, "When is Daddy coming back?" Of course, many wartime children suffered these deprivations, but Marietta's preoccupations were elsewhere, and she could not compensate for the child's sense of loss.

Frankie's response to her mother's emotional absence was to grow much closer to her grandmother Peabody, just as Marietta herself had found a home with her grandmother Parkman. Much later, Frankie published an article, entitled "My Most Unforgettable Character," about "Ga-ga," in which the author recalled, among other things, those summers in Northeast Harbor when her grandmother, who swam daily in the icy-cold Maine ocean, taught the four-year-old to do the same. The love and admiration Frankie felt for this strong-minded, uncompromising woman came through most powerfully in this essay.

Desie came home for a short leave in January 1943, and his Peabody in-laws came down from Syracuse to see him. "This time more than ever I feel like a vacuum," Marietta said after he left. "And the apartment seems more empty without Desie. I hope all of this outside stuff will help. Taking your mind off yourself and your sadness always does."

Meeting Orson Welles helped. Talking to Wendell Willkie helped, whom she met at a cocktail party at the David Selznicks'. Introductions to Pierre David-Weill and Lord Beaverbrook helped. Dinners at the Astors where she met movie stars like Tyrone Power helped a lot. Parties with the Paleys filled many vacuums. At one of their evenings she met the distinguished Oxford philosopher Isaiah Berlin. He was then first secretary of the British Embassy in Washington, and she described him as "a brilliant Jew, who knew more about the Episcopalian church here than any layman I've ever met. You should have heard him and Eddie Warburg discussing Jewish politics. They both express themselves so well and so amusingly that I wish it could have been reported."

Her own dinners had become greatly in demand, thanks to her connections, through Mary Warburg and Dorothy Paley, with people like Dr. Rudolph ("Kaetchen") Kommer, the mysterious Austrian man-about-town; Raimund von Hofmannsthal, son of the famous poet; theater people; and various foreign envoys who graced her table. (Those painful nights of nervousness and faux pas in the kitchen were ancient history.)

But even these stimulating encounters failed to eradicate the gnawing frustration eating away at this "top glamor girl," as the society columns called her. In February 1943, she hit a particularly low point. She poured out her feelings in a letter to her Peabody grandparents in Groton. "I am going through a period of standing aside watching myself go by, and it's not a very satisfactory experience," she told them. "I am a terrible flop at the office, I think as they check me up so much, and in the so-called social life, I feel that although I am busy and seeing people every minute, I am a bore and a parasite and contribute nothing. Please advise, it is desperately needed. Even though people ask me around, I don't feel as if I mattered much (enough) to anybody to have them think of me as a real friend."

Part of the gloom stemmed from her latest assignment at work, which was to get advertising for the Arbitration Association's new magazine, *Arbitration in Action*. Her task was to go directly to the heads of companies rather than through the normal departments. Her employers obviously thought that her impressive connections could be well used in this way, but Marietta felt like a "worm of the lowest order" practicing this high-pressure exploitation. (She never became good at asking people for contributions.) But her distaste was only a symptom of a deeper malaise and concern about her own worthlessness.

These mood swoops between bouts of frenzied gaiety and self-abasing despondency had already marked Marietta's childhood, college, and early married life. Each swoop seemed to etch itself more deeply on her psyche, like an engraver's tool on a piece of jade. It is a tribute to Marietta's strength of will at this time that with each swing, the marks were somehow filled in, the surface buffed, and the jade restored to an apparent state of purity.

That summer Desie and Marietta were reunited twice in quick succession. In June, she was allowed a week off to visit him in Alabama. She lay around the pool during the day, they partied at night, and she declared that the visit had greatly restored her spirits. His next leave was planned for September, after which he believed he would be going overseas. He was given another six days leave in August, when he planned to come to New York. As in 1942, Marietta had arranged for Frankie and Isabel to spend the summer with her parents, and with what was already becoming a habitual lack of maternal feeling said, "Isn't it a pity that Frankie can't see him!"

In July, at the urging of Frances Kellor, Marietta took an intensive typing course. Desie and Marietta managed to arrange to go to Northeast Harbor from August 12 to August 27, so that Desie could be reunited with his daughter, as well as with the Peabody grandparents. While Marietta declared that this vacation was the best ever, and that Northeast Harbor was the happiest thing in her life, there were a few problems to be faced, the most urgent being the departure of Isabel, who wished to call it quits after two strenuous years. (Perhaps thankless years, also. Desmond FitzGerald, who conceded that the job was "unusually tough," realized at the end of her tenure that he did not even know her last name.)[5] Marietta's many absences had required Isabel to play a more important role with her little charge than most nannies are expected to play. She also must have sensed Frankie's loneliness, because she told Marietta's parents she thought Marietta should have another baby. Marietta was enraged at this suggestion: "As to having another baby, I am not going to do it, just to please her."

Whether other stresses were apparent during that last summer together is not clear. Was Desie becoming uneasy at the hectic social life his wife was leading? Or was he simply proud of her as she rushed from office to dinner party to nightclub? He had written to his in-laws that during his leave he suspected that "there will be the curious experience of sitting drone-like at home while Marietta grabs her lunch-pail and what she nicknames a hat and dashes for the office." Did these lighthearted comments conceal a note of resentment? Did he communicate his disapproval to her when they were together?

Desmond's family was certainly less than enthusiastic about Marietta's activities. Desie's sister, Eleanor Francke, disapproved strongly of Marietta taking a paid job, when all right-thinking women were doing volunteer work with organizations such as the Red Cross. Eleanor was also appalled when Marietta missed one of Frankie's birthday parties, owing to a previous assignment in Washington. Such a heinous crime was unforgivable then (and perhaps somewhat startling even now). Marietta's name and photograph appeared altogether too frequently in the society pages of the newspapers and glossy magazines. Both FitzGerald *père* and the Franckes, with their two children, Albert and Nora, would call on Marietta at home, keeping an eye on her.

The picture that emerges of Marietta during the first two years of the war is of a woman pulsating with pent-up energy, curiosity, and excitement about the world, a woman whose restrictive background and reserved emotional upbringing, combined with a heavy dose of religious piety, had driven her into a hurried marriage. New York, particularly at the beginning of this extraordinary decade, could hardly have been a more seductive place for such a person. The temper of the great metropolis, with its political and social turmoil, its mix of intellectuals and bohemians, was like an aphrodisiac to this naive new resident. Tension was inevitable. Her eagerness to improve herself and her wish to be involved drove her into the world, just as her built-in sense of inadequacy and lack of confidence drove her back to the feet of the Peabodys, so that at times she seemed ready to snap. To sober observers like the Franckes and some of her old school friends, her turbulent behavior was unseemly and intemperate; to Marietta, it was the inevitable expression of her confused ambition.

In September, to his great relief, Desie was finally sent abroad as liaison officer in the Burma-China-India theater. Also in September, Frankie started nursery school with a new nurse in tow, a German called Miss Engelhard. As her two family members bravely embarked on their journeys into the unknown, Marietta herself finally achieved her desperately sought goal. That winter, she was hired as a researcher for *Life* magazine.

From this point on, the distance between Desie and Marietta as he steamed across the ocean toward the Far East could no longer be reckoned in miles. The separate trajectories the couple had commenced blazed a path that led one way only. When the fire had burned itself out, there was merely a heap of ashes for the homecoming.

# CHAPTER *II*

# *"In a kind of fever of happiness"*

The search was over. At last Marietta had found herself, her place in the working world. All her energies were harnessed finally to the pioneer magazine of photojournalism, *Life*.

Her friend John Hersey had tipped her off that the executive who hired for Time-Life was not to be found in Personnel (they rarely are), but in the person of Bernice Schrift, who was the head of the magazine's research department. Hersey made the appointment, and Marietta did the rest. Although apprehensive about her lack of experience, and as always desperately conscious of the crimson flush of nervousness that spread up her neck to her cheeks during the interview, she won the day. When she received the telephone call telling of her appointment, "I sang, hugged myself, danced around the room, and must have frightened the people in the apartment below with my entrechâts."

Initially she was hired at $50 a week to be a general researcher in a group overseen by Schriftey, or "Red," as Bernice Schrift was known (because of her red hair), but very soon it was apparent where Marietta's interests lay, so she was promoted to research the articles written by the leading political journalists on the magazine, with a raise to $75 a week.

Schriftey, the most important woman on the thirty-third floor, was like a headmistress with her class of researchers—stern but protective, as Marietta later explained:

Most of us researchers, still wet behind the ears, felt that the world was divided very simply into New Dealers and Fascist Beasts, and that the more conservative writers in Time Inc. fell into the latter category. In the battle between these writers and most of the researchers, Schriftey sided unobtrusively with the liberals, assigning to the crustiest right-wing ideologues the scrappiest and most resourceful researchers. For a writer who wanted to exhort the readers to vote for Governor Dewey against FDR, or who tried to prove that the whole CIO was Communist-dominated, copy-checking by a *Life* researcher was a hellish experience. He was often arguing dates and disputing conclusions until 4 in the morning with a calm, smiling girl who seemed to have the whole encyclopaedia in her head and infinite time and patience to wear him down.[1]

Then as now, the schedule was intensive for three or four days until the magazine "was put to bed," as journalistic parlance describes the printing. On Tuesday, Marietta's editor would give her the weekly assignment, and point her to the most useful sources. "Find them, read them. Go through the Morgue and read all the clips you can on the subject. And Mr. So-and-So, who works on *Fortune,* is a great expert in this field. . . ." So Tuesday, Wednesday, and Thursday, Marietta would immerse herself. On Friday, the writer would produce the story, and Marietta would meticulously check it. The finished piece would probably not reach the copy room until the very last minute on Saturday night or even early morning. Sunday and Monday were her days off, then the process would start all over again.

How the work pleased her!

In this way, she learned an enormous amount in a very short space of time. She had to read six newspapers a day. She had to read the relevant books and interview experts on all subjects from the rise of the British Empire to the death of Bismarck. She had to learn the voting records of all the House committee chairmen in the Senate on important issues. She researched information on subjects such as tax reform, the economics of the New Deal, and the structure of world peace. She fact-checked for a widely disparate pool of writers, including ex-Germans, ex-Trotskyites, ex-Stalinists, ex-advisers to Chiang Kai-shek, and with characteristic zeal challenged them all—the "calm, smiling girl" counteracting this impertinence—on their stories for the magazine.

She shared an office with Earl Brown, a highly regarded black writer who specialized in city politics, baseball, and unions. Initially, Marietta was "sweatily polite" to him, as she put it, to show her lack of prejudice, but the breakthrough came when he chastised her for failing to pass on an important telephone message from labor leader Walter Reuther. Marietta responded hotly, and "in my anger, I suddenly saw a person—Earl Brown, not a black man. The miracle happened. I never saw his color again nor did I ever see anybody's color after that. Our little argument had pierced the veil of my prejudice and at last I could see the whole person beyond."

Through her association with Brown, she first personally experienced the color bar. Only a very few restaurants (mostly French) would allow him to eat lunch with her. Chock Full O'Nuts opened their doors to blacks during the early forties, but very few others. Thanks to Dorothy Paley and the work for Sydenham Hospital, Marietta had begun to understand the injuries being done to American blacks, but for a senior colleague at *Life* to endure such humiliations aroused Marietta's sympathy to a fever pitch. Brown invited Marietta and Dorothy Paley to a party in Harlem, where she met many black professionals—doctors, social workers, lawyers, actors, journalists. "These are the people who will contribute much to forging the future," she declared. At that time, hers was a provocative position, and many friends, including her mother, did not agree with her. "Are you sure, dear, you're not doing something that's too radical?" Mrs. Peabody once asked her. "I don't see how you can be a Christian and say that," Marietta retorted. Later, of course, Mrs. Peabody was brought into the forefront of the struggle.

Marietta met many talented colleagues at *Life* who went on to greater accomplishments, such as the science writers Gerard Piel and Dennis Flanagan, who founded *Scientific American* (fifty years later Flanagan remembered Marietta's great looks and efficient ways. "We loved having her work there").[2] Historian Theodore H. White, playwright Robert Sherwood, photographers Robert and Cornell Capa and Douglas Duncan were among other stars of the Time/Life organization. Sometimes she fact-checked for the editor of *Life,* John K. Jessup, a man she greatly admired. She saw her sessions with him as having the intellectual power of an Oxford tutorial, and was grateful. "To Jack Jessup I owe my real education," she said. (Jessup found her equally intriguing. "She was very bright, very handsome and always dining out in well-connected areas," he said.)

She even did research for Henry R. Luce himself, the legendary founder and editor-in-chief of *Time, Life,* and *Fortune.* She had already met him at a party, and sometimes she traveled up in the elevator with him in the Rockefeller Center building. "Occasionally, if forced to recognize my nervous presence," she recalled, "he would bark out some question such as, 'What does the Field of the Cloth of Gold mean to you?' or 'Name the three most influential men in the world today?' Before I could blurt out, 'Churchill, Stalin and Roosevelt' (knowing he would hate my mentioning Roosevelt), we would have arrived at the 31st floor. As the doors clanged shut, a senior editor, puzzled by this exchange, would ask, 'Say, who was that jerk you were talking to in the elevator?' "

Marietta violently disapproved of Luce's politics (he once told her that he would "vote for a yellow dog if he was a Republican"); with him, however, she could not deploy the ruses the researchers used to sabotage wrong-thinking stories elsewhere in the magazine. If a Fascist Beast who was the subject of a story was to be photographed, for instance, the researcher would ask the photographer to take the picture with the said FB looking *down* into the camera—a pose "which would make even Gary Cooper's face look bloated," Marietta said gleefully.

Luce would not have appreciated his staff's subversive activities. He would not have appreciated, either, the militant union activity within his organization. One day an editor came into Marietta's office and pointed out that her salary, working conditions, and benefits depended entirely on union solidarity, whose members put themselves on the line, jeopardizing their jobs to win these concessions from the management. Would she therefore care to join the Newspaper Guild? Although Marietta, like many people from her background, had been brought up to believe all unions were Communist-run, her work at *Life* had taught her that left-wing politics were not so simple, and she eagerly agreed to join. In no time she had become the shop steward for her floor, collecting dues and attending meetings with all the fervor of a new recruit. (Today, the Guild's power has almost totally evaporated, thanks to the New York newspaper wars of the eighties and nineties.)

While Marietta was constantly polishing up her political opinions, she was never close to becoming a Communist. As Isaiah Berlin observed when he first met her at that time, "She was a progressive, liberal figure who was mixed up with a lot of naive left-wing sympathizers. She saw herself practically as a Trotskyite and was very proud of the fact." [3] In fact, much of Marietta's work with the Newspaper Guild was to prevent Communist infiltration by young radicals who wanted to take control of the union, both locally and internationally. The Guild's strategy involved the usual primitive techniques of bureaucratic powerplays, such as outsitting the Communist rebels at all meetings, so that votes could not be pushed through behind the executive committee's back, and so on. Staying up late hours in this fashion, Marietta felt involved in political action at its most elemental.

There were, of course, many Communists at Time/Life in those years. In the thirties and early forties, Communism still retained something of the ideological virility that had originally attracted so many American intellectuals to the party. At that time, Russia was still an ally against Germany in the war, and the bitter sense of having been betrayed was yet to erode the commitment of these idealists. On one occasion, when Marietta was researching one of Jessup's editorials on economics, she found a sentence she did not understand, so she called out to the pool of her research colleagues, "Who's an economist here?" About six hands went up out of ten. Marietta went from one to the other of these six, and none of them understood the sentence. "Well," Marietta said to them, "I thought you said you were all economists here." "Oh," one said. "We thought you asked, 'Who's a Communist here?' "

Because of Marietta's Guild connections, she was appointed a vice chairman of the CIO's national political action committee in the presidential election of 1944. She modestly attributed this appointment partly to her new-found loyalty to FDR and partly to her politically correct name—Marietta FitzGerald, half Italian, half Irish. She attended a huge CIO PAC luncheon for Eleanor Roosevelt that summer, where she sat on the dais between a leader of the young Democrats and Frank Sinatra. She also invited top union officials, such as Walter Reuther, Jack Conway, and Philip Murray to her apartment to discuss the campaign. Exposure to American blue-collar politics provided Marietta with education no university could possibly have given her, and she threw herself into this new, tough, grass-roots world with characteristic ardor.

As well as late night research assignments and union meetings, there were late night parties, both within the office and out on the town. Marietta admired her colleagues, felt comfortable with the guys, no longer had to pretend to be dumb, would have worked all through the night if asked, and was, as she told an interviewer much later, "in a kind of fever of happiness the whole of the two years I was there."

Work over for the day, she would rush home to give a dinner party for foreign visitors arriving in New York or new political or reporter friends, or go out with the Warburgs, Paleys, or Astors. She sometimes went dancing at El Morocco as much as four nights a week. Henry Luce was always sticking his head in the office of her boss, Jack Jessup, and saying, "I dined out again last night with that researcher of yours."

Her assignments sometimes made the crossover into her social life. To celebrate the first general election in Britain after V-E Day, Marietta was asked to produce a history of British democracy. Some of the issues baffled her, and when one night she found herself at a small dinner in the Colony restaurant next to the duke of Windsor, she was enchanted. He could answer the questions which she had been unable to check.

"Sir, could you describe to me the process of the Salic Law?"

"No, not really."

"Oh. Did the laws of British royal succession start with the Empress Sofia of Hanover?"

He gave her a piercing look. "You know, I really couldn't answer that. But why don't you get in touch with my mother, she knows all about that kind of thing."

"Wouldn't it be difficult to approach her?"

"Well, I can do it if you like—but no, why don't you just wire the Palace?"

But Marietta was not yet through.

"Sir, is Eire a member of the British Commonwealth?"

"Yes, I think so." (He was wrong.)

The duke asked her why she was asking these strange questions.

"Because, sir, we are doing a story on the rise of British democracy in connection with the British General Election next week."

"Well," said the duke, "if Churchill wins, that's fine. But if Attlee and the Socialists win, that is the end of democracy in Britain."

"Why, sir?"

"Don't you know the Socialists are the same thing as Communists, and the Communists in power will do away with British democracy!"

Marietta did not think much of this source. She found him stupid, anti-Semitic, and generally prejudiced, conceding, however, his "ner-

Marietta in the bathtub at 563 Park Avenue. On the back of photo she has written, "Medaeval [*sic*] plumbing." (This was one of several pictures she sent to Desie in Burma in 1943 of her and Frankie in the apartment.)

Sharing a joke at 563 Park. This, along with other snapshots with Frankie at home, originally taken when Desie was away at the war, was enclosed in a letter from Marietta to Ronald Tree in England in 1946.

vous charm, and elegant manners and dress." She was more impressed with the duchess of Windsor, in particular her prodigious memory. In a later meeting, she recalled, "When the Duchess commented that the color of my dress was more becoming than the black one I wore last year, or the aquamarine one I'd worn the year before, I expostulated quite unconsciously, 'My, if you could only put that memory to some creative use,'—thinking what a wonderful reporter she would have made. She assented and five minutes later she did a double-take and came across the room to say, 'You know, my dear, my memory has been so useful in the kind of life I lead *now!*' "

With her fatter paycheck (worth $700 a week in 1997 dollars), supplemented by weekly overtime pay and Desie's allowance, Marietta was beginning to live quite luxuriously. The new duplex apartment at 563 Park Avenue which Marietta and Frankie moved into in October 1944, had ten rooms and gold fixtures in the bathrooms. It was looked after by Helen, the housekeeper, and Alice, Frankie's latest nanny. Marietta gave receptions and dinner parties every week, sometimes for as many as thirty. All food was catered and delivered to the apartment, and her housekeeper did the household and personal shopping for the family. During this time Marietta's wardrobe was greatly expanded with clothes carrying labels like Hattie Carnegie, Valentina, and Fulkenstein. More closets were needed. More clothes were bought. More parties were planned.

She admitted later that some of her colleagues at the office must have felt she lived in a different world. Not many researchers, after all, wore designer clothes to work. But many barriers were being broken during the war, and she continued to rush from office to nightclub, from "cabbages to kings," as she put it, relishing her freedom.

Meanwhile, Desie wrote saying he was "somewhere in Burma." (In fact he was with a regiment of Chinese troops on the march to China.)[4] In the summer of 1944 he managed to get a leave, which he spent in Calcutta. He sent Marietta some lovely Indian scarves during that visit. After the leave, he was sent away to a place he was not allowed to name, and Marietta, reading about the heavy fighting of American and Chinese troops, feared the worst. She kept all his letters, and sometimes read them aloud to friends. As usual, Frankie spent much of July and August in Northeast Harbor with Alice. Marietta managed to get up for two weeks, again expressing her love, gratitude, and dependency on her parents.

In July 1944, Marietta's eldest brother, Endicott, who was in the U.S. Navy submarine service, married Barbara (known as Toni) Gibbons, a beautiful young woman who had been born and raised in Bermuda. Though Marietta had firm friendships with women, this new entry into the Peabody family was another matter altogether. Marietta had become quite used to being the only female, and her competitive spirit was galvanized by this introduction of a pretty, blond, green-eyed rival to her throne. Toni, a highly strung young woman, was awed by her beautiful sister-in-law and felt the antagonism keenly. Insecure in her new family, she also felt that Bishop and Mrs. Peabody looked down on her.

Toni borrowed Marietta's wedding dress for the New York ceremony, since water damage had ruined her own during its journey from Bermuda to New York in Endicott's submarine. This apparent exercise in generosity provoked a mist of resentment in both borrower and lender, and symbolically marked the beginning of what was to be a tortuous relationship.[5]

The other major family event that year was the death in November of Marietta's grandfather, the former Rector of Groton, at the age of eighty-seven. Magazines and newspapers filled columns with praise for

At the 1944 wedding of Marietta's brother Endicott to Toni Gibbons, with the retired Rector of Groton, Endicott Peabody, and his wife, Fannie.

the pioneering educator and legendary headmaster who had inspired so many boys to a life of Christian values and public service. That month also saw the reelection of Franklin Delano Roosevelt to an unprecedented fourth term, living proof of the power of the Groton ethos, even if the Rector himself had not in this case been on the side of the angels.

Marietta's increasing visibility as a successful working journalist brought her offers of other employment. Through the influence of the playwright Sidney Kingsley, one of the Warburgs' inner circle of friends, Marietta was invited to join a literary agency. She was also offered a job by *The New York Times* as a political reporter. She refused both, the first for lack of experience, the second because she had no confidence in her ability to write. Anyway, she was happy at *Life*.

In the early part of 1945, Desie, now in China, was promoted from captain to major. Later that spring, there was a flurry of excitement that he might be coming home to spend the summer in the United States and return to China in September. "Naturally, there is a storm of butterflies in my stomach, and I feel I ought to go to the hairdresser every day, just in case he should suddenly appear," Marietta wrote to her father. Meanwhile, she made sure the apartment was looking good for his first sight of it (she had sent him photographs). But the hope turned out to be false, and they were not reunited until after the war ended.

Marietta had little time to mourn. She was given a flying lesson by an RAF pilot, met the Czechoslovakian leader Jan Masaryk, teased Lord Beaverbrook, and gave a party for Lord Cranborne, whose wife came instead, dressed so sloppily that Marietta wondered why Englishwomen had so little style outside a tweed suit. Perhaps her favorite moment was a dinner conversation with Lord Lovat, the dashing British former commando and Tory cabinet minister, whose Churchill-led government had just been defeated in a shocking Labour landslide, the consequences of which Marietta had been researching for a seventeen-page story for *Life*. "I sailed into him all evening long, stressing mainly that the accident of his birth had brought him all these benefits . . . and he'd better get educated quick, as he had a large debt to pay back to society, and painted in blackest colors the misery and uselessness of his life if he simply sat back and went to Ascot. . . ." This tirade evidently silenced the arrogant laird, who became "as meek as a persecuted mouse," Marietta exulted. "I was amazed, but boy was it fun!" (Shimi Lovat also thought so. Smitten by this gloriously preachy goddess, he remained an admirer for the rest of his life.)

How different Marietta sounds now from the tentative young woman who started out in 1941 to find a job. As with many women, she had been transformed by the war. *Life* had given her what she craved—work of substance, of significance, work that stretched her intellectually, that was always renewing, relevant. With this work and the financial freedom it allowed her, she discovered a sense of confidence and independence unimaginable to prewar women of her generation. The gender rules were being rewritten, and Marietta's hand was on the page.

A draft letter she composed later to describe her days at *Life* contained the following final paragraph: "My entire life was indeed changed by the job. I would never have become militant in the opening battles for civil rights, never become a shop steward in the CIO, never become a Democrat, never known the difference between a Trotskyite and a Stalinist, a Stakhanovite and a Henry Georgeite, a paradigm and a paradox, and never fallen in love."

In this unfinished manuscript, the last five words have been crossed out. Crossed out, but not erased. They live, still clearly legible, in her tall, wide-spaced, breathless hand. However urgently Marietta wished to excise that last phrase, either because of its indiscretion or for her own peace of mind, it remains on the faded pad, stubborn testimony to an event that happened in 1945, in the last year of the war, an event that brought this young woman, already in a maelstrom of change and growth, to a new frontier. The man's name was John Huston.

Marietta pretending to be a bank president while researching a story about big business for *Life,* July 1945.
*(Herbert Gehr for Life)*

# CHAPTER *12*

# *From "Miss Boston"*
# *to "Miss World"*

Marietta first met John Huston in late 1942, at a dinner party given by
Sidney and Madge Kingsley at the "21" Club in New York. There were
two extra men at the dinner, so when Mary Warburg, who had been
originally invited, asked if she could bring Marietta, Madge Kingsley
was delighted.

Marietta sat next to John Huston. "I couldn't think of anything
to say," Marietta said later, "so I said, 'Are you any relation to Sam
Houston?' He thought for a bit. 'Who's Sam Houston?' " It did not
matter what they said. The encounter was electric. They never looked
at anyone else the whole evening.

It ended equally dramatically. Marietta had felt "perfectly awful"
that day and had taken two pills. They drank bourbon on the rocks
and wine with dinner. At some point great purple welts started appearing all over her face (her complexion once again letting her down).
"John," Marietta said, "I'm getting chicken pox or measles, and I
must go this very minute." Huston volunteered to take her home.
Shortly after, she fainted. When she opened her eyes, John was nowhere to be seen. The headwaiter helped her downstairs, where John
reappeared and took her home. John disagreed with this version of the
story. He said he helped put a cold compress on her head and did not
disappear at all. "She got up and one of the first things she said was,
'I'm not drunk.' "[1]

At thirty-six, Huston was the country's newest cultural hero,
thanks to his first feature film, *The Maltese Falcon,* which had been

released in 1941 to huge critical and commercial acclaim. But he was at this time deeply involved in war work. He had gone to the Aleutian Islands earlier in 1942 to document the war there (mostly a messy and expensive series of air battles), and at the time he met Marietta, he was working on its final editing.

During the winter of 1943 and spring of 1944 he went to Italy to film the progress of the American forces on their way from Naples up to Rome before being finally ordered back to the United States in the early summer of 1944. On his brief leaves, he would go to New York and call on Marietta. At this time, he was still married to his second wife, Lesley Black, and carrying on a tumultuous affair with Olivia de Havilland. But he found time for Marietta, and he took her all over New York, spending night after night bar-hopping, enthralling her with tales of his movies, his adventures, his childhood, the brutal scenes of war he had witnessed overseas. Wide-eyed, she listened to his stories, breathing in the strange magic of this Irish spellbinder.

And all the time, he was falling in love with her: "I would steal glances at her. The slope of her neck from shoulder to ear; the angle of her jaw, as though drawn by Piero della Francesca. . . . She was the most beautiful and desirable woman I had ever known."[2]

John Huston's moviemaking talents were matched by his colorful private life. Already married twice, he was a hard drinker, an obsessive gambler, a compulsive womanizer, and a wildly attractive man who lived a bold, spontaneous, and free-wheeling life. Marriage meant little to him, his own or his lady friends'. In 1943, he met a young woman in London whose husband was away in the RAF. When he invited her to his apartment, she had the temerity to tell him she was faithful to her husband and wanted to keep the relationship platonic. His response so scared her that she fled the apartment while he was fixing drinks.

John Huston was intensely exciting to the still stage-struck Marietta. Huston at this point was war-weary, cosmopolitan, eleven years older than Marietta (always an attraction for her), and his friends in the movie and writing business were mostly in their thirties and forties, thus to her exemplars of wit and sophistication. She was meeting famous authors, movie stars, and directors, on the inside of this glamorous world for the first time.

But for a while, like the young wife in London, Marietta also resisted this brazen suitor. "I felt it was very important to be faithful to my husband, or faithful to the man at the front," she declared later. This was no great sacrifice on her part. Her upbringing had trained her to indulge in chaste flirtations. She and the other women of her class and generation knew how to entertain men without provoking messy entanglements. Although the war had relaxed some of these conventions, Marietta did not succumb so easily. Her sexually chilled background and strict parental values were powerful inhibitors. There-fore, while she was fascinated by John Huston, she was less than totally infatuated. For John, of course, as for most philanderers confronted with such a challenge, her restraint was wildly tantalizing.

After the completion of his film *The Battle of San Pietro* in 1944, Huston began a film for the army, *Let There Be Light,* an in-depth examination of the psychological impact of the war on men in combat. The Mason General Hospital on Long Island was his prime location, and since he was living more or less permanently in New York for the duration of the movie, he was able to see Marietta more regularly—among other women, of course, including Olivia de Havilland, and Doris Lilly (inspiration for Holly Golightly in *Breakfast at Tiffany's*).

In April 1945, Lesley divorced John, so he was a free man. His attention to Marietta intensified, with the idea of marriage firmly in his mind. They used to stay at the Warburgs' White Plains farm on weekends, where Marietta often took Frankie to escape from the city and play with Mary's son, David. The first mention of Huston (un-named) to her parents occurs at this time. "Tonite," she wrote, "to Mary W's for the weekend with Frankie, a British Air Marshall [*sic*], and a delightful movie director, now doing movies for the army."

Delightful? There might have been more explicit adjectives, but they would hardly have been suitable for her parents' ears. Marietta had never experienced such physical intensity in a man. No wonder she fainted that first night she met him. None of her well-bred New England liaisons had prepared her for this stronghold of testosterone. The range of emotions pitched by the men in her life, including her husband, seemed like matchsticks compared to the lofty struts of John Huston's erotic exuberance. Thus, after three years of persistence on the part of this famously experienced Don Juan, Marietta, disciplined for so long, finally entered the forbidden portals.

"That summer was a time of enchantment," John Huston wrote in his autobiography nearly forty years later. "I'd have moments of wonder at my good fortune; I was alive with the most desirable woman in creation at my side."

Huston was a devoted companion. When Marietta worked late into the night putting the magazine to bed, he waited patiently outside in his army uniform. He encouraged her in her work, discussing poli-tics, art, literature. He taught her her most important lesson: "That I was not Miss Boston. I was instead Miss World."

He frequently came to the apartment on Park Avenue and made friends with Frankie, who loved him. "He used to tell stories and sing songs, and pay a lot of attention to me. He gave me a toy I still have." Since her father had left for the war, Huston was the first man in Frankie's life to show affection to her, and she never forgot it.

All that summer at the Warburgs', Marietta and John played tennis, rode horses, swam, and loved each other. One morning, Mary had to leave early for New York, and left a note for them adding an old western saying, "Yours till the bedsprings break." Marietta was mortified. It turned out that the bed she and John were in had collapsed that night. "I was only kissing him good night," she insisted uselessly to her knowing friend.

Marietta's dinner parties now regularly featured Huston. Friends remember how he never took his eyes off her. She blossomed under the intense light of his love, irradiated with a new sense of power and confidence. Like him, she was jubilant. "I just went head over heels."

For Marietta, John Huston was the missing link. She had achieved so much in terms of social and career experience. But in one area she was still almost totally unversed. She had had sex with only one man, her husband, whose personality and background did not promise great expertise in the complex arena of pleasing a woman, particularly a woman who had been taught that touching, hugging, stroking, and kissing were almost as distasteful as sex itself. With even the inexperienced couplings with Desie now reduced to abstinence since he left three years earlier, Marietta, twenty-eight years old, and having flirted more or less outrageously with men for over ten years, was ripe indeed for the plucking.

For those last few months in the late summer of 1945, she and John had a glorious time together. He made her lighten up, forget her solemn politicking. He would make her sing. "Summertime," for instance. "Summertime . . ." she would begin. "Higher," he would command. Out would come "Summertime . . ." a little higher. "Higher still." "Summertime . . ." And up and up until they collapsed with laughter.

She met John's beloved father, so different from her own father. Walter Huston took to her at once but was anxious about her and John's future together. What would happen when her husband came back? "Why, we'll tell him how we feel about each other and he'll give Marietta a divorce and we'll get married," said John blithely.

In August, she went up to Northeast Harbor for her annual visit to Frankie (who had been there since the beginning of July) and the family. She slept and rested and again expressed to her parents how restorative Northeast Harbor was—"the long picnic days, the pleasant foggy afternoons by the fire—everything in short there is to being in Northeast and with one's family was just the way I hoped it would be."

But although the war was finally over that August, the vacation was not an easy one for Marietta. No wonder she slept and saw few people and hailed so earnestly the meaning of family. For Marietta FitzGerald, child of the Puritan tribunal, had finally broken the faith.

They say that the first time a woman sleeps with a man other than her husband is like losing her virginity all over again. Sleeping with John Huston put Marietta beyond the pale. That decision separated her from her past far more definitively than any formal rejection. Short of murder, she had committed the ultimate sin against God and betrayed every value the Peabody family had indoctrinated in her. It *was* murder, in a sense. She had killed any hope for the pure and blameless life her parents had expected of her. In the last judgment, she would be found guilty.

When Marietta came back to New York, the pace with John picked up, but with an edge of panic. She had finally received word from the Far East: Desie was coming home.

The rumor mills had already started to churn. Various friends had heard about John Huston, and were trying to be kind. "Desie has been away so long," they murmured. "It's not really surprising." Whether her parents had picked up any of this gossip is not clear, but they both wrote to her as though sensing trouble in the marriage, urging her to be affectionate to Desie when he came home, and to enlarge her family soon. Marietta responded violently:

> I am 28 years old now, and if I haven't learned these obvious things by now, there's no point telling me anything. What I would like every once in a while is a little approval from you both—as a matter of fact, that is what I have wanted all my life from you, and never felt—or certainly rarely felt that I had it— as compared to what you give Endicott and Mike, for instance. You have done so much more for me than most parents, that I have no cause for complaint, and overflow with gratitude—but I do get approval from others (even in the family) and can't be entirely wrong—and naturally, I would rather have it from you two than anybody else—except Desie.

This outburst shows the extent of her emotional turmoil. Guilty, she became angry. Defiant, she begged for her parents' sanction.

Desmond arrived home in mid-November 1945. Marietta told him immediately about John Huston. In his autobiography, *An Open Book,* Huston writes: "I didn't hear from her for three days after Desmond arrived. Then she came to my hotel. I could see that she'd been through an ordeal: her face was drawn and her eyes swollen. Desmond had agreed to give her a divorce but only on condition that she see an analyst and undergo therapy before starting proceedings."[3]

This is Huston's version. Huston's lawyer, Henry Hyde, confirmed that he thought Marietta had confronted Desie with the request for a divorce as soon as he stepped off the dock. It is difficult, however, to imagine Marietta making this demand so precipitously. It seems doubtful that she could have been sure about her wish to end the marriage at this time. She had not seen her husband for three years. The idea of her demanding a divorce at this early stage seems to have been something Huston invented for himself. Or perhaps she let Huston think it was true. It is almost certain that she never mentioned to Desie any idea of *marrying* Huston. The thought of separation was dramatic enough, "divorce" a word she was only just beginning to articulate, and that with difficulty.

Although Marietta had kept up the conjugal front with family and friends during Desie's absence, it is possible that by 1945 he had heard some rumblings of trouble. Some letters he wrote from China to his in-laws that year were signed rather pointedly, "Frankie's father." But he was also making plans to buy the Parkman house in Northeast Harbor (which had been sold at the beginning of the war) on his return, and in late September wrote how greatly he was looking forward to Christmas in Syracuse with the whole family reunited.[4]

He was obviously not expecting serious marital trouble, and being a very stubborn man, it is inconceivable he would have agreed to give Marietta up without a fight.[5] Moreover, he was deeply attached to his daughter, whom he was just connecting with again after a long absence.

If indeed it was Desie who suggested the therapy (which would have been a desperation measure for him, given his background and temperament), it was probably because, like many people at that time unfamiliar with the complexities of aberrational behavior, he saw her as temporarily deranged, and in need of treatment to bring her back to her former "real" self.

Marietta's entry into psychoanalysis in early 1946 (she began seeing a woman doctor on Park Avenue) was also encouraged by her friend Dorothy Paley, who was a passionate convert. Marietta's view of psychoanalysis became equally affirmative, and for the rest of her life she would assert that therapy was one of the best experiences that had ever happened to her.

But therapeutic treatment is time-consuming. Its effects are long term, and Desmond and Marietta needed a much quicker-acting medicine to ease their malaise. They began having rows almost immediately. Desmond demanded that Marietta quit her job. He wanted to know what she was doing about Frankie's education. He wanted his friends in the apartment for dinner parties. He wanted his closets and his clothes back. (Marietta had given away some of his suits.) Having suffered long and courageously in a terrible war, he wanted his share of a life that Marietta had enjoyed without him for over four years. Above all, he wanted *her*.[6]

Thus in one fell swoop, Marietta was being asked to surrender many of the things she cared about—the job which she adored and in which she had learned so much, the attractive, artistic, witty older friends she so preferred to Desie's right-wing Harvard buddies, the free-spirited day and night life of New York, the admirer who had opened her mind and heart to love and laughter, not to mention the closet space.

Although Desie had hoped for a reunion with his in-laws, the FitzGeralds spent Christmas 1945 in New York. Her parents were very hurt they did not come to Syracuse for Desie's first holiday home from the war, but Marietta explained to them that she had been feeling poorly, with fainting spells and exhaustion. "So both Desie and the doctor didn't want me to go away at this time."

The fainting spells and exhaustion, as symptomatic as a Victorian woman's vapors, reflected the extreme tension between the couple trying to patch up their lives at 563 Park Avenue. Like many an ex-war widow, Marietta found that she was expected to slip back enthusiastically into the role of a good wife—in every sense of the word. (Rose Parsons Lynch, a Peabody cousin, stayed with Marietta during the war and remembered Marietta sitting on the bed filing her nails, and telling those present, "In wartime, it is very important to remember that men miss their women. So they will be very eager when they come back. Especially if you are a married woman, you must take this into account and hold them off.")

Like many husbands back from the war, Desmond FitzGerald found himself in a time warp. He had left a world where things were in a certain place and people behaved in a certain way. His brief leaves, treated like celebrations rather than real life, shored up that belief. Four years ago, he had said good-bye to a wife who was an eager, attentive homemaker and hostess. He came back to find a woman he hardly recognized. Not only was she a confident, independent, elegantly dressed career woman, but she was "holding him off" while having betrayed him beyond the limits of his comprehension.

Meanwhile, Huston's instructions were to leave her alone. He returned to California. In his book he says he "lived from one call to another." This is no doubt true, but he was not suffering alone. He continued to go to parties and enjoy the company of women, while he worked on the script for *Treasure of the Sierra Madre*. But it was a time, he said, of great frustration.

After Christmas had lurched to its unhappy conclusion, the Fitz-Geralds went on a trip together. Mary Warburg, also coping with a husband back from the war, had invited the couple to join them on a vacation in Mexico after Christmas. At the last minute, Marietta called Mary and suggested they change their plans and go to Barbados instead, where Ronald Tree had invited them to stay at Sir Edward Cunard's house in Glitter Bay. Mary willingly agreed.

Ronald Tree, a sophisticated, urbane Anglo-American who lived in England, was well known to many of Marietta's New York friends. Dorothy Paley had met him in England through her first husband, Jack Hearst, and had later introduced him to Bill Paley. During the war, while Paley was visiting London, he stayed with Ronnie and his stylish American wife, Nancy, at Ditchley Park, the Trees' magnificent Georgian country house in Oxfordshire. Mary Warburg's sister Edwina D'Erlanger, also knew the Trees well and for a time lived on the Ditchley estate. Ronnie's war work with the British Ministry of Information brought him frequently to New York and to dinner at the Paleys, which is where he probably first met—and fell in love with—Marietta.

The FitzGeralds and the Warburgs set off in January 1946, driving down through Virginia, stopping at Mirador, Nancy Tree's family home where she and Ronald had first lived after their marriage, and then at the South Carolina plantation of the Trees' cousins, Marshall III and Ruth Field. Their final U.S. destination was Palm Beach, where the FitzGeralds stayed with Desie's father and stepmother, and the Warburgs stayed with Mary's in-laws. (Marietta came back complaining furiously to Mary about Desie's ultraconservative family.) From Miami, they took a little plane that island-hopped down the Caribbean until it reached Trinidad, where the couples spent the night.

"There was an earthquake in Trinidad," Mary Warburg remembered. "We slept through it, but Desie and Marietta argued all night long. That was when I first sensed something was wrong." Marietta later said she did not even know there was an earthquake, thinking it was her anger that was causing the room to shake.

They finally reached Sir Edward Cunard's house in Glitter Bay, on the west coast of Barbados. Ronnie Tree was there to welcome them, along with his friend George McCullough, an amusing but rather drunken Canadian newspaper proprietor. Tree offered his visitors a choice of bedrooms, one with a double bed, the other with two singles. The Warburgs chose the two single beds (Mary was recovering from chicken pox), leaving the FitzGeralds the double, a padded cell for dysfunctional couples. From the start of the vacation, Desie slept on the floor, until Ronnie tactfully set up a cot in the room.

They stayed in Barbados for three weeks. From Marietta's point of view, apart from time spent in the bedroom, the holiday was magical. She had never been to a tropical island, and the clear turquoise water, hot sun, soft sand, and whispering palm trees were a revelation. Trips to Italy and England had not prepared her for the intoxicating atmosphere of the Caribbean in January—the perfect antidote to the chilly Bostonian landscape of her childhood.

The six swam and walked on the beach, drank a lot of rum, were serenaded at night by strolling bands. Marietta and Ronnie went off sailing together almost every day. Occasionally, Mary would ask plaintively if she and Eddie might go along. "No," they were told firmly. "The boat is too small."

The vacationers returned to the United States in February, back through Trinidad and Palm Beach, the latter again for Marietta "solid nausea." On February 19, en route to South Carolina, where the FitzGeralds were finishing up their vacation, Marietta wrote a thank-you letter to their host in Barbados. "Darling Ronnie," she wrote in her upright, eager hand. "It seems about 52 years since I last saw you, and that's about 52 years of ache, and 52 years of living in memory. . . ." Three days later, back in New York, she wrote to him again, "For a confirmed non–letter writer, I find myself wanting to write to you every day—practically any conversation or reaction or event has the corollary: Ronnie must be told. Darling, I do hope you are feeling somewhat the same way."

Ronnie was. He sent her a welcome home telegram to New York, followed up by two letters that became worn almost to shreds from Marietta's reading and rereading them. "They have been my only happiness since leaving you," she told him.

But what of John Huston? Wasn't he in California waiting for her to get her divorce and decide to marry him? Wasn't he desperately longing for the telephone to ring? "Sometimes she'd be late calling and I'd sweat blood, waiting," was the way he described his enforced banishment.

The wind had changed, with startling suddenness.

Who could have guessed that while John continued to sweat it out in California, Marietta was bewitched by her island Prospero, reliving those weeks in Barbados, "lying on the beach, or watching the flying fish from the top of a green wave," declaring with reckless certainty, "The single important thing in my life is darling, extraordinary you and the longing to be with you forever and ever."?

While rumors of Marietta's giddy New York life had drifted north to Boston and south to Philadelphia, most of her friends from home would have been astonished that Marietta Peabody could be writing such letters to a totally new and unknown figure in her life. And so soon after her husband had returned from the war? It was inconceivable.

Yet few knew just how much those war years had changed her. Very soon after Desmond's return to 563 Park Avenue, she saw how hopeless their marriage was. The contrast between them now appeared irreconcilable. If he had changed through his war experiences, it was not in the way she wished. But even more significantly, it was her experience with John Huston that exposed with such devastating clarity the barrenness of her relationship with Desie. She had become in the modern term "empowered," and there was no turning back.

The switch from Huston to Tree is perhaps the most intriguing aspect of this drama. Marietta always asserted that John Huston was not someone she ever thought of marrying, in spite of his claims. Whatever she felt for him, she knew that his wildness, his financial unreliability, and his sexual fickleness would have made him a disastrous husband. In a novel called *The Big Girls,* written by Nancy Holmes almost forty years later, the romance between Delphine and Ryan is based on Marietta and John. The affair collapses, in spite of its intensity, because Delphine discovers Ryan in bed with another woman.[7] Ms. Holmes, a society journalist, later declared that Marietta was the only woman Huston ever really loved, but that Marietta could not accept his infidelities and that she had other plans. Ms. Holmes was right. Marietta had other plans. In spite of his undeniable charms, John Huston was not the right person to inhabit the future she wished for herself, and thus, turning on a dime, with cool resolve she set her face against him.

But although John Huston was not the man to lead her out of the desert, he had prepared the way. It is almost impossible that Marietta would have had the ability, either emotional or financial, to move out and live on her own. In those days, it would have required a trust fund and a more unconventional spirit than Marietta's to take such a drastic step. But now her saviour was at hand: Ronald Tree, whom she had met socially a year earlier, was suddenly transformed during that glorious three-week vacation in Barbados into the prince she had once dreamed of as a child. Just as Desie had done seven years earlier, Ronnie would rescue her and offer her the world—not only the world that Huston had prescribed for her, but an even greater one, promising the fulfillment of all her ambitions.

# CHAPTER *13*

# *Anglo-American Relations*

In January 1946, at a party given for Mrs. Randolph Churchill (later Pamela Harriman), a young ex-war-reporter just back from Europe was approached by a tall, beautiful blonde, who said, "Are you Bill Walton? I was a researcher and read all your war dispatches and cables and would love to talk to you." Walton was dazzled by Marietta's introduction, and very soon they became close friends. Walton remembered particularly a benefit ball at the Waldorf they both attended later that spring. Marietta said to him, "Can I bring a British friend of mine?" It was Ronald Tree. Walton knew Ronnie and had visited Ditchley, so they had an enjoyable evening and then the three of them went on to a nightclub. "I thought it would be a good thing to get rid of Ronnie at this point," Bill Walton said ruefully, "until I realized it was me they wanted to get rid of!" [1]

Ronald Arthur Lambert Field Tree was born on September 26, 1897, in a handsome English house called Ashorne Hill in Warwickshire. He was the only child of Arthur Tree, also an only child and heir to a large Chicago real estate fortune accumulated by Ronald's paternal grandfather, Lambert Tree, a judge and one-time ambassador to Russia. Ronnie's maternal grandfather was even richer; he was the Chicago millionaire department store founder, Marshall Field.

Arthur fell in love with Marshall Field's only daughter, Ethel, on the hunting field in England. Both had rejected the United States for the delights of British fox-hunting and polo. When they married, she was seventeen years old and heiress to part of a fortune that, when

Marshall Field died, was estimated at over $120 million dollars, an astronomical figure in those days.

When Ronnie was three, his mother bolted and his parents divorced. The scandal was greatly heightened by the circumstances: Ethel Tree had been spotted out hunting by a dashing naval officer, David Beatty, who fell madly in love with her. Without a backward glance, Ethel left her husband and child and ran off with her glamorous suitor.

Bitterness flowed. As the only child of a very rich man, Ethel had heedlessly committed large sums of money to very expensive additions to the house she so blithely abandoned. After the divorce, of course, and her marriage to Beatty, who was later created an earl for heroism in World War I, her funds were no longer available, and Arthur, whose father was very ungenerous with his allowances from the United States, was reduced to straitened circumstances. Ronnie conceded that they still lived well, with servants and polo ponies, but his child's heart was scarred by the sense of anxiety that permeated the household. Adding to this insecurity was the realization of how much his father had been hurt by the divorce. As he wrote later, "From the time my mother left him, it seems to me in retrospect, he changed completely. Except for a few friendly neighbors and a handful of old friends who would occasionally come and stay, his contacts with others seemed to atrophy; he dropped out of the world in which he had been brought up."

The little boy suffered the companionship of a lonely and disappointed father with protective fortitude. Occasionally, his mother, "looking very beautiful and smart," would drive over to see her son, having declared an interest in gaining custody, but he treated her coldly, conscious of the pain her visits inflicted upon his father. Arthur took Ronnie to visit his grandfather in the United States, and on other occasions Judge Lambert Tree would come to England and take them on grand trips to meet European royalty. The old man was disappointed that his son was living what he regarded as a wasteful expatriate life, and regarded his grandson as the hope of the family. Lambert Tree died in the late summer of 1910 when Ronnie was thirteen. In his will, Tree left the income from his considerable fortune to his son for life, thus relieving Arthur of any financial worries. The judge also expressed his wish that his grandson would return to take up a career in public service in the United States, a wish that was to influence Ronnie's future.

The following September Ronnie went to Winchester, one of England's most academically demanding and distinguished boarding schools. He loved it. Like many children from lonely or broken homes, the structure, social life, and security of boarding school gave him confidence and allowed him to make friends and enjoy work and sports in a way that up until then had been denied him. Sadly, this experience was cut short.

In 1914, war broke out, and that year, Ronnie's father, fifty-two years old, was struck down with a perforated appendix. Ronnie rushed to be with him in the hospital. In despair, he realized his father was not going to recover. "A few days before he died, when I was at his bedside," Ronnie related, "a message was brought to me: there was a lady wishing to see me in the waiting room. When I got there, a woman whom I had never seen before rose with outstretched arms to greet me with the words, 'Your mother has sent me to take you away.'"

Ronnie was sixteen years old, and had not seen his mother since he was seven. His horror at the appearance of this nightmarish messenger can only be imagined. "I burst out with a refusal and went back to my father's bedside." Arthur Tree died the following day.

Ethel Beatty made another attempt to reclaim her son, this time appearing in person before him at the home of the American consul in Southampton. Again the boy refused to go with her.

Thus Ronald Tree had no parents and no home. His American trustees urged him to return to the United States, in accordance with his grandfather's wishes, so Ronnie went back to Chicago, where he met his relations and promptly joined the navy, signing up to train as a pilot. He was posted to Brest in France, and spent the rest of the war flying submarine-spotting patrols. In 1918 he became attaché to his uncle Thomas Nelson Page, then U.S. ambassador in Rome, and when that assignment ended a year later, he returned to London by boat. On the boat was another relation by marriage, Nancy Perkins Field, widow of his cousin Henry Field (Marshall Field III's brother), who was traveling to spend Christmas in London with her aunt, Nancy Astor. Ronnie fell in love with her at first sight.

Nancy had married Henry Field in 1917. Five months after the marriage, he died from a pulmonary embolism, a tragic and unnecessary complication after a tonsillectomy. Owing to the brevity of the marriage, the disbursement of his will caused some dispute, but a settlement was ultimately made upon his young wife.

The following May, 1920, Nancy and Ronnie married in London.

Ronnie did not invite his mother or stepfather to his wedding. But in the late 1920s, as neighbors in England, Ronnie, Ethel, and David Beatty became reacquainted, and Ronnie became deeply attached both to his stepfather and to his two half brothers, David and Peter.

History will not be kind to Ronnie's mother. She abandoned her firstborn son, and was a sick and unhappy woman most of her life. She gambled, frequently ran away abroad, had affairs (Peter, her second son, was born of another father), and seemed in her later years mentally disturbed. Today, she would probably have been diagnosed as a manic-depressive and helped by medication.[2]

Ethel died in a deep depression in 1933 at the age of fifty-eight. Earl Beatty wrote to his stepson Ronnie with a generous epitaph, "There never was a more truly generous minded woman when she was not afflicted, and it is as such that we have to think of her."

Ronnie's emotional life had always hinged on male caregivers— his grandfather, who had offered him his only real experience of af-fection; his father, whose private despair and loneliness had inhibited his ability to express love; finally, his stepfather, who had shown him the sort of kindness he had been mostly starved of during his upbring-ing. So when in 1936 Earl Beatty died of pneumonia, Ronnie felt his death deeply, and remained in close touch with his two half brothers. (Peter was born with an infection caught from his mother that later made him blind. Ronnie looked after him, taking him to medical expert after expert, until Peter died by his own hand in 1950.)

With his marriage, Ronnie began a new life with a woman who outshone many of her class and generation. Nancy was a Langhorne from Virginia, with all the beauty, wit, and energy that the family possessed in such abundance. The couple decided they wanted to live in America, and with Ronnie's considerable wealth from his grandfa-ther's trust fund, plus Nancy's money, they bought Mirador, the beau-tiful country house in the Blue Ridge Mountains of Virginia that had belonged to Nancy's grandfather.

At Mirador, Nancy found expression for the first time for the talent that later made her famous. She completely redecorated the house, adding a gracefully curving main staircase, an upstairs landing spacious enough for a chamber group to perform at parties, and a skylight. She designed wonderful gardens in the English style, with perennial borders, arbors, ponds, and fountains. With their combined wealth, Ronnie and Nancy turned Mirador into a mecca for parties, hunts, and balls.

But the fun did not last. In November 1922, Nancy gave birth to an infant daughter who died the same day. By this time, Ronnie had discovered he was prevented from pursuing a career in American poli-tics because of his English birth and accent. Restless with his sybaritic life, he was anxious to pursue a career in public service, as his grandfa-ther had wished.

In 1926, the Trees returned to England. Nancy always said Mira-dor meant more to her than any other house she ever lived in; leaving Virginia was perhaps not what she would have wished. But she and Ronnie soon found satisfaction in their adopted country. They rented Kelmarsh, a Georgian house owned by the Lancaster family in Northamptonshire (some of the best hunting country in England), where Ronnie became Joint Master of the Pytchley Hunt and Nancy set about redecorating with the same flair that she had exhibited at Mirador.

The house became a social center for London weekenders, and their guestbook reads like a litany of England's most distinguished titles. The famous English artist Sir Alfred Munnings visited Kelmarsh and painted Ronald Tree on his horse as Master of the Pytchley, and later Mrs. Tree and her young son, also on horseback.[3] The paintings capture wonderfully the arrogant, elegant style of the Tree family during those years.

In spite of his country gentleman's life, Ronnie continued to pursue his dream of a political career. To achieve this, it was important to live in a district likely to adopt him as a parliamentary candidate, so in 1933, thanks to the Marshall Field legacy Ronnie received on the death of his mother, they bought Ditchley Park, near Blenheim Palace in Oxfordshire. The house, designed by the eighteenth-century architect James Gibbs, had been owned for over a hundred years by the Dillon family. "I can see [the Trees] now," recalled underhousemaid Edith Bridges, fifty years later. "They came to look at the place and they had lunch under a tree. Mrs. Tree had on a yellow backless dress with a picture hat. They had two dogs with them so the Dillons would not let them into the house."

The estate had fallen into disrepair, but with Nancy's talent for interior decoration, and their combined inheritances, the eighteenth-century house and park were transformed. Ronnie shared her knowledge of and interest in furniture and paintings (indeed, Nancy herself later credited him with a much greater feeling for architecture and art than she had), and between them they restored the house to its original beauty.

To top it all, by good luck a parliamentary vacancy occurred almost as soon as they had bought Ditchley. Relinquishing his post with the Pytchley, Ronnie was proposed as Conservative member for Market Harborough in August 1933. While press reports at the time seized on confusion over his American nationality (Ronnie had to assure them of his English birth), they also noted his useful connections in Parliament via Lady Astor, and his millions. The combination was evidently irresistible, and he was adopted unanimously. In the ensuing by-election, aided by a whirlwind visit by Nancy Astor, Ronnie beat the Labour candidate by a modest majority of 6,860 votes.

So Ronald Tree was now a member of Parliament. As he said, "I had done what my grandfather had hoped of me, and I had done it in my father's adopted country."

The alterations at Ditchley took two years, and the Trees moved in in 1935. The house soon became famous for its dinner parties, shoots, local cricket matches, and the classic country-house weekends enjoyed by the upper classes in those last carefree years between the wars. The enjoyment depended, of course, on money and servants. It must be remembered that while Ronnie and Nancy were turning Ditchley into a brilliant re-creation of eighteenth-century living, both their countries, in contrast, were mired in a crippling economic depression.

The Trecs, however, felt none of the constraints suffered by so many others. Ronnie happily bestowed his fortune on Ditchley, and the consequences were spectacular.[4]

Ronnie brought material pleasure to the household; he also brought Collins. Edmund John Collins had been in the Life Guards before he became Ronnie's personal butler at Kelmarsh in 1927. Perhaps no butler since Jeeves has made such a name for himself in the circles who knew him. He was the highest-paid butler in England; but he was more than a butler to his master, he was also his friend, and he would stay with Ronnie to the end.

From 1935 to 1939, the Trees lived in the political and social spotlight, enjoying a style of life that harked back to the heyday of this almost-vanished world. Thanks to Nancy's Astor relations, they were on friendly terms with the highest echelons of English society, including many of the royal family. The Trees spent weekends at Cliveden, the beautiful country house outside London owned by the Astors, where Ronnie met the most influential Conservatives of the day, and where he made lasting friends of Anthony Eden and Bobbety Cranborne (later marquis of Salisbury).

In 1936, Ronnie was given his first political post, as parliamentary private secretary to Robert Hudson, minister of pensions, and later of the Department of Overseas Trade. In 1937, Neville Chamberlain became prime minister. Early in 1938, when Anthony Eden resigned over Chamberlain's perceived obtuseness on Italian and German aggression, Ronnie supported Eden against the prime minister. Although he is not generally given credit for it in the history books, throughout 1938 Ronnie held secret meetings at his London house in Queen Anne's Gate for those opposed to the "appeasement" policy promoted by the government.

In the spring of 1939, Ronnie and Nancy attended two of the grandest parties of the decade—one at Holland House, attended by the king and queen, and the other a ball at Blenheim for the coming-out of the Marlboroughs' eldest daughter. For this occasion, the Trees had a large house party at Ditchley, including among the guests the American ambassador, Joseph Kennedy, his wife, and their two older children, Joe and Kathleen. It was the last of the great parties to be given before the war.

Early in September, immediately following Germany's entry into Poland, Chamberlain declared war. The prime minister invited Anthony Eden to become secretary of state for the Dominions, and Winston Churchill, as in World War I, was made first lord of the Admiralty. Ronnie was asked to go to America immediately and prepare a report on the British Information Services.

On the strength of it, and of his impressive U.S. connections, he was made parliamentary private secretary (PPS) to the minister of information, Lord Reith. When Churchill became prime minister in the winter of 1940, he dismissed Reith, and appointed Ronnie's friend Duff Cooper to the post. Cooper immediately asked Ronnie not only to stay on as PPS but also to assume the duties as adviser to the minister on American affairs. Ronnie traveled across the country as a propagandist for the British position against Hitler, reaching as far as Hollywood, where he met David and Irene Selznick. (Because of David Selznick's very vocal anti-U.S. involvement in the war, Ronnie punched him in the jaw at a party. "The only man I ever hit," he used to say with satisfaction.)

But perhaps the most famous contribution Ronnie made to the war effort was his house, Ditchley. In November 1940, Winston Churchill called Ronnie in to his office in the House of Commons to ask him if Ditchley might be made available at weekends "when the moon is high." (The Germans had taken reconnaissance photographs of the prime minister's official weekend home, Chequers, and his advisers were alarmed that on a clear night the house might be a bombing target.) Ronnie was delighted; in all, Winston Churchill made a dozen visits to Ditchley between 1940 and 1942, the trips ending when the threat of night air raids diminished. It was an extraordinary honor for the Trees, who not only entertained the most important man in Britain but saw him with his hair down, so to speak, with his cigar and his whiskey and his anxieties all laid out for inspection at two o'clock in the morning. He always sat on Nancy's right at dinner, where she exerted her considerable skills to distract the frequently taciturn war leader with her wit and repartee.

Perhaps these responsibilities acted temporarily as a bandage to bind up deeper wounds festering behind the gilded enclaves of Ditchley. For after Churchill's visits ended, Ronnie hardly ever returned there. He was often in the United States for the Ministry of Information, or in London—first at his Queen Anne's Gate house, and then, after it was damaged by bombs, at the Ritz Hotel.

With Nancy alone at Ditchley, there began to be visits from Colonel Claude G. Lancaster, whose family owned Kelmarsh, the house the Trees had rented after their move to England. Lancaster, known as "Jubie," was member of Parliament for the district of Fylde in Lancashire. Educated at Eton and Sandhurst, he was a bluff, hearty, anti-intellectual fellow, who felt most at home at White's, his club in London—very different from the refined and cultured Ronnie. Lancaster's rough masculinity, and his beautiful country house which meant so much to Nancy, proved irresistible.[5] They say that it was Collins, the perfect gentleman's gentleman, who took it upon himself to tell his master that when Mr. Tree departed from Ditchley, the colonel moved in.

In 1943, Ronnie's work at the ministry came to an end, and he helped found, with a group of younger, more liberal-minded Tory colleagues, the Tory Reform Committee. He continued to work closely with American journalists visiting London to cover the war and to visit the United States. On a speaking tour in the West, he met a young lawyer in his hometown, Chicago, who, as he put it later, "was to play a large part in my life." This was Adlai Stevenson.

Meanwhile, Nancy collapsed with what she termed a "breakdown," and returned to the United States, staying in a mental institution in Connecticut for treatment. When she went back to England, she never visited Ditchley. Later, she explained that the stress of living a political life, far away from her beloved Virginia, and of the loss of her daughter, as well as other problems, had made her leave Ditchley —and Ronnie—forever.

In 1945, with the war almost over and Churchill running a caretaker government, Ronnie attended a dinner party given by Bill Paley in New York. Present at the dinner was his friend Isaiah Berlin, whom Ronnie had first met in 1941 at a dinner in Washington. After the party, Ronnie went back to Isaiah Berlin's hotel and said he wished to speak to him urgently. Finding the only drugstore that was still open, "We sat until one in the morning," Sir Isaiah recalled, "while he told me how deeply he was in love with Marietta FitzGerald."

But it was not until that January 1946 in Barbados that Ronnie had the opportunity to be alone with Marietta. Her response perhaps surprised even him. From that moment, his purpose was to secure a divorce from Nancy and marry the woman with whom he had fallen in love in New York. That spring, after a month of parties, seeing Marietta both publicly and privately, Ronnie flew to Chicago for family trust business, on to Mirador in Virginia, and once again to the Fields' plantation in Charlottesville, South Carolina, where Desie, Marietta, and Frankie joined him.

Ronnie and Marietta's moments alone confirmed their feelings for each other. They agreed everything must be kept a secret while they decided how to proceed. At that time, there was little opportunity to do more than swear eternal love. Breathing not a word to anyone about her new hopes, Marietta wrote a cheerful letter to Susan Mary Patten (now at the French Embassy in Paris), referring only to the fact that Ronnie Tree had been in town, "which is a colossal joy."

In early May 1946, Ronnie sailed for England and Ditchley. Nancy had decided she wanted to marry Colonel Lancaster, but because of her frail health, her children and friends urged her to wait. "In effect, my mother and father became separated," her son Michael Tree said later.[6]

Not knowing at that time the existence of Marietta in his life, many of Ronnie's friends were surprised at the rapidity with which he began pursuing a divorce. Certainly, Nancy's affair with Colonel Lancaster was damaging, but the Trees had enjoyed a striking affinity of styles and interests for over twenty-five years, and one little peccadillo, in the typically English attitude toward extramarital affairs, would not normally provoke such an extreme reaction.

But Ronnie's past gave him little confidence in the loyalty of women. His mother's betrayal of his father had proved to him that marriage was a flimsy thing when one party wished to leave it. His wife's infidelity was, like a replay of his childhood trauma, an act of treachery that could not be overlooked, and he found solace as soon as he could. Marietta was an American, like Nancy, but her beauty, youth, and eagerness to learn made an attractive contrast to his difficult wife. At the same time, Marietta seemed deliciously strong, a fearless warrior for good causes, and her high spirits struck a spark in him that lit the way to end his marriage.

# CHAPTER 14

# "A happy married life"

All of Marietta's energies were now focused on the new purpose in her life. She thought of nothing except the moment when she might see Ronnie again. She sent him a stream of impassioned love letters. She rushed to the "morgue" at *Life,* where she mooned over photographs of the "handsome Conservative candidate." When he arrived in New York City in March 1946, she talked to him without reserve about divorce, remarriage, and children. The last subject raised the issue of his age, for Marietta later sent him a newspaper story with the headline: "Father for 20th time at 81!"

Meanwhile John Huston, unaware of Marietta's change of heart, continued to wait for instructions. She telephoned him in February, after Barbados, but it was a stalling call. Her brother George, staying at the apartment, overheard her on the phone to California, at the end of which she said, "Oh, George, it hurts so to turn him off. He loves me so much."

Some time that spring, John Huston's father came to see her. Walter and Marietta had always got on well together. The day he arrived, Marietta was sick in bed. "I looked so terrible and I wanted him to see me at my best." Huston talked a while, and then asked if there was anything he could do for her. On an impulse, she asked him to sing "September Song," the song he had sung so memorably in the film *Knickerbocker Holiday.* In a scene worthy of one of John's movies, while the beautiful young woman lay in bed and listened, Walter Huston stood in front of the window and sang for her.

Forced by Desie to resign from her job at *Life,* Marietta picked up her volunteer work with Dorothy Paley. Sydenham Hospital in the Bronx was by now integrated from the board of trustees downward, an astonishing accomplishment at that time. During 1946 and 1947, Sydenham, in financial crisis, took up much of the energy Marietta had so happily expended at *Life.*

She was still invited to almost every journalistic and diplomatic party in New York, mostly without her husband. Desie, returning to his law firm, had become involved in the American Veterans Committee, and took to working late, or preferred to excuse himself from his wife's entertainments. Old friends like John Hersey and Jack Jessup (her old boss at *Life*) kept her abreast of political gossip.

She was becoming exposed, too, to the fledgling civil rights causes that were to come to fruition in the sixties. She met many Negroes (as blacks were still called) in Harlem, who told her painful tales of racism across the country. Her conscience was further inflamed by her work at the Wiltwyck School in upstate New York (a school for troubled boys, supported by Eleanor Roosevelt), where she worked with a new black friend, Marietta Dockery. (There were jokes about the black and white Mariettas.) Encouraged by Dorothy Paley, Mrs. Dockery enrolled her daughter in the Dalton School as the first black child, where Frankie was now a student.[1]

Marietta was invited to be an observer at the United Nations for the National Council of Women, and began to meet European foreign ministers at UN parties. This early introduction to the UN would later be parlayed into some of her finest work.

Her hunger for a serious career was made more acute by the plethora of jobs that were offered to her—features editor for *Junior Bazaar,* head of the women's division of the CIO Political Action Committee, her old job at *Life.* Bill Paley asked her to be Ed Murrow's research assistant (Dorothy, however, did not like the idea of her friend working for her soon-to-be ex-husband). She was offered a job at the Museum of Modern Art, and most enticing of all, the position as assistant to the managing editor of *The New Republic.*

But, because of Desie, all had to be turned down. "I am feeling more parasitical than ever," she wrote to her parents. "My only activities seem to be sitting next to people at dinner. I hate myself and long for a regular job." She took out her resentment and frustration, naturally enough, on the FitzGeralds. During occasional obligatory dinners with her father-in-law at the Union Club, she had to keep herself under tight control and not launch into a fiery speech in favor of communism. "My, what evil, self-indulgent, stupid, smug faces— both men and women overdressed and over-alcoholed (naturally there would be nothing to talk about if they weren't tight)."

Her hostility, of course, was to some extent displaced defensiveness. She knew her Boston and Philadelphia friends would be appalled at her duplicitous marital behavior. She would be a leper in the eyes of the women she had grown up with who had "kept the faith," and for whom divorce was unthinkable. Occasionally, these friends would be invited to dine at the FitzGeralds'. It was immediately obvious that things were terribly wrong, with bitter remarks tossed between Desie and Marietta at each end of the table. Albert and Nora Francke, the children of Desie's sister, remembered overhearing violent rows between the couple and knew how much their mother worried about their beloved uncle.

Marietta clung to Dorothy Paley and Mary Warburg, whose company was free of censure. Mary, after all, was enjoying her second marriage, and Dorothy was in the middle of a very contentious divorce from Bill Paley. During 1946, Marietta had noticed Bill's increasing attentions to Babe Cushing Mortimer, whose marriage was also a casualty of the war. Babe kept appearing with new and fabulous jewels, and once when Babe was in the hospital with phlebitis, Marietta found her friend and Bill in what was called in those days a compromising position. Dorothy had not been totally faithful during the war either, having become involved with Anatole Litvak, a movie director friend of John Huston's. In the characteristic double standard of the time, Paley used that as a justification for the breakup of the marriage.

Marietta, not surprisingly, followed Dorothy's situation closely. She became Anatole's ("Tola's") confidante as Litvak waited and hoped in vain for Dorothy to agree to marry him. To add to Dorothy's emotional stress, in January 1947 she was diagnosed with breast cancer and had a radical mastectomy. She was only thirty-eight years old. She remained in the hospital for about a month, recovering very slowly. Marietta spent nights in the hospital with her, sleeping on a chaise longue, and looking after her when she came home from the hospital.

In spite of their closeness, Marietta still could not bring herself to talk to Dorothy about her own situation. Dorothy suspected something was going on, but Mary Warburg was accidentally given proof when one day a beautiful blue-enameled Fabergé box with "M" inscribed in diamonds arrived. It was from Ronald Tree. "I received a phone call saying it was meant for Marietta," Mrs. Warburg said later. "It was a dead giveaway!"

Mary Warburg was not entranced by the romance. She was fond of Ronnie, but could not imagine that Marietta was seriously contemplating divorce. "If there's any letting down to be done," she said to her friend, "I hope you will try not to hurt Ronnie too much." In a conversation a little later, Mary asked her friend what was the most important thing in life. Marietta replied, "A happy married life, which involves being the best possible wife and mother and then trying to help the community—with one's husband, if possible." Mary agreed, but added pointedly that you couldn't do this by changing husbands.

In late May and early June, Marietta and Desmond had a series of long and painful talks about their future. Although Marietta's first request for a divorce had not included remarriage to John Huston, she now had to tell him she wanted to marry Ronnie. In their arguments one of Desie's most entrenched positions was that Frankie must never be allowed to leave New York. He also took advantage of Marietta's therapy, saying he would not let Marietta go until she had a clean bill of health from the analyst, for Frankie's sake. Desie was not going to give up on the marriage. Thousands of others had had these troubles, he told her, and he considered that he and Marietta were just as capable as they at solving them. Marietta responded by saying that she could only try to show him that it was hopeless. "Oh, dear, the pain and the hurt involved cuts very deep in both."

Desie also confessed that he might have to seek some "emotional release," which, he assured her, would have no effect on the marriage. Marietta had already suspected this. Those repeated late nights could not all have involved work. "Heaven knows," she admitted to Ronnie, "he needs a little solace." She then burst out, "These conversations are ghastly, aren't they, and leave me, I'm afraid, with feelings of guilt and sorrow, and a little ashamed."

She went to a party for her old friend Gordie Palmer's wedding, and met many of her companions from her debutante years. She was apprehensive about meeting them after so long, but she stayed up till four-thirty in the morning with her old beaux Antelo Devereux and Bob McCormick—Desie having left early, as usual. These vivid encounters with her past only emphasized the distance she had traveled, and filled her with nostalgia for a life that once had given her so much pleasure and seemed so simple compared to the present pain and confusion.

The death on March 4, 1946, of her grandmother, Fannie Peabody, at the age of eighty-five, provided another wrenching reminder of those heedless years, and represented the end of an era. Although never so close as to her grandmother Parkman, she loved Mrs. Peabody. Leaving Groton after the funeral, Marietta could not help comparing her grandmother's pure and saintly life with her own.

Meanwhile, in England, Ronnie was having his own problems. Although many friends had noticed the happy change in him since the beginning of the year, he was tormented by Nancy, who was still seriously disturbed and under doctors' care. Geographical distance took its toll. Ronnie and Marietta could communicate with each other only by letter (which often took nearly a week) or by international telephone, a poor medium of communication at that time, full of noise, interference, and cutoffs.

When Marietta caught a whiff of faintheartedness from the other side of the Atlantic, she quickly moved to deflect it, constantly reaffirming her love for Ronnie, for his strength, courage, humor, and attractiveness to her. "Happiness breeds happiness and productive lives," she said firmly, "so we best get married soon in order to help the general situation." Ronnie showed his appreciation by sending her more presents (properly directed this time), including a gold cigarette case, diamond earrings, a St. Christopher pendant, a belt, and a diamond cross (which someone admired at a dinner party and she had to lie, saying it was a family heirloom). Her psychiatrist commented that Marietta was becoming symbolically bound to Ronnie by wearing all his gifts.

Ronnie's wealthy cousin, Marshall Field III, and his third wife, Ruth, became close friends, and Marietta used to take Frankie to visit their huge estate in Caumsett, on Long Island's north shore. Ruth Field had been a supporter of Marietta from the beginning (they worked together for the Wiltwyck School), and Marshall, founder of the *Chicago Sun* and publisher of the liberal evening newspaper *PM,* was probably more politically in tune with Marietta's views than Ronnie. (Field gave her a large percentage of the funds needed to keep Sydenham Hospital afloat.) They shared not only political sympathies but also a belief in a life of public service, and faith in psychoanalysis.[2] Marietta appreciated the luxuries offered by the Fields and enjoyed the liberal friends they invited to Caumsett. On one occasion she met Adlai Stevenson there, "one of our delegates to the U.N., an unusually intelligent man from Chicago," she wrote to Susan Mary Patten in Paris.

Ronnie's friends from England were becoming curious about Ronnie's new love and began to get in touch, including Anthony Eden, who telephoned Marietta in her New York apartment to suggest dinner. Marietta's brother George was in the apartment when "Tony" rang, and was mightily impressed. The meeting was a great success, at least according to Marietta, who found Eden very amusing and much less stiff and humorless than she had expected—"and good-looking besides!" To Marietta's annoyance, because she had been longing to talk to Eden about Ronnie, Desie on this occasion decided to show up.

In the middle of June, Marietta made her first major step toward the divorce. At Ronnie's suggestion, she consulted Louis S. Weiss, Marshall Field's personal attorney, adviser, and partner in Field's liberal politics. (Weiss's wife was also a fervent Democrat and a colleague at Wiltwyck.) Weiss, who had helped Ruth Field in her divorce from

Ogden Phipps to marry Marshall, advised Marietta that she should tell Desie about the consultation, but that she should keep Ronnie's name out of any discussions.

Ronnie, meanwhile, was struggling with Nancy's increasingly erratic behavior. She refused to cooperate on a divorce. She was afraid she was going insane. Colonel Lancaster was able to offer little or no support. Ronnie's own political future seemed equally uncertain. Churchill's caretaker government had been dismantled in the general election of July 1945, and Ronnie had lost his Market Harborough seat in the Labour Party landslide that ensued. Since that time he had felt shut out of any role in the Opposition. Churchill, now in bitter banishment, ignored him.

Marietta, desperately worried by Ronnie's expressions of anguish, suggested he see a psychoanalyst (two names, including that of Anna Freud, had been recommended by Victor Rothschild). She argued, like many believers, that if one party to a marriage was being psychoanalyzed, as she was, it was a good idea for the other also to enter treatment, "because the analysis might produce a personality change in becoming adjusted that the other might not accept." Perhaps, she added somewhat disingenuously, Nancy might get better if the divorce were speeded up.

Ronnie returned to New York in July 22 after visiting Paris, where he met Susan Mary Patten (who was becoming an important diplomatic hostess) for the first time. By dint of much careful planning (Desie was in Canada, Marietta supposedly staying with friends), Ronnie and Marietta met at the Seascape Inn in Provincetown, Massachusetts. Then Marietta went on to Northeast Harbor (Frankie had already been there for a month) for her annual summer visit with her parents. A few days later, Desie joined them. Ronnie stayed in Dark Harbor with the Fields and Ronnie's two sons, Michael and Jeremy, over from England. Michael, sensitive to the strain between his parents, was suffering fainting spells, another worry for Ronnie. To muddy the waters still further, Nancy announced that she was going to come to the United States to see her family.

Marietta and Ronnie stole one more meeting at the Bucksport Toll Bridge before he flew to Chicago. As Marietta then picked up her life of sailing and picnicking, the insidious charm of Northeast Harbor once again began to threaten her wavering resolve. She confessed to Ronnie that "the power of the Peabodys is still strong, but feel sure this will be worked out and understood soon."

Another link from her past was severed that summer. In August, John Huston, tired of waiting and increasingly disillusioned, suddenly got married. It was an impulsive move, inspired by a vivacious young actress, Evelyn Keyes, who swept him off to Las Vegas after a drunken dinner party. He regretted it almost immediately. Evelyn overheard a conversation between John and his father about the marriage in which Walter mentioned the name "Marietta." "I don't know what . . . I doubt if she'll . . ." John's voice trailed off. Evelyn, who had not heard the name before, knew at once that this one was different from all the others.[3]

Ronnie spent a month in Chicago before returning to England. For him, the next few months saw the crisis of his separation from Nancy. She continued to refuse to consent to a divorce, and most of her friends, including one of the most powerful women in England, her aunt Lady Astor, supported her, making Ronnie's life almost unbearable. Not only was his wife a daunting opponent, but the Labour Party had imposed crippling taxes on foreign trust funds, and Ronnie was beginning to realize that he might no longer be able to afford to live in England. "I felt my life shattered," Ronnie said later. "I was frightfully depressed."

Marietta's letters during November and December poured out support for him and praise for his adaptability and talents. She urged him to consult a doctor, and tried to suggest ways out of the divorce impasse, pointing out that "the gentleman in question [Lancaster] remains in full attendance," which surely could be used as evidence ("loathsome word").

Although she expressed optimism, Marietta's confidence was at an equally low ebb. Reports from the front by friends were of little help. Eddie Warburg, for instance, freshly returned from England, told her that he had heard Ronnie had moved in with Edwina D'Erlanger (Mary Warburg's sister), and that Ronnie was forever locked with Nancy. At home, Desie continued to refuse to consider divorce until the doctor gave her clearance; as a result, the atmosphere at 563 Park was increasingly hostile. Marietta, writing letters to Ronnie twice a week, worried that his letters back would be intercepted, and asked him to address them in care of Dorothy Paley.

To add to her emotional strain, John Huston showed up in September in New York to direct Jean-Paul Sartre's play, *No Exit*. John and Marietta met again at a party at the River House, an encounter which Evelyn Keyes described with some acidity in her autobiography: "I couldn't help noticing John talking to a willowy blonde, almost as tall as he, smartly dressed, class oozing from every pore. Their conversation was terribly intense. Sparks were flying, people were whispering, sneaking looks at them and at me. Even as I watched, John took her hand, pulled her into another room and closed the door."[4]

Marietta went to the play, and later she and John had several lunches together. She was careful to tell Ronnie of these encounters with her old flame. Provocative, perhaps, but then she followed up with a ringing declaration in Ronnie's favor: "It's good to know in my heart that although I am very fond of John, I am also detached, and of course that is due to my strong love for you."

As is always the case with families in disarray, Christmas was particularly awful. Nancy came back to visit Ditchley. Ronnie, feeling sick and nervous, finally made an appointment with a psychiatrist. Marietta, with Desie and Frankie, went to Syracuse to spend Christmas with her parents and two of her brothers, George and Sam. Marietta's stomach was a knot of nerves most of the time. "Coming home at this point in my analysis only sets up another pattern of tension—probably the pattern I was working so hard to evade in New York."

To feel better, she relived the bright days she and Ronnie had had together during the past tumultuous year—the miracle of Barbados, the romantic moments in Bucksport, the beaches in Provincetown. "But I have to confess that after being in [the family's] bosom for five days and continually hearing divorce decried as a sin worse than pride or any other, my spirits quailed. . . ."

Marietta was bracing herself for the big battle she would have to wage in order to become Mrs. Ronald Tree.

# CHAPTER *15*

# *"You have let down your family and your society and your God"*

Marietta once said to Evangeline Bruce how glad she was she had been the "one who got away" from John Huston. "How did you do it?" her friend asked. "He must have been irresistible."

"Oh, it was simple," Marietta answered; "I could never have told my parents." (In fact, twenty years later she could still not admit to her parents that she even knew John Huston. After visiting him in Ireland, she told them she had been staying with "an old friend.")

Did she think it would be easier to tell them about Ronald Tree? Ronnie was twenty years older than Marietta. He was not very tall, but handsome and cultivated. He had money, a beautiful house in the country, friends in politics, journalism, and the arts, and perhaps most interesting of all, since it cannot be bought, access to the grandest, oldest, most aristocratic families in England.

The bishop and Mrs. Peabody had long been Anglophiles—a legacy of the Rector, who had so loved his years in England, and who had founded his school on the English model. There was even a connection with the Tree family; during the Peabodys' 1924 trip to England, they went to tea at Cliveden with Lady Astor. On the face of it, Ronald Tree would seem a very acceptable son-in-law.

But in the end, what Marietta was planning separated her from her parents for ever. Her decision to embark on the long, lonely journey to divorce inflicted a wound on the family psyche that never completely healed.

In January 1947, Marietta's mother came to New York on the first of her trips to see her daughter about the marriage. "For the first time I saw the good results of my analysis," Marietta told Ronnie. "We were able to talk intimately for the first time ever on a realistic basis. Mostly about Desie and this general situation and to my great surprise, she was quite sympathetic. But naturally wants me to go on working on it as hard as possible."

Meanwhile, Desie was beginning openly to admit his discouragement about the possibility of a reconciliation. Marietta proposed a separation. "Anything would be better than this destructive wearing-down process." But Desie's sad change of heart forced down her guard and she was jolted by a paroxysm of guilt. "If I could change emotionally, all would be well. He is so decent and intelligent in every way, what can be wrong with me?" she asked herself. (In the middle of this wave of remorse, she met Salvador Dali at a dinner party, who asked her to pose for him as an angel.)

Desie came up with a new plan—that they should move to Boston. That might have been the perfect solution for him, Marietta tartly observed, but was disastrous for her, who hated the sporty weekends with his friends. "I gave up my flask and raccoon coat years ago."

At the end of January, Ronnie's half brother David Beatty came to New York, and he and Marietta met and talked freely about her future with Ronnie. Ronnie, meanwhile, had left Ditchley after Christmas, taking his other half brother Peter, now increasingly ill and blind, to a specialist in Switzerland. He then went on to stay with the Fields in Charlottesville, South Carolina, where Marietta joined him.

This meeting was the turning point in their relationship.

Up until now, there had been moments of panic on both sides. They had spent so little time together. Ronnie was in despair about Nancy, his sons, and his career. How could he ask Marietta to share her life with him? What was going to happen to him in the future? Depression, arthritis, and an increasing sense of personal futility had plagued him as the months dragged on.

But his doubts were as nothing compared to hers. Marietta was fearful of family retribution, of Frankie's reaction, of giving up the life she had made so satisfying for herself, and of her ability finally to make the emotional commitment to a man she sometimes, as is clear from her letters, doubted was right for her. Ronnie's Tory career, his right-wing stance on many issues, his anti-liberal friends and his anachronistic lifestyle were hardly what Marietta's political conscience had prepared her for.

In Charlottesville, the tide turned. Somehow, their talks during that week at the end of February convinced her that she was doing the right thing, that Ronnie was indeed the one for her, and that all barriers to their future would be overcome. Ronnie's ardent love for her and his conviction that they could have a fine life together inspired her with his vision and gave her the courage to pursue it.

It is tempting to think there was a sexual breakthrough on this occasion, because Marietta referred afterwards in letters to him that he had made her feel "utterly female." Her analyst described Marietta's change of attitude in characteristically clinical terms. "Heretofore," Marietta reported to Ronnie, "my pattern has been to get emotionally involved with a character, and then tick him off at a certain point (one of those mistaken revenges against the father). . . . You made me feel like a female (psychologically) for the first time in my life."

Marietta explained to him that according to the analyst, she now knew what it felt like to be a complement to a man, instead of a competitor. This mindshift was regarded by both doctor and patient as highly desirable. Marietta's only worry now was that since Ronnie's wife had been an aggressive, competitive woman, was he going to be able to adjust to living with the utterly female, submissive woman that Marietta, largely thanks to her therapy, had become?

The doctor, in Marietta's eyes clearly promoting the liaison with Ronnie over Desie, also observed that Marietta's "suspicious over-interest" in politics was a "fine displacement of emotion." Presumably, from now on, with her emotions properly focused on Ronnie, politics could be banished to the back seat where they belonged.

Without the doctor's own notes, it is impossible to know how, if at all, Marietta misread or reinterpreted these encounters. The emphasis on the patient's discovery of "femininity" certainly reflects the general thrust of Freudian analysis in the 1940s and 1950s to return women to their traditional roles. Marietta's enthusiastic descriptions to Ronnie indicate her belief in the doctor's diagnosis, and she declared herself much more confident after these revelatory sessions. Bathed in her analyst's support, Ronnie's love and understanding, and her newfound submissiveness, she felt sure they would succeed brilliantly together, and that "our deep and enduring happiness is something most of your dominating women friends will never know from the womb to the tomb."

The couple agreed that for divorce purposes, they must not see each other again until they were free. The weeks that followed were filled with practical issues. Marietta, thinking her way into the move to England, started researching a progressive school near Oxford for Frankie. She also began talking to Edith Entenman, a child psychiatrist who had studied under Anna Freud and was a longtime friend and consultant of Dorothy Paley, about how to lead Frankie through the months to come.

In early April, Mrs. Peabody came again to New York and told Marietta that her father was deeply distressed about the failure of the marriage, and that all her friends and family could never give their approval for her behavior. "This news had only the effect of making me feel rather defiant."

On April 12, 1947, Marietta was thirty years old. Her father wrote her a long birthday letter, setting out his feelings. Although sympathetic to the problems between her and Desie, especially following the war (was he remembering his own difficulties on returning to Lawrence in 1918?), he urged her to reconcile. "The alternative of course is almost too terrible to contemplate."

He pointed out that she had pledged her word, that she should not even consider failure since she had been brought up to such high standards, that the damage to Frankie would be irreparable, and that "failure at home would go far to disqualify one from any authentic influence in [the field of social ideals]." He quoted British army chaplain Studdert Kennedy's remarks to the men in the trenches in 1916: "For to do the best he can, Is to be an Englishman, not a rotten 'also-ran.' Carry on!" The bishop also quoted Henry V at Agincourt: "Now God be praised who hath matched us with this hour." (In fact, Mr. Peabody got this wrong. The quote is another World War I source, Rupert Brooke's poem, "Peace": "Now God be thanked who has matched us with His hour, / And caught our youth, and wakened us from sleeping.") Finally, the bishop urged Marietta to go and see Sam Shoemaker, the rector of Calvary Church in Gramercy Park and an old family friend.

What Marietta made of her father's strangely inappropriate exhortations has not been recorded. That he used British sources was an extra irony. Shoemaker saw Marietta on two occasions, and Desmond once. He told Malcolm he thought Marietta had lots of spirit, and that she would never be content if she felt she had not done her duty as a Christian. However, he also sensed that she rebelled against family tradition, although at the same time admiring its values. Shoemaker seems also to have implied that she saw in Ronald Tree some of these values, and was attracted to him for that reason.

The cleric's efforts on the Peabodys' behalf were inconclusive. Marietta at least promised to pray. But these continuing demands eroded her confidence once again, and her letters to Ronnie at this time are filled with an overanxious boosterism: "I *love* you so! You are such an extraordinarily good and darling and cozy man with such sensitivity and humor and understanding and *attractive* for me. God bless you and keep you as strong-fibred as you are."

Pressure came not only from her family. Her closest friends were deeply disturbed by her contemplated divorce and remarriage. Ronnie had confided to Mary Warburg about his hopes and plans. Mary was shocked and astonished at how far the situation had progressed. She returned to Marietta, urging caution. Could you not wait a little, she begged, not act so hastily? Wait another year. "I can't wait," Marietta told her. "I am terrified of getting pregnant again."

Some time that spring, returning from a business trip to Germany, Desie's law associate, Peter Kaminer, went to dinner at 563 Park Avenue. Marietta was not there. In her place, Frankie, then six years old, asked him if he would like a martini. During dinner, Desie asked Peter about his trip, and Peter described the voyage over to England on the *Queen Mary* (the ship's first voyage after service as a troopship during the war). At his table in the dining room, Peter said, were Allen Dulles, Kathleen ("Kick") Kennedy, Philip Toynbee, and Ronald Tree. "That is the man who is going to marry my wife," Desie said grimly.[1]

Frankie could not be protected from these painful exchanges. Now a bright young student at Dalton, she hardly saw her mother. But while playing hostess for her, Frankie was witnessing the disintegration of her childhood world. She began to display signs of distress, and her mother vowed to try to spend more time with her. One night, when Marietta was putting her to bed, the six-year-old said to her mother, "The child is much closer to the mother than the father. For after all, I was borned from you and you married the father. The mother may marry again, but the child will always be with her." Marietta wondered whether Frankie had picked this up from Edith Entenman, whom Frankie had been seeing, but the psychologist denied it. Frankie's observations made Marietta feel less guilty, but it was only a temporary respite. She was wrenching Frankie away from her father, and she knew it. One night Marietta heard Desie weeping, "and it just about carved me in two."

By law, Marietta had to set up residence for six weeks in Nevada in order to get a quick divorce. Her lawyer, Louis Weiss, suggested that she move to Lake Tahoe in June. Dorothy Paley was also getting her divorce from Bill, and the two friends decided to take up residence together. Marietta told all her friends, loathing the lie, that she would be in Northeast Harbor as usual that summer.

In May, Ronnie finally got his divorce, and suddenly everything looked very different. Freedom seemed just around the corner. Delightful questions required immediate attention. For instance, should she and Ronnie go to Italy together after their marriage, or Barbados? Did Marietta need hunting clothes, or was a riding habit enough? What did a woolen tea gown look like? The couple was overtaken with a frenzy of planning, shopping, and lists for a new life together.

Ronnie's divorce also forced Marietta into clarifying her own position. Up until this moment, she had avoided making a public commitment, giving both Desie and her parents the impression that no decision had been made. But on May 21, she wrote to her mother and

Marietta's paternal grandparents, Endicott and Fannie Peabody, on their honeymoon, 1885. *(Photo courtesy of Groton School)*

Marietta's maternal grandmother, Frances Parkman, 1925. *(Courtesy of Samuel P. Peabody)*

Proud parents, Reverend Malcolm E. Peabody and Mary E. Peabody, at Marietta's christening, May 3, 1917, Lawrence, Massachusetts.

With her eldest brother, Endicott, c. 1923. *(Photo courtesy of Back Bay Studio, Lawrence, Massachusetts)*

The Peabody family, June 1937. From left: George, Malcolm, Mike, Marietta, Endicott, Mary, Sam, and Spotty the dog. *(H. Rohn)*

Marietta on the arm of her brother, Endicott (her father was officiating), before her marriage to Desmond FitzGerald in Northeast Harbor, Maine, September 2, 1939. *(Ira L. Hill's Studio, New York City)*

Frances, Marietta, and Desmond FitzGerald, summer 1942, before Desie left for the war. *(Brown's Studio, Hulls Cove, Maine; courtesy of Nora Cammann)*

"One of the prettiest young set New Yorkers," at La Rue in New York, 1940. (*King Features Syndicate, photo by Michael Caputo*)

Frank Sinatra admires his companion on the dais at the National Citizens' Political Action Committee lunch chaired by Eleanor Roosevelt, summer 1944. (*Life*)

Desmond FitzGerald (left) and Ronald Tree in Barbados, January 1946. (*Eddie Warburg*)

Penelope Tree with her parents, early 1950.

Ronnie and Marietta Tree (at right) with Michael and Lady Anne Tree in Venice, 1949.

OPPOSITE: Aerial view of Ditchley Park, near Oxford, England. *(English Life Publications, Ltd.)*

Portrait of Marietta Tree, châtelaine of Ditchley. *(Condé Nast Publications, Ltd.)*

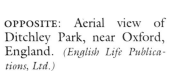

Marietta as head of New York's Volunteers for Stevenson, introducing the candidate, 1956. *(George Zimbel)*

With her mentor, Eleanor Roosevelt, outside the Economic and Social Council Chamber at the UN, March 1961. *(United Nations)*

At her post at a UN meeting, 1963. *(Inge Morath, Magnum Photos, Inc.)*

The UN Ambassador and his protégée outside the UN, September 1963. *(A. Rickerby for Life)*

Grief-stricken, with her brother, Endicott, in London, as the funeral cortège of Adlai Stevenson passes on its way to take him home, August 1965. Behind her are Ronnie Tree, Mr. and Mrs. William Benton, and, on the top step, Hubert Humphrey, Eugene McCarthy, and Ambassador David Bruce, among others. *(The Times)*

Penelope dancing with her father, New York, c. 1957. *(Freudy Photos)*

**BELOW LEFT AND RIGHT**: Heron Bay, Ronnie Tree's beautiful Barbados creation.

The Tree family at dinner on East 79th Street, New York, 1963. *(Steve Schapiro, Black Star)*

Marietta with Richard Llewelyn-Davies in Barbados, 1966.

With William Paley and Henry Kissinger (left) at the Family of Man dinner in New York, 1982.

Dorabella and Fiordiligi (Evangeline Bruce, left, and Marietta) in Tuscany, 1989. *(Frederick Eberstadt)*

Good friends (from left): Mary Warburg, Kitty Carlisle Hart, and Marietta, 1972.

Mother and daughters at Richard Avedon's show, 1978. *(Henry Grossman)*

Three generations of Peabody women, during the shooting of *The Female Line* in Northeast Harbor, Maine, 1979. *(Jimmy Moore)*

Sparks still fly: Marietta and John Huston with Sam Peabody and Danny
Huston (standing left), during the shooting of *The Dead* in California, 1987,
six months before Huston died.

A royal encounter: Marietta in her favorite silver lace, Nancy Reagan also in
silver, at the White House, Washington, D.C., 1986. *(Photo courtesy of Ronald
Reagan Library)*

Odd couple Marietta and Andy
Warhol at 1 Sutton Place, November 1986. *(Henry Gillespie)*

With her grandson, Michael,
1990. *(Stuart MacFarlane)*

Gallant beauty, 1990, off to see the world. *(Eben Pyne)*

father announcing that having tried everything, Desie and she had agreed to divorce.

Immediately after receiving this letter, Mrs. Peabody stormed down to New York, this time armed with all the wrath of the Peabodys. "You have let down your family and your society and your God. No matter how you may try to do good again, you will never achieve it— as you'll never have the respect of others. You're weak. All you care for is admiration. You are ruining your child's life. You never even tried to give Desie a chance. You will never find happiness, as you will repeat the same pattern in your next marriage. I hope you don't suffer. No, I take that back. I hope you don't suffer as much as I know you will." And then, in the unkindest cut of all, she added: "You are even worse than my mother, as she at least stood by us and my father, instead of marrying the man she always loved."

Mrs. Peabody spoke for an hour, and then left. As soon as she had gone, Desie appeared, looking embarrassed. He admitted he had been with his mother-in-law most of the morning, providing ammunition, and as he said, "She was out for your scalp." Desie then also turned to bitter invective, saying he felt sorrier for Ronnie than anyone in the world.

After the visit, Mrs. Peabody wrote to Desmond: "You and Marietta loved each other once and it is possible that you might love each other again. . . . She had had too much flattery and perhaps not enough of the little affectionate marks of devotion. I know I failed there, for I am not good at that. . . ." She also wrote to her daughter that day, castigating her once more for her failure to create a home for her husband and child. "A Reno divorce with a quick marriage afterwards puts you in the class with the movie stars. It is an added crime to take Frankie to another country, away from her father and all her relatives. The whole thing is fantastic and if your attitudes toward life had not been warped by the life of excitement you have led in N.Y. and the adulation you have received for the impressive qualities that you have, I think you would see it yourself."

Marietta staggered under these assaults, all confidence, all self-esteem draining away. There had never been a divorce in the Peabody family. Only Naughty Sam had committed the vile act in the Parkman family, to everlasting opprobrium. In Marietta's parents' circle, the horrors of divorce were described in movies such as *Children of Divorce* (shown in Northeast Harbor in 1927), "Taxicabs their cradles, blaring saxophones their lullaby, sophisticated at sixteen, jaded at twenty!" Was this what Marietta was wishing on little Frankie?

The final punch came the following weekend, when Marietta, Dorothy Paley, and their children went on a picnic with Gerry Warburg, Eddie's brother. Gerald F. Warburg had just been in England where he visited Ditchley, and he regaled the company with malicious stories about how furious Ronnie had been when Gerald shook hands with Collins, the butler, mistaking him for a guest, how Ronnie had said that vulgar Americans were ruining Venice, and so on, all the stories making Ronnie and his way of life sound snobbish and out-of-date.

None of Marietta's friends could stop him, and of course he was unaware of the circumstances, but the effect on Marietta was devastating. Gerald's remarks had tapped into one of the most fundamental anxieties Marietta had about her future husband. Was he in fact an elitist fuddy-duddy, a reactionary old-style Tory? Was she simply exchanging the establishment country-club existence she so scorned in the United States for an equally stultifying one with Ronnie in England?

When Ronnie first met Susan Mary a year earlier in Paris, he had talked about Marietta's pro-Jewishness and had remarked to Susan Mary that "she was getting better." Marietta wept when she heard this. Did that mean being liberal and liking Jews was "not quite nice"? Ronnie hastily reassured her, but these little revelations cut deep.

As soon as she got home from the picnic, she rushed into her room and reread some of Ronnie's letters. They calmed her a little. "I realized . . . that you were a man capable of adjusting to the times, far better than most—that our life together *could* be purposeful rather than a frivolous routine with people who were made from so-called upper class English life in 1910."

But she had lost her footing. Her mother and Desie despised her. She despised herself even more. "You have had one bad experience lasting 25 years," she cried to Ronnie, "why should I burden you with another when you deserve the best? How can you believe in me ever, when I don't believe in myself?"

Ronnie responded instantly with a telephone call and a letter so effective that they pulled her out of her "dark dungeon." In this moment of crisis, he brought to bear all the weight of his experience, age, and authority, and, enthralled, she bowed to his mastery. Just as in the previous year it was she who had encouraged and supported him with her love, so now he returned the favor, and the balance of power between them swung slowly back to an equilibrium.

On Friday, May 29, she flew to Syracuse for the day to tell her parents that she was going to Reno to divorce Desie, and that she was then going to marry Ronnie and move with Frankie to England. Her brother Sam was outside with his father when a plane flew over and the bishop said grimly, "That's Marietta's plane." There was a tension-filled tea, then Marietta went into her father's study. When she came out, her mother blurted out, "You're disgracing the family."

Like Hester Prynne, Marietta was branded now with the scarlet

"A." Nathaniel Hawthorne, married to a Peabody, described a bitter judgment for the adulterous woman from her "iron-visaged" peers; the same retribution was now to be endured by a Peabody daughter nearly one hundred years later. "All the light and graceful foliage of her character had been withered up by this red-hot brand," wrote Hawthorne. For Marietta, too, a light was extinguished by the severity of her condemnation.

After her daughter had left, Mrs. Peabody tried one more appeal. Think of your brothers, she wrote. Think of your father. "I don't see how he can preach about marriage as I have heard him do so often when this thing has happened in his own family." Think also, she might have said, about Marietta's grandfather, the Rector of Groton, who, in his many pitiless sermons denouncing divorce, described it as "the beginning of hell on earth."

But Marietta knew there was no going back now. Desie himself had come to the end of his love for her, and told her so. She said to her parents how desperately unhappy she was, and that her unhappiness was due to the fact that "I am stabbing you, that I am a serpent in your bosom. I am afraid you've always suspected this, and now here is your proof. . . ."

With a kind of numb determination, she started to close the apartment, pay bills, collect tickets, get clothes fitted, write to all her many relations informing them of her divorce. On June 6, her parents and brothers came to New York to say good-bye to her. They behaved magnificently, never referring to the pain of the occasion, just hugging her farewell. "I was so overcome by their kindness and the terrible wound that I was inflicting, that I burst into heaving sobs—all to the amazement of the people around me on the corner of 5th Avenue and 44th Street." Then her mother said, "I am glad to see you suffer, darling, for only suffering will bring the expiation of your sins." Later that night, her father called to wish her good luck and again she wept.

Suddenly without her family, she felt bereft. She asked her brother George to go with her to Tahoe, but he could not. Marietta was on her own.

The trip to Tahoe was an ordeal. The party consisted of Dorothy, with her two children, Jeffrey and Hilary, aged nine and eight; Marietta, with Frankie, aged six; and Edith Entenman, the psychiatrist. The flight went first to Los Angeles, which took twelve hours, with the Paley children and Frankie behaving like mad things and screaming uncontrollably throughout. Then they flew on to San Francisco where no hotel rooms were ready for them. The children were exhausted and Frankie became convulsed by wild sobs. They could not sleep because of the time changes, and when they finally chartered a plane to Tahoe, all were in a state of collapse.

Marietta described this to Ronnie in one of the last letters she would ever write to him as Mrs. FitzGerald. "Oh my darling," she wrote, "I am so looking forward for our life to begin."

After the horrendous journey, Tahoe turned out to be a happier time than expected. They found a cabin on the lake that delighted them all. (Bill Paley paid the rent.) Even Frankie found the tension had gone. None of the children was told about their parents' divorces until they reached Tahoe. Perhaps learning of the decision temporarily banished their anxiety and uncertainty about what was happening to them. "There was an atmosphere of freedom," Frankie said. "We had a lot of fun riding and singing." There was a puppy to play with, they played card games, swam in the lake, and had daily sessions with Mrs. Entenman. The two divorcing women ran the house, did the shopping, and went gambling together at the casino, promising each other a twenty-dollar limit. Marietta lost hers in ten minutes.

There was also a lot of telephoning. Ronald Tree telephoned. Anatole Litvak telephoned. John Huston telephoned. The children went to a secret place and had fun discussing whom they would like best as their new stepfather. They had no idea who was supposed to belong to which mother. Hilary chose Tola Litvak because he had given her a charm bracelet. Jeffrey chose John Huston because he made movies. "I was divided between John Huston and Ronnie Tree," Frankie said, "Ronnie because of the black pony with a blue ribbon he promised me."

Dorothy Paley felt that even at this late hour, Marietta had moments of doubt. John Huston was continuing to put on the pressure, in spite of his marriage. One day, Walter Huston telephoned. Marietta told him she was marrying Ronnie. "Do you love him?" the old man asked. Marietta said she did. "Do you *really* love him?" Marietta said she thought they were going to be very happy together. "Well," Walter Huston said, "I'm sure you and John will meet in the third act."

Dorothy later said that John Huston thought she, Dorothy, had influenced Marietta in her decision to marry Ronnie. In fact, Dorothy knew that John was not a candidate for Marietta's hand, but for her, as for many, the decision to marry Ronnie seemed difficult to understand.[2] It was hard for them, knowing and loving Marietta's liberal leanings, to see past his fortune. When Marietta telephoned Mary Warburg from Tahoe, asking her if she would give the reception for her wedding to Ronnie, Mary once more tried to stop her going through with it. She urged Marietta to rethink her decision. Don't marry him for money, she said. We can give you money. Please reconsider.[3]

Marietta received her divorce decree on July 25, 1947. The settlement gave Frankie's parents joint custody. Marietta would have Frankie with her during the school year and Desmond for vacations until she reached the second year of high school, when this arrangement would be reversed. Desmond agreed to pay $3,000 a year into a savings account for Frankie, and $2,000 a year to Marietta for child support, plus travel expenses, and a one-time payment to Marietta of $1,500 in lieu of alimony, which she did not request.

The day after the divorce, on Saturday, July 26, 1947, Marietta Peabody FitzGerald married Ronald Tree.

Two days before the wedding, a report was published in the newspapers of a dispute in the Episcopal Church about divorce, provoked by the remarriage of the wife of Elliott Roosevelt (son of the former president and old friend of Marietta's) to an Episcopal minister. Dr. Manning, retired bishop of New York, made a strong statement condemning the divorce, and various bishops from around the country chimed in.[4] One voice noticeably absent from the debate was the bishop of central New York, Malcolm Peabody. While he did not publicly comment, he was overheard privately saying that he would rather have his daughter live in sin than divorce.

The marriage took place in the town hall of Huntington, Long Island, near the home of Marshall and Ruth Field. The reception was given by Mary and Eddie Warburg in their house on the Field estate. Bishop Peabody and his wife attended the ceremony but left, without a word, before the reception. (Marietta later asserted that they had not been there at all.) Her youngest brother, Mike, remembered his father as "drained of color, looking like death." Mrs. Peabody was equally strained, particularly with Mary Warburg, whom she regarded as one of the New York influences who had "warped" her daughter. Mary Warburg wore shorts to the wedding. Three of Marietta's oldest friends—Louise Roberts, Mezzy (now Hickok), and Patricia Scull—showed up. They all wore black. Ronnie's son Michael was there. Frankie and the other children behaved badly and were removed. Just as at Marietta's first wedding, it rained.

Meanwhile, in another part of Long Island, Bill Paley, having received his freedom from Dorothy at the same time as Marietta had received hers, on that day married Babe Cushing Mortimer in Manhasset. *The New York Times* published a report of the two marriages on the same page.

Immediately after the wedding, Frankie was sent away to spend the month of August with her grandparents in Northeast Harbor, and Marietta and Ronnie went off, together at last, to Barbados, stage of their recognition scene. Their plan was then to return to New York and pick up Frankie before sailing for England.

The deed was done. Ronnie wrote to Mrs. Peabody, thanking her for coming to the wedding, and promising that he would take care of Marietta. "She is a very precious person, with such great potential for good and helping others that it must be fully developed and matured. I am quite sure that together we can create a good and useful life."

He added that he hoped the Peabodys would consider Ditchley to be their English home. "I'd like you to see Marietta in what will be her own setting—and I'm pretty sure she will be happy there."

Ditchley was indeed to be a new setting for Marietta for the next two and a half years. Home, however, was not quite the right word.

CHAPTER *16*

# "*Whose Puss is in My Boots?*"

The *Queen Mary,* carrying Mr. and Mrs. Ronald Tree, Frances Fitz-Gerald, and her nanny, Anne Rheinwald, sailed for England from New York on September 11. One night during that last week before she left, Marietta telephoned her old friend Mezzy Hickok, who was living in Pittsburgh. With anguish in her voice, Marietta asked Mezzy if she would come to New York. "Couldn't you help see me off to England?" she begged. Mezzy was hundreds of miles away, at home by herself with a new baby. To leave was impossible.[1]

It was Marietta's final moment of panic, her last surrender to doubt about the tremendous undertaking ahead of her.

A few days later, Ronnie's car, with twenty-two pieces of luggage, was carrying its passengers from Southampton to Oxfordshire. After passing close to Blenheim Palace, and slowly traversing a long avenue of beech trees to a circular driveway in front of the house, Marietta entered Ditchley Park as the second Mrs. Ronald Tree.

Marietta's arrival was greeted by the butler, Collins, and a staff of about thirty lined up in the hall to meet them. Ronnie introduced her to each one of them, and then led her and Frankie on a tour of the house. It took a long time. There was the White Drawing Room (decorated with Lely portraits of Charles II and Barbara Villiers, and two Kent mirrors brought from the Trees' former house, Kelmarsh), the Tapestry Room (named for its two large Flemish tapestries), the Velvet Room (hung with Genoese red and yellow velvet), and the Green Silk Room (its green-patterned silk wall coverings made in Lyons).

Ronnie took them through the Stucco Room, probably not referring to the fact that it was his first wife, Nancy, who had discovered and restored the unusual ocher and orange color of the wall.² They looked at the Library, extended by Ronald and Nancy to make a fifty-foot-long room (a decision Nancy later regretted); the Dining Room; the Music Room; the Breakfast Room; and then they went upstairs to all twenty-nine bedrooms, including the one where Winston Churchill slept during the war. Ronnie also showed them the gardens, entered from the stuccoed hall, flanked by two large stone lions he had found in Venice. They visited the formal garden with its stone-edged beds and Italian terra-cotta vases, the semicircular stone-tiered pool containing a fountain, the three-hundred-yard terrace overlooking the lake, at the south end of which was a temple, and the kitchen garden with blue plums espaliered against red brick walls, where they also met all the gardeners.

Ronnie then took them to the stables, where a new black pony called Beauty was waiting for Frankie. In Marietta's version to her parents, this gift put Frankie "in such a fever of excitement that she had to retire to her bed where the poor babe has remained the last week with a cold. However, all is well now and she'll start school next Monday."

In fact, Frankie's retirement to bed may have had other causes. For her, this grand new world was less fairy tale than nightmare. The beautiful eighteenth-century house may have been one of the finest examples of the work of James Gibbs, William Kent, and Henry Flitcroft, but to a small child the place was terrifying, with its echoing corridors, high ceilings, and endless rooms stuffed with antiques. Frankie's own bedroom was at the top of the house, far from human contact. She could not find her way to her mother's room, let alone find her mother.

Even at mealtimes they were not together. Her food was often brought to her on a tray by a maid or by Collins, while the grown-ups, in the traditional English manner, dined separately. She was the only child in a house filled with servants, and apart from the pony, Beauty, and the groom, Jack, saw no way to be comforted. She did not even have a doll to talk to, since Marietta refused to give her daughter dolls. (Marietta's explanation for this deprivation was odd. It had nothing to do with later feminist opposition to gender-biased toys. Marietta said she remembered too painfully how her own dolls, having lost arms or legs, would be taken away from her—supposedly to go to doll hospital —and would never come back.) Looming ahead for the child was the prospect of entering a local progressive school full of progressive English children. It is not surprising that Frankie caught cold that first week of her new life at Ditchley.

September is partridge season in England, and that September was no different. Ditchley had a very popular shoot, which meant from nine to fifteen people to every meal including tea, and perhaps a dozen men to shoot every Saturday and Monday throughout the month. Marietta was plunged immediately into her new role as chatelaine of a famous country house.

She discovered that while she was titular head of a small city-state, like the British monarchy she had well-defined but very limited constitutional powers. The young sons of estate workers came in every day to keep the fires stoked in all the fireplaces. There were horses in the stables and cars in the garages, looked after by estate employees. The flowers were arranged twice a week by the head gardener. There were two chefs (one French) and four kitchen maids. There was a still room, where all the breads, cakes, and pastries were made. There was Ronnie's treasured old Nanny Weir, who had brought up his two sons, in permanent lodgings on the top floor.

The rituals of the house were equally well defined, following traditions created many years ago when the Trees first moved into Ditchley. While the rest of the immediate postwar world was struggling on survival rations, Ditchley's pheasant, partridge, venison, sweetmeats, clarets, and port, offered in a surrounding of priceless art and furniture, were a triumphant declaration that at least some standards still survived.

The house, in short, ran itself, thanks to Collins and the very efficient staff. How could Marietta, eager to take charge, hope to be welcome in this closed shop of domesticity, perfected by the first Mrs. Tree? A friend remembered visiting Ditchley and sitting with Marietta and Ronnie in one of the grand drawing rooms. It was a sunny day, and at some point in the afternoon Collins came in and closed the curtains. When Marietta questioned the loss of sunlight, Ronnie said, "This is the way we always do it." [3] Marietta did not even dare make changes in her own bedroom, whose huge proportions gave her agoraphobia and whose heavy taffeta curtains prevented her from getting enough light to read in bed. "I was too young and uncultivated in the decorative arts to make suggestions about changes to Ronnie. I knew he admired the room and I didn't want to hurt his feelings or rouse his scorn about my ignorance of these matters."

Ronnie presided over his empire with serenity. He would hunt or ride almost every day, and there were local duties that had to be fulfilled, such as bazaars and fetes held on the grounds, visits to the local Conservative Association, pony clubs, cricket matches, and the other feudal obligations of a major landowner. A restless man, he got bored quickly, and after the last of the many weekend guests had gone and his local duties completed, he would go up to London with

Marietta until Thursday or Friday, when they would return to Ditchley and the next round of weekend house parties.

Those early days were still touched with the roseate glow of romance. Having lived together hardly at all, they were happily learning each other's foibles and habits. Ronnie, much more set in his ways than his young wife, wrote out a helpful list of his likes and dislikes which she preserved in a scrapbook. Among his dislikes he noted "Rows," that is, arguments, which was perhaps the most significant item on his list. Completely in character for a man brought up in the scene-averse society of upper-class England, it was also the characteristic most congenial to the Peabody culture of his new wife. Otherwise, Marietta soon discovered that she had entered an alien country, whose similar language to her own belied its difference. Indeed, language turned out to be a treacherous ally. She never forgot an early faux pas over the English expression to do "damn all," assuming it meant that a person had done his best. Thus, at one party, during a lull in the conversation, Marietta said to her dinner partner, "Ronnie tells me you did damn all in the war! I'd love to hear about some of your exciting experiences." Ronnie could not protect her from these linguistic landmines.

She discovered that the English preferred their children to be seen and not heard. Frankie would be allowed to appear at hunt breakfasts along with the silver chafing dishes, and at teatime. At Marietta's insistence, she would sometimes have her supper behind a desk in the Great Hall while the grown-ups gathered before dinner. But she was kept so isolated from Marietta that she never even saw her mother get dressed for dinner, a ritual that she had counted on, dating back to those intimate days in New York when her father was away at the war. (And how she missed him, back home in New York, three thousand miles away.)

Marietta fretted about Frankie's loneliness, and how she would fare in her new school at Oxford. (She had not forgotten her own misery when she was plucked out of her school in Lawrence and deposited in the jungle of Chestnut Hill.) But these worries were overshadowed by her anxiety about her daughter's performance in front of the English. All parents feel they are to blame when their children behave badly in public. Marietta was terrified that somehow Frankie would let her down in this new child-unfriendly environment. Was she wearing the proper clothes (an issue Marietta also remembered with mortification from her own childhood)? Frankie was suddenly showered with new outfits, such as grand leather riding boots from Savile Row. Marietta continually dreaded Ronnie's disapproval of his American stepdaughter. Ronnie after all was so much older, and unused to a young child in the house. On one occasion, when the doctor came to give Frankie a shot, she ran away from him in terror and it fell to Ronnie to try and catch her. Such scenes did not inspire confidence.

While praying that Frankie would not commit some social sin, Marietta also had to face the hostility of Ronnie's two sons, Michael and Jeremy. She was only a few years older than they were, always a difficult situation for a stepmother. The atmosphere was made far grimmer by their mother, Nancy, who, in Marietta's view, poisoned the boys against her. Michael and Jeremy excluded her, ignored her, talked to themselves in their own English slang, and observed her awkward mistakes with amused scorn.

As for Ronnie's friends, the reception was not much better. The English are masters of the subtle put-down, the delicate ostracism, the surgical elimination of someone who does not pass muster socially. Marietta, to many of the Ditchley circle, was a fortune hunter, a social climber. In spite of her beauty, she appeared pretentious and humorless, a pushy American who had the audacity to be photographed for *Vogue* at Ditchley in a ballgown, as though she owned the place. But Marietta's greater crime, in English eyes, even than this act of presumption was that she was an ideological bore. Her forays into political discussions with the old Tory lords who dined every weekend with Ronnie were greeted with pained politeness. Her contributions on matters such as communism and the postwar world did not impress. Her efforts to lecture Lord Salisbury on the weaknesses of British democracy made even supporters cringe with embarrassment.

Marietta's political position by this time was firmly established, and she had no hesitation in declaring it. After her youthful abandonment of Hoover in favor of Roosevelt's liberalism, she had ultimately found a home with the politics of the leftist journalists and writers she met in New York in the early forties, and had gone further than many of them in her commitment to civil rights. Her association with Jewish and interracial causes in New York at that time was both instinctive and deliberate. While so many New York intellectuals had become cynical, burned out after the radicalism of the thirties, disillusioned with communism and frustrated with socialism (crystallized in Mary McCarthy's telling story, "Portrait of the Intellectual as a Yale Man"), Marietta's social activism, in contrast, retained the freshness of a schoolgirl's.

That was why Ronnie's old Tory friends, with their reactionary attitudes, were so deeply dispiriting to her. She did not understand their sardonic commentary. Their fondness for irony left her blushing in confusion. Their cynicism made a mockery of her girlish earnestness. Moreover, she soon found out that English women did not put themselves forward as she did. If they were to speak, they were expected to be witty and frivolous, not weighing in about British foreign policy in the Middle East or Russia's intentions in Europe. Only a brilliant woman like Nancy could carry off that sort of thing. "If only the second wife had not been another American," sighed an old friend of Ronnie's. "It would have been so much easier if she had been French or English."[4]

Perhaps the most graphic example of Marietta's stumbling at this time was over the first postwar ball given in Paris by the then ambassador to Paris, Duff Cooper (Ronnie's wartime boss), and his wife of legendary beauty, Diana. Held in December 1947, it was going to be the social event of the season, indeed of the decade, a sign that the war was over and everyone could bring out their new-look Diors and ancestral diamonds and drink champagne until dawn. Large contingents from England were going over for the event. But Marietta hesitated. She worried about the influence of the Communist Party in France, and how poor the people were, and how tactless this ball would appear to them. She even telephoned her old friend Isaiah Berlin, now back at Oxford, to ask his advice. The philosopher, like Ronnie, said it was up to her. In the end, she stayed home at Ditchley. When people in England heard this story, they shrieked with laughter at what seemed to them a wildly inappropriate case of condescension mixed with an equally tiresome Puritanism. Isaiah Berlin justified Marietta's position to their friends by comparing her to a Henry James heroine, a remark that deeply hurt her. (Isaiah Berlin later did not remember this.)

Not all Ronnie's friends were so critical. Ronnie's old bachelor crony, Brendan Bracken, told Marietta how pleased he was to see Ronnie so happy. Of course, like others, he may have had an ulterior motive, wishing to establish good terms with the new wife in order to continue enjoying Ronnie's exceptionally lavish hospitality at Ditchley. Other friends of a less traditional background also took to Marietta, including David Niven, who stayed at Ditchley soon after Marietta's arrival and welcomed her warmly.

Winston Churchill's wife, Clementine, had always been in favor of Ronnie's remarriage. She told Ronnie she had long wished that "some lovely gift from Heaven" should come to him, and that now it had happened.[5] Marietta's first meeting with the great war leader, however, was not auspicious. About ten days after her arrival in England, the Trees were invited to dinner in London with the Churchills. They were joined by Sarah Churchill, Winston's actress daughter; John Colville, Churchill's private secretary; and Lord Lambton, among others.

As Marietta told the story later, for much of the dinner Churchill addressed his remarks to the table, as was his wont, and everyone listened respectfully to his observations about British politics and the future of the country. Marietta sat quietly, not understanding all his references, but eager to ask questions. Meanwhile a lot of champagne was being passed around.

At one point, Churchill begin to inveigh against the rationing system in Britain after the war, which he condemned as being a drag on the free market. This was Marietta's moment. Here at last was a subject that she could understand. She broke into the conversation, explaining to Churchill and the rest of the table that rationing was obviously necessary due to shortage of goods, and that if the free market were allowed to flourish, then only the rich could buy their needs and luxuries, and the poor would not only be deprived of essentials but could become revolutionary when they saw the rich luxuriating in their comforts.

Churchill stared at her, noticing her for the first time. His daughter, Sarah, sitting on his other side, said to her in a loud whisper (which she knew her deaf father would not hear), "Go on, give it to him! It's good for him!" Encouraged by Sarah and the champagne, Marietta enthusiastically pressed her point. "I was like John Calvin addressing the sinners," she said afterwards.

However, no one around the table took up her fervent arguments. The subject was dead in the water. "I realized my mistake in challenging the great man," she recalled, "and subsided in a rush of blushes, staring remorsefully at my plate for the rest of the meal."

After coffee and farewells, Ronnie and Marietta walked home across the park. "Oh, Ronnie," Marietta said. "I am so very sorry. Was I terrible? Did I embarrass you? Will we ever be asked again?" Ronnie replied unconvincingly, "Oh, that was all right."[6] (In fact the Churchills remained in touch, meeting the Trees in the Caribbean occasionally, until Churchill died in 1965.)

But was it all right for Ronnie? Loving Marietta as he did, he must have wanted so much to protect her from these clannish British critics, so skilled at cutting the upstart down to size. Yet there was so much she had to learn. Friends remembered humiliating moments, for instance, when Ronnie would reprimand Marietta in public for not writing a note to Lady So-and-So.[7] In those first months he must have been intensely aware of the contrast between his old wife and his new. Nancy had always been so wonderful with Churchill.

Nancy. Always Nancy. Of all the assaults Marietta had to defend herself from during her tenure at Ditchley, the most devastating by far were those launched at her by Nancy Tree. In Daphne du Maurier's novel *Rebecca*, the second Mrs. Max de Winter is brought home to the family house, Manderley, only to discover she has to live with the ghost of the dead first wife and beloved mistress of the sinister housekeeper,

Mrs. Danvers. The experience of the second Mrs. Tree was strikingly similar.

Marietta did not ride. (Nancy was a wonderful horsewoman.) Marietta did not shoot. (Nancy was a splendid shot.) Marietta did not know how to run a stately home. (Nancy had lived in such houses since she was a child in Virginia.) Marietta had little talent for interior decorating. (Nancy was famous for her taste.) Marietta did not have a sophisticated sense of humor. (Nancy was a wicked wit.) But most distressing of all, Marietta did not understand the English, at least not the ones she met at those testing weekends at Ditchley. (And how they had all loved Nancy!)

The psychological warfare, as Marietta described it to Susan Mary in Paris, began almost immediately. The first Mrs. Tree called her coarse names such as "Nigger Lover" and "Coon Queen." She made remarks that immediately spread all over town such as "How can Mrs. FitzGerald live in *my* finery when she's a socialist who should be selling posters for the Jews on Fifth Avenue?" She left a note in one of Marietta's bedroom bureaus which read: "Whose Puss is in My Boots?"[8] (One version has it that this was sent to Bishop Peabody in Syracuse, but Nancy refused to confirm or deny the story.) Nancy came over to Ditchley (always at weekends, when there were guests), ostensibly to reclaim objects that were hers, but stayed on to create a scene. Susan Mary, as a guest at Ditchley, remembered a house party when Nancy suddenly arrived wishing to see the old family nanny. After making a terrible row, she was taken upstairs. The guests were quickly conducted by a white-faced Marietta into the library where they plunged into a game of backgammon, trying not to hear the sounds of hysterical screaming and shouting upstairs.

In November 1947, two months after Marietta's arrival in England, she received a call from a woman whose voice seemed disguised, but which she recognized as that of Lady Astor, Nancy's formidable aunt.

"Why did you marry Ronnie?" the voice said.

"It was for sex," Marietta replied provocatively.

"Sex causes divorce," Lady Astor retorted. "I hate sex and I hate divorce. You are bad and Ronnie is a weak man. You have to tell him what to do."

"It seems to me that you are divorced, Lady Astor."

"Yes, but not for sex, for drunkenness."

At this point, Marietta hung up. She scribbled down the key phrases of this exchange later, its hostility over time losing none of its power. The climax of this hate campaign came the following year. Nancy continued her assault of telephone calls, name-calling, and threats, throughout the winter of 1947 and spring of 1948, until one

Friday night she showed up at Ditchley with her psychiatrist. Marietta described the event to Susan Mary:

> I was really frightened lest she disturb Frankie, but having posted Alice (the maid) with her (she slept through it all, thank God), I herded the guests into a room, and when the coast was clear on the stairs, got them to dinner which was eaten to the accompaniment of slammed doors and running feet. . . . Poor Ronnie was left to face the sluttish language and fury of a demented woman. She changed back all the little changes I made in the rooms and wrecked [sic] havoc in my room, destroying and tearing up all my pictures in R's room—slapped him black and blue, while the psychiatrist said to him, "It would be embarrassing for you if Mrs. Tree tried to annul your marriage, wouldn't it?"

Perhaps fortunately, in smashing the glass of a picture in the hall Nancy cut her leg, and after the psychiatrist had examined it, Nancy agreed to leave to see a physician.

The weekend was salvaged.

But if Marietta was hurting, she did not show it. Marietta Peabody had never shown her feelings—not when she came home from a day of ragging at Shady Hill, nor when her brother George hit her too hard. She held her head high then, and she held it high now in defiance of Nancy's spite, the duke of Marlborough's coldness, her fear of offending Ronnie, and, as always in the back of her guilty mind, her family's malediction. Refusing to be beaten, she summoned up the old spirit that had led her to this point, and took charge.

One of Marietta's first moves was to fire the housekeeper, who said, "The first Mrs. Tree always did it this way," one time too many. However, before she fired this Mrs. Danvers figure (complete with black bombazine dress and bunch of keys at her waist), Marietta managed to shock her quite terribly. Nancy Tree's maiden name was Perkins, thus on the impressive collection of linens she left behind at Ditchley was embroidered the monogram "NPT." Marietta, lacking a trousseau of her own and always alert, as a true child of her mother, to thrift, sent for a seamstress to come to the house and change all the monograms from "N" to "M."⁹

The next action Marietta took was to improve the conditions of the staff, which seemed to her medieval. She raised all the wages. She tried to bring together the workers, who lived in various cottages over the 3,000-acre estate, by opening a community center in one of the empty rooms in the house. She started a small library and invited people in to give lectures and otherwise entertain the staff. It is doubtful that any of these moves (except the financial one) was very successful. Those in service in England at that time knew their place, and did not expect to be offered educational advancement, especially from an American lady. They probably found it insulting.

But Marietta also found an ally in an unexpected quarter, perhaps the most useful ally she could have acquired under the circumstances. Ronnie's man, Collins, came out on her side, and in the thousand little ways available to such a powerful person in the Ditchley hierarchy, gradually helped change the atmosphere. Even Mrs. Peabody realized the importance of this vote of confidence. On a picnic during the summer of 1948 (after the Peabodys had visited Ditchley), she confided to Marietta's friend, Trishy Scull, "A very fortunate thing has happened to Marietta. She is going to be all right because, in spite of everyone else, the butler has championed her."

Mrs. Peabody's shrewd assessment of the power structure at Ditchley was correct. But neither she nor her daughter could have foreseen that this hard-won peace was so soon to be shattered.

# CHAPTER *17*

# *"I could hardly believe such beauty existed in the modern world"*

Marietta soon found herself adapting to the time-honored routine of Ditchley. After a weekend house party, the Trees would set off for London with Reg Duvall, the chauffeur, at the wheel, to stay at Ronnie's suite at the Ritz. Although it sounded grand, Marietta did not like the Ritz, which was very run-down from the war. The rooms were freezing, the carpets were worn, the lighting was dim, and the gilt on the moldings had turned black. Breakfast, when it came, was cold. By December 1947, Marietta had persuaded Ronnie to rent a flat at 15 Grosvenor Square—"lovely, hot, small, American-furnished and chintzed"—where she, at least, was happier. While Ronnie attended business meetings, Marietta went from hospital to public clinic volunteering her services as a secretary or extra pair of hands, but the newly flourishing National Health Service had no place for her offers and she found little welcome.

Life in London had its moments of pleasure. In spite of a postwar depression, there were still very rich people hanging on to their inherited wealth, and Ronnie's connections to royalty and the aristocracy gave the Trees entrée to some of the best parties thrown each season. When Marietta was in London, she would often join Ronnie for lunch at Wilton's, a fish restaurant patronized by London's *gratin*, and then they would visit four or five antique dealers, or a museum, or the art galleries of Mayfair. These excursions formed the basis of Marietta's education in the decorative arts.

"What made Ronnie's blood course was buying," Marietta said later. "Our houses and their closets were stuffed with objects and furniture. Eventually I had to implore him not to buy more, but he always said, 'My greatest regrets are the things I *didn't* buy,' and kept on buying. It is said that in every marriage one of the couple is the spender and one the saver. After my mother's continual disapproval for my spending on a new hat or a good pair of shoes, I felt strange being forced into the position of the nagging saver in our marriage."

At Ditchley, the weekend would be as meticulously choreographed as a Fokine ballet. Before lunch the guests gathered in the hall, where Marietta mixed the martinis. Ronnie thought the American formula, which featured a great deal more gin than vermouth, superior to the British version. "In fact on the day of our marriage he cleverly asked me if I would give him a wonderful present—would I make the drinks for the rest of our lives? Thrilled that I could give him pleasure with this simple (I thought) request, I eagerly assented, and thus spent a great deal of our social life with my head in the ice bucket, while Ronnie had interesting conversations with the guests." Afternoons were spent playing tennis, taking walks in the formal gardens, or visiting great houses nearby such as Blenheim or Heythrop. In the evening, the guests were served drinks by Collins and his assistants in the Green Silk Room. Friends from Oxford would join the house party for dinner, such as David Cecil, Isaiah Berlin, and Rhodes Scholar Charles Bolté (whom Marietta had known in New York as the founder of the American Veterans Committee). Dinner was served in a room decorated with English portraits and a huge Tiepolo painting of a halberdier (later owned by Gianni Agnelli).

While Marietta learned to take these grand entertainments in stride, thanks to Collins, the perfectionist, and Alice Butler, who became Marietta's lifelong personal maid and friend, there were moments when the irony implicit in her changed circumstances struck her very forcibly. At one dinner party she was seated next to Henry Ford, chairman of the Ford Motor Company, who started to complain to her about his troubles with labor in his Detroit factories. Marietta's experience as a vice chairman of the CIO Political Action Committee for the reelection of Franklin D. Roosevelt, and her friendship with Walter Reuther, head of the United Automobile Workers, were suddenly relevant again, and she was able to assure Mr. Ford that Mr. Reuther was a fine man, and that thanks to Reuther's firsthand knowledge of factory conditions in the USSR, Mr. Ford would find him an ardent supporter of collective bargaining and the free enterprise system. "Mr. Ford looked at me, and then down the table of dazzling, bejewelled ladies and well-dressed men, with some surprise."

At the same time, Marietta's new role involved exposure to such extremely grand people that she could not help being impressed by them. Meeting Princess Elizabeth's private secretary, and getting gossip about what to wear for the Royal Wedding (of Elizabeth and Prince Philip); the trip to the British Embassy in Paris with Diana and Duff Cooper, where Ronnie took her to all the couture collections as well as a private viewing of Versailles and dinner at Maxim's, plus encounters with Rothschilds and Gaston Palewski (de Gaulle's éminence grise and Nancy Mitford's longtime paramour); attending a royal ball in which Princess Elizabeth "didn't smile all evening" and Prince Philip had a "rather mean and immature expression," were episodes that dazzled the rector's daughter, and were relayed with breathless excitement in letters home.

Marietta had always been a diligent letter writer to her parents, and from England her correspondence (which she asked to have typed up and passed around to the family) demonstrates with aching clarity the conflicting pressures that once again beset her. The almost weekly letters are a fascinating mixture of name-dropping, political commentary, and the expressions of an uneasy conscience. Her intentions were obvious. Her parents on one hand wished for assurances of their daughter's good behavior, and on the other found titillating her tales of princes and palaces—as she perfectly well knew. Thus one paragraph would describe her efforts to find volunteer work or her teaching Sunday School to the estate children, the next would relish in glittering details of dinners with Princess Margaret and Emerald Cunard, a third would offer an analysis of British Labour Party policies, and a fourth would describe Frankie's new life.

The first Christmas was spent at Ditchley. Marietta asked her mother to send Crisco oil, lard, rice, a ham, cheese, and soap, items still lacking in ration-bound England. The annual Christmas party took place with all the estate workers coming in to see the Christmas tree and celebrate. Frankie was an angel in the nativity play, but was disappointing, according to her mother, in that she had no feeling for the mood, and when one of the little shepherds coughed, collapsed in a fit of giggles.

The giggles did not last long. Her nanny, Anne, who had been her closest companion since arriving in this strange new country, resigned. Even Marietta could not deny this loss, and she and Ronnie whisked Frankie off to London the week after Christmas to take her mind off her grief.

By this time, several members of the family were beginning to show up to examine Marietta's new life in England. Her aunt Penelope Griswold visited Ditchley in December, and wrote a long letter to Malcolm and Mary Peabody about it. She found the house overwhelming. "We just couldn't take it. I have seen luxury before but never in such beautiful surroundings. The bathrooms were the last straw. Beside each john there was a lovely old table with a basket on it and in the basket the toilet paper laid out neatly betwen sachets!" They were also overwhelmed by the service. "Invisible housemaids laying out everything and drawing your bath and two men waiting on the four of us at table. It's all wrong, of course. But I hope it can be preserved—it's all so perfect."

Another of Marietta's aunts, Dot Davison, visited Ditchley early in 1948. She reported back with a perceptive evaluation of Marietta's first five months: "To live there as a new member of the family must be a bit trying at times for the place is full of traditional splendor and old retainers. It is his house and not hers yet but she has many friends there for weekends and handles herself well." Mrs. Davison added that she would have liked to have a more intimate family chat with her, but she sensed Marietta wished to avoid this.

Marietta had good reason not to sit down for a family chat with her aunt. While Marietta's letters home were as loving as always to her parents, and also referred eagerly to her brothers, she was still suffering not only from the condemnation of her parents but also of her eldest brother, Endicott, who had written her a letter when she divorced that so upset her that she sent it back to him. In the letter he told her that it was clear she had been having an affair with Ronnie while still married to Desie—an act he could not condone. The letter caused an estrangement from her eldest brother that was to last until almost the very end of Marietta's life. (Sam had also written her a letter expressing his dismay at her divorce, but when he found out how much he had hurt her, he withdrew it, and they reconciled.)

Dot Davison, Ronnie, and Marietta traveled together on the *Queen Elizabeth* to the United States on February 19, 1948. Frankie stayed behind in the hands of Collins and Alice, Marietta's maid, who after the departure of Anne, also became the nanny. Her mother would be away almost two months, visiting in the United States and Barbados. Marietta asked Frankie if she wanted to join them in Barbados, but she said she did not want to go there, preferring to wait until the summer when she could go to Northeast Harbor with her grandparents.

The reason was that her father was coming. Desmond FitzGerald had married Barbara Lawrence on February 25, 1948, and they were visiting England on their honeymoon. Frankie went up to London to see them, and then they came to Ditchley. It was a wonderful reunion for father and daughter, and, according to Marietta, Frankie immediately liked her new stepmother, saying, "She loves to play and is not the kind who says, 'Watch out, you might tear my stocking.'" (That this might have revealed something about Frankie's own mother seems not to have struck Marietta.) Alice, who was to sustain a long and interesting correspondence with her mistress throughout her life, confirmed Frankie's happy time with her father and Barbara. "You will Madam be pleased to know that Frankie has taken a great liking to Mrs. FitzGerald."

Ronnie's trip to the United States had darker motives. He was confronting serious money problems. Owing to the Labour Party's confiscatory tax on foreign trust funds coming into Britain, Ronnie's income had been drastically reduced. But according to the terms of his trust, he could not touch the capital. He went to Chicago several times during 1948 and 1949 to see if he could somehow renegotiate the distribution of the trust, of which he was the major beneficiary. The trustees were adamant. As a last resort, he brought suit against them, but failed to win a judgment in his favor.

While Ronnie wrestled with these problems, Marietta visited her New York friends, and saw her brothers Sam, George, and Mike. Afterwards, she and Ronnie went on to Barbados, where the glorious Palladian house that Ronnie had been building was almost finished, and his plans for real estate development on the island began to take shape. Returning briefly to New York, the Trees were given a wonderful farewell party at the Marshall Fields, with the Herseys, the Murrows, the Warburgs, and others, before returning, exhausted, to Ditchley at the beginning of April.

At Ditchley, Ronnie began to look for ways to live on his much-reduced income. He imposed stringent economies by cutting down on staff and household expenses. He tried to expand the produce of the kitchen gardens as a commercial venture. The architect of their Barbados house came to visit in order to discuss ways of turning one wing of Ditchley into a self-contained space where the Trees might live (an idea vehemently opposed by Ronnie's sons). There was also talk of closing down part of the house and moving into a smaller cottage on the estate. There was even some discussion of selling Ditchley altogether.

Ronnie was also grappling in earnest with his future. If he were to stay in England, he needed a job. Politics at the moment were out. He saw no hope at his age and stage in life in looking for a constituency where he would have to start all over again in a very anti-Tory climate. A general election, in which his old friends might be returned to power and give him a post, seemed a long shot. What else could he do? There seemed to be no outlet for his particular talents, and he became very disheartened. "I am hoping that the answer will be some kind of small factory here (perhaps frozen foods)," Marietta wrote to Susan Mary, "which would be a creative and useful job, enabling us to live in the country most of the time."

Meanwhile, the round of social events continued. They lunched with the aesthete Lord Berners ("now a crumbling pederast who is quite charming and wears a crocheted doily on his head"). Dorothy Paley came to stay and they all went to Paris for a week. Marietta's parents arrived on June 19 and stayed for over a month. Marietta put herself out in a major way to please them. She arranged for her father to preach at the local church. She laid on elaborate sightseeing trips, including a Shakespeare play at Stratford on Avon, the Oxford colleges, Cotswold villages, and a panorama of English architecture. The high point for the Peabodys, however, was undoubtedly the garden party given for Queen Elizabeth by Lord and Lady Salisbury at Hatfield, one of the crown jewels of the English stately homes. Her Majesty was gracious, and Bishop Peabody was given the honor of sitting next to her at tea.

Marietta felt the visit was a success and good relations had been restored. Families, however—and particularly Peabodys—do not reconcile so easily. With Endicott estranged, George, Marietta's second brother, also remained a feisty contestant in the family rivalry stakes. George had yet to inspect his sister's palatial new home. That summer of 1948, he was sitting in his office in New York and saw the cover of *Time* magazine, which showed a picture of the Matterhorn. "In ten minutes I had my ticket to go climb it." On his way, he stopped off at Ditchley for the first time. The Peabody parents had left (taking Frankie back with them), and Marietta and Ronnie were about to set off for Europe. George joined them. They went first to Paris, then drove on through France and Switzerland, where they left George "to find truth on a mountain peak in Switzerland," as Marietta put it cuttingly. Ronnie and Marietta drove down to Venice, and spent a magical week at the Gritti Palace (Marietta's stepdaughter-in-law, Lady Anne Tree, thought Marietta's happiest times with Ronnie were in Venice). To add to their cheerful mood, they learned that during their absence, Nancy Tree had finally married "her tired old beau," as Marietta described Colonel Lancaster. Marietta and Ronnie journeyed back through the Loire Valley and Burgundy, and took the boat back to England at the end of August.

George climbed the Matterhorn and returned to Ditchley in triumph. But Marietta's early disparagement of her brother's achievement was only the prelude. Staying at Ditchley at the time was Henrik Kauffmann, Danish ambassador to the United States, who, Marietta found out, had also climbed the Matterhorn. "That was the kind of data Marietta clung to," George said later. " 'Here's George, poor George, he's only twenty-six, coming back boasting about climbing the Matterhorn and here's a fifty-year-old man who's done it and never mentioned it!' " It was the old sibling competitiveness once again, a competitiveness they would never grow out of.

Shortly after returning from Europe, again Ronnie and Marietta flew to the United States. Marietta's agenda included buying supplies for the Barbados house, buying clothes, and taking Frankie to doctors and dentists, plus a visit to the psychiatrist Edith Entenman. Ronnie went again to Chicago to continue his battle with the trust.

Then back once more to Ditchley in late September, where Frankie returned to school, and the social round continued unabated. For Marietta, by far the most thrilling event that fall was Harry Truman's success in the American presidential election. Her letters to Susan Mary and her parents bubble with excitement and joy. "So many first rate men elected to Congress and to the governorships (amongst them R's great friend Adlai Stevenson in Illinois), and the New Deal program affirmed! . . . Can't see any future for the Republicans now —with such good material for Democrats to choose from in 1952."

Later that month Marietta danced with the duke of Edinburgh at a party at the American Embassy and had a very sticky time, "as all the questions I wanted to ask him I had to suppress such as 'How do you like your life'—'what do you think of Socialism,' etc. . . . so we danced in a languid way giving each other frosty smiles." In early December, Susan Mary and Bill Patten came to stay, and Franklin D. Roosevelt, Jr., also visiting from the States, said to Susan Mary, "You and Marietta have certainly got around plenty since I was cutting in on you at the Kimball House in Northeast Harbor."

But the skies were darkening over Ditchley. At some point during the winter, Ronnie decided it would have to be sold. It was a wrenching blow. Nearly thirty years later, when he published his memoir, *When the Moon Was High,* the pages devoted to his work with Nancy on restoring the house and gardens at Ditchley resonate with nostalgia. "Whether I was there alone or had a mass of guests staying in the house," he wrote, "it never frightened me or made me feel lonely. Looking back over my years there I remember nothing but sunlit days and the great satisfaction derived from living in an atmosphere of such beauty and such balm."

Marietta's view of the impending change in her life was, not surprisingly, more optimistic. She told her parents that Ronnie's spirits were good, considering, and that he was encouraged about a future business possibility in New York that would keep him in close touch with England. "I'm sure it's wrong, but I feel better than I ever have in my life," she said.

The year 1949 was a memorable one for the Trees. The English countryside had never looked more beautiful. The festivities of the season were unusually brilliant. Ronnie and Marietta attended the Trooping of the Colour and Ascot. Many visitors came to Ditchley, including Marietta's aunts Betsey and Margery Peabody. There were two quick trips to Paris for couture fittings and dinner parties. In May,

Ronnie and Marietta flew back from France the same night that Kick Kennedy Hartington was killed in an airplane crash. A later trip had to be postponed because Marietta caught cold and felt so low that several important social engagements had to be canceled.

What aggravated this uncharacteristic weakness on Marietta's part was that she was pregnant. Dorothy Paley, who visited Ditchley at this time, thought Marietta was less than pleased about this development, and said later it was the only time she saw Marietta out of sorts. In spite of her discomfort, Marietta attended two balls in June in Paris, one for Lady Diana Cooper, and one at the Pré Catalan restaurant, where "the Duchess of Kent was by far the grandest and most handsome person there, with a large tiara, miles of organdy and a dozen or so diamond orders on her dress."

Meanwhile, potential buyers flocked to Ditchley and dealers and appraisers combed the place for its art and antiques, while Ronnie and Marietta began the huge task of sorting out and packing up a lifetime's treasures for removal to the United States. In late June, Ditchley was sold to Lord Wilton, a wealthy twenty-eight-year-old bachelor with a weakness for grand houses. He agreed to keep on most of the staff, and buy much of the furniture and farm and garden equipment. The Trees were lucky to find such an agreeable buyer so quickly in those hard times. (Lord Wilton later called the purchase a *folie de grandeur*, and sold it almost immediately to Sir David Wills of the tobacco family, in favor of a slightly smaller eighteenth-century palace called Ramsbury.)[1]

The Trees' final gesture to their vanishing way of life was the Ditchley Ball, held on July 22, 1949, to which four hundred people were invited. There was dancing, fireworks, and the house and gardens were awash with floodlights. In each room there were huge flower arrangements by the famous London florist, Constance Spry. Two Hungarian violinists serenaded groups in the garden, and people danced in the William Kent drawing room under the gaze of an approving Charles II. The food consisted of hams and rice imported from Macy's in New York, with kedgeree, chicken terrapin, and raspberries and ice cream. At four o'clock in the morning, eggs and bacon were served. Never had the house looked more glorious. Marietta herself looked radiant, softly pregnant, in a floaty sea-green dress. As the fireworks cascaded across the English summer sky, people were silhouetted against Ditchley's magnificent facade as though partaking in a dream.

Twenty-four guests stayed the weekend at Ditchley for the ball. Princesses Elizabeth and Margaret both attended. In fact, Marietta's only reservation was having to sit next to the duke of Edinburgh at dinner. One is not allowed to leave a member of the royal family until he or she gets up first. Unfortunately, Marietta found herself feeling increasingly faint until she finally had to bolt from the room. "This is the only time I have had a baby symptom," she told her parents afterwards.

Over a hundred letters poured in after the ball. "I could hardly believe such beauty existed in the modern world" (Victor Cunard). "A great joy" (Princess Elizabeth). "A really perfect evening" (Princess Margaret). "It was far and away the best party that has ever been given in England" (Pamela and Michael Berry).

Mixed in with these encomiums were letters that conveyed a more elegiac tone. "I know how sad you will be to leave that lovely place, after all you have done to make it beautiful," Lord Salisbury wrote. "It made a most fitting and dazzling finale to a great epoch at Ditchley," Cecil Beaton summed up. Ronnie's sons, for whom in part the ball was given as a farewell party, most particularly felt the loss of their family home. Not only had they lost Ditchley, wings and all, but they had lost their father to New York. Michael (who had become engaged to Lady Anne Cavendish, the duke of Devonshire's daughter), and Jeremy (who never married), would remain behind in England.

Frances FitzGerald, the other stepchild of this Anglo-American tableau, was not present to see her mother's triumph at the ball. She had already left for Maine with Alice, where she would stay for July, August, and most of September with her father and grandparents. Frankie was not told anything about the sale of Ditchley or the move to New York, the theory being that she would be upset and it would spoil her holiday. In fact, her new stepsister, Barbara Lawrence, three years younger, let the cat out of the bag in the blunt way that children have. "You're not going back to Ditchley," she announced as the two little girls stood on a rock one day above Northeast Harbor.[2] Stunned, Frankie stared at the ocean, refusing to cry. But that night she wept, pleading with Alice to say it was not true.

At the age of nine, Frankie was once more uprooted, unsure in what direction she was headed, the sense of bereavement compounded by the lack of explanation or reassurance from her mother, who was not to be with her daughter at all during those critical three months. Frankie had not been able to say good-bye to anyone—even to her beloved pony.

Meanwhile, after the ball, Ronnie took Marietta for a holiday to the Scottish Highlands, where they went shooting, ate grouse, and slept long hours. They then returned to Ditchley to complete the packing up, to give a farewell party for all the estate workers (with two tents and much weeping), and to attend many farewell parties in their honor, before sailing away for the last time, on October 1, on the

*Caronia* to New York. It was a terrible leave-taking for Ronnie. Marietta conceded that she had come to consider England her home, and "though a lot of the agony of leaving was due to my worry over Ronnie's loss, a great deal was due to my root-entwined attachments to the very place and the people who lived on it."

Bravely spoken. At that moment she could, of course, afford the sentiment. Although she had had moments of great joy and excitement during her two and a half years in England, what was she giving up? A society of chilly, superior beings who made her feel a stupid outsider, a political system dominated by birth and breeding, and a lady-bountiful role that went against all her instincts of democracy and egalitarianism.

Marietta and Ronnie arrived in New York on October 7, 1949, and settled for a few weeks in a rented house at 16 East 72nd Street. There Ronnie contemplated his future while Marietta awaited the birth of their child and rushed eagerly to pick up the reins of her New York life.

# CHAPTER *18*

# *"On weekends we have a heavenly, cozy time together"*

On December 2, 1949, at the age of thirty-two, Marietta gave birth to a daughter, Penelope, in New York. Marietta had not enjoyed her second pregnancy. Dorothy Paley had noticed this in England, and it was equally clear to Mary Warburg in New York. Mary thought her friend was frustrated at the loss of her figure and of her freedom. (Mrs. Warburg was also pregnant, and she gave birth to her daughter, Daphne, three weeks after Penelope was born.) A new baby was also a difficult adjustment for Ronnie.

When he and Marietta moved back to a rented house in New York, he had just celebrated his fifty-second birthday. He had lived only briefly in New York as a young man after his father's death. He had not felt comfortable then in the noisy, hungry city. This time was no easier. He could not ride his horses, run the farm, walk through his lovely gardens as he used to. He had no job, no function, no connection to the city.

Shortly after arriving that fall, he suffered another loss. His half brother, Peter Beatty, committed suicide at his home, Mereworth Castle, in Kent, just before Ronnie's son, Michael, was to marry Lady Anne Cavendish. Ronnie, returning to England that October for the wedding, instead found himself attending a funeral. It was a distressing event, with Peter's friend Aly Khan "in floods of tears," as Ronnie told Marietta, and Ronnie's ex-wife, now Nancy Lancaster, "looking frightfully haggard and drawn." (In fact, Nancy, who very soon left her husband, was still mentally unstable, so much so that her sons feared she would take the same tragic course as Peter, causing Ronnie further anxiety.)

Ronnie missed Marietta desperately during these weeks, longing for her "calm, wonderful self to give us all a necessary sense of balance." He returned briefly and sadly to Ditchley, before flying back to New York, where he had taken up a temporary position with an investment banking firm. He also began looking for a permanent home to buy for his family, and worked on plans for the extensive work still to be done on his house in Barbados.

His ties to England remained strong. Both his sons and his oldest friends lived there. He remained in touch with his old political cronies, now once again in power, making suggestions, offering ideas, lobbying for an appointment. He saw Churchill several times, bringing back amusing stories of the grand old man in his declining years. These intimate evenings with Winston and his wife Clementine (who was eager to visit Barbados) helped Ronnie feel he was still an insider.

He visited friends and discussed possible career moves in both the United States and Barbados. He talked to Peter Thorneycroft at the Board of Trade about Anglo-American business opportunities. However, this campaign of knocking on doors and eagerly offering help was not well received. When he asked Anthony Eden if his name might be put up as a delegate to the United Nations, Eden dismissed the idea out of hand, saying that it presented "real and formidable difficulties."

Ronnie's continued efforts throughout the 1950s to lobby his still influential friends were cruelly rebuffed. In spite of his generosity to Churchill in the war, the great man never gave Ronnie a single honor in thanks for his past loyalty and service. Even when Anthony Eden became prime minister in 1955 after Churchill finally resigned, silence continued to emanate from Downing Street. (Ronnie bore these humiliations ungrudgingly, and remained a good friend, helping the Edens buy a house in Barbados after Anthony's resignation over the catastrophe of Suez in 1956.)

After each visit to England Ronnie returned, crestfallen, to New York. The house at 123 East 79th Street, which he bought in May 1950 for $115,000, was a large double-fronted structure, with fine proportions and a splendid central staircase, and Ronnie filled it with relics of Ditchley that he could not bear to part with. They included English paintings by Constable, Augustus John, and Sir Thomas Lawrence, French and English eighteenth-century furniture, Georgian silver, Sevres porcelain, and two Italian marble busts of blackamoors. There were other reminders of Ditchley. Collins, Alice Butler, Mabel O'Dell (Penelope's nanny), and the chauffeur, Reg Duvall, with his wife and young son, also followed their master to America. Still handsome, if a little overweight (Marietta had tried in vain to limit his diet), Ronnie restlessly roamed his new domain, so familiar and yet so strange, while he waited for some sign from Downing Street. None came.

Barbados in the end became for Ronnie the substitute for his life in England. Under British colonial rule, the island remained hospitable to white expatriates, and many rich exiles from Britain had made homes there. The house Ronnie built in St. James's, on the west coast of the island, became legendary for its elegance and refinement. The site was just down the coast from Sir Edward Cunard's Glitter Bay, where Marietta and Ronnie had first started their romance. Ronnie chose the Palladian style of architecture, like that of Glitter Bay, with gardens designed by the man who had transformed Ditchley's gardens, Sir Geoffrey Jellicoe. (In fact, Jellicoe never visited the house during the construction, sending his design orders from England. This explains the odd position of the vista *behind* the house away from the ocean. "I had no idea the house was on the beach!" the great landscaper remarked on finally seeing his handiwork.)[1]

Every detail of the house was meticulously thought through, from chandeliers to side tables. Ronnie made trips to Portugal to find tiles for the floors, he bought lacquer furniture from Venice, and shipped pictures and furnishings from England. Traces of Ditchley also found their way there, including statues, furniture, and the graceful iron gates. Ronnie had invited all his English friends to stay, including members of the royal family, so the house was required to be up to royal standards of hospitality. It would be a mini-Ditchley in the tropics, a West Indian stately home teeming with the same interesting people who used to flock to Ditchley for those summer weekend parties.

The price of this venture was lavish by modern estimates. In contrast to today, when the oceanfront land would be astronomically expensive, the construction cost more than the real estate. Ronnie had acquired most of the land and an existing house (the Pink Cottage) back in 1947 for just over £5,000, or four cents a square foot.[2] The cost of the construction of Heron Bay—including furniture, furnishings, landscaping, and outbuildings—came to just over $125,000.

At the beginning of the Barbados venture, Marietta threw herself into the project with her customary energy and enthusiasm. She went on shopping trips with Ronnie to find treasures to decorate their new vacation paradise. He included her in meetings with the local politicians and bankers to discuss the island's economic potential, giving her her first taste of business, which she found, to her surprise, she very much enjoyed. She also began working with Ronnie on starting a Planned Parenthood organization on the island, with top government support.

In 1951 they spent their first winter, six weeks of January and

February, at Heron Bay, in an exodus that was to become an annual ritual. For the first year, they took Frankie with them (taking her out of school) as well as baby Penelope. Many friends came to stay. The house was beautiful, the scenery romantic, and guests were enchanted with Ronnie's architectural masterpiece.

But there were difficulties. Frankie was ten years old and grappling with yet another strange new world at home and school. She was also having to adjust to a new baby sister after nine years of being the only one, a baby sister with whom she had to share her mother, and with whom her stepfather was clearly besotted. Having spent one year at Dalton, reentering in the fourth grade, and finally becoming accustomed again to an American school and making new American friends, she was wrested away, missing the whole winter term. Instead, she was plumped down on an exotic island and sent to a local church school, run by Episcopal nuns, where she learned multiplication tables but was often bored.

There were even fewer children to play with on the island than on the Ditchley estate. Charlotte Carstairs (later Woollett), whose father was a British civil servant based in Barbados, was one of the few children the same age as Frankie, and she was invited over occasionally to play. Once, when the Trees were away the whole weekend, Charlotte was summoned to Heron Bay for the night to keep Frankie company.

"There was just a Barbadian servant there," she remembers. "No nanny. Frankie had this huge bedroom all to herself. I was so unhappy I wept and wept and my parents came and took me home. Poor Frankie!"

The household staff also turned out to be a problem. Ronnie demanded a very high level of service at Heron Bay, and, as at Ditchley, Marietta had to learn to satisfy him. Guests were offered every attention imaginable. Picnics were served by the chauffeur and servants, who carried the hampers of food and wine, laid out the napkins and silverware, and packed everything up again afterward. Clean towels appeared by magic; suitcases were unpacked by invisible hands.

But many of the black islanders were indifferent to the British standards expected of servants. Marietta had great difficulty in explaining to them how she wanted things done. "Have spent most of the week trying to train the help who all act as if they had just been born, and continue to do everything wrong after three patient and detailed explanations," she complained to her parents.

Marietta still had few instincts as to how to handle this most subtle of relationships. She had had a crash course at Ditchley, but there she had been protected by Collins and a staff that needed little or no instruction. In Barbados, there was no Collins to shoulder the responsibility. (Interestingly, Collins never went to Barbados. By private arrangement with his master he took his annual vacation when the family left for the Caribbean.) Marietta was on unfamiliar territory. She talked to the staff with her head held high in a way that seemed to them aloof and demanding, and she never smiled.[3]

It is likely that her consciousness about race complicated the situation for her. In Barbados she worked hard for civil rights, and yet she gave orders to black servants. How was one to reconcile that seeming contradiction? When Frankie, on meeting the black prime minister of Barbados, Grantley Adams, rushed to her mother saying, "Is he a cousin of my Mr. Charlie Adams of Dedham?" Marietta was delighted at this demonstration of her daughter's color-blindness. Back in New York, her old friend from *Life* days, Earl Brown, had become a city councilman from Harlem, and had contacted her about working on a project there. What would he think of her colonial existence at Heron Bay?

In contrast, Ronnie, like many Englishmen born into his social class, knew how to communicate with the servants, and in return they loved him. At Heron Bay, Ronnie called on Osmondo Tull, a hardworking Barbadian native, to replace Collins. Tull started as a driver and then took on the English butler's duties, in the end becoming as beloved and necessary to Ronnie's life as Collins. Heron Bay was famous for its rum punches, and much later Tull described with delight how Lord Linlithgow, for instance, would signal Tull by the way he punched the air with his fist how strong he wanted his drink that day. This kind of camaraderie with servants was completely foreign to Marietta. She was not at ease with them, and it caused much friction with Ronnie, who always took their side. On one occasion, when Marietta complained that one of the waiters was drinking on duty and should be punished, Ronnie was appalled, pointing out that Barbadians grew up on rum and to penalize them for it would be absurd.[4]

Once upon a time, Marietta had disappointed Desie in her failure to be a good hostess. Now with Ronnie, she was once again trying to live up to her husband's demands for a smooth-running house, and her combination of imperiousness and gaucheness indicates her continuing insecurity in the role. Indeed, her attempts at being a convincing chatelaine sometimes verged on the ridiculous. Friends visiting Heron Bay remember wanting to play tennis, but when Marietta discovered there were no ballboys, she called off the game.

Gradually, the geographical fissure between the Caribbean and the United States took on a psychological dimension. Ronnie spent more and more time in Barbados, hoping to build a new career for himself promoting the island economy. He visited the Colonial Office in London, for instance, to try to drum up interest in starting a handi-crafts industry on the island. Later he became a major player in the transformation of Barbados's west coast into one of the most luxurious and expensive resort developments in the Caribbean.

Ronnie also realized an intense joy in his little daughter, Penelope, and wanted a secure family life for her. (Perhaps in addition to his natural paternal pride, there was the fleeting sense that this waiflike, wide-eyed child finally assuaged for him the memory of the infant daughter he and Nancy had lost so long ago.) "I like to get into bed every evening and before going to sleep think of what you all look like," he wrote Marietta from England. "Penelope's hair and her wist-fulness and Frankie doing her homework by the fire and Jody barking and all the hundred and one things that go to make my life with you such a blissful one." He loved buying things for his little daughter: "Tell Mabel I bought [Penelope] a coat and material for leggings and two cotton and two viyella dresses—so she ought to be alright for the winter." And he continued to give his wife gifts—a fur stole for her trip to England because "it's often cold in England in July." Four years after their marriage, he wrote to her with gratitude "for the great happiness you have brought me . . . I didn't know how utterly dependent I had become on you—and consequently how horrible it is to be alone."

But Marietta, while promoting family values ("On weekends we have a heavenly, cozy time together," she assured Susan Mary), was beginning to feel the pinch of marital disenchantment. The split from her family, the wrenching divorce, those dire warnings of a future of hellfire, had had one golden compensation: Ronnie and Ditchley and world politics. That promise had almost overnight been dashed. Now, what was she left with? An exiled husband, who instead of finding a new career in New York was retreating more and more to a Caribbean island as alien to Marietta's spirit as any Conservative Party fête. She was watching the man she had hoped would save her from a dreary domestic existence become transformed from a senior political insider into a bridge-playing expatriate, surrounded by wealthy people lying about drinking gin while black servants fanned the tropical air. The sybaritic, indolent life of the West Indies' white community ran con-trary to every fiber of her Peabody background and instincts. Had she gone through all those searing changes to give dinner parties for rich Brits and be agreeable to the locals and waste her life away in the irrelevancies of a far-flung vacation paradise?

In New York, she pursued her friends with zest, seeing Bill and Babe Paley in Long Island, dining with the Irwin Shaws, dancing on the St. Regis Roof, and lunching with Mary Warburg. (One lunch included Pamela Churchill, who announced that the only interesting

Ronnie and Marietta with Isaiah Berlin (right) on board the *Queen Elizabeth* in 1953. *(Cunard Line)*

life of the nineteenth century was as a *poule de luxe*. That Marietta thought this worth mentioning to Susan Mary at the time indicates how even then Mrs. Churchill's career aroused certain suspicions.) Mezzy Hickok and Coupie Kernan, with other friends and relations, came at various times to 123 East 79th Street and admired the Chinese Coromandel screen, the George III gilt mirror, and the needlework carpets from Ditchley, in the home where Mrs. Ronald Tree reigned —dressed by Dior, surrounded by servants with English accents, guarded by two Italian marble blackamoors, and conveyed about town in a Rolls-Royce driven by an English chauffeur.

Impressed by her regal beauty and rich surroundings, they wondered if perhaps their old friend seemed a little more stiff and less spontaneous. Some of those who remembered her antics as Brownie Captain at St. Tim's, or dancing the night away at El Morocco, saw an almost imperceptible shift away from that unguardedness in her new role as wealthy, international socialite. Had her elevated position made her more formal and self-conscious? Had Marietta, with her new, carefully modulated accent, changed?

Her English experience had certainly chastened her. She had picked up a new style of presenting herself that would be more accommodating to her critics. Englishisms crept into her speech that never left her, such as "terribly pleasant," "awfully amusing." As she observed the way society worked in England, she learned how many of its rituals were in effect subtle protective mechanisms to conceal emotional weakness or vulnerability. This aspect of the English psyche was not unfamiliar to her, for the repressed approach to setbacks was one of the most enduring legacies of her grandfather, the Rector (along with the English accent). Thus she easily adopted the distancing manner practiced by Ronnie's social circle. A touch of aloofness concealed really quite well the old insecurities that churned inside her voluptuous frame. But this emotional sealant was applied at a price. A mask was slowly being created to protect her and ease her way into the political and intellectual world to which she so keenly aspired.

There were more pleasurable, if superficial, lessons. She learned to stay in the grandest hotels of Europe, order food and wine such as never graced the Peabodys' table, and travel in the lap of luxury. Ronnie took her to the Paris couture shows and chose her wardrobe. No more "making do" with one black party dress.

During her years in England she had mixed with the highest levels of English society, going to parties with kings and queens, dukes and earls, in beautiful houses filled with treasures. She had been showered with caviar and danced "hip-deep in champagne," as she put it, encountering a way of life that in at least one other European country had provoked a revolution. That she felt guilty about the social divide is evident from the many defensive references to it in her letters home; that she enjoyed her new position of privilege is also indisputable.

She had been taught to despise material wealth. Self-sacrifice and public service were the keystones of her Peabody upbringing. Yet, like many offspring of patrician but impoverished families, the lure of financial security was extremely potent. After all, English aristocrats had been marrying American heiresses for years for precisely this reason. And even her grandfather, Endicott Peabody, manipulated his wealthier Groton boys with a clear conscience. The money promised power; but in Marietta's eyes, perhaps more important, it promised access.

Now those difficult days of England were behind her, already transformed into tolerable legend. She had made some English friends during those two and a half years, friends to whom she would return regularly over the years. But it was a place of the past for her, as indeed it was in historical terms. Weakened by the war, haunted by a rapidly vanishing empire. Britain was experiencing a decline. America, by contrast, was a country in political flux, with a vital liberal resurgence in the postwar years, reflected in Truman's stunning win over Dewey in 1948—on a ticket that included an official civil rights platform—and in the number of new young Democratic senators sent to Washington such as Paul Douglas from Illinois and Hubert Humphrey from Minnesota (whom Marietta thought the most outstanding of all). Marietta responded to this invigorating Democratic movement with excitement, and was determined to share in it.

In late 1951 and early 1952, Ronnie embarked on a speaking tour of the United States sponsored by the English Speaking Union. His subject was the "new" Britain and its importance as America's ally. He and Marietta traveled together to Louisville, and then on to Springfield, Illinois, to stay with Adlai Stevenson, Ronnie's old friend. They were delighted when Stevenson finally accepted the Democratic nomination that summer in Chicago. Ronnie sent him a modest $200 and Marietta signed up in New York as a volunteer, with Ronnie's support. This was a political issue that they could both agree on.

Adlai Stevenson's presidential run in 1952 was a critical piece of timing for Marietta. She had a beautiful New York town house to live in, her daughters were in the hands of expert caregivers, and her husband had become preoccupied by his own projects. She was bursting with energy, surrounded by interesting connections, financially secure, and committed to a kind of political activity that had, as yet, no focus. But she would not have to wait any longer. With the emergence of Stevenson as the Democratic Party's most inspiring and enigmatic leader, Marietta's search for personal fulfillment seemed over. Adlai Stevenson would replace all the others in her life as the repository of her highest ideals.

CHAPTER *19*

# *"Adlai knew all the right questions"*

Marietta's first political move on returning to New York was to join the Lexington Democratic Club, named, according to its cofounder, Richard A. Brown, for its first headquarters on 60th Street at Lexington Avenue. The Lexington Democratic Club was one of several pioneer reform clubs formed in New York after the war with the purpose of overthrowing the old political machinery that was centered in Tammany Hall and dominated at the time by the old-style "boss," Carmine de Sapio. Several similar clubs had sprung up in other major American cities. The impetus came from idealistic young liberals and intellectuals, who had watched in horror the disintegration of political systems in Europe during World War II and were determined to prevent similar catastrophes back home. As George H. P. Dwight, a member of the Lexington Democratic Club when Marietta joined (he later became president), explained, "We were a group of people—mostly lawyers—who wanted to make local politics more acceptable to their constituents. We supported the universal principle that local political clubs should be *democratic,* as opposed to being controlled by an acknowledged boss in the traditional way."

The manner in which these young reformers attempted their revolution was also democratic, that is, from within the system, by putting up candidates to contest Tammany Hall candidates in primaries where district and county leadership was at stake. The Lexington Democratic Club was signally successful in its campaign, winning the 9th Assembly District (the Upper East Side, known as the Silk Stocking District) with its own candidate, Jean P. J. Baltzell, and in so doing, setting in motion the movement to dismantle Tammany Hall.

There was another important distinction between these new groups and the old party clubs. Whereas de Sapio's Tammany Hall circles were strictly male, the reform clubs welcomed women as potential district leaders, club presidents, and candidates for the assembly. Marietta Tree was one of those women.

The Lexington Democratic Club could have been designed for her. Its members consisted of volunteers, bright young intellectuals and professionals, who had burning ideals and the energy (and funds) to pursue them. The cause that united them was as pure as that of destroying Nazism. The means—getting signatures to support candidates to run against the enemy—was simple to understand and execute. It took legwork (ringing on doorbells), paperwork (collecting signatures and filling out forms), and much late night discussion of strategy. Thanks to her eclectic work at *Life*, Marietta had become proficient in all these activities.

Within two years of joining the club, she was persuaded to run as a county committeewoman for her district, and won. She replaced Dorothy Schiff, owner and publisher of the *New York Post*, who knew Stevenson and whose former husband, George Backer, was a loyal Stevenson supporter. In 1954, Marietta was elected to the Democratic State Committee, a position of more style than substance, but which required attendance at national Democratic Party meetings and representation on local party platforms. (She would be reelected in 1956, 1958, and 1960, quitting only when she was appointed to the United Nations in 1961.)

In February 1952, Governor Adlai Stevenson came to New York to tour the new housing developments in Harlem. Among the entourage in New York that February were Bill Blair, Stevenson's executive assistant and Marietta's old friend from Northeast Harbor; Earl Brown (her former deskmate at *Life*); and Marietta herself. Feeling particularly confident in the presence of these familiar faces, and with Ronnie's connection to Stevenson, she participated eagerly in the discussions and emerged exhilarated by the experience. "Adlai knew all the right questions and the answers were very exciting," she wrote to Susan Mary. "We are in the process and well on our way to erasing all slums in New York City, and all this since the war. It is a miraculous achievement."

Dick Brown, who, among other responsibilities, was in charge of organizing Stevenson Clubs in New York in the 1952 election, said that in a campaign it was often difficult to find something for volunteers to do. "You can't rely on them to be there to make phone calls at eight o'clock in the morning, and if there's a sale at Bergdorf's, they aren't going to show up at all. So you give them a research project." In particular, he added, women with money in campaigns were (a) notoriously unreliable, and (b) temperamental. Marietta was neither. She was always reliable, and completely temperament-free.[1] She became chairman of research for the New York State Democratic Committee, and in this capacity she was allowed to attend the convention in Chicago. Ronnie went with her.

Working girl she may have been, but nobody by this time would ever have mistaken her for an ordinary foot soldier. Mary Bingham, wife of Stevenson's close friend, the Kentucky newspaper publisher Barry Bingham, remembered Marietta's first appearance that summer in Chicago. "We were supposed to meet Adlai for lunch in the stockyards," she recalled. "It was terribly hot and we were all pouring with sweat. An open car drove up to the restaurant, and out stepped this vision in a cool lacy dress twirling a parasol that seemed made of lingerie. It was as though a goddess were descending from the car."[2]

A couple of nights before the convention, a group of friends had dinner at Bill Blair's house in Lake Forest, and Marietta sat next to Stevenson. "Instead of being neurotic and over-pressured, he talked about the Middle East and poetry," she told her parents. Present that evening was Adlai's close friend Alicia Patterson, the rich, handsome, and tough-minded daughter of Joseph M. Patterson, co-editor of the *Chicago Tribune* family and founder of the New York *Daily News.* Adlai had first met and become fascinated with Alicia during his bachelor days, but he went on to marry another socially prominent woman, Ellen Borden. When he met Alicia again in 1947, his marriage was almost over. Although Alicia was married at the time to her third husband, the financier and philanthropist Harry Guggenheim, she and Adlai began seeing each other, and the friendship turned serious. Marietta summed up the situation immediately: "They were very clearly together, he had brought her and he was taking her home." Alicia was wearing black taffeta, which Marietta, goddess of cool, thought unsuitable for the hot night. Was this mere idle criticism on Marietta's part? She was clearly sizing up the dynamic and powerful woman at Adlai's side. "She was very conservative politically, you know," Marietta confided to Stevenson's biographer, John Bartlow Martin, later. "She scorned my liberal views."

Marietta was thrilled by her sudden proximity to the candidate, drinking in the political gossip, delighted that she was included in the talk as though she were a legitimate cabinet official instead of worthy only, as she put it, to sweep the floors of the convention hall. Marietta was on the podium seated behind Stevenson when he made his famous (or infamous) "Let this cup pass from me" acceptance speech. (Ronnie had gone back to New York for business reasons and missed the great moment.) Clayton Fritchey, newspaper editor and Stevenson adviser, leaned over to her and said, "Your candidate is pretty good." Marietta, looking at Stevenson from the back, remarked how the candidate was shaped like a pyramid.[3] She and Ronnie sent a joint telegram to him the following day, saying: "Our prayers, our hopes and our wishes are with you on this great day in American history."

When Adlai Stevenson accepted the nomination to run against Dwight D. Eisenhower in 1952 (with Alabama senator John Sparkman as Stevenson's running mate), the political temperature skyrocketed. In particular, the generation of young reformists who had joined the clubs in the late 1940s saw at last a leader who genuinely reflected their doubts, hopes, and yearnings for a better world. Stevenson's patrician background, intelligence, wit, and modest public persona spoke to these eager minds like the voice of a messiah. George Dwight said he was listening one night to Adlai talking over the radio and realized tears were coursing down his cheeks.

This quality Stevenson possessed to inspire people came from sturdy roots. His paternal grandfather, a high-ranking Democratic politician from Illinois, was vice president under Grover Cleveland; his maternal grandfather was an adviser to Abraham Lincoln; and his father, Lewis, was in turn journalist, farmer, and politician. Thus the seeds of Adlai's career were sown early.

Although Stevenson's childhood was marred by the incompatibility of his parents, the single most traumatic event to happen to him took place in 1912, when he accidentally shot and killed Ruth Merwin, a distant cousin and school friend of his sister, Buffie. The effect of such a tragedy on a sensitive twelve-year-old boy can hardly be imagined, and many observers later attributed to it some of Stevenson's insecurity, self-doubt, and fatalism. "It must have been something he thought about every day of his life," Arthur Schlesinger, Jr., said.[4]

The most significant influence on the young Stevenson was his mother. Regal, elegant, and immensely charismatic, Helen Stevenson soon lost interest in her disappointing marriage and lavished her energies on her only son, going so far as to move to Princeton when Adlai was admitted as an undergraduate, so that she could be closer to her "dearest laddie," as she called him. (Perhaps it is not an accident that the mother of another political legend, Franklin D. Roosevelt, was equally protective and possessive.)

Boys who grow up with powerful, adoring mothers have predictable conflicts when they reach adulthood, especially in their choice of mate. Adlai, after several years of popular success, finally decided to marry a young woman who had many similarities to his mother. Helen Stevenson liked to make an impact when entering a room. Ellen, Mrs. Stevenson's daughter-in-law, was equally competitive, so much so that when Adlai began making a name for himself in public life, she became fiercely jealous. If he told an amusing story at a party, she would jump up and insist on going home.

The couple had three sons, Adlai III, Borden, and John Fell, before Ellen's increasing mental instability and erratic behavior forced Adlai to give up hope for the marriage. Ellen's psychological collapse grieved him deeply, and he never remarried. (The scar was permanent. A week before he died, he was still talking about his former wife with deep concern.) [5]

Meanwhile, after an undistinguished start as a lawyer in Chicago, Stevenson found the spotlight as a speaker at meetings of the Chicago Council on Foreign Relations. Attracted by public affairs, he went to Washington after the outbreak of World War II in the office of the secretary of the navy, Frank Knox. After helping promote Senate ratification of the United Nations Charter in 1945, he was appointed a delegate to the UN General Assembly (he was to return twenty years later in a far more exalted role). From there it was a short step to the governorship of Illinois, where he served an effective four years before winning the Democratic presidential nomination in Chicago in 1952.

For many, this new Democratic leader provided a call to arms. Hundreds of volunteers flocked to their local Democratic clubs to work for him. But some close friends of Stevenson and many moderates felt ambivalent about the nomination. They regarded Eisenhower as a very attractive candidate and doubted that Stevenson could defeat him. Adlai's friend Marshall Field came out for Eisenhower, and even Marietta saw the appeal of the fresh-faced, wide-smiling war hero and Republican centrist as he rode in to rescue the American people from a tired, corrupt Democratic regime. (When Republican Party workers waved their campaign banners at Stevenson, he responded by saying, "I like Ike too!") "Time for a change," always a cogent campaign slogan, seemed particularly powerful in 1952.

On August 4, the Trees went to Northeast Harbor for two and a half weeks. Marietta kept up on the campaign with Walter Lippmann, Sumner Welles, and the Finletters (Tom Finletter was a close Stevenson aide), who summered there. On her return to New York, she plunged into action. She had been appointed vice chairman of Volunteers for Stevenson in New York. Using her contacts, her money, and her house to raise support and votes for her candidate, she worked hard as the campaign progressed.

Ronnie was also involved, and wrote to Adlai in August offering help. "To all of those who believe that a democratic party is the one best fitted to carry this country through the next crucial years, your nomination to carry the banner was more than heartening. Particularly as it looks as if Eisenhower would be driven more and more into a corner by his isolationist supporters. . . ." Adlai responded at once with gratitude for Ronnie's support and encouragement. "I think you have put your finger on it—the greatest hazard is the isolationist influences which dominate the Republican party and must inevitably temper the General's attitude. . . . My love to Marietta."

In September, Ronnie went to England, leaving Marietta to concentrate on her campaign duties. He visited the Pattens in Paris, and Susan Mary took him to Dior, where he bought a skirt and stole for Marietta. Marietta, meanwhile, was collecting names of Women for Stevenson, entertaining, and helping organize rallies. She enlisted Frankie, now almost twelve years old and already catching her mother's political fever, to stamp envelopes and help canvass Park Avenue apartments. Marietta even persuaded her mother to support Stevenson (with a modest check), but the bishop remained firmly in the Republican camp.

One of her major triumphs was getting an advertisement in *The New York Times* proclaiming one thousand Women for Stevenson. Another triumph was the Women Volunteers for Stevenson lunch she helped organize at the Waldorf-Asotria in New York on October 28. She expected eight hundred people and three thousand showed up. Marietta, speaking publicly as a Democratic Party official for the first time, introduced Eleanor Roosevelt (a key Stevenson ally) and Jane Dick, co-chairman of the National Volunteers for Stevenson Committee and a close friend of Stevenson's. Marietta was very nervous about the speech but discovered she enjoyed it. "This must be a strong inheritance from my parents," she wrote, complimenting them.

Perhaps equally exciting for Marietta was the dinner she gave at East 79th Street that evening for thirty-five Stevenson campaign insiders from Springfield, Illinois, prior to a Stevenson rally at Madison Square Garden. This party exposed Marietta to Adlai's most powerful and intimate associates, and they were dazzled by her. (Of those present, both the journalist Clayton Fritchey and the historian Arthur Schlesinger, Jr., had something of a crush on this bewitching Democrat; Arthur, who had first met her in Paris in 1948, never forgot that first vision of a "stunning blonde girl in a smashing red dress," and became a lifelong friend.) Later that week Marietta dined with the Springfield group alone, while they thrashed out matters of policy and strategy, the war in Korea being a major issue.

For Marietta, it was wildly flattering to be accepted in the inner cabinet like this, sitting in on the campaign strategists' most confidential discussions. When asked her opinion as to whether they should accept Hamilton Fish's unlikely conversion to Stevenson (Fish, a Republican congressman from New York, was notorious for his pro-Hitler, "America First" position in the early 1940s), she felt like saying,

"Who, *me?*" Needless to say, this humble reaction did not prevent her from giving her reasons why Fish should not be accepted, especially so late in the campaign.

During that October visit, Bill Blair told Marietta that the governor wanted to see her. Again, she thought, who, *me?* "When I went to see him he said, 'Dulles has just said that Eastern Europe should be liberated. What do you think of this?' Well, I was so staggered to be asked what I thought of this. I went on about it and how I thought this should be denounced and all that sort of thing, but I was really staggered."[6]

In the English satirical magazine *Private Eye,* the code phrase for a couple meeting for nefarious purposes is "to discuss Ugandan affairs." That Stevenson invited Marietta to come to his hotel room to discuss American foreign policy was surely not quite plausible, even to his naive guest. She rationalized why he should have done so by explaining that Eden and Attlee did the same thing—asked the advice of people whose opinions they did not value on large questions. She thought it was a technique to ingratiate oneself with the person questioned—and not a very nice technique. In fact, Stevenson discovered several interesting facts that night, but not about Dulles. He had no idea, then, that Marietta was a committed campaign worker, or that she had been a vice chairman of the CIO Political Action Committee and a shop steward in her *Life* days. "He thought of me as the wife of the stylish Ronald Tree."[7] A wife, however, who had aroused his curiosity enough to probe further.

Much has been written about Stevenson's political chances against Eisenhower in 1952, and in hindsight it is clear that they were slim. The election was in the end a Republican sweep. Stevenson carried only nine states, and received 89 electoral votes to Eisenhower's 442. In spite of the fervor the governor aroused in the young, many thought he ran an amateurish campaign, appearing too high-minded, an unconvincing "man of the people," and paying too little attention to local party leaders. The ethic of noblesse oblige that sounded like an obbligato throughout the campaign was not music to the ears of the blue-collar voters. And Stevenson's "soft" position on communism, plus the liberalism of some of his staff, offended the right wing of the party.

Some believed that his lack of a conventional domestic background harmed him. His former wife Ellen became increasingly irrational as the campaign progressed and made embarrassing scenes in public; and rumors, thought to have originated with the Republicans, circulated that Stevenson was a homosexual. But perhaps the single most damaging aspect of Stevenson's candidacy was his waffling on the issue of the Korean War, which, like Vietnam later, had become an increasingly unpopular engagement, and one which Eisenhower promised to end.

However, the huge following Stevenson inspired across the country surprised many people, including himself. One particularly influential group of supporters, who gained little public attention at the time, were women voters. Just as the reform clubs had accepted women as equals in the political battle for democratic representation, so Stevenson's appeal touched the women of the United States in a very profound way, and Marietta could take credit for having played a role in summoning them to the ballot box. Following the 1952 defeat, she helped organize a group called the Democratic Women's Workshop, founded in 1954 for the purpose of bringing together the women who had worked for Tammany Hall to vote for Stevenson and Democratic candidates. James Rowe, who worked on both of Stevenson's presidential campaigns, reported that when he worked on Lyndon Johnson's campaign in 1960, he was struck by the high caliber of young Democrats in county offices across the country. He asked how they got there, and their answer was always the same: During or after the 1952 campaign, their wives, inspired by Stevenson, had urged them to go into politics. (Today the women would have gone into politics themselves.)

Ronnie returned to New York on November 1, in time to watch the election results. For Marietta, while the defeat of her candidate was disappointing, it was somehow mitigated by the excitement of the campaign, in particular meeting people in politics who were to be lasting friends.

"What was good about the election was that on November 5, there was no bitterness or hard feelings," Marietta wrote to Susan Mary in Paris. "Everyone felt that Stevenson had done his best (and it was a remarkable best), that this Republican tide had been gathering since 1940, and we were glad that the vote affirmed Eisenhower and his policies rather than that of the irresponsible right wing. . . . As for Stevenson, my hope is that he will remain the *real* leader of the Democratic party, evolving a new concept in American politics—that of the loyal and constructive opposition. How that can be worked out when he holds no office, will be difficult."

On November 10, Ronnie wrote to Adlai, deploring the result from an international point of view, comparing it to Britain in 1945. "Then a party that had been many years in power and had allowed its machine to become rusty and lazy, found itself confronted by new personalities and a desire for change. . . . From what Marietta and others have told me, you are confronted by the same inertia and lack of organization not only in New York but in many of the other areas of the country as well." Ronnie, who had sent Stevenson's speeches to

Brendan Bracken, Churchill's adviser, also told Adlai that Winston had been touched by Stevenson's references to him, and hoped they might meet in England.

Adlai wrote back nine days later, a characteristically quick and personal response in spite of having received up to eighty thousand telegrams and letters. "I have read and re-read your thoughtful and gracious letter," Stevenson wrote. "I think your analogy about the moribund Conservative party is quite right. But must I dedicate years to the painful job of reorganizing and revitalizing across this endless land? I don't know and it is not an engaging prospect. Of this we must talk sometime, together with your remarkably wise and versatile and lovely Marietta."

Meanwhile, wise, versatile, and lovely Marietta was composing a letter of her own. "You have lifted politics into another sphere where I hope they will stay," she wrote Adlai on November 21, "sustained by you as leader of the Democratic Party. You have done so much more for this country than merely running for President—for you have elevated us all and the spirits of the world by your mind and heart and character. I pray you will continue to lead and give hope, not only to us loving Democrats, but also to Republicans and people all over the globe. And we are going to need you badly." She had learned that he was traveling to the Orient in March 1953, and invited him to come to Barbados for a few weeks at the beginning of February to prepare for the rigorous trip. "With all our gratitude to you for your glorious campaign, and all best wishes and prayers for your future molding our future! Ever affectionately, Marietta Tree."

Adlai's response came a week later: "I have read and re-read your thoughtful and heart-lifting letter of November 21" (an opening sentence he obviously liked). "Actually, my heart needs little lifting and I feel more like the victor than the vanquished. But I am distressed by the disappointment of so many friends. Your own heroism I shall never forget. Indeed it would be hard to forget you regardless of campaigns! I shall live in hopes of the Barbados, but the future is misty."

The Trees spent a busy fall season in the city, attending parties for the Bennett Cerfs, the Sam Goldwyns, Irene Selznick (who had become a passionate Stevenson supporter), and dinners with other luminaries, including Clare Boothe Luce, whom Marietta described to Susan Mary: "Clare, at 50, is unbelievably beautiful, without a line in her face or a change of expression, and speaks continuously in a grey monotone about mysticism."

The weekend of December 7, the Trees traveled to Chicago and stayed two nights at the Governor's mansion in Springfield. That this invitation should have been extended by Stevenson so soon after the grueling experience of the election indicates the increasingly warm friendship between them. Jane Dick (wife of Edison Dick, one of Stevenson's oldest and closest friends from Lake Forest, Illinois, who had often played Adlai's hostess during the campaign) was also a guest, and they played charades, the original version of "The Game" that Marietta always so enjoyed and played throughout her life. (As well as being an amusing test of literacy, charades allowed her to indulge in her old passion for acting.) Ronnie was not an enthusiastic player, preferring bridge and Scrabble.

During this weekend, encouraged by Arthur Schlesinger (who warned her, however, that Adlai was hopelessly resistant to the idea of vacations), Marietta again urged the Gov (friends' nickname for Stevenson) to come to Heron Bay after Christmas. Her powers of persuasion worked. On January 20, 1953, at almost the hour of President Eisenhower's inauguration in Washington, Adlai, Marietta, and Jane Dick flew together to Barbados. (Ronnie had gone ahead to open the house.) Stevenson, with a last farewell to public office, had just moved out of the Governor's mansion in Springfield and was facing his "misty" future. Bennett Cerf at Random House wanted to publish a selection of his campaign speeches, and his plan was to work on these while vacationing at Heron Bay. Stevenson had also announced his plan to make a world tour sponsored by *Look* magazine, so the Caribbean getaway was all the more precious. For a few weeks, the exhausted campaigner could rest and recover from the last six months.

Marietta had invited other close friends to keep him company, including the Finletters and the Binghams. But Adlai was not in the mood to party. He stayed in the Pink Cottage most of the day working on the speeches, shunning the rum punches and the tennis games. On one occasion he did, however, manage to surprise his attentive hostess. "Suddenly he took off his swimming trunks and ran naked into the surf. I was shocked. I ran up to the house to get a big bath towel and take it down to him so he could use it both to dry himself and cover himself with. He had absolutely no modesty." The almost palpable tone of disapproval with which she related this story to John Bartlow Martin reveals how deeply Marietta's Puritanism was etched in her character.

Stevenson left Barbados on February 11. After making several speeches and visiting the White House, he took off for the Far East on March 2. He would not return to the United States for almost six months.

Stevenson's departure acted like a magic potion on Marietta, transforming her from political barnstormer into belle of the ball. Forgotten were those hardworking days at the Lexington Democratic Club. Abandoned were the money-raising drives and musty mailings that had governed her time throughout much of 1952. Now, with Adlai gone, she could pick up the strings as wife of Ronald Tree, assuming once more her role as socially prominent friend of the British aristocracy, former mistress of Ditchley, relation by marriage of the duke and duchess of Devonshire, intimate of Lord Salisbury, and dinner companion of Winston Churchill. She was returning to take part in the 1953 London season, and in particular to celebrate the high point of this historic year, the Coronation of Queen Elizabeth II.

# CHAPTER *20*

# *"The great spectacle of our lives"*

Ronnie, restive in New York, had rented a house in England for the summer of 1953. They were to be away almost five months. Since returning from Barbados, Marietta had been busy with work for the Urban League and for the Wiltwyck School. But her most serious political accomplishment at this time was helping organize "A Day of Political Education" for the purpose of luring women and independents who had worked for Stevenson into the Democratic Party. (This was the fledgling movement of what in 1954 became the Democratic Women's Workshop). Averell Harriman and Joe Clark, mayor of Philadelphia, and other Democratic National Committee members came to speak to the group (about 320 women turned up), and Marietta had to introduce them, which as usual left her nervous but ultimately triumphant.

Parkfield House in Surrey, which Ronnie had rented from the earl of Drogheda for the summer, had a pretty garden and a tennis court, and it backed onto Windsor Great Park. From there, the Trees launched into a series of parties and social events. Dinner at the Dorchester for thirty friends included diplomats and politicians, the playwright Robert Sherwood, and the English newspaper proprietor Michael Berry (of the *Daily Telegraph*) and his wife Pamela. Barry Bingham was there, just back from a stint with Stevenson's world tour, and he reported glowingly on the governor's visits to Vietnam, Indonesia, Malaya, and Thailand. The art historian Kenneth Clark gave a party for the Trees in Hampstead, with composer William Walton, ballet dancer Moira Shearer, and her journalist husband, Ludovic Kennedy. The Berrys gave a dinner and a lunch for them, inviting top diplomats and members of Parliament.

But most British eyes were trained on the upcoming Coronation. Thanks to Ronnie's daughter-in-law Anne Tree, whose mother was the duchess of Devonshire, Marietta attended the rehearsal in West-minister Abbey. The night of the rehearsal, Marietta and Ronnie went to a ball given for the queen by the Guards Regiments at Hampton Court. In addition, there were several more parties leading up to the Coronation itelf on June 2.

The Trees watched the procession to Westminster Abbey from the Whitehall office of Anthony Head, who was minister of war and a great friend of Ronnie's. Marietta reported to her parents that "The bagpipes, flags, 12,000 marching men . . . royal coaches, air force gen-erals and admirals . . . made it the great spectacle of our lives." That night the couple went out on the Thames on a boat chartered by the duke of Devonshire to see the fireworks.

The celebrations continued. June is England's big racing month, and the Trees went to Epsom for the famous Oaks, which was won that year by William Astor's horse. They also went to the Derby, supporting the queen as she examined her runner in the paddock. (It came in second.)

They spent a weekend in Norfolk with Judy Montagu, where one of the guests, Prince Nicholas of Yugoslavia, told Marietta that his father was so afraid of germs that he pushed doors open with his elbows. They went to an exhibition of Venetian pictures and porcelain. In the midst of all this prewar-style partygoing, Marietta tried on tiaras for the gala opening of a new opera at Covent Garden, the premiere of Benjamin Britten's *Gloriana,* written especially for the royal occasion.

Marietta and Ronnie repaired briefly to Parkfield House, where Frankie played tennis and croquet, and Penelope, wearing a gilt and red paper coronet, called herself "Queen Celeste" after her favorite storybook character. But the season was in full swing, so there was no rest for the popular Trees. There was Ascot to go to—the Royal Enclosure, of course, with Lord and Lady Salisbury, Bill Astor, and Michael, Anne, and Jeremy Tree. (Jeremy was to make a career of training horses.) In describing this event to her parents, Marietta pre-ferred not to mention that divorced people were prohibited from entering the Royal Enclosure unless they were the "innocent party," and Marietta had been hurriedly required to send for her divorce papers from Nevada to prove her eligibility.

She noticed that most of the women at Ascot (where dressing up is de rigueur) were swathed in mauve or white organdy, which seemed unfortunate, considering the freezing weather. But her own wardrobe seemed hardly less appropriate. "My sartorial splendour was always wrong," she sighed to her parents, "either underdressed, or another day taking a tip from other ladies, would wear a big hat and lots of jewelry, only to find in some mysterious way, that I was tragically overdressed and all the ladies in grey flannel suits." Sometimes she seemed sick of all the society hoopla. "Seeing so many people and talking about nothing much," she admitted, "as invariably happens when you see people at spectacles, makes me nervously exhausted." These signs of stress were not surprising. Her hateful experiences as a young bride at Ditchley only five years earlier were still fresh in her memory. In spite of ultimately making a good impression on some of Ronnie's English circle, she still felt vulnerable to their critical glances. Moreover, her political seriousness remained an issue. Even if she had learned to throttle down her democratic conscience, sometimes her American friends betrayed her. Marshall Field, visiting the Trees that summer in England, infuriated Marietta's stepdaughter-in-law by asking her if White's Club (a men's club in London) had any charitable purpose.[1] For the Fourth of July weekend the Trees stayed with the Agars, where Senator J. William Fulbright was also a guest. Marietta thought him charming, idealistic, and a first-rate politician. She asked him if he thought a Citizen's Committee should be formed to fight Senator Joseph McCarthy, whose anticommunist witch-hunts were increasingly effective. He replied he thought it would be wiser to wait to see whom they should fight—Ike or McCarthy—for Eisenhower could down the latter whenever he wanted to.

Social commitments continued to distract her from the political scene back home. There was the opening of the Sadler's Wells Ballet at Covent Garden. The queen was there too, wearing white with a high diamond tiara, and this time she came over to speak to Ronnie "and acted as if he were the only man she wanted to see." There was a ball at the American Embassy, a visit to Yorkshire, a fête in Oxford, and finally the big weekend of July 26–27 at the Salisburys. The most exciting guest that weekend was Adlai Stevenson, just arrived with Bill Blair from Paris, where he had fielded questions about McCarthy, China, and the Soviet Union.

"Adlai, despite increased avoirdupois, is in extremely good and relaxed form," Marietta reported to Susan Mary, "which is a miraculous show of strength after the arduous last six months—indeed six years." She noticed that Stevenson and Lord Salisbury (currently foreign secretary in Anthony Eden's Tory government) got on very well, and spent a lot of time together talking in private.

Adlai did almost as well socially as the Trees while in England, attending a garden party at Buckingham Palace, meeting the queen, going to Goodwood Races in the Royal Box, visiting the House of

Commons, dining with Lady Astor, and having lunch with the ailing Winston Churchill. Apart from that weekend at the Salisburys, however, Marietta and Ronnie did not see their old friend, for the following Friday they took off on an extended trip to Europe.

The children did not accompany their parents. Frankie flew to New York and on to Northeast Harbor as usual, while Penelope stayed in England with a nurse. Ronnie and Marietta left by automobile for Germany, where they visited the Baroque churches and King Ludwig's castles in Bavaria, then on to Vienna and lunch in a fifteenth-century schloss with Lady Elizabeth and Raimund von Hofmannsthal. They finally arrived at the Gritti Palace in Venice, where they stayed for a week. The couple went sightseeing in their private boat, swimming at the Lido, "buying heavy silk shantung, and risotto and gallons of wine at Harry's Bar and gazing at Santo Spirito lit up against the dark sky from our balcony window."

After Venice, they drove up to Lake Garda to have lunch with the Duff Coopers and the von Hofmannsthals (Elizabeth was Diana Cooper's niece). Diana, whose beauty Marietta greatly admired, wore a silk scarf over her head and tied under her chin, with a peaked straw hat on top, an idea that in later years Marietta copied. After Garda, the Trees drove to Cap d'Antibes for a weekend with the Paleys at their villa. Greta Garbo was an intriguing neighbor, "giggly and full of sympathetic sighs, and Ronnie fell hard for her." The Trees drove on through Provence to the Dordogne region, spending a few days with Pierre de Montesquiou in his eighteenth-century château. They ended up at the Ritz Hotel in Paris, after a trip of such luxury that Marietta was overwhelmed with guilt and determined to work very hard in New York that winter "as part payment."

Readjusting to life in New York that fall was not easy. Ronnie made a lecture tour in Texas on Anglo-American relations, and organized the move from the Fields' Winter Cottage in Caumsett, which they rented, to the Summer Cottage (with their blessing), thus allowing him to indulge his passion for redecorating houses. But this was not enough. His unhappiness with New York was such that he intimated to Marietta that he thought they should move to Washington. Panicked at the thought of leaving New York, Marietta responded, "after we have retired."

A priority that fall was to find a boarding school for Frankie, who was just turning thirteen. Marietta's firstborn was not an easy teenager. From her earliest years she had been shunted from place to place, country to country, with a beautiful and dynamic mother who was as elusive as quicksilver. ("Nobody had a mother like mine, who worked all the time and who looked like she did," Frankie said.) Her daughter was fitted into her mother's schedule, but only just. Marietta was an early articulator of the post-feminist parenting notion of "quality time," declaring defensively to her old school friend Weasel Roberts that she could give Frankie more attention after work than Weasel could give her child in a whole day.

There were frequent weekends at the Fields' cottage at Caumsett, where Frankie and the two Field daughters, Phyllis and Fiona, were fine company for each other. Frankie spent much of her time on horseback. (She was a passionate rider and competed in major horse shows, including one at Madison Square Garden.) The Field children also went to the Dalton School in New York with Frankie. Most of the children of her parents' friends went to largely WASP-dominated educational establishments. At Dalton there were only three non-Jewish children in Frankie's class. She loved the school and thrived there.

There were also the regular summers in Northeast Harbor. But if the young girl was looking there for the enveloping warmth and affection she missed at home, Bishop and Mrs. Peabody were not about to provide it. Malcolm was, as always, distant and stiff. Her grandmother was strict and quick to criticize. (Other grandchildren felt the same way. Endicott Peabody's daughter, Barbara, said that at times she hated her grandmother for her coldness, while recognizing her strength of character.)[2] Mrs. Peabody thought Frankie should be out rowing with the other children and generally learning physical toughness. But Frankie disliked rowing class, hoped daily for fog, and like all lonely children, preferred to read.

Her father could not always help. The FitzGeralds lived in New York until 1951, when Desie joined the CIA and moved to Washington. In 1954, he was posted to Japan, and the family moved there for two years. During that time, Frankie did not see them. Apart from those years, however, she regularly spent part of the summer with Desie and Barbara in Northeast (where the FitzGeralds had a house), moving over from the Peabodys. Barbara FitzGerald tried to be a good stepmother, sending back reports to Marietta of the child's progress.

Barbara's daughter, Barbara Lawrence (later Train), showed less sympathy. Young Barbara, whose own father was an alcoholic, had come to love Desie and saw him as her defender against the world. She bitterly resented Frankie's right to sit on his lap, which was how she first set eyes on her new stepsister. Being suddenly the younger daughter added to Barbara's sense of displacement. From the start, the two girls were jealous of each other and competed for Desie's attention.[3]

If the role of stepsister is notoriously tricky, that of stepfather is no easier, and Ronnie Tree had little affinity for it. Like Desie, he came from a culture in which parenting was a distraction rather than a delight. His age, background, sensibilities, and, most important, his focus on his own daughter, all conspired to leave Frankie in the farther reaches of isolation in the big house on 79th Street. Interestingly, it was in the charged exchanges with Ronnie (he disliked her habit of wearing red kneesocks, for instance) that Frankie and her mother grew closest together. "I was her ally against Ronnie and Ronnie's devotion to Penelope," Frankie said. "My mother would shield me from Ronnie's disapproval. She tried to umpire. My survival depended on her when I was young."

Christa Armstrong, Hamilton Fish Armstrong's second wife, who was staying in Barbados once when Frankie was small, remembered an occasion on the beach when a man swimming off a cruise boat drowned. Witnessing this terrible event, Frankie, with tears streaming down her face, cried, "I've got to get my mother. *She'll know what to do.*"[4] Marietta was the strong protector of her daughter—when she was there. The fact that she was so often not there created in the child feelings of dependency mixed with resentment. The result: profound ambivalence.

Meanwhile, Marietta wasted no time in extending her political connections. She became involved in a survey being conducted for the National Urban League on careers in business for black women, attended meetings of the Lexington Democratic Club, and became co-chairman of the Women for Wagner in support of Robert Wagner's run for mayor of New York. (Against the odds, Wagner won.)

The Democratic Party held a conference in Philadelphia on the weekend of December 12, 1953. Marietta took the train down from New York with Averell Harriman and Arthur Schlesinger. At the conference she took part in many of the workshops and meetings, enjoying her encounters with local district leaders, old southern congressmen and key Stevensonians, such as former senator Archie Alexander of New Jersey and Mayor Joe Clark of Philadelphia. Adlai gave one of his more stirring speeches at a fund-raising dinner on Saturday night, touching on the nation's beleaguered freedoms in the face of McCarthy's red-baiting. Marietta, filled with admiration, told Susan Mary she found Adlai "much calmer and stronger now, because he seems to have accepted the mantle of leadership in his *own* mind, thank goodness."

Returning on Sunday from Philadelphia to New York, Adlai invited Marietta to travel back with him in his compartment. Bill Blair, having hoped that the governor would do some paperwork on the journey, instead once again held open the door to usher his beautiful childhood friend into Adlai's lair.[5]

Marietta had several times remarked to Susan Mary and her parents how pleasing it was to see Bill Blair grow in maturity and tact as he continued to work in Stevenson's entourage. This unusual emphasis on Blair's character seems odd, until one realizes Marietta had special reason to be grateful for his impeccable discretion. He was always present when Adlai asked for her, and the silent sanction of her old friend on these delicate occasions made them acceptable, and gave her confidence to allow the relationship with Stevenson to develop.

That night in her diary, Marietta wrote simply, "travel back with Adlai," but it seems likely that the train ride was a milestone for both of them. In Adlai's eyes, she was no longer "the wife of the stylish Ronald Tree," but a woman he wished to know better. Her political commitment, combined with her admiration, encouragement, and belief in him, acted like a corrective to his unsteady soul. For her, traveling back with Adlai was a compliment of overwhelming proportions, joining her even more firmly to the cause of his leadership, and with it, the promise of a closer friendship.

The Tree family spent Christmas in New York, then traveled to the Fields' Chelsea Plantation in Ridgeland, South Carolina, for New Year's, where Ronnie spent his time shooting. On January 28, 1954, it was time again for Barbados—"two months of the life languid ahead," as Marietta put it. After the exciting political events of December, the regular winter stay in Barbados had taken on a slightly less appealing cast. As Marietta was to become more and more involved in the Democratic Party and Adlai Stevenson's career within it, those two months of "life languid" in the Caribbean, like annual crabgrass, threatened to creep up and suffocate her.

# CHAPTER *21*

# *"We'll use Marietta's house"*

Throughout the four years between Adlai's two presidential runs, the dual commitments of Marietta the political animal and Marietta the social hostess run through her appointment book like two radio stations tuned too close together on the airwaves.

There had been some of this scrambling at *Life,* when she would leave her research desk for dinner at El Morocco with the duke of Windsor. But now the clamor of interference noise is almost audible. She rushed from fittings with Charles James, the designer known for his extravagant ballgowns, to meetings with the black leaders of the Urban League. She moved from lunch with Babe Paley at fashionable midtown restaurants to dinner with Clayton Fritchey or Tom Finletter for updates on Democratic Party strategy. She flew in Marshall Field's private plane from the charmingly decorated Summer Cottage at Caumsett, Long Island, to late night meetings at the scruffy headquarters of the Lexington Democratic Club. On at least one occasion, she stepped into the Rolls-Royce after a dinner-dance, told Reg, the chauffeur, to turn aside the rearview mirror, and wriggled out of her designer ballgown and into a modest black dress. A few moments later she stepped out of the car in suitable attire to attend a political meeting.[1]

In between platform conferences and registration drives, weekends on Long Island, theaters, benefit dances, political fund-raisers, and meetings of the Junior Fortnightly (a select club of distinguished women she had been invited to join in 1950), she managed to steal a quick hour for her regular hair appointment at Saveli's Beauty Shop on East 55th Street, dates with the skin specialist Laszlo, and most important of all, the weekly visits to her therapist, Dr. Sara Bonnett, in her office at 895 Park Avenue.

Marietta had found a psychiatrist almost as soon as the family moved back to New York. At first, the appointments were sporadic. She was busy, Penelope was a baby, the house had to be made ready, she had to pick up with all her old friends. But by 1952, she was seeing Dr. Bonnett as often as three times a week. (Dr. Bonnett, a woman in her fifties, was supervising analyst at the New York Psychoanalytic Institute, one of the most rigorous psychiatric training schools in the United States.) Ever since the therapy during her divorce, Marietta had been a believer, and from 1952 through 1956 she found time for the sessions, regardless of her hectic schedule.

Why was therapy so important to Marietta over the years? To many, she seemed the symbol of sanity—cool, calm, and always in control. To attain that level of serenity, of course, she had to pay a price; in her case, that price was suppression of emotion. Raised in an atmosphere dedicated to keeping feelings under the severest discipline, the only outlet she permitted herself was in the psychiatrist's office. There she could let off steam, rail at the world, declare her most wicked sins, and rather than receive in return the warping, asphyxiating cloud of disapproval, find instead understanding and acceptance. Anonymous, protected by the pledge of confidence between doctor and patient, Marietta could reveal to this practiced, nonjudgmental listener what she could never reveal to anyone else. Emerging refreshed and energized, as she always said she felt after these sessions, she could face the conflicts in her life with new heart. The irony is that, ideally, psychotherapy releases inhibitions and awakens emotions that allow for more open and honest relationships outside the doctor's office. For Marietta, the reverse was true. She exposed herself during the therapy sessions only to emerge afterwards more in control of her feelings than before; which was, of course, precisely the way she wanted it. At that time, what was on her mind was challenging enough to her emotions, God knows; her divided life, her increasingly unhappy husband, her anxieties as a mother, her alienation from her family. Enough to keep any couch warm.

Marietta rarely visited her parents in Syracuse. She met them at Easter when the Davisons hosted the clan at Peacock Point, Long Island, and at Thanksgiving, when the family congregated at Groton with aunts Betsey and Margery Peabody, the unmarried sisters of the Rector. Otherwise, parents and daughter kept a distant connection by writing to each other. These letters were regular, often once a week. In Marietta's, like a child writing letters home, she drops names she thinks will impress them (particularly all those wonderful English titles), describes work she thinks they will approve of, and stresses her continuing feelings of inadequacy and moral weakness.

Her mother counters by describing the good works she is doing around the region, and occasionally her father writes about his duties as bishop of a disparate diocese. Other than these small exchanges, little of a personal nature is revealed. Gifts are given and received, but the ever present ache of disapproval and criticism is not assuaged. Marietta dutifully declares an interest in their doings, occasionally showing just a little irritation at her brother Endicott for his ungrateful behavior to her unless he wants something.

In the summer of 1954, Endicott Peabody wanted something quite badly. He asked his sister for money to back him in his campaign for state attorney general of Massachusetts. This was the first step of a lifelong attempt for Endicott to attain, in the Peabody tradition, public office. It was also the first step of a new journey for Marietta, a journey she thought she had completed when she divorced Desie and married Ronnie. Her eldest brother, the All-American football hero, who had from the beginning usurped her supremacy within the family and siphoned off her parents' love and approval, was now once again annexing her territory, this time her hard-won position within the Democratic Party.

Marietta's feelings for Endicott had been cool ever since the letter of disapproval he wrote her when she divorced Desie. When she saw him at family gatherings she spoke to him politely, and indulged in their three children's playing with Penelope at Easter or Thanksgiving. She gave his wife Toni expensive but unsuitable clothes (too ostentatious, Toni felt) as Christmas presents, and sometimes her own designer castoffs, which as gifts often smacked of condescension. Under the circumstances, the request for money from Endicott infuriated her. She urged Ronnie (who wrote the checks) not to give him more than $500 (and that in monthly installments).

Her feelings toward George had grown more friendly. During the 1950s, Marietta saw him from time to time in New York. He had entered the ministry, and from 1954 to 1956 was associate rector at Grace Church in Silver Spring, Maryland. Marietta was supportive of her brother's calling, and once went with friends to hear him preach. During the sermon, George recalled, she "stared continuously at a nonexistent spot on the floor." (She gave a good report, however, to her parents.) She also invited him to Barbados, and he went five or six times. He always liked and got on well with Ronnie.

Sam, the brother closest to her, having taken a degree in sociology from Harvard, started working in a bank in New York. When he became engaged to Judith Dunnington in 1950, Marietta took him aside, and to his great amusement, tried to educate him about sex. The couple married in 1951, with Marietta as matron of honor.

Although Marietta, always a furious family competitor, tended to have a tense relationship with her sisters-in-law, she accepted Judy more easily. Judy at the time was an aspiring singer, a career sympathetic to Marietta. Judy had inherited money, which also gave them something in common, particularly with regard to clothes, a major interest of the young Mrs. Peabody. (Judy remembered what Marietta was wearing when they first met—a rich red taffeta ball gown by Charles James.)

Mike, the youngest, was at Harvard Business School and saw his sister mostly at the annual family reunions. His significance in her life was to come later.

If Marietta was somehow keeping her family ties neatly knotted, her role as mother had some loose connections. After much calendar-juggling, on July 6, 1954, Marietta and Frankie set off together for the Lazy K Bar Ranch at Big Timber, Montana, for three weeks, while Ronnie and Penelope stayed in the Summer Cottage at Caumsett. Probably both Dr. Entenman, whom Frankie still saw regularly, and Dr. Bonnett had urged this course of action to effect some much-needed bonding between mother and daughter. "Marietta had promised me this for a long time," Frankie remembered. "I was so amazed she had managed finally to find time for it."

The trip was not quite what everybody had hoped. Marietta found herself the sole single parent in this vacation place for horse-minded families. At least Frankie was able to get involved in the activities of the ranch (although the children of the mostly Republican families taunted her for her Democratic leanings), but Marietta had no outlet for her interests or energies. The owner of the ranch was a violent anti-Democrat and thought women shouldn't have the vote. Yet this was the man Marietta had to be nice to in order to get a ride into the depressing local town, which for some reason she thought might cheer her up. She was wrong. Like babes in the wood, one night "we just stayed in our room and cried," Frankie remembered.

The result was a premature departure, but a renewed closeness between mother and daughter. Marietta did not hide from Frankie her misery at being stuck in such a dismal hole, and as they fled together, cheering, the unlamented vacation, the experience became an amusing memory to share. The following week Frankie was again on a plane, this time alone to Northeast Harbor for the rest of the summer, while Marietta, after a week of politicking in New York, joined Ronnie and Penelope in Barbados.

Marietta went to Barbados six times between 1954 and 1956, sometimes for as long as three months, more often for quick visits of two weeks. Barbados offered its familiar charms—sultry weather, white orchids blooming in the garden, and a constant flow of guests. While partly vacation, Ronnie worked on plans for the formation of the

Federation of the West Indies, and Marietta continued to help establish a Planned Parenthood clinic for the island. In the spring of 1955 the high point was a visit from Princess Margaret, who was touring the British West Indies. The princess liked Heron Bay and returned unexpectedly the next day.

It was a long way from the austere confines of the rectory at Chestnut Hill to the colonnaded terraces of Heron Bay with a member of the British royal family as a house guest. But these impressive distractions could no longer conceal a truth that Marietta was only just beginning to face: Her second marriage, for which she had risked her family name and the judgment of God, had turned into something she could not have possibly foreseen.

Because of his changed circumstances, Ronnie had altered the compass of their marriage in a major way, and in consequence, Marietta had lost her bearings. Not belonging in Barbados, did she then not belong any more to him? It was noticeable that Ronnie was beginning to spend more and more time away from New York, while Marietta stayed behind. Apart from the long trip to Europe in 1953, and the three months together in Barbados at the beginning of 1954, for much of the rest of the following two years he was in Barbados, Chicago, or Europe—alone. (His tax position, presumably, partly directed his peripatetic life. A British citizen, now resident of Barbados, he could avoid income tax and thus maintain his lifestyle, only by periodic short stays in the United States or England.)

Marietta complained about the emptiness of the house when he was gone, but in truth it was not empty for long. Indeed, Russell Hemenway, one of the leading Lexington Democratic Club members, said that they used 123 East 79th Street as an adjunct to the club. "We'll use Marietta's house," was the refrain. (Hemenway met Stevenson in Athens. Stevenson told him that one of the most exciting Democratic organizations was one that his friend Marietta Tree was involved with in New York, so as soon as Hemenway returned to the United States he left the Foreign Service and started work at the Lexington Democratic Club.)[2]

Marietta was digging deeper and deeper into her New York life. In 1954, she was elected to the Democratic State Committee for the 9th District. She was co-chairman for the Committee to Elect Anthony Akers to Congress. In 1955, she worked on the campaign to elect Averell Harriman as governor of New York. She spent time with the Democratic Women's Workshop. She even had several meetings with Tammany boss Carmine de Sapio to enlist his support for this work, and by all reports she charmed him off his little gangster feet. (She kept a note he wrote her later from jail, thanking her for her "cheery letter" of support.)

Since Stevenson's defeat in 1952, an inner group of advisers had been formed under Tom Finletter's name, including at various times Paul Nitze, John Kenneth Galbraith, Arthur Schlesinger, Jr., Chester Bowles, Averell Harriman, and Clayton Fritchey. These men met frequently to discuss strategy, and helped Stevenson compose the speeches that were to keep him in the public eye until his second presidential run in 1956. Stevenson (who had started a law firm in Chicago with partners Willard Wirtz and Newton Minow) stressed the dangers of McCarthy's anticommunist activities, and also questioned Secretary of State John Foster Dulles's newly articulated hard-line policy of "massive retaliation" in the face of Communist aggression. The heating up of the Cold War, already fraught, in the public perception, with the dangers of atomic weaponry held both by the Soviet Union and the United States, was deeply alarming to the Democratic leadership.

On June 5, 1954, Stevenson gave a televised speech at Columbia University. In it he warned against ignorance and fear, "the most subversive force of all." The night of June 4 and the following week he stayed in William Benton's apartment at the Savoy Plaza (former U.S. Senator Benton, chairman of the *Encyclopaedia Britannica* and a longtime supporter, put Stevenson on the board of the *Britannica* later that year), then moved to the Trees (with Bill Blair) for Saturday and Sunday. This was the first time Marietta had seen Adlai since the train ride six months earlier. For Sunday lunch, Ronnie and she invited the Fields, the Finletters, the Guggenheims, John and Aliki Russell (he was a British Foreign Service officer), and Barbara Ward. Wife of the planning expert Sir Robert Jackson, Barbara Ward, an economist, foreign affairs adviser, and prolific writer, became another of Stevenson's influential friends and admirers, and co-wrote some of his speeches over the years.

For the rest of the period up to the presidential campaign, Marietta saw Stevenson only rarely. He found time to write affectionately to Alicia Patterson, and kept at arm's length with postcards the latest passionate admirer, Agnes Meyer, wife of Eugene Meyer, publisher of *The Washington Post,* whose motherly ministrations were a source of strength until his death. On his campaign trips to New York, Marietta was usually included in the entourage. When he gave a speech at Cooper Union in late 1954, for instance, attacking Eisenhower and calling for a politics of reason rather than innuendo, there was a party afterwards at William Benton's apartment and Marietta helped compile the invitation list.

Stevenson returned to New York on November 26 and Tom Finletter gave a dinner party for him, which the Trees attended. Afterward, Marietta had a drink with Stevenson (apparently alone) and they discussed his presidential prospects in 1956. "I had learned not to give him advice. It maddened him that I wouldn't. I told him, 'You already know what you want to do.' "[3] On December 2, Stevenson returned to New York once more to receive an award at the Weizmann Institute before going on to New Orleans for the Democratic National Committee meetings. He made a speech that night about the Arab-Israeli conflict, being careful not to offend either side. The day before the award ceremony, the Senate voted to censure Joe McCarthy, an act that started the final winding down of a painful period in American history. That night, Stevenson dined privately with the Trees. The friendship was never stronger.

February 5, 1955, was Adlai's fifty-fifth birthday, and since he was going to be in New York that weekend, Bill Blair asked Marietta if she would throw a birthday party for him. (Ronnie had already left for Barbados.) Marietta was thrilled but anxious. Everybody would want to be invited, and she could easily alienate important Stevenson voters by excluding them. But her skills as a hostess had been finely honed by this time, and the party was a great success, running on well into the small hours with parlor games, poems, charades, speeches, and plays.

It was a happy time for Marietta. Putting out of her mind the

Ronnie with Princess Margaret in Barbados, 1955.

problems of Ronnie and Barbados, she worked hard at a cause she believed in with her whole heart. There was the excitement of being on the inside, with the secrets and the jokes, and the tremendous camaraderie both with the New York group and Stevenson's staff. And of course, "it was wonderful working for a man with genuine inspiration and creative political talent."

Frankie started boarding school at Foxcroft in the fall of 1955, although Marietta had wanted her to go to St. Timothy's, her old school. They decided on Foxcroft, in Virginia, because, Frankie thought, the school allowed horses and she could ride there. Frankie enjoyed her years at Foxcroft, although she found the lessons unsatisfactory. The school offered her a secure berth in face of her fractured home life. Penelope was less fortunate. Following in her clever sister's footsteps, she was enduring a difficult adjustment to Dalton.

During this frenzied period of American political activity and English frivolity, a surprise meeting brought into sharp relief the magnitude of the decision Marietta had made in New York in 1947. In early 1955, while Ronnie was in Barbados as usual, she went to a dinner party with Irene Selznick, and one of the guests was John Huston, just back from the Canary Islands after completing the film *Moby Dick*. "To my surprise, it was v. pleasant seeing him again and we had a good long talk mostly about his life and what he'd been doing," she wrote to Ronnie. "It was a new John—calm, serene, responsible, however, as Irene noted, I wouldn't trust this phase to last." The following afternoon, Huston went to see her at 123 East 79th Street, and they talked again, "about his life, hunting in Ireland, etc.," as she casually reported to her husband.

The last exchanges between John Huston and Marietta FitzGerald had not been pleasant. Each had in some ways betrayed the other, Marietta perhaps more than John. But now she could not quite keep the pleasure out of her voice. Just as they had ten years earlier, they found it wonderfully natural to talk to each other. And also, however uneasy she was now beginning to feel about her second marriage, there were some accomplishments in her life she could point to with confidence. These encounters with John took place just at the time when she was organizing Adlai's birthday party, so she was preoccupied, exhilarated, flushed with the compliment of being Stevenson's hostess. When Huston came to see her in that rich and beautiful town house, surrounded by servants and the accoutrements of wealth, he saw in her lovely face a mixture of seriousness, enthusiasm, and excitement, precisely the characteristics that had delighted him in the first place. After that afternoon, Walter Huston's prophecy hung in the air. It was not likely that John Huston would wish to stay entirely out of her life ever again.

# CHAPTER *22*

# *"I hope you miss me just a little"*

Ronnie spent much of 1956 abroad. While many Americans, including his wife, were focusing on the presidential election that fall, Ronnie was becoming more and more detached from his country of origin. His New York work was perfunctory, and the Manhattan social whirl failed to interest him. Barbados, with its British roots and large British expatriate colony, was now the center of his life.

He revived his efforts to be recommended for the governorship of Barbados. Again he was rebuffed, and this time he asked his old friend Lord Salisbury whether his divorce had anything to do with it. Lord Salisbury assured him that divorce was not the issue. No, Ronnie's problem, apart from the fact that he was not a career diplomat, was his age. The current governor was not due to retire until 1958, at which point Ronnie would be "upwards of 60," as Salisbury put it. (Actually, Ronnie would be sixty-one.)

Failing an official post, Ronnie began turning his energies to other activities in Barbados, in particular, land development. His idea was to buy as much beachfront property as he could and build a hotel and ancillary buildings on the land. He hoped to enhance the tourist prospects of Barbados, while protecting the island from the hideous type of cheap hotel and condominium development he had seen ruin other coastlines in the Caribbean and Mediterranean.

While drumming up funds for this project, his own financial situation was deteriorating. Although a nonresident of the United Kingdom, he was still a British citizen, and the British government had found a way to slap a new tax burden on his estate. He appealed the ruling, and in spite of pulling strings with Tory officials, was turned down flat. To pay this penalty, he once again requested access to the capital of the Lambert Tree Trust, and was once again turned down.

The trust at that time was valued at about $8 million (about $21 million in 1996 dollars), which gave Ronnie an income of approximately $320,000 a year (or roughly $1.5 million in 1996 currency), enough, it would seem, to support the family. Marietta was not an extravagant woman. In fact, she continued to attempt to make Ronnie economize, both in travel (she traveled coach while he flew first class), and in running the house. But Ronnie had expensive tastes. His trips to Europe always involved the most de luxe reservations. His buying sprees resulted in huge bills. He was used to living well.

He also supported three households. In New York there was his driver, Reg Duvall, as well as Duvall's wife Bella and their fourteen-year-old son Michael. (The move to America by the Duvalls had not been easy. Bella could not drive and was often lonely on Long Island while her husband was in New York chauffeuring the Trees around town. Thanks to Peabody connections and support from the Duvalls' neighbors, the Trasks, Michael Duvall was accepted at Groton, with Ronnie paying two-thirds of his scholarship.) Collins, Alice, and Mabel were also on the New York payroll. In Barbados, he kept an equally large staff. The house on East 79th Street, the Summer Cottage at Caumsett, and Heron Bay were all high-maintenance homes.

Both of Ronnie's sons liked to be looked after in the way they had been used to at Ditchley, and when they came to stay, along with the tensions, expenses seemed to Marietta to escalate. "I do think it isn't fair to us," she complained to Ronnie on one occasion after they left, "as we are so strapped." "Strapped" may seem a rather strong word in the face of the Trees' lifestyle, but it is clear that at this time Ronnie was truly worried about money, and Marietta, raised in an atmosphere of permanent financial anxiety, was quick to respond. When Ronnie impulsively bought a new Rolls-Royce, Marietta was furious, saying they did not need it and could not afford it. "We have got to cut down somewhere," she told him, "and I'm trying to do it in little ways, such as no wine at lunch, no flowers downstairs unless we have guests, etc. Do you think you could cut out one of your N.Y.C. clubs?" she added.

These attempts at economy did not work very well. Visitors to East 79th Street never failed to notice how the house always smelled like a flower shop, thanks to the huge fresh flower arrangements everywhere. Ronnie did not resign from any of his clubs. Instead, he came up with the surprising solution of putting the New York house up for sale. Marietta was horrified. "Oh, how I love it here!" she wrote to him in desperation. "I feel that it's home and unless it's violently over-expensive, *couldn't* you reconsider?"

Ronnie reconsidered. Having never learned to economize, he seemed as little able as Marietta to think of seriously starting now.

Meanwhile, the presidential campaign of 1956 had already begun to preoccupy Marietta. She and Lloyd Garrison, former president of the National Urban League and longtime Stevenson supporter, had been reelected as state committee representatives for the 9th District. She also became a member of the executive committee of the New York Stevenson for President Committee, and was full-time co-chairman of the New York Volunteers for Stevenson. Her responsibilities seemed to pile up daily. As early as April, Ronnie was writing plaintively from Barbados, "I hope you miss me just a little, and have a thought for something else but Democrats and their politics."

In June, Stavros Niarchos, a Greek shipping magnate, lent the Trees his Cartier-designed yacht, as he had done the year before. But this year, even these Greek enticements failed to seduce Marietta away from politics. So Ronnie went on the cruise alone, accompanied by his old friend Odette Pol Roger (a longtime admirer of Ronnie's) and Susan Mary Patten, whose husband, Bill, was becoming increasingly ill with asthma.

The group sailed round the coast of Sicily, ending up in Rome. They were in St. Peter's when the pope was carried in to give a blessing. "If only Marietta were here," was the refrain. Susan Mary felt so sorry for Ronnie that she urged Marietta to take a short holiday with him later.

After Rome, Ronnie went on alone to Paris and London, continuing to miss Marietta dreadfully. "Darling—I do love you deeply. I wish wish wish we could be together more and do more things together. Do get the political life a little subordinated by next year is my earnest prayer. God bless you, Ronnie."

In London, Ronnie suffered a serious bout of depression. "I wake up at six in a suicidal mood and twist and turn about. I only hope I didn't show it to Michael or Anne. When I get to New York I must try to find out the cause and deal with it as it really is nightmarish when it comes on—the brightest days seems black—and all news is bad. Surely science with all its strides *must* have some palliation."

When he reached Paris in October, there was no letter waiting for him. He was deeply hurt. "How revolting politics is," he wrote in an uncharacteristic outburst. "Sometimes please give me a thought." He tried to think of ways to bring her back to him. "I went to Grès this morning," he told her, "and ordered you two lovely dresses . . . also —un petit cocktail at the Dior boutique. I hope you like them."

Returning alone to London, Ronnie found himself in the midst of the Suez crisis, which involved both his close friends, Anthony Eden (who resigned over the issue) and Lord Salisbury. But in spite of these moments of connection with his old political life, the depression lingered. All his friends seemed to be ill (Brendan Bracken died that fall), and the mood of the country was bleak. He again expressed his sadness at missing both Marietta and his adored Penelope. "I miss her dreadfully. I think of that little upright figure and her loving affection all the time." Ronnie could not conceal his profound unease. "God bless you, darling—I hope when all this is over, we can get down to the same cosy life we used to have. . . ."

The tone of these letters has a far more melancholy quality than those he wrote to her earlier in the marriage. The image of the warm, happy home around the fireside he had conjured up for her after their return to New York in 1949 has dimmed, leaving a confused picture. Like Marietta, he sensed the widening distance between them and could not disguise his misgivings. "Sometimes I get dreadfully worried about the future. . . ."

Marietta compensated as best she could with words of love. "With all dearest love my dearest. I miss you so terribly. . . . Penelope misses you terribly too. All we do is talk about you and she makes kissing noises after mentioning your name. . . ." In the early days during their divorces, their letters flew across the Atlantic almost daily carrying messages of support for each other. Now Marietta attempted to recover that tone of hope and encouragement as he traveled through Europe alone that summer. "I miss you really, really terribly, and have been so depressed and needed your affection and wise advice desperately. . . . I just don't know how I could be so lucky as to be married to you. I am so blessed, and only hope that you feel a fraction of the joy that I do in our marriage."

But as with one hand she stroked her sad husband, with the other she ministered to the beleaguered candidate. For Adlai also was in need.

By all accounts, Adlai Stevenson's second presidential campaign was a disappointment. The thrill had gone. Author Eric F. Goldman said he had "none of the platform wizardry" of 1952.[1] Anxiety spread within the governor's inner circle. Bill Blair and Barry Bingham complained to Marietta that the candidate seemed to be spending what energy he had writing endless letters late at night to neurotic females instead of focusing on the issues, and also putting on weight, thus increasing his exhaustion. One of many recognizing the power of the incumbent, Jim Fosburgh, suggested that they should let Averell Harriman run and save Stevenson for 1960.

In early April, Marietta flew to meetings in Chicago. "Everything seems to be wrong with the candidate and his chances, with his organization and ours in New York," she wrote to Ronnie from the plane.

Since Minnesota [the primary in which Stevenson was defeated by Estes Kefauver], there has been a bad dropping off of volunteers, no new reservations for the dinner [a fund-raiser in New York she was helping organize], Republicans raising large sums for Kefauver, and people like Bennett Cerf, Goddard Lieberson etc., saying Stevenson now is not the man they were for in '52 —his magic has become blurred to one and all. Even Tom and Arthur are exasperated with him. All of this has hit me like a ton of bricks, and not for many years have I been in such a depression. Today, lunching with Dorothy at the Colony, I came close to fainting . . . and had to lie down in the ladies room.

As her emotional state indicates, Marietta's identification with Stevenson was by this time all-consuming. She attended various rallies and occasions with him, and continued to speak out ardently in his favor. On her thirty-ninth birthday, alone in New York, she said angrily that "they" were "murdering" Adlai, "and he is so physically exhausted that he hasn't had time to think or to organize (which was never his forte) and the results are poor."

At the invitation of Bill Blair (was he as usual thinking of his boss?), Marietta flew to Los Angeles in June for the California primary. In a fever of excitement she witnessed Adlai's victory by a huge majority. In high spirits, the following day Adlai, Marietta, and a group of California politicians, friends, and supporters of Stevenson were taken on a tour of the MGM lot by Dore Schary, where they saw Marlon Brando filming *Teahouse of the August Moon*. (Marietta was thrilled; she always loved movie stars.) When Brando met Adlai, he said, "As I come from Libertyville, I hope I will be called the Stevenson of acting." To which Adlai, never having heard of the actor, replied, "I hope I will be known as the *Marlo* Brando of politics!"

The exhilarated group then drove up the California coast to the San Ysidro Ranch, a resort near Santa Barbara popular with politicians and movie stars, where Adlai was inundated by congratulatory mail. He was very tired, and Bill Blair worked at protecting the candidate, even from Marietta. "He would give the Gov a whiskey and tell me, 'Let's you and I go out on the porch,'" Marietta said. This was perhaps the most satisfying moment in the campaign for Stevenson and his supporters. His surprise showing in the very important California primary for a moment boosted hopes that he had a chance to defeat Eisenhower in November. (Later, commentators felt that the California result in fact was a hollow victory, since after it Stevenson stopped campaigning in the energetic way he had prior to the primary and lost the valuable momentum gained since Minnesota.)

Back in New York in July, Marietta found temporary distractions from the campaign. Ed Sullivan did a TV show on *The John Huston Story,* and Marietta went with John to the show and dinner afterwards. She also saw Adlai briefly in New York, and Frankie sat next to him at the popular musical *My Fair Lady.* (Stevenson was with Mary Lasker, the New York philanthropist who was currently a front-runner in his ever-fluctuating private life.)

Marietta also stepped up her visits to Dr. Bonnett. Every time she returned to the city, she made appointments with her therapist, but now the pressure was heightened, not only by the upcoming vacation of Dr. Bonnett, who, like most New York psychiatrists, abandoned her patients for the month of August, but also by Marietta's increasingly demanding schedule. Yet this time of all times was when she needed help, what with Ronnie's cries of loneliness from abroad and Adlai's plummeting pulse at home. For much of late June and July Marietta saw Dr. Bonnett four times a week.

In August, Stevenson again won the nomination at the Democratic National Convention in Chicago, defeating a challenge from Senator Estes Kefauver. Kefauver was nominated as vice president, over the young senator from Massachusetts, John F. Kennedy. Stevenson's acceptance speech was disappointing to many, a pale shadow of the brilliant rhetoric of 1952 and perhaps a foretaste of the campaign to come.

It was clear by this time that Marietta's presence had become more than decoration for the candidate. His advisers had begun to reckon with her as a useful influence and conduit to their overworked and elusive master. She seemed to be able to get to him in ways that others could not, and on at least one occasion, Tom Finletter and New York Volunteers adviser Jack Shea asked her to push certain views and projects on their behalf. After California, she saw more and more of the candidate, both in New York and in Chicago, where she spent several weeks throughout August.

She had begun to share the role assumed by other women close to him, in particular, his sister Buffie Ives and close confidante Jane Dick. Long divorced, Stevenson often needed a wife-replacement for all the receptions and dinners he was required to attend. Buffie, Jane, and now Marietta were called in to do this duty. When Stevenson's staff opened their suite at the Hilton for the convention, Marietta and Helen Stevenson (a cousin of Adlai's who was to marry Governor Robert Meyner of New Jersey) acted as hostesses. "We washed glasses and saw that there was enough soda and gave messages to Bill Blair," Marietta told John Bartlow Martin. She wore a Stevenson costume and arranged for pretty girls to be photographed with the candidate. It was the sort of job at which Marietta excelled.

When not attending to Stevenson, she was a vital player in the

New York Volunteers office. The 1956 volunteers were an engaging mixture of rich Park Avenue matrons who had their lunches brought in from fancy restaurants, people with grand operating titles because they had been big donors, and eager students. All were equally inexperienced. One day a man arrived at the office saying his name was Eddie Arcaro, the famous jockey, and he wanted to give a lot of money. Thrilled, the volunteers held a press conference. It turned out the man was mentally disturbed.

One of the volunteers was Meg Greenfield, then just back from three years in Europe, who later became a distinguished political journalist in Washington. When Meg joined the group, she thought Marietta was the most glamorous person she had ever met. "She called us 'Dear girl,' and every time she breezed in it was an event." Meg thought the early organization of the Stevenson volunteers very chaotic, but admired Marietta's professionalism. "Marietta tightened it up and made do out of a motley crew."[2]

Like the other workers, Meg knew that Marietta had a husband who took little interest in the campaign and who seemed to spend most of his time in Barbados. The staff also knew that Marietta lived in a grand house and that there was a chauffeur around the corner. "We used to talk all the time about her clothes. We had sometimes to wear name tags, which didn't matter to us, but Marietta wasn't about to put pins through her beautiful silk shirts!" Helen Stevenson told Meg that when she went to stay with Marietta at the Summer Cottage in Caumsett, the maid washed Helen's hairbrush. But Marietta was never snobbish, never standoffish. "She was always plain-spoken with people like me and kids on the staff just out of college," Meg Greenfield said.

By October, nobody in the office (except Meg) expected their candidate to win. Dick Brown, head of public relations for Stevenson in New York, ran an office pool that said Ike would win. Brown tried to give Stevenson a more common appeal by having him photographed with a baby—"It was a disaster." "Adlai was the worst candidate imaginable," Meg agreed. "He kept shaking hands with us instead of the voters. He hated every minute of it, you could see that."

Stevenson picked up the pace with a whistle-stop train journey from New Haven to New York, and again two weeks later through the Midwest. Marietta went on both trips. She saw him once more in New York, where he addressed a crowd at Madison Square Garden, before flying back to California and ending the last week of the campaign in Boston. Marietta made a speech to a women's group in Westchester, then went to Philadelphia for a dinner, to Brooklyn for a rally, and finally settled in New York with Ronnie for the election itself.

Frankie also came home from Foxcroft for the election. Her letters through this time tend to ring with the refrain, "You sound as if you were having a heavenly time . . . I hope you'll write if you ever get a moment though I don't expect a letter . . ." For her sixteenth birthday, she asked Marietta to get her a gray or black cardigan, adding, "preferably cashmere of course." (Truly her mother's daughter.)

Eisenhower's remarkable recovery from surgery for a heart attack in the summer of 1956, the Suez debacle, fears of a depression, the new Republican policy offering moderation and "co-existence" with the Soviet Union, vice-presidential candidate Richard Nixon's strange appeal to the ordinary man, and Stevenson's failure to counteract these pressures with a clear enough platform of his own, all conspired to defeat him in 1956. He lost even more overwhelmingly than in 1952, carrying only seven states.

He heard the election results in Boston (where his son, Adlai III, had presented him with his first grandson), and flew back to Libertyville the next day. Marietta dropped everything and flew to join him. "Oh, it hurts so badly," he told her. "It's even worse than in 1952." Marietta reported seeing him as "a man in torture, bleeding from his wounds. In public he was sporting and gay, but it was a private agony that was worse than '52."[3]

Two days after the election, on November 8, Marshall Field, who had been diagnosed with cancer of the brain a month earlier, died at his estate in Caumsett, Long Island. He had been in a coma for two days, and did not know that his friend Adlai Stevenson, whom he had so loyally supported over the years, had once again been defeated. Field's cousin Ronnie was immediately called in to help make arrangements for the funeral. Marietta arrived back in New York to attend the funeral service at St. James's Episcopal Church. Immediately afterward, the mourners took the funeral train with Field's body to Chicago, where he was buried in his hometown. Adlai Stevenson joined the ushers. When he saw Marietta, he said, perhaps reflecting the melancholy mood, "I hope you will wear a beautiful hat with a veil like that at my funeral."

On Sunday, November 18, Marietta went with Marshall's widow, Ruth, the Finletters, and Adlai to the Fields' Chelsea Plantation, in Ridgefield. Ronnie arrived after the weekend in time for Thanksgiving. During the evenings in South Carolina, Marietta held Ruthie's hand, and in the days she kept her eyes on Adlai. "The men get up at five and bang away at various forms of wildlife, with tennis sandwiched in between," Marietta wrote to Susan Mary. "It's wonderful therapy for Adlai and Tom, as they are so exhausted and yawny by dinner. . . . Adlai looks very well and is full of jokes, but I don't know if this isn't just a noble facade."

For eleven days the party rested and played in "this white-pillared cocoon." "Ruthie and I ride a lot, sleep a lot, and join the others for picnic lunch—hot roast quail under the glittering pines, and large amounts of white wine."

The glow of her description can be attributed to something more than the agreeable routine of plantation life. That week, something happened between Adlai and Marietta, something that seven years later, in the same place, Adlai recalled with a charming verbal caress. The two had found themselves together in a blind, watching for quail. "It was frosty, but so warm and tender in the blind," Adlai wrote to her in 1963.

And so it was. And so he remembered it.

# CHAPTER *23*

# *". . . In gratitude, respect, and love for Mr. J."*

On January 18, 1957, Helen Stevenson and Robert Meyner were married in Oberlin, Ohio, and spent their honeymoon at Heron Bay. (Helen had hesitated about marrying Meyner, but Marietta's arguments in favor were both revealing and compelling: one, Meyner had money, and two, Helen would otherwise be lonely.) Ronnie, already in Barbados, missed the wedding, but Marietta, Meg Greenfield, Millie Robbins, and other colleagues of Helen's from the New York Volunteers office flew on a wintry day to Oberlin. They found their way to a country inn where they all changed and assembled at the bar. "There were two things I remember about Marietta Tree that day," said Meg Greenfield. "One was that she looked more elegant than anybody, and she had a hat on with a net veil, and she was smoking with a cigarette holder through the veil. And I thought, how cool, nothing fazes Marietta."

The other thing Meg remembered took place at the wedding. "Adlai Stevenson joined us at some point and we walked across the snowy common to the church. Marietta and Adlai were leading, arm-in-arm, and then they saw the photographers all set up, and Marietta suddenly fell back and said to Meg, 'Dear girl, we mustn't have these pictures taken, you go ahead with the Governor. . . .' " So Meg, astonished, was pushed up to walk with Stevenson the rest of the way.[1] Of course Meg did not understand until later the meaning of this gesture, but Marietta's precautions indicate how sensitive, at least in her own eyes, the relationship had become.

Ever since Marietta had become reacquainted with Stevenson before his presidential run in 1952, the connection between them had gradually intensified, finding expression in the blind in the Chelsea Plantation that Christmas of 1956. From then on, it was only a matter of time before some kind of consummation took place. Meanwhile, Marietta returned to Barbados that winter in a state of suspended anticipation.

"I am glad to be returning to my old life," she asserted to Susan Mary. "Ronnie has been truly angelic this past year, and now I am going to devote myself to him, and lie back on a chaise longue and read Proust and eat sugared violets. . . ." She could keep this theme up very effectively. "Am sitting at the blue and white venetian desk in my bedroom," she rhapsodized, "overlooking a little star-shaped garden full of geraniums, which is surrounded by a sweet lime hedge. . . . All's perfect with this aquamarine and golden world. . . ."

Returning for a quick trip to New York, she told Ronnie how empty the house was, and how much she looked forward to coming back to Heron Bay. Looked forward to coming back? Not Marietta's usual response, these days. But this time Heron Bay was indeed bathed in aquamarine and gold, for the simple reason that Adlai Stevenson was to join them there on March 6 for almost three weeks, with the Schlesingers and Binghams along as support.

The visit was brilliantly successful. They chartered a plane and made trips to the Dominican Republic and St. Vincent, where "we ate hearts of palm, wild strawberries and frogs from the mountain streams, bathed in deep pools from high waterfalls, gurgled rum punch, and drove through endless coconut groves bathed in a green light." Adlai was full of laughter and long, funny stories. "I remember one time Arthur and Adlai and I were out on the water and we started to laugh and nearly drowned." The high spirits were infectious. Ronnie, according to Marietta, was never happier, and Stevenson told Agnes Meyer it had been the perfect holiday. He was planning an extended trip to Africa that June, and Ronnie and Marietta decided to join him for part of the journey, taking Frankie with them.

When Stevenson returned to the United States after his vacation, he wrote to the Trees, "My woes I forgot, my work I neglected; and certainly I am brown, baked, peach-fed and rum soaked, in short, edible!" A month later he wrote again, asking the Trees (his "dear, dear friends") if they could arrange for him to stay with the Salisburys at Hatfield for the weekend in May when he was receiving an honorary degree at Oxford.

A week after writing this letter, he wrote another one, to Marietta alone. It was dated April 12, Marietta's fortieth birthday. In the letter was a coin. He explained that the coin had been given him a couple of years previously by a classmate of the class of 1922. "(You were *six* when I graduated from Princeton, which will always upset me!) I looked at it, caught my breath and slipped it into my pocket—hurriedly. Later, that night, when I emptied my pockets I looked at it again. Yes, there it was!" The point was that the head on the coin startlingly resembled Marietta. He had kept it in his pocket ever since.

"I began to live when it came to live with me. Now you are 40 and the richest part of your life is beginning. So I want it to live with or near you for a while . . ." He added that it was very valuable—"It is worth $1.00. A."

This was one of the first of Stevenson's many letters to Marietta, written in the articulate, droll manner so characteristic of his speaking gift. Stevenson at this time was fifty-six years old, with much of his career behind him. Yet there was still a sense of potential in his words and actions, and his many admirers still had hopes vested in him.

Now enduring a political time-out, however, he was able to concentrate on his private life, which he had always indulged in with a flourish. Ever since his divorce in 1949, he had attracted a stream of women to his side, whom he played off against each other. The women had similarities: they tended to be rich, elegant, socially adept, and all had strong personalities. They were invariably married, thus *safe;* for it seemed Adlai was never ready to make a serious commitment. Burned by the painful breakup of his marriage, and fearing the possibility of a repetition of that kind of anguish, he kept his women friends at arm's length. Always looking to them for the support and devotion he had inspired in his mother, of course he was invariably disappointed by these pale copies, and thus found it impossible to make a lasting alliance with any of them. Alicia Patterson had been a longtime solace; Agnes Meyer and Mary Lasker had also been reliable companions. But there were always new candidates looming on the horizon, and he welcomed them greedily. That tender moment in the blind had produced yet another player, rich, beautiful, adoring—the familiar story. Ever hopeful, Adlai once more pulled out his little bag of tricks and set the spells in order.

He went to England and duly stayed with the Salisburys. After receiving his Oxford degree (in the presence of Barbara Ward), he then set off for his three-month tour of Africa. For some time, Stevenson had been fending off rumors that he was about to marry Mary Lasker. (Marietta's Lexington Democratic Club colleague, Dick Brown, reported it to her.) On June 6, when Ronnie, Marietta, and Frankie arrived in Johannesburg to join him in South Africa, his group consisted of his son Adlai III and wife Nancy, Alicia Patterson, and Bill Blair. Mary Lasker was not of the party.

The trip, which included South Africa, North and South Rhode-

Adlai Stevenson's African trip in 1957. From left: Nancy Stevenson, Frankie, Alicia Patterson, Marietta, Ronnie, Bill Blair, Albert Schweitzer, a nurse, Adlai Stevenson, Adlai Stevenson III.

sia, the Belgian Congo, and French Equatorial Africa, was dominated by wrenching encounters with apartheid, interspersed with visits to diamond mines, shanty towns, the caves where *King Solomon's Mines* was filmed, and meetings with local and national political leaders. The culminating moment was a visit to Albert Schweitzer at Lambaréné.

There were mixed feelings about the famous doctor's hospital. Marietta was shocked by the primitive and unsanitary conditions endured by his patients, while Frankie observed that one had to understand Schweitzer's philosophy to explain his "seeming unwillingness to accept progress." She thought his idea was to keep close to the essentials of humanity; that all modern devices were distractions.

Frankie was sixteen and had had an exceptionally good year at Foxcroft. She kept an extensive diary of the trip, unlike her mother, who, typically, would have loved to but didn't get round to it. Instead, Marietta wrote long descriptive letters to her parents and asked that they be saved. Of the two records, Frankie's observations are of a more raw political nature, but their analyses were remarkably similar. (This was a strong bond between mother and daughter; Frankie admired Stevenson enormously and shared her mother's progressive political values.)[2]

From Lambaréné the party traveled back to "the little Europe," as Frankie called it, of Leopoldville and Brazzaville, then on to Nigeria.

The journey finally ended with Ronnie, Frankie, the young Stevensons, and Marietta flying to Lisbon, leaving Adlai and Bill to conduct more business in Guinea.

The trip had been a huge success. Frankie produced a 48-page diary of her exposure to what she called "the real world" that was an early tryout for her later reporting of the Vietnam War. Marietta found in the trip something to please her parents: the vital importance of the foreign missions (of all faiths). Ronnie, although long-suffering about the lack of creature comforts, provided some acid comments about African dancing and the food. But the star, of course, was Stevenson. "Adlai's restless and probing curiosity," wrote Marietta, "and concern for all for their problems, *made* the trip for his fellow voyagers, and all the rest of us, though I do say it, were v. good travellers—neat, polite, energetic, intelligent and on time!"

However, there was tension. Frankie, always the acute observer, noticed electricity between her mother and Adlai during the trip, and later thought this was when they started their affair. If Frankie had noticed something, how much more must Alicia (or for that matter, Ronnie) have noticed? But if Alicia and Marietta knew that the torch was being passed, not a word was ever said about it. Alicia was "my shrewd, nice, humorous friend," Marietta told Susan Mary.

It was business as usual for Marietta in the fall—helping Democrats in local New York races and working for Averell Harriman's reelection for governor (he lost to Nelson Rockefeller). The winter months, however, found Marietta once again trying to coax down a few sugared violets in Barbados, as she sat at her blue and white desk and stared dreamily out of the window.

"Soon, we'll all swim and look at fish through goggles. . . . Then Oliver Messel and two gentleman friends come to lunch—rum punch, cold soup, eggs valenciana, lime ice. . . . Then at 8.30 dinner of dolphin, chicken casserole, and coconut pudding, more bridge and gossip, and bed at 11—sleep from 11.05 to 9.00 am without moving. . . ."

But these sweet morsels could not satisfy her hunger. She told Susan Mary that when she dined with Democratic senators Hubert Humphrey, Mike Monroney, Clint Anderson, and William Fulbright in Washington before her return to the Caribbean, "I was like an art lover gazing in the Louvre." How could the idle bridge players at Heron Bay compete with such masterpieces? Averell Harriman, Dick Brown, and Clayton Fritchey wrote to her in Barbados keeping her posted on Democratic Party matters. And by 1958, she was writing to the leader of them all in a way that could not be misinterpreted.

Mr. J showed me another part of his vast garden the other day, and tho I had already seen a great deal of it, and loved intensely what I knew, the new vistas and parterres and fountains were of beauty and wonder. But *no* wonder really, as we know he is full of care and responsibility and knowledge, his taste, passion and sense of proportion remarkable. I rate him higher than Pericles, with whom he shares so many qualities, realizing that only he can be a great steward over the public domain, who can make his own garden splendid.

He sweetly gave me an armful of roses, which I have made into a wreath, and fancy it gives a mature look, its v. becoming in any case, and I will keep it all my life in gratitude, respect, and love for Mr. J.

This letter crystallizes Marietta's feelings for Adlai: her worship of his public personality, his high-minded politics, his intellect, combined with her delight in his romantic qualities—the scribbled notes and sonnets, and the invention of a private world (including code names) that they created for themselves to counteract the glaring spotlight in which he, and to some extent, she, permanently dwelled. Their secret names for each other were variously Mr. and Mrs. Johnson and Mr. and Mrs. Richardson. (Choosing Johnson is curious—perhaps a private joke—considering it was the name of that very contentious senator from Texas, Lyndon Baines Johnson, who gave Stevenson all kinds of trouble within the Democratic Party.)

There were certain places the Johnsons could be fairly sure of meeting in safety. Barbados and the Fields' Chelsea Plantation in South Carolina both became regular trysting spots. The other safe havens were Democratic Party meetings of various kinds. But Stevenson was a frenetic traveler during the years before he went to the United Nations, and as Marietta herself was constantly in flight, much of their affair was conducted by letter.

Between 1958 and 1960 Adlai wrote to her from Russia, from Sweden, from Chicago, from everywhere. He wrote also to his other women friends, Alicia, Agnes Meyer, and Ruth Field (Marshall's widow, who was becoming more and more focused on Stevenson). He even wrote to his women friends' children. He liked to be liked, even by the very young, and both Frankie and Penelope were the beneficiaries of his attentions. (Among other notes to Frankie, he wrote a letter to Radcliffe, for instance, in support of her application. With Penelope, he invented the name she then called him, "Yo Yo"—a diplomatic word, he explained, a combination of Yes and No.)

Like a good business manager sending follow-up notes after meetings, Stevenson was a brilliant purveyor of the billet-doux. Hundreds of little notes and poems in his small, flowing hand flitted through the mails during the years after the 1956 defeat. Adlai, as they would say in the jargon of pop psychology, was working on his relationships. For the first time since his divorce, he had the time to do so.

He was earning money from his law firm, from the Field Foundation (of which he became president after Marshall Field died), and from the *Encyclopaedia Britannica*. He sat on the Democratic Advisory Council, attended meetings, gave speeches and lectures. But for the moment, there was no pressure. Apart from continuing problems with his ex-wife, Ellen, Adlai was relieved of responsibilities. Always harboring a sybaritic streak, he put on weight from wining and dining and flirting his way through the four years of Republican rule that came to an end in 1960.

Marietta's calendar shows a remarkably similar schedule. Between 1956 and 1960 she was executive chairman of the New York Committee of Democratic Voters, which raised money to support the Democratic Advisory Council. She became a member of the Advisory Council's Civil Rights Committee, of which Mrs. Roosevelt was chairman. (With their support among others, Mayor Robert Wagner, a keen civil rights activist, passed the first Fair Housing Law in America.) She was also on the executive committee of the Women's Division, New York State Democratic Committee. She raised funds for another Anthony Akers campaign for Congress. And she was out at dinner parties almost every night.

In 1959 she was given what was by far her most important voluntary post so far: a position on the newly formed Commission of Inter-Group Relations of New York City (later the Human Rights Commission), founded by Mayor Robert Wagner to attempt to come to grips with the racial issues dividing the city. Resigning her post as a director of the National Urban League (which had given her invaluable insights into the problems of the inner city), Marietta, as the only Protestant and only woman, found herself deeply involved in questions of integrating education and housing, matters that had always been close to her heart.

Meanwhile, Adlai's letters confirmed their increasing commitment to each other. "Brussels will be forever blessed; not one, but three [letters]," Adlai writes to her after a luncheon with King Baudouin of Belgium. "I am reminded of some other words; So few who live have life. I think [we] are blessed because we have *life*, in so many dimensions." People in love often indulge in a kind of self-absorbed appreciation of their relationship. The form it took with Stevenson and Marietta—a sense of enlarging each other's experience of the world—fed brilliantly into Marietta's appetite for embracing life to the full.

Often using the stylistic conceit of writing in the third person, Adlai describes his meetings with important officials and poses rhetorical questions about the political problems that face the countries he visits. There are many scheduling arrangements, hopes of meetings. "J's pains acute—time, distance endless". . . "If Mrs. J could be ex-

actly precise about Paris it would be welcome"... There are complaints about not hearing from her. "No intelligences waiting here,"
he writes from Berne in the summer of 1958, "although this is spy
capital and poor Mr. J is even more disturbed, but he seems confident
there will be some *comfort* at next stop. Always says that, mumbling
meanwhile about waste and living without life. Pity—with such a sure,
solid type." He signs this letter: "Ivan the Tired." However, he often
defuses his expressions of need. "I'll pray all is well—and that's what
I said to Gromyko at end of long anguished session yesterday. . . ."

"The poor J is a mess," he writes to Marietta from Stockholm.
"He can't sleep. . . . But I know what's wrong and it rather serves him
right. After all he'd been master of heart and head a long time, and
then *thought* he was a long time longer than he was, if you can understand that sort of sentence. But now his defenses are crumbling and
the poor fellow is weak with wanting. . . ."

He sometimes makes jealous references to her other admirers,
including his "rival," Arthur Schlesinger, who continued to be Marietta's close friend. He likes to remind her precisely whom she is causing
to suffer in this way, pointing out that he is under considerable and
sustained pressure and "constantly exposed to public scrutiny."

He also returns frequently to the theme of his own triumphs, such
as in Sweden, when he tells her, "But . . . under trying circumstances
[he] occasioned much public mirth by his sallies, all recorded at length
in press with photos." Like a small boy proudly sending his mother
good reports from school, Adlai includes clippings of his speeches or
flattering articles about him published in foreign newspapers. From
time to time he takes his own political temperature in rambling, self-
absorbed paragraphs of doubt and despondency. In some letters, the
personal messages to Mrs. J have to be sucked out of these pages of
discursive prose like marrow from a bone.

They met in Paris, New York, Chicago. Adlai felt young, admired;
Marietta felt extended, enriched. In the summer of 1959 they spent a
delicious time in the Mediterranean on Bill Benton's two-hundred-
foot yacht, *The Flying Clipper*. Since Bill Benton's expressed goal was
that the cruise should please Stevenson, Marietta was not his only
female companion on the trip. Adlai's latest friend, a good-looking
young divorcée called Susie Zurcher, heiress to the Morton salt fortune, traveled part of the way. Marietta met and was charming to the
new favorite at a party she gave for Bill Benton at 123 East 79th Street
while Ronnie was in Portugal in October 1959. ("Susie Zurcher!" her
diary exclaims cryptically.)

Marietta was on board *The Flying Clipper* the first eleven days of
the cruise, joined by Frankie, Adlai III, and Nancy. (Frankie had won
a scholarship to Radcliffe the previous fall, to her mother's delight,

although she worried about paying the tuition.) For those glorious hot days they sailed, toured museums, visited Moorish castles, swam, were entertained by ambassadors, and dined in wonderful restaurants.

Marietta and Frankie then flew to Rome before going on a tour of the Middle East. Before she left, Adlai urged Marietta to come back via Florence and stay with his sister, Buffie Ives, at the house she had rented, the Villa Capponi. Marietta and Frankie duly arrived on July 27, exhausted after their journey through Jordan and Israel, to find Adlai and his son Borden there to welcome them. Another delightful week ensued, this time filled with the unmatched beauties of Florence and the Tuscan towns. Then Adlai and Borden left for Athens and the South of France (where they stayed at Mary Lasker's villa), and Marietta and Frankie took the train to Paris. Four days in the French capital passed quickly with visits to the couture houses of Grès and Balmain, and dinners with Charles and Jayne Wrightsman and Frank and Kitty Giles (Frank was the Paris correspondent for *The Times* of London). Frankie stayed on in Paris while Marietta flew off, this time to Barbados, where Ronnie and Penelope were waiting to meet her.

Once more she assumed her duties as "cruise director and traffic cop," as she called it. Once more she gazed out of her window and wrote letters, but this time it was not Susan Mary who was the recipient. "I am sitting at my blue and white desk overlooking a geranium-bright garden with the aquamarine beyond longing to be alone with J —if only for a few hours. . . ." The yearning is almost palpable. "But what of AES? Full of Turkish accomplishments and/or Turkish delight? Mrs. J wrote to say that she still awakes to the pearly light over the Duomo. . . ."

The moon is a participant in their bliss, as that pale voyeur so often is on these occasions. "I saw that jewelled star set in the crescent of the moon on the flight down here, and had 2 wishes (on 1st star seen, and 1st sight of new moon over left shoulder) or a double wish for a permanent view of Richardson. . . . Mrs. J dreams always of the northern week, and now swings on that moon and dances through the stars. . . ."

During the visit to Paris that summer of 1959, Marietta had lunch with John Huston. Frankie came too—a chaperone, perhaps. He charmed them both. After meeting again in New York in 1956, Marietta and John had rendezvoused several times for drinks, but Marietta needed now more than ever to establish the ground rules. John would never stop wanting her, but over that lunch in Paris she talked to him in a way that allowed him to accept her conditions and remain friends. She confided to Susan Mary the conclusion of this encounter. "Very rewarding and satisfactory. Feel blessed, as I think this kind of thing happens rarely. No responsibility—no strain—no decisions—oh, joy!"

Not even to Susan Mary, however, could she confide the responsibility, strain, and decisions she was in fact beginning to encounter elsewhere—the responsibility, strain, and decisions of an adulterous relationship. Given her personal history and background, they created a particularly complex burden. The joy Marietta expressed in the straightforward connection she had established with Huston would be far more difficult to sustain in the illicit link she was forging with Adlai Stevenson.

# CHAPTER *24*

# *"Who are these blighters?"*

In 1957, Bishop Peabody was approaching his seventieth birthday and thinking about mortality. In preparation for updating his bequests to his family, he wrote to his son-in-law asking how Ronnie was providing for Marietta in the event of his (Ronnie's) death. Ronnie told Malcolm that Marietta would inherit Heron Bay with all its contents (which he estimated conservatively at that time at $150,000, or roughly $800,000 in 1996 dollars). He was also leaving her 123 East 79th Street with all its contents, some of which were very valuable. Ronnie's life insurance was the maximum: $250,000 ($1.35 million in today's currency).

But he could not give her more. His grandfather's trust, which he had so often tried and failed to break, specifically excluded any beneficiaries except Ronnie's children, who would inherit one half, and the St. Luke's Hospital in Chicago, which would inherit the other half. "I have made it very clear in my will," Ronnie told his father-in-law, "that the Trustees should pay Marietta a large portion of Penelope's income—as I have been unable to provide for her in the way I would have done had I not been tied down by the trust." (He did not say how the trustees would effect this.)

Meanwhile, Ronnie's hotel venture was beginning to take shape. His investors included Henry Breck, Lord Kindersley, Canadian businessman Bud Reger, and Lord Astor, with Ronnie only a modest shareholder. Jack Dear, a Barbadian lawyer who had worked with Ronnie, put the U.S./U.K. corporation together.[1]

Ronnie threw his energies into the Sandy Lane Hotel, the opening of which was set for February 1961. But while working with Sandy Lane's architect Robertson ("Happy") Ward distracted him, Ronnie was increasingly lonely. In Barbados, he became fearful of having to dine on his own. He would insist on calling people over to play bridge or tennis. "He *made* people come," said Jimmy Walker, who also helped build the resort.

Ronnie especially missed his daughter, who was now at Dalton. Roaming the grounds of Heron Bay alone, he kept hoping Penelope might come around a corner and surprise him. Penelope, too, grieved. Not an academic star, in contrast to her brilliant half sister, Penelope was only slowly beginning to make friends. She was as devoted to her father as he to her, and her childhood letters are full of love and loss during these long separations.

In 1958, Jack Dear, who had become a close friend of Ronnie's, was instrumental in getting a group together to propose that Ronnie be appointed Governor-General of the Federation of the West Indies. "I got local politicians to ask the British Government to consider him," Jack Dear recalled. "Grantley Adams [prime minister of Barbados] also tried." Yet once more Ronnie was turned down. This time Tory cronyism was the excuse—the job went to Patrick Hills, an old friend of Winston Churchill's.[2]

The fact of the matter is that Ronnie was never in the running for any of these posts, for in political life, though considered an honest and dependable fellow, he was also regarded as a lightweight, given temporary ballast by Churchill's exploitation of his wealth and hospitality during the war. By his apparent abandonment of his country after the war, any chances of support from within the Tory party became increasingly slim.

Ronnie's continued efforts in this regard reflect his profound sadness at not being more useful in the world, and he must have judged Marietta's increasing political responsibilities in light of his own failed career. Still, in many ways he was able to maintain the upper hand in their relationship, and exert his authority over her at times. For example, Marietta was always careful to ask his permission when she was offered some new job in the Democratic Party. (He never refused.) Or he would criticize her seating arrangements at dinner, or draw attention to her habit, as he saw it, of talking about things she did not know anything about. On one occasion, in front of Mary Bingham, he chastised his wife for her ignorance, saying, "Mary is a Virginian, she understands."

Ronnie and Marietta had always shared an interest in politics, and Ronnie's knowledge of world politics was greater than hers. But as he grew older, he became less and less comfortable in her New York milieu. He confided once to Mary Warburg that he could not abide the "awful people" who frequented the house on 79th Street. Russell

Hemenway overheard him grumbling to Collins on one occasion, "Who are these blighters?" Feeling increasingly alienated, he turned more and more away from her and toward his old life, where once he had been involved and happy.

In the autumn of 1959, for instance, in England as usual at that time of year, Ronnie spent a weekend shooting with the Salisburys at Hatfield. The October day reminded him of Ditchley—"root fields, small coverts, the whirr of pheasants and all the delights of English country life." He also saw his ex-wife Nancy Lancaster, as he sometimes did on his trips to England.

Perhaps it was partly these nostalgic reminders that drove him to make the following confession to his wife:

> I must say the account of your life as described in your last letter sounds pretty fearful, and I'm only glad I avoided the parties. I'm afraid as I get older, I can only take a very few people altogether and prefer them to be friends. A crowd—or the very idea of it—gives me acute claustrophobia and I don't think I can ever again go to those mixed or mixed-up parties. It takes years off my life and gives me a deep inferiority complex.

Unfortunately for Ronnie, this painful revelation could not have come at a more inappropriate time. For 1960 meant yet another presidential election year, and Marietta was slipping away faster and faster into its swirling current.

The year started slowly. Although Adlai urged Marietta to start working for Hubert Humphrey as the Democratic candidate, the governor was once more toying with the idea of seeking the nomination. It was, after all, definitely his last chance. He wrote letters to the Democratic Advisory Council recommending strategies. The old faithfuls who had campaigned with him in 1952 and 1956 urged him on. Agnes Meyer offered a large sum of money to support his nomination (including, with Mary Lasker, paying for a writer, William Attwood, to take a leave from *Life* to work full time for Adlai). George Ball, Senator Mike Monroney, and others set up a small group in Monroney's Washington office to further the Stevenson candidacy. A New York Stevenson for President Committee was organized with leadership from Russ Hemenway, Ruth Field, Tom Finletter, and Marietta. Many other old Roosevelt liberals, including Mrs. Roosevelt herself, still hoped Stevenson would become president.

But this year, there was a new mood abroad in the Democratic Party. Several other contestants were jockeying for position. The Republican competition, Richard Nixon, caused many on all sides of the political spectrum to feel somewhat queasy. Who was the candidate most likely to defeat him?

Adlai, concentrating on his role as foreign policy expert, distanced himself from the early primary races by going on a tour (for *Look*) of Latin America. He then joined Marietta and Ronnie in Barbados. (Four days later, Ronnie departed for Portugal, leaving the two of them alone.) The day Adlai arrived, Kennedy won the Wisconsin primary, defeating Humphrey by just over 100,000 votes. A week later, with all eyes on him, Stevenson gave a press conference in New York, in which he demonstrated once again his evasiveness about the nomination.

It was 1952 all over again, but on this occasion the patience of even his most loyal friends was wearing thin. Arthur Schlesinger was beginning to struggle with a divided conscience as he increasingly recognized Kennedy's potential. Reporter John Steele, who saw Stevenson in Washington, described him as "an utterly harried, put-upon, almost distraught person. He was not the picture of a man, even in the eyes of his friends, who should be in the White House. . . . He spun from useless cocktail party to cocktail party, disheveled and breathless. He submitted to the back pounding of people who can help him not at all. He affronted editors who sought to shake his hands as he bolted for an exit. . . ."[3]

For one supporter, however, there was no doubt. From the blue and white desk in Heron Bay, encouragement flowed:

> Happily no one realizes that Mrs. Rich lives in a world entirely bounded by J. So much joy and energy is generated that it illumines all the people seen, ideas propounded, books read—a rum punch, a moon-filled sea, because J. is interested and involved with everything and everybody. One of the strong reasons why she loves him. (—Is this all crystal-clear?) I do hope that your colleagues are keeping up, and your speeches—fraught with depth—come easily, and you are feeling useful and delighted. Time diminishes nothing—rather time strengthens. The cup runneth over.
>
> M.

From Barbados that spring, Marietta followed with devoted concern Adlai's progress toward the Democratic Convention. She wished she had been with him in Latin America, and worried that he was doing too much. She reported to him what people were saying about the Democratic candidates, such as the hateful remark of his friend Malcolm Muir of *Newsweek,* who said to her, "How can the Party give [the draft] to a defeatist?"

She was temporarily diverted from foreign affairs by the arrival in Barbados of Winston and Clementine Churchill. The Churchills were guests on board Aristotle Onassis's yacht, the *Christina.* Onassis was exceedingly generous to the Churchills, and Marietta was touched by how the Greek shipowner played up to the aged British statesman. Onassis had trained a parakeet called Toby to sit on Churchill's shoulder, which temporarily brought a light to the old man's clouded eyes. Onassis also allowed Churchill to beat him at the card game called bezique. Onassis and Churchill sometimes took a ride around the island in an open car. Since Churchill was always slumped in the back seat, Onassis would wave vigorously, and Marietta was certain that many of the cheering crowds thought the great British prime minister was a deeply suntanned man with a head of thick and wavy white hair.

The Trees had dinner on the *Christina,* where Churchill downed whiskey or sank his head on his chest "either through titanic gloom or boredom." Marietta took a great interest in the facilities of the yacht, such as the mosaic-lined swimming pool with mermaids frolicking, Onassis's private toilet which was a huge glass box, and the fully equipped operating room should Churchill need an emergency operation.

But even these distractions failed to keep her from feeling she was virtually a prisoner at Heron Bay. She wrote to Adlai that "For six weeks now, it seems that around 30–50 people a day have come to this house on business, for drinks, for meals, for tennis or croquet or just to see the house, and I am very very tired of it—tired from lack of privacy and solitude (this letter has been interrupted 4 times already), tired of eternal small talk, tired of that logey afternoon feeling when you've had a drink before lunch, and purposelessness."

She begged Adlai to forgive her self-indulgence in pouring out her complaints, and added, "Thank God for your creative energy, and your intelligence and force and loving nature—M."

In June, she went with Ronnie, Penelope (now aged ten), and Mabel on their annual visit to England for a month of high society. The list of parties read like "Jennifer's Diary," the ultra-social column in *The Tatler:* a coming-out party for Lord Lambton's daughter; a weekend at Hatfield House with the Salisburys and the Churchills; and dinners with Kenneth Clark, David Niven, Victor Rothschild, and Isaiah Berlin.

None of the distractions worked for long: "80,000 leagues from reality and Johnson . . . I want to know what's happening in the 1st District North Manhattan, and the result of the school redistributing on 81st Street, and most of all what's happening to J. Richardson . . . the most-cherished."

John F. Kennedy had won the West Virginia and Oregon primaries, and was beginning to look unbeatable. Humphrey had withdrawn from the race. Lyndon Johnson was determined to stop Kennedy, which meant preventing Humphrey and Stevenson voters from throwing their support behind the Massachusetts senator. Many still doubted Kennedy's ability to beat Nixon (both his youth and his Catholicism were seen as major obstacles to victory) and Stevenson remained a front-runner in many polls. (In a straw vote taken at Groton School, Adlai beat Nixon by 72 to 60. "Bless those Peabody trained moppets!" Adlai wrote, sending on the results to Marietta.)

Yet even Stevenson knew that the original fervor of his presidential hopes was gone. "You can only be a virgin once," he reportedly said about the 1956 campaign. The best idea that spring was that if Stevenson would endorse Kennedy, Kennedy would make Stevenson secretary of state, thus offering a compromise that would please a large section of Democratic voters.

In the aftermath of the U-2 incident—in which a U.S. pilot flew over Soviet air space—coming as it did just before a USSR-U.S. summit meeting, Khrushchev and Eisenhower faced off with some of the most militaristic language of the Cold War, and people again looked to Stevenson as the voice of reason and calm. Stevenson made several good speeches about the nuclear threat, but still evaded any questions about his own or anyone else's candidacy. Kennedy, recognizing the importance of Stevenson's endorsement, met with the governor at Libertyville, but the results were inconclusive. Now several of Adlai's closest allies, including Arthur Schlesinger and John Kenneth Galbraith, finally announced they would support Kennedy.

Schlesinger's defection was a serious blow, although hardly unexpected. Arthur repeatedly said that if the governor had declared his candidacy, he would have supported him. Mrs. Roosevelt and Agnes Meyer, amongst many dedicated Stevensonians, were very angry at Schlesinger's change of horses, but Marietta was sympathetic.[4] He wrote her two anguished letters explaining his position, reiterating his love and loyalty to Stevenson and to her. Their friendship survived and flourished.

Yet, as always in Stevenson's political career, there remained many Americans who dreamed of his presidency. Eleanor Roosevelt endorsed him publicly and became honorary chairman of the New York Draft Stevenson Committee, which collected thousands of volunteers and signatories. Alicia Patterson came out for him in her newspaper, *Newsday*. "I imagine the pressure on you is worse and worse and worse," Marietta wrote to him from London, "and everybody in various nominal camps beginning to behave rather badly. How I wish I could help, and pray there's a chance for that in the future. Time does not assuage. M."

Marietta returned from England on June 29. The next day, the *New York Post* endorsed Stevenson for president and Kennedy for vice president. The Democratic Convention, to be held in Los Angeles, was just over a week away.

"Darling," Marietta wrote to Ronnie from the Ambassador Hotel in Los Angeles on July 11,

> Have been here two days and gone so hard that I feel I've been here for 2 months. Los Angeles is a terrible place—takes forever and $5 in a taxi to get anywhere, and it's so bland and synthetic.
>
> Also I dislike it because from the beginning it has been clear that Jack K. would win. Most of the delegates are saying, "he's going to win anyway, so we might as well vote for him," but all are without any fire or belief in him. Barry Bingham and Averell, in fact, told me that Kennedy was good *because* he had no integrity—like Roosevelt. On this basis, we should all vote for Nixon, because I bet he has even less integrity than Kennedy.

Three days later she wrote again:

> I'm so tired now I can hardly direct this pen, my voice is gone, my complexion is like tapioca and my hands are fountains of sweat from weakness. . . . The big night was last night where Jack got elected easily on the first ballot. There was never even a remote chance for anyone else. That Kennedy machine is the coolest and most efficient in anyone's memory.
>
> But what was wonderful was when Adlai was nominated by the flamingly eloquent Gene McCarthy. The whole place went mad for cheering "We want Stevenson," and the demonstrations and the clamor went on and on and on. There was no feeling or fervor at all for Kennedy in contrast. . . . So at least Adlai is the most loved of the Democrats—that was made abundantly clear—I think that made a great difference to Adlai, and all in all I think he's quite relieved. But I guess Jack and his type are the reflections of our time, and we might as well adjust to it. I only hope that he has all the ability he is purported to have to deal with the worst problems of all history, and I only wish he had a heart. He has none.

Less biased observers felt that Adlai Stevenson performed poorly in Los Angeles. In spite of many spontaneous demonstrations, it was clear that Stevenson had no chance of being nominated, and was simply being a spoiler by keeping his hat in the ring. On the night before the convention, he joined the Illinois delegation, and amid a riot of cheering, was invited to the rostrum. As Arthur Schlesinger, Jr., describes it in his book *A Thousand Days*, "Again he seemed to recoil from the occasion. Instead of speaking two or three sober sentences which might have rallied the convention, he tried a pleasantry ('after going back and forth through the Biltmore today, I know who's going to be the nominee of this convention—the last man to survive'). The demonstrations quieted down almost instantly. Leonard Lyons said afterward, 'He let out all the air with one bad joke.' "[5]

His supporters were appalled. Agnes Meyer said, "I could have murdered him. He should have told us he wouldn't fight." Yet the following day Stevenson still canvassed behind the scenes, almost begging for a sign of commitment from the Illinois delegation, and was given a categorial thumbs-down from Richard Daley in response. Hubert Humphrey declared for Stevenson. There were more pro-Stevenson demonstrations.

Delegates were confused. Having earlier refused the Kennedys' plea to withdraw his name from nomination, Stevenson then declined their invitation to nominate the young senator, a childish gesture that aggravated the already damaged relationship between the two men and that was to have lasting consequences for Adlai's later years in politics. Finally, on the last day of the convention, Stevenson introduced Kennedy as the Democratic presidential candidate, and a new era of Democratic politics began.

Immediately afterward, a group of Adlai's close friends, as in 1956, went to Santa Barbara to recover. Marietta joined them. The party then moved to Lake Tahoe, after which Marietta went on for a weekend in Chicago and more private consolation with Adlai. On Monday, July 25, she flew back to New York, and three days later on to Barbados, where she stayed for three weeks. She wrote to Adlai from Barbados: "Please thank Rich. eternally for the Elysium of Tahoe, Chicago, N.Y."

Marietta's political goal was now to start working to achieve Adlai's hoped-for appointment as secretary of state in a Kennedy administration. Thus she started campaigning for Kennedy with a will. She took on the leadership of the Citizens for Kennedy group in Manhattan (her contacts in Harlem and with the Puerto Rican districts were very valuable), as well as becoming chairman of a $100-a-plate dinner in October for Kennedy where Adlai would be the only speaker.

Late that summer she returned for another weekend to Libertyville, writing to Ronnie that she played tennis with Adlai and that there were a lot of parties. She also went on at length about Jane Dick's porch furniture, which she felt sure Ronnie would like and she would get addresses of the manufacturers for him. Clearly Marietta was juggling again.

Ronnie came back to New York for three weeks in the middle of September, and Marietta, wearing her conjugal hat, arranged dinners for him with old friends like Cecil Beaton, Sir John Russell, Pamela Berry, the Wrightsmans, and the Brecks. After Ronnie went back to Barbados, Marietta was free to hit the campaign trail with Kennedy. She flew to Raleigh, North Carolina, and spent four days attending rallies across the state.

In early November, Marietta and Dorothy Hirshon organized a fund-raising breakfast which Kennedy attended. They raised $80,000. Kennedy then asked Marietta to go campaigning with him for the day, "which was sweet of him," she wrote to Ronnie disingenuously. (When did John Kennedy ignore a pretty face?) They barnstormed through Connecticut, Massachusetts, Vermont, and New Hampshire. Kennedy made roughly the same speech in each spot. "There seemed to be the same crowd of hysterical teenagers cheering him on. Let's hope they reflect their parents' views." Marietta had a marvelous time, as many of her old friends were with the press, "and it was all v. jolly. Jack seemed extraordinarily relaxed but trenchant." A whirl of parties and fund-raisers led to the climactic day in November when John F. Kennedy, with Lyndon Johnson as his running mate, wrested a very narrow victory from Richard Nixon.

So it was done. Kennedy was in the White House. The question of secretary of state was immediately addressed. Marietta asked Adlai to write down arguments in favor of his appointment that she could use in discussion with people, and he wrote her a penciled three-page list of his qualifications. ("1. Decisiveness—as Gov. of Illinois . . . 2. Competance [sic]—lifetime interest in foreign affairs . . . 3. Influence, respect, popularity—unequalled abroad by any American, including Ike! 4. Position at home. Twice nominee virtually without opposition . . . 5. What has he done for me? Between 60–75 speeches in 11 states during campaign. Keeping out of the contest and strictly neutral for 4 years; doing *nothing* to encourage draft.")

But these did not, apparently, convince. After much awkward dickering with the new president, Adlai was passed over in favor of Dean Rusk, and offered instead the ambassadorship of the United Nations. The failure to be appointed secretary of state was one of Stevenson's greatest humiliations, and he did not at first accept the booby prize with grace, further infuriating an already alienated Kennedy. But by the end of the year, Stevenson had assumed his new mantle of international statesman. He would wear it responsibly, if at times reluctantly, until the day he died.

# CHAPTER *25*

# *"Give my love to Mummy"*

During the 1960 convention in Los Angeles, Marietta saw John Huston, who was in town to film Arthur Miller's *The Misfits*, starring
Marilyn Monroe, Clark Gable, and Montgomery Clift. Huston invited
Marietta to visit the set, so while the Stevenson party was recovering
from the convention in Santa Barbara, she flew to Reno to watch the
filming. "Nobody had heard of the convention there," she told Susan
Mary, "and it was fascinating to be transported into a completely
self-enclosed world . . . to watch the cameramen in action (in 116 degree heat), to see Marilyn Monroe falter over the same two lines 23
times in a row. . . . She wears a wig, I'm sorry to tell you, having very
little hair of her own."

    While on the set, Marietta was picked by Clark Gable for a small
part as one of Gable's girlfriends. She was thrilled. This was suddenly
a dream come true—Marietta the actress. In late August she went
back to Reno to shoot the scene, which involved her saying one line
to Clark Gable at the train station: "And remember, I have the second
biggest laundry in St. Louis." Huston told her to remember to pronounce the name "Saint Lewis," not "Snt. Looey," which was how
Marietta would naturally pronounce it. Otherwise he gave her no
instructions. Maybe he should have, for her performance was very stiff;
no great talent emerged from this movie debut.

    The experience on the set was more arduous than she had ex-
pected. For three days, she had to stand embarrassingly close to Gable
and make polite conversation with him until the shot was finally filmed.

Meanwhile, Marilyn Monroe, by then a sick woman, was taking vast amounts of barbiturates, and filming often had to be delayed until she had leveled out. "In her terror," wrote Marietta later, "she clung to Mrs. Lee Strasberg, who was always dressed in black, and from whom she was never parted. Even on the set, Mrs. Strasberg sat beside her, one inch out of camera range. Then John would say, 'Now, Marilyn, do it or say it this way.' Marilyn would turn to her black-robed companion and if she nodded assent, Marilyn would then do it as best she could."

Frank Taylor, the producer of *The Misfits*, witnessed at close range the three days Marietta spent on the set. "She and John had a very warm relationship," he recalled. "Every evening, there would be a lot of drinking and gambling at the tables in Reno."[1] After the shot was finally completed, Marietta went on to Chicago and Libertyville for the weekend. She was disillusioned by the Reno experience. "It seemed a little squalid and rather shoddy," she wrote to Ronnie, adding that the atmosphere was not helped by John and friends "becoming rather bibulous."

However, she cheerfully described her foray into movie stardom to reporter Inez Robb, who made it the leading anecdote in an article that appeared in the *Saturday Evening Post* a month later. Entitled "The Democrats' Golden Girl," this five-page profile of Marietta finally put the "green-eyed blonde" on the national map. Descriptions of her good works, her exquisite private homes, her involvement with Democratic candidates, her parties in New York, her impressive family background, her "two adoring children," and the secret ingredient, Collins the butler, accumulated like coins in a slot machine, until the combination came together in a triumphant last paragraph: "And win or lose, the Democrats will still have a dedicated worker who is also beautiful, brainy, rich, gay, mistress of a salon—and soon to be seen in a movie, kissing Clark Gable. What other political party can make that claim?"

And all this publicity was *before* she received the appointment that was to propel her into a different league entirely. For in early 1961, Marietta was recommended by Adlai Stevenson to be the U.S. Representative to the Human Rights Commission of the United Nations. He also nominated two other close women friends, Jane Dick and Gladys Tillett, for UN jobs, the former to the Social Commission, the latter to the Commission on the Status of Women.

Having discussed it with Adlai, Marietta was not above doing a little modest hustling on her own account. "You forced me to say that I wanted the job more than anything else in the world," she wrote to him, "—which is true, as it would enable me to work with total dedication to the peace of the world and for you. I had not wanted to say this so you would not feel in any way obligated. . . . However," she added, with a shrewdness born of longtime exposure to local politics, "if you and Jack [Kennedy] plan to appoint me, it ought to be done soon, perhaps, before the opposition mounts (from your 941 girl friends and others). Once an appt. is delayed, people think it's possible, by putting on pressure, to get their own candidate in. Viz, if Jack had appointed Fulbright promptly, there probably would have been no trouble. . . ."

She need not have worried. Kennedy was "amused," as Arthur Schlesinger put it, by Stevenson's recommending all his women friends, but being a man who grazed in somewhat the same pastures, he found no difficulty in giving his approval.

The New Year, 1961, exploded in a frenzy of activity. Marietta went to Washington for the inauguration, staying at the Georgetown house of Bill Walton, her old friend from the 1940s. Walton, a close confidant of JFK, had been the head of the Kennedy campaign in New York. Kennedy was also staying there in preparation for the inauguration. Marietta arrived in the Trees' chauffeur-driven Rolls-Royce and passed through the Secret Service barricade without trouble. When she found out that Walton and Kennedy were having a quiet lunch together in the dining room, she made one of her spectacular entrances and said to JFK, "I'm so proud to have you as president." To which he replied, "I'm so proud to have you as one of my subjects."[2]

After attending many celebratory dances and parties, Marietta finally left for Barbados on January 30. On February 6, Adlai sent a telegram telling her that she had the UN job. "Love, congratulations, and regards to Ronnie." Ronnie may have had mixed feelings, but he congratulated her warmly, and she returned to New York a week later. Throughout the next months, she shuttled between New York and Washington in a whirlwind of briefing meetings, introductions to the Washington officials with whom she would be dealing, and social receptions.

She reported to the Human Rights Division of the International Organizations Department of the State Department and the Human Rights Division of the Labor Department, both of which were in Washington. Marietta said that Stevenson had no idea of what she was doing at any time during the four years she served with him at the United Nations. Neither did the top ambassadors. "They were interested only in their own agendas on their own committees."

Marietta was succeeding Mary Pillsbury Lord, a Republican who had served under Eisenhower. The most distinguished holder of the post, however, was the first U.S. Commissioner for Human Rights, Eleanor Roosevelt. While traditionally the post was given to women, Mrs. Roosevelt had exerted an authority that went far beyond gender

Being sworn in as U.S. representative on the United Nations Commission on Human Rights, New York, March 1, 1961. "Dear Marietta—I was proud to be a witness!" Adlai Stevenson wrote on this photograph. *(George Brown)*

lines, and her shadow was still felt in the corridors of the United Nations. "Marietta had a difficult time because theoretically she was inheriting the mantle of Eleanor Roosevelt, which is a tough mantle to inherit," said Sir Brian Urquhart, one of the United Nation's most distinguished civil servants and the biographer of U Thant. "But Marietta worked very hard and after a certain amount of smirking everybody admitted that Marietta was somebody in her own right."

The Human Rights Commission met every March, either in New York or Geneva, and during the prior summer, the relevant U.S. or government people would cover the questions raised and issue policy statements. It was Marietta's duty to articulate these when the meetings were in session. The Human Rights topics would come up on the agenda of the Economic and Social Council, which met in July every year, and finally, if they survived these meetings, would appear on the agenda of the Third Committee of the General Assembly for ratification.

The Human Rights delegates to the Third Committee rotated. The first year, Gladys Tillett was appointed to the Third Committee, with Marietta and Jane Dick as special advisers. (Marietta did not warm to Gladys. Mrs. Tillett was a tough political professional from North Carolina, who did not feel it necessary to consult with Mrs. Tree, whom she regarded as a lightweight.) In 1962 Marietta was the delegate, with Mrs. Tillett and Mrs. Dick as advisers; and in 1963 Mrs. Dick was the delegate.

Marietta was confirmed by the U.S. Senate on February 16, 1961. She admitted openly that she knew nothing about the job. The senators asked her all sorts of questions she couldn't answer, such as, "Are you for conventions as against declarations?" But she answered smartly enough: "I don't really know what you're talking about, but I'll let you know in a week. I was just appointed." The senators seemed perfectly satisfied with that, and the confirmation went through. (They never asked her back to find out what she thought.)

One of Marietta's brightest moves after her confirmation was to go immediately to ask the advice of Mrs. Roosevelt, whom she revered. They had first met when the Roosevelts went to Groton for the school's fiftieth anniversary. Marietta, then sixteen and watchful of the great lady, thought the president's wife ungainly and shy. "I remember she left a pair of gloves behind in her bedroom. . . . I went in and took those gloves and then I was divided about whether to send them back to her or not. I'm sorry to say that I decided to keep them as a souvenir of her because, of course, I looked up to Mrs. Roosevelt very much at that time. . . . So I had those gloves for years in my top drawer to remind me of her and what she was doing." Over the years, Marietta had encountered the former first lady during Stevenson's presidential campaigns and appreciated her support. Most recently, Marietta had worked directly with her over the movement to legislate open housing in New York City.

Mrs. Roosevelt gave Marietta invaluable advice. "First, she told me to learn the language of the resolutions. That was the hardest part of the job-training, as I was not used to precise legal language and had to memorize it. . . . Second, she said you must learn to know your fellow delegates well and learn who will vote what way in certain situations; who, although he may come from a small country, has enormous influence in his group—say the Islamic group or the African group; who can be relied on to lie; who will go back on his word; and who will always stick by his word."

She told Marietta that the only way you could learn these things was by making friends, and you did that by inviting the delegates to dinner (better than lunch) in your own house in threes and fours, rarely in large groups. Delegates from abroad loved to be in someone's house because in the United States they were generally in some bleak hotel or committee room. "Just the meal and personal contact turn you into friends." One final word was that while it was only rarely that you could change a country's vote from yes to no, often you could change their vote to "abstain," and that helped a great deal when the final count came.[3]

Marietta's first task on the Human Rights Commission concerned the framing of the Declaration of Human Rights, a contentious document long under consideration to be ratified and made legal worldwide. Marietta spent a lot of her time trying to lobby Congress to pass simple conventions on the subject of genocide, for instance. She discovered that her own country, and in particular southern senators, were far more intolerant about the idea of the United Nations having legal powers over national sovereignty than the Soviet Union was. She also took part in discussions about racial discrimination and religious freedom, familiar subjects before the commission.

The job was tailor-made for Marietta. As at *Life,* she was learning new things without the responsibility of originating ideas. The duties of UN diplomats in fact demand the opposite, in that the delegates must speak for the governments they represent, not for themselves. (This job requirement was precisely what Stevenson found so difficult to accept, and what almost drove him to resignation during the famous Bay of Pigs incident in 1961. Inadvertently misled by the White House about the botched invasion of Cuba, he had to deliver statements to his UN colleagues that turned out to be lies.) On all the issues before the Human Rights Commission, Marietta received instructions directly from Washington. She was a good researcher and a willing recipient of advice. Her State Department handlers (whom she called her "Nannies") had no trouble with her.

However, later on, in the spring of 1964 after Lyndon Johnson had replaced the assassinated JFK as president, she found she had to take the initiative. She and her colleagues were working on a last-minute check of the language of a declaration against religious intolerance. On studying the preamble, she realized that while most forms of racial intolerance were included, no mention was made of anti-Semitism. Horrified, she called her State Department supervisors to ask their permission to add a sentence against anti-Semitism. But everyone was out to lunch (literally). She then called Stevenson and others in the mission, but again found no one home. Since the declaration was to be introduced immediately, Marietta would have no other chance to amend the preamble afterward, so she spoke up and recommended the clause herself.

Immediately the Arabs and Soviets rose up in a rage, and although Marietta had answers ready for them, she did not have an answer for the deputy assistant secretary of the International Organizations Department of the State Department, who came up to New York the next day in a fury. He said, "If you do another thing like this without instructions, you're going to be fired."

But Marietta had the last laugh. *The New York Times* reported on March 13, 1964, that Marietta P. Tree had raised the issue of anti-Semitism and "in a speech that appeared clearly directed at the Soviet Union . . . she asked the United Nations to go on record as opposing the 'violent and hateful disease of anti-Semitism.' "[4] Two weeks later, a conference was organized in Washington by twenty-four major national Jewish organizations to focus attention on the rising tide of anti-Semitism in the Soviet Union. On Wednesday, April 8, President Johnson and Dean Rusk held meetings with these groups to discuss the problem, during which Rusk reaffirmed the concern expressed the previous month at the United Nations by the United States Representative to the Human Rights Commission, and also reaffirmed the proposal made by Mrs. Marietta Tree, the United States Representative, that United Nations members "pledge themselves to eradicate anti-Semitism in accordance with their obligation under the United Nations Charter." Marietta's words precisely. This too was given full treatment in *The New York Times*.[5] Marietta cut out both the stories and sent them to the assistant secretary of state who had threatened her. "I never heard from them again."

Marietta was justly proud of this episode. It might have caused more trouble than it actually did, and someone more cautious would not have pressed the issue. But if she had been irresponsible, she had shown courage, and the risk paid off. She was also proud of her efforts, toward the end of her time at the United Nations, to get the commission to create a World Commissioner of Human Rights. "This was readily adopted by the State Department, but I had been long enough at the U.N. to know that anything that came from an American initiative, particularly in the Human Rights Commission, would be defeated automatically. So I got my friend who was the Costa Rican ambassador and very liberal, to put it forward." In fact, the idea remained on the agenda but was never voted upon.

In 1964, Marietta was promoted by Stevenson to the post of U.S. Representative to the Trusteeship Council of the United Nations with the rank of Ambassador. This was a more responsible job than Human Rights, and Marietta shrank from accepting it, citing her inexperience and lack of knowledge. Again, Stevenson encouraged her, but it was her old friend Clayton Fritchey, then press officer at the United Nations, who convinced her. "It's a challenge," he said; "besides, it'll be so useful later on when you're traveling." He meant it would give her a diplomatic passport, and indeed it did. Marietta used it for the rest of her life.

She replaced Jonathan Bingham, who had been promoted to the Economic and Social Council (ECOSOC). Jonathan's wife, June, Marietta's friend from their Barnard days, saw a lot of her during this time and was fascinated to watch how Marietta had been transformed from that unhappy, insecure, pregnant student she knew in New York to the radiant woman gracing the corridors of the United Nations.

Marietta was attached to the Committee of Twenty-Four, which was devoted to colonial problems and non-self-governing territories, in particular in the Middle East and Africa. Her instructions were to work with the colonial countries in achieving self-government as soon as possible. This was an issue she could wholeheartedly support. In 1964 and 1965, she traveled to Africa to hear petitions from the various shadow governments presenting their cases for independence. Both the United Kingdom and the United States were closely involved in these issues, and Marietta found herself working with diplomats she had known from her days at Ditchley.

While she proceeded with her official duties, she also remembered Eleanor Roosevelt's recommendation that she get to know the delegates. This task of course employed one of Marietta's most conspicuous talents, and social life at the United Nations was greatly enhanced in the Stevenson years by the presence of this tall, beautiful woman with regal carriage and designer clothes, her blond hair beautifully done (every week, by Kenneth), tirelessly giving dinners, attending parties, crossing every language and color barrier with her enthusiasm and interest in people's lives. "I got to know them by asking questions about their childhood," she recalled. "If you ask about the childhood of somebody from Upper Volta, it is in striking contrast with the childhood of somebody from Colombia or France. As a result . . . I have at least five or six friends in every country of the world." She illuminated UN events, dancing the night away with representatives of Third World countries, who had never encountered anything like this dazzling American Valkyrie, and who never forgot her.

Much of this work was not paid. Marietta's official salary was $19,800, but, like the two Human Rights commissioners before her, Marietta was paid on a "when actually employed" basis. Thus, when the Human Rights Commission was not meeting (which was much of the year), Marietta's activities behind the scenes went financially unrewarded. Stevenson attempted to rectify this, pointing out her many contributions to the mission aside from the commission itself, but to no avail.

Not that money was a problem: it did not go unnoticed that the

U.S. Human Rights delegate arrived every day in a chauffeur-driven car, or that her wardrobe was haute couture. On one occasion, she was having a fur coat made and the furrier came into the office to fit it. Nor did Marietta's other life fade away. Her forty-fifth birthday was celebrated with Ronnie on Onassis's yacht, once again with the Churchills on board; Onassis presented her with a beautiful cake and many toasts were drunk. She was seated, as usual, beside Churchill. "He is even slower than last year—there are v. few flashes coming from that almost extinct volcano. Pam Hayward [later Harriman] sat on his other side and we really worked."

Marietta's ex officio duties also included a great deal of public speaking, a task to which she never felt adequate. In October 1961, on one of her earliest public assignments, she had returned to Philadelphia, her childhood home, to address the World Affairs Council at their annual lunch for UN Day. "You can imagine how I quaked," she told her parents, "especially when I heard that May Clark was organizing a table of all my old girlfriends." Mezzy Hickok came from Harrisburg with her daughter. Louise Roberts, Antelo Devereux, Stewart Rauch, and Teddy Roosevelt all turned up to see dear Marietta in her brilliant new role. On the dais she sat next to friends George Clark and Edgar Scott (whose introduction included the remark that when an ambassador was appointed to the moon, it should be Marietta), and she reckoned she got through the speech all right. Afterwards, the University of Pennsylvania gave her a reception with faculty and students in attendance. "I felt such a fraud," she confessed, still haunted by the lack of a college degree.

These reminders of her Philadelphia childhood did not, however, translate into greater attention to family values. Frankie, at Radcliffe, was finally settled in a world where her intellectual spirit could be properly nurtured. One of her closest friends there was Alice Albright, the niece of Alicia Patterson. Frankie was twenty-one on October 21, 1961, and Marietta found time to organize a dance for her at 123 East 79th Street a month later. (She had had a big coming-out party in 1958.) Adlai Stevenson was there, and it lasted until 4 A.M. Although Ronnie was co-host, he remained in Barbados. He sent Marietta a check to cover the party's expenses and Frankie a telegram for her birthday.

As Frankie became a young woman, new sources of tension arose with her mother. Frankie's striking intellectual abilities were now apparent, and that discovery, while making the mother proud, made her aware of her own inadequacy, which in turn drove Marietta to find other ways subconsciously to assert herself over her daughter. What to wear, for instance. Frankie still had the gaucheness of youth, and Marietta compounded it by buying her clothes of the most inappropriate kind. Bill Walton was present when Marietta gave Frankie a fluffy ballgown as a Christmas gift that even he could see was totally unsuitable. One could say this was simply a lack of attention, but psychology leads one to a harsher interpretation.

As she grew older, Frankie found in herself the ability to fight back. Sometimes she made a joke: "My diamond earrings [they were costume jewelry] are the biggest and the best. I will never take them off—once I get the cranes and cement to put them on. . . . The sweater is beautiful, but made, I am afraid, for a Sino-Portuguese humpback with very short arms." But the light tone occasionally turned darker. "I do thank you for the thought of sending that dress," she wrote at one point. "Unfortunately I can't think of four occasions on which to wear it. Only two come immediately to mind—a nice, private lynching or a Come As Your Worst Fears party. . . . All love from your unfashionable daughter."

Frankie's battle for separation and independence eventually was to take an even more damaging form. At Radcliffe, she grew slender and became increasingly good-looking. She loved to dance (like her mother) and enjoyed parties. She also noticed that when she brought boys home, they all fell for Marietta. This was a form of aggression Frankie could not fight, and it remained a thorny issue between them for a long time. Frankie's male friends over the years witnessed humiliating scenes where Marietta would sweep in, talk animatedly and charmingly through the evening with her daughter's friends, and generally force the most invidious comparisons. (How relentless were the repetitions that shaped this family: One recalls the bitter poem Mary Peabody wrote her mother, "When you and I are seated here,/ And beaux on me come calling,/ They much prefer to talk to you,/ All interest in me falling . . .") Thus does the compelling inheritance of an unloved, competitive childhood play itself out in the next generation.

Penelope also suffered the consequences of this tough legacy. Armed with that terrible Peabody instinct, Marietta would invariably point out to her younger daughter how brilliant Frankie had been at Dalton, and refer to the IQ test in which Frankie had scored off the charts. Thus, nine years apart in age, and with vastly different temperaments and childhood experiences, the two girls, who might otherwise have become allies, were given little opportunity to become friends during those years.

Like Frankie, however, Penelope became very fond of Adlai Stevenson. She would write him letters from school. "I adored him," she said later. On one occasion, she added to the bottom of a letter, with a child's innocence: "Give my love to Mummy." How telling a request. For Marietta's life at the United Nations, with all its excitements and dramas and homework, was entirely colored by her proximity to her ambassador, who was now permanently in New York, installed in apartment 42A of the Waldorf Towers on Park Avenue at 50th Street.

In 1961, when Stevenson arrived in New York, Marietta was forty-four years old. Not only was she now the nationally recognized golden girl of the ruling Democratic Party, as well as a brilliant hostess and power behind the throne, but she had been thrust upon a world stage that surpassed even her most grandiose childhood dreams. To cap the triumph, she was working alongside the man she idolized, loved, and hoped would become more and more a part of her life.

How surprising, then, when one morning in December 1962, Marietta's secretary Cecilia (known as "Ceil") Wentz went into her boss's office to find her lying on the couch, crying. This was so unusual that Ceil was alarmed, but Marietta told her secretary to leave her alone and close the door. After about ten minutes, Marietta got up and called one of Stevenson's drivers, saying she had to go to the doctor. Word of this later reached the ambassador, who called to find out what was wrong. Nobody knew.

What was wrong was that Marietta had been to see Dr. Arnold Seligman, tumor expert and specialist in experimental chemotherapy for cancer. Marietta had a lump in her breast, and Dr. Seligman wanted a biopsy. It seems likely that Marietta came back to her office after this examination and collapsed before deciding abruptly to seek a second opinion, or simply to flee.

The day after receiving this news, she had a psychiatric session with Dr. Bonnett, but no other medical arrangements could be made because she was due to fly to Barbados two days later. In fact, the biopsy did not take place until February 1963, a delay of two months. A woman has to have nerves of steel to wait that long. Marietta revealed her fear only when she came back for the procedure, and then only to her secretary. By chance, Ceil had also had a breast biopsy, and she was able to reassure Marietta that the procedure was not too painful and that she, Ceil, had completely recovered.[6]

The tumor turned out to be benign. Of course. Peabodys were never sick. But it was a wake-up call that she was to remember later. Meanwhile, exhilarated by the reprieve, she returned to her duties. Her energy level had never been higher. That little hiccup behind her, she had more important things to take care of. For with a husband allowing her freedom, enough money to bankroll her increasingly public position, and her children settled in school, Marietta was sailing into a magnificent middle age.

# CHAPTER *26*

## *"The greatest honor ever accorded me"*

With Adlai Stevenson's female entourage following him to New York, the earth tilted a little toward the eastern seaboard. He was comfortably installed in apartment 42A of the Waldorf Towers. He brought with him from Chicago his longtime housekeeper, Viola. The apartment was unprepossessing to start with, but within a short time it was filled with furniture, paintings, and flowers from his admiring women friends, in particular Mary Lasker, who had peeled off thousand-dollar bills to Stevenson supporters during past campaigns, and now produced artworks worthy of a museum for the new ambassador to enjoy.

The current front-runner for Stevenson's hand, according to gossip, was now Ruth Field, Marshall's widow. Marietta reported nonchalantly to Adlai in the summer of 1960 that "all Dark Harbor says you and Ruthie will be married after the election." Upon Adlai's appointment, Ruth moved from an apartment on Park Avenue to a much larger one on 79th Street in anticipation of the entertainment needs of the new U.S. Ambassador to the United Nations. She was to be disappointed.

So was Susie Zurcher, a constant companion to Stevenson for the previous two years, who finally called it quits during the spring of 1961. Marietta told John Bartlow Martin that Stevenson had broken it off because "she thought she was the only one." Mrs. Zurcher said she disliked the many women who paid court to him at the United Nations and had found someone else. A less clean break was made with Mary Lasker. Mrs. Lasker had served him long and faithfully, with financial and emotional benefits that were beyond price to him. But in the end he "let her down," in Marietta's words.

There were always others ready to fill the abdicated shoes. The beautiful Elizabeth Paepcke (Paul Nitze's sister and recent widow of Walter Paepcke, with whom she founded the Aspen Institute) became a frequent visitor. Another glamorous friend was Lauren Bacall. Evelyn Houston, a new acquaintance from California, often saw him when she came to New York. Jane Gunther, wife of author John Gunther, dined with him at 42A. He escorted movie star Joan Fontaine to several New York functions. Elizabeth Taylor excited him enormously. (Like Marietta, he was always drawn to show business people.)

And Marietta? With Adlai suddenly so accessible in New York, their relationship took a more intimate turn. While many of his other women saw him only in hurried moments stolen out of his busy schedule, Marietta was with him almost daily at work, and also during many evenings. Throughout Stevenson's UN years, the last entry in his daily calendar is frequently: "M.T. later." In Marietta's calendar, she just puts "J." She had the keys to his apartment (which she kept in an envelope until the day she died). She bought his shirts and socks for him; her notation of his neck, sleeve, and sock size was transferred to each of her yearly calendars throughout 1961–65. She stocked the Stevenson refrigerator, organized his social life. Thus did domesticity arise like a soufflé between them, embracing them in its frothy warmth.

They also traveled frequently together on UN business. The meetings of ECOSOC in Geneva every summer extended deliciously into other places in Europe: the Aga Khan's villa in Gstaad; Buffie Ives's Villa Capponi in Florence; Rome; Paris; Copenhagen, where Bill Blair was now U.S. ambassador. For Marietta, those summers in Europe with Adlai and the other delegates were unforgettable. "We would go off to small restaurants on the lake, and drink a great deal of wine and laugh and tell national jokes and get to know each other. It was a thoroughly delightful period."

And when they did not see each other, they continued their intimacy by letter. Adlai was a compulsive letter writer, and Marietta was eager to match his output. She marked her envelopes to him "Personal Please," to mask the incriminating messages pulsating within. They frequently harked back to the many lovers' memories, code words, and gifts that had accumulated between them since 1958. From Barbados at the beginning of 1961, she wrote, "Mrs. J writes that she is a perfect vise [sic] of sentimentality. Worse than ever. She puts on the same Palm Sunday dress and makes a pilgrimage to the Temple. She never removes S.F. and twirls it dervishly. She dreams of J. *all* night—not to speak of the day. . . ." (Letters frequently referred to "the Temple"—

in Barbados—and "S.F.," evidently jewelry of some kind.) In one letter she signed off, "I know a bank where the wild thyme grows, and keep enclosing myself in the dream of it."

She continually sounded the familiar theme of her unworthiness, and marveled at her good luck. Humble in the presence of Adlai's idealism, as she was humble once in the presence of Ronnie's worldliness, she poured out her gratitude. ". . . On arrival here, thank heaven, was missive from J, suggesting coordination of all matters ec. soc. and pol. I am serious when I say it's the greatest honor ever accorded me, and I hardly dare to think of my blessings as I want to deserve them. With R's [Richardson's] inspiration and help I can try, because as you point out, it is more than a need, it's a necessity. . . ."

For both of them in their busy careers, meetings were critical. ". . . Mostly I want to know," Adlai wrote, "if you know whether Mrs. Johnson is planning to go to Desbarats, Ontario, over Labor Day, with Richardson and Hermon Smiths [lifelong friends and supporters of Stevenson]. I was thinking of August 31–Sept 4? There's a cabin in the pine woods by the blue lake she wanted to see sometime, and I could arrange it with the others. . . ." Marietta was more specific about her longing to be with him. "Don't know if Rich. can survive next 12 days, but she's sustained by state of N.J. [New Jersey, a code expression for being alone with each other] last week. . . ."

On Marietta's forty-fifth birthday, in 1962, he wrote to her:

45—! For *me* it was a beginning—San Francisco, London, New York, Illinois—and you.
    For you—I dream it is a beginning too—for *us*. And that I must be away hurts so. . . .

Adlai kept a stockpile of poems and meditations on love that he would send to (and receive from) his women friends. (He also kept their love letters. Some were found in a drawer by his bed in the Waldorf Towers after he died. "Tender bits," he called them.) "M— In the anguish of that sleepless night I took refuge—as I sometimes do—in my golden books. I found this—which I wanted to read to you—in the joy of *last* night." He then quoted some lines from "Burnt Norton"—the first of T. S. Eliot's *Four Quartets*—that Adlai cited several times, often underlining it: "Human kind cannot bear very much reality." (At Christmas that year he sent the lines to her again, asking, "Have I sent you that before?")

Sometimes he sent her little observations on love by famous people: "Nietzsche: There is always folly in love. But there is always reason in the folly. . . . Have you never said yes to joy? Then, my friends, you have said yes to all suffering. All things are enchained, entangled, united by love." He would add his own amusing stanzas:

*Hunger perhaps may cure your love,*
*Or time your passion greatly alter;*
*If both should unsuccessful prove*
*I strongly recommend a halter.*

". . . It is hard to work—I can't set paper to pencil or vice versa —or subdue the desire to read—unless it be to write bits to you. Is the price of rich reverie poor production? A."

He once sent her a Valentine with two attached hearts, adding the note: "Curious malformation, giving rise to acute pain and great exhilaration . . . probably incurable." Copying Adlai's writing style, Marietta would also find quotations to impress him in her letters, such as this one from E. M. Forster: "Life is indeed dangerous, but not in the way morality would have us believe. It is unmanageable because it is a Romance, and its essence is Romantic beauty."

There are few overtly sexual references in his letters, and none, not surprisingly, from modest Marietta. Occasionally, Adlai would feel pleased enough with himself to make an allusion to the physical side, ending one letter, for instance, "Johnson—who shrinks day by day— and loves it." On another occasion, a penciled poem rhymes "con- cupescent" with "recent," adding, "And this I'll now confess—Let us forever concupess!" They also had a private joke about three French hens and a rooster. But more often the communications are romantic rather than erotic in nature.

Adlai's sexual orientation has often been called into question. Though his homosexuality has generally been ruled out as a political canard, there is no question that he gave ambiguous signals at best. Harold Nicolson went to a reception for him in London in 1953, and made this note in his diary: ". . . A heavy man, with slim body, but heavy appearance, reddish face, alert eyes, a rather prancing manner— in fact a deception."[1] Isaiah Berlin was also uneasy in his presence, remarking, "He was vain. I felt he was embarrassing."[2]

Adlai had a strong exhibitionist streak. Marietta was only one of many who saw him take his clothes off in an unexpectedly uninhibited fashion. He liked other people's nakedness, too. Mary Bingham re- membered once when Stevenson was visiting Louisville, he was work- ing on a speech in the garden when her daughter teasingly told him there was a naked woman in the drawing room. Stevenson dropped everything and rushed inside, only to find she was referring to a Fujita painting of a nude. Arthur Schlesinger agreed with Marietta that he was curiously "free" in that sense; "really an 'inner-directed' type, but of course, doomed to the self-questioning, conscience, Calvinism, etc., which goes with this type; so that the 'freedom' is superb when attained, but either comes at the end of a struggle or else breeds feelings of guilt."

Guilt was surely at the heart of much of Stevenson's behavior. Schlesinger believed that the childhood shooting accident left him with a profound feeling of unworthiness that he could never eradicate. His hesitancy about running for office, despite proven support, was a symptom of his low self-esteem. Guilt about his divorce and the effect on his children haunted him throughout his life. And although no reference to it ever appears in his letters, one wonders how he felt about his long affair with the wife of one of his friends, Ronnie Tree. "I don't think Adlai was ever happy," Dorothy Schiff said. "He was fundamentally a very discontented man—discontented with himself—and no matter how much adulation he got from the people he admired, he still lacked self-confidence."

For many men suffering from this malaise, chalking up female conquests is at best a temporary therapy. That he enjoyed occasional physical intimacy with his women friends is indisputable. But the importance of their presence seems to have been more psychological than physical. Betty Beale, a Washington journalist, who revealed in her memoirs *Power at Play* that she had been an intimate friend of Adlai's from 1962, said that her nights with him were as often celibate as sexual.[3] Alicia Patterson told Dorothy Schiff that "with Adlai, sex is not urgent."[4]

Yet Stevenson had one outstanding quality that set him apart from most other men of his class and generation—he took women seriously. Thanks in part to the powerful influence of his mother and sister, he had always been comfortable in the company of women, whom he treated as equals. He listened to them, encouraged them, and respected them. Whenever possible, he gave them jobs and then promoted them. In those sexually repressive years of the 1950s and early 1960s, such lack of prejudice was both rare and refreshing, and that is largely why so many strong, intelligent women found him irresistible.

In one of his longest letters to Marietta, Stevenson described a dinner at the White House where he sat next to Jacqueline Kennedy, who admired him greatly. At this dinner, even Jackie felt at ease enough in his company to confide in him. She told Adlai how her Catholicism was very indifferent until she married into the Kennedy family. ("Daddy only went to church to see if he could find a pretty girl.") And she added, "Lee and I always talked about divorce as practically something to look forward to." She also said she didn't care how many girls Jack had, "as long as she knows he knows it's wrong [Adlai added two exclamation points here] and I think he does now. Anyway, that's all over for the president. . . ." Adlai was the kind of man on whom such confessions were often bestowed, and he clearly enjoyed the intimacy it implied. (Stevenson and Jackie kept up a lightly flirtatious correspondence throughout the UN years.) The point is, of course, as well as the mutual respect, this was also safe sex. His epistolary romances were as satisfying as the real thing.

Adlai's sexual blandness seems to have suited Marietta. Like many of Adlai's married women friends, Marietta was (conveniently) not always available, and thus their relationship hinged more on romantic yearnings than on physical pleasure. Nor is there evidence that she pushed for a more erotic relationship. Raised to prudishness about sex, Marietta remained squeamish to the end of her days. This is borne out most vividly in her inability to grapple with the subject with her children. Having failed to help Frankie out with the birds and the bees, she was hardly more forthcoming with Penelope, who remembered being in her bath in the company of Mabel, when Marietta swept in wearing an evening dress. "What is the difference between boys and girls?" Marietta briskly asked her daughter. Penelope, who always felt stupid around her mother, could not think of an answer, and muttered something about girls having longer hair. "No! Boys have penises and girls have vaginas." And with that, Marietta swept out again. "That was my sex education," said Penelope.

Bill Walton, who was one of Marietta's closest friends, used to go to the movies regularly with her, and at the promise of any steamy flesh scenes she would insist on leaving. He remembered going to a film with her in which Gérard Depardieu appeared as a transvestite. Marietta nudged him. "We have to go. Can't stay here." Bill dutifully got up and they went across the hall to another movie, about the Argentine ballet. After a while the heroine lifted up her tutu and a man began to fondle her. Came the nudge. "Bill, we must go." (At this point he called it quits and they went home and had dinner.) Walton volunteered more evidence why he felt she was not a sexual person. "Most people you are cozy with you touch, hug, cuddle sometimes. You never touched her."[5]

But then there was the wild card, John Huston. Frank Taylor, who observed the two during the days of Marietta's filming on *The Misfits,* thought they were clearly sleeping together. "This was completely understood by the crew. Of course," he added, "every woman who visited John Huston on the set was assumed to be sleeping with him." It's doubtful that Taylor was right on this occasion. At the time, Marietta was totally focused on Stevenson and had just left his side. But Huston drove up the temperature between them in a way that was almost palpable.

Adlai's attitude was the opposite from Huston's: cerebral rather than physical, introspective rather than extrovert, doubt-filled and self-conscious rather than confident. Writing to Marietta from New York in April 1963, after a week spent together in Spain, which included her birthday, Adlai remembered: "M—tomorrow is Easter—and the memory is vivid. I've relived it all this Holy Week. Palm Sunday I walked in the fields at Crawfield, warm with the first hint of spring in the thickening treetops—and wondered where you were at 11.30— on a hill bathed in hotter sun?" At the end of this letter, he urged her to return from Barbados, saying, "Besides, there are still unused cans and jars in the cupboard. Why did you get that jar of [illegible] pears? I think I'll sneak down tonight and eat them—a sort of communion."

A year later, Easter once again heightened the emotional climate between them. From Barbados on Palm Sunday, Marietta wrote: "I have just returned from the shrine at Porters swamped with emotion. Something must be done to bring the Richardsons together for ever. Present circs. are not good enough. . . ."

By the middle of 1963, they had reached a point where their future was becoming the critical issue. On June 19, 1963, Adlai wrote to Marietta: "Darling mine—thank God for your letter. . . . I was beginning to get that awful panic again. . . . Think of little else save Mrs. J in spite of vigorous, cruel, mental exercises to prepare for all eventualities. . . ."

Adlai, in this letter, also felt vulnerable enough to write, "Repeated talk about MT's divorce and marriage to Mr. Clark by 3 new communicants." ("Mr. Clark" was Blair Clark, the handsome, witty former campaign manager for Averell Harriman, then running CBS News. He was quite frequently an extra man for Marietta, while more seriously wooing Lillian Hellman, a very different lady, who was as irked by Mrs. Tree as Adlai was by Mr. Clark.[6] "Can't stand it much longer," Adlai went on. "The divorce residence—Mexico only quick one, valid in N.Y. if there is consent to divorce by other party, property settlement and no contest."

This sounds like a couple on the brink. But they did not jump.

On July 2, 1963, Alicia Patterson died. Stevenson was in Paris. He sent a telegram to her husband, Harry Guggenheim, saying, "She was my oldest dearest friend. Returning if possible." He did not return, however, and the funeral took place in Chicago without him. If Marietta hoped Alicia's death would release him in some way, she was disappointed. While in Paris, he telephoned a new friend, Sarah Plimpton, and they arranged to meet two weeks later in Milan. Sarah, a young poet and artist working on a magazine in Paris, was a friend of Frankie's (Sarah Plimpton's father, Francis T. P. Plimpton, was Adlai's closest colleague at the UN), and Adlai had become very taken with her. (". . . A couple of delicious hours on the lake in the afternoon with that extraordinary Sarah—who just might be a unique writer," he told Marietta with his usual tact.)

Meanwhile, on July 1, Marietta arrived in Geneva for the ECO-

SOC meetings. Adlai joined her on July 4 and they spent the weekend together at the Aga Khan's chalet in Gstaad and then another two days there during the following week. Then Adlai went on to Francis Plimpton's villa on Lake Como, having joined up with Sarah Plimpton in Milan. He spent a brief two days with this new interest before he was called back to Washington to discuss Angola and South Africa with Kennedy.

Marietta went on to Florence to meet Ronnie and Penelope, then the family moved on as usual to Venice. At the end of this crazy month, she received a little dagger from a disgruntled Adlai: "You are in Venice . . . and full, no doubt, of comforting memories of conjugal felicity. For me it has been a bad fortnight. . . ."

That Adlai and Marietta could have carried on this kind of war of nerves as well as fulfilling their political and social responsibilities at the United Nations is extraordinary. Between September 1962 and May 1963, Marietta was on four different committees of the United Nations—U.S. delegate on the Third Committee of the 17th General Assembly (and chairman of the western caucus of the Third Committee, which met nearly every day for the three and one half months during the 17th General Assembly); U.S. Representative to the UN Human Rights Commission; Acting U.S. Representative to the Committee on Non-Self-Governing Territories; and chairman of the UN subcommittee on the celebration of the fifteenth anniversary of the Universal Declaration of Human Rights.

In these months, she gave thirty press interviews and made approximately fifty speeches live, on radio or television, including addresses to the Council of World Affairs, the United Church Women, the League of Women Voters, the Colony Club, the *Herald Tribune* Forum, the YWCA, the National Women's Democratic Club, and the National Urban League. She gave a dance at the U.S. Mission for five hundred delegates, press, and advisers, and entertained hundreds more at her home. She was on the road for much of the year.

With the escalating war in Vietnam, Adlai, meanwhile, was involved in one of the most serious political and international crises his country had ever faced. Yet in the midst of these compelling problems, he could pause to scribble a poem to one of his female correspondents. Shuttling between New York and Washington, he found time to entertain Elizabeth Taylor and Archibald MacLeish and go to endless late night parties. George Ball called those last years of Adlai's in New York, surrounded by women and going through the motions of doing his UN job, "an unhealthy business."

After President Kennedy was killed, Adlai's position deteriorated. Although hopeful of good relations with Lyndon Johnson, Stevenson discovered that the new president had little respect for the UN Ambassador. ("The trouble with Adlai is that when he goes to the bathroom he has to squat," was one of Johnson's observations.)[7] The parties and late nights continued while Stevenson's health and political career slowly declined. Yet in 1964, in spite of the disdain emanating from the White House, Stevenson once more started toying with the idea of high office. Vice president? Senator from New York, Illinois? Although many of his friends found these suggestions inappropriate, he seemed to wish seriously to consider such options.

But as the problems in Southeast Asia began to build, Stevenson removed himself more and more from the crises confronting him at the United Nations. In January 1964 he went to Jamaica to stay with the Dicks, taking with him Sarah Plimpton. (Jane Dick was very unhappy with this visit, witnessing her beloved friend paying court to someone over thirty years his junior.) In March, Stevenson vacationed on Agnes Meyer's yacht in the West Indies, and in May, Marietta joined him for a cruise around the Mediterranean with Ricardo Sicre as host. Also on board was Ava Gardner, to whom Stevenson, needless to say, took a fancy—"Strange, lovely, lush girl." The press learned of their time together and quickly claimed they were an "item," which Stevenson laughed off, but was obviously flattered by it. At the end of the cruise, Marietta and Adlai flew to Rome. They spent one night there before Adlai went on to Stockholm, where again he met Sarah Plimpton, and Marietta traveled on alone to Teheran, Kabul, Beirut, Cairo, and Algiers, on Human Rights business.

It is not clear if Marietta knew that Stevenson was having this rendezvous with Sarah, but it would be in character for him somehow to have let the information drop. Anyway, now for the first time, she seems to have begun to unravel. Stevenson's persistent liaisons with other women, and in particular with one only four years older than Marietta's daughter, combined with the endless separations and the continued uncertainty about the future, finally began to take their toll. Arriving at the Park Hotel in Teheran, Marietta revealed her insecurity with uncharacteristic pathos: "Feel like a child who has left home for the first time, homesick and lonely, worried about Penelope, deprived of her and all my family, and above all nostalgia for J. and the week that was. A week that was joy unconfined and happiness distilled, and only marred by the knowledge that it had to end."

In spite of being well entertained in Iran, meeting junior cabinet officials and attending conferences, she could not shake her feeling of abandonment. It became so acute that she begged Adlai to send a wire requesting that she return home from Cairo instead of going on to Algiers. Not hearing from him, she became desperate. She sent a telegram saying that Mrs. Richardson missed him, and followed it up with another: "Please cable Kabul information on Mr. Richardson."

Adlai never sent for her. His response was, as usual, a masterpiece of solipsism:

> Your letter from Persia has come and if you have felt miserable and alone so have I—and now I feel desperate, frustrated, angry and irritable. To think of all those adventures in places I've never been—without me!! It seems such a waste. So does every day—every moment. . . . Then my mind goes leaping back over the years, not to the things we've done *together,* but to the things *you've* done without me and *I* without you, and all the little things we've done *together* get crushed under the weight of the other things,—and I feel worse. I guess I *really* am *sick*—perhaps for the first time. . . .

Stevenson wrote this letter from London, another place haunted for them both. "I went to the Bensons for 20 minutes and inspected the rooms where you are to live! Oh, hell, I'm going through it all again, and it never gets easier—only worse and worse. What are the limits of endurance? What is reason? Madness?" He then described some of his London activities, ". . . and here I am writing you, as usual, and nursing my perpetual malaise. . . . I dream of summer seas, without Ava Gardner, and eternity with Mrs. R. . . . A."

He wrote a postscript to this letter: "Just read foregoing and am embarrassed. Please disregard all plaintive moaning—I was weary yesterday. . . ."

Not entirely reconciled, Marietta pressed on dutifully to Cairo and Algiers, and ended up in London (missing Adlai), where she was with Ronnie and Penelope until mid-July. Then she flew to Sweden to stay with Lars Schmidt and his wife, Ingrid Bergman, before going on to Geneva for ECOSOC. But to her great disappointment, owing to the political situation at home, Adlai could not attend the meetings. At this time of tension and strain in their relationship, Adlai's decision not to go to Geneva caused one of the most serious rifts between them. Marietta sent him a telegram: "Town ghost ridden please exorcize. Mary E." She also telephoned him, which was a disaster. Adlai wrote her a long angry letter at 2:00 A.M. "I'm desolate, lonely and tired—and the *last* thing I should be doing is writing this to you. But there is one thing I must say—when I said I wasn't coming to Geneva —that I thought it best for both of us. . . ." He went on to explain that with Plimpton leaving, Charles Yost (Stevenson's deputy in the Security Council) away, the financial negotiations with the Russians starting again, there were very practical reasons for not coming.

"I think you know—or *thought* you knew what's in my heart— so I asked you to please, please write me every day. Your sharp and petulant reply—a note I've often heard before—that in view of what I had said you didn't think you should, stunned me. I knew you would be disappointed (and what do you think *I* feel!) but I assumed you would sense and respect my reasons and give me understanding and love, not resentment. . . ."

Marietta was filled with self-recrimination. "I am so v. sorry we put ourselves and each other through these ghastly black pits from which there never seems to be egress when one is in them. . . . I imagine with such heights, there are bound to be depths, but I wish the depths could be better understood at the time and thus lose their horror. . . ."

Adlai in his turn then rushed to conciliate, telling her how much he would love to come to Geneva after all. "But I mustn't—I can't go on plotting, planning my whole life around our meetings. For so long I've dreamed of living with you all the time; yet for more than a year now I've *known* I had to *learn* to live without you for long stretches; I've got to learn now *not* to count days, weeks, hours. . . ." He told her how busy he was, how tired all the time, how the mail piled up, how the Russia, Cyprus, Congo issues were escalating. And he added a desperate P.S.:

> I haven't needed you so much in at best 4 years! But please don't worry about *anything*—just pet the heart that's in your hand from time to time—and *write! write! write!* Also account for *every* evening—and try to spend an occasional one *alone* in bed reading and asleep early. Don't remind me of the ghosts, *they've devoured me already. Telephone calls are shattering—but again please!*

Thrilled by this letter, which Harlan Cleveland delivered personally in Geneva, she felt confident of his love once more. "It's so nice to feel that you need me as well as Arethusa and the girls" (a joke between them referring to Adlai's many other female admirers). She was again concerned about his complaints of exhaustion. *"Be sensible, darling heart, I need years in the future with you. . . ."* So Marietta wrote every three or four days from Geneva, describing the meetings and holding Stevenson's heart tight. Then, in a state of emotional exhaustion, she returned to the Villa Capponi, where she somehow resumed her role in her other life with Ronnie and Penelope.

The end of 1964 saw Adlai and Marietta once more united in New York and Libertyville. In late October they flew to Santiago, Chile, together, as official representatives at the inauguration of President Eduardo Frei. They returned on November 6 and between meetings and parties there were a few stolen nights of "N.J. with Johnson." On November 21, Ronnie returned from a long trip abroad. That morning, Marietta had an appointment with Dr. Bonnett, her first for over two years. On December 19, Marietta flew to Barbados, and Stevenson spent Christmas with his family in Libertyville.

During a brief respite over the holidays, Adlai went shooting with his son Borden at the Field plantation in South Carolina, and remembered that happy moment seven years earlier with Marietta. Afterward, he wrote to her telling her how much the memory meant to him. "I was beneath the pine tree—giving thanks for her love and loyalty, her comfort and counsel, her goodness and gallantry; and thanking God for these years of joy and peace that are only sharpened by doubt and despair."

How vividly the ambivalence of his feelings emerges from these words. The push-pull of their relationship, the endless meetings and partings, the demands of their other lives, created a fault line between them that seemed always poised to erupt. They were so alike in some ways: they were both insecure; they both liked to laugh (although Adlai's humor seemed to vanish in most of his letters to her); they both loved the admiration of the opposite sex; and they both resonated to the energy and joie de vivre in the other. "Why is it you vibrate even when you're still? Are you really ever still?" he wrote to her in 1964. "I don't think so—except in those dead sleeps. The fires are always burning in your restless mind, tireless body and troubled heart. Serenity, peace at the end for us; the thought is soothing, the prospects disturbing." How did he and Marietta think they could pull off a life together in the midst of such turmoil and complexity, with the country stumbling headlong into a disastrous war and their own lives beginning to spin out of control?

In the event, they never got the chance.

# CHAPTER *27*

# *"Keep your head high"*

An avalanche of press coverage followed Marietta's progress at the United Nations. Apart from the anti-Semitism episode, it was not human rights that gave the journalists their stories. It was the society and feature writers who had a field day with the fascinating Mrs. Tree. "Our Glamor Lady at the U.N.: Promoter, Hostess, Linguist" . . . "Stamina, Empathy, Beauty at the U.N." . . . "Patrician with a Mission" were some of the headlines. Reporters on the women's pages doted on her slender elegance ("a fresh island of beauty in that great sea of men," as quoted by one UN delegate); her designer clothes ("Classically draped, green silk jersey gown, designed in Paris by Mme. Grès, is typical of timeless fashion she prefers"); and her hair ("Her coiffure is a modified bouffant style, not unlike that of the President's wife").

The photographs accompanying these profiles showed her either looking serious in a suit and a three-string pearl necklace (a favorite piece of jewelry) or smiling in a glamorous ball gown with a spray of diamonds (another favorite) pinned at the low point of her generous cleavage. In the photographs she was often the only woman in a sea of men, her bare shoulders and fair features making a striking contrast to the black African diplomats on her committee with whom she frequently posed. If the diplomats were short of stature, as they invariably were, she would tactfully kick off her shoes during the picture taking to minimize her height. Occasionally she would pose at home with Penelope seated charmingly in the background, and she often made the "best dressed" or "most influential" lists of women concocted by newspapers to amuse their readers.

The journalists loved to hear about her dinner parties: "I like small dinner parties—six, eight or nine. Nine's the classic number, you know. Because that's the number of the Muses. And the ninth person determines the conversation." They devoured her menus: "First we have some sort of fish bisque or soup, or a fish entree. Then a casserole, chicken or veal with vegetables, something that won't dry up if some of the guests are late, and ice with fruit for dessert, or perhaps a deep-dish fruit pie." (Marietta was learning the importance of party food. In the back of her yearly calendars she kept recipe ideas for her cook: "smoked trout mousse with thin smoked salmon on top; green noodles, mushrooms, ham, onion . . . ; fillet of sole, shrimps, mushrooms cut fine, white sauce with cream and put in pancakes, gruyere sprinkled on top . . .")

Then there was commentary on her Episcopalian background, and her commitment to human rights and civil liberties. Ronnie was rarely mentioned except as the rich husband behind the scenes. In one interview, however, the reporter asked Marietta in Ronnie's presence if she aspired to replace Perle Mesta as the champion party giver of the Democratic Party. " 'Over my dead body,' broke in her husband."

She was invited endlessly to reveal the secrets of her success, and she obliged. "A U.N. delegate needs such qualities as massive endurance, patience and humor. . . . And we also have to learn how to live on sandwiches, coffee and nerves. . . . The simply heavenly part of my job is the chance I get to know people from iii different countries. . . . My sex has also been a help. Diplomats are very gallant by nature."

But not a word was breathed in the newspaper columns about anything more titillating. Nobody questioned her about Ronnie's absences, or her evidently close friendship with Adlai Stevenson. (Many UN delegates had their suspicions. "It was hands off Marietta because she was Adlai's," recalled Iraqi ambassador Adnan Pachachi much later. "We all knew.") If people at the United Nations knew, most of the outside world, including close friends, had no conception of the extent of Marietta's double life.

It was easier to be discreet in those days, and Marietta's public image as aristocratic diplomat, along with her composed and haughty bearing, represented for the press the essence of Yankee probity. Moreover, Marietta was very careful. She always feared gossip. (What would her parents say?) There were the occasional inevitable rumors. While Adlai was receiving the gossip about Mr. Clark, Penelope, to her horror and shock, overheard at school a remark about her parents divorcing. But these murmurs never reached the gossip columns, and they never named Stevenson.

It is almost impossible for us today to accept that Marietta's presence at Adlai's side at almost every UN event, both official and private, both at home and abroad, did not arouse the tabloids' interest. Yet it must be remembered that the newspapers also remained silent about John F. Kennedy's noisy private life. The culture of personal revelation was simply not yet as developed as it became by the end of the century. The English journalist Ernestine Carter probably summed up best the image that Marietta projected at that time: "Mrs. Tree combines her enjoyment of life with a genuine dedication to service. 'What I would like to do some day is to teach but now I'll give you a lift. I've got to dash home and change for a reception.' "[1]

But beneath this breezy facade, the tormented affair continued to haunt the participants' sleep. The parties and trips were so demanding that in her 1965 diary, Marietta began to make tiny notations of what nights Stevenson would be busy (i.e., unable to see her privately).

In 1965, the Vietnam crisis escalated. There was a flurry of diplomatic maneuvering, led by Stevenson and Secretary-General U Thant at the United Nations, but it did not amount to anything. Adlai left for a vacation on Avery Island with Marietta, and during that spring they managed several evenings at 42A, including Easter Sunday. On May 23, Marietta went to Africa for meetings with the Committee of Twenty-Four and did not return to New York until June 17.

Meanwhile, that June, Stevenson went to the UN twentieth anniversary celebrations in San Francisco. President Johnson also attended. According to Brian Urquhart, who was present in his role as assistant to U Thant, Stevenson foolishly told *New York Times* reporter James Reston that LBJ had been advised by Stevenson's staff members to make a speech shifting his Vietnam policy. This story, needless to say, appeared in the newspaper of record. "LBJ was incandescent with rage," recalled Urquhart, "and stayed on Air Force One to be too late for the speech, to show contempt, and also in the process to ruin a lunch in his honor." Later, Johnson called a meeting with U Thant, and as the Secretary-General and Brian Urquhart arrived, "Stevenson flew out, practically in tears." The president had thrown him out of the meeting.[2] From this humiliation Stevenson flew back to New York and then Libertyville, where Marietta joined him for two days on the farm. "He always went from these bruising experiences to a strong woman," Urquhart noted.

On July 3, Marietta flew to England for the annual summer in Europe with Ronnie and Penelope, missing the ECOSOC meetings. On July 9, Adlai flew from Geneva to Paris to have dinner with Sarah Plimpton and the Harrimans, at which Sarah felt he ate and drank too much. He asked Sarah if she would go with him to visit his sister at the Villa Capponi in Florence after his trip to London, but Sarah had arranged a trip to Brittany and could not go. She never saw him again.

The next day Stevenson flew to England, spent the day with Prime

Minister Harold Wilson at Chequers, then on to Oxford for the night. On Sunday, he drove to the American Embassy in London. That night, Katharine Graham, proprietor of *The Washington Post,* who was also staying at the embassy, arranged to meet him after he had appeared on a television program and attended a buffet supper given by the BBC. She said later that he had a crush on her and had come to London partly to see her.[3] (Another mother/daughter twist: Mrs. Graham's mother, Agnes Meyer, had been closely connected to Stevenson for years.) He went to her room that night and stayed "for at least an hour," in Mrs. Graham's veiled recollection, leaving behind his tie and his glasses.[4] On Monday, Marietta canceled a lunch with Pamela Berry and Kay Graham to have lunch with Adlai in a pub. On Tuesday, she walked with him in Hyde Park, and they dined together at the Berrys'. On Wednesday afternoon, the 14th, she went to Claridge's Hotel, where Bill Benton was staying, to pick up Adlai for a walk. Benton was leaving for New York, and Stevenson asked him if he could have the key to Benton's suite "for some afternoon appointments."

When Marietta met Adlai at the hotel, he was reading a letter from Jane Dick. (After he died, Marietta generously thought to tell Jane that. Twenty-four years later, Jane still remembered and was grateful.) As they walked out of the hotel together, Adlai turned in Benton's key, saying he did not need the suite after all, and would save Benton some money.

Marietta told Stevenson's biographer, John Bartlow Martin, what happened next in a carefully worded letter, clearly aware that it would be the story of record.

> At the beginning of our walk Stevenson wanted to show me the house where he had lived during the war in a mews near Grosvenor Square. The house had been demolished and in its place was rather a modern building. Stevenson looked at it and sighed, "That makes me feel very old." We then proceeded toward Hyde Park past the American Embassy on Upper Grosvenor Street. A lot of people were walking slowly on the sidewalk impeding our progress. I ducked around them walking in the gutter as did he. When we got in front of the strollers, he asked me to slow down as he felt very tired and then said, "Keep your head high." I don't know why.
>
> We were then a few feet away and he said to me, "I am going to faint." I looked into an open back door of a building hoping to find a box for him to sit on until the faintness passed, and I felt his arm brush mine and he fell backward on the pavement like a felled forest oak. The crash was so terrible I thought he had fractured his skull. I first ran into what turned

out to be the Sportsmen's Club and asked them to telephone for a doctor. I then returned to him on the street and tried to give him some water and had covered him with a blanket or coat that had been given me.

I knelt beside him helplessly until a stranger came along who said he was a heart doctor and started massaging his heart and instructed me in mouth-to-mouth resuscitation. After a while, he started breathing again. I then asked a stranger to send for David Bruce [U.S. ambassador] but did not say who had fallen because I did not think Adlai would want it published that he had fainted. When a guard from the Embassy finally appeared without Bruce, I told him to send for Philip Kaiser [a minister at the embassy] and that Marietta Tree wanted him to come as soon as possible.

Kaiser arrived about the same time as the doctor and the ambulance that I had sent for. Stevenson was put into the ambulance and we all got in after him. He was still breathing. Just as the ambulance started to go off, I looked at the spot where he had fallen and saw a good many pink Confidential State Department papers and rushed back to get them. A few minutes after we had arrived at St. George's Hospital, the doctor told Phil Kaiser and me that AES had died.

Then Kaiser and I returned to the U.S. Embassy and met Kay Graham and [Eric] Sevareid on the steps, who obviously had already heard the terrible news. We all went up silently to David Bruce's office where I described what had happened to him and his wife Evangeline.[5]

In her diary, she simply wrote, underlined: "5:30. Adlai is dead. We were together."

Later, Marietta returned to the flat Ronnie had rented for the month. David and Evangeline Bruce had dinner that night with the Trees. "Marietta had perfect control," Evangeline recalled, "although we knew her heart was broken. Penelope asked a question about Adlai and Marietta gave her a gentle résumé of his life and work. It was extraordinary." However, in front of Ronnie and Penelope alone she wept uncontrollably. "I felt so sorry for my father," Penelope said.

The news spread swiftly. Frankie, in Athens, could not reach her mother by telephone so sat down and wrote a letter full of love and understanding: "It must have been worse for you than anyone." Sam Peabody was sightseeing in Siena when he saw newspaper photographs of Adlai and Marietta with the huge headline: "MORTE!" He thought his sister was dead. Endicott Peabody flew to London to accompany Marietta home. He went on the presidential plane with

Vice President Hubert Humphrey, Richard Daley, George Ball, Willard Wirtz, and Stevenson's three sons. In her need, Marietta for a moment let down her guard when her brother arrived. Desperate for reassurance, she described for him the place where Stevenson had fallen. "She felt she should have caught him." Endicott visited Grosvenor Square and talked to the nearby building staff. He then returned and assured his sister that she could not have saved Stevenson.

There was a brief ceremony at the American Embassy with Marietta looking frozen with grief. "Beautiful, black and stricken," was how Sir Philip Adams (later director of the Ditchley Foundation) put it. The following day the body was flown back to Washington. There was a funeral service at National Cathedral, with President Johnson and other senior officials attending. In Washington, Marietta stayed with the Schlesingers, along with two other of Adlai's "widows," as Arthur Schlesinger called them—Jane Gunther and Lauren Bacall. (Even Marietta managed a laugh at "Arethusa and the girls" collected round the funeral bier.) Then Stevenson's family and friends took his body to Springfield, where he lay in state before being buried in Bloomington. Marietta followed him every step of the way on the long journey to his final resting place.

After the burial, Marietta flew back to New York with Ruth Field and went to Caumsett, Long Island. As soon as she got there, with typical thoughtfulness, she invited Stevenson's three UN assistants— Norma Garaventa, Roxane Eberlein, and Judy Davidoff—out to the Marshall Field estate for a picnic. "There was a lovely swimming pool but we didn't feel like swimming," Norma Garaventa remembered. "Mrs. Tree told us that she had tried to drown her sorrows with drink, but could not get drunk. Her doctor explained that drink did not work in these situations."[6] Perhaps the worst moment in the aftermath of that terrible week was returning to 42A, a painful task she accomplished that Saturday in the company of Roxane, Viola, and Adlai III.

For the next few days, she found comfort in the presence of Clayton Fritchey and stayed up late grieving with him. She had a drink with Jane Gunther, lunch with Dorothy Hirshon, and meetings with Arthur Goldberg, who had already been named as successor to Stevenson at the United Nations. She asked her loyal friend and secretary Ceil Wentz to come back from vacation. But perhaps the friend who helped her most was Susan Mary ("S.M. so sweet and helpful," she noted in her calendar). Susan Mary's presence was particularly important. Bill Patten had finally died after a long fight with asthma in 1960, and a year later Susan Mary married Patten's close friend, the political journalist Joseph Alsop, and moved to Washington. Alsop was no great admirer of Stevenson's and had written some controversial columns about the governor, which did not sit well with Marietta, and for a while the friendship between the two women had cooled. But now, Susan Mary rushed to her friend's side and any bad feelings vanished.

On Monday, July 26, Susan Mary accompanied Marietta to Paris to spend a few days there before joining Ronnie in Florence. She stayed at the U.S. Embassy. Evangeline Bruce was also a guest at the embassy, and she and Susan Mary spent nights staying up with Marietta as she talked and talked about Stevenson. That icy self-control had finally cracked. "She was deeply shaken," recalled Susan Mary. "I had never seen her so completely without her armor. There was even talk of suicide. For the four days she was in Paris, I never took my eyes off her. I thought she would jump into the Seine."

On Saturday, July 31, Susan Mary and Marietta took the day flight to Florence. Marietta was still distraught. "It was awful," Susan Mary said. "She stayed in her room all the time, writing letters, while a house party went on outside. It was very hard on Ronnie. I thought it would be the end of the marriage." Other visitors vividly remember that ghastly summer. Sam Peabody, who went to see his sister, was shocked at the sight of her. "She was skin and bone. She never left her room. Ronnie was very patient."

On July 19, at the memorial ceremony for Stevenson held at the Assembly Hall of the United Nations, Adlai's friend, the poet Archibald MacLeish, said: "What we have lost, as he said of his friend Mrs. Roosevelt, is not his life. He lived that out, if not to the full, at least more fully than almost any other man. What we have lost is himself. And who can name the warmth and richness of it?"

What had Marietta lost in losing Adlai? There were several basic differences between them. Right from the start, his political position, while stemming from the same elitist origins, appeared conservative in comparison to hers. ("He thought I was just misled," she said.) His fuzzy morality on issues such as race remained discouraging to someone of her clear-eyed commitment. "I was irritated," she admitted later, "because of his views on civil rights and Arab-Israel affairs—they were not my views."

Marietta early scented a whiff of anti-Semitism in the governor and called him on it. "Why do you always have to say a 'Jewish' banker?" she would ask him. (He was careful with her after that, but in a letter to Ronnie, who had asked him if he knew any financial backers for business in the British West Indies, Adlai wrote, "I occasionally run into people with investment curiosity about B.W.I.—frequently Jewish (and I would not dare mention that to Marietta!)."

But just as she had closed her eyes to the disturbing aspects of Ronnie's way of life, so she ignored these trivial flaws and concentrated instead on the hero of her dreams and hope of her future. Would they actually have married? After six years of intimacy, they seemed no closer to it at the end than at the beginning. Mary Warburg once said to him, "Why don't you marry Marietta?" To which he replied, "I would if she were free." Mrs. Warburg then added as an aside, "But of course he wouldn't."[7]

Did he really want to marry anyone? Adlai's sons recalled their father going over a list of potential wives with them. Adlai III thought Marietta was a front-runner. Adlai's second son, Borden, had more concrete evidence. When staying in his father's apartment at the Waldorf Towers, he overheard his father and Marietta discussing marriage. They discussed wedding dates and how to tell Ronnie, a problem that Adlai in particular flinched from. Marietta said she would give up Ronnie's money, and that she had $20,000 in the bank.

Ah, money. The familiar stumbling block. Ronnie was a gentleman in the old-fashioned sense, and would probably allow her to divorce him. But owing to the terms of Ronnie's trust, there was no hope of a large payoff. In 1964, her father made over to her a gift of $6,000 in addition to an earlier gift that year. She was grateful, first, "because I realize that it is quite a sacrifice for you and Mother. . . . Second, you know my need for security or capital in the future." She went on to tell them how she had invested the earlier sum and "I have about 13 or 14 thousand dollars in my account. This is remarkable to me, having had *no* capital a year ago, rather like the parable of the talents. . . ." So, by 1964 she was trying to save. Was this for some particular purpose?

Adlai liked money and the lifestyle it offered. He proposed marriage once to Brooke Astor, on a mountain climb in Northeast Harbor, Maine. "I knew he was hard up," she recalled, amused. "I told him he did not love me. He agreed, but said we were good friends and he hoped we might take it a little further." Mrs. Astor declined, but they remained friends. "I still walk past the rock where he talked about it."[8] As a married man, how could he have gone on enjoying the free ride given him by his rich women friends—the cruises, the plantations, the villas throughout Europe where he was always so welcome? He was tight with money. He never paid for anything if he could help it. In this way, he shared the Peabody frugality gene, and together, he and Marietta might have come to some agreement. But the sacrifices were very great.

Perhaps too great. Even with Marietta, Adlai was frequently distant. His selfishness emerged in all sorts of little ways. For instance, he escorted Marietta to President Johnson's inauguration, but at the inaugural ball he found there was only one seat left in the presidential box, which he took, leaving Marietta to fend for herself.

His chief manipulative weapon, of course, was his womanizing.

As long as he was with Marietta, he still could not resist the pursuit of other women, keeping them on the boil with his scribbled notes, apologies for neglect, and incessant charm. And if as he got older, the standards began to slip a little, who noticed? How many did he need? On the last afternoon of his life Marietta accused him of having Pamela Berry's face powder on his jacket.

But perhaps the cruelest technique he used to keep Marietta constantly on edge was his relentless disclosure to her of these romantic encounters. With a little boy's cocky pride, he couldn't help mentioning how someone put a hand on his knee at dinner or monopolized him at a party or danced with him all night. "It's Mon. a.m. and I haven't even told you about the extraordinary young woman who rode in with me from the airport," he boasted once. Marietta tried to make light of his provocations. "You *are* mean to tease Mrs. J," she complained on this occasion.

Agnes Meyer once said of Adlai, "The secret of his life was that he was a mother's boy." Marietta had not started out mothering Adlai. In her first encounters with him she was the wide-eyed, blushing schoolgirl, tongue-tied in the presence of her hero. But Adlai helped her become strong. In the presidential campaigns, he included her in the decision making and gave her responsibilities; and most significantly at the United Nations he not only gave her the career opportunity of a lifetime but helped her do a good job, overcome her nervousness, understand the issues, learn how to face up to questioning.

This was Adlai's great strength. After listening to Marietta make a speech, for instance, he wrote her a penciled note of congratulation: "M—Excellent! And from one so young and beautiful! It's not fair that you could have so many talents and most so few. I protest—on behalf of the common man! But 1) the word is "administer"—not "administrate." 2) With larger type could you forgo the glasses? Or are they a "property" to reduce dazzle?"

But gradually the balance began to tip the other way. As she became more and more closely involved in Adlai's career, he began to depend on her for encouragement and protection from the blows that befell him over the years. When LBJ gave Hubert Humphrey the nod for vice president in 1964, Marietta knew how disappointed Stevenson was. "I wanted it for you, first because of the U.S. and our country's future . . . and then I wanted the cup of your career to overflow as it so well deserves to. I pray you are not hurt and am sure you are too gallant on the surface."

She gave Stevenson shrewd advice about his work habits. "Have strong intuition that you should be on the telephone to Washington with your political friends more and more—asking their advice—or for information on what do they think about x or y situation. It's a great pity that Bill Blair is not there to do it for you. It was his great contribution. There's now the impression in some quarters that you have no men friends in public life any more. . . ."

She worried constantly about his health. "Please take a small nap after lunch every day," she would urge. In late 1963, she wrote three magisterial pages to him:

> . . . A. Now will you please *take care of yourself,* and stop taking on things you don't have to do—such as sitting up with Aunt Mary, one more Roosevelt Foundation task, another cocktail party. . . . You have got to get more mature quickly, because *your very survival is at stake.* Maturity is knowing what the priorities are. Your top priority and indeed only responsibility between now and Dec. 20 is your work at the U.N. and keeping fit for it so you can do the best possible job for the U.S. Are you going to do that or fritter yourself away? . . .
>
> I would not write this if I didn't worry about you always, but especially *now.* If you get diverted from your main responsibility I think you ought to face the fact that your ego or your vanity is involved in peripheral matters or people who must be peripheral until you have accomplished your main purpose for existence.
>
> And I wouldn't be so stern or so mean in this letter unless you were the main purpose and responsibility of the Johnsons.

Adlai liked this nannying. He frequently provoked it: "Temp today 100 degrees—so of course I played tennis at noon . . ." He would insist that he wished to leave politics, waiting for the predictably gratifying response from his audience. Marietta and Arthur Schlesinger exchanged letters noting the contrary trait in him "of saying something so that people (women) will tell him that he can't do that and must do what he intends to do anyway." (For instance, going to Mrs. Roosevelt in 1952 and saying he would step aside for Symington or Johnson, knowing that she would scold him for such faintheartedness —which of course she did.)

But was this what Marietta wanted? She may have emulated Mrs. Roosevelt in many ways, but was the role of scold one of them? Was Marietta once more to be the nursemaid, counselor, hand-holder to her man? Wasn't that what happened to Ronnie, who had started out so full of command and ended up with his energies dissipated in a tropical exile? Adlai had also started out full of promise, and yet by the end was surrounded by sycophants, filled with doubts, sliding toward obscurity. (By the time he died, he had almost certainly decided to resign from the UN.) Ronnie was twenty years older than Marietta;

Adlai was seventeen. Beside this energetic Amazonian goddess, the older men dwindled and faded. Was this the glorious future she was once again mapping out for herself?

In what was probably Stevenson's last letter to her, when she was in Africa that spring of 1965, his wasted spirit comes through with devastating clarity. Enclosing several newspaper clippings reporting his triumphant appearance in Ottawa (where he received an honorary degree from the University of Toronto), he told Marietta of his equally great success making a speech in Atlantic City, and how pleased he was with the receptions and ovations. But the childishly boastful tone rapidly turns melancholy. "When—oh God!—when can I roll in the grass and look at the sky thru the leaves—with a hand in mine for the fullest measure!" Once again he asked the unanswerable questions. "What am I doing all this for—for me? for you? for who?" The letter grows increasingly elegiac. "I'm done at last—with nothing except these blank pages and a speech to do for Arkansas the day after tomorrow—and no true tomorrow. . . . But this whimper of self-pity is unworthy—and all I wonder and worry about is Africa and my hostage. . . ."

His last paragraph was full of questions about her movements in June and July. "Must you plane for England at once? Or shall we go to—Bloomington? or the Adirondacks? or?—or somewhere absolutely *alone*? Or is it all nonsense—as I suspect?" Thus with this last sentence he cruelly threw the medicine ball back to his "hostage" while withholding the ultimate imprimatur of commitment.

Marietta was in effect gambling on someone who, in the words of Brian Urquhart, was "an incomplete man." Did she begin to see that by the end? Perhaps she no longer dreamed of public glory, although there had been moments of great hope for both of them, and her last letters to him in 1965 were still as fond as ever. From Dar-es-Salaam she wrote to him counting her blessings, of which the first one was, "The Richardsons and Johnsons have been to N.J. 28 times since Jan.!" And once more the old insecure refrain came through: "My only complaint—and it's a fierce one, for it involves such horrible dreams—I have not heard from my boss—no instructions, no advice, no encouragement. But then I know how busy he is."

As it turned out, there were to be no more trips to "New Jersey." No more advice, no more encouragement. As it was, Adlai Stevenson died a beloved national figure and a respected international statesman. Although most obituaries sounded the theme of disappointment ("A tragic figure in American history," said *The Times* of London), he was still admired by many, and given a hero's funeral. Even though his self-destructive behavior during the last years was commented on by many, Marietta refused to admit the sadness and loneliness so many sensed in him. She was confident that she could nurture him back to strength. Hadn't they been discussing a vacation together at Desbarats that last afternoon in Grosvenor Square?

Marietta was with him when he died. She gave him his last embrace. The closest she ever got to being his wife was at the moment of his death. When she ascended the steps of the plane bearing the coffin back to the United States, she was alone, in grieving black widow's weeds. None of the other women in Adlai's life could claim such status. That last afternoon, in those terrible moments when he hit the ground at her feet, Marietta Tree's name became forever linked to his.

# CHAPTER *28*

# *"In you I have so much to be grateful for"*

When Stevenson died, Ronnie Tree was sixty-eight years old. For four and a half years, while his wife co-starred at the United Nations with Adlai, he had played an almost invisible supporting role. He took pride in Marietta's achievements at the United Nations, and remained in touch with her office life. When Marietta was away on a trip, Ceil Wentz had a slipped disc operation and Ronnie visited her in the hospital. But he hardly ever saw his wife.

In 1961 he oversaw the opening of the Sandy Lane Hotel, which was a huge success. People were delighted by its architectural elegance, beautiful gardens, elegant interior decoration, and dazzling position on the water. Sandy Lane was a strikingly original world-class resort; and it is to Ronnie's credit that many others later emulated his standards. He also threw himself into the task of finding a house in Barbados for his old colleague (and fair-weather friend) Anthony Eden, who had decided to buy a property on the island.

With Marietta increasingly involved in work, and justifiably pointing out that she could hardly leave Penelope, who was in school in New York, for long periods, the marriage inevitably suffered.

Ronnie soldiered on alone. But he was beginning to slow down. Though he continued his annual rounds of Barbados, London, and Italy, he began to suffer from painful headaches and liver problems. He had high blood pressure and giddy spells. His loneliness was diverted into work, his illnesses, and a busy travel schedule. He continually worried about money, not only the liquidity of the Sandy Lane Corporation but also his own diminishing fortune.

He also found distraction in the companionship of Michael Teague, a handsome young photographer whom Ronnie had first met in Portugal. Teague went to Barbados to work on a story about sugar plantations in the Caribbean, and later took the photographs for a book Ronnie was putting together on the history of Barbados, which was published in 1972. From their first meeting until Ronnie's death, Michael came every year to Heron Bay. They liked to travel together, always Ronnie's best remedy for sadness or boredom. They went to the Far East, to the Soviet Union, and to Baden-Baden, the fashionable health spa of the European elite, where Ronnie made an annual pilgrimage to the Brenner Park Hotel to take the waters. "Michael Teague is delightful," Ronnie wrote to Marietta. "I'm very lucky to have him as a travelling companion. . . . He . . . likes everything and has a host of friends everywhere."

But in spite of these interests, a more troubling issue was brewing. During this time, Ronnie's tender relationship with his daughter began to unravel. Penelope was showing all the signs of a classically rebellious teenager, and since this was the sixties, rebellion meant serious business. In 1962, at the age of thirteen, she started wearing pale lipstick, black clothes, and dark glasses. During the spring of 1963 when Marietta was in Geneva, Penelope went down to Greenwich Village with a friend, chaperoned by Mabel, and started singing and dancing with some guitar-playing "beatniks" in Washington Square. Mabel wrote to Marietta describing the scene with some trepidation, worried that "Penel was getting too much city life. . . ." (Penelope's own hilarious version of the adventure took a different tack. ". . . When Mabel went to the Village with us it was *just* awful. I'm not kidding. She refused to pretend she didn't know us and was prudish the whole time because some men had beards and wore blue jeans. . . .") There were still light moments, such as when Penelope taught her father to dance the "hitchhiker," but Ronnie, who had depended so much on his daughter for solace, now found that communication between them languished.

The only time Ronnie vented his anger directly to Marietta about what was happening to the marriage was through Penelope. He blamed Marietta for bringing her up badly and allowing her to wear such outrageous clothes. (Marietta's cousin Rose Parsons Lynch overheard Ronnie saying to Marietta, "You're not going to let her out looking like that, are you?" To which Marietta retorted, "She's *your* daughter.")[1] Penelope felt sad for her father and humiliated by her mother, who, in the middle of cocktail parties, would sweep up to her daughter and whisper how terrible she looked.

In 1964, Penelope was sent away to Concord Academy. It was a virtual prison sentence. She found the work difficult, she missed the teachers and friends from Dalton, and she was desperately homesick. Her letters home would have caused the hardest parent's heart to melt. ("Dear Daddy: This is a cliché, but so true: The only thing that gives me comfort in being here in this dark school is seeing the same sun that shines so brightly in Barbados watch and warm me here. . . .") Ronnie could not bear his daughter's unhappiness, and urgently sought ways to help her overcome her misery, writing her long, encouraging letters.

Marietta took the tough approach—Penelope should stick it out in true Peabody fashion, just as Marietta had done in Chestnut Hill and at La Petite Ecole. She seems to have completely blocked out her own unhappiness and rebelliousness, even when Penelope confessed to having been caught smoking (although the tone of shame and self-abasement is astonishingly similar to her mother's). Thus, instead of showing sympathy with her daughter's emotional problems, Marietta offered no comfort to the teenager. "I cannot decide myself whether it's the normal sensitive period that all poor 15-year-olds undergo. Shall wait and watch," she wrote coolly to Adlai.

After much soul-searching, in 1965 Ronnie and Marietta decided to send Penelope back to Concord Academy for a second year. That year proved worse for her. Penelope grew depressed and anorexic, thus finally persuading her parents that she must be allowed to leave. She was taken out at the end of the spring term in 1966 and placed instead at the U.N. International School in New York, where she immediately felt more at home and did better academically.

Powerful mothers cannot help having their power, but they can help their children live comfortably within it. Frankie's intellectual brilliance and early career success gave her a head start on her young half sister, who was at this time at an emotionally low ebb. After graduating from Radcliffe magna cum laude in 1962, Frankie went to Paris to work for the Congress for Cultural Freedom (CCF), under the directorship of Nicolas Nabokov. (The CCF was funded by the CIA, a fact that nobody—including Frankie—knew until the early seventies, when it was revealed in *Ramparts* magazine.) She spent two years there, editing articles on international affairs, reading and writing. In December 1964 she returned from Paris and began to publish articles, joining the growing group of intellectuals and political observers who were by 1965 voicing serious doubts about the Vietnam War. Many reporters began to make their way to Southeast Asia, and Frankie left for Vietnam in January 1966.

During Stevenson's last years, the Trees' marriage teetered on the edge of disintegration. The veneer of politeness so carefully maintained over fifteen years was beginning to splinter. Marietta was increasingly cold. "I'm so sorry you've been having such a miserable, lonely time.

At least I'm relieved that we aren't all in debtor's prison and that you have achieved your goal in getting the financial problems under control. . . . There is no *need* to be lonely there, unless you want to be alone. . . ." Ronnie responded in kind. On one occasion, when Marietta arrived for one of her flying duty visits to Barbados, he suggested she go straight back to New York. In a letter to Adlai, Marietta wrote: "R. is well, avoids Mrs. J assiduously. . . ."

Then suddenly, in an afternoon, the balancing act came to an end. Ronnie's tact over Stevenson's death was exemplary. On her arrival back in New York after the funeral, Marietta found a generous and deeply sympathetic letter from her husband waiting for her: "I only hope that the shock is gradually passing and with the passing the remembrances of all the happy times will begin to emerge and take the place of the numbness that comes with death."

He continued to support her throughout the terrible period in Florence, during her grieving over Stevenson, and later, when she lost her job. The new U.S. Ambassador to the United Nations, Arthur Goldberg, replaced most of Stevenson's appointees by the end of 1965, including Marietta. She was not surprised, but the changeover was done with surgical speed, and left some bad feelings. One of the saddest aspects of the dismissal for Marietta was having to say good-bye to her assistant, Ceil Wentz. Ceil and Marietta had enjoyed a closeness that went far beyond an office relationship. By sharing Marietta's panic over the cancer scare, Ceil had become one of Marietta's few intimates, and Marietta had come to lean on her in ways she probably did not even recognize. The parting was painful for them both. In fact, they never lost touch, and toward the end of her life, Marietta was to call on her again.[2]

When Marietta learned that she was to be dismissed from her UN post, Ronnie was in Florence. He wrote at once: "I've been thinking of you all day—since your telephone call of this morning—and worrying about you. Penelope dissolved into floods of tears and said, 'poor Mummy, poor Mummy.' I only wish I could be with you to help and be of some comfort." He went on to remember the day he was defeated in 1945—"it suddenly felt as if the bottom of my life had fallen out, and I was bewildered as a child is, and didn't know where to turn." He suggested she have a good rest for two or three months, and that perhaps she would go to Baden-Baden with him—"the brooding Black Forest might be just the thing."

Marietta passed on the brooding Black Forest. Perhaps she feared the intimacy the vacation might entail. Besides, she was desperate to find another job. Arthur Schlesinger had written to Robert Kennedy asking if he would give her a job in his New York office, but nothing came of it. Instead, Marietta hastily grabbed the offer of a job on U

Thant's staff at the Secretariat. It was not a good choice. Her position was unsuitable and humiliatingly low-level after her ambassadorial career with the mission. Her specific assignment was to raise $3 million for the U.N. School.

Marietta was not a good fund-raiser. She hated giving money herself (not only was she naturally parsimonious, but the money had to be wheedled out of Ronnie in the first place), and she found asking other people for money to be embarrassing. Moreover, she thought the Secretariat very badly run, and U Thant a poor administrator, so that morale was low and efficiency even lower. "It was a great let-down after the U.S. Mission, which was such a tight team and ran so beautifully," she said later.

What she was too discreet to add was that any post-Adlai position would have been joyless for her. She was working very hard to recover the motivation and enthusiasm that had drained out of her that July afternoon in London. Her method was to throw herself into frantic activity, and the job, however unpleasant, was one way to revive her energies. Going out every night was another distraction. Her calendar through the end of 1965 is filled with visits and dinners with Stevenson's friends, attendance at Stevenson memorials, receptions for Ambassador Goldberg, farewell teas with delegates, and so on.

Although the new UN job meant she stayed in New York, Marietta was also intent on another important piece of business—the repair of her marriage. Ronnie's extraordinary consideration throughout the mourning period gave her the opening she needed. At this time her letters to him were filled with a new interest in and affection for her husband.

In January 1966, after a visit in Barbados, she wrote: "Darling, it was heavenly to hear that the hols. made you as happy as it did me —and evidently Penelope. All the credit is due to you, because you have created the most beautiful ambiance in the world there, and the measured pleasure of our routine in that beauty is better than lotus-eating on Mt. Parnassus. Thank you with all my heart for all that happiness. . . ." She added that she was grateful to have her new job "that fits in with our family life. Naturally I plan to be with you in England for the rest of the summer. . . . All best love, I *miss* you!"

That spring, Marietta was invited by the State Department to make a six-week fact-finding lecture tour, with special emphasis on human rights, the status of women, and the United Nations peacekeeping operations. The State Department had suggested several trips, but Marietta demurred. Had she not promised to be with Ronnie all summer?

The one trip she agreed on was Asia, "because I had never been."

Also, Frankie was in Vietnam, reporting on the war for *The Atlantic Monthly* and the London *Daily Telegraph*, among others. Frankie planned to leave Vietnam later that summer and hoped to link up with her mother, perhaps in Singapore, at the end of her stay. Marietta drew up a list of subjects about which she would lecture, including "The New Age of Human Rights," "World Problems Facing the U.N. Today," "The Changing Role of Women," and "The New Internationalism versus Nationalism in the Atomic Age." (She also enlisted a lecture agency, W. Colston Leigh, in New York, to get her bookings on the U.S. lecture circuit with these topics.)

She flew to Japan on April 30, 1966. Ronnie was very anxious when he said good-bye to her, thinking she seemed at the end of her tether. The itinerary alone was staggeringly crowded, but as well as the travel there were the question-and-answer "talking papers" she had to master on the subjects of national liberation, issues having to do with Vietnam, communism, and so forth. (*"Question:* Why is the United States waging war against North Vietnam? *Answer:* The U.S. is not doing that at all. We are helping the free government and people of the Republic of Vietnam [RVN] defend their freedom and independence against attack, directed and in part supplied from North Vietnam.")

Once on the road, Marietta soon recovered the old spirit. She started in Tokyo, staying with U.S. Ambassador Edwin O. Reischauer. She then did a two-week tour of Kyushu, the southernmost island of Japan, speaking in small towns and dining in the local geisha houses with the mayor and other dignitaries. The officials' wives were very excited that Marietta gave them entree to these places, which they would never have been able to penetrate on their own. "Apart from the geishas, I was the first woman who'd ever entered most of these houses. . . . All those exquisitely dressed little modern geishas, with white enameled faces, bee-stung lips and exquisite embroidered kimonos were about the age of my daughter Penelope [around sixteen] so I felt quite at home playing silly games with them at the table like baseball with bread pellets."[3]

Marietta was at her best on these occasions, charming the Japanese officials out of their formality as they downed sake and told her all about their lives, and making the women feel comfortable in her dazzlingly tall and glamorous presence.

She wrote about Japan in glowing terms to Ronnie. She referred to things that would interest him ("Ronnie, why can't we get that feathery Japanese bamboo for Barbados?"). She described Hiroshima as a "vulgar, bustling metropolis, the only reminder of the ghastly bomb is a badly organized Peace Museum and the American-Japanese Institute for Research on the Survivors, where the whole terrible reality is lost in the hum of IBM computers." On her last day in Japan she gave a report of her experiences to Reischauer. The ambassador was only marginally impressed. He remarked to her that neither McGeorge Bundy (who was also in Japan traveling for the Ford Foundation) nor Marietta had found the "mysterious East."

Whether or not she had found it, Marietta's whole mood at this time was one of exhilaration. She was back in the saddle, working at what she loved, swinging enthusiastically between glittering embassy receptions and intimate Japanese family dinners. "Oh, how I wish you could enjoy this with me," she cried to Ronnie. "We've all got to come together again and soon . . . Please take such good care of yourselves. I miss you terribly and love you, love you, M."

From Japan, Marietta traveled on to Hong Kong. She dined with Hong Kong diplomats and art dealers, and visited a Chinese refugee settlement in Macao, before flying on to the Philippines, staying in Manila with the U.S. ambassador, her old friend Bill Blair. On May 30, Marietta met Imelda Marcos, an occasion which she later described at length, but in her diary she merely wrote, "Mrs. Marcos prettier than Jackie. v. cozy. Told me she met and married her husband in ten days. Family furious."

On June 1, she received an unexpected telegram from the American Embassy in Saigon. It said that Miss Frances FitzGerald was being operated on for chronic menorrhagia, which had not responded to several weeks of medical treatment. "Felt rather ill and dizzy all day," Marietta wrote, "but telegram from her at 8. pm helped me recover for large dinner Bill gave for me in the Embassy. . . . Great fun." (Frankie's telegram read, "All's over and well.")

Marietta flew on to Singapore and finally, on June 15, two weeks after the news of Frankie's surgery, she arrived in Saigon. Stepping off the plane, immaculate in her lightweight traveling suit, Marietta found Frankie in shocking physical and mental shape. "After a few hours there, don't see how she has survived this long," Marietta wrote in her calendar. "The city . . . is one big traffic jam, garbage piled high, no water and the necessities of life require bribery to get them."

However, since the U.S. Embassy had arranged a trip by special plane for Marietta to see the countryside, she dashed off to tour hamlets, military installations, Special Forces firebases and the like. Photos were taken of her looking splendid in a white dress with a huge hat.

Frankie went some of the way, but her friend, the journalist Ward Just, was badly wounded in Saigon and she wanted to return to him. On the way back, she witnessed a U.S. Army truck run over a young Vietnamese. Unable to get through to Saigon, she rejoined her mother's party and spent that night sick in bed while a dinner dance for Marietta took place downstairs. The small plane Frankie finally found next day to take her to Saigon lost its landing gear, and when she looked down as it circled, she thought she saw Marietta taking a swim on the beach.

At this point, Frankie completely collapsed, forcing Marietta to confront the extent of her daughter's illness (which was due to a postoperative internal infection and exhaustion). After three more days of hectic touring, she scooped Frankie up and flew with her to Singapore and the comforts of a first-class hotel. Frankie began to mend, but was intermittently feverish, with nightmares and dizziness. During the week, Marietta attended UN functions, made speeches, and fitted in a trip to Djakarta, where Frankie joined her, before flying on to the Erewan Hotel, Bangkok. After lunch with new English friends, Gordon and Peggy Richardson (he was a distinguished investment banker, who later became governor of the Bank of England), Marietta left Frankie at the hotel for more rest, and flew on with the Richardsons to Teheran, Persepolis, Isfahan, and Shiraz. On Friday, July 1, she flew to London and met up with Ronnie and Penelope. (Her European clothes had been sent on, with occasional instructions to Ronnie winging in from the East. "Please tell Alice to be sure to pack my blue silk suit [Balmain] for London.")

From London, Marietta wrote a report of her trip to the Far East for Charles Frankel, assistant secretary of state for cultural affairs. After some rather effusive opening words ("Every day was filled with learning, beauty and pleasure"), she made some sensible, if modest, recommendations.

> In all these Asian countries, I felt the lack of an under-pinning of democracy, stable government and the orderly transfer of political power. Throughout there seemed a real lack of citizen responsibility. . . . Therefore, I would advocate more work by the Embassy and the U.S.I.S. in helping local citizen groups to organize and become more effective. . . . I also think there should be an increase of teen-age exchange programs, both in the public and private sectors. I myself learned more by going into people's homes for meals and chatting informally with families and their friends than from any other experience. . . .

Meanwhile, Frankie slowly grew better. "I'm not sure what I would have done if you hadn't come when you did," she wrote to her mother from Bangkok. While in Vietnam, to Frankie, in the grip of blood and death, her mother's appearances had seemed absurd. But in neutral territory, the dea ex machina had once again plucked her from the jaws of death. How could Frankie possibly escape the thrall of her omnipotent mother?

After a wonderful summer in England, Paris, Florence, and Rome (with a side trip to Ireland to stay with John Huston), Marietta left Ronnie and Penelope sightseeing in Italy and flew briefly to the South of France (where she spent a day with David and Hjordis Niven), to Paris (for clothes), and to Turin (to ask the Agnellis for a contribution to the U.N. International School), before returning to New York on September 8. She had been away almost six months.

Ronnie stayed on in Italy before flying out to Beirut and then Bombay with Michael Teague. In his absence, that fall in New York Marietta picked up her friendship with Gordon Richardson, dining with him at the Italian Pavilion and going to parties with him. She went to meetings for the U.N. School, made speeches, attended a UN seminar in Albany, and was asked to run for New York lieutenant governor. Flattered, she turned the offer down, telling Ronnie that she refused because Penelope was still at school and she could not leave her. "I thought you would be relieved that I am not running full tilt . . . ," she added pointedly. Frankie had an interesting take on her mother's refusal: "What will you do when Penelope is no longer willing or able to sit in as the potentially motherless child? Confess. What you lack—[Endicott] must have got it all—is the gambler's instinct."

Ronnie and Marietta spent Christmas 1966 in Barbados. By that time, John Bartlow Martin had embarked on his biography of Adlai Stevenson. He interviewed Marietta several times that fall, and she showed him Stevenson's letters and allowed him to Xerox a selection. Was this opening up of the past painful to her? There is no reference in her letters or in the interviews with Martin at this time indicating any distress about the reliving of her life with Stevenson, nor is there any notation in her diary marking the anniversary of his death. Her major concern conveyed to Martin was that nothing be said in the book to offend or upset Ronnie.

Over a year had gone by—a year of traveling immense distances, both literally and psychologically. Marietta always looked forward. She had a new and difficult job, and a marriage to take care of. That other part of her life was over, and as the pain wore off, there was nothing more to be felt about it. "Maturity," as she had told Adlai, "is knowing what the priorities are."

After Marietta left Italy that summer of 1966, Ronnie wrote to her saying that "This year was certainly the best we've had and I only hope we can have many more. . . . Fondest love, my darling, I love you so much." Marietta fervently agreed with him. "How I loved it, because we were together and in beauty. . . ." After the winter vacation in Barbados, she wrote on her return to New York, "You have given me the best life of any female in the world, and you and Penelope, and Frankie too, have made me feel a Fulfilled Woman in the basis or well-spring of my life. . . . Thank you my darling for the most perfect holiday and my most perfect life."

The year that letter was written, 1967, was Ronnie and Marietta's twentieth wedding anniversary. The marriage, it seemed, was as good as it had ever been.

# CHAPTER *29*

# *"Hysterical amiability settling on me"*

Marietta was not the only Peabody to hit the headlines in the 1960s. When Malcolm retired as bishop of central New York in 1960, he moved with his wife from Syracuse back to a small house in Cambridge, Massachusetts. Mrs. Peabody wasted no time in getting involved in local community service, in particular raising money for a school for black children in the parish of Brookline. Her consciousness was raised, in the parlance of the time, by the continuing reports of the Freedom Riders and the rising tide of the civil rights revolution in the south. A member of the church, who was also a member of the Southern Christian Leadership Conference (SCLC), told Mrs. Peabody he'd asked the bishop to attend a demonstration he was organizing in St. Augustine, Florida, over Easter 1964 (when students would be on vacation).

"My husband couldn't go," Mrs. Peabody recalled. "It was Easter week, and he'd been left in charge of the church by the rector. . . . I said to them, 'Are you recruiting women?' And they said, 'Yes, we want women too.' So then I said, 'Well, would I be any use?' "

Endicott Peabody was governor of Massachusetts at the time. (After failing in two runs for attorney general, he won the governorship in 1963.) His mother carefully avoided telling him anything about her plan. "I didn't want to have arguments with him about it." She flew to Jacksonville with Mrs. Rowe (Mike Peabody's mother-in-law), Mrs. Donald Campbell (wife of the dean of the Episcopal Theological Seminary in Cambridge, Massachusetts), and Mrs. John Burgess (wife of the first black Episcopal bishop in the United States). They spent the night in St. Augustine, and were told to report the following day after a good breakfast.

The next morning, the four ladies sat down at a lunch counter in a drugstore and waited to be arrested. But the waitress did not notice that Mrs. Burgess, who was light-colored, was black. "As we weren't making much progress there," Mrs. Peabody related later to Michael Teague, "I called the waitress and I said to her, 'It's fine that you serve both blacks and whites here.' She almost turned a somersault and quickly went to fetch the manager, who said, 'Ladies, please leave immediately. I will refund your money.' "[1]

After failing to be challenged at other lunch counters, Mrs. Burgess finally refused to leave and was arrested. The newspapers chose to put the spin on this story that once again the black had been persecuted while the whites had escaped. The white ladies did not like this, and although anxious about their families, decided they should also go to prison. Mrs. Peabody telephoned Endicott to warn him. Endicott, loyal son, said, "It's all right, Mother, what's right there is right here. Let your conscience be your guide." (He did, however, ask Florida governor Ferris Bryant to keep an eye on her.) So Mrs. Peabody and a small party of blacks and whites returned to the restaurant and the sheriff came and read an injunction, and finally, on March 30, 1964, they were led away to jail. (Mrs. Burgess was taken away separately.) On the way out, a Philadelphia friend saw Mary Peabody and said, "Mary, what are you doing here?" Mary said, "I'm getting arrested." Her friend said, "Can I do anything for you?" And she said, "Yes, you can get in touch with Malcolm and tell him."[2]

Herded into a cell already crowded with young demonstrators, the elder women were given two bunks for them to sleep in and Mrs. Peabody reported she managed to sleep very comfortably. In the late evening George Peabody appeared. He was traveling in Florida and thought he'd better stop and check on his mother. He was allowed to see her, and she told him she was having a good time. The next day, she and her friends were allowed out and they all went home.[3]

Mrs. Peabody was seventy-two years old when this event took place. It became a big story in the newspapers. Of course, some people were shocked, thought it unconscionable of her to put her son, the governor, in such an awkward position, and saw her behavior as the wife of a bishop unseemly. But for many others she became a role model, the epitome of Boston Brahmin courage and spunk.

Marietta was in Barbados when her mother went to Florida. During those suspenseful days, news of Mrs. Peabody's progress was communicated by friends and family over the telephone. Marietta felt strongly that her mother's trip to St. Augustine made no sense unless she was arrested. One day, the Trees were lunching with the queen mother at Government House. According to Sam Peabody, on leaving, the queen mother said to Ronnie, "I do hope Marietta's mother gets arrested soon!"

Although Marietta supported her mother's activism, the incident was rife with irony. Marietta had been a passionate civil rights advocate ever since her years at *Life* in the early 1940s, whereas her mother had only recently shown more than a passing interest in the subject. Yet now, after one splendid public gesture, Mrs. Peabody had seized the limelight that escaped Marietta all those years. After this episode, Marietta could never again compete with her mother in the field of civil rights. Even when, with the support of Marietta Dockery, her old friend from Sydenham and Dalton days, she was elected an honorary member of the black sorority, Alpha Kappa Alpha, in 1980 (one of few whites so honored), who was also similarly honored that same year? Mary Peabody.[4]

Marietta fought back as best she could. As always, she used the envy card. "I am on the way back from Barbados after a 5-day visit to see the Queen. . . . Last week Ronnie, Penelope and I spent in Paris— me working for the Secretary-General and trying to buy a few clothes. . . . We also swilled Mouton Rothschild '45 and '26 with the Rothschilds and returned to the Dutch pictures in the Louvre. . . ."

Mrs. Peabody received these enticing snatches of her daughter's life with serenity. She regularly replied with a description of her own community good works, which, while lacking the impressive names, needless to say created their own damage. Marietta's defensiveness comes through clearly in many sarcastic little remarks: "I have greatly enjoyed your letters and the accounts of your many doings—frivolous, and familial, and freighted with social significance. . . ." Sandwiched between the expressions of devotion, bitterness sprouts like rue. "Incidentally, Mother," she wrote on one occasion, "would you be an angel and send me a p.c. giving the date of your birthday? I think it is either July 18th or 24th. But I want to think of you especially hard on that day."

With her father, a more gentle affection prevailed. When he began distributing his legacies to his children, Marietta's gratitude struck a chord in him, and he expressed his love for her in fulsome prose. He liked writing to her about money (it must be remembered that Mike had said he would have been a good businessman). He also understood his daughter's wish to be financially independent. He reminded Marietta how, when his sister Dot married a rich man (Trubee Davison), her husband gave her a large sum all her own, "and thereby set up her own self-respect and confidence in her independence." (The implication being that it was a pity Ronnie could not go and do likewise.)

The Peabody family reunited at Bishop Peabody's 80th birthday, June 1968. *(Photo courtesy of Pamela Peabody)*

He found pleasure in Marietta's rounds of parties and good works, praising her for her commitment to "the welfare of oppressed people." In a moment of confessional candor after Marietta had expressed regret over her inadequacies in adolescence, Malcolm admitted his own great failing—self-blame for wrongs done, "or even more, for stupidities and immaturities committed long ago." He said he dwelled on his ineptitudes already forgiven by God. "This procedure is like the act of a man who manacled to his dead brother insists upon lugging him wherever he goes! . . . The hard thing for me has been accepting forgiveness. This shows a terrible lack of Faith in God. . . ." With these admissions of weakness, Malcolm urged his daughter to strengthen her own faith.

But just as these exhortations remained as difficult for Marietta to gratify at fifty years of age as at five, so the sibling issue remained equally intractable. In the fall of 1966, while governor of Massachusetts, Marietta's brother Endicott ran for office again—this time as senator, running against the black Republican attorney general, Edward W. Brooke. Marietta's support for her brother had always been muted. She felt she could not criticize his political positions or statements because of, as she put it to Arthur Schlesinger, "the sister-brother biz." Then there were always his pleas for money, of course. "I'm afraid the sister's role (if she doesn't agree or violently uphold) is to pay up and shut up." Ronnie was equally unenthusiastic, sometimes groaning as the next request for money would arrive.

During the years when Adlai was alive, although Stevenson made occasional appearances on Endicott's behalf at fund-raisers, some of her family felt Marietta could have persuaded him to do more. "She was running around with the top dogs of the Democratic Party," George said. "Chub [Endicott] was counting on her and she wouldn't even see him." Sam also felt that the Peabodys compared very unfavorably to the Kennedys in supporting their family members. On one occasion at 79th Street, Sam felt Marietta was being so negative that he left the house in disgust.

Endicott lost his bid for the Senate. He was to lose many other contests in his efforts to regain political office. Perhaps what made his loss in 1966 even more vexing than usual for Marietta was the fact that her own career was faltering. Gone were the glory days when she strode through the corridors of the United Nations, greeting diplomats, attending meetings, and being welcomed as an important member of the UN community. Now she was in a backwater, the U.N. International School's Development Fund was going nowhere, and she could not raise the money she needed. In one moment of bitterness, after describing to her parents a weekend with the Wrightsmans amid French furniture, Pisarros, and gold and ivory beds, she said, "If the ladies of this party would just give me their engagement rings the U.N. would be solvent forever."

The Ford Foundation, a major backer of the United Nations, was so dissatisfied by the failure of the fund-raisers to approach their goal, and in particular by the failure of the U.S. government to make a commitment, that it threatened to withdraw funds to other UN projects if the money was not raised soon. Marietta openly criticized Washington and by implication U.N. Ambassador Arthur Goldberg for their lack of support, and her complaints reached the ears of Goldberg, who was not amused. He told her that she was causing him trouble, and to "lay off Washington."

Marietta responded with some asperity to him, explaining the urgency of the situation. But her "over-zealousness," as she called it, caused even more bad feeling between them. Soon after this fracas, she was invited to be nominated as a delegate-at large to the New York State Constitutional Convention in Albany in the summer of 1967. To her surprise, she was elected high on the list of forty delegates. The offer could hardly have come at a better time. Jumping at the opportunity to leave the United Nations and continue her involvement with politics, albeit local, she tendered her resignation, effective March 1967. It was accepted. "Perhaps some of the results for which you have

At the New York Constitutional Convention, 1967. "For Marietta, Probably the only woman at the Constitutional Convention who reads the *New Republic*," wrote Robert F. Kennedy in his autograph. *(Bill Burlingham)*

been striving so hard may be realized later on," Secretary-General U Thant said kindly in his farewell letter.

The convention would take six months, starting in April and ending in October. This meant spending the summer in Albany instead of in Europe with Ronnie. Marietta spent some anxious days over this issue, which Penelope interpreted with her usual perceptiveness. Saying Marietta "looked as if she was a piece of laundry put through an old fashioned wringer to dry," she thought her mother had accepted the job too hastily because she was honored and flattered, and had lost her sense of perspective, not realizing how it would eat into the family summer. "I personally can think of nothing worse than sitting in an unspeakably air-conditioned hall in hot Albany with a lot of grotesque senators breathing down my neck," Penelope remarked. In the end, reluctantly responding to the new mood of marital harmony, Ronnie agreed to forgo Italy and stay in a hotel in Saratoga for the month of August, so he could be with his wife while she attended the sessions.

Marietta was put on two standing committees: the Bill of Rights and Suffrage, and Education. As in her other political endeavors, some of the professionals regarded her as just an Upper East Side WASP, a beautiful token liberal to decorate the corridors of power. Her departure every evening in a chauffeur-driven car from the seedy Albany hotels to elegant Saratoga did not help this impression, but since she flew up to the opening of the convention in Robert Kennedy's plane (at his invitation), there were also those who realized she had powerful Democratic Party connections.

Jon Margolis, a young reporter for the convention, saw how gradually she won her colleagues over with her hard work and enthusiasm. On one occasion, she argued against a measure and won. Margolis, later on the *Chicago Tribune,* recalled talking to her afterwards. "As we stood in the baroque anteroom of the State Assembly chamber discussing her success, the chief sponsor of the measure walked past— an Italian Democrat from Brooklyn. Mrs. Tree broke off our interview, explained to her colleague with great vigor and charm why she had been forced to oppose him, assured him that it had pained her because of her respect and affection for him . . . and expressed the confidence that they would be allied on many matters on days to come. Entirely pleased and mollified, he thanked her and walked off. When she was sure he was gone, she turned back to me, rolled her eyes heavenward, and said simply, 'Good God.' "[5]

Just as she had flung herself into her job at *Life,* so in Albany she eagerly studied the issues involved in framing a constitution, including state and city domestic policies, the education system, urban planning, and legal questions of all kinds. She hung around with the judges and lawyers, picking up information and taking direction about how to vote. She went out to dinner with the borough politicians, Italians one night, Irish the next. Every day she would be briefed by her administrative assistant, Preston Brown (a member of the Lexington Democratic Club and lawyer friend of Frankie's), on the subtle political and social issues prior to a vote, and listen to debates, at the same time making invaluable contacts with state and city politicians. It was all very lively and great fun.[6]

At most of the sessions, Marietta sat next to plenary delegate Hortense Gabel, a state and city housing expert. These two women became close friends, and Marietta learned a great deal about local politics from her more experienced colleague. Horty Gabel was a fierce women's rights activist, and she remonstrated with Marietta for not putting her name to three resolutions about women's rights that the other eight women delegates had agreed to. Marietta's objection was that the resolutions were too long, and that the word "sex" in the Bill of Rights resolution would take care of women's rights. (She was shying away from being identified with the issue, as she did all her life.)

In July, Marietta took three weeks off and went to England with Ronnie, meeting up with Penelope. The trip ended with a visit to John Huston in Ireland with Frankie. Just after her return to Albany, a link with her old life was finally broken. On July 23, Desmond FitzGerald died on the tennis court at his country house in Virginia, the result of a heart attack. He was fifty-seven years old. As part of the patrician group who entered the CIA in the 1950s, Desie's role would present some difficulties later, although the extent of the undercover operations he and his colleagues were engaged in, particularly in Cuba, during the 1950s and 1960s, was not known at that time. In spite of his CIA involvement, Desie had remained close to his eldest daughter, supporting her, fearful for her safety in Southeast Asia (she could have been a hostage for him), generally keeping track of her.

Frankie, who was still in Ireland when she heard of her father's death, "cracked like an egg," according to her cousin, Albert Francke. But in emulation of her mother, her control was impeccable. She flew to Washington, where there was a big funeral in Washington Cathedral with all Desie's old friends from Boston and New York. Frankie stayed a few days with her stepmother, Barbara, before returning to Ireland. "There remains a sense of unreality and a vacuum that is hard to comprehend," she wrote to her mother.

With Marietta back in Albany, Ronnie sat out the intense heat of Saratoga in furious discomfort. There was a short respite at the end of July when he and Marietta flew to Paris for three days to celebrate their twentieth wedding anniversary. Penelope, Michael, and Anne Tree joined them, also Bill and Babe Paley, who were married on the same day twenty years before. They had a splendid banquet at the Grand Vefour, went to the Tutankhamen exhibition, as well as several dress shows. Then it was back to the smoke-filled debating rooms in upstate New York—from Balmain to the Bill of Rights, Marietta's bifurcated fate.

But after returning to Saratoga, Ronnie's fretfulness grew worse. He had a bad attack of gout and remained in his hotel room in bed. Friends such as the Selznicks and Whitneys visited, and they went to the Saratoga race meetings and outdoor concerts, and laughed at W. C. Fields movies at the local cinema. But there was not much of interest for Ronnie in that culturally challenged region.

Marietta was distracted and tense, longing to be away from this gloomy sickbed and back where the fun was. The contrast was disturbing. In Saratoga she was with an aging, depressed man who found everything she talked about boring. At the convention she was learning new things, meeting influential people, and was one of only eight women (and by far the most fetching) in a crowd of one hundred seventy-eight men, all jammed together day after day in intense intimacy and camaraderie. It wasn't Groton, but it had almost the same effect.

When Penelope visited, she hated the atmosphere between her parents so much that she left for New York after a few days. Helpless in Saratoga, Ronnie saw his daughter inexorably slipping away. Penelope's life was indeed changing dramatically. Graduated from the U.N. School and accepted at Sarah Lawrence, Penelope had met the fashion photographer Richard Avedon earlier in the year, who had asked her to model for him. (She had already had a modest sensation in December 1966, when she was just seventeen, making a much-photographed social debut at Truman Capote's famous masked ball, wearing a see-through black dress with angular holes cut out of the sides and amazing eye makeup.) She was photographed in *Look* that year as an up-and-coming representative of Youth, and in June 1967, *Women's Wear Daily* did a story that would send shivers down any anxious parent's spine: "While Twiggy is the face of '67, Penelope could be, not only the face of '68, but the face of the decade."[7]

But it was Richard Avedon's spectacular fourteen-page spread in the October 1, 1967, issue of *Vogue* that catapulted the leggy, waiflike beauty to stardom. Ever desperate for a new face, the media picked her up with murderous enthusiasm. By the end of 1967, stories on "fantasTree" had appeared in *The Washington Post, Time, Newsweek*, the London *Sunday Times, Queen*, and a thousand gossip columns. Penelope went to Sarah Lawrence for a couple of months before quitting to go and live in London with the other great sixties photographer and rival to Avedon, David Bailey. College never really had a chance.

Marietta was furious. Her daughter was doing exactly what she had done—passing up a college degree. On this occasion, repeating the pattern was not to be tolerated. When David Bailey came to New York to fetch Penelope, Marietta tried to refuse him entry. "Bailey firmly wedged a pointed toe of one of his Cuban boots into the open crack of the front door through which we were communicating," Penelope recalled, "and said to Marietta, 'Just be thankful I'm not a Rolling Stone!' "

Ronnie brooded over his lost daughter and waited for the Constitutional Convention finally to come to a close. His relief was Marietta's regret. "I am getting to love everybody," Marietta sang to the journal she was keeping, "even Republicans. Hysterical amiability settling on me, so perhaps it's time for the Convention to be over. . . . I shall miss living in this big, lively, friendly group."

Not much was achieved by the convention, since its implementation was voted down in the November elections. However, for Marietta it was such a positive experience that eight years later she wrote to Judge Anthony Travia, one of the 1967 delegates and speaker of the convention, to suggest a reunion. Travia thought poorly of the idea, since in 1977 the question of yet another Constitutional Convention was to be placed on the ballot and he thought a call for a reunion would create the wrong impression. Also, the failure of the 1967 convention was not likely to find many delegates as eager as Marietta to get together again.

But for Marietta the convention had been anything but a failure. Although she came out of it without a job, she had begun forming a new career for herself. In particular, her interests were moving in the direction of housing and urban planning. To this end, in the fall of 1967, she registered for an urban planning course at Columbia University under the direction of Charles Abrams. Abrams, a friend of Marietta's, allowed her to take the two-year course in a year, without having to take the studio part (which entailed practical drafting and design).

Once more, Marietta was making a course correction in her life. But whereas before, there had always been a consistent theme in her trajectory—that of Democratic politics—now she was turning away from these old allegiances. She still kept up connections with the Democratic Party, and campaigned vigorously for Bobby Kennedy, becoming a delegate, with Theodore Sorenson and Robert Low, for the 17th Congressional District. Bartle Bull, Kennedy's New York campaign manager, remembered her sitting down in his tiny office, crossing her long legs, encased in their trademark black mesh stockings, and asking him to put her to work. He did, sending her out to the housing projects to recruit volunteers. (That was Marietta's way—not to sign checks, but to do the legwork.) Every night she would go back to Bartle Bull and make her report. Bull, twenty-eight years old at the time, was utterly captivated by this energetic, enthusiastic, and attractive woman. They became lifelong friends.

But after Robert Kennedy's assassination, Marietta was doubtful about which candidate to support. She attended the Democratic Convention in Chicago, which she found very depressing, given the riots and the deep divisions in the Democratic Party over Vietnam. She campaigned modestly for Hubert Humphrey, whom she admired and with whom she had kept up a sporadic correspondence since the mid-1950s. (She flattered him, as she flattered many others, by asking him to send her copies of his speeches, which he did, signing himself, "Your Minnesota boyfriend.") But by the end of 1968 her attentions were elsewhere.

It is possible to argue that with Nixon winning the election and the Democrats banished from Washington, it was pointless for people like Marietta to huddle on the sidelines in frustration. Committed party workers, of course, simply sit out the time and hope that four years down the road the game will once more change in their favor. But predating the Nixon victory, in fact ever since Stevenson's death, Marietta's interest in politics had waned. Apart from her visit to Vietnam in 1966, she rarely referred to the conflict or got involved in any political action concerning the war and its increasingly tragic consequences. (The only time she seems to have taken a serious interest was when the Columbia University students staged their revolution in 1968, preventing her—and the whole class—from graduating. Once again those academic credentials she craved eluded her.)

Although she claimed her motives for pursuing her new interest in urban planning had derived from the knowledge and insights about public policy she had acquired that summer in Albany, there was another element that undoubtedly played a role in her decision. Marietta rarely made major career moves entirely alone. As in all her professional choices, a man seemed to appear at the crucial moment. At this point, now fifty years old, as she cast around for ways to harness her formidable energy and continue her goal of public service, she found her "bliss," as Joseph Campbell would have called it, in the form of a tall, charming, intellectual English aristocrat. He was an urban planner, and within a few years his life and work would become inseparable from hers.

# CHAPTER *30*

# *"Astral company"*

Marietta met Richard Llewelyn-Davies for the first time in March 1967, in Barbados, where he and his wife Patricia were staying as guests of their close friends Victor and Tess Rothschild. He and Marietta got on so well that they arranged to meet in early April in New York. They had dinner there and went to the movie *Ulysses*.

Richard Llewelyn-Davies was born in 1912 and had spent much of his childhood in Ireland. He was educated at Cambridge, the Ecole des Beaux-Arts in Paris, and the Architectural Association School in London. It was a privileged, intellectual upbringing. He used to say that Bertrand Russell pushed his pram. His cousins were adopted by J. M. Barrie and immortalized as the Lost Boys in Barrie's *Peter Pan*.

At Cambridge, Richard had belonged to the elite left-wing group of undergraduates and young dons called the Apostles. This all-male secret society was founded in the nineteenth century to promote philosophy and literature, but by the 1930s the Apostles had become politicized, and consisted largely of disaffected public school–educated young men (many of them homosexual, which at the time was illegal in Britain), who felt alienated from the establishment and the Church of England, and who, like many young people during that unstable decade between the wars, idealized the Soviet Union.

There were some notorious products of this closed society. The Apostles nurtured several of the Cambridge-fed group of spies such as Kim Philby, Guy Burgess, and Anthony Blunt, who later shocked the country with their treason. According to Andrew Sinclair, author of

*The Red and the Blue,* Richard Llewelyn-Davies had been a Marxist during those years.

Llewelyn-Davies qualified as an architect in 1939. His early achievements were in the field of hospital design. He became professor of architecture at University College, London, in 1960, and later of urban planning at the Bartlett School of Architecture, also in London. As well as teaching, he built up a successful architectural practice. His radical urban planning format for Northwick Park in the Cotswolds and Milton Keynes in Buckinghamshire in particular were widely praised as offering a visionary response to the social and economic pressures of urban growth. In 1963, he was given a life peerage for his contribution to architecture and planning. His wife Pat, a senior Labour politician, was also given a life peerage in her own right five years later. They had three daughters.

When Marietta met him, Richard Llewelyn-Davies and his partners were involved in several master plans for so-called new towns in Great Britain, but his firm was also hoping to expand its business abroad. Furthering these international ambitions, Richard had been made president, in 1965, of the World Society of Ekistics—ekistics being a theory relating to the interplay of environment and human settlements originated in Athens by the millionaire developer Constantinos Doxiadis.

That spring of 1967, when they first met, Marietta had scant interest in or knowledge of urban planning, but she immediately responded to Richard's work and wasted no time in furthering the connection. She wrote to him, telling him she was reading about ekistics and asked him to send her information about new town design. She met Constantinos Doxiadis and opened up a correspondence with him. When she started work at the New York State Constitutional Convention in April, she told Richard about some of the relevant issues. She invited him to go with her to Expo '67 in Canada in September, with her friends Roy and Lee MacLaren (Roy MacLaren was a former member of the Canadian Mission to the UN, and had become a good friend of Marietta's during the ECOSOC meetings in Geneva).

This was aggressive pursuit for a woman of that pre–women's liberation era, and especially one of Marietta's background. But by this time Marietta was inventing her own rules. She was fifty years old and an early convert to hormone therapy replacement. She radiated good health, looked wonderful, and was filled with energy that currently found no satisfactory outlet. It seemed a striking example of serendipity that this upper-class, remote Englishman, just the type she had always found attractive, not only entered her life at this point but responded so willingly.

Richard was gratified by her interest in his work. He invited her and Ronnie to dinner in London that first summer after they met, to introduce her to the minister of housing and local government, and other leading British economists and planners. He also suggested that Penelope and his daughter, Melissa, might meet, since Melissa was going to be a student at Harvard in 1968. Even their families were going to get along. (His wife Pat, meanwhile, had a demanding career in the House of Lords and was rarely around.)

The relationship blossomed. In September, Marietta abandoned Albany for Washington, where she met Richard and his English partner, Walter Bor. They toured a new town and then she and Richard flew on to Montreal to stay with the MacLarens and visit Expo. The MacLarens liked Richard and noticed Marietta's bright face in his presence. ("Perfect weekend," she told her calendar.)

It is unquestionable that the entrance of Richard Llewelyn-Davies into Marietta's life had a profound influence on her decision to enroll in Columbia University's urban planning program in November 1967. Following in the steps of her ancestor, George Peabody, who had pioneered low-income housing in London in the late nineteenth century, she responded warmly to Richard Llewelyn-Davies's high-minded approach to societies and habitats. The issues were not unfamiliar. She had encountered them during her years as a founder of Sydenham Hospital, as a member of the Fair Housing Practices Panel of New York under Mayor Wagner, and as a UN Commissioner of Human Rights. Now, with Richard's encouragement, she plunged into the Columbia course work with enthusiasm, keeping up a killing schedule that for Marietta was the means whereby she derived her strength.

But Richard Llewelyn-Davies had a more ambitious agenda. He had always been fascinated by the United States, and dreamed of opening an office in that country of zone-free real estate. Now he saw his opportunity. Marietta, with her money and her impressive contacts, would be the perfect person to help transform his British planning firm into a global enterprise. What better person to become a partner in the expanding venture he envisaged for his firm?

Throughout 1968 Marietta continued her studies, visited new towns, and went with Richard on his various trips around the United States checking out possible projects. She had to cut short some of her social and political obligations in New York that summer because Ronnie, alone in London, lost six pints of blood in one night and was rushed to the London Clinic. Ronnie's hemorrhage was diagnosed as having been due to the medication he was taking for his arthritis. He stayed in the hospital for almost three weeks, and was still there when Marietta left London in July to go on her first of the annual cruises around Greece organized by Constantinos Doxiadis.

These highly sought after cruises were designed to bring an eclectic group of scholars together for the study of ancient civilizations and to hold symposia on human settlements. Doxiadis, who helped build Islamabad, the new capital of Pakistan, structured the cruises with great care, with each morning devoted to seminars and each afternoon to private excursions. The last day's destination was always Delos, where a "proclamation" on the results of the seminars was held in the amphitheater. The other members of the 1968 cruise included Martin Meyerson, Jonas Salk, Buckminster Fuller, Margaret Mead, Arnold Toynbee, and the Llewelyn-Davieses.

Marietta was in her element, listening to experts expound on social psychology, architecture, urban planning, population, anthropology, and political science. She compared them to movie stars in the presence of a high school freshman. "I can't imagine why I was asked with this astral company," she wrote to her parents.

Martin Meyerson paid particular attention to Richard and Marietta during that cruise. Meyerson, a professor of urban planning and public policy, was at that time president of the State University of New York at Buffalo, and had been a close friend of Richard Llewelyn-Davies since 1960. Meyerson first met Marietta in New York, at a dinner given for them both by her teacher at Columbia, Charles Abrams. They entered into a friendship that was to last her lifetime. Perhaps one of his greatest gifts to her came in 1971, after he had become president of the University of Pennsylvania. He helped arrange for her to receive her bachelor's degree. She was by then, also thanks to Meyerson, a trustee of the university, and at the graduation, when the B.A. students rose, she was so pleased that she jumped up from her seat beside the trustees to share in the acclamation.

For that 1968 cruise, Meyerson had flown from London to Athens with Pat and Richard Llewelyn-Davies to join the Doxiadis party, and noticed Pat's response when she realized Marietta was going to be on board. "I could see Pat's face fall, feeling perhaps that this was real competition." On the last night of the cruise, the boat ran into a terrible storm, and Marietta and Martin stayed up talking till four o'clock in the morning. The group spent a night in Athens before Marietta and the Llewelyn-Davieses then went on to Israel for four days, visiting settlements and religious sites with Mayor Teddy Kollek, before finally returning to London. Although Ronnie was still recuperating, the Trees then left for their annual visit to Paris and on to the Villa Capponi in Florence.

Martin Meyerson, recipient of those 4:00 A.M. confidences on Doxiadis's yacht, believed that the romantic spark between Richard and Marietta was ignited that day in Athens after the glorious cruise through Greece. Just as Frankie had sensed something between her mother and Stevenson in Africa, so in Athens Martin picked up the unmistakable vibrations of two people falling for each other.[1] It is almost certain, however, that just as in Adlai's case, the vital connection had already been made. A month earlier, on June 5th, Bobby Kennedy was assassinated in Los Angeles. Richard Llewelyn-Davies sent Marietta a telegram from London that day. It read: "All my love and sympathy. Thy Richard." It would be difficult to misinterpret those seven words stamped in purple by Western Union.

By late 1968, Marietta was deeply involved in almost every aspect of Richard Llewelyn-Davies's business activities. She was passing possible clients to him, suggesting new projects to him, getting to know the partners in his English firm. At the end of that year, Llewelyn-Davies Associates (LDA) was established in New York (a second office was subsequently opened in Houston, Texas), with Llewelyn-Davies, John Weeks, and Marietta Tree as founder/partners, along with several young executives imported from England.

Business partners Marietta and Richard Llewelyn-Davies flank Los Angeles Commissioner Kenneth Hahn, 1968.

The business was precarious but full of potential. In those years, the idea of new towns had become fashionable as a possible solution to urban overpopulation, and developers were hungry for the huge real estate deals the building of new towns would engender. The office was soon humming with activity. Within the first two years of its incorporation, LDA was involved in the planning of thirteen new towns. The company also became involved in the restoration of several areas devastated by the race riots that marked that period in the United States. Llewelyn-Davies and his young English planners went in and attempted to rebuild communities in various strife-torn districts in New York, Detroit, and Los Angeles.

LDA expanded rapidly throughout the United States and points east. Work was embarked upon in Bogotá, Mustique, and many parts of the Persian Gulf. In 1971, the first Middle East office opened in Bahrain. Projects in Australia and Southeast Asia emerged, as well as in Thailand, Malaysia, Brunei, Indonesia, the Philippines, and Burma. By 1975, commissions in Asia were so successful that Llewelyn-Davies joined up with an Australian firm and became Llewelyn-Davies Kinhill (LDK).[2]

During these years, Marietta's contribution was incalculable. She wrote, or told Richard to write, to hundreds of people who might hire the firm or, if they could not, point them to real estate planners or developers who would do so. Her targets included old friends such as Bill Benton (who told Richard, "I will do anything for Marietta. Indeed, I will do anything to the point where she won't let me!"), and new ones such as Imelda Marcos. She gave lunches, dinners, made telephone calls. She even suggested to Ronnie that they rent out the rooms in East 79th Street that Penelope had vacated to the LDA office staff. "Only three people would use the rooms—they can go through the basement to the elevator and up. . . . The rent and the amount you get off the tax on the house might make it well worth while."

This idea was not palatable to Ronnie, who felt he had already made enough of a contribution to Marietta's new career. When she became a partner, she not only agreed to take no compensation but also put $25,000 (of Ronnie's money) into the firm. It needed every penny. While the ideals and talents of the group were considerable, they had almost no administrative skills. As the jobs came in, they had to find architects, economists, land use experts, plumbers, designers, and so on, and then pay them. Very soon it became clear that this would prove impossible. The office was hopelessly mismanaged right from the start. Even Marietta admitted she had no idea how to run it —"I just thought you took the money in and you paid people their salaries and kept the rest." Richard Llewelyn-Davies was no better at the practical side of things, and so the firm lurched from crisis to crisis in a mass of inefficient paperwork. As London partner Robert Trew commented later, "New York was high-profile and low bank balance."

To add to the firm's difficulties, there was a great deal of tension between London and New York. The London office felt that Richard was going out on some crazy limb in New York, spending all the firm's modest capital on deals that had no hope of bearing fruit. At least one senior partner in the London office also felt that Marietta Tree was a bad influence on Richard, distracting him from their increasingly serious financial problems, and deflecting him from his true course. The New York representatives in their turn felt that London was a brake on their ambitious ventures, and resented the criticism that emanated from across the Atlantic.

By 1972, Marietta's personal debt as a partner to Llewelyn-Davies Associates was over $33,000, and if the company was liquidated (as some were already predicting), her responsibility might be more. Ronnie's accountant began making anxious noises, so Marietta proposed to Richard that she be recompensed in some form for work done, and that from now on she be paid according to her time spent on the various projects as director of market research for the firm.

She redoubled her efforts to get business. Llewelyn-Davies Associates had a foothold in Manila, but the projects were not going well, and Marietta was called upon to reactivate her relationship with Imelda Marcos. So she made a trip to the Philippines with her colleagues, and although at the beginning relations between the visiting planners and Mrs. Marcos were slightly strained, the entire team ended up in a motorcade with the Philippine president's wife, their projects approved.[3] A year later Marietta went back, and again got on well with Imelda, leaving the country with a shopping list of possibilities, including being added to the short list for the World Bank development project of low-cost housing in the Tondo area of Manila.

Thanks to Marietta, all these overseas trips were marvelously well organized. She and her party could always stay at an embassy, since she knew many ambassadors either socially or from her State Department days (her old Indian diplomat friend Natwar Singh, for instance, had become ambassador to Poland). A car and driver were always put at her disposal. Thanks to Marietta, dinners were given to meet the crucial players. Tours of the areas in question, meetings, drinks, and sightseeing trips were laid on at the highest level.

Back home, the networking continued. She would invite important developers or corporate executives to dinner at 123 East 79th Street to meet Richard. Tall, lean, and intelligent, he acquitted himself well. People were impressed by his aristocratic demeanor, although he didn't particularly like his title, and only very reluctantly allowed the office to use it for the purposes of acquiring business. His left-wing sympathies made him hostile to such elitist panderings, and he was very sensitive to the class issue, particularly in the United States. On one occasion, he and Marietta were attending a government conference reviewing a study of poverty in Nassau County, New York. One of the key problems was lack of access to transportation. "Oh, I quite understand it," Marietta remarked. "Why, just a week ago, my driver was ill and I couldn't get around at all!" Richard was appalled, and warned her afterwards to be more careful.[4]

Marietta did not often make such blunders, although she was walking a tightrope between two worlds—one, the world of poverty, overcrowding, disease, and homelessness; the other, the world of Bill and Babe Paley, Venetian gondolas, and daily deliveries of fresh flowers. But by this time, she was accustomed to the dichotomy. Richard himself, after all, bridged these chasms with perfect aplomb.

It was a fine time for her, corraling, as it did, so many of her talents. Like her father, she enjoyed business, and said she wished she had started earlier. Visiting the City of London, Wall Street, and other business centers, she announced she wanted to become a merchant banker in her next career. "They seem such a wise and delightful lot." She had carefully learned the language of planning and prospectuses and had accumulated a certain amount of financial knowledge. But it was the people she met who stimulated and fulfilled her—and most of them were men.

It must be remembered that in the late sixties and early seventies, Marietta was a pioneer woman in a largely male profession. Builders, real estate developers, architects, chartered surveyors, were almost without exception men. Some women, such as those first law partners or corporate officers in all-male bastions, found this gender isolation daunting or irritating. Marietta loved it. Accustomed by now to being the only woman attending a business meeting, she played it for all it was worth. She was still nervous at having to make a speech or presentation; in spite of her accumulated experience, she never got over this nervousness, and would sometimes break out in hives. But for the most part those long, black mesh-encased legs were enough to distract her clients from any signs of anxiety, and she knew it. If the intensity of the relationships made during the New York Constitutional Convention had had a touch of Groton about it, her urban planning career was Groton writ large, this time with grown-ups instead of schoolboys gazing at her across the conference tables.

Moreover, the job gave her peripatetic life a sense of purpose. Her trips to England now had some justification, since they always involved meetings with Llewelyn-Davies Weeks, the London firm. Her glamorous dinners and trips abroad, always now with the purpose of hunting up business, qualified for an expense account. Not since the years with Adlai at the United Nations had she felt so morally grounded.

Her experience in the business world reaped another dividend. In

1973, Marietta was invited by her old friend Bill Paley to join the board of CBS. This was a time of increasing feminist militancy within the boardroom and in business generally, as more and more women moved up the corporate ladder and found no representation at the top. There had been pressure from inside CBS to hire a woman, and a 1973 CBS policy note recommended that "further progress and faster progress was essential." Bill Paley, like most chief executives, had no mind to offend the climate of the times, and Marietta was a perfect candidate. She had ambassadorial rank, she had an impressive background of foreign affairs, she had powerful friends; above all, she was loyal.

Her reputation began to spread in other quarters. In 1974, her old friend Susan Mary began working on a book of the letters she and Marietta had written to each other since the 1940s. Ken McCormick, the editor at Doubleday who worked with Susan Mary on the book, recognized that both women had led interesting lives, and thought each should produce separate memoirs. So both collected their letters saved over the years and had them typed up for publication. Susan Mary's letters to Marietta turned out to be wonderfully lively and illuminating about life at the U.S. Embassy in Paris between 1945 and 1960, and there seemed no reason why Marietta's in turn should not provide an equally fascinating mirror-image story about postwar life on the other side of the Atlantic. *To Marietta from Paris, 1945–1960,* was published in 1975 with great fanfare and lots of parties. When completed, Marietta's book was expected to enjoy the same enthusiastic reception.

Thus, by the mid-seventies, Marietta's loss of position at the United Nations had been effectively transformed into a new career. There were obvious similarities to her old job. She had an office with company letterhead, and loads of homework. She was required to travel a great deal, meet new people, inspect installations, and write reports. But the bottom line was very different. She had moved from the government to the corporation, from non-profit to for-profit, from public service to private gain. Although perhaps not apparent at the time, this shift represented one of the most critical preoccupations for Marietta during her last twenty years—financial independence.

# CHAPTER *31*

# *"Where was Marietta?"*

Ronnie's birthdays mostly went uncelebrated by his wife. She did not note them any more in her calendar, but on his seventy-third, in 1970, which he celebrated alone as usual at the hotel in Baden-Baden, she remembered to send him a telegram. In thanking her, he said he couldn't understand her ending, which read: "the happiest day for me." "Did it refer to my increased age!!" he asked, "or had you got a new town?"

The acidity of his remark was telling. For by this time, Ronnie had swallowed the bitter pill of recognition: he had lost Marietta again. There had been a brief respite after Adlai Stevenson died, when she returned to the fold, expressing devotion, missing him when apart, lyrical about their times together. But now all that was once again dissipated in a flurry of career duties, and, more crucially, in the maelstrom of romantic attraction.

Richard was not the only one. There was William S. Schlamm, a journalist who had met her in the 1940s and, like Arthur Schlesinger, had never forgotten her; Jack Cates, her UN colleague; William Hewitt, the handsome owner of John Deere farm equipment. All these men wrote to her during the years before and after Adlai's death with varying degrees of subtlety, longing for a speck of encouragement from that Belle Dame Sans Merci of East 79th Street.

Meanwhile, Ronnie mourned a double loss. For in 1968, just before his seventieth birthday, Collins retired and went home to his wife Nellie in England. (Few people knew that Collins had a wife. She

Playing "The Game."

was left behind when Collins went to America with Ronnie.) For his last vacation, the butler for the first and only time visited Barbados, seeing finally the tropical paradise that Mr. Tree had so often described.

As far as Marietta was concerned, Collins's retirement simply meant finding a replacement if possible (they still had a cook, a maid, a nurse, and a driver, in New York), although she conceded that the household missed him. Others also missed him. The art historian Kenneth Clark, who often stayed at 123 East 79th Street, used to say he only stayed there because of Collins. Bishop and Mrs. Peabody were deeply fond of Collins, and often sent their love to him in letters to Marietta. But for Ronnie, losing Collins meant more than losing an extraordinary butler. It meant losing his closest friend. The two had been together for over forty years. For Ronnie, New York had never really seemed like home. With Collins gone, his heart left the city forever.

Ronnie's mood darkened. Like many people as they age, he became increasingly disenchanted with the world. In his European travels, as he encountered the destructiveness of mass tourism and the crumbling of the buildings he loved, he grew nostalgic. "My memory keeps going back to the 20s and 30s, when it all shone with gaiety and light." By the early 1970s, Ronnie and Marietta were separate for longer and longer periods. When they were together, the bickering between them was noticeable. If Ronnie was in the middle of a story, Marietta would interrupt with one of her own. Playing "The Game," Ronnie would suggest the word "guilt" and add, sotto voce, "Marietta would be good at that one."

But this time, he turned elsewhere for succor. Deserted by Marietta, and with Penelope no longer living at home, he felt he could revert to a safe haven he had experienced as a much younger man and now found again gave him some kind of peace, a haven that excluded women altogether.

He was very discreet. In fact, many people would not believe that Ronnie was bisexual. "Double-gaited? I never saw it," Hope Scott, Ronnie's neighbor in Barbados, said.[1] But Hope Scott was Marietta's friend, and many of her friends closed ranks on the issue. Ronnie's own friends felt differently. A considerable number of young men of their generation, who were steeped in the values of the classical education purveyed at traditional British public schools, had had homosexual experiences as boys. Most moved on to heterosexual love and marriage, but many never lost the romantic glow of Greek love instilled in them as adolescents. Ronnie's bitter childhood, bereft of female warmth or comfort, and with only a sad and lonely father for companionship, would have made him a ready candidate for the intense consolation of Winchester, where he found an aesthetic and emotional home, and which he later described in a torrent of gratitude.

Ronnie's other life remained secondary to his marriages, but it did not disappear. Bill Walton, longtime friend to both Trees, remembered a night in England in 1943, in the middle of the war, when he was invited for the weekend to Ditchley. Going down in a train during the evening blackout, he found himself in a pitch-dark compartment wtih one other person, whose army boots were the only identifying feature. Both travelers alighted at the Oxford station, where a voice said, "Ditchley, sir?" It was Collins. To Bill's surprise, the army boots followed him to the car. They belonged to an American soldier.

They arrived at Ditchley, where a glamorous dinner party for four was prepared for them by Ronnie with Edwina D'Erlanger (Mary

Warburg's sister, who was staying on the Ditchley estate) as the only other guest. After dinner, it was made perfectly clear to Bill that he was to disappear to one side of the house while Ronnie and the young American captain retired to the other.[2] (Ronnie's marriage to Nancy broke up at about this time, and in this context it is interesting that Nancy said much later about Ronnie, for whom she retained a deep affection, that she "wished to God" he were her brother.[3] The sexual implication may well have had a bearing on her flight from him into the arms of the earthy Colonel Lancaster.)

At the beginning of Ronnie's relationship with Marietta, he was totally in love with her. Nor is there any evidence she had the slightest inkling of his sexual otherness. But sensitivity to the subject emerged early in their relationship. During the two years before their marriage in 1947, her letters are filled with remarks such as, "Everybody's a little queer but thee and me, dear," or about a friend with a "new pansy husband, both looking tortured . . ." When she met Joe Alsop, she ascribed his sweeping political cynicism to his latent homosexuality. About Harold Nicolson, whose book *Some People* she had just read, she said, "he reveals himself as a rather frivolous, intellectual snob with a great streak of homosexuality." She described a dinner party with a "loathsome homosexual." She suspected a friend of being a homosexual "as the only girl he has ever been interested in is a wildly promiscuous type and this is his way of mentally getting contact with other men. . . . This is a very well-known pattern." Back in New York, her bias continued to show. In 1960, campaigning for John F. Kennedy along West 55th Street, she complained to Ronnie about the "squalor and sordidness of people's lives there. Most of the people we saw were homosexuals, and glad to say they were mostly Republican."

Homophobia was undoubtedly part of Marietta's Peabody background. The Rector of Groton, having founded his school on the English model, was hypersensitive to the dangers endemic in such places, and he made quite sure that the English public schoolboy's experience would not infect his own institution. Hence the sleeping cubicles with flimsy curtains, showers with no doors, no dorm visitations, and, in perhaps a more subtle show of prejudice, the almost total lack of emphasis on art in the school curriculum. Marietta, who, like most of her class and generation, grew up in a society where most gays were still locked in the closet, had little conscious exposure to homosexuality and even less knowledge of its observances. Indeed, Lionel Trilling wrote a biography of E. M. Forster in 1943 without ever realizing that Forster was a homosexual.

But even taking into account the period in which she was living, a period of extreme naïveté on the part of most educated Americans, her references to homosexuality, emerging from the very beginning of her affair with Ronnie, seem odd. It is difficult not to conclude that her unease stemmed from a deep subconscious suspicion about her future husband. Her insistence on mentioning homosexuals to him in such a derogatory fashion, and her repetition of stories proving how Ronnie shared her opinion, seem to confirm that the doubt was pressing on her mind. For instance, in 1949, while still living at Ditchley, Ronnie and Marietta went to a party given by Noël Coward, at which Ronnie, according to Marietta, was so appalled by the overwhelming number of "pansies" there that they left within the hour—even though Marlene Dietrich was present! The most revealing aspect of this story is that she reported it to her parents, indicating how much she needed this kind of "correct" response from Ronnie to show the world there was nothing to worry about.

As the marriage progressed, Marietta's apprehensions diminished. But her aversion to homosexuals did not disappear. She rarely had openly homosexual friends, and unlike many women, did not enjoy their company. Frank Taylor had become a top publisher at McGraw-Hill after his stint in the movies and had remained friendly with Marietta, inviting her to be a literary scout for him. But when Taylor came out of the closet in the late 1970s, Marietta never spoke to him again. Her old friend from the Stevenson days, C. K. McClatchy, also turned out to be gay. According to his former wife, Grace Warnecke (George Kennan's daughter), he could never have told Marietta.

When Evangeline Bruce remarked that she would rather her husband go off with another man than with another woman, Marietta disagreed, saying she would prefer another woman, for then one could at least be jealous.[4] On another occasion, Marit Gruson (a friend and frequent guest at Heron Bay) and Marietta were discussing a mutual friend, whom Marietta said was very interested in her. "But surely you realize he is a homosexual?" Mrs. Gruson said. Marietta was horrified.[5] At Marietta's parties, the single men around the dinner table were invariably divorced. Marietta would not invite single males unless she was confident they were heterosexual.

Thus, when Ronnie later began to surround himself with homosexuals, the old fears came back to haunt her. Of course the very fact that Ronnie had chosen to take up residence in Barbados was, in sophisticated circles, something of a signal. For in the early postwar years, Barbados was becoming like Tangiers a mecca for English homosexuals. (Homosexuality was illegal in Britain until the 1960s). Famous residents such as Edward Cunard and Oliver Messel had established in the British West Indian island an expatriate circle that was well known in the artistic and fashionable world of London.

A few visitors to Heron Bay during Ronnie's last years saw the signs—young male guests, late night bedroom assignations—but it is not certain when or how Marietta realized what was going on. It is a fact that on one occasion in the 1970s when two flagrantly gay friends of Ronnie's arrived in Barbados, Marietta pointedly announced she was leaving for New York. Her way of dealing with the problem was simple—get the hell out. Ronnie's exclusion of her in this way was also, of course, her ticket to freedom. He had in effect granted her license to pursue her own interests.

Always experts in the practice of discretion, they kept up a united front. They regularly wrote to each other with fondness, declaring that they missed each other. Marietta still asked Ronnie permission to do things—to go to Africa in 1968, for instance. In 1972 they celebrated their silver wedding anniversary in London with one hundred guests (Ronnie did not mention it in his calendar).

They also shared an increasing anxiety about Penelope. Marietta's relations with her second daughter had continued to disintegrate. As Penelope grew up and learned how to uncover her feelings, Marietta's remained concealed in more and more layers of impenetrable wrapping. The problem was compounded by Penelope's success as a model. Mothers with a history of beauty often feel threatened by the youthful progress of an equally beautiful daughter. Penelope's face and body splashed across fashion magazines and newspapers all over the world presented a real challenge for her mother. Articles about Heron Bay would be entitled "Penelope's Tree House." Marietta might appear in a token snapshot alongside her daughter.

Marietta was not pleased by this publicity. "I must say, I am getting a little fed up with her cosmic pronouncements about bosoms and legs," she wrote testily to a friend. When pressed, she would make disparaging remarks both privately and to the press about Penelope's "grotesque" clothes and eye makeup. Like many parents in the sixties, Marietta was bewildered by the extent of her child's alienation, which she could neither understand nor sympathize with. Ronnie's indulgence of their daughter only aggravated Marietta's hostility.

Penelope's continuing cohabitation with the very famous David Bailey was equally upsetting. Marietta was accustomed to co-opting the male friends of her daughters, and Bailey's stubborn rejection of her charms was extremely irritating. When the young couple visited Barbados, Marietta retaliated with condescension. If they played The Game, she would say, "Do you think Bailey will understand this word?"

But in 1972, the year of the Trees' silver wedding anniversary, Penelope gave them a particularly unwelcome present. That October, she was arrested in a flat in London with drugs in her handbag. The police treated her very badly and refused to allow her to make a phone call until David Bailey turned up to post her bail. "Suddenly they became charming and took my fingerprints as if teaching me piano."

Penelope at home in Barbados, 1972.

She was tried at the West London Magistrates Court, conditionally discharged for two years, and ordered to pay £15 costs. Ronnie supported Penelope throughout the proceedings, and stayed by her, undaunted by the publicity he received from the press.

Marietta had been in New York when Penelope was arrested and did not fly to her side. "Penelope trouble," she wrote in her calendar. Moreover, although she was in London immediately prior to the trial, she did not stay. Leaving Ronnie and Penelope to cope together, she went back to New York. Lunches and dinners with friends had been arranged for that week in New York, but in fact there was no urgent appointment she could not miss. Under these circumstances, it is difficult to justify Marietta's abandonment of her daughter. For Penelope, her mother's absence was duly filed away in the drawer marked "Heartlessness."

Meanwhile, Frankie was a paragon of daughterhood. Having worked for several years on a monumental essay on the history of the war in the Vietnamese context, in October 1972 she published the book *Fire in the Lake*. It was a stunning critical success. But although Marietta was intensely proud of her daughter's sudden fame, again her reaction was laced with rivalry. Penelope's power over her mother pertained to her beauty and celebrity. Frankie's threat was intellectual, and just as problematic.

And then Frankie won a Pulitzer Prize for *Fire in the Lake*. Although Frankie's time in Vietnam had liberated her to some extent, the honor gave her enormous assurance, and the strength to loosen the bonds by which she was "hopelessly wedded," in a friend's phrase, to her mother. For Marietta, pride and jealousy fought for ascendancy. She told friends how she wished she could write like Frankie. (Her own book was going nowhere, which intensely frustrated her.) "I am now either Mrs. Peabody's daughter or Frances FitzGerald's mother," she said. Nor was she entirely pleased with the discovery that when she could not get a table at a restaurant, if she said, "I am Penelope Tree's mother," a table magically appeared.

Meanwhile, although Marietta and Ronnie lived mostly apart, she was still attentive to his moods and was anxious not to make a bad situation worse. Ronnie published his book about Barbados in 1972, and encouraged by the response, he now began to write his memoirs. The writing of this was more difficult, however, than he had thought, and he grew discouraged. Marietta was determined that the project go forward. Earlier in London she had met the author and journalist Kenneth Harris, who was writing a biography of Clement Attlee, the Labour prime minister who succeeded Churchill in 1945. "Ronnie's period," Marietta told him, and asked Harris to stay with them in Tuscany and help Ronnie with his book.

Ronnie and Harris worked together on the book all through August. Harris then went back to England to his own writing. But in January 1974, he met Marietta again in London and she told him that Ronnie was very depressed and said she would pay Harris's fare to Barbados if he would go out and help Ronnie finish the book. So Harris and Ronnie started work again, and with a typist and a tape recorder managed to complete a draft by the summer of 1974.[6]

On June 20, 1974, Marietta's father died in his sleep in Massachusetts General Hospital, eight days before his eighty-sixth birthday. The bishop had been ailing for four or five years with Parkinson's and what was probably a condition of pre-Alzheimer's. Mrs. Peabody nursed him almost entirely herself. Marietta found this self-sacrificing behavior wildly irritating, seeing it as yet another example of her mother's martyrlike strength, and her one-upmanship. Marietta grew enraged, for instance, when Malcolm took a bad turn and Mrs. Peabody would not call the doctor because their regular doctor was on vacation.

Mrs. Peabody did in fact find the long decline of her husband painful and debilitating, hating to witness his weakness. On occasion she would grow abusive, for instance saying, "Go on, tie your tie, old man," to the enfeebled bishop. One day she was talking to a friend in her husband's sick room, and remarked that they'd had a lovely life together. "We've always been happy." At which the bishop raised his head and said, "Says you!" and fell back on the pillow again.

Marietta was in London when he died, and flew to Boston the following day, where a huge family gathering took place at All Saints, Brookline. The ceremony had been mostly planned by the bishop himself, with some assistance from his son George, now the family's senior cleric. There was a lunch in the parish house for about eighty members of the family, and the following morning, once more playing the bad daughter, Marietta flew back to England, thus missing the burial. Endicott wrote to her describing the scene. It was a glorious spring day. "George requested that a spade be left at the grave site and during the prayers we all sprinkled some dirt in the grave. . . . Mother was like a rock—I'm sure immensely relieved for Daddy to be liberated."

The only son (amid five sisters) of a legendary educator to thousands of boys, many of whom themselves became distinguished public servants, Malcolm Peabody was handicapped from birth by the weighty presence of his father, and never escaped the psychological burden. Malcolm had been a good bishop in a second-level diocese. He had been a careful businessman and an excellent administrator, and he acknowledged his weaknesses.

As a father, he was never strong enough to share power with his wife, thus creating an imbalance in the family dynamic that had lasting effects on all his children. Even at the end of his life, Malcolm had not come much closer to sensing his children's needs. Sometime before he died, he revised his will, and asked Sam whether, knowing of Marietta's wealth compared to the other members of the family, he should leave any money to her. Marietta heard about this and flew into a fury, making sure she got her share. That Malcolm should have contemplated such a classic error indicates his lack of understanding about his children, whose relentless competitiveness was the benchmark by which he would ultimately be judged as a parent.

As the father of Marietta, this failure of nerve was particularly damaging. He was her primary model of manhood. But the fact that he was a bishop, and yet at the same time unable to redeem his only daughter, presented her with an insuperable paradox. Throughout her life, her choice of older men was to a great extent predetermined by her experience of Malcolm Peabody as both God and wimp.

Malcolm represented another paradox, which also cut deeply into the consciousness of his daughter. The clerical profession involves by its very nature a series of deceptions, both moral and ethical. While most jobs have responsibilities during the day that can be shed in the evening, the job of a priest is to be a holy person all the time. The priest's family, *who know the truth,* must sustain the myth and keep the reality from the world. For Marietta, the outward and visible sign of her father the bishop as man of the cloth was counteracted on a daily basis by the imperfect individual whom she knew at home. She, like her brothers, grew up as a co-conspirator in the family secret.

This early training in deception was aggravated by Malcolm Peabody's social circle, a diocese of mostly rich people. Particularly during the years in Chestnut Hill, the pressure of an impoverished parson to keep up with the standards of wealth of his flock, while at the same time teaching the Christian values of humility and unselfishness, was made painfully clear to the young Marietta. The anxiety over appearances engendered by this conflict played an important role in her later years.

In the end, after leaving most of his tangible possessions to his wife and small gifts to various Episcopal institutions, Bishop Peabody bequeathed to each of his children roughly $37,000 in cash (with Endicott receiving less, in recognition of the bishop's contributions to his son's many political campaigns). Marietta also received thirty shares of IBM common stock to add to the gifts of stock he had already made her—a respectable legacy, but not enough to relieve her of fears about her financial future.

Three months after Marietta's father died, Ronnie had a stroke. Sam and Judy Peabody had seen him in August in Venice, where he seemed pathetically sad and lonely (Marietta, perhaps feeling a twinge of guilt, had asked Judy to keep him company there). He was staying at the Cipriani, where he had always felt at home, and yet this time he seemed not to know anyone. Judy's last memory of him before his stroke was of him with his cane, standing alone on the boat taking him from the Cipriani back to the mainland.

That September, in Asolo, as usual, with Michael Teague, they decided to take a trip into the mountains. As they drove over the Alps, Ronnie began to feel strange (he had high blood pressure and the air was very thin). By the time they returned home, Ronnie was paralyzed and was taken immediately to the hospital in Asolo. Marietta arrived the following day with Penelope. Ronnie stayed in the hospital in Asolo for three weeks, then he was flown to the London Clinic for further treatment. He stayed in London until the beginning of December, when he finally went home to Barbados.

Many friends rallied around, sending gifts and offering help. Marietta spent the month of September commuting between London and New York, organizing therapy, finding someone to read to Ronnie, making appointments for visitors, and always urging him on to recovery. Once back in Barbados, a routine was arranged for him, which involved speech therapy, physiotherapy, and swimming every morning, aided by his close friends and family, including Frankie, Christa Armstrong, Michael, Anne, Jeremy, and Penelope, who had now broken up with David Bailey.

Another element contributed to his slow but sure improvement. In early 1975, thanks to the good fortune of Kenneth Harris's availability and Ronnie's perseverance, Ronnie's memoir, *When the Moon Was High,* was published in England. It was serialized in December 1974 in the London *Sunday Times*—a wonderful Christmas present. The book was very well received and provoked a lot of interest and comment. There are some curious omissions, however, for those with biographical instincts. Ronnie dwells long and lovingly on the purchase and restoration of Ditchley with Nancy, and on his first wife's contribution to Churchill's enjoyment when the great war hero spent weekends there during the war. The author does not mention Marietta; the last chapter ends before Ronnie left England in 1945, and the dedication is to Kenneth Harris.

Much of the spring of 1975, Marietta commuted. Sometimes it would be a week in Heron Bay, a week in New York, then back to Barbados again, to London for a week, back to New York. This backbreaking schedule was interspersed with trips to Caracas and Toronto, a gala week entertaining Roy Jenkins, then British home secretary and a new friend, plus regular attendance at meetings of CBS, the Asia Society (which she had joined in 1967), the Junior Fortnightly, and the University of Pennsylvania.

In this period of business activity for Marietta, perhaps her most significant new appointment was to the board of Pan American World Airways. She had met Najeeb Halaby, then chairman of Pan Am, in the early 1970s. Halaby had expressed more than a passing interest in her, and as the friendship developed, it was an easy progression to get her introduced to William Seawell (who replaced Halaby as chairman and CEO of Pan Am in 1972). Marietta was elected to the board in March 1975. This was an ideal matching of individual and interest, for, apart from the added financial benefits, she could now travel almost anywhere in the world free.

While Marietta sped about her business, Ronnie was still nearly immobile in a wheelchair. There were two full-time nurses at Heron Bay. Tull, the faithful servant, carried his master three times a day into the ocean to swim. "It was a real sorrowful time," Tull recalled later.[7] The stroke had damaged Ronnie's speech, and like many stroke victims, he grew exasperated at not being able to find the right words. As she watched him, so reminiscent of her grandmother, Mrs. Parkman, after her stroke, Marietta reacted, typically, by trying to push him harder, harder. Her reports home to parents and friends were always about how brilliantly he was improving, as if by mere force of will she could cure him.

In June, Ronnie was deemed well enough to make the annual trip to London. Marietta stayed with him just four days before returning to New York for five days, then back to London again. In London she saw a lot of Richard Llewelyn-Davies, of course, for business reasons, and there was the usual round of social events, most of which Ronnie could not attend. James Montanari, a member of the Llewelyn-Davies firm in London, used to escort Marietta to some of these parties ("when it was indiscreet for Richard to go with her," he observed), including the duke of Buccleugh's ball for his son's twenty-first birthday.

When Ronnie returned to Barbados, Marietta's hectic schedule continued. She now had monthly meetings of four major boards, as well as travel for Llewelyn-Davies. Literally every other week she commuted between Barbados and New York, a trip that takes almost a whole day under the best conditions. The effect was that both places suffered. "I feel I have to collapse a month's work in two weeks to justify being there only half a month every month, so I do everything badly," she confessed to her mother.

Ronnie's Barbados friends shared this opinion. Jack Leacock, a doctor and scion of one of the oldest families of the island, felt so strongly that Marietta was deserting her husband that he told her so in a letter. "The place was beginning to deteriorate," he said later. "There were no more parties to cheer him up. Where was Marietta?"[8]

Two years after his stroke, in May 1976, Ronnie left Barbados again for New York and Europe. Although still weak and barely mobile, he made the journey from Barbados alone. Just before he left, he arranged for a photograph to be taken of himself and all the staff on the steps of Heron Bay. He stood on the colonnaded staircase he had designed with such care, surrounded by his beloved staff, and wept. "We all cried," Tull remembered. It was as though he—and they—knew they were together for the last time.

Ronnie stayed in New York for a month. He was ill and tired there, but Marietta had made many engagements and tried to arrange for friends such as the Brecks to distract him. On June 10, they went together to London, where they had rented the Glendevons' flat in Chelsea. However ill and tired he was, the relentless social schedule had to be kept up. They went to the opera, attended an antiques fair, spent the weekend with the Linlithgows.

On June 18, Marietta's favorite aunt Betsey Peabody died at the age of eighty-one. Marietta hurriedly flew back to Groton for the funeral, then returned to London for two weeks before flying back again to New York. The weekend of the Fourth of July she rested at the Paleys' pool at Kiluna Farm on Long Island. Her old friend Babe Paley, who had been diagnosed with the cancer that was to kill her two years later, was recovering from the removal of her right lung. (Marietta was equally brisk with Babe, encouraging the sick woman with her energy and positive thinking.)

Back in New York, Marietta attended a Pan Am meeting, went to a dinner party for the British publisher George Weidenfeld, and attended a farewell party for the queen on the royal yacht *Britannia*. On Sunday, July 11, while Marietta was again enjoying the Paleys' pool, Ronnie had another stroke. This time it affected the brain stem, and he went into a coma.

Marietta flew to London, arriving on Monday morning. She was furious. In her absence, Michael, Jeremy, and Penelope, after consultation with the doctor, had decided that their father should not be returned to the hospital but that he should die peacefully in his bed. They knew he wanted to go. The two years since his first stroke had been mostly a time of deepening despair. But Marietta would not release him, not even during those last days. "You have let him die," she railed at them. "He could have lived."

Ronald Tree died at noon on Wednesday, July 14. He was seventy-eight years old. It was while Marietta was gone that he had slipped away.

# CHAPTER *32*

# *"Ronnie full estate to me"*

Ronnie's funeral service was held at the American Church in North Audley Street, Mayfair. Marietta sat in the front pew, heavily veiled. At the end of the ceremony, an anonymous prayer was read, sent in by a friend of the family. People afterwards learned it had been written by Nancy Lancaster.[1]

After her divorce, Nancy had moved to a house not far from Ditchley called Haseley Court, which was much admired and photographed for its fine interior decoration. For the rest of her life, although refusing ever to reenter Ditchley, she kept a close eye on her former home. When Ditchley was bought from Lord Wilton by Sir David Wills and turned into a conference center (the Ditchley Foundation, formed in 1958 to promote Anglo-American relations), Nancy was often consulted about redecoration and furniture acquisitions for the house.

As she remained close to Ditchley, so the first Mrs. Tree had remained close to Ronnie. Even at the worst time after their divorce Ronnie had maintained a connection, urging her to buy the design firm founded by the well-known English decorator and socialite, Sibyl Colefax, which later became Colefax & Fowler, and with which Nancy did her finest work as a decorator.[2] Over the years, Nancy and Ronnie sometimes saw each other on Ronnie's annual trips to England, and they occasionally corresponded. When she heard Penelope was moving to London, Nancy proposed that Penelope rent her London flat. She could not help adding a characteristic dig: "It is no funnier than

Marietta being photographed at Ditchley in my rooms and going to Mirador. . . ." Nancy Lancaster did not believe in bygones being bygones.

After Ronnie's stroke, Nancy sent him flowers. "I won't come and see you," she wrote, ". . . our past goes so far back that it might emotionally upset you until you are stronger." A Christian Scientist, like her aunt Nancy Astor, Nancy assured him that she was getting help for him in Christian Science. Later she visited Ronnie in his London flat. Marietta, having let her in, left the house and wandered around South Audley Street, growing more and more agitated. On one corner of the street there was a negligée shop, so, filled with revenge, she went in and bought herself a totally outrageous satin nightdress. "Just send the bill to Mr. Tree," she told the salesperson.[3]

In December, after Ronnie had returned to Barbados, Nancy wrote to Marietta, telling her that the doctor had said he wanted Ronnie to relax, "and not try with exasperation to strain to get better." Nancy knew that the doctor's opinion went directly against Marietta's own preferred course of action, otherwise she probably could not have brought herself to write to her nemesis in this way. (The first Mrs. Tree outlived the second. When Nancy finally died in 1995, at the age of ninety-six, she was buried in the place she loved best, the family home of Mirador, in Charlottesville, Virginia.)

Ronnie's death was treated honorably in the newspapers. His connection with Churchill and his friendship with Tory politicians such as Anthony Eden and Lord Salisbury were referred to with respect. *The Times* noted that his happiest times were with his first wife Nancy at Ditchley during the war. The obituary writer did not mention Ronnie's children, and only glancingly named Marietta as his second wife. Ambassador David Bruce wrote a tribute in the same newspaper which mentioned Ronnie's hospitality, kindness, and genius for friendship, adding that before Pearl Harbor, "with the exception of Winston Churchill, Tree was the most effective British official associated with Public Relations aspects of Anglo-American Affairs."

Ronnie's contributions to Barbados were the most keenly felt and his buildings there remain as monuments to his artistic sensibility. Isaiah Berlin expressed this in a letter to Ronnie in 1965: "I have never admired anything more than your taste, courage, confidence, creative capacity, above all fearless self-confidence and perfectly justified reliance on your infallible aesthetic sense in creating that magnificent palazzo. . . ."

But Ronnie gave much more to Barbados than beautiful architecture. His lawyer and friend Jack Dear listed in the *Barbados Advocate* Ronnie's many contributions to the island, apart from the Sandy Lane Hotel, including the Family Planning Association, fund-raising for the

University of the West Indies, the founding of the Barbados National Trust, and the rescuing of many parts of the island from development or destruction—the Trents Playing Field and Welchman Hall Gully among them.[4]

What Dear also knew but did not mention was a letter Ronnie had given him five years earlier. Dated April 21, 1971, it was marked, "To be opened in the event of my death." In it, Ronnie told Jack that he wanted to be cremated in New York and his ashes scattered over the cliffs at the east end of St. John's Church in Barbados. He asked that none of the family attend. "It is too hard on my family to do this." These instructions were not carried out as Ronnie died in London, but they indicate the love he felt for the island he had come to think of as home.

Instead, Ronnie was buried on Monday, July 19, 1976, in All Saints Church, Spelsbury, in the parish of Ditchley, in Oxfordshire. A small group of friends as well as the immediate family attended. The Peabodys had pooled their resources and sent Sam over from the United States to represent the family. ("He is a good one to do it, for he knows how to communicate better than some of us, myself included," said Mrs. Peabody.) Richard Llewelyn-Davies did not go, telling Roy Jenkins that he had stayed away on grounds of privacy. Perhaps he meant tact.

As an odd footnote, a year later almost to the day, some of the same people found themselves in that church again, this time to attend the funeral of Ronnie's closest aide and longtime servant, Edmund John Collins. Collins was two years younger than Ronnie, and as always, he saw that his master went first. The legendary butler's funeral was attended by his wife Nellie, Michael and Jeremy Tree, and Marietta's former maid Alice Butler, who had in Collins's final years moved near him and helped nurse him at the end.

Collins was buried next to his master in the cemetery of All Saints. The two graves are almost identical, with matching engravings on the stones, and they lie together, like a longtime couple, protected by a box hedge enclosure. Thus in death, class distinctions vanished. ("No room for me," Marietta remarked wryly some time later on viewing the neatly enclosed plot.)

There was a memorial service for Ronnie at the Grosvenor Chapel in South Audley Street, attended by representatives for Princess Alice (the queen's cousin) with whom Ronnie had worked closely in their roles as trustees of the University of the West Indies, the earl and countess of Avon (Ronnie's old friend Anthony Eden), and other friends. On this less private occasion, Richard Llewelyn-Davies showed up. There was also a memorial service at St. James's Church in Barbados, which was overflowing with Ronnie's friends and those who had worked for him.[5]

The distinction of Ronnie's condolence letters perhaps reflects best the qualities of the man. They ranged from messages from the queen mother at Buckingham Palace to the former warden of All Saints' Church at Spelsbury. Many mentioned his sweetness, generosity, and human decency. Perhaps the most moving was from Tull, Ronnie's loyal Barbadian servant. "I was very sad when I heard the sad news of Mr. Tree death," he wrote to Marietta. "It leave me limbless without saying nothing. . . . Mr. Tree was a father to me, almost everything I achieved is through him. I am sure that I could never find no one after God to be like him to me. . . ."

Many referred to Marietta's role in Ronnie's life, his immense pride in her, her life-enhancing qualities, and her contributions to his happiness. Harold Acton, after referring to Ronnie's exquisite taste, tolerance, and vitality, wrote to her, "Coraggio e avanti! Life must be lived, not endured, as Norman Douglas used to say." Anne Tree affectionately recalled her last memory of Ronnie and Marietta together at Michael and Anne's country house, arm-in-arm in the garden on a lovely June night.

For Marietta, these sentiments were overshadowed by a bruising personal crisis. Ronnie's death presented her with perhaps the biggest challenge of her life. For the first time, she was on her own. That in itself, of course, was not so significant. She had been living on her own, in a sense, for years. But now she was on her own financially—a very different matter indeed. The first realization of it terrified her. She had had maids, chauffeurs, clothes from Paris, the best hotels, the best restaurants, flowers, champagne. Without a thought, weekly bills had magically been paid by the limitless supply of Ronnie's cash. Now where would the money come from? It had vanished almost overnight. Vanished also was her composure. For a short while after Ronnie's death, Marietta almost went out of her mind.

Penelope was the first to suffer. After her mother's furious accusations that Penelope had not done enough to save Ronnie, there was no repairing the damage. Devastated at the loss of her father, Penelope found herself grieving alone. Michael and Jeremy were close by, but they were half brothers, not mothers. Frankie and Sam were there to comfort Marietta, but who was to comfort Penelope? "It was one of the worst moments of my life," she said later.

Raw with rage and pain, Marietta and Penelope grew increasingly distraught with each other. Even Michael Teague, a constant presence during those anguished days, saw the tension and tried to make some fragile peace between them, to no avail.[6] Penelope wept and her mother screamed until nothing more could be said, and then Penelope fled. She hardly spoke to her mother again for over a year.

Ten days after Ronnie died, Marietta returned to New York with Sam and Frankie. In New York, she met with Coudert Brothers' senior partner James B. Sitrick, her lawyer, and old friends Mary Warburg, Martin Meyerson, Christa Armstrong, and Calvin Plimpton. She then flew up to Northeast Harbor for a week, to see her parents, aunts, and Frankie. In Maine, Marietta climbed Acadia Mountain, attended a big family lobster and clam party, went to church, and slept badly. After another week in New York she flew to Barbados. Susan Mary and her son-in-law, George Crile, accompanied her. Staying in the Pink Cottage were the Llewelyn-Davieses.

At Heron Bay, Marietta withdrew. Facing the hundreds of condolence letters that flooded in, she was paralyzed. Susan Mary, faithful friend, sorted them for her and tried to urge her to respond at least to the most important ones. Even Eppie Lederer, Marietta's old friend from Chicago, was enlisted to encourage her. As the columnist Ann Landers, she knew what was required. "You must let friends who wrote know that their letters were received and appreciated." Marietta, like a child who has been naughty, apologized. "I realize that it's good for others as well as for myself, and I also want to get your approval. . . ."

Those close to her were shocked at her loss of poise. Michael Tree, who had witnessed her collapse firsthand, implored her to keep a cool head. Evangeline Bruce, learning of Marietta's breach with Penelope, wrote from the heart (her own daughter, Sasha, had been murdered in 1975 after a period of alienation from her parents): "That Penelope share some of your present time in Barbados is my fervent prayer. Nothing is more bitter than a loving child's face turned against one. . . ."

But that month in Barbados, Marietta could barely function. There was tension with the staff of Heron Bay, who were reluctant to continue working for their mistress. She had never been able to win them over. Her insecurity translated as arrogance. They also were deeply loyal to their beloved Mr. Tree, and they did not like it that Mrs. Tree kept photographs of Governor Stevenson in her bathroom.[7] When Marietta was at Heron Bay without Ronnie, they had often been openly hostile—even insolent, Lee MacLaren remembered. With Ronnie's death, all joy left the house at Heron Bay, and there was little sympathy left for the woman they had never really trusted.

Marietta stayed in her room, tired and anxious, talking obsessively to her lawyers and accountants about finances. She found no respite in the presence of Richard Llewelyn-Davies, for his alert wife kept a strict watch and made acid asides about the grieving widow that only aggravated the tension. It was left to Susan Mary to smooth ruffled feathers, keep the place running, and to show the house to prospective buyers. When she finally returned to Washington, she, too, was exhausted.[8]

For the two years between Ronnie's stroke and his death, the issue of money had loomed larger and larger in Marietta's mind. She started making inquiries about her tax situation. In May 1976, two months before Ronnie died, she wrote in her calendar, almost as though to reassure herself, "Ronnie full estate to me."

What was this estate? In spite of his early efforts, she knew she would not inherit any capital from Ronnie's trust, which gave a one-sixth share to each of his children, but none to his wife. After Ronnie's stroke in 1974, Marietta and he had decided to sell 123 East 79th Street and buy something smaller. Ronnie would never wish to be in New York for long again. Penelope had left home. The house was obviously too big for Marietta alone, even counting the live-in servants who remained; they included Alice, Mabel, and a cook. In early 1976, a controversial millionaire named John Samuels agreed to buy the house. (Samuels had made his fortune on one huge coal deal in the early 1970s that netted him $500 million. Intent on crashing the top levels of New York society, he was busy purchasing three major New York houses to reflect his rapidly elevating social position.) Meanwhile Ronnie bought, for $295,000, a small but charming two-bedroom apartment on the ground floor of 1 Sutton Place South, with views of the river and a grand living room that would work well for entertaining. The title deed was in Marietta's name. The only unfortunate piece of timing was that the closing on 123 East 79th Street had not taken place when Ronnie died in July.

Ronnie owned another house in Syosset, Long Island, which he had bought for his chauffeur Reginald Duvall in 1949. The Duvall family had turned out to be more of a financial burden than expected. Their son, Michael, after graduating from Groton, began to have serious psychological difficulties. He had several breakdowns and was hospitalized repeatedly. Ronnie paid for most of his hospital and medical bills over these years. (For Michael, being the son of an English chauffeur at a place like Groton was not an easy experience, and probably aggravated his mental problems.) Marietta sold the house to Reg Duvall as soon as she could after Ronnie's death.

Ronnie had made over to Marietta the ownership of Heron Bay and all its contents in the early 1960s. Thus, after his death, Marietta's financial security rested almost entirely on the realization of the value of the two houses. She had to close on 123 East 79th Street and sell Heron Bay as quickly as possible. But speed is rarely to be recommended in real estate dealings, and Marietta suffered badly in her need to unload the properties. Not only was 1976 a depressed period in the U.S. real estate market, but John Samuels scented blood when he understood the changed circumstances of the seller of his prospective property, and reduced his offer.[9] Althought *The New York Times* reported the sale price to be "well over a million dollars," in fact Marietta was forced to sell the house to Samuels for $450,000. In 1981, Samuels sold it to the Brazilian Embassy (which still owns it) for $4 million. (Samuels later went bankrupt, ending up in jail in Bahrain.)

Heron Bay was equally problematic. She was anxious to sell it for over $1 million, but initially there were no takers. In November, desperate for some income, she rented the house for six months at $4,000 per month to Barron Burgen, representative of Broadlands International, who was interested in an eventual purchase of the property. Marietta wrote an elaborate list of instructions to the housekeeper at Heron Bay to try to sweeten the deal. "Be sure that Howard [the cook] uses the menus I have written in the menu books, and that she uses different dishes and table ornaments every day for lunch," Marietta ordered. "Enough wine—we can drink up the rest at Christmas. See the upholstery is clean, flowers in all the rooms, including bedrooms. Put out writing paper and envelopes everywhere." This four-star treatment was effective. During his stay, Burgen agreed to buy Heron Bay for the sum of $1.325 million. However, the deal fell through, and by mid-1977, Heron Bay was back on the market.

But by far the most pressing problem Marietta faced during these long-drawn-out negotiations both in the United States and Barbados was that she could not get her hands on any ready cash. All these real estate deals took time. Moreover, the settlement of Ronnie's estate was complicated by the fact that although he was a British citizen, his trustees, for tax reasons, wished the will to be probated in Illinois. Much effort had thus to be expended in establishing his Illinois residency, delaying distribution of funds from the will.

There was a further burden on her cash flow. In 1975, Ronnie had decided that extensive improvements had to be made to Heron Bay, including a new roof. These alterations, still continuing throughout 1976, amassed enormous bills, and since funds from the Lambert Tree Trust had dried up instantly at Ronnie's death, Marietta was faced with the responsibility herself. Other debts, including bills from lawyers, accountants, and nurses who had been with Ronnie through the months before he died, piled up and made her hysterical with anxiety. Suddenly her childhood fears of an impoverished life reappeared, with the specter of a poverty-stricken old age looming ahead. For almost thirty years she had lived without thought of an income, or of who would pay the bills. She had never even seen the checkbooks. At the reading of Ronnie's will, she declared she would be living in the poorhouse. Appalled, both Michael and Penelope said they would lend her money. She unthinkingly borrowed small amounts from them. She also borrowed $10,000 from Bill Paley. "You are a friend in need and a friend in deed," she wrote, returning the loan nine months later.

Meanwhile, she called on every possible contact to give her financial advice. She had an excellent pool from which to draw: James Wolfensohn, John Heimann, Arthur Ross, Maurice Tempelsman (who had doubled Jacqueline Onassis's portfolio), Bill Paley were all consulted. On top of the frenzied rounds of meetings over Ronnie's will, tax issues, probate problems, and selling both properties, she also had to get out of the house and move to Sutton Place. Dismantling a house as large as 123 East 79th Street and sorting out all the contents that were to be sold at auction was a huge and exhausting task. Finally, having packed her own personal possessions, she moved on September 20, 1976, just over two months after Ronnie's death, taking with her a few precious pieces of furniture and paintings that would stay with her for the rest of her life.

In October, there was a two-day sale at Sotheby Parke Bernet of the contents of the East 79th Street House. Most of the over 350 lots had come originally from Ditchley, and included works by Géricault, School of Tiepolo, Constable, Augustus John, and Berthe Morisot, as well as some exceptionally fine examples of English and French furniture. But the timing was bad. Not only was there a recession, but the style that came to be called the English Country House Look was not yet popular with American decorators. Today, a collection from a house like Ditchley in all probability would break auction records; but in 1976, the total from the two days of sales came to just over $550,000, a very disappointing sum for Marietta.

There were those who said Ronnie was not generous, and could have made more over to Marietta in his lifetime through gifts of jewelry and other tangible property or stocks that she could have sold after his death. With their marriage at a low ebb, it was possible that he felt disinclined to protect her further, although it is difficult to imagine what he could have done to make a major difference.

By January 1977, it seemed that Marietta had come out of her panic. Most people thought that by then a considerable portion of Ronnie's wealth had found its way satisfactorily into her bank account, although Roy Jenkins, who stayed with her just before Christmas, recognized that as usual she was concealing how difficult her life still was. With Heron Bay still unsold, she was writing letters to all sorts of real estate developers, as far afield as Germany and Venezuela, and including Club Med, offering the property for sale. Although she knew Ronnie would have hated the thought of Heron Bay being developed, the debts were piling up.

In October 1977, bills for the insurance, house repairs, and taxes on Heron Bay came to over $73,000. Marietta called in Jack Dear to try and wrest some of this money out of the Lambert Tree Trust, a task not made easier by the resistance of Michael's and Jeremy's lawyers, who of course argued that any diminution of the capital would lessen their clients' inheritances. Marietta's lawyer, James Sitrick, once told Marietta she could probably sue Ronnie's children for $3 million (later Sitrick could not remember on what grounds he had based this advice), but even in her most anguished moments, she never seriously considered it. Nor was there ever an open rift between her and the English side of the family. Over the years, although Jeremy retreated from Marietta's life, Michael and Anne remained in touch, and Marietta often stayed with them on her visits to England.

In 1978, Anthony Bamford, an Englishman who had made a fortune through agricultural equipment, made an offer for Heron Bay. The Bamfords had rented the Pink Cottage for six weeks that winter and fallen in love with the place. They bought Heron Bay for $1.425 million, agreeing to pay in U.S. currency, plus $208,000 for the contents. (Although this was an excellent deal, Marietta, still frantic, asked Roy MacLaren if he could get the Bamfords to up the bid.) The Bamfords kept on all the staff, and they also allowed Marietta to stay at Heron Bay over Christmas for the following two years. At last relieved financially, Marietta expressed no emotion at saying good-bye to the beautiful place Ronnie had created. She was grateful, however, that it would not now be developed, and thus Ronnie could sleep more peacefully in his grave.

The next hurdle was how to get the money out of Barbados. Normally, the removal of such a large sum was fraught with red tape and currency restrictions. Here again her connections proved invaluable. After receiving permission from the Governor-General of Barbados, Sir Winston Scott, as a personal favor, Jack Dear helped her negotiate a very generous deal with the Central Bank of Barbados whereby she was allowed to take the money out in three-year installments. (The head of the Central Bank later said this favor was granted because of Ronnie's contributions to the island.) Her advisers helped her invest this money wisely, and it became the basis of her income for the rest of her life.

The two years following Ronnie's death saw a series of memorials raised in his name. At Ditchley, a little temple was built and named in his honor. His friends in Barbados set up the Ronald Tree Memorial Fund for the purposes of acquiring a center for the Barbados National Trust, which Ronnie had founded. After a five-year search, the Ronald Tree House was purchased and named for the man who had cared so much about the natural beauty of the island. A plaque was installed in the East Wing of the Sandy Lane Hotel, Ronnie's visionary development, and also in Welchman Hall Gully, which Ronnie had helped save from destruction. The plaque at Sandy Lane reads: "On 25th August

1977 Marietta Tree named this terrace the Ronald Tree Terrace in honour of her late husband who founded Sandy Lane Hotel in 1961."

When Marietta first returned to New York after Ronnie's funeral, she telephoned Christa Armstrong, one of Ronnie's oldest friends and a woman of great sympathy, asking if she could come to see her. Christa was surprised at this unusual call from Marietta, who so rarely asked anyone for anything. "It was difficult seeing her, she was so helpless," Christa remembered. "She was confused. How should she behave? Should she get on with her life, do something else? The fact was, she didn't know how to mourn."[10]

Much later, in admiring author Susan Crosland for the way she was coping with her MP husband's death, Marietta said she wished she had spent more time alone to work out her grief, instead of rushing headlong into things. "They say it is therapeutic to return to work as soon as possible," she wrote to T. F. Bradshaw, president of Atlantic Richfield, a month after Ronnie's death, "but it is difficult to believe that this kind of grief or shock can be alleviated."

She knew grief of a sort—grief for a lost protector, for a vanished lifestyle, and for some marvelous memories. After all, Ronnie and she had been married for nearly thirty years. When she returned to Italy, she described the streets of Florence as infused with Ronnie's presence. Revisiting Ditchley to see Ronnie's grave filled her with nostalgia. Evangeline Bruce once came upon her alone in her room. "I was thinking of Ronnie," Marietta said.[11]

After the deaths of both Adlai Stevenson and Ronnie, Marietta suffered a period of collapse. This helplessness shocked those who knew her as a person lacking in self-pity and always under control. But it is these little glimpses behind the door, so to speak, that reveal the strain that she was under much of the time in order to keep her vulnerabilities invisible.

But Marietta was not cut out to grieve. Every fiber of her being resisted the sentiment, weakness, and immobilization that grieving entailed. So now, once again, she found her bearings and pushed out to sea. Soon she was able to express her progress to Natwar Singh: "The main thing is now I am on a stable keel, after a year of horror and grief after R's death. I had no idea how terrible it might be, but now I do not wake up sobbing. I greet the day."

There speaks Marietta's true voice. Of course she greeted the day. There were powerful motives for her to rush back into the fray, motives that perhaps were not available to many widows. For as well as coping with her financial crisis, Marietta also had a career that engaged her personal life very directly, and that required her presence more urgently than ever.

# CHAPTER *33*

# *"I love LLD more than ever"*

The year Ronnie died, 1976, was an *annus horribilis* for Richard Llewelyn-Davies. All three of his partnerships reported disappointing projects, management errors, and defections at the top. The firm's balances in London, Australia, and New York were all in deficit, with LDA's overdraft in New York amounting to hundreds of thousands of dollars. In October that year, the gravity of the situation was such that the firm practically closed down. The only areas of potential business seemed to be overseas, in particular the Middle East, the Philippines, and Iran. To realize this end, the partners created yet another company, Llewelyn-Davies International. They hoped this restructuring would help solve their operating problems.

There was in fact some cause for optimism. In 1975, Llewelyn-Davies Associates had been commissioned to prepare a master plan for Shahestan Pahlavi, a new center for the city of Teheran. This huge commission, which involved a capital center, a city hall, and other ceremonial spaces, came about thanks to the introduction by Jacob Rothschild of Richard Llewelyn-Davies to the Shah. In an international competition for the project, Llewelyn-Davies won. There were other major projects under discussion in Bahrain and Riyadh, which also promised vast financial rewards.

There was another factor that made 1976 challenging for Richard. With Ronnie's death, Marietta had become a free agent, available. This new configuration instantly changed the balance of power between Richard, his wife Pat, and Marietta. What had been a safe hand to play in the years before Ronnie's death was now thrown into confusion.

Richard had continued to be somewhat guarded with Marietta. They went to movies together, discussed work endlessly, spent nights together, but he remained uncommitted, even faintly condescending. When some people in Washington invited him to dinner, he said he would like to bring his assistant. "Oh, we'll dress down," they thought. The assistant turned out to be Marietta.[1]

By the mid-1970s, however, his feelings began to change. Love notes accumulated, some on House of Lords stationery. He began to show his feelings. Marietta responded. Tension was now in the air when they met in public. On one occasion, when Marietta went to lunch at Claudette Colbert's house in Barbados with Bill Walton and the Grusons, Lady Llewelyn-Davies and Lady Rothschild also showed up. Marietta was so disturbed that she refused to eat with them, retiring to a chaise longue in another part of the garden while the guests tried to enjoy their meal.

Yet most people did not guess there was anything more between Richard and Marietta than a business partnership. Richard's distant demeanor and Marietta's coolness precluded the kind of speculation that attended more ostentatious pairings. They worked to sustain this illusion. (When Marietta borrowed Jack and Grace Warnecke's ranch outside San Francisco so Richard and she could be together, she made it clear to Grace they were on a *working* trip to the West Coast.) But Christa Armstrong, astute observer, remembered seeing them at the Guggenheim Museum, Marietta looking up dreamily at Richard as he dilated on some painting or other. "She was hanging on his words." In Richard's thrall, Marietta shared his anxieties about the survival of the firm. Although mired in her own financial crisis, in late 1976 she found herself lending Llewelyn-Davies Associates $50,000, with the Australian branch of the firm acting as guarantor.

On November 30, 1976, Marietta and Jacquelin Robertson, the firm's distinguished architect and project director, flew to Teheran for a week to discuss their plans for the development of Shahestan Pahlavi. They toured archeological sites, had lunches and dinners with the prime minister and other government officials, real estate developers, and contractors, and at 11:30 A.M. on Monday, December 6, they had an audience with the Shah's wife, Farah Diba. On her return, Marietta wrote a flowery letter of gratitude to Her Majesty, looking forward to creating the new city: "It will characterize Iran's contribution to civilization, and proclaim its progress from a developing country to a great power in our time under the leadership of His Imperial Majesty."

Meanwhile, Marietta continued to write solicitation letters to the possible clients, sometimes stretching her integrity for the cause, such as her note to Mr. and Mrs. Louis Haggin of Keeneland Racetrack, in Lexington, Kentucky: "After seeing your lovely house, the beauty of your rolling country, the elegance of the Keeneland racing establishment, I now, as a Northerner, understand the reason for the Civil War. People wanted to keep the South *just* that way!"

She asked Jim Wolfensohn, who had become a good friend as well as adviser, how she could bring in more business, and he introduced her to the Australian real estate developer Dik Dusseldorp, who was setting up business in the United States.[2] Dusseldorp put Marietta on the boards both of Lend-Lease, his insurance and land investment company based in Sydney, Australia, and of his new U.S. company, International Income Property. Although initially these positions only paid her approximately $10,000 a year, by the mid-1980s they were to prove an enormous income producer for her, and both companies also became useful connections for LDA.

Still the firm's troubles continued. In November 1977, there was a crisis of the partners in London and Marietta flew over to help try to patch things up. Richard's despairing business manager, Maurice de Rohan, confided to Marietta that Richard was near bankruptcy, and that his high-handed management style had irrevocably damaged the firm. Marietta was advised that she was accumulating serious financial liability by her continued support of LDA. But by this time, she was beyond reason when it came to Richard's affairs, and she ignored the warnings, telling her accountant there was nothing to worry about. She also advanced another $25,000 to the firm.

Marietta's calendars throughout the late 1970s reflect her increasing dependency on Richard. She made her plans around his trips to New York, and whenever he left, she would try to leave too, to take a trip somewhere. As always, her solution to her personal problems was to lose herself in a grueling travel schedule. Mexico, Hungary, Salzburg, Northeast Harbor, Hong Kong — she flew from one destination to another, settling for only a few days in any one place, like a restless butterfly, returning for a moment's rest before taking off again. Her stamina was astonishing.

When Richard was in New York, she blossomed. She wanted to take care of him, keep him healthy (as she had with Ronnie and Adlai). She made him go to a dentist to have his teeth fixed, and paid the bill. Richard liked to cook (Marietta never knew how to boil an egg!), and they enjoyed evenings together alone at Sutton Place, catching up and taking in a movie. ("Oh, bliss," she confided to her diary after one such weekend.) They were invited everywhere, a popular couple. "They *looked* so good together," Kitty Carlisle Hart said.

But the many separations while Richard was in England became more and more painful for Marietta. "It's so sad when you can't live with someone you love," she said wistfully to Mary Warburg, whose own life now permanently in the country with her family, having once seemed boring to Marietta, now seemed wonderfully settled. Over the

Christmas and New Year's vacations, famously lonely times for the "other," Marietta began going again to Ruth Field's South Carolina plantation. She had continued to keep in touch with the Stevenson family and supported Adlai III in his political campaigns. When the highly praised biography of Stevenson by John Bartlow Martin came out in 1976–77, she was once more in the limelight as Adlai's great friend and "kiss of life" heroine at his death. But her heart was now in other realms. Democratic politics had been displaced by global planning.

Richard found Marietta more and more splendid. Now, on his frequent visits to New York, he stayed at her apartment on Sutton Place South. He kept his clothes there. Sometimes he was there without her, waiting for her to come back from a trip. He would write notes to her on her signature blue writing paper, telling her how he was longing for her, setting out for her his daily list of appointments, with the last notation, "6.30: Home and my love."

Some friends thought this was the first truly physical passion Marietta had known since John Huston. And yet here too, as always in Marietta's sexual dealings, we find ambiguity. While some thought of Richard as a passionate man, others called him dry, as cold as ice. His schooling and Apostolic career at Cambridge left him open to the possibilities of other preferences. One close friend once confided that sex was "not Richard's thing." His acknowledged pleasures mostly involved walking and reading at home at his country cottage at Tring —not the pursuits of an erotically charged nature.

Marietta's celebrated discretion would never have allowed further enlightenment of this issue. But for the greater part of 1978 she kept a diary—not the yearly calendar of appointments she always kept, but a private journal. Not that she had suddenly become confessional, but in light of her failure to produce a companion volume to Susan Mary Alsop's collection of letters, she felt increasing pressure to write her memoirs. To this end, super-agent Irving ("Swifty") Lazar urged her to keep some kind of personal record that would enliven her yet-to-be-written manuscript.

In these intimate 1978 diaries, written in her large upright hand, mostly in pencil, she—occasionally—managed to put down her feelings for Richard. "July 3. Dined at White Tower with LLD. All well until he said that some charmers would make one give up everything. I replied without thinking, 'Not you,' and turned cool on him. Didn't realize that I cared. It hurt the evening but made him protest love for quite a few days." Later that month she confessed, "I love LLD more than ever."

It was a love that was sorely tested by the endless separations. In late September he arrived in New York after over a month's absence and they had a tense evening that was happily resolved—"but not forever," she noted darkly. Shortly afterward, she confronted him directly. "Drama when I point out that I want to become more involved and therefore he must move out permanently. Of course this ends in the situation ante and a lot of making up."

Even though Marietta was now free, Richard made no move to disengage further from his life in England, which frustrated her. "Englishmen never divorce, do they?" she sighed to Evangeline Bruce one night. "Would you marry him?" Mrs. Bruce asked. "Of course," Marietta answered.[3]

Of course. Marietta was a third-generation Anglophile, and Richard Llewelyn-Davies, this upper-class, cultivated Englishman, had become the newest repository of her hopes and desires. His craggy handsomeness was exactly the look that had always pleased her. Although he had no money, she did not care. His natural-born superiority and high-minded ambitions were sufficient compensation. As she saw it, only one obstacle stood in the way of her future with Richard. She used to refer to Pat Llewelyn-Davies as "Nanny," perhaps, as Martin Meyerson suggested, because Marietta feared being regarded as a nanny herself. The image of Pat became etched in Marietta's subconscious mind so deeply that a year after his death, she still dreamed of her rival—a terrible dream in which Pat, corseted, slim, wearing a long dusty rose crepe dress, followed Marietta out of a urinal and started to scuffle with her in an elevator.[4] When Richard went back to England again after a visit in November 1978 she told herself sadly, "I do not ask enough of him and appear too strong and independent."

What woman in Marietta's shoes has not reproached herself with these terrible faults? Yet she had in fact misread Richard's psychology. Unlike her first two husbands, both of whom were in effect motherless, Richard had a powerful mother, whom he deeply admired, and an equally strong, career-driven wife. Adlai Stevenson also had a dominating mother, which led him similarly to strong women. "If nothing else," Richard once told Tom Finletter's wife, Eileen, "Marietta has a very clear sense of who she is."[5]

The irony was that what made Marietta so attractive to Richard was not only the opposite of what she thought he wanted, but also the opposite of what she felt. On the surface, she was a commanding, confident woman; inside, she was still a little girl longing for love, approval, and guidance. The deception she had so carefully and successfully built up over the years was in this situation now working against her. Because of Marietta's background, training, and commitment to the unexamined life, she could not delve beneath this layer of contradictory messages to get at the truth. And Richard was the last person who might help her try.

That there were other men around was no consolation. Marietta had always been surrounded by men with whom she flirted with that cunning mixture of promise and denial that kept them permanently on edge. In her diary she refers to someone kissing her wetly on the lips and saying, "Suppose we fall madly in love." She comments that she didn't enjoy this much, especially when she discovered she knew his wife. Another left a love note in her purse. Such overtures from men are endured by all beautiful women (although not so often after sixty, Marietta's age at this time), and she accepted them as her due. On the other hand, she never ceased to flirt, either. It was an instinctive reflex with her. In her 1978 journal, on one occasion she asks herself why; but does not pursue the question.

One new friend was Dr. Calvin Plimpton, her old UN colleague Francis Plimpton's brother, who was president of Amherst College and later president of the Downstate Medical Center of the State University of New York. He was also chairman of the board of trustees of the American University in Beirut. Each one of Dr. Plimpton's various hats was valuable to Marietta, who recruited him for his hospital administration expertise to help Llewelyn-Davies in his design for a hospital in Bahrain, and for his Middle Eastern contacts to find further planning projects in the region. She also asked his advice about doctors for herself.

Arthur Ross, a very wealthy widower with a strong personal interest in her, escorted Marietta to several New York occasions during the late 1970s and invited her to his house on Long Island on summer weekends. Rumors of marriage proposals were floated. As well as providing her with free advice on her investments, he was instrumental in getting her on three more boards, the Dreyfus Corporation, S. G. Warburg, and the Cooper-Hewitt Museum. Through him she became involved with the art gallery he founded at the University of Pennsylvania (where she failed to win reelection on the board after her major supporter, Martin Meyerson, left the presidency).

But perhaps the most persistent suitor was Najeeb Halaby, who had waited patiently for her and now hoped for something more. Marietta saw him frequently during the 1970s, when Halaby, after his abrupt departure from Pan Am, had become a consultant to Middle East airlines. Jeeb was pro-Arab and Marietta violently pro-Israel, a problem that caused coolness between them when they visited the Middle East together. But Jeeb remained an ardent admirer, and many people found him a sympathetic candidate for her hand. Once Kitty Hart urged her to be nicer to him. She brushed off the notion. She was already answered for.

It was Halaby, however, with whom she shared one of the more momentous episodes in her life. In April 1978 she went with him to the Middle East to visit Jordan and Israel. She flew first to Amman,

With Najeeb Halaby, 1970.

where she was met by Jeeb and his daughter, Lisa. After a few days of sightseeing, the three Americans were granted an audience with the king (Lisa had not particularly wished to attend but was urged to by Marietta), and they talked to him for about three-quarters of an hour.

King Hussein invited Lisa to lunch the following day, "and as she stayed with him for 7 and a half hours and was driven home by him in an exotic car," Marietta wrote, "I think it might be the beginning of a romance." She was right. Later, claiming responsibility for the marriage, she wondered privately if she had done Lisa a favor by "forcing" her to attend that original audience with the king.[6]

Also in 1978, Marietta made her first trip to Australia. In her new role as board member of IIP in New York and Lend-Lease in Australia, she would attend annual meetings of Lend-Lease in Sydney for the next nine years. In typical fashion, she wrote to friends before she left asking for contacts. The Australian writer Shirley Hazzard arranged for her to meet a famous but reclusive author, Patrick White, and Isaiah Berlin gave her the names of interesting academics.

Later, Richard and Marietta went together with Jacquelin Robertson to Teheran to make the final presentation of their new city design to the Shah. Thierry Despont, a young architect working in Iran, had been invited to join the project and was present at this critical moment. Robertson and Despont held a dress rehearsal of the presentation in front of the mayor of Teheran, during which a major problem was discovered. The reviewing platform where the Shah would stand to watch his troops march by was in the wrong place. It would require the troops to salute from right to left, instead of from left to right. "I can't present this to the Shah," said the mayor. The team rushed to consult with Richard and Marietta. "But Richard," Marietta said, "how does the Queen of England take the salute?" "She takes it from right to left, as we have designed it." If it was all right for the queen of England, the mayor concluded it was all right for the Shah. The team was given the green light, and the presentation was a huge success. Shortly after, however, the Shah was deposed, taking with him all of LDA's hopes in the region.

In spite of these reverses, by the end of the decade, Marietta herself had completely recovered from the widow's panic that followed Ronnie's death. Her own financial position had stabilized. She lived in an apartment that suited her, filled with choice pieces from Ditchley, including the eighteenth-century giltwood overmantel mirror above the fireplace in the drawing room, the giltwood overdoors, and some fine English and French furniture. On the wall hung the beautiful watercolors of Ditchley by Serebriakoff that Ronnie had commissioned for her after their marriage. What a distance she had come from the austere ecclesiastical houses of her childhood to these interiors with their lush colors, flounced pillows, satin damask upholstery, and lashings of leather, rosewood, and gold.

Some aspects of the rooms were oddly familiar to those who knew the first Mrs. Tree's decorating style. The gauze balloon blinds in the drawing room, for instance, were identical to those designed by Nancy for the Games Room at Ditchley, and the Ditchley collection of blue and white porcelain on giltwood brackets in Marietta's bedroom was mounted in almost precisely the same configuration as that created originally by Nancy. Marietta, the least sentimental of women, had no qualms about using what worked, whatever its provenance.

With Alice retired, Mabel, Penelope's old nurse, remained on the staff as housekeeper. Marietta's invaluable part-time secretary, Mrs. Lillian Klotzer (who had started working for Marietta in 1968), came to the apartment one morning a week to go over the accounts and correspondence, take dictation, write the checks, and help make lists for parties. Marietta planned her parties with thrift and the menus were simple—casseroles and fruit salads. "I serve for dinner what other people serve for lunch," she declared without embarrassment. (At Heron Bay, in Barbados, guests used to complain that there was never enough food. Ronnie was always on one of Marietta's diets, and people joked that they would eat a meal first before going on to dinner at the Trees.)[7] She had good financial advisers, and she was now free to travel, meet people, and generally pursue her interests—except for the tantalizing, frustrating, delightful Richard.

In 1978 she was sixty-one, but looked twenty years younger after a little help from a face-lift done by Robin Beare at the London Clinic early that year. She had begun using wigs when she went on some of her longer trips abroad, finding it almost impossible, with her hectic schedule, to have time to go to the hairdresser or even to depend on finding one in some of her out-of-the-way destinations. She retained a continuing vulnerability to two problems she had suffered since she was a young girl. One was the hives, which caused her face and neck to flush like a teenager. The other was also a stress-related problem: high blood pressure and a tendency to high cholesterol. To treat this condition she embarked on regular cardiovascular checkups and a three-mornings-a-week exercise regimen, that she was to follow for the rest of her life.

A small portent of mortality flickered before her in the summer of 1978. On July 6, the day after her sixty-third birthday, Babe Paley died after a long battle with cancer. In her will, in an extensive list of personal bequests to friends, Babe left Marietta a pair of gold and white enamel earclips and a triple-strand necklace set with coral and lapis beads.

Babe had always been a role model for Marietta. Ever since she had first met the glamorous young Cushing sister in New York as a debutante, Marietta had emulated Babe's elegance and style, seeing in her friend's reserved way of conducting herself the ideal technique for a successful life. Like Madame Merle in *The Portrait of a Lady,* Babe Paley seemed to Marietta to have been determined, through the pursuit of reason over impulse, to learn the secret of life—"as if [it] were some clever trick that she had guessed." That Babe had to suffer the slow corruption of cancer was a capricious flaw in this otherwise lacquered life. In her journal, after writing, "Today Babe finally slept her life away. It must be a relief for them all," she added her own cry of defiance: "But she did not want to die."

Meanwhile Marietta's days and nights with Richard were more and more fulfilling. They traveled to Houston where business was coming in, to Aspen to attend the institute's seminars, to Barbados, and to Italy, where Marietta and Evangeline Bruce began what was to become an annual event, renting a house together in Tuscany for the month of August and inviting friends to stay. For the first year, 1979, they rented the Griersons' house in Castellina in Chianti for two weeks.

There was the occasional dark note in this inspiriting symphony. "Determine to leave Richard," she announced firmly to her journal in November 1978. "I want to belong to someone instead of rattling

With Joseph Brooks of Lord & Taylor in 1979, eating "Strawberries Marietta," thus fulfilling a dream—to have a dessert named after her.

around." The next day, she reported, "After telling Richard the above, I felt better than I have for weeks. I don't know if there is any connection. Anyway, he is coming over next weekend (from England)— rather good of him and I don't deserve it." And so "the oldies waltzed on," as Penelope later described the antics of her mother at this time.

In late 1979, Marietta wrote to her friend from the 1940s, Charles Bolté, describing her life: "What am I doing? Running 800 million miles a hour and working mainly at Llewelyn-Davies and for seven corporations. Therefore, on Monday morning, I have a list of 35 telephone calls to make in connection with at least 20 different activities. Yes, I am doing too much, but shouldn't I at this age when I only have about 40 more years of work ahead of me?"

And so she strode on toward the millennium.

# CHAPTER *34*

# *"Well, there'll be nothing"*

Ever since Mrs. Peabody's arrest in St. Augustine, Florida, she had been a media favorite. This feisty old Boston lady, bishop's wife, mother of a fascinating daughter, and grandmother of two equally fascinating granddaughters, made good copy. Pictures appeared regularly in the press of Mrs. Peabody, Marietta Tree, and Frances FitzGerald, on one occasion showing them receiving honorary degrees together at Skidmore. Mrs. Peabody herself expressed impatience with this constant attention. "I have nothing of interest to contribute, either about myself or other women," she said briskly. ". . . I have been interviewed ad nauseam. Everyone must know by heart my trip to St. Augustine—so I hate to mention it again."

But interest remained high. Two television documentaries were made about the women who represented the three generations of this Peabody line. The first, which appeared in 1975, was with Eric Sevareid, an admiring and respectful interviewer. Frankie, dressed in red, and her grandmother, dressed in blue, were seated together on a sofa, while Marietta, dressed in black and white and beautifully made up with bouffant hair, sat by herself in an armchair.

In spite of her experience over the years, Marietta was still nervous on these occasions. Her comments often sounded as though she were reading lines. Her answers to Sevareid's questions about politics, the future of liberalism, and international relations lacked substance. She was at her most relaxed when discussing the role of women in politics. This was a subject on which she had made speeches throughout the world during her UN term of office, and when pointing to Golda Meir, Indira Gandhi, and Margaret Thatcher as models of twentieth-century feminism, she was fluent and convincing.

As it came to the more personal questions, nobody's guard slipped one iota during the hour's interview, except for three revealing exchanges. One concerned Sevareid's question to Mrs. Peabody and Frankie about their reactions to Marietta's appointment as a UN ambassador. "We were certainly very impressed," Mrs. Peabody said in heavily ironic tones, with Frankie echoing her. "I don't think any of you were at all," Marietta murmured, laughing lightly off camera. Later, Mrs. Peabody said that she realized she had not been a good mother after Marietta had made public announcements that her mother had not been loving and affectionate. Marietta tried frantically to wriggle out of the accusation, but Mrs. Peabody was unmoved. "There's nothing like being on TV to learn what your family thinks of you," was her wry comment. But it was Sevareid's probe into the question of family support for Marietta's second marriage that caused the most violent exchange between mother and daughter. "No support," Marietta declared. "Nobody came to the wedding." "I *did!*" Mrs. Peabody almost shouted, with more agitation than at any other time during the interview. "Didn't see you there," Marietta replied, smiling coolly.

The second documentary was a TV debut for the producer, Pamela Peabody, wife of Marietta's brother Mike. Directed by the Englishman Robin Hardy and shown in 1979, this was a much more controversial affair, revealing an angry Frankie, a self-effacing Mrs. Peabody and Marietta at her most artificial. Marietta looked marvelous, but shown in settings that, as *Newsweek* said, "fairly scream 'limousine liberal,' " she came off as a frivolous airhead. Marietta, who later regretted agreeing to the film and privately acknowledged yet again her lack of achievements compared to these two extraordinary women, took the high road and never complained to Pam about the negative slant of the film. (Frankie, however, flew to her mother's defense, and when the program was shown again, the film was re-edited to show Marietta in a more favorable light.)

Penelope was excluded from all this Peabody brouhaha. As much a Peabody as Frankie, as a child she had loved the Peabody relatives. But her Peabody grandparents disapproved of her life with David Bailey and this caused a rift. She felt much more at home in England with her half brothers, Michael and Jeremy Tree, who accepted her.

In 1981 she married a "coloured" (in apartheid law) South African musician, Ricky Fataar, further alienating Mrs. Peabody, for all her civil rights protests. (When her son Sam called her on this, "I believe in justice, not intermarriage," she snapped.) After a spell in Los Angeles, the couple moved to Australia. Marietta, lacking her mother's soph-istry, firmly supported her daughter's choice. She was disturbed instead by the fact that Penelope was seven months' pregnant. Marietta was anxious that the baby not be born out of wedlock (both for the child and for how it would look to her friends).

By the mid-1970s, Mrs. Peabody slowly began to fail. She refused to seek medical help, and continued her activities as long as she could. In 1978, she had a heart fibrillation while staying with Marietta in Barbados, and Sam Spiegel's private plane flew her back to Boston. Her doctors told her she should have a heart bypass operation, but on hearing that it would take a year to recover, she decided against it. She told her old friend Mary Bundy she thought a year's convalescence was too much for her.

In August 1980 in Maine she had another heart attack, and was taken to the Bar Harbor Hospital. This time it seemed to be the end, and the family collected at her bedside. But she recovered and shortly afterwards was back home sailing. She hung on for another six months, living mostly alone, independent and fearless. She broke her hip in February 1981, an accident that required an operation from which she barely regained consciousness. Mary Parkman Peabody died on February 6, 1981, at the age of eighty-nine, which was the way she wanted it. (She once told a friend she was terrified she might reach ninety.)

The last days had not been easy. Her salient characteristics of emotional control and antipathy to weakness combined to repulse any attempts at medical intervention or personal sympathy. Thus, when her tough old heart finally began to fail, she raged furiously, like her only daughter, against the dying of the light. Ironically, it fell to Toni Peabody, who lived nearby, to do a lot of the nursing of her mother-in-law during the last months—Toni, who had received such little warmth from her Peabody in-laws over the years, and who had always felt they scorned her because of her "inferior" island background.

The last Christmas of her life, Mrs. Peabody was too ill to go to New York to Sam and Judy Peabody's annual party, so Toni fixed up the house in Cambridge with lights and decorations and invited neighbors to a Christmas Eve party. The night before, Mrs. Peabody and Toni were in Mrs. Peabody's bedroom eating dinner off trays, when Toni's mother telephoned her from her home in Bermuda. Toni, always an emotionally outspoken person, spoke fondly to her mother, saying how much she missed her, especially at Christmas time. "I love you, Mother," she said. When she put down the phone, Mrs. Peabody was beating on a chair and screaming at her, "How can you talk like that about love? It's horrible! It's cheap!" Toni ran from the room in tears. Later that night, Mrs. Peabody asked Toni to come back, and

Toni remembered her saying, "You don't understand. That word was never said in our family. We thought it was cheap to show your feelings."[1]

But people loved Mary Peabody. Letters poured in after her death, ranging from Ralph Abernathy and the Southern Christian Leadership Conference, who saluted her struggle "to make justice and equality a reality for all mankind," to the ladies of the Cranberry Club in Northeast Harbor, who recalled how she had one summer hat and one woolen shawl (perhaps in a lifetime) "and wore them like a queen." Obituaries invariably referred to her high sense of obligation to public service (to which one friend responded, "That explains Marietta").

There were also the famous stories of her extreme thrift, such as when Toni Peabody visited Bermuda, she asked Mrs. Peabody if she would like her to bring her back a sweater. Her mother-in-law said, "Oh, no, dear, I already have one." Once in Cambridge, Mrs. Peabody was shocked when Frankie's friend Kevin Buckley asked for two lumps of sugar in his coffee. When she and the bishop traveled overnight by train, Malcolm took a berth; Mary sat up all night.

This carefulness with money was reflected in her will, in which she left small legacies to her godchildren and grandchildren and her house in Cambridge to the Episcopal Divinity School. (The Northeast Harbor house had already been given to Endicott, George, and Mike in 1978, with Sam and Marietta refusing their share, Marietta saying she preferred to stay with Frankie or Susan Mary.) The rest of Mrs. Peabody's estate came to roughly $500,000, which was divided equally among the five children.

She left them, however, another, more ambiguous legacy. Her four sons admired and respected her, but even though she always paid the most attention to them, they felt starved of affection. Her constant urge to make them compete, even as little children, took its toll. Sam said she knew how to find your weakest point and then tease you about it. All the sons were victims of this weapon. She once remarked disparagingly to Kevin Buckley that during the war when her son Endicott was on a submarine, he slept through depth charges—"a rare disclosure turned into a weakness," as Kevin Buckley saw it. When Mike told his mother that he would be able to be taken in as an air force officer straight out of business school to serve in the Korean War, Mrs. Peabody responded, "Oh, I was hoping you'd serve in the front line."[2] What did they have to do to wrest a drop of fondness from that ungiving frame?

In the early 1970s, Mike Peabody started organizing a series of psychiatric sessions with his family in Washington. His mother gamely went down and attended some of these encounters. The doctor had his own prejudices against WASPs, "so we'd sit there," Mike remembered, "and glower at each other and he'd say, 'Real people don't act this way.' " Mrs. Peabody took a beating for her contribution to the family's emotional troubles. The revelations led her to suspect that she had not been a good mother. "You see, I wasn't aware that my children were having problems when they were growing up. I've come to realize, with them as well as the young, that it's important to keep the line of communication open. . . . I don't talk easily. I don't have that skill."

For Mary Peabody's sons, however, successes in work and sports gave them some respite and commendation. The daughter's attempts to please never succeeded, ever. To the end of her life, Mrs. Peabody retained dominion over her most rebellious child. People remember witnessing telephone conversations in which Marietta disintegrated at the sound of her mother's voice. When together, they bickered incessantly. "I'm afraid we are too much alike," Marietta once wrote to Ronnie, "and hate our own characteristics in the other." But Mrs. Peabody outfenced her daughter at every turn. When Marietta told her mother she was going to write a book, Mrs. Peabody said, "Oh, and what will you write about? Your parties?"[3]

Two nights after Mrs. Peabody died, her five children had dinner together and stayed up until midnight talking about her. They all report that it was an unusually close time. But Marietta could not sustain the intimacy. After the funeral, she immediately flew back to New York (where Richard was waiting for her), and did not return to help her brothers with the house or cleanup afterwards. Later that week she was on her way to Egypt with the Fritcheys.

"She didn't want to recognize the death," observed her brother Endicott. There was more to it than that, of course. A lifetime of anger was written in that hurried departure from her dead mother's house, a lifetime's inability to find forgiveness. As the praise-laden letters about Mrs. Peabody piled up on the antique desk in her Sutton Place apartment, Marietta responded to them gracefully. But she had not taken care of her mother when her mother needed her. Nor would her mother ever have expressed that need. Thus the two women were doomed to play out to the end their roles in this fierce family drama. Even in death no hands reached across the abyss, and there was no reconciliation.

But Mrs. Peabody died with a secret, a secret that would have shocked many of her friends, parishioners, her Peabody in-laws, and perhaps her late husband most of all. It was a deception that, like so many of the other Peabody deceptions, went to the heart of the family mythology. Her third son George, for whom religion was both inspiration and burden throughout his life, revealed it with a wry laugh: "Our mother didn't believe in the afterlife."[4]

When Bishop Peabody died, George helped put together the funeral service. Going through the hymns with him, Mrs. Peabody would object to some as being "too religious." As she grew weaker, George used to take her by boat to visit her old friend Edith Drury on Cranberry Island, and they would all go sailing together. Mrs. Drury was a born-again Christian, and tweaked Mary for her irreligiousness. "Now Mary, you're not going to live too much longer. What's going to happen after you die?" And Mrs. Peabody would say firmly, "Well, there'll be nothing." And Mrs. Drury would pounce on her, saying, "What do you mean, 'There'll be nothing'?" And Mary, truculent, would stand her ground.[5]

When Endicott went to see his mother in the hospital in 1980, they too began to talk about religion. "Do you believe in the afterlife?" she asked her eldest son. "Well, of course I do, Mother," Endicott said. "I'm not sure I do," said Mrs. Peabody.[6]

What was it like for Mrs. Peabody, who conducted her life in a spirit of moral and political correctness, to have suffered such heretical thoughts? It makes her more human, of course, perhaps even more admirable. For her children, however, immersed from their earliest years in the most devout atmosphere of dedication and duty to God, to realize their mother was in effect at the end of her long life giving the lie to this commitment was tantamount to calling their upbringing a fraud. Whom could they trust after such a disclosure? They had seen their father, as God's representative, reveal his human frailties behind the ceremonial garments. Now their mother, whom they had always regarded as the very icon of Christian faith, had stripped away the rest of their illusions.

Thus the generational torch was passed. Marietta was now the senior member of this branch of the Peabody family, and the oldest female. When Mrs. Peabody's mother died, the daughter was released from a subtle oppression and became more confident, outspoken, independent. In her turn, relieved of her mother's judgmental presence, Marietta perhaps could chart a course less calibrated to please. Freed from that particular form of guile, she could sail on with a lighter heart and an easier conscience.

But there were legacies of family blood that could not be escaped so easily. On June 16, 1981, Marietta paid a visit to the office of the distinguished cancer specialist, Dr. William Cahan. Marietta knew Dr. Cahan socially. He was married to Grace Mirabella, the editor of *Vogue,* at the time. They had visited 123 East 79th Street several times and he had occasionally been Marietta's escort during what he called her "interregnums." This, however, was not a social visit. Marietta was worried about a lump on her breast.

Dr. Cahan immediately ordered a mammogram, which recorded a small tumor on the upper outer quadrant of her left breast. A biopsy revealed it as malignant. Three days later, a lumpectomy was performed by Dr. Cahan at Memorial Sloan-Kettering Cancer Center, and with a classic small incision on her left breast he removed the tumor. To accommodate the surgery, she had to cancel two cocktail parties—for the U.S. Trust and at the Asia Society—a dinner given by Arianna Stassinopoulos (now Huffington) for Anne Getty, and a weekend in the country with Arthur Ross.

How could those splendid breasts, which had been admired by so many over the years, have betrayed her so badly? Although over the years she had been heard to complain about their size, and even considered having them reduced, only recently she had entered into a spirited correspondence with Roy Strong, then director of the Victoria and Albert Museum, over the modeling of a Charles James gown that Marietta had donated to the museum.

On seeing her evening dress on display at the V & A, its owner had been horrified at the lack of balance between the bosom and the bustle, which was the point of dresses of that kind. "Indeed," Marietta wrote to Sir Roy, "I think Charles James, the designer who made it, would try to kidnap the dress rather than have it seen in this condition." Marietta suggested stuffing the bodice of the dress with tissue paper. She also added, with evident pride, "When you tell the curator in charge about the stuffing, please tell him or her my bust measurement is (and was) 39 inches. I assure you that will make the dress look 100 percent better."

No wonder, then, that when Dr. Cahan had given her the choice of a lumpectomy or a radical mastectomy (the latter then, as now, considered the more extreme procedure), Marietta never for a moment hesitated. She wanted to "maintain her cosmetic appearance," as Dr. Cahan, who knew of her involvement with Richard Llewelyn-Davies, put it.

The day of the surgery, Marietta telephoned her brother Sam, saying she had to go into the hospital immediately, and would he take her, and would he promise not to tell anyone. On the way, she remarked how ironic it was that she had just had lunch with Grace Mirabella and now was about to be operated on by her husband. Sam took her to the hospital, never said anything (except to his wife Judy), and, as instructed, put it out of his mind.

The day after the lumpectomy, Marietta came home. Follow-up radiation therapy (she refused chemotherapy) continued from June 29 until she went to Italy in August, with frequent checkups by her surgeon. The operation was declared a complete success.

The speed and silence with which she dealt with the experience was typical of Marietta. She was supposed to be in London during those first weeks of July when she was undergoing radiation, and told friends with whom she had arranged parties and dinners there (Evangeline Bruce, Jayne Wrightsman) that she was undergoing a minor operation (unspecified) and sadly must cancel the trip, but that she would see everyone in Italy.

Behind this bravado, she was scared—scared enough to start seeing a psychotherapist again. The Monday after her surgery she made her first visit to Dr. Mildred Newman, who had been recommended by Frankie. Dr. Newman was well known, and with her husband, Bernard Berkowitz, had written a best-selling self-help book, *How to Be Your Own Best Friend.* Marietta was to go on seeing Dr. Newman to the end of her life.

There were special reasons for her troubled mind. The "C" word was never allowed to be spoken by members of the family, although one of Marietta's aunts died of breast cancer. Marietta's cousin Trubee Davison had died of leukemia as a teenager. He was kept in a room and nobody was told of his illness. His brother Daniel, nine or ten at the time, never knew his adored older brother was dying. "There was massive suppression of this grief," said Harry Davison, Trubee's nephew.[7] Marietta too found herself afraid. How unfair that the death of her mother, far from freeing her from her Peabody bonds, had within months confirmed the daughter's continued subjection to her origins.

Marietta hoped (or talked herself into believing) that by denial the damned spot would go away. One of the more remarkable things about this episode was that even to Dr. Cahan she did not tell the whole truth. When he interviewed her about her health history, she mentioned smoking a pack of cigarettes a day until fifteen years earlier, when she gave it up. In fact, she occasionally still smoked, as photographs attest. She told him about the radiation treatments she had undergone for her acne in her teenage years, and about the program of hormone replacement therapy she had embarked on in 1969 and recently discontinued. She even mentioned the deaths of her two aunts. But she could not bring herself to mention the biopsy for the tumor in her breast she had undergone when she was at the United Nations. Although of course it was benign, she could not admit that frightening appointment with cancer, even to her surgeon. She simply mentioned that in 1960 (in fact it was a year later) she had had "an injury to her breast." She didn't say what it was, and Dr. Cahan supposed it was a minor trauma that had no relevance.

For Marietta, the battle, waged alone, in gritted-teeth silence, was won. Or so she thought. But 1981 was not going to let her off so easily.

In 1980, Richard Llewelyn-Davies and his partners decided to close down Llewelyn-Davies Associates. The fall of the shah that year had been a catastrophic blow, in a trice depriving the firm of the prospect of millions of dollars, plus the investment it had already made in the project. After shopping LDA around, a Houston-based company run by Randhir Sahni bought its assets, with Richard and Marietta remaining on the new board.

But Richard's enthusiasm for the New World had not waned. In the fall of 1980 he became a Director's Visitor at the Institute of Advanced Study in Princeton, largely thanks to the influence of Jim Wolfensohn and the institute's director, Harry Woolf. A year earlier, he had given a lecture there, and a young woman named Patricia Danielson went to hear him and met him afterwards. She was then in charge of community affairs for the Meadowlands development in New Jersey. She showed him around the Meadowlands and other projects being built along the expanding Route 1 corridor, which greatly impressed and excited him. He said he would like to open a one-person office in Princeton, and he appointed Patricia as office manager, giving her an expense account and a credit card. "All we need is one commission along Route One," he told her.[8]

Although his enthusiasm was genuine, these efforts were a far cry from the glory days of Llewelyn-Davies Associates. Route 1 was hardly a serious alternative to Teheran, and Richard's forlorn drives with the eager state employee were as removed from the glamorous trips with Marietta as the Meadowlands from Manila.

Moreover, unknown to most people except his family and partners, Richard had been sick for several years. By 1980, the prostate cancer that had been diagnosed and suppressed had recurred. He was often stricken with fevers and back pain, and retired to his country house in Tring for long periods of rest. But with typical British stoicism, neither his wife Pat nor he acknowledged the seriousness of his illness. Like Marietta, they refused to recognize the imminence of death, and just as Marietta kept Richard from sharing her cancer scare, so Richard never allowed Marietta to know the truth about his medical history. If at times he suffered from pain in Marietta's presence, he brushed it off and pushed on, as did she.[9]

In the summer of 1981, Richard, as usual without his wife, joined Marietta in Italy. Guests in the house thought he seemed thinner than usual, although as charming as ever. Only Evangeline Bruce knew something of his condition. He and Marietta had talked to Evangeline about his severe stomach and liver problems, and Evangeline wondered if it might be hepatitis. Once again, in supreme denial, Richard made no mention of the cancer he probably knew was killing him.

Richard stayed in Italy for just over a week and then left for New York, where he saw Thierry Despont, who after the shah's fall had moved to New York. The two discussed prospects for Thierry's practice, and Richard complained—as usual—of back pain. He told

Thierry he would be returning in September and would continue their discussions then. He also saw Patricia Danielson on that trip. She thought he looked very yellow and shaky. Richard assured her that he would soon be coming back.

But in late September his secretary telephoned his New York partners and friends to tell them that Richard was in St. Bartholomew's Hospital in London. Everyone was shocked. Nobody seemed to be able to reach him by telephone. His secretary explained it was because he was in a public ward where there were no phones. She did not add that Pat was there, a tiger, guarding her husband's bedside. Marietta, preoccupied with engagements, and preparing for her regular visit to Australia for the Lend-Lease board meetings, insisted that Richard was doing wonderfully in the hospital. But as time went on and he was not released, she began to fret. She begged Mary Warburg, who was in London, to go and see him for her. She sent a huge bouquet of flowers to the ward. That was all she could do.

On October 15, Marietta flew to Australia, returning on October 25. While in Australia she received a telegram from Richard that said, "Not waltzing yet slow foxtrot more my line phone you New York, love Richard." On Monday, October 26, she attended a U.S. Trust meeting and went to the Heinzes for a dinner in honor of Gavin Young.

The following day, Richard Llewelyn-Davies died. He was sixty-eight years old. Marietta was stunned. She later told Christa Armstrong that she had no idea how sick he really was.[10] Although other friends had sensed Richard's grave illness toward the end ("How could she not have known?" Christa asked), Marietta had steadfastly refused to see the face of death upon him, and he had died without her.

*The Times* obituary was thought by his friends to be insensitive and petty, mentioning his failure to support the organizations to which he belonged, and how his colleagues found him a "somewhat enigmatic and puzzling figure." *The New York Times* was more admiring of his contributions to architecture and the field of urban planning, and Marietta, burying her hostility, sent the obituary to his wife in London. Pat wrote a grateful letter back, allowing her old rival a few morsels to treasure about Richard's death; how good the nursing had been, how all the other patients on the ward had called him "the Prof," and how he had not been in pain at the end. She generously added how much he had loved Marietta, and that the times in New York were wholly life-enhancing for him.

Marietta deliberately began divesting herself of Richard's memory. She gave away the clothes he had kept in Sutton Place—some to Thierry Despont, some to Arthur Schlesinger. On December 17, she invited close friends and colleagues of Richard's to a sort of "wake" or informal memorial celebration in her apartment on Sutton Place. After everyone had assembled, Marietta stood in front of the fireplace and talked about Richard's life and work with a calm demeanor that greatly impressed her listeners.[11] Her control in front of this audience was exemplary. She told them about plans to keep his work known, including a lectureship in his name at the Institute for Advanced Study, proceeding under the aegis of Harry Woolf. The elegies spoken that evening by Mrs. Edward Larrabee Barnes, Susan Braybrooke, and Martin Meyerson were published and circulated to friends.

After this evening, Marietta closed another book. Not one of those books she so diligently listed in the back of her calendars every year (by authors like Ronald Steel, Shirley Hazzard, Paul Fussell, V. S. Naipaul, Olivier Bernier—the eclectic works a well-educated New Yorker should read), but a text about an emotional journey with a man she had loved for over ten years. At his death, the book snapped shut. It would not be opened again in her lifetime.

# CHAPTER *35*

# *"The ultimate WASP"*

There were several crises over the winding up of Richard Llewelyn-Davies's estate. The confused state of his various partnerships at home and abroad (including a large amount of unpaid taxes) forced the estate to be frozen. Marietta herself, as a partner and shareholder, had certain rights to assets from the firm, but debt reimbursements and litigation over the taxes seriously depleted the estate. After it was settled, Marietta's disposition came to about $20,000.

By that time, it hardly mattered. Throughout the 1980s, Marietta's financial situation improved dramatically. Her success was based in part in her having searched out and accepted good advice. This had always been one of her most appealing and sensible qualities. When making speeches, for instance, she often sent a draft to Arthur Schlesinger and asked him to rewrite it for her. ("Could you possibly put in large chunks about the President's role in Human Rights?" she requested on one occasion.) In the 1960s she had followed the suggestion of Millie Robbins Leet (a Stevenson volunteer and later founder of the poverty program "Trickle Up") and taken public speaking lessons to prepare her for her UN job.[1] Now, at the suggestion of Jim Wolfensohn in the 1980s, she took courses on finance in order to understand something of balance sheets and bottom lines. She also relied on Arthur Ross and Maurice Tempelsman, both of whom counseled her well.

But like Thursday's child, Marietta worked hard for a living. Her major source of income was from directors' fees, and by far the largest money-spinner was Lend-Lease of Australia, which in 1987 paid her $45,000. She received roughly $20,000 from CBS and Pan Am. She had a large stock portfolio, managed by Neuberger & Berman, the U.S. Trust Company, and Warburg, Pincus, plus stock in International Income Property, Apache, Krupp Realty, and Smith, Barney. Starting in 1985, she was also a consulting editor for *Architectural Digest*.

She attended board meetings almost once a week, for which she had to do extensive homework. She did not shine at these intimidating meetings, where she was often the token woman. Sometimes, when she volunteered a comment, it made little impression. But on other occasions, her wide knowledge of people in the financial and diplomatic world proved useful. She was also refreshingly different to look at across a boardroom table.

There were other perks, besides the money she received from these appointments. "Marvellous dinner at '21' for Salomon Bros partners (60 people)," she wrote in her personal diary for 1978. "I have just been made a limited partner, and felt like Queen of the May being the first woman in the firm. . . . Everything laid on—the best champagne and caviar, pheasant, silver caddies for each guest. . . . John Gutfreund, the new senior partner, took me home."

Marietta was now moving with a far faster set than at any time since Ronnie's death. Surrounded by Renoirs and whisked about in chauffeur-driven cars, she was once more in that comfortable world Ronnie introduced her to all those years ago. Her photograph appeared with regularity in the "Eye" section of *Women's Wear Daily*, the bible of New York society, alongside both the old-money families represented by such women as Brooke Astor, Drue Heinz, Nin Ryan, Grace Dudley, and Lily Auchincloss, and the new-rich entrants who included Gayfryd Steinberg, Ivana Trump, Carolyne Roehm, Susan Gutfreund, and the other wives whose husbands had made quick and spectacular fortunes on Wall Street during the hectic eighties. Marietta bridged that gap with expertise, her professional status and lack of snobbery making her as popular with the new guard as with the old.

Among these fashion plates, Marietta's appearance grew steadily more flamboyant. She would attend the meetings of the Junior Fortnightly in red stockings. Rosamond Bernier remembered a meeting of the board of overseers at the School of Architecture at the University of Pennsylvania. It was to be a working dinner with real estate developers. "Marietta appeared in a Thea Porter orange chiffon with glittery patterns of the Orient," Rosamond recalled. "It was terribly inappropriate, but of course the men were thrilled."[2]

After all those tailored Dior, Balmain, and Grès years under Ronnie's tasteful tutelage, Marietta's own preference had emerged for a kind of youthful, bohemian exuberance. She loved lace, taffeta, and

Guests at Marietta's round table for dinner at 1 Sutton Place, 1986.

sequins, generally in bright, clear colors that distinguished her in a crowd. (She traveled to China and Eastern Europe in a bright orange padded down coat that stood out like a tropical plant in those drab gray surroundings.) She gravitated toward floating rainbow-colored caftans like those designed by Zandra Rhodes and Thea Porter; pink suits and red jackets by Oscar de la Renta; easy-to-pack silk shifts by Zoran; satin trousers; startlingly short skirts; black, silver, and gold ballet slippers (to conceal her height); and those signature black-patterned tights that had made men breathe faster for fifty years.

She would never become extravagant about clothes. Once she found something she liked, she wore it for years—the silver-gray lace, the taffeta blouse, the sequinned top. In Barbados, the neighbors had sometimes made catty jokes about the turquoise caftan in which their hostess so frequently appeared. When she bought a new white lace dress from Thea Porter, "I love it," she wrote in her journal, "so I wear it every night." It is interesting that after suffering the humiliation of having to remake the same frock over and over during her debutante years in Philadelphia, now, when she could afford to stuff her closets with dresses, she was not seduced. The old Peabody values were still strong in her.

Similarly, her jewelry did not consist of precious diamonds, sapphires, and rubies like those owned by her rich friends. She had a few good pieces from Ronnie, but she mostly wore costume jewelry, strings of pearls or waist-length beads, with dashingly long earrings that dangled from her earlobes like chandeliers, accentuating her long neck.

Thanks to her increasingly photographed appearances at charity balls and mentions in the gossip columns, the charge of being a limousine liberal, which had haunted her ever since TV viewers saw her dilating on the wonders of paying taxes in New York as she sat in the back seat of a chauffeur-driven car on the way to work, was now for the first time an accusation that might have stuck. For by the 1980s, while her politics remained firmly liberal, her lifestyle belied that stance. She was still an ardent Democrat, and would strike up an argument with the many Republicans with whom she spent her working days at board meetings. Jim Sitrick used to love watching her passionately defend Democratic politicians to bemused businessmen at the IIP and Lend-Lease meetings.[3] She also continued to support Democrats running for office, including Adlai Stevenson III and Senator Claiborne Pell. She gave money to Common Cause, Amnesty International, the Fund for Free Expression, and other liberal causes.

But her friendship with the Kissingers (along with Kitty Hart and Phyllis Cerf she sang for his seventieth birthday, "I'm just wild about Henry, and Henry's wild about me"), and other well-known Republicans, and her frequent attendance at parties for the Reagans, for instance, was viewed by some of her family and friends as a betrayal of lifelong political principles. The first time she ever got invited to the White House (apart from her childhood attendance at Roosevelt's inauguration in 1933) was by the Reagans. It was a trophy invitation she had hungered for. Too bad if it finally came from the wrong party.

There was still something of the bedazzled schoolgirl in Marietta. She had always been impressed by stars—whether movie people, academics, politicians, or, at this stage in her life, the Republicans in Washington. Of course Marietta could argue that since one of the duties required of women such as herself was charitable fund-raising, it was important to keep in good standing with the rich and powerful, whatever their political leaning. Marietta used entertaining as her contribution to the world's needs; and if she had to entertain famously right-wing individuals in order to raise money, she saw that as a necessary part of the job.

"In the last eight months," she wrote to Gloria Steinem in 1984 in response to a plea for money, "I have given a large party for the Schlesinger Library, a large dinner (65 people) for the restoration of

Carnegie Hall, a dinner for 700 in the ballroom of the Waldorf for the Citizens Committee for New York City, of which I am Chairman, and now am about to give a dinner for new additions to the Cooper Hewitt Museum as I am a Council member there. People rush away screaming when they see me on the street, as you can well understand. . . ."

The letter gives some idea of the scope of Marietta's institutional involvement at this time. In addition to her directorships, during the 1980s she became a member of many other institutions, including the Cooper-Hewitt Museum, the Council on Foreign Relations, the Council of American Ambassadors, the Council for the United States and Italy, the Franklin and Eleanor Roosevelt Institute for Freedom Foundation, the Churchill Foundation of the U.S., the American Ditchley Foundation, the Arthur Ross Gallery at the University of Pennsylvania, the Marconi International Fellowship, the Pilgrims Society, and the National Council of Inter-Action. She also continued to attend meetings of the Junior Fortnightly and the Forum for Women Directors, a networking organization for women on company boards.

Never having liked music (except for singing show songs), she avoided getting involved in that world, aside from Jim Wolfensohn's Carnegie Hall campaign. There was one other major exception. At the urging of Jim Sitrick, she agreed to be a director of the U.S. board of the English Chamber Orchestra Society. At first she demurred, saying how little she cared for classical music. But Sitrick persuaded her, and every two or three years when the orchestra came to New York, Marietta diligently attended their concerts. She never missed one, even in the last year of her life.

She also loyally continued to try to find business for Llewelyn-Davies Sahni. Randhir Sahni wrote her enthusiastic letters about the efforts of the firm in Houston, and she responded by writing to many of her friends, including officials of the Rouse Company, the Ford Foundation, Pan Am, General Reinsurance Corporation, and other potential clients, promoting the firm's reputation in real estate development and making personal appointments for Sahni. She even contacted Mrs. Marcos on his behalf. Most of these efforts failed, but by 1985 Sahni was able to report billings of over $1 million (the profits were less dramatic, however). During a further crisis in 1987, Marietta pledged $25,000 in MAC bonds as collateral for the firm's debt. She faithfully attended meetings each fall in Houston, staying just one night before flying back to New York.

But perhaps the job that was most suited to her abilities was the chairmanship of the Citizens Committee for New York City, which she assumed in 1981, succeeding John E. Zuccotti. Founded by Jacob Javits during the city's financial crisis in 1975, the Citizens Committee was made up of concerned New Yorkers devoted to helping the city's poorer inhabitants who suffer most directly from the city's economic cutbacks. The committee organized a network of block associations in scores of neighborhoods in the five boroughs, focusing on the problems of poverty, homelessness, and crime. Its vigorous efforts showed how volunteer services could, through programs and projects directed at specific targets and by funding small outreach programs, enhance the quality of life in the inner city.

An unsalaried position, the chairmanship nonetheless allowed Marietta to put her skills to the very best use. Her board members included Betty Chapin, Peter Duchin, Tom Guinzberg, Anne Hartwell, and Mollie Parnis. She was reliable, hardworking, and "did not treat it as a lark," in the words of board member John Trubin (later vice chairman of the New York City Housing Authority). She ran the meetings well and efficiently, and they always ended on time.

Perhaps her greatest strength, as always, was her fund-raising "outreach." Nobody could turn her down. Although she could hardly bring herself to pick up the phone and ask foundations or individuals for money ("I can't bear to be rejected," she told Citizens Committee director Michael Clark), the annual fund-raising dinners were always peopled by Marietta's friends. She would add four hundred or more handwritten notes to invitations, and after the party, the same number of handwritten thank-you notes. This was care and feeding of a high order, and her friends appreciated it.

Not all her staff were convinced by their chairman, finding it hard to see past the socialite facade. Board member and former chairman Osborn Elliott suspected that some regarded her as a lightweight, but John Trubin thought they respected her, and Michael Clark, who worked most closely with her, found her an excellent chairman and colleague. "I think she really cared," he said, "and she had the talent to directly engage one. That kept the staff together."

During the 1980s, the Citizens Committee was by far Marietta's most important responsibility. Roughly once a week Michael Clark would go to Sutton Place and they would meet in her red sitting room to go over the balance sheet, agendas, program proposals, and progress reports. He found he had to educate her about some of the committee's principles. "Like a lot of people who don't understand nonprofit finance," he said, "she thought all our programs were liabilities, and in a deficit situation would say, 'We'll have to cut one of our programs.' Saying this was like saying Dior should stop making dresses. It was the programs that generated the money."

Marietta had no qualms about asking the much younger man's advice on upcoming board meetings. As always, she wished to learn from an expert, and was entirely humble in her desire to understand better the problems arising before the committee. Originally intimidated by her, Michael found this openness both admirable and very flattering. "With her family credentials and personal charm, she was the ultimate WASP," he said.[4]

Oz Elliott, who was her contemporary and less awed by her background, sensed that underneath her confident exterior, Marietta was often scared. When she ran the board meetings, he was aware of her fear before she made a speech. John Trubin also picked up on this insecurity. "You could see the tension and anxiety in her face."[5] Yet with that mixture of personal attractiveness and careful preparation, she always measured up. In 1987, the fiscal year ended with a surplus of $80,000, with all financial goals accomplished. Like Vartan Gregorian at the New York Public Library, Marietta made the Citizens Committee glamorous, and thus a hot charity ticket. (After her death, the Citizens Committee created an annual award in her name.)

She was now receiving the honors (degrees, awards, invitations to speak) appropriate for a woman who had paid her dues to society. People found her more relaxed, playful even. She embarked on a lively correspondence with Henry Steele Commager about oxymorons (one of Commager's suggestions for a company was "United Diversified"). At one of Brooke Astor's dinners, she and Ashton Hawkins (legal counsel for the Metropolitan Museum of Art) found themselves greatly admiring the place cards, which Mrs. Astor's English butler, Paul, had hand-painted. The capital letter of each guest's surname was in the form of an animal. After dinner, Marietta beckoned Ashton back into the dining room and, like naughty children, they scooped up five or six cards as mementoes.

Summers in Italy still beckoned. After two years of renting Ronald Grierson's house in Tuscany, Marietta and Evangeline Bruce found a better one in Poggio al Pozzo, outside Siena, a wonderful old farmhouse with a terrace and pool. The house belonged to the Englishman Edward Millington-Drake and had been decorated by the designer John Stefanides.

These August vacations became an important part of Marietta's schedule through the 1980s. Starting in January, she and Evangeline would go over lists of guests, discussing who would mesh well with whom, when and how long people should stay, every detail thought out with the greatest care. Johnny de Faucigny-Lucinge, a visitor one year, remarked to Bill Blair that they ran it like a hotel: "Your room won't be ready till three p.m."

Certainly Mrs. Tree and Mrs. Bruce kept their establishment on a tight rein. Some years, Kitty Hart joined them in renting the house, but in general it was the two original hostesses who ran the show. Their roles were carefully delineated: Evangeline did most of the inviting; Marietta, whose Italian was a little better, dealt with the staff. They planned menus for the week together. Marietta cared much more than her partner about having an equal number of men and women in the house at all times. Sometimes Evangeline protested about some boring male Marietta proposed to invite, but Marietta would insist, saying that otherwise the house would be like a girls' boarding school. Marietta did not shrink from asking people to leave who she felt had stayed too long, and was equally firm if she thought someone should not be driving home after dinner after enjoying too many bottles of wine. "She was better at that than I was," Evangeline said.

Both tall, lean, handsome women, with their wide-brimmed straw hats, splendid bearing, and global connections, they created an indelible impression during those Italian years. Zandra Rhodes, who designed clothes for them both, remembered seeing them coming toward her at the Uffizi in Florence wearing huge summer hats and floaty dresses, and said it was as though the two women had stepped out of a Gainsborough portrait.

They were in great demand for these enchanted summer weeks. People jockeyed for invitations, competing with each other for the chance to stay with Dorabella and Fiordiligi, as the art historian John Pope-Hennessy called them. Marietta's regular English friends were an eclectic mix of political and literary types, including the Roy Jenkinses, the Nicholas Hendersons, George Weidenfeld, Stephen Spender, the Ludovic Kennedys, the Frank Gileses, the Grusons, and the Anthony Quintons. When Jayne Wrightsman came to stay, she arrived by private plane and stretch limo, bearing gallons of caviar as a house gift. For Jayne, Marietta always gave up her bedroom.

Every year there would be a de rigueur visit to Harold Acton at I Tatti, and to John Pope-Hennessy in Florence, for some invigorating injections of high culture, as well as frenetic sightseeing. Speaking a workable Italian, Marietta took guests to churches and galleries with the energy of a young girl.

Marietta kept careful records of everything they spent. She and Evangeline had no squabbles over money, each being scrupulously fair and appreciative of the other's attention to detail. They had local staff problems, needless to say, as their Italian servants were required not only to clean the house after the endless stream of visitors but also to wash and iron for the demanding Americans. After five years, the two maids complained and were relieved of these extra duties. But apart from these small domestic problems, the annual Italian idyll was one of Marietta's happiest experiences, and she looked forward to it with eagerness every year.

Marietta also uncovered a new seam of enjoyment in Australia, where Penelope now lived. On each of her twice-yearly visits, she collected a host of new friends and admirers. She became vice chairman of the American Friends of the Australian National Gallery, and threw herself into this cause. Her own most successful contribution to the gallery was arranging, through her friendship with Fred Hughes, Andy Warhol's executor, for the Andy Warhol Foundation to donate three silk-screen portraits of Henry Gillespie, the Melbourne lawyer and art patron, to the gallery.

The connection between Marietta and Andy Warhol led to one of the more curious episodes in her later life. Henry Gillespie, who had known Warhol in the 1980s, had become a friend of Marietta's during her trips to Australia. On a visit to New York, he proposed bringing Warhol for a drink at Sutton Place with some other friends. But Marietta was oddly resistant. "If you bring him, Henry," she said, "you don't need me." Henry assured her that he did. Later, Marietta told Henry that Andy Warhol had committed a faux pas with Jackie Onassis by coming to one of her dinners not only inexcusably late but with an uninvited boyfriend, and that Jackie had asked Marietta and her other friends to punish Warhol for this rudeness by not inviting him to their parties.[6]

In Australia, Marietta felt once more as she had as a young girl entering Groton, cynosure of a thousand eyes, as titillating as a brightly colored bird. Even better, in Australia she was free to do and say whatever she wanted. Australians were not accustomed to women who mixed an erotic charge with a cool head, and who had perfected the "knack of charm," as Henry Gillespie described it. She bestowed on Australians a kind of "grace," as Frick director Charles Ryskamp put it. She was the "ultimate status symbol for Lend-Lease," commented the *Australian Financial Review*. In Australia, Marietta Tree could be entirely the person she had created for herself and at the same time receive validation for her work.

Validation was beginning to come as well from other quarters. Honorary degrees poured in—from the University of Pennsylvania, Drexel, Hobart, Russell Sage, Bard, Franklin Pierce, the College of New Rochelle, and Skidmore. Prior to 1980, Marietta's yearly diaries, always the same pocket-sized, leather-covered notebooks printed by Frank Smythson of Bond Street, were bound in navy blue. Starting with 1981, she chose instead a bright scarlet. With this cheerful color Marietta strode through the weeks and months, and her life revealed within those pages reflects her mood as she entered her eighth decade. They describe almost hourly appointments with various boards and associations. Interspersed were trips abroad, visits to the doctor, the dentist, the dermatologist, the hairdresser, three-times-a-week exercise classes, regular Monday morning sessions with her secretary Mrs. Klotzer, and of course companions for almost every lunch, cocktail hour, and dinner.

If anything, the pace picked up as she raced toward seventy. In 1986, she went to Turkey, Texas (twice), Portugal, Paris, London (twice), Miami, and Australia (twice). Between July and October she traveled to England, Maine, Italy, New York, Boston, and Australia. Even her remedy against jet lag was almost as demanding as an Outward Bound course: "For every hour that you are in the air you have a glass of water. If you are flying to Australia this means . . . glug, glug, glug. When you reach your destination do some really vigorous exercise like walking 20 blocks."

On the last page of her calendar for 1986, Marietta wrote with a flourish: "1986—the most satisfactory year so far!" What an enviable comment for a woman about to celebrate her seventieth birthday.

# CHAPTER 36

# "I am going to try
# to keep a journal"

In 1987, Marietta declared a gross income of almost $340,000, double that of the previous year. This figure reflects a remarkable performance from a woman who had no college degree, no professional training, and who ten years earlier had practically no personal income whatsoever. Moreover, she had achieved all this between the ages of sixty and seventy, when many women were thinking of wrapping up their table linens in preparation for the retirement home.

But while to many people $300,000 a year for a single woman without dependents, rent, or a mortgage seems delightful, for Marietta this income was laughable in comparison to that of her friends like Jayne Wrightsman, Brooke Astor, the Kissingers, the de la Rentas, and the Wolfensohns. Unlike these people, whose wealth was vast and stable, Marietta's cash flow depended on continued income-producing activities. At any moment, if she lost a seat on a board or the stock market took a nosedive, she would be in serious trouble.

In 1987, her fears were almost realized. That year, so financially rewarding, she was seventy years old, the age at which, under Australian law, one must retire from corporate boards. Thus, at a stroke she lost a major portion of her working income. Reluctantly retiring from Lend-Lease, she received a director's retirement benefit (which partly explains her high income for 1987). In thanking the board for their generosity, she said that this was "one of the most important relationships of my life." Aware that other retirements would soon be required, she asked members at a CBS nominating committee meeting if they might not explore the possibility of retirement provisions for their directors, as was the case with Australian companies.

As it happened, her panic was unnecessary. Although Pan Am also had an age limit for directors, the company was in such financial and managerial turmoil at this time that the rule was waived and Marietta remained on the board until she died. In the more wrenching struggle for CBS's future that took place in the mid-eighties, Marietta remained staunchly loyal to Bill Paley, who was ousted in a coup in 1983 by Thomas H. Wyman. When Laurence Tisch took control in 1986 and reinstated Paley, Marietta was once more in the right camp. She had never been in the inner circle of directors who plotted the various changes of power during those years. She was in Italy during the most crucial negotiations, and received information by telephone. But her position as a Tisch/Paley supporter stood her in good stead, and Tisch kept her on the board after the new management had taken over, although, as at Pan Am, in a diminished role.[1] She was scheduled to retire in 1992.

But as these crises occurred, she felt once again the cold wind of financial insecurity. When Martin Meyerson told her he wanted to endow something at the University of Pennsylvania in her name, she laughed and said he should simply leave the money to her. She also began hustling (often quite openly) to find new sources of income. She wrote letters asking her Australian friends to find her consulting jobs. "I feel sure that my network of friends, business experience and business associations in the U.S. could be useful to some Australian company with American interests. . . ." At parties, she would hunt out influential businessmen, such as Anthony Solomon, the ex-chairman of the Federal Reserve Bank, who was looking for a woman to join two of his boards, the United Kingdom Fund and Europe Fund. "It was clear she was eager," he said. She became a director of both in 1990.

She also became a consultant for Hill & Knowlton, and a trustee of the company's foundation. Hill & Knowlton was something of a departure. Most of Marietta's boards had been financial or culture-oriented; Hill & Knowlton was a public relations firm, whose success or failure depended almost entirely on contacts—hence the directors' desire to recruit someone like Marietta, with a major Rolodex. Marietta saw her role in somewhat elevated terms: advising business clients, dealing with America's place in the world, upcoming problems in U.S. politics, as she hopefully described it to Robert L. Dilenschneider, chairman of the company. In fact, her job was to get clients. (There were other, more subtle ways in which Marietta could serve. For instance, Dilenschneider asked her to recommend him for the Council on Foreign Relations.)

In 1990, Dilenschneider got into hot water for taking on an anti-abortion campaign sponsored by the National Conference of Catholic Bishops. His employees were outraged, two resigned, and the resulting controversy caused the firm, supposedly the ultimate public relations professionals, a great deal of damage. (Dilenschneider later left.) Marietta, normally an outspoken supporter of the pro-choice movement, remained silent during this time. She took on another PR position as consultant for Taylor International in Washington.

Were these new PR jobs suitable for Marietta? Was it really necessary for her to write these letters to find more and more work, or to take on responsibilities where her contacts would be exploited so ruthlessly for economic gain?

A woman of her age, living alone, without either inherited wealth or wealth acquired through marriage, is never entirely free of fear. Marietta had no qualms about asking for assistance in securing work, but having to ask for financial help was something she would have hated above all. It was vital, therefore, that she remain in control of her financial destiny. Unlike many women then or now, she was practical, keenly aware of her situation, and determined to be self-sufficient.

She continued to serve modest meals at her parties. A typical dinner menu would be fish soup with shrimps and scallops, veal scallopini in butter and lemon with purée of carrots and potatoes, followed by peach tart; or mushroom soup, fish soufflé with salad, and apple pie. (She always planned menus well in advance; at Heron Bay she wrote them out for a whole year.) Some found these meager rations; others thought them brilliantly simple. On one occasion, for a benefit for Carnegie Hall (Jim Wolfensohn had put Marietta on the Special Events Committee), she produced boxed suppers, which aroused some criticism for their simplicity.

If one looked very carefully at the decoration of her apartment on Sutton Place, one might find fabric stapled to the wall, or wall covering discreetly peeling. For many of her friends, a limousine at the door was a given, as it had been during her marriage; now it was never an option. She would manage to get lifts in her rich friends' cars, take taxis—or simply walk.

As well as the permanent anxiety about money, there was another issue that still nagged at Marietta: her inability to produce her memoirs. She once said to an editor at Houghton Mifflin, "The idea of sitting down to write a book in the usual fashion scares me to death because I have neither the talent nor the time." George Weidenfeld had wanted Richard Llewelyn-Davies, Martin Meyerson, and Marietta to do a book together. Marietta was the first to beg off. In her role as editor-at-large, she managed to write an article for *Architectural Digest,* but it was not a success, and, while being kept on as a scout, she was not asked to write any more. As the years passed, she came no nearer to producing a manuscript. On one occasion, inspired by seeing the names "Martin Marietta" together (the name of a corporation), she got the idea that Martin Meyerson would help her write her book, but changed her mind when she realized they wouldn't make any money.

At a party in 1985, someone said to her, "You've had the most interesting life of anyone here." She wrote this down, almost like a mantra, in order to give herself encouragement. But nothing worked, even after Swifty Lazar got her a book contract. She eventually turned to Frankie for help. Frankie suggested she try the diary form, and encouraged her to make her observations as personal as possible. So in April 1986, Marietta started again.

"*April 27.* I am going to try to keep a journal," she stoutly announced in a small, unlined book with an Italian paper binding that already contained a couple of menus. She managed to keep it for precisely two days, writing fourteen and a half pages, before giving up. But even these fragments are revealing. At a dinner given by Sir John Thomson (then UK ambassador to the UN), for instance, she cites a conversation with Robert Goheen (former U.S. ambassador to India): "He and Elaine Wolfensohn and I talked about what our parents wished us to become and what we had become, and what we had wished for our children. His parents had wished that he had become a doctor. Hers a physicist. Mine were wiser, or perhaps less hopeful, they merely wished that I be a good girl and educated."

Diarists edit their entries, of course, and Marietta did a little editing of her own. For example, as she wrote on seeing John Fairchild (editor of *Women's Wear Daily*) in the lobby of her apartment building: "I was cordial despite the fact that he deemed me on "Out" list of W. at end of 1985. But I am too"—here Marietta had crossed out "old" and replaced it with "sophisticated"—"to care, and I think that he knew that which gave me the upper hand."

Marietta had invited her old friend Bill Walton to stay with her at Sutton Place while he recovered from a heart operation: "He has been staying here since the hosp. has no room to look after him in his filthy loft, and he is in the best of spirits. . . ."

> *April 28.* Had a fairly interesting lunch with . . . Maurice Tempelsman. He . . . is currently Jackie Onassis's best friend. He is v. dependable, which is a quality she obviously likes in a man, having seen it so seldom. . . . Lars Schmidt . . . just arrived from Sweden and asked me to lunch with him tomorrow. Accepted —it means chucking a lecture on the gulf states. Don't want to go with Schmidt and wish I weren't so enthusiastic.

*April 29*. Breakfast 8 a.m. Carnegie Hall with Jim Wolfensohn and Sandy Weill and Co, for fund-raising of new tower and refurbishment of Hall. Lunch Jockey Club with Lars Schmidt just over from France. Terrific flirt, but we are old enough friends dating from days when he came with Ingrid Bergman (then his wife) to B'dos. We are both physically well and engaged in work we liked and vowed to meet again in 20 years for a night on the town.

Mary Warburg came to see Bill and it was most enjoyable reliving a dinner party at her apt. when we were young (and I was married to Desi) and she had Joan Bennett and Walter Wanger to dinner and I in a fringe dress that didn't work as I sat in my slip with the fringe beside me plus overwhelmed by being in the presence of a *star* for the first time.

Dinner dance: Prentis and Denise for Zubin Mehta's 50th birthday at L'Orangerie of Le Cirque. Perfect dinner—lobster in a broth etc. Sat next Danny Kaye who cut up all night and was only interested in you when you turned away. Kept whistling in a piercing way at people who came in like Henry Kissinger so the whole room was forced to stop and watch them embrace. On other side a really nice man, a magnate (171 companies, he said) called Dave Murdock. He was fascinating about his world-wide activities. The key was getting the best man possible for that kind of business and paying him enough to come and to stay. I liked him a lot as he didn't seem to be playing on a lot of levels—nor did his ego seem over-inflated.

And that was just about all she wrote. The tone is touching in many ways, schoolgirlish in her enthusiasms and in her obvious plea-sure in name- and place-dropping. Her expressions of affection for Bill Walton and Mary Warburg and her ability to laugh at herself probably come as a surprise to many of her friends, who rarely saw this side of her. The conflicted references to work and play reflect the never-ending battle she struggled with between the "good" and "bad" sides of her nature. Yet even in this new and sadly short-lived writing effort she found it difficult to do more than record social encounters.

Thus the book project remained stalled. She made lists on slips of paper reminding herself of anecdotes ("Trip to Niarchos yacht, Henri Bernstein tango, lunch with Churchill"), and instructions such as "household details," "a minister's daughter," "background of Rich-ard," and so on. She wrote and had typed up several chapters with specific subjects like meeting Imelda Marcos, work at *Life,* filming *The Misfits.* She collected the letters she wrote to her parents from Ditchley and had them typed up. But the prose did not sing. Like her movie performances, these little essays were formal, stiff, and did not capture the spirit of the author. How one longed for some of that reckless buoyancy of her early letters home, or of those sparkling essays at Penn. Yet, like flat champagne, the spirited literary style of Marietta's schooldays had been eliminated by a lifetime of circumspection, and she could not now reach back and recover that unselfconscious eloquence.

Hope for a solution to the impasse came from an unexpected quarter. She was invited to record an oral history of her life for the Arthur and Elizabeth Schlesinger Library's series on the History of Women in America at Radcliffe College. She had already contributed to oral histories of Eleanor Roosevelt and Adlai Stevenson, but this was the first with Marietta herself as subject, and it was a signal honor. The work was completed, with interviewer Nina Cobb, in late 1985. Yet, flattering though the experience was, the results did not please her, and she requested the director of the Schlesinger Library, the late Patricia M. King, to destroy the manuscript. Ms. King could not bear to destroy historical evidence, however flawed, and returned to Marietta the only copy intact. Ms. King agreed, however, that the transcript did not present the "complete and thoughtful perspective on your activities that should be preserved for posterity," and hoped that at a later date Mrs. Tree would incorporate the material into her autobiography.

These comments confirmed Marietta's worst fears. Not only had she emerged from the oral history as a frivolous and incomplete person, but she was also assumed to be producing an autobiography that would finally prove her worth. The oral history—flighty and girlish— may have sounded more like Marietta, but it contravened Marietta's view of herself as the person she had become, with so much travail, and at such a cost. How could she be sure she would be fairly judged without some affidavit for posterity? Even as the awards and honors continued to come her way, insecurity ate away at her confidence.

She tried through other means to secure her reputation. She wrote to Fred Friendly at *The Washington Post* protesting about the word "socialite" next to her name, declaring she had not only been a reporter but had spent most of her life "working in the civil rights movement, and in grass roots politics." When she wrote a letter of recommendation for Robin Hambro, she said, "like me, she is a career woman." She tended to use her title of "Ambassador," although United Nations ambassadorial titles are occupational only, and strictly speaking should be dropped when the term of office is over. (Hoping to transform hers into something more permanent, in 1977 Marietta had applied to be ambassador to Sweden. Anne Martindell, a St. Timothy's alumna, who had been appointed ambassador to New Zealand by President Jimmy Carter, was at that time a member of the board that reviewed ambassadorial appointments. The board's response to Marietta's application, Mrs. Martindell said, was negative.)[2] At her old friend Bootsie Morris's twenty-fifth wedding anniversary, when Mr. Morris introduced her simply as Marietta Tree, she corrected him, insisting that he add the word "Ambassador." This was not really typical of Marietta, and it indicates how deeply she needed recognition for her achievements.

In 1989, as though willing it to be true, Marietta announced to gossip columnists that she was writing a book. But at the very same time she wrote—and underlined—in her calendar, "after a week of palpitations, sciatica, etc. postponed book until Fall." She told Swifty Lazar about her decision, adding that she could not accept an advance for the book. He wrote a consoling letter, assuring her that this was perfectly common for authors who wished to feel free of financial constraints.

In the early fall of that year, she called on her old UN secretary, Ceil Wentz, to help her work on the book. She would dictate or mail material for Ceil to type up. But Ceil could tell Marietta was anxious about it.[3] There were others snapping at her heels. Why, even Marietta's friend Evangeline Bruce was deep into a book—about Napoleon and Josephine. Marietta *had* to produce. The project lurched on.

Meanwhile, driven by work and social demands, she maintained her usual heavy schedule. At least she could continue to produce the life, if not the book.

# CHAPTER 37

# "I don't think
# she wanted to be alone"

Private anxieties notwithstanding, as the 1980s continued, Marietta still looked radiantly young (there had been a second face-lift in 1984 and some collagen injections for wrinkles in 1985). Her complexion, with occasional treatments (and in 1989, the removal of a little skin cancer), was vibrant, her green eyes often enhanced these days by bright blue or green eye-shadow. Her health and energy were astonishing. She continued to carry herself with head held high, shoulders back, firm figure—causing people to turn and gaze in admiration when she walked down the street.

She sometimes exhorted herself to slow down just a little, noting in her calendar, "Better to get control of my life and obey H. Breck's rules of health: 'Never get tired and never get cold.'" But the pace did not slacken much. Why did she run so fast? Close friends wondered about the continued frenzy of activity—the parties, the travel, the nights out. "Marietta never refused an invitation," Sir Brian Urquhart said. "It didn't matter how obscure it was, she always turned up. This disposed one very much in her favor. But I don't think she wanted to be alone."[1]

For a woman who never really ceased to question her value in the eyes of the world, the hectic social life was essential reinforcement. Marietta could point to the hundreds of invitations she received as a confirmation of her identity and status. And in return, by pulling together such well-known and stimulating people as she invariably did at her own parties, she enjoyed, albeit briefly, a sense of achievement that otherwise seemed often to elude her. "Gen con" (general conversation), a term Marietta used for singling out an individual to address the table during dinner, was a mechanism that allowed her to place the burden of intellectual discourse on others rather than on herself, thus concealing her own lack of confidence. The custom also flattered her star-studded guest list, although it could be abused, and some visitors found it contrived. But her parties became famous, representing not only her contribution to society but testimony to her place in it.

Was there something else that made her compulsively pick up the phone to arrange another lunch? Was it loneliness, as Brian Urquart suggested? Some friends sensed that that lay behind the cheerful, busy facade. If so, if was not the loneliness that comes from lack of companionship or social activities. No, Marietta's loneliness stemmed from another source. She had begun, belatedly, to realize what a great deprivation she had suffered, not only as a daughter and a sister but as a mother. When Michael Clark talked to her about raising his children, she admitted sadly how much she had missed. "Children are the most important thing in life," she declared to Elaine Wolfensohn at this time, as though making a surprising discovery.

She became a grandmother twice over. During Penelope's marriage to Rick Fataar they had a daughter, Paloma. That marriage had ended, and Penelope was now living with an Australian psychotherapist, Stuart MacFarlane. In 1989 they had a son, Michael. Marietta was transported. She began filling her scrapbooks with pictures of Paloma and Michael. She talked to people about Paloma, saving her school reports, longing to see her and the new baby, who lived so far away in Australia. She often said that the best part of her Australian boards was not the money but the opportunity to see her daughter and grandchildren.

Yet when she visited, things did not necessarily go well. Penelope always felt that her mother was making a token call, whirling in and out, dressed in some sparkling outfit, ready to go on to some fancy dinner with her Australian businessmen. Although Marietta noted in her calendar the pleasant evenings she spent with Penelope's family, Penelope never remembered them like that. "Actually, she would stay at the Regent Hotel for ten days, and we would have lunch once and dinner once. She was always too busy to spend more time with us." Jim Sitrick was with Marietta in Sydney one year for the IIP board meetings when she begged him to stay on one more night to see Penelope. "She wanted an escort to see her daughter," Sitrick said. "It was as though she did not want to see her alone."[2]

In 1984, Penelope needed money in a hurry to send Paloma to visit her father in South Africa. Rather than lend the money, Marietta sold an emerald and diamond ring at Christie's and gave her the

Paloma's ninth birthday, with her mother and aunt, New York, 1989. *(Suzy Drasnin)*

proceeds. But the ring had been Ronnie's, and was supposed to have gone to Penelope. Marietta had enough money then to pay the air fare without selling this precious memento. In Penelope's eyes, the money hardly made up for the loss of her father's gift to her. It was the kind of unfeeling transaction that continued to keep mother and daughter apart.

When Penelope visited New York, Marietta, hoping to compensate with her granddaughter for what she had failed to accomplish with her daughter, would volunteer eagerly to baby-sit, but the experience was usually disastrous. "She loved Paloma but couldn't stay with her more than five minutes." Although Marietta had found great joy with her own grandmother, she could not find the necessary language, spoken or unspoken, to pass down that deep, rich bond to the next generation.

Her firstborn could not fulfill this new need either. Frankie, who invariably referred to her mother as "Marietta," which some saw as a distancing mechanism, was in her own way remote, particularly in withholding information about her work. On several occasions friends would mention hearing Frankie speak, or reading an article by or about her, of which Marietta knew nothing. "I love to get a report of her," Marietta wrote to her cousin "Torchie" Parkman with some bitterness. "Naturally, she tells me nothing and she generally speaks in far-flung spots so I have not heard her myself in years. . . ." Penelope in Australia, Frankie in "far-flung spots"—the geography was telling. "Isn't it wonderful that your children all want to be near you," she wrote wistfully to Charles Bolté, who had retired to Maine.

Her own family was equally distant. Except for Sam, she had kept her brothers at arm's length all her life, and now they were beyond her reach. At family Thanksgivings, Marietta could not help picking at the old wounds of Peabody rivalry, such as lining everybody up and demanding, "Now who is the real star here?"

Even at major gatherings of the clan such as Aunt Margery Peabody's ninetieth birthday, held at Endicott and Toni's house in Hollis, New Hampshire, in December 1987, feelings were hurt. Marietta swept in and arranged herself carefully at the foot of her aunt's chair, posed to be at the center of the photographs and movie cameras recording the historic event. But she did not stay for the group meal, racing off instead to a dinner in Boston. The family would never hold her.

Three of her brothers bore private grievances against their sister. Mike never forgave her, for instance, for the time she came to Washington when he was working at HUD, and she went to his office building and did not even call on him. He learned of her visit from a colleague. This cruelty made Mike so angry that he telephoned her, insisting she leave a meeting, so he could tell her how angry and humiliated he had been.[3]

George, although having trained himself to receive her "hits," never became thick-skinned enough to ignore her snubs to him in front of friends, such as—after he had carefully described his work to her—"Now what is it exactly, George, that you do?" Yet George tried over the years to make a rapprochement, apologizing for his insensitivity, declaring his love for her, and pleading for the occasional evening together.[4] Endicott, who also tried many times to reconcile with her, found her brisk and dismissive of his efforts. When he suggested he come to hear her speak at St. Timothy's, for instance, she told him to stay away. Toni, always at the opposite end of the emotional spectrum to Marietta, made little effort to hide her anger at what she regarded as her sister-in-law's lack of support for Endicott and relentless condescension to her.

But this detachment was Marietta's only defense against what she saw as her brothers' power. Her reaction to criticism from them was always excessive. When George, Sam, and Mike started seeing a psychiatrist in New York in the 1970s, Marietta refused to go. "It was at that time I realized she was frightened of us," Mike said. "It was bad enough taking us on one by one, but all of us together . . ."

Marietta had lived most of her life protecting herself from her brothers. Now, although surrounded by friends, acquaintances, and admirers, she began to feel like an exile, and sensed that her family mattered to her after all in some way she had not been willing to recognize. She started to make deliberate efforts to restore family relations, such as putting her brothers' birthdays in her calendar—something she had never done before. She was looking for a way home.

She found consolation by keeping in touch with some of the friends she had grown up with. She would have lunch with Coupie Kernan and Hope Scott. She attended the fiftieth reunion of her boarding school, St. Timothy's, where she spoke to the graduating students. There were four main rules of life, she told them: "1. Exercise. 2. Keep out of the sun. 3. Be punctual, and 4. Always do what you say you are going to do." She spent the night before at a hotel with her chum Bootsie Morris, and Bootsie remembered with joy how Marietta that evening abandoned her formal posture, let her hair down, and became her old, fun-loving self.[5]

Marietta (second from left) at her St. Timothy's School fiftieth reunion, 1984.

She began to make regular visits to Roy and Lee MacLaren who now lived in Toronto. Roy MacLaren had left the diplomatic service for a career in business, and they had a wide circle of friends. She loved relaxing with the MacLarens and their children, going to summer theater at Stratford, Ontario, and regularly going to church. "Time to get on your knees," Roy MacLaren would say on Sunday morning, tapping on her door.[6] Here was the cozy family life she found herself missing, the affectionate routine that eased for a while the chill that crept up on her unawares as she roamed her apartment alone before dashing out into the New York night.

Marietta also began to look elsewhere for the comfort that most naturally springs from family feeling. It was not easy for her. For her old and close friends, she had painstakingly built up a persona over the years that would have been too painful and complicated to dismantle. (Only with her therapist, Mildred Newman, whom she saw regularly throughout the last ten years of her life, could she be more relaxed and open.) Yet with more recent acquaintances Marietta found she could begin again, so to speak. They had no preconceptions about her, and conferred on her the freedom to open up more frankly.

In 1986, William Luers, formerly U.S. ambassador to Czechoslovakia, was named president of the Metropolitan Museum of Art. Marietta had spent a little time with him and Wendy, his wife, in Prague in 1985. In New York, Wendy, a native of San Francisco, found herself exchanging diplomacy for the back-stabbing world of the New York social circuit. She was frantically redoing their new apartment when Marietta called and said, "I need to talk to you." Wendy was terrified she had committed some awful faux pas, and nervously invited Marietta to tea. But the call had another motive. In the midst of construction dust and packing cases, Marietta sat down and told Wendy a story. It was about the memorable first occasion at which she met Winston Churchill. She did not elaborate on the horrible errors she had made at the table, but described to Wendy how hurt and angry she was that Churchill ignored her and talked only to the men on each side of him. She said that she only found out later that Churchill never talked to women unless he knew them well and found them amusing. "I would never have made this mistake," Marietta declared, "if I had had a friend in England who could have explained this to me." She then turned to Wendy and said, "I want to be your friend in New York."

Wendy, very touched by this gesture, made full use of the offer over the years. "I remember I wanted to give a dinner for a Human Rights monitor and I asked Marietta, and of course she knew exactly who to invite and how to make it a wonderful party. She was both a socialite and substantive. She espoused liberal causes and yet was elegant. Few women could be as comfortable both in a drawing room and in a political meeting as Marietta."[7]

How these women appreciated Marietta's small devotions! She wrote notes, sent little gifts, inquired after children, listened to their problems. Her cheerful high spirits were infectious, and they loved every encounter with her. Hortense Gabel was one who had remained a friend after the Constitutional Convention. As a housing expert, she worked with Marietta on projects for Llewelyn-Davies. Horty had a troubled daughter, Sukreet, about the same age as Penelope, and the two mothers sometimes compared notes. Later, Marietta went to immense pains to write reference letters to graduate schools for Sukreet, and when Sukreet got married, the wedding took place at Marietta's Sutton Place apartment. (In 1987 Sukreet denounced her boss, Bess Myerson, and implicated her own mother in a sensational trial that destroyed Myerson's, and Hortense Gabel's careers.[8] Marietta stayed out of the headlines.)

With most women, Marietta seems to have provoked almost no hostility, quite an achievement for a single woman who had often inspired sexual excitement in other women's husbands. "Hello, Beauty!" she would greet the females she met at parties, flattering them into a rosy cloud of self-esteem. This talent for friendship with women was unusual in a city where competition, rivalry, and envy marked so many social encounters, and Marietta was one of the few women who could pull it off. In a society of suspicion, she was entirely trustworthy. Hating gossip, she revealed nothing. If, sometimes, this meant revealing nothing of herself, that was part of her identity. One of her oldest friends, Mary Bingham, realized with chagrin one day that "We've told her all our troubles but she's never told us hers." But this was Marietta's way, and her friends respected it.

Arthur Schlesinger described her in an interview as the most *reliable* friend. "You can tell her anything and she will protect it," he said. June Bingham (now Mrs. Robert Birge), who had known her ever since they had been young pregnant wives driving to Barnard together, thought this was perhaps Marietta's unique characteristic, her ability to be trusted by both sexes. "In a world where some women are wonderful with men and some with women, she was wonderful with both," Mrs. Birge said.

The secret, of course, was that while most men thought she *might* be available, women sensed that she was not. Marietta's sexual responses had remained consistent over the years. "Of all our games," Marguerite Yourcenar wrote in *Memoirs of Hadrian,* "love's play is the only one . . . in which the player has to abandon himself to the body's ecstasy." Marietta could never be such a player, differing in this way most radically from the woman to whom she was sometimes compared, Pamela Harriman. Another Golden Girl of the Democratic Party, Mrs. Harriman had, like Marietta, succeeded in achieving wealth and status through her connections with men, but her conquests included a lively and enthusiastic sexual component. While Marietta could perform well enough in bed when necessary, the idea of bodice-ripping *voluptas* filled her with fear, whether she saw it in movies, in books, or in real life. She did not like John Updike's novel *Couples*— "I find as middle age creeps over me that my Puritan roots have a good firm hold. Therefore, it told me more than I wanted to know about the sex lives of his characters."

If women knew this about her and felt safe, many men felt just as comfortable, particularly those who were growing older along with her. Erection-free seduction—the perfect solution for the sixty-somethings. Putting such men at their ease, Marietta now began to reveal a charming delicacy that drew upon her long and rarefied experience in so many worlds. She had lunch, for instance, with her former *Life* colleague, Earl Brown; who had become old and depressed. "So I got him talking about the old days during the war, when he knew and reported on all the labor leaders, gangsters, politicians and athletes." Donald Rivkin recalled how he arranged a luncheon table so that Marietta would be seated on his left, explaining to her with some embarrassment that it was because of his deaf right ear. Marietta immediately assured him that it was fashionable to be deaf in that ear— many gentlemen had that affliction from a lifetime of shooting. Rivkin was from that moment an admirer for life. "All women should go to Marietta Tree School," said George W. Goodman, the economist known as "Adam Smith."

She also began now to build on her newer friendships, confiding in ways she never had before. Publishing consultant Parker Ladd first met Marietta in Barbados and in 1982 he plucked up courage to call and ask her to lunch. From then on they had lunch together almost every three weeks until she died.

"Our friendship was based on those lunches," Parker recalled. "I very rarely went to her dinners. We'd go to the Positano and talk about our lives." Marietta talked to him about growing up with a disapproving father and a critical mother. She asked his advice about her book. They talked about health. She confessed she had a serious cholesterol problem and Parker recommended some pills. Although she also worried about her weight, Parker noticed she ate like a truck driver, always finishing her plate. She loved ice cream and ordered it although she knew it was bad for her, insisting Parker help her eat it so she would feel less guilty.

Marietta told Parker that she and Desie fell out of love with each other at the same time. She told him that she had met Ronnie *after* she had divorced Desie. She said she had been an unorthodox mother but that that was what her children had wanted. She also denied to Parker that either John Huston or Adlai Stevenson had been her lovers.

It seems clear that Marietta wanted to rewrite the parts of her history of which she was not proud. She was trying in her way to seek approval yet again, by whitewashing aspects of her past. Always the bishop's daughter, she knew in her heart that she was a sinner. Perhaps by this method of storytelling, she might be forgiven.

Parker Ladd lives with the designer Arnold Scaasi. Marietta never asked Parker anything about Scaasi and would not go up to Scaasi's quarters when she visited Parker in the apartment they shared. With Parker, she maintained what he called a "capsule" relationship. They always met separately. After lunch she would rush off to a meeting, desperately trying to find a cab. (Parker, like her other friends, could not understand why she didn't get a car.)[9]

Although she obviously felt uncomfortable about Parker's private life, by this time she had begun to accept the homosexual world and even enjoy it. A woman who was still of the generation and mind-set that required a male escort, she finally realized what hundreds of women on the social circuit had known forever, that homosexuals served this purpose admirably, and moreover were often more amusing companions than their heterosexual counterparts. The city was full of such men, and Marietta in the end found their flattery and admiration pleasing.

Her Australian friend Henry Gillespie was another new companion. Henry squired her around when she visited Australia, introducing her to local society. In return, Marietta took him to parties when he came to New York. She enjoyed his youthful energy and curiosity. He was impressed by the wide circle of friends she introduced him to, such as Nin Ryan, Jayne Wrightsman, and Evangeline Bruce. She would call him before he left Australia, telling him of the social engagements she had organized for him, and they would both be frisky with anticipation. He was thrilled by her, and she knew it. Henry, like many gay men, admired women who had in some way created themselves. He saw Marietta's performance as larger than life. "She worked at being even bigger," he said. "She needed the acclaim."[10]

Perhaps the person with whom she had the most intense friendship during the last years of her life was Joe Armstrong, an attractive Texan in his forties who, having moved very successfully through the New York media scene, was now a consultant for Gannett Newspapers and a regular single man at top-level parties. Joe, like Henry, was fascinated by Marietta. Her curiosity and interest in people reflected his own. "She went into parties like a gold miner," he said. He was also impressed by her modesty. "This is a town where everyone tells you what good they do. She never talked about it," he recalled. "She'd offer her help when nobody was looking."

Marietta was equally taken with Joe. He had charm and enthusiasm, and his admiration for her was palpable. They went to museums together, had lunches on Saturday and went to the movies afterwards. "We talked about people, politics, values, and priorities—nothing personal," he said, again comparing her favorably to so many people he knew in New York. "She was always purposeful." He remembered how she liked the quality of being eager, which she differentiated from enthusiastic, defining eagerness as being "moved by a strong and urgent desire or interest."[11]

Her new friends did not only come from the gay world. She often had lunch with Thierry Despont, who had worked with Richard Llewelyn-Davies and then created a highly successful architectural practice. Marietta helped him by introducing him to important clients. Thierry loved Marietta for her support and encouragement. She would come to his office downtown and admire his work, a proud parent sharing in her child's success.

Harry Davison, Marietta's cousin Danny Davison's son, was another young admirer. He first talked to her properly at a family Easter in 1984. Harry was young, handsome, and promising, and Marietta readily turned her attention to this Golden Boy. He had recently graduated from Yale and was planning a bicycle trip with a friend across Europe that would include Italy. Marietta invited the two young men to visit her in Tuscany.

For Harry, the visit was an epiphany. He had never met a woman like Marietta. She went out of her way to include him in the conversations with her famous guests, charming him, enlightening him, encouraging him, showering her attentions upon him like sparks from a Catherine wheel. He felt she was taking him by the hand and admitting him into adulthood. It was a classic case of "boy comes of age," and as he ate his figs and toast with honey every morning on the terrace, Harry embraced the rite in a state of rapture. Although the sexual element was missing, typically, as in most of Marietta's dealings with the opposite sex, it made no difference. "I learned from her how to become a man," he said later.

Whenever Harry returned to Italy, he could not stay away from this priestess of warmth and wisdom. She arranged for him to come to work for the Citizens Committee, and Harry, who was by that time working for J. P. Morgan, started his own pioneer community projects with block organizations. Marietta would make phone calls to influential people for him, to further his career. She loved his clothes, and they would laugh as he modeled his latest Italian purchases for her. For Harry, this was home. He compared this embracing, giving woman to his own parents, who, in true Peabody fashion, were "not given to excessive physical expression," as he put it. This was indeed a new Marietta. She had reconfigured herself yet again for her infatuated young cousin.

Bartle Bull also became a close companion of Marietta's at this time. Having met during Bobby Kennedy's 1968 campaign, they continued to see each other over the years. He felt she was a mentor to him, encouraging him in his writing and publishing career, although mentors, as he said, were normally of the same sex. As with Harry, she was to Bartle a delicious mixture of the maternal and the erotic. The age difference (over twenty years) did not seem to be an issue. Marietta's sexual style as usual allowed the two to flirt without complications. "She was my best older friend," Bartle said. "We were windows for each other."

Bartle was a good addition to Marietta's dinners, and a perfect escort for her. He was attractive, literate, single, and in touch with what was happening in New York. Bartle's son went to Groton, another bond. Bartle and Marietta went together to Groton's one hundredth anniversary celebration. Her return to Groton was not merely a courtesy call. She was on a course back to her roots, roots that still lingered, despite her efforts, like the faint ache of an extracted tooth.

She started cultivating her role of godmother, focusing on Malcolm MacLaren, the young son of her old friends Lee and Roy MacLaren. She would speak to him on the telephone in Toronto, making jokes to his parents about waiting only a few more years before taking him on travels with her. The MacLarens felt that their son's name held some magic for her—Malcolm, the name of her father. Marietta even gave the boy the silver porringer that her godfather, Jack Crocker, had given to her at her birth in 1917, adding her young godson's name to hers.

"I felt like I was her son," Harry Davison said of their relationship. "Marietta made me feel like her child." Joe Armstrong also experienced this connective tissue. "It was as though I were her younger brother," he said. And now, by adding young MacLaren to these new relationships, Marietta was creating a second family to replace the one she had repudiated, bestowing on them that affection and interest a mother naturally pours on her offspring. Her brothers and children might still rule from a distant kingdom, but with her new champions she could counter that Peabody tyranny. Thanks to these willing substitutes, she was re-creating her lost past.

Nothing illustrates this desire more clearly than her choice of beau with whom she shared her last years. His name was Eben Pyne. His wife had recently died, and he and Marietta began seeing each other after a party for John Pierrepont in 1987. There had been a consistent male type in Marietta's life to whom she was attracted, a type represented most perfectly by well-educated, upper-class Englishmen—tall, lean, and emotionally reserved. (The Oedipal school will compare the type to her father, Malcolm Peabody.) Adlai Stevenson was an obvious aberration from this model physically, but he had other compensating qualities.

Although American instead of English, Eben Pyne fit the requirements. He might not have the wit of Adlai Stevenson or the intellectual vigor of Richard Llewelyn-Davies, but he was tall, trim, and handsome, and he and Marietta looked wonderful together. He also offered something deeper and more important to her than this superficial allure. Eben went all the way back to her childhood. As a boy at Groton, he, like his fellow students, had sighed over Marietta's young form as she sat at the Rector's table in the school dining room. He had gone to the same debutante parties in New York. He had even gone to Ditchley when Ronnie and Nancy (a family friend) lived there. With Eben, Marietta did not have to explain her past. With him, she felt she was finally coming home.

"We were both disciplined," Eben recalled. "We both were brought up with the same obligation to society. We had an enormous amount in common. We were both on boards and I knew the issues that came up with CBS or Dreyfus and could help her deal with them. She was very careful with money and I respected her wish to be independent. My mother was raised the same way. Marietta loved Old Westbury, where I lived, and we'd go to Caumsett and she'd tell stories about Marshall Field."

Eben was also a willing and adventurous traveler. "I wanted to go to places like India and Istanbul, so we went together." Eben responded to Marietta's increasing interest in background and family. She began going back more frequently to Northeast Harbor, sometimes late in the fall, staying with George and Peggy Cheston in their spectacular house at the end of Somes Sound. Peggy, originally Peggy Seyburn, was Marietta's old ally in rebellion at La Petite Ecole in Florence, another powerful link to her past.

In Maine, Marietta would lead Eben up the mountains she had climbed as a girl (taking particular pleasure in climbing the one named Parkman), and they would go on picnics like the ones she remembered from so long ago when boatloads of parents, cousins, and friends would find an island and spend the day eating lobsters, climbing rocks, and taking brave plunges in the cold Maine water. With these expeditions, Marietta was gathering up the strings of memory for her own private purpose.

As a rich, good-looking widower, Eben was in great demand by many glamorous women. Most of his time, however, was spent with

With Eben Pyne in Santo Domingo, as guests of the de la Rentas, 1989.

Marietta. They went to parties together. (Sometimes Eben would respond just a little too agreeably to an attractive guest and Marietta would jump up and announce that they had to go home.) He loved classical music and the opera, and often on weeknights in New York Marietta found herself ensconced in Eben's box at the Metropolitan Opera, once more listening to that pesky music she had never quite managed to come to terms with. On weekends, she would travel out to his Long Island house and they would spend quiet days working together.

Eben sometimes talked to her three times a day on the phone if they were not together, and although some of the Pyne family felt that Marietta was chilly and kept Eben away from them, he said he would have willingly married her. But she did not want to marry again. She told this to many of her friends. "It is so wonderful," she said to her brother Sam, "not to have someone tugging your arm at a party wanting you to go home." Susan Mary had seen how much she cared for Eben, sometimes waiting by the phone for him to call. But when

Susan Mary asked whether Marietta would marry him, the answer was negative. "I know I'm taking a chance, but I just prefer my independence."

Independence, yes, but it was of a certain kind. She was independent in that she lived alone and paid her way. But she had always moved in the lee of male companionship, and that was not about to change now. She was never so independent that she could comfortably go out at night alone. She still required escorts for public events in the way of well-bred women born and brought up before World War II. Nor did she ever feel at ease if the male-female ratio was uneven at her parties. (At a dinner party for Claudette Colbert given by Jerry Zipkin, Marietta noted all her friends were there, "but too many ladies.")

Thus to say no to Eben was an act of considerable courage. Unlike Pamela Harriman, whose attachments to rich men helped her career, Marietta, who also had rich admirers (William Hewitt, Arthur Ross, Eben Pyne among them), did not marry any of them. Now in her early seventies, she was again saying no to financial and domestic security and the safety of a predictable companion. At this late age, as she acknowledged to Susan Mary, she was taking a major risk.

She was still a magnet for men, of course, not only from the old circle but the countless colleagues with whom she had worked over the years, both at home and abroad. Natwar Singh and Amjad Ali would have dropped everything to be at one of her dinners. Charles Bolté wrote to her from his home in Maine proposing marriage. Many others would come to her side at the slightest call. That she was able to resist them all was not only impressive, but an exhilarating example of a woman's vote for personal freedom.

There was one man, however, who still had the power to move her more deeply: John Huston. The love letter to her he published in French *Vogue* in 1982 said it all: "When I have doubts, I go to see her, and naturally, she is the same charming young girl. I fall in love all over again." From 1949 on, Huston had continued to write to her. He often used to dream about her. After an absence, he would write saying, "I long to see you and be with you once again." Gladys Hill, Huston's secretary, and Henry Hyde, his lawyer, kept Marietta posted about his itinerary and she stole meetings with him all over the world. There was often a wife and/or children around him, and he was usually about to make or complete a movie, but their time together was always treasured.

Whether their relationship was physical at all after the initial affair in 1942–44 is unlikely. There were opportunities, certainly, and Huston surely was not a man to repress his feelings. But his letters, while full of affection, never make any sexual references or innuendoes. Henry Hyde believed that "they were lovers and then lifelong friends

—the best way to be."[12] Part of Marietta's appeal to Huston was surely her unattainableness, her Peabody guard. She was the one who got away, and he would never get over it.

However, when John's father, Walter Huston, had telephoned Marietta in Reno during her divorce from Desie, and said to her that he was sure she and John would meet in the third act, he spoke with the force of prophecy. By 1987, John Huston was very ill with the emphysema that was to kill him. He wrote his last script, *Mr. North,* and worked as an adviser (attached to an oxygen tank) while his son, Danny, directed the movie. Once again Huston arranged for Marietta to have a small role, this time more suitably playing a society matron welcoming guests to a ball. On July 30, 1987, Marietta went to Newport, where the filming of *Mr. North* was taking place, to find John in the hospital. "Deathly ill," she wrote in her diary, but "still witty, writing notes." She spent two days in Newport, then flew back to New York, making a note to buy him Guerlain's Imperial Cologne as a gift.

On August 5, she returned to Newport for the filming. That night there was a birthday party for John, with cake, doctors, nurses, John's last wife Maricel, his children Danny, Allegra, and Anjelica—and Marietta. Marietta spent time alone with him talking about his sons, and she also talked separately to Maricel. Although it might have been awkward, Henry Hyde observed how Marietta, always the experienced tactician, won the younger woman's trust.

The following day when Marietta arrived on the set, Huston made her official technical adviser on balls, as no one else on the set had ever been to a ball. She filmed her part without much more conviction than her earlier performance in *The Misfits,* saying her few lines stiffly. But Huston did not care. On Sunday, when she went to see him again in the hospital, it was noticed that the electrocardiogram to which he was hooked up started jumping with excitement as soon as she entered the room.[13] In her diary she wrote presciently: "v. loving farewell." That night she flew to Italy, where Eben Pyne joined her.

On Thursday, August 27, John called her in Italy and said that he was out of the hospital and feeling much better. They made a date to meet in Newport over the Labor Day weekend. On Friday, August 28, as Marietta was on the way to Pisa with Eben, John Huston died. Marietta and Eben went on to Rome and spent two days there, finally coming back to New York on September 4. She spent Labor Day, not in Newport with John, but at the Brooklyn Museum with Eben.

Marietta Tree and John Huston—the lady and the lady's man, the aristocrat and the artist, the doer and the dreamer; an unlikely romance that outlasted their several husbands and wives, and that was as highly charged at the end as at the beginning. But Marietta could not bring herself to talk about him, even to close friends, and many had no idea of the relationship until she appeared briefly on a TV documentary about Huston that was broadcast after his death in 1989. (Her only comment about the program was typically unsentimental: "I was good but v. badly lit and looked awful!")

John Huston, brilliant talent though he was, could never meet her standard of male integrity. She had remained faithful, in her fashion, keeping in touch with him, admiring of his movies, at the end trying to find new kinds of oxygen equipment to help him breathe. But now, all these years later, she could still hear the footsteps of her Peabody ancestors pacing restlessly, waiting and watching for her to fulfill her family destiny. At the start of her 1987 calendar, she wrote, "Be ashamed to die until you have won some victory for humanity." What had she won, exactly, so far? Summoned by those Boston shadows, she resolutely pushed on toward the finish line.

# CHAPTER *38*

# *"I'm just trying*
# *to sort things out"*

In April 1989, Jayne Wrightsman gave Marietta a party. There were seventy-five guests, with dinner and dancing. (Marietta requested dancing.) Although her birthday was in April, it was not really a birthday party, at least not recognizably so. If that had been the case, Marietta would never have agreed. The problem with birthdays is that they tend to raise the question of age, and Marietta's age by now provoked a certain amount of testiness. When Bill Blair remarked to her that 1992 would be the Big One (their seventy-fifth), and why didn't they do something together, Marietta was furious. "I'm nowhere near there, Bill!" she said, to his astonishment.[1] Louis Auchincloss, an old friend of the Peabody family and chronicler of WASP ways, recalled her obfuscation on the subject. Talking about his days at Groton, she said to him, "Oh, you big sixth formers, I was so in awe of you." To which Louis Auchincloss replied, "You can't get away with that, Marietta, we are only three months apart!"[2]

Most people would have been amazed that she was seventy-two in 1989. Not only did she keep a schedule that to many seventy-two-year-olds would have been physically and mentally impossible, but she seemed never to be tired, never sick, never even to have a cold. In spite of this robust health, however, Marietta had a deeply concealed fear of sickness. When Judy Peabody began her work with AIDS patients, Marietta could not bear to hear about it. When Kitty Hart and Evangeline Bruce had conversations about illness, Marietta refused to take part. The anxieties she expressed to Parker Ladd over lunch about her weight and cholesterol were not the lighthearted comments of an urban health freak, but the expression of a woman who dreaded what might befall her. On several occasions she phoned Martin Meyerson in the middle of the night, thinking she was having a heart attack. (Meyerson was a discreet confidant, who also in his position as head of the University of Pennsylvania had access to a large pool of doctors for Marietta to consult.)[3]

By 1989, a few more signs of vulnerability emerged. On May 18, a month after Jayne Wrightsman's party, she wrote in her calendar, "ill all day from overdose of antibiotic," medication probably being taken for a recurrence of the bronchial infection she had had a year earlier. She continued to have regular checkups. Her internist at the time, Dr. Jeremiah Barondess, who saw her mostly in order to give her the shots required for all her trips to exotic lands, noted that, as with most patients who had had a cancer alarm, there were times when she "ran a little scared" with symptoms.[4] "The one thing we must do is keep our health," Marietta declared to Evangeline Bruce in Italy that summer of 1989.

Perhaps with a vague sense of unease, that same summer she changed her will. The only significant difference from the one she wrote in 1982 was in favor of Penelope, now pregnant with her second child. Maybe Marietta was looking for ways to reach out to her second daughter. Having originally left her whole residual estate to Frankie, Marietta now bequeathed the Sutton Place apartment, tax-free, to her elder daughter, and the residual estate in equal shares to Frankie and Penelope. She signed the will on August 3, 1989, and that night she flew to Italy. In September, Penelope gave birth to Michael, and Marietta proudly wrote in her calendar how her daughter had had "no pills, stood or squatted for 5–6 hours, then went home with the baby afterwards!" That was the kind of physical toughness bred in the Peabody family for generations, and Marietta was delighted to see it in her daughter.

In the same sturdy spirit, Marietta urged herself on. Well into 1990 she hardly stopped for breath. After Christmas in Barbados, she flew to Australia for two weeks. Then she went with Eben Pyne to Hobe Sound, and at the end of February on to Santo Domingo and the de la Rentas. On March 16, she had another face-lift, this time with Dr. Daniel C. Baker. She recuperated for a week, doing the books with Mrs. Klotzer and taking part in a Pan Am meeting over the telephone before launching off into the usual round of parties, exhibitions, and trips abroad that punctuated the New York spring season.

On April 24, 1990, she fitted in an office visit with Dr. Cahan. He felt a lump behind the scar tissue of the upper outer quadrant of her left breast, where the lumpectomy had been performed. Although the

X-rays were negative, Dr. Cahan did not like what he felt. Having retired from surgery, he referred Marietta to his son, Anthony. The younger Cahan immediately ordered a biopsy at Doctor's Hospital (now Beth Israel). The biopsy took place on May 4, and the malignancy was identified immediately. Frankie happened to be with Marietta at Sutton Place when the news came through. Her mother froze. On this occasion, she used the word "cancer." Frankie, of course, was immediately sworn to secrecy and told the matter was not to be discussed again. "I couldn't find a way to comfort her," Frankie said.

On May 8, Mrs. Klotzer went with Marietta to Doctor's Hospital, where Dr. Anthony Cahan performed a modified radical mastectomy, which meant the complete removal of the left breast, plus a portion of glands in the underarm. No muscle was taken out. Dr. Cahan had given Marietta the option of reconstruction, but the idea repelled her, and without hesitation she turned it down.[5] Just like her mother, she did not want to spend the time. She would deal with a prosthesis, although she despised it.

Frankie was with her mother when she woke up, and saw her leave the hospital in three days. On May 14, the drains were taken out at Sutton Place by Dr. Cahan. That afternoon she had a checkup with Dr. Baker to make sure her face looked well. She was not surrendering. She did not even note in her calendar what had happened that week, preferring to leave the meetings, cocktails, and dinner engagements intact, as though she had attended every one.

Then she leaped into action. On May 15 she had an appointment with a specialist bra maker, then went to a meeting at the Cooper-Hewitt and attended a dinner given by Patsy and Lou Preston. On May 16 there was a party for writer Dominick Dunne at Mortimer's and a concert at Carnegie Hall. On May 17 she went to Washington to attend another party given by Kay Graham for *The Washington Post*'s Ben Bradlee. On May 18 she and Sam flew to Boston to visit Sam's nephew in Brookline before going on to Groton for the weekend. They arrived in Boston very late, and got lost in the dark, finally ending up after midnight at a Howard Johnson's where they spent the night. This grueling journey, taken just ten days after the mastectomy, temporarily unraveled Marietta's composure and she became very agitated, telling Sam her doctor had told her to take care of herself. Sam, of course, had no idea what she really meant.

On May 23, she had her first appointment with Dr. Anne Moore, the oncologist at New York Hospital recommended by Dr. Barondess to provide Marietta with chemotherapy. For stage-two breast cancer, which meant high risk of metastasis, aggressive treatment was recommended. (Radiation was not an option, since it is not possible to re-radiate the same tissue.) Given her schedule, on which she refused to compromise, this treatment was something of a challenge. Dr. Moore was amused by her patient's elaborate consultations with the little red leather calendar, as they attempted to fit in the treatments over the summer.[6]

One of the first lunch dates Marietta made after surgery was with Elaine Wolfensohn, who had recently undergone a similar experience. They had lunch four times in all, with Marietta asking all the right questions, wanting the specifics about chemotherapy and how one should deal with it. Before she embarked on her own program, Marietta, always the diligent researcher, wanted to make sure she knew as much as possible about it. In addition to Elaine Wolfensohn, there were others for her to consult. There was Dorothy Hirshon, an early victim of the disease, yet full of health forty years later; Mrs. Klotzer, Marietta's longtime secretary, had a mastectomy in 1988 with Dr. Cahan as her surgeon; Marietta Dockery was equally robust twelve years after her operation.

All those women told Marietta how they had fared. Not one of them, however, knew that Marietta was suffering from the same affliction. Although asking them searching questions about their ordeal, she never once shared with them what they so generously shared with her. At least one of her confidantes found it hard in retrospect to forgive this secretiveness. "I felt exploited," Elaine Wolfensohn said later.[7]

Marietta arranged all the chemotherapy appointments herself. No possibility of a leak was to be tolerated. She had her treatments twice a month at New York Hospital through the summer. She was always put into a private room, under the name "Mary Tree," so that nobody saw her, and she was never accompanied. Patients tend to feel weak and nauseated after the treatments, but Marietta took to them wonderfully, emerging cheerful and full of energy. "She was usually going straight from chemo to a board meeting," Dr. Moore said with admiration. Worried about her hair falling out, Marietta had icepacks put on her head and began using Rogaine, a commercial hair-loss product. But in fact she suffered little from this symptom, and with her beautifully designed wigs, could appear in public without the slightest suspicion of anything amiss.

Her summer was frantically busy. In June she was in London, New York (time for one treatment), Barbados, and Northeast Harbor. On Monday, July 9, she returned again to New York for three days (and a treatment) before flying to London to stay with Evangeline Bruce and attend the Ditchley meetings. She stayed in London a week, returned to New York, and then back again to Northeast Harbor. Frankie and her friend James Sterba, a *Wall Street Journal* writer, were also there for the summer in the cottage Frankie and her FitzGerald siblings had built on their father's land along Somes Sound.

There was one more stopover in New York to fit in another treatment, plus a weekend in East Hampton with Time-Warner CEO Steve Ross, before the annual trip to Poggio al Pozzo. She picked up her routine of swimming every morning before breakfast, sightseeing, and arranging dinners with Evangeline. "Everything perfect as always," Marietta wrote in her calendar.

But it is difficult to conceal everything about one's body, particularly in front of very old friends. Kitty Hart was staying that summer and sensed something slightly wrong. "She was always the first to get out of the sea and put on her robe. I felt she did not look quite even. But of course I didn't say anything." Marit Gruson thought Marietta seemed unusually thin. But when Kitty remarked on it, Marietta laughed it off. "My dear, my mother was a *stick* at seventy. So was my grandmother. It runs in the family."

Back in New York, Marietta occasionally noted a little fatigue, and turned down the odd invitation out of "prudence," but in general her activities seem to have been stepped up. In October, after one of the last chemotherapy treatments, she admitted that she felt weak and trembly. The following day, she was fine again. On October 8 she had a bone scan that was normal. The doctors were very pleased, agreeing that she was healthy and looked terrific.

That fall, Marietta went to London and Toronto and committed to a seemingly endless procession of nights out. She was beginning to run, one might say, for her life. Her only concession was her resignation as chairman of the Citizens Committee of New York, her favorite cause. "I don't want so many demands on me," she told Parker Ladd. But he sensed other, darker reasons.

In September, Sir Crispin Tickell, British ambassador to the United Nations, gave a farewell dance at the ambassador's residence on Beekman Place before his return to England. Sir Crispin remembered Marietta that night with special vividness. "She came down the stairs, sparkling in a new and beautiful Oscar de la Renta gown. She was the queen of the party." She seemed to some to have lost a little weight over the summer, but many people who saw her then said, on looking back, that she never looked more radiantly luminous than that winter.[8]

On October 26, Bill Paley died at the age of eighty-nine. Marietta had seen him frequently since Babe's death, and for a time was one of the women on Bill's "next wife" list. But he never married again. Marietta was asked to give one of the eulogies, which terrified her but made her feel very proud. The other speakers were Henry Kissinger, Frank Stanton, Walter Cronkite, David Rockefeller, Jeffrey and Bill Paley, Jr. The memorial service at Temple Emanu-El was on November 12, and Marietta spent the weekend before working on her speech. She had it typed up the way that she had done during her UN years, in very large type so that she did not have to wear her glasses, with words underlined to remind her to pause or make an emphasis.

The eulogy was one of her most polished performances. It was filled with anecdotes and wry, self-deprecating humor, such as the story of going to a famous restaurant with Paley and being ushered to a banquette with shaded lights and glittering silver. When handed the menus, "Bill leaned towards me, took my hand and looked deep into my eyes with a seductive smile and said, 'Darling, doesn't your heart beat faster—when you see a new menu?' "

She also gave credit to her old friend Dorothy Hirshon, Bill's first wife, mentioning how Bill and Dorothy had shared such an interest in art. "Here it is appropriate to give Bill full praise for his choice of Dorothy and later, Babe," Marietta declared. "Although quite different, they were both remarkable and talented women who gave him strength and comfort as well as bringing great luster to his life and all around them." It took some courage to say those words in front of that assemblage in the Temple Emanu-El. Dorothy was very touched.

In late November she had "tummy flu" for a day, but was on the move through December, making a flying visit to Houston before preparing for Christmas. She called Michael and Anne and Jeremy Tree with Christmas good wishes, had dinner with Joe Armstrong, then flew to Barbados, where on Saturday, December 22, Frankie and Jim Sterba were married in St. James's Church. "Father Hatch's service *perfect,*" Marietta noted; ". . . 26 friends afterwards for a glass at Claudette's [Colbert]." Kitty Hart, Bill Walton, and the Grusons were also on hand to celebrate the occasion. It was a welcome event for Marietta, who now saw both daughters possessed of what she had always deemed advantageous in conducting a successful life—a male companion.

As 1990 came to an end, her calendar was so crowded with appointments that it is almost unreadable. The writing begins to be scrawly and thin, with crossed-out entries and hasty lists of names of people she met or invited to dinner. It would not take an expert writing analyst to suggest that these were telling signs of loss of altitude. Kitty Hart, who often compared calendars with Marietta, began to notice that sometimes she seemed confused. "It was so unlike her."

At a party in December, before she left for Barbados, she slipped a present into Joe Armstrong's hand, "like a little girl," he recalled. It was a traveling clock. "Just a stocking-stuffer," she told him. Joe sent her in return a small wooden sculpture entitled *Peaceable Kingdom,* and in the accompanying letter he wrote out the words of the song, "I'd like to teach the world to sing, in perfect harmony," telling her to go and sing in the sunshine and have a wonderful holiday. On January 1, 1991, Marietta wrote back from Barbados, "It is like you to send the heavenly 'Heavenly Kingdom.' Of all my friends you are the one who would fit in the best there. If I am canonizing you, I mean it." She then added what seemed to Joe at the time a mysterious sentence, "and so I trust you will lend a helping hand later."

The day after writing that letter, Marietta returned to New York to prepare for the new year's engagements. As always, she had already made a list in her calendar of the monthly Pan Am and CBS meetings through 1991, as well as other important obligations. (Never having had a full-time secretary, she noted these vital dates for herself well ahead of time.)

But while in Barbados that winter, she had begun to feel weak and suffer dizzy spells. Frankie observed her mother's distress, putting it down to the aftermath of the chemotherapy. Once back in New York, Marietta began to complain of headaches. She saw Dr. Cahan on January 10, who ordered bone and CAT scans. The results were the worst possible. The scans showed widespread metastasis of the cancer, both in the bones and the liver. To make doubly sure, Dr. Moore did a bone marrow examination, but there was no reprieve. The mastectomy had come too late.

Marietta received the news without emotion. When the doctors recommended further chemotherapy, she simply whipped out her little red calendar to start fitting in appointments for treatment. "We couldn't start right away," recalled Dr. Moore, "because she had an important lunch date." The only noticeable reaction to this terrible blow was a bout of depression that Frankie picked up in her mother during January. But she shook herself out of it, and started the new course of chemotherapy in February.

This time, it did not help. As the cancer spread, her back began to hurt and her liver became enlarged. "By March and April, she was desperately sick," Dr. Moore said. "We were working hard to keep her up and running."

Up and running? It is almost impossible to believe what Marietta accomplished that last year. She made her annual trip to Santo Domingo, and spent much of it on Oscar de la Renta's dance floor. "She kicked off her shoes and danced like a professional," Jayne Wrightsman said. "You'd have thought she'd been called in to entertain us." She had canceled a trip to Australia at the end of January, telling her Australian friends that she would come in March. That date also passed. She bought some new clothes to fit her slimmer figure. Someone said to her at this time, "You look so great, Marietta, I want to do what you do." "No, you don't," Marietta said quickly.

In April, she went to a dinner with Roy Jenkins on one of his regular New York trips, but wanted to go home early and said she would not be able to see him again during his visit. Roy thought this odd.[9] She attended a Junior Fortnightly meeting where Christa Armstrong thought she seemed too thin. Christa was worried. She had seen Marietta coming out of her doctor's office "looking ravaged."

Marietta began putting her affairs in order. In March, she invited the art expert and collector Khalil Rizk to tea with her and Susan Mary Alsop. When he arrived, she took him around the apartment, asking what everything was worth. "I'm just trying to sort things out," she said. She made what turned out to be her last visit to Penelope's old nurse, Mabel, in her nursing home on Long Island. "Mabel has half a million dollars," she told Henry Gillespie in New York later that spring. "That's nice for her," Henry said. "That's what comes of having good employers," Marietta said proudly.

She continued to write her monthly check to charities and paid her estimated taxes. She paid her contribution to Teddy Millington-Drake for July's rental of Poggio al Pozzo. She accepted an invitation to speak at the College of the Atlantic in Bar Harbor in late July. She and Eben went to a concert of the American Friends of the English Chamber Music Society, coming in from Long Island to attend. (They left early.)

But close acquaintances gradually began to observe a loss of control. Joe Armstrong went with her to a lunch at the United Nations for the ex-ambassador to Syria, and was delighted how everyone at the United Nations remembered her and wished to speak to her. But at the end of lunch, she suddenly looked at her watch and said she had to rush to a doctor's appointment. The urgency in her voice and her abrupt departure were very unsettling. After a dinner at Khalil Rizk's, she called in distress to say she'd lost an earring. "We hunted and hunted and then it turned up in her bag." Michael Clark was walking her to a taxi after lunching at the Century when she discovered to her panic that she'd lost her glasses, and they had to return to the Century to try to find them. In almost anybody else, this kind of absent-mindedness would have been quite normal. But because it was Marietta, these tiny glitches were remembered.

In May, her old school friend Alice Spaulding Paolozzi called to invite her to come to Spoleto. "She sounded strange and said she couldn't come," Mrs. Paolozzi recalled. "I wondered if I had done something wrong." Henry Gillespie, in New York that month on his annual visit from Australia, went to several parties with her and noticed that she often asked to sit down. She also ate sparingly and wanted to leave early. But these were small signs of what he thought was probably a perfectly natural fatigue, considering her schedule. More often, she was her usual exuberant self. After a ball at the Plaza for the United Nations Association, she turned to him and said, "Don't you love New York, it's so stimulating!"

A photograph of her at the ball appeared in *The New York Times,*

The two Mariettas, Tree and Dockery, at a party at 79th Street, 1950s. *(Bill Anderson. Photo courtesy of Marietta Dockery)*

looking splendid in caftan with lots of pearls and dangling earrings. Marietta Dockery saw the photograph and telephoned her. "Were there any PITAs at the party?" she asked. (Long ago they had invented this acronym for pains-in-the-ass.) These two women of different color had sustained a remarkable friendship over the years. Marietta Tree had urged her friend to become a Representative of Negro Women at the United Nations. Marietta Dockery had followed her friend's progress as she, too, moved up in the political hierarchy. That evening when Marietta Dockery telephoned, the other Marietta invited her to tea. But Mrs. Dockery's husband was sick and she could not go. "We must get together *very* soon," Marietta Tree said.

At the beginning of June Marietta complained to Dr. Moore of headaches again and of double vision, a well-known symptom. The cancer was on the move. A brain scan was immediately ordered. It showed multiple metastases. There was only one possible course now: radiation to the brain. Once again, Marietta plucked out her red leather calendar. "Will my face get fat with the cortisone?" she asked.

On June 3, Marietta went to the Cooper-Hewitt spring benefit with Henry Gillespie. On this occasion, she danced as though she would dance forever—twenty minutes on the dance floor, in her favorite lace dress, kicking up her heels in a frenzy of energy, "defiance, rather," Henry concluded, in hindsight. At the end of the evening, in the pouring rain, Marietta said to Henry something she often said to him, "Let's get one of our rich friends to drive us home."

Marietta was in fact rehearsing for one last great effort. With Australia having slipped through her fingers, she was determined at least to see one more time the other country that had played such an important part in her life—England. In spending so much time there (a visit every year of her life since her marriage to Ronnie in 1947), Marietta had finally learned how to present herself in the European manner, how to handle social situations with confidence, and how to convey a sense of irony. These lessons, never taught in American schoolrooms, were hard-won, but by the end, her skills were honed to the point where the seamless ability to engage with others while withholding oneself came as easily to her as singing to a skylark.

Isaiah Berlin had once allegedly observed that Marietta was a Henry James heroine. Disliking the remark then, as she grew older she could not have denied its validity. This gauche, impressionable young American beauty had grown into an experienced player, as she moved from drawing room to garden party each summer with her titled friends. Certainly Marietta wanted to go to England one last time. She had finally gained acceptance there, as her annual piles of engraved invitations proved. Although she never talked about the place with the affection she expressed for Maine or Italy, recalcitrant England was perhaps her most prized conquest.

The radiation treatments were put on hold. On June 6, Marietta gave one of her classic dinner parties at 1 Sutton Place, in honor of the Indian ambassador. Among the guests were Jacqueline Onassis, Maurice Tempelsman, Alan Pakula, Chessy Rayner, and Judy and Sam Peabody. She ran the party in her usual way, insisting on "gen con" at the end. "Now let's hear what the Indian Ambassador has to say. . . ." Afterwards Mrs. Onassis wrote to her in lyrical appreciation of the evening. "Your living room looked so beautiful—with the window open and the great summer breeze blowing in and all the green outside —and the mirrors and shadows and gleam at all the magical things inside. . . ." She added that next fall she was going to have a dinner and do "General Conver," as she called it, and everyone would have to name their most ravishing evening—"and mine will be last night."

The day after that party, on June 7, 1991, Marietta flew, with Eben Pyne, to London.

# CHAPTER *39*

# *"Terribly sorry, I have the flu"*

Marietta had asked Sir Nicholas Henderson to arrange a big dinner for her at the Garrick Club in London with Polly Fritchey and Evangeline Bruce, insisting that they would share expenses. Henderson brought together a group of about thirty friends. Jayne Wrightsman came early, and was surprised to see such a large number. Marietta usually preferred small groups of six to eight. Marietta and Jayne did the placement together, putting Isaiah Berlin on Marietta's right, Henderson on her left.[1] A noticeable absence was Roy Jenkins. Why did Marietta not invite him? "My guess is because I would have known she was seriously ill," Lord Jenkins speculated later, "and she could not have stood that."

Marietta wore her white lace dress to the party. Eben Pyne thought she did not look well. The Hendersons remarked that she looked a little "piano," as they put it. They asked her to dine later in the week, but she called saying she could not come. "I have the flu, but I'll see you in Italy."[2]

Isaiah and Aline Berlin gave a lunch for Marietta and Eben in Oxford. She looked thin but wonderful, they thought, in a pink suit. The two couples drove back to London together and promised they would meet again when Marietta returned to England for the Ditchley Conference in early July. Aline's last recollection of her was a glimpse of her legs in those wonderful black stockings as she stepped out of the car.[3]

Marietta spent just under a week in London, returning to New

York on June 13. She was exhausted and in pain. "I don't know what was the matter with me in London," she said to her brother Sam. "I couldn't get my energy up." On June 18, she went to see Dr. Moore, who for the first time saw her patient flagging.

Marietta had hope, of course. She was still as strong as a horse. But under the hope was frustration now, and under the frustration, fear. Like many facing later stages of cancer, she began looking at alternative medicine. She attended a seminar on aromatherapy where she saw Steve Ross, another sufferer in search of magic potions. (Ross outlasted Marietta by a year, dying of prostate cancer in December 1992.)

By this time, in spite of her prodigious efforts, she was unable to maintain her normal schedule. Bill Walton said that usually it was impossible to get her to lunch or dine less than three weeks in advance. Suddenly, she seemed available. "I thought she'd broken up with Eben." She took Bill and little groups to lunch at Mortimer's, one of her favorite places. Khalil Rizk saw her there once and noticed how her appearance was less than immaculate. What was wrong with her?

Antibiotic poisoning, she told people. When Rosario Gonzalez, her maid, went with her to the hospital for the treatments, "Don't tell anyone," her mistress would instruct her. "To callers, say it is a cold." "But Madame, it is not a cold." Madame was adamant.

Throughout the rest of June she had a daily treatment of radiation to the brain. She became extremely anemic, and started receiving an injection of Erythropoetin to elevate her red blood count. There was no fuss. She learned to inject herself three times a week in the thigh. How she must have hated it. But she had to be up and running. For there was still one more journey Marietta wanted to make, perhaps the most important of all, before it was all over. It would mean stopping the radiation. But she had to find the strength, and the time, to go back to Maine.

But how? She knew by this time she could probably not get through the trip alone. At the same time she could not ask any of her close friends to accompany her and see her fail. Frankie—apart from her doctors the only person who knew the truth—would travel up with her, but Frankie was planning then to stay for the rest of the summer with her husband Jim. Marietta could not ask her daughter to accompany her back to New York so soon. Desperate, she tried a long shot. She had recently had dinner at Mortimer's with Russell Hemenway, her old friend from the Lexington Democratic Club days. Perhaps she could ask Russ? "It's just going to be family," she said to him. But he could not go (he later sadly regretted it), and she had to turn elsewhere.

There was always Eben. But Eben had been kept in the dark ever since the first diagnosis. On his own admission, he never even knew she had had a mastectomy (Marietta proudly confirmed this to her oncologist), let alone the chemotherapy and radiation treatments. (His wife had died of cancer, and it is possible that in some part of him he was denying the possibility of a repetition.) So, when Eben was asked to attend an anniversary party with his family in New Jersey the weekend she planned to go to Maine, Marietta encouraged him to go.[4]

She had told Joe Armstrong many times how she wanted to take him to Northeast Harbor to meet her family. This, then, was the moment. The remark about "a helping hand" in her Christmas letter to him, he realized later, made perfect sense. She had foreseen everything. As soon as she got back from London, she telephoned him to tell him about the trip and that she had decided to go a few days early to get some air "to revive me." She suggested Joe travel up with Sam at the weekend.

On Wednesday, June 26, Frankie, Jim, and Marietta flew to Bangor, where Susan Mary met her and drove her to the house that had belonged to Susan Mary's mother, Mrs. Peter Jay. High on a hill overlooking Northeast Harbor, it was filled with family mementoes and portraits that Marietta had grown up with. Susan Mary thought she seemed tired, but she said she was looking forward to the weekend. Susan Mary had invited Trishy Scull and Peggy Cheston, both women who had known Marietta from her youth, to come to dinner. It was just the four of them. Marietta appeared in a pants suit made of a multicolored satin material that looked like stained glass. But Trishy could tell she did not really want to come down to dinner. "I'm fine," Marietta assured her anxious friend. "But how are you *really*?" Trishy insisted. "I am very ill," Marietta said. "I think I am being killed by antibiotic pills."[5]

Sam and Joe arrived on Friday, renting a car from Bangor Airport, and got to the house just as Marietta, looking very wan, was waiting for a taxi to go to the hairdresser in Somesville. (The hairdresser in Northeast Harbor was much closer, but what if she were seen and recognized?) She insisted on going in a cab, and asked Joe to go with her. It is clear she was afraid she might collapse on the journey, which took about thirty minutes. Marietta told Joe to explore the village while she was in the beauty parlor, and he did, buying postcards while he waited.

They were four for dinner that night—Susan Mary, Sam, Joe, and Marietta. Susan Mary served lobster, as she always did when guests first arrived in Maine. As they came to the table, Marietta stood behind her chair and put her head down. "I don't think I want anything," she said. "I think I'll stay on the sofa and we'll just talk." So she lay on the chintz-covered sofa in the living room (which opened into the dining room), and the other three went through the motions of eating their dinner. "Tell Joe about the painting," she would tell them. "Describe to him the story about . . ." She never came to the table at all. The next day, she stayed in her room.

On one of her last visits to Babe Paley, when the cancer had taken control, Marietta described her friend as "beautiful as ever in bed with a turban (most of her hair has gone) but holding up a hand to one eye. I fear the disease has gone to her head." By now Marietta knew she was in the same desperate plight. When Sam went into her room the next morning to see her, "Her back was to me, and she was looking at her hand, and I felt she was facing something she didn't want to face."

The day dragged on. Marietta told Susan Mary she wanted Joe to take a walk, see the top of Cadillac Mountain, thinking up ways for him to enjoy the glories of Mount Desert Island. She kept saying she would be down shortly. Frankie came over. Marietta was complaining that the antibiotic poisoning was giving her double vision. Susan Mary, horribly worried like the others, was convinced that it was a brain tumor, and offered Marietta an eyepatch (Susan Mary had had eye problems for some time). Joe visited her, and she said she would be down later. But all that day and night, she never left her room.

On Sunday, June 30, she was to fly home with Joe. As he helped her into the cab to drive to the airport, he saw something in her face that terrified him. "Marietta, we don't have to go," he said urgently. "You can stay on here." "No, no, we must go," Marietta said.

She began sinking then, in the cab, during the long hour's drive to Bangor. "Let's pull over and get a drink," she murmured at one point. They stopped at a service station and bought a soda. At the airport she was so weak she could not get out of the cab, and Joe had to find a wheelchair. When he returned, she was lying on the back seat. He held her hand while they waited for the wheelchair to arrive. There was a long line at the check-in, and no one would allow them through early. She sat in the wheelchair, her hand on her head, looking down. For those terrible hours, perhaps for the first and only time, she could not obey Adlai Stevenson's last ringing words to her to keep her head high.

On the plane, Joe held her hand the whole way. She thought food might help, but she could not eat. Finally, he got her to Sutton Place. She walked into the apartment unaided, sending Joe home, saying, "I must just get to bed." When he got back to his apartment, there was, unbelievably, a message from her on his machine, saying how sorry she was for not saying thank you.

She had done it. But the price was very high. In early July another CAT scan revealed more cancer. She still looked remarkably well, even with the severe loss of weight. Surely the illness could be arrested, even for a little while? Marietta, always the optimist, artist of denial, was hope personified. Her doctors encouraged this spirit in her. Knowing her belief in exercise, for instance, they urged her to try to move around as much as possible, although walking was increasingly difficult. The radiation made her lose her balance. A friend saw her at this time trying to walk in the lobby of her Sutton Place apartment and had to avert his eyes from the pitiful sight.

She plunged once again into feverish activity. She attended board meetings by telephone. She called Charles Ryskamp at the Frick Museum, worrying about preserving letters she and Ronnie had received from Winston Churchill. She started a letter-writing campaign to get Susan Mary's book *To Marietta from Paris* reissued. She continued to accept invitations through the fall. She called her old friend Lee MacLaren in Toronto and said wistfully, "When are you coming down again, Leesie?" (How Lee later wished she had dropped everything at that moment and flown to New York.)

Eppie Lederer, her Chicago friend from the Stevenson days, came to New York and she and Marietta had lunch together as they always did at La Grenouille. "I thought she looked quite thin, but we had our usual time together, talking politics. As we parted, she asked me to drop her off as I had a car. Of course I agreed, although it was the opposite direction. When she hugged me to say farewell, 'Oh, Eppie,' she said, 'I have loved you so much. You've brought so much joy to my life.' "

She telephoned the Berlins, saying that owing to antibiotic poisoning, she could not return to Ditchley. Sad to miss her, the Berlins left for Paris and then Scotland. Kitty and Frank Giles had asked her to dinner after the Ditchley meetings. Again, that familiar bright voice came over the telephone: "Terribly sorry, I have the flu. Next time . . ."

She managed a trip downtown to have lunch with Thierry Despont. When they parted, she said she would see him when she returned from Italy. She telephoned Jim Sitrick, who was in France on vacation, and asked his advice about a new contract she had received from Swifty Lazar. The book project was still alive. She also wanted to go over her will with him. She had dinner with the Grusons. To Marit, she seemed hectic. She had to go home abruptly, obviously in pain.

There were other faithful monitors of this last journey. Michael Clark, missing her at the Citizens Committee meetings, telephoned her. "I just wanted to call you," he told her, "and talk about the Committee. What would you like to know?" "I want to know about the young people," Marietta said. "Tell me how they are doing." Bill Walton visited Marietta at Sutton Place toward the end of July. She was wearing the eyepatch, looked desperately thin, and hardly moved. No reference was made to her health. "I burst into tears on leaving the apartment," he said afterwards.

All through July, the goal was to get Marietta to Italy. "We made and remade the plans a dozen times," Frankie said. But by the beginning of August, Marietta was increasingly frustrated by her lack of progress. She complained about her vision to Martin Meyerson, who was about to leave for a trip to Japan, and asked him, as she so often had, whether she should consult another doctor. Her blood count became dangerously low and she was put on a course of blood transfusions. Kitty Hart was in East Hampton when Marietta told her over the telephone that she had a blood problem. Kitty got on a plane from Long Island and flew back to New York to see her. "I knew then she had leukemia." But between them no name was given to her sickness.

The new plan was to fly to Rome with Eben on August 8 and then go on for the rest of the month to Poggio al Pozzo as usual. Shortly before everyone was to take off for Italy, Marietta telephoned Evangeline Bruce, telling her she would not be able to make the trip. Evangeline, dejected, went on to Italy without her. Marietta instructed Jayne Wrightsman, who left for Italy shortly afterwards, to call every night and tell her who the guests were and how Evangeline was arranging the table. (That summer turned out to be the last at Poggio al Pozzo. A year later Teddy Millington-Drake sold the house, and Evangeline went instead to Provence.)

Bill Blair, perhaps fittingly as one of Marietta's oldest friends, was one of the last people to go out to dinner with her. She wanted to take him and the Schlesingers to Mortimer's. Bill Blair went to pick her up. "I had to help her out of the car," Blair recalled. "But we never alluded to it." The dinner was difficult for everybody. Marietta was on edge and asked for the check while people were still eating dessert. Arriving at Sutton Place, she was so frantic to get inside her apartment that she insisted the driver go the wrong way into the driveway in order for her to get home sooner. "As we parted," Bill said later, "I hugged her and she said, 'I love you, Bill.' "[6] Arthur Schlesinger was also disturbed by the appearance of his beloved friend. He telephoned Frankie, who, keeping her terrible secret, was forced to evade his questions.[7]

Frankie had finally taken charge. She was now the sole bearer of her mother's wishes and needs. In these last weeks, Marietta, who had always been Frankie's saviour in times of trouble, had relinquished that magical power in favor of her patient daughter. Frankie was given power-of-attorney. Together with a lawyer, they rechecked Marietta's will. Frankie read to her mother things she thought would please her, such as an essay by Joseph Brodsky on Isaiah Berlin. She went with her mother to her doctor's appointments.

Fending off inquiries from countless concerned friends was equally difficult. Yet sharing her secret was Marietta's most precious gift to her daughter. In extremis, Marietta had been compelled to bestow upon her daughter the key to her heart, a heart that had for so much of both their lives been locked away. Unlike Mrs. Peabody, who had displayed only a few moments of weakness in her dying months, Marietta was forced by the progress of her disease to allow Frankie inside the fortress, where the child saw her mother plain, revealed, without defenses, and could finally make peace.

The irony of these generational forces playing out against each other was not missed by either participant. On one of the many visits to the doctor, Marietta turned to Frankie and said, "I am not sure that I would have done this for *my* mother." Frankie replied, "Don't be silly," but then thought, "My God, she is probably telling the truth." Frankie said, "Well, you are a much better mother than your mother was to you." Marietta responded, "I am afraid that isn't so. I would love to do it all over again."

For her second child, there were no such touching disclosures. Penelope had called her mother before leaving Australia for her annual visit to Europe and the United States with her children. Speaking to Frankie instead, she sensed something was terribly wrong. But Frankie, still not knowing the extent of the illness, thought it would alarm Marietta if Penelope came to New York early—so much deception was at stake. Thus Marietta's own denial was transmuted into a denial of her younger daughter. When Penelope got to London, she spent an uneasy time waiting for news, and finally arrived in New York in late July. "When I got there it was quite clear she was dying," she said. "Part of her had gone already."

Penelope and the children sat through the heat of July and August, trying to cheer Marietta. Several agonizing dinners took place with Marietta's friends, while Marietta sat in her usual place at the table, attempting to hold on. On one occasion, blood streamed from her nose and she went on eating until Penelope finally said something and her mother left to lie down. Penelope would listen to her mother on the telephone, promising to see friends in Italy or making lunch dates well into the future. "Wouldn't it be better to be honest?" Penelope asked the doctors. But they had accepted their patient's decision to keep up the deception. Marietta had never asked them, "How long?" and they never volunteered a guess. (Afterwards, the doctors were astonished, considering her tenacious vitality, at how thoroughly the cancer had ravaged her body by the end.)

Although both Marietta's daughters were now with her, there was still unfinished family business. Her four brothers knew she was sick. She sent a message to them through Frankie saying she wanted to see them. Sam, of course, had seen her as regularly as he always did. After the distressing visit in Maine, he visited her in New York and some-times found her on the couch, reading business papers, which encour-aged him. But later, he was less hopeful. On one occasion, "I've got to get out," she said to him urgently. They went out to the little garden outside the apartment, but she had to sit down twice before they got around that tiny lawn.

Sam went off to Venice as usual at the end of July. Marietta telephoned Judy, who was still in New York, and asked if she thought Sam would come and visit her when she got to Poggio al Pozzo. "I know how much he loves Venice," she said, "but it would mean a lot to me." So Sam arranged to meet Jayne Wrightsman in Florence and the two of them would drive up together. "I love you," Sam said on the telephone from Italy. "I love you," she replied. Thus, from a distance, goaded by premonition, these two could finally express their feelings for each other. But the meeting never took place. Marietta called Sam in early August and said, "I'm not going to Italy. I'm just going to stay here and get well."

Mike came up from Washington. He hadn't seen her since Thanksgiving the year before, where she had been her usual bright self. This time he was greeted by his sister in her nightgown, wearing an eyepatch. She got herself together and they had lunch. It was clear to Mike that she had cancer. When the rumor first surfaced that Mari-etta was ill, George and Mike had discussed the idea of a family plot, and both agreed they wanted to be buried in Northeast Harbor. Mike mentioned this now to his sister. "Oh, I would like that too," she said. "It was clever of her," Mike said later. "She was not admitting any-thing. I did not think, of course, that that would be the last time I ever saw her."[8]

Endicott came down from New Hampshire. Marietta and her oldest brother had had perhaps the most difficult relationship of all the siblings. Endicott was not a brilliant competitor, either within the family or in politics, but Marietta could never forgive his easy progress through her world. Something, however, moved them both during this last visit. After he left, he wrote her a letter expressing his sorrow about the loss of the closeness they once had, so long ago, and regret that the rift had never properly been repaired. He hoped very much they could now become close again. "You are my only sister and I have missed you for so long."[9]

When the letter came, Marietta was able to read and accept its loving, conciliatory message. George was not so lucky. He had just arrived in Northeast Harbor when he received the phone call. "She's very sick," Frankie said. "How sick?" George asked. "Very sick," Frankie said. "Shall I come down?" George asked. Frankie could not say any more, insisting only that he not say anything to anyone about it. Frustrated by the familiar, infuriating game played by his sister, and fearing that if he made the effort he would be snubbed again after a lifetime of snubs, George stayed away. It was a decision made in anger and bitterly regretted. At the last minute, he wrote her an impulsive note declaring his love for her, "my beautiful and caring sister, strong in body, clear in mind and so splendid in spirit . . . I pray for thee, I hope for thee, dearest sister." He sent it by Federal Express on August 14, but it was too late. By the time it arrived, his sister was already dead.[10]

Marietta kept up her own correspondence to the very end. As more and more expressions of concern began to arrive from friends, she dictated letters back in sprightly tones, promising future meetings. Indeed, so punctilious was she that some of her letters arrived at their destination after her death, like a voice from beyond the grave. On August 7, she wrote to Henry Gillespie in Australia, "thrilled" at the prospect of his arrival in the fall. "Be sure to reiterate your date for New York nearer the time so we can make good plans. At the moment I am laid up," she added, "but expect to be on my feet by Labor Day."

Two days after writing that letter, on August 9, she was due for a blood transfusion. Instead, "I want to go to the hospital," she said. Frankie and Penelope took her to the emergency room of New York Hospital. The admittance procedure was a nightmare. The paperwork took forever and her daughters were not allowed to be with her. Dr. Moore came in to examine her and saw how near the end she was. Penelope thought she should be brought home, but Frankie dissuaded her. Finally Marietta was settled in a private room. She did not want to see anybody or talk to anybody on the phone, even Eben, who would have realized from her voice how bad things were. ("When she was in the hospital I never thought it was final," Eben said later. "I wasn't even very worried." How pleased Marietta would have been.)

She never left the hospital. Blood transfusions were given in an attempt to stem the anemia from the cancer that had decimated her bone marrow. There were round-the-clock nurses, and one day she was in enough pain for Frankie to urge them to give her morphine. After that, the pain was less. Penelope played tapes to her and held her hand, but after a while Marietta moved her daughter's hand away. One and a half days into the morphine, the scheduled night nurse did not show up, and a replacement came who had not been on duty before. Frankie and Penelope saw that their mother had more morphine, and then went home. Later that night, "let go," in the language of death, by her children, Marietta died with only a nurse to witness her departure.

CHAPTER *40*

# *"Always look as if you're having a wonderful time!"*

Marietta died in the early morning of August 15, 1991, at the age of seventy-four. Many of her friends were away. The Schlesingers were in Sun Valley. The Meyersons were in Japan. The Berlins were in Austria. Sam Peabody was in Italy. Harry Davison, just back from a business trip to Jamaica, eagerly picked up the phone to confirm a tea date with his glorious cousin later in the afternoon, only to hear she had died that morning.[1]

The news of her death sent shock waves through the city. "How could this be?" people asked. "I just saw her at a party looking as youthful as ever"... "She was walking down Park Avenue, radiant in a pink suit".... "She was a Gibson Girl at a Century celebration the other day".... "We had just arranged to meet in Italy." People remembered her leaping impatiently out of a taxi in traffic jams, swimming disciplined lap after lap on vacations.

For Marietta, it was the greatest performance of her career. In January that year, as soon as she knew her fatal prognosis, she had made her decision. She was not going to go out lying on pink, fluffed-up pillows, receiving the bouquets of acquaintances and tears of relatives and old beaux. Such sentiment was not for her. She would exit after the show-stopping song had been sung, the applause still in her ears, leaving behind the image of Marietta Tree, head held high, beautiful, gallant, and strong.

She had covered up much during her life—her lack of education, her inadequacy in the eyes of her family, her vulnerability to criticism, her emotional isolation—but this cover-up was the most challenging of all. How could she conceal her illness when she led such a public life? For Marietta to become a recluse would be to raise questions she did not want to answer. She had to create a foolproof front that would carry her through party after party, meeting after meeting, until she could discreetly disappear forever. Hadn't her best advice to her school friend Coupie once been, "Always look as if you're having a wonderful time!"

Yet from January until August, as she brilliantly impersonated herself, the strain must have been almost unbearable, not only of keeping up the fiction but also of suffering alone. For some deprived of human solace, the presence of a comforting God can alleviate that last desolation of death. One would have thought it particularly tempting for a bishop's child to be seduced by the Church's teachings of forgiveness and redemption. But Marietta was not a candidate for this ideology. Although a regular churchgoer, she seemed more concerned with appearances than with salvation. Her brother George never got over the shock of seeing his sister with a house party of guests at a service at St. James's Church in Barbados, standing up and insisting they all walk out before communion. "I never thought she took seriously the mysteries of the Church," he said later.

In the last two years, she had begun going to services with Sam more frequently, but like his brother, Sam did not believe she had any more use for notions of the afterlife than their mother had. "She was knocking on wood," he said afterwards. Frankie confirmed this view. "There were no talks about God," she said about her mother's last weeks. Thus Marietta, well known by all her friends and family to be terrified of death, was now facing it in solitary confinement.

It was a choice, some felt, that was cruel to those she left behind. Elisabeth Kübler-Ross describes a terminal patient's journey to death as a series of stages through denial to acceptance. Marietta refused that journey with its transcendent destination, and thus refused the beneficence that accompanies such a journey. For by denying those close to her the truth, she had disdained E. M. Forster's famous axiom "Only connect," and denied them their connectedness to her. By keeping them away from her, she deprived them of intimacy at a time when they most wished to express it.

The consequence for some was a feeling of great hurt. She left them empty-handed, so to speak, abandoned. When Jacqueline Onassis died, with almost the same startling speed as Marietta, she spent her last days at home, with a stream of loving friends and family pouring into her New York apartment to say good-bye. This is what the death experts call "closure," or resolution. Marietta invited friends to dinners or visits to her apartment in what they *afterwards* realized was an intentional last encounter. But she did not allow most of them the satisfaction of saying how much they loved her. Like a well trained soldier, Marietta held the line, even in the last hours of her life.

Others, however, took the opposite position, regarding her final months as of a piece with her life, knowing how she would have hated deathbed scenes. Her evasion of intimacy was merely a response to her Boston background, her wish for privacy the natural reaction of a woman of Peabody blood. Her death reflected, for these witnesses, not a kind of exclusionary selfishness but courage, stoicism, and an unshakable integrity.

The funeral after her cremation was a small family ceremony at St. Mary's-by-the-Sea, Northeast Harbor, where Marietta had so many times heard her grandfather and father preach, and where she had been married to Desmond FitzGerald. Her brother George conducted the service, taking it from the Book of Common Prayer. Sam requested a reeading of "Life Is Eternal," by John Masefield, a metaphorically apt evocation of Marietta's spirit, which had been read at their uncle George Parkman's funeral.

In a final salute, Frankie and Penelope taped her 1991 red leather calendar to the box containing her ashes, before it was buried in the new family plot in the Northeast Harbor cemetery. (Who would have guessed that she would be the first tenant?) A speckled rock called popplestone, common to that part of Maine, was hastily plucked from Frankie's doorstep and placed by the grave as a temporary marker. Later it was succeeded by a simple flat stone with Marietta's name and dates engraved on it.

There was a huge memorial service at St. Thomas Church in New York, attended by Mayor David Dinkins, who made a graceful speech about Marietta's contributions to the city. The list of those present read like a diplomatic and social *Who's Who*. Susan Mary, Arthur Schlesinger, Roy Jenkins, and Frankie spoke. Frankie's tribute was the most spirited, describing her mother's energy, her jampacked instructions for a "normal" day, and her famous response, when asked whether she would prefer to go to a boring dinner party or to stay home and read a good book, volunteered without hesitation, "The boring dinner party." "For her," added Frankie, "there was no such thing as a boring dinner party." Her cousin Danny Davison wrote a special prayer, which George Peabody read to the congregation. It said, in part, "She was such a vision of vitality and purpose and beauty that we were bewitched into belicving that, for her, time stood still."

A memorial service was also held at the Grosvenor Chapel in London, organized by Roy Jenkins. Nicholas Henderson addressed the congregation, which included the Tree family, Lady Avon (Anthony Eden's widow), Lady Llewelyn-Davies, Mrs. Raymond Seitz (representing the American ambassador), and a large gathering from the British aristocratic, arts, and business worlds. Sir Nicholas spoke of Marietta's commitment to civic duty, but also stressed her attractiveness, with details such as her exercising in a pink leotard. Exemplifying once again Marietta's polarized life, some found this emphasis inappropriate, while others thought it expressed perfectly their perception of her.

There were many glowing obituaries and articles, mentioning her energy, her parties, her Democratic loyalties, and her Peabody background. Letters flooded in from all departments of her life: old school friends from St. Timothy's, Lexington Club Democrats, Stevenson supporters, UN officials, New York politicos, diplomats, businessmen, socialites, admirers. Many expressed their shock at the suddenness of her passing. "She was so vital and buoyant and purposeful that I thought she was immortal," wrote John Pope Hennesssy. "They don't make them like that any more," was another consistent theme. "New York is unthinkable without her." But perhaps the writer Ward Just caught the spirit most graphically in describing the last time he saw Marietta, in Ireland, "standing on that Dingle Peninsula promontory, face to the wind, looking as if she was about to set sail for the new world, and the new world better watch out."[2]

She would have liked all that well enough. But the old competitiveness would not have let her off so easily. In the larger historical picture, how did she really rate? Some of her women friends had achieved so much—people like Kitty Hart, Katharine Graham, Millie Leet, Alice Paolozzi, Susan Mary Alsop. Others had enjoyed long and happy marriages and close family ties, such as Mary Warburg, Bootsie Morris, Mezzy Hickok, and Louise Roberts. What had she *done*?

Inspired by Ronnie, an inveterate scrapbook keeper, Marietta had joined him in producing scrapbooks of their yearly activities, including photographs of parties, travels, people, and relevant press clippings. As their lives separated, so did their scrapbooks. Marietta would put in a drawer in her bedroom all the pictures and newspaper stories that followed her career from the 1960s on, and Mrs. Klotzer and her daughter would stick them into handsome leather-bound volumes engraved with the year and Marietta's initials in gold.

But the 1991 scrapbook is different. The album starts out with photographs of her two grandchildren, Paloma and Michael, and an obituary of her old friend Lord Rothschild. There is an invitation to the queen's garden party at the British Embassy in Washington, held on May 15. (She carefully wrote on this invitation, "Didn't go—too much of a hassle, 1999 others invited.")

In this scrapbook, Marietta has saved an article written by Frances FitzGerald for *The New Yorker* on Jim and Tammy Faye Bakker, and the 1990 program of the Citizens Committee for New York City awards dinner, with Barbara Walters as mistress of ceremonies and Marietta as chairman. Included also is the April 1991 *Groton School Quarterly*, which happened to have the famous Sargent portrait of the Rector on the cover, and inside a collection of reminiscences of him by old friends such as McGeorge Bundy, Douglas Dillon, and Danny Davison.

There is a postcard from Penelope (dated May 1991 in Marietta's hand) in which Penelope thanks her mother for sending her some childhood pictures. "They gave me so much insight into what I was feeling at the time. Are there any more? They're like gold in the inner world. . . ." There is a *Wall Street Journal* article by her son-in-law James Sterba. She has included, too, a letter from Frankie written to Ronnie in 1957, thanking him for his generosity in taking her to Africa that summer, but also expressing her gratitude to him for all his guidance and support over the years.

One page of this last scrapbook displays a letter written to Marietta by another of Adlai Stevenson's biographers, Porter McKeever, pointing out that on December 28, 1962, Adlai had sent her the following poem:

> *Beauty crowds me till I die.*
> *Beauty, mercy have on me.*
> *But if today my life should flee*
> *Let it be in sight of thee!*

McKeever had written on the bottom, "it is an eerie coincidence—but also a consoling one."

The scrapbook also holds a collection of salutes to Richard Llewelyn-Davies spoken at the memorial evening Marietta held in November 1981.

There are other poignant entries here. She has saved a paper she wrote on King Michael of Romania for the Council on Foreign Relations. There is an article on Jerry Zipkin by Christopher Buckley, a photograph of King Hussein and Queen Noor of Jordan, and a profile of the Philippine educator and philanthropist Helena Benitez. There are also invitations to two big 1991 events, Zubin Mehta's farewell concert with the New York Philharmonic and Carnegie Hall's Centennial Gala.

The penultimate entry is the complete text of an essay Harry Davison wrote for his application to the Stanford Business School. In it he lists the three most significant institutions in his life: Groton School, the J. P. Morgan Bank, and the Citizens Committee for New York City. He goes on to describe the three most influential individuals at these institutions who were his role models: Endicott Peabody

(Harry's great-grandfather); Pierpont Morgan—and Marietta Tree. In extolling her virtues, "she has taught me compassion for others," he wrote, "and given me an enlightened conscience."

The last entry is a little poem in the form of a get-well card from the Oxford scholar Anthony Quinton, regretting she will not be attending the Ditchley meetings.

In sifting through the fragments of this archive, one does not need the skill of an archeologist to extract their meaning. Marietta was in her last months putting together a scrapbook of her life, but in a very specific way—the way that she hoped to be remembered. Since she had never been able to get the words she wanted into a written autobiography, perhaps she could make the scrapbook, with its immediacy and visual impact, create instead the record she wished to leave behind for posterity. (How modern, in retrospect, she was to invent this form of memoir.)

Every entry had been selected toward this end. There are documents referring to Marietta's best moments, from her political appointments to her romantic attachments. There is proof of her social prominence and her intellectual connections. The notes from Penelope, and the grandchildren's photographs, show the world that Marietta's family relationships were close and affectionate. The letter from Frankie, with its warm words to Ronnie, strongly vindicates her mother's second marriage, damned by so many all those years ago. And with Harry Davison's hymn of praise to a woman who taught him not only the value of volunteer work but that good business skills can be combined with compassion, Marietta presents her final case for absolution.

The 1991 scrapbook ends abruptly midyear, but the material in it leaves the reader with a clear picture of the person who compiled it. She did not have to fill it with any more proof of worth. She had already found the most relevant evidence and painstakingly put it together. Although she ran out of time that summer, the scrapbook was complete. Marietta could raise these pages to the skies and declare once and for all, just as her parents had hoped, "I was a good girl and educated."

# Epilogue

In Marietta's Sutton Place apartment after she died, eighteen cookbooks were found, along with a looseleaf folder of typed recipes and menus dating from the 1960s, testament to her constant desire to make a good dinner party even better. Hanging on the walls in the back of her apartment were over thirty plaques and awards she had been given over the years for her good works in politics, civil rights, and urban affairs. In a series of faux panels under the main book-lined wall of the big living room, a cache of almost every letter, invitation, school report, or other personal document she had ever received, including those her mother had kept, was discovered, all neatly filed and labeled. This was an astonishing find, considering that Marietta had been regarded by most as an unsentimental observer of life. Even her daughters had no idea how carefully she had been stockpiling her past.

Christie's auctioned the contents of the Sutton Place apartment nine months after her death. The sale, enclosed in a bigger auction, was not a major social event, but the prices for many of her possessions skyrocketed, proving how much she was loved and missed. Marietta, that frugal financier, would have been delighted at the results, which far outpriced the auction house's estimates.

Several other memorials for Marietta were initiated after the services in new York and London, including the creation of a prize in her name awarded annually by the Citizens Committee for New York City. But perhaps the most vivid tribute to her is in the form of a leaded glass window bought in her memory by the American Friends of the

Australian National Gallery Gordon Darling Fund. The window, installed in the National Gallery in Canberra, was designed by Frank Lloyd Wright, and its clear colors and graceful shapes not only seem to sing out Marietta's name but also indicate how, in her never-ending search for new horizons, she continued to make a brilliant and joyful impression.

The image of light persists. In people's memories, it is Marietta's incandescent presence that lingers, lighting up a room. Perhaps it is fitting, then, that there is another tribute to her memory that New Yorkers enjoy every night in the city. Inspired by seeing models of the 1964 World's Fair, Marietta wondered why the bridges of New York that Robert Moses had so spectactularly built were not lit up after dark. The strings of lights that now decorate the city's bridges are a sparkling memorial to a woman who believed in the best of all possible worlds.

# Acknowledgments

I wish to thank Marietta Tree's daughters, Frances FitzGerald and Penelope Tree, for bestowing upon me their mother's papers without restriction in order to write this biography. I also wish to thank Marietta's four brothers, Endicott (and his wife Toni) Sam (and his wife Judy), George, and Mike (and his wife Pamela), who were drawn into reliving their sister's past, and thus compelled to talk openly about their family to me. This was not easy. Yet they helped me at every turn, patiently responding to my questions while making no judgments. No biographer could have been better served.

One of Marietta's attributes was her enormous circle of friends and acquaintances on several continents. It would have taken a lifetime to speak to them all, and I beg the indulgence of those I had to exclude. The following people made major contributions to the book, and I offer my thanks: Charles F. Adams, Susan Mary Alsop, Christa Armstrong, Vera Armstrong, Brooke Astor, Louis Auchincloss, Joan Avagliano, Carolyn Barrow, Robert Becker, Sir Isaiah and Lady Berlin, Rosamond Bernier, Mary Bingham, June Birge, William McCormick Blair, Bill Blass, Sarah Bradford, Edith Bridges, Richard A. Brown, the late Evangeline Bruce, Kevin Buckley, Bartle Bull, Harvey H. Bundy, Dr. Anthony Cahan, Dr. William Cahan, Nora Cammann, Edward Lee Cave, Peggy and George Cheston, Blair Clark, May and George Clark, James M. Clark, Michael Clark, Minette Cummings, Patricia Danielson, Gordon Darling, Daniel Davison, Henry P. Davison, Jack Dear, Annette de la Renta, Pat Derrian, Thierry Despont, Antelo Devereux, Marietta Dockery, Robin Duke,

George H.P. Dwight, Frances Edmunds, Inger and Osborn Elliott, Cora Peabody Emlen, Mrs. Walter Foulke, Eileen Finletter, Albert Francke, Clayton and Polly Fritchey, Norma Garaventa, Aretha Gibson, Frank and Lady Kitty Giles, Henry Gillespie, Rosario Gonzalez, George W. Goodman, Katharine Graham, Penelope Griswold, Marit and Sidney Gruson, Kenneth Harris, Kitty Carlisle Hart, Ashton Hawkins, Jerome Heimann, Russell Hemenway, Sir Nicholas and Lady Henderson, Mary Isabel Hickok, Derek Hill, Dorothy Hirshon, Henry Hyde, Lord Jenkins of Hillhead, Tony Kaiser, Peter Kaminer, Moira and Ludovic Kennedy, Leslie Kernan, Evelyn Keyes, Lillian Klotzer, Parker Ladd, Margaret and Jack Leacock, Eppie Lederer, Millie Leet, Bernard Leser, Wendy Luers, Rose Parsons Lynch, Lee and Roy MacLaren, Maude March, Anne Martindell, Ian McGregor, Charles McVeigh, Margy and Martin Meyerson, Anne Milliken, Phoebe Milliken, Minot Milliken, Jim Montanari, Dr. Anne Moore, Mrs. DuBois Morris, Rachel Nachman, Anne Griswold Noble, Diane Nutting, Mrs. R. More O'Ferrall, May Osborne, Mitchell Owens, Adnan Pachachi, Alice Paolozzi, David Parker, Nancy and John Pierrepont, Dr. Calvin Plimpton, Sarah Plimpton, Dr. Curtis Prout, R. Stewart Rauch, Zandra Rhodes, John Richardson, Khalil Rizk, Louise Roberts, Arthur Ross, John Russell, Charles Ryskamp, Arthur Schlesinger, Jr., Patricia Scull, Natwar Singh, James B. Sitrick, Hannah Stapleton, Patricia Sullivan, Michael Teague, Evan Thomas, Sir Crispin Tickell, Michael and Lady Anne Tree, Robert Trew, John Trubin, Osmondo Tull, Sir Brian Urquhart, the late Nicholas Wahl, Harold Wakefield, Jimmy Walker, Barbara Walkley, the late William Walton, Mary Warburg, Grace Warnecke, Benjamin Welles, Cecilia Wentz, Edith Williams, Marnie Williamson, Elaine and James D. Wolfensohn, Charlotte Woollert, the late Paul Wright, and Jayne Wrightsman.

I would like to thank Helen and Brian Williamson for their hospitality when I was visiting Mirador, in Virginia, and Hope and Paul Burghardt for taking me around the house that Nancy Lancaster loved so much. Jeremy and Holly Treglown offered me the same generous hospitality at Ditchley. I am particularly grateful to Sir Philip Adams, who agreed to see me there at short notice, and to Sir John Graham, who gave me a very informative private tour of Ditchley Park. I am deeply grateful, too, to Sir Anthony and Lady Bamford for arranging for me to meet the staff of Heron Bay in Barbados.

I would like also to thank William Polk, headmaster of Groton School, and Douglas Brown, the school archivist, for allowing me to examine the Peabody Papers at Groton. Ben Primer, of the Seeley G. Mudd Library at Princeton University, kindly agreed to house temporarily the seventy-four volumes of scrapbooks belonging to Marietta and Ronald Tree, and made them available to me at all times. I would also like to thank this library and its librarians for allowing me to examine the Adlai

E. Stevenson Papers there. In particular, I thank Susan Illis and Nancy Young for their meticulous work in extracting photographs from Marietta Tree's scrapbooks for illustrations. I am grateful, too, to Robert Pyle, librarian of the Northeast Harbor library, for directing me to materials pertaining to Mary E. Peabody.

I would like to thank my editors: Michael Korda for his support and wonderful title and Chuck Adams for his concentrated work on the book. I would also like to thank the rest of my editorial team: David Frost for being so extraordinarily patient and agreeable in all crises, Ann Adelman and Eva Young, for spotting a lot of my mistakes, Edith Fowler for her elegant design, and Cheryl Weinstein, for coordinating everything.

# Source Notes

The principal sources I have used for this book are Marietta Tree's correspondence, scrapbooks, notebooks, calendars, and diaries. All are housed in the Arthur and Elizabeth Schlesinger Library on the History of Women in America at Radcliffe College, except for the scrapbooks, which have been retained by the family. An oral history conducted by Nina Cobb for the Schlesinger Library was invaluable. Unpublished letters from Marietta Tree to Susan Mary Alsop from 1945 through 1961 were very useful. Where no source reference is given in any chapter, the information comes from these collections.

Other important information came from the Peabody family, in particular the correspondence of Mary E. Peabody, whose papers are also to be housed in the Arthur and Elizabeth Schlesinger Library. In addition, the Public Library in Northeast Harbor, Maine, contains source material about Mrs. Peabody and her family. Other Peabody papers, in particular concerning Endicott Peabody, the Rector of Groton, are in the archives of Groton School in Massachusetts.

Every page of the book is enriched by the information unstintingly given me by Marietta Tree's daughters, Frances FitzGerald and Penelope Tree, and by Marietta's brothers, Endicott, Samuel, George, and Mike Peabody, whose names I therefore shall not always repeat in each chapter.

Unless otherwise indicated, the remaining principals I have interviewed are named at the beginning of each chapter in which they have contributed major information. Other important interviews (some by telephone) or source materials are specifically cited.

## CHAPTER 1

For information about Groton School, I am indebted to the late Paul Wright.

1. *Peabody at Shiloh,* unpublished study by Carlton L. Smith (1983).
2. Louise Hall Tharp, *The Peabody Sisters of Salem* (Boston, 1950).
   Edwin Palmer Hoyt, *The Peabody Influence* (New York, 1968).
3. Frank D. Ashburn, *Peabody of Groton* (New York, 1944), p. 36.
4. Malcolm E. Peabody, *The Story of My Life,* unpublished memoir, April 1970.
5. Interview with Endicott Peabody, Oct. 17, 1992.
6. Peabody, *The Story of My Life.*
7. Francis Parkman, unpublished history of the Parkman family (1633–1984), 1984.
8. Louise Hall Tharp, *Mrs. Jack* (Boston, 1965).

## CHAPTER 2

1. Michael Teague interviews with Mary Peabody and Katherine Putnam, Dec. 20, 1978.
2. Mary Peabody's diary, April 7, 1916.
3. Letter from Reverend Charles Lawrence to MT, March 5, 1981.
4. Peabody, *The Story of My Life.*

## CHAPTER 3

For information about MT's childhood, I am indebted to Louise Roberts, Mezzy Hickok, Phoebe Milliken, and Susan Mary Alsop.

1. Documents from St. Paul's Church, Chestnut Hill, Philadelphia. Interview with Reverend Charles A. Carter III, March 8, 1993.
2. MT University of Pennsylvania essay, Dec. 3. 1936.
3. Interview with Penelope Griswold, June 10, 1993.

## CHAPTER 4

For information about MT at boarding school, I am indebted to Mary Derby Morris, Edith W. Williams, Alicia Paolozzi, Marnie Williamson, Coupie Kernan, and the Alumnae Office, St. Timothy's School, Catonsville, Maryland.

1. Victoria Glendinning, *Trollope* (New York, 1993), p. 56.
2. Interview with Harvey H. Bundy, July 21, 1992.
3. Mary Brannum and the Editors, *When I was Sixteen* (New York, 1967), p. 22.

## CHAPTER 5

1. Interview with Peggy Cheston, July 30, 1992.
2. MT letter to parents, March 10, 1935.

## Chapter 6

1. MT University Of Pennsylvania essay, 1936.
2. Interview with George Peabody, Oct. 22, 1992.

## Chapter 7

1. Interview with Harvey H. Bundy, July 21, 1992.
2. Letter to the author from Martin Meyerson, March 10, 1997.
3. Interview with Mezzy Hickok, June 8, 1993.
4. Interview with George Cheston, July 30, 1992.
5. MT oral history transcript with Nina Cobb, June 29, 1982.
6. Glendinning, *Trollope,* p. 42.
7. Interview with R. Stewart Rauch, May 12, 1993.
8. MT University of Pennsylvania essay, 1936.
9. Ibid.
10. Interview with Dr. Curtis Prout, Sept. 9, 1992.

## Chapter 8

For information about Desmond FitzGerald, I am indebted to Albert Francke and Nora Cammann.

1. Interview with Maude March, July 20, 1992.
2. Interview with George Clark, April 10, 1992.
3. MT oral history transcript with Nina Cobb, June 29, 1982.

## Chapter 9

1. Interview with Louis Auchincloss, Sept. 22, 1992.
2. MT oral history, op. cit.
3. Ibid.
4. Interview with June Bingham Burge, April 5, 1995.

## Chapter 10

For information about MT's early life in New York, I am indebted to Mary Warburg and Dorothy Hirshon.

1. Interview with Charles F. Adams, July 18, 1993.
2. Sally Bedell Smith, *In All His Glory, The Life of William S. Paley* (New York, 1990).
3. Letters to MT from Desmond FitzGerald, 1942.
4. Letter from MT to her parents, Nov. 1, 1942.
5. Letter from Desmond FitzGerald to Mr. and Mrs. Peabody, Aug. 28, 1943.

## CHAPTER 11

MT wrote a memoir (unpublished) of her years at *Life*, from which much of the material in this chapter is drawn.

1. MT unpublished memoir, undated.
2. Interview with Dennis Flanagan, Nov. 10, 1993.
3. Interview with Sir Isaiah Berlin, July 1, 1992.
4. Evan Thomas, *The Very Best Men* (New York, 1995).
5. Interview with Toni Peabody, July 6, 1993.

## CHAPTER 12

1. Lawrence Grobel, *The Hustons* (New York, 1989), p. 238.
2. John Huston, *An Open Book* (New York, 1980), p. 121.
3. Ibid.
4. Letter from Desmond FitzGerald to Mr. and Mrs. Peabody, Sept. 21, 1945.
5. Interview with Nora Cammann, Oct. 20, 1993.
6. Interview with Evan Thomas, Nov. 3, 1993.
7. Nancy Holmes, *The Big Girls* (New York, 1982).

## CHAPTER 13

I have drawn on two books, *When the Moon Was High* by Ronald Tree (London, 1975) and *Nancy Lancaster, Her Life, Her World, Her Art* by Robert Becker (New York, 1996), for much of the information in this chapter.

1. Interview with William Walton, June 8, 1992.
2. Charles Beatty, *Our Admiral: Biography of Earl Beatty* (London, 1980).
3. Interview with Eben Pyne, Jan. 6, 1993.
4. John Cornforth, *The Inspiration of the Past* (New York, 1985), p. 125.
5. Interview with William Walton, June 8, 1992.
6. Letter to the author from Michael Tree, Dec. 9, 1992.

## CHAPTER 14

For information on Marietta Tree's divorce, I am indebted to Mary Warburg and Dorothy Hirshon.

1. Interview with Marietta Dockery, Feb. 4, 1993.
2. Stephen Becker, *Marshall Field III* (New York, 1964).
3. Interview with Evelyn Keyes, Nov. 3, 1992.
4. Evelyn Keyes, *Scarlett O'Hara's Younger Sister* (Secaucus, NJ: 1977), p. 104.

## CHAPTER 15

1. Interview with Peter Kaminer, Dec. 16, 1993.
2. Interview with Dorothy Hirshon, Aug. 26, 1992.
3. Interview with Mary Warburg, June 1, 1992.
4. *The New York Times,* July 26, 1947.

## CHAPTER 16

1. Interview with Mezzy Hickok, June 8, 1993.
2. Tree, *When the Moon Was High.*
3. Interview with Lady Berlin, July 7, 1992.
4. Interview with Mrs. Roderick More O'Ferrall, July 5, 1992.
5. Letter from Lady Churchill to RT, June 20, 1947.
6. MT unpublished memoir of Ditchley, undated.
7. Interview with Louise Roberts, May 29, 1992.
8. Interview with John Richardson, June 27, 1993.
9. MT oral history, op.cit.

## CHAPTER 17

1. Interview with Sir John Graham, July 6, 1992.
2. Interview with Barbara Train, July 21, 1993.

## CHAPTER 18

1. Interview with Jimmy Walker, March 16, 1994.
2. Interview with Jack Dear, March 18, 1994.
3. Interview with Osmondo Tull and Aretha Gibson, March 18, 1994.
4. Interview with Lady Anne Tree, July 8, 1992.

## CHAPTER 19

For background on the Lexington Democratic CLub, I am indebted to Richard A. Brown, Russell Hemenway, and George H.P. Dwight. See also James Q. Wilson, *The Amateur Democrat, Club Politics in Three Cities* (Chicago, 1962).

For information about Adlai E. Stevenson in the following seven chapters, I have drawn extensively upon the biographies, *Adlai Stevenson,* by Porter McKeever (New York, 1989), and *Adlai Stevenson of Illinois* and *Adlai Stevenson and the World,* by John Bartlow Martin (New York, 1976–77).

1. Interview with Richard A. Brown, May 7, 1994.
2. Interview with Mary Bingham, Dec. 12, 1992.
3. Interview with Clayton and Polly Fritchey, April 10, 1992.

4. Interview with Arthur Schlesinger, Jr., Nov. 21, 1994.
5. Conversation with Robert Pirie, March 15, 1995.
6. Martin, *Adlai Stevenson of Illinois,* p. 623.

## CHAPTER 20

1. Interview with Lady Anne Tree, July 8, 1992.
2. Interview with Barbara Peabody, July 20, 1994.
3. Interview with Barbara Train, July 21, 1993.
4. Interview with Christa Armstrong, Oct. 27, 1992.
5. Interview with William McCormick Blair, June 18, 1992.

## CHAPTER 21

1. Inez Robb, "The Democrats' 'Golden Girl,' " *Saturday Evening Post,* Oct. 20–29, 1960.
2. Interview with Russell Hemenway, Jan. 14, 1993.
3. Martin, *Adlai Stevenson and the World,* pp. 148–149.

## CHAPTER 22

1. Eric F. Goldman, *The Crucial Decade* (New York, 1973), p. 221.
2. Interview with Meg Greenfield, Oct. 22, 1992.
3. Martin, *Adlai Stevenson and the World,* p. 392.

## CHAPTER 23

1. Interview with Meg Greenfield, Oct. 22, 1992.
2. Unpublished African Diary by Frances FitzGerald.

## CHAPTER 24

1. Interview with Jack Dear, March 18, 1994.
2. Ibid.
3. John Steele file, quoted in Martin, *Adlai Stevenson and the World,* p. 475.
4. Interview with Arthur Schlesinger, Jr., Nov. 21, 1994.
5. Arthur Schlesinger, Jr., *A Thousand Days* (Boston, 1965), p. 38.

## CHAPTER 25

For information about MT's UN years, I am indebted to Sir Brian Urquhart, Natwar Singh, and Adnan Pachachi.

1. Interview with Frank Taylor, March 12, 1993.
2. Interview with William Walton, June 8, 1992.

3. MT unpublished essay on her years at the UN.
4. *The New York Times,* March 13, 1964, p. A8.
5. *The New York Times,* April 8, 1964, p. A2.
6. Interview with Cecilia Wentz, Oct. 6, 1992.


## CHAPTER 26

1. Harold Nicolson: *Diaries & Letters Volume III:* The Later Years 1945–1962 (New York, 1968), p. 243.
2. Interview with Sir Isaiah Berlin, July 7, 1992.
3. Betty Beale, *Power at Play* (Washington, D.C., 1993), p. 140.
4. Quoted in Jeffrey Potter, *Men, Money and Magic: The Story of Dorothy Schiff* (New York, 1976), p. 253.
5. Interview with William Walton, June 8, 1992.
6. Interview with Blair Clark, Dec. 3, 1994.
7. Conversation with Paul Resnik, Oct. 20, 1994.


## CHAPTER 27

1. Ernestine Carter, *Sunday Times* (London), Nov. 8, 1964.
2. Interview with Sir Brian Urquhart, May 6, 1992.
3. Interview with Katharine Graham, June 16, 1992.
4. Katharine Graham, *Personal History* (New York, 1997), pp. 377–378.
5. Martin, *Adlai Stevenson and the World,* pp. 862–863.
6. Interview with Norma Garaventa, Nov. 8, 1992.
7. Interview with Mary Warburg, June 1, 1992.
8. Interview with Brooke Astor, July 15, 1994.


## CHAPTER 28

1. Interview with Rose Parsons Lynch, Feb. 11, 1993.
2. Interview with Cecilia Wentz, Oct. 6, 1992.
3. MT oral history, op.cit.


## CHAPTER 29

1. Michael Teague interview with Mary Peabody, Dec. 20, 1978.
2. Harriet Belin oral history with Mary Peabody, Feb. 8, 1979.
3. Michael Teague interview with Mary Peabody, Dec. 20, 1978.
4. Interview with Marietta Dockery, Feb. 4, 1993.
5. Letter to the author from Jon Margolis, April 26, 1992.
6. Interview with Preston Brown, Oct. 8, 1995.
7. "A New Face," *Women's Wear Daily,* June 19, 1967.

## CHAPTER 30

For background information on Richard Llewelyn-Davies and his work, I am indebted to Martin Meyerson.

1. Interview with Martin Meyerson, Jan. 14, 1993.
2. Interview with Robert Trew, Nov. 20, 1992.
3. Ibid.
4. Interview with James Montanari, Feb. 8, 1993.

## CHAPTER 31

1. Interview with Hope Scott, June 10, 1992.
2. Interview with William Walton, June 8, 1992.
3. Becker, *Nancy Lancaster,* p. 295.
4. Interview with Evangeline Bruce, July 8, 1992.
5. Interview with Marit Gruson, Dec. 7, 1992.
6. Interview with Kenneth Harris, Nov. 20, 1992.
7. Interview with Osmondo Tull and Aretha Gibson, March 8, 1994.
8. Interview with Dr. Jack Leacock, March 17, 1994.

## CHAPTER 32

1. Interview with John Richardson, June 27, 1993.
2. Cornforth, *Inspiration of the Past,* p. 127.
3. Interview with Diane Nutting, Nov. 17, 1993.
4. Interview with Jack Dear, March 18, 1994.
5. Ibid.
6. Interview with Michael Teague, Nov. 12, 1992.
7. Interview with Lady Bamford, Nov. 5, 1992.
8. Interview with Susan Mary Alsop, April 10, 1992.
9. Interview with James Montanari, Feb. 8, 1993.
10. Interview with Christa Armstrong, Oct. 27, 1992.
11. Interview with Evangeline Bruce, July 8, 1992.

## CHAPTER 33

1. Interview with Richard A. Brown, May 7, 1994.
2. Interview with James Wolfensohn, March 22, 1994.
3. Interview with Evangeline Bruce, July 8, 1992.
4. MT note on extra page at end of 1982 calendar.
5. Interview with Eileen Finletter, Oct. 17, 1992.
6. MT unpublished journal, 1978.
7. Interview with Margaret Leacock, March 17, 1994.

## CHAPTER 34

1. Interview with Toni Peabody, July 16, 1993.
2. Interview with Mike Peabody, Oct. 22, 1992.
3. Interview with Martin Meyerson, Jan. 14, 1993.
4. Interview with George Peabody, Oct. 22, 1992.
5. Ibid.
6. Interview with Endicott Peabody, Oct. 17, 1992.
7. Interview with Henry P. Davison, Aug. 24, 1994.
8. Interview with Patricia Danielson, Sept. 10, 1994.
9. Interview with Martin and Margy Meyerson, Feb. 26, 1993.
10. Interview with Christa Armstrong, Oct. 27, 1992.
11. Interview with Brooke Astor, July 15, 1994.

## CHAPTER 35

For information about MT's work with the Citizens Committee for New York City, I am indebted to Osborn Elliott, John Trubin, and Michael Clark. For information about her trips to Australia, I am indebted to Henry Gillespie.

1. Interview with Millie Robbins Leet, Feb. 4, 1992.
2. Interview with Rosamond Bernier, March 20, 1995.
3. Interview with James Sitrick, Feb. 15, 1995.
4. Interview with Michael Clark, March 5, 1993.
5. Interview with John Trubin, Dec. 7, 1993.
6. Interview with Henry Gillespie, June 2, 1995.

## CHAPTER 36

1. Ken Auletta, *Three Blind Mice* (New York, 1991).
2. Interview with Ambassador Anne Martindell, Nov. 13, 1992.
3. Interview with Cecilia Wentz, Oct. 6, 1992.

## CHAPTER 37

For information in this chapter, I am indebted to Sir Brian Urquhart, Wendy Luers, Parker Ladd, Joe Armstrong, Thierry Despont, Henry P. Davison, and Eben Pyne.

1. Interview with Sir Brian Urquhart, May 6, 1992.
2. Interview with James Sitrick, Feb. 15, 1995.
3. Interview with Mike Peabody, Oct. 22, 1992.
4. Interview with George Peabody, Oct. 22, 1992.
5. Interview with Bootsie Morris, Aug. 20, 1992.
6. Interview with Roy and Lee MacLaren, June 11, 1995.

7. Interview with Wendy Luers, April 4, 1995.
8. See Shana Alexander, *When She Was Bad* (New York, 1990).
9. Interview with Parker Ladd, Feb. 18, 1993.
10. Interview with Henry Gillespie, June 2, 1995.
11. Interview with Joe Armstrong, March 4, 1993.
12. Interview with Henry Hyde, May 24, 1993.
13. Conversation with Anjelica Huston, March 20, 1996.

## Chapter 38

1. Interview with William McCormick Blair, June 18, 1992.
2. Interview with Louis Auchincloss, Sept. 22, 1992.
3. Interview with Martin Meyerson, Jan. 14, 1993.
4. Interview with Dr. Jeremiah Barondess, April 27, 1995.
5. Interview with Dr. Anthony Cahan, Sept. 30, 1993.
6. Interview with Dr. Anne Moore, March 3, 1993.
7. Interview with Elaine Wolfensohn, Feb. 14, 1994.
8. Interview with Sir Crispin Tickell, Nov. 18, 1992.
9. Interview with Lord Jenkins of Hillhead, Nov. 18, 1992.

## Chapter 39

For information in this chapter, I am indebted to Joe Armstrong and Susan Mary Alsop.

1. Interview with Jayne Wrightsman, April 30, 1992.
2. Interview with Sir Nicholas and Lady Henderson, Nov. 17, 1992.
3. Interview with Sir Isaiah and Lady Berlin, July 1, 1992.
4. Interview with Eben Pyne, Jan. 6, 1993.
5. Interview with Patricia Scull, Sept. 23, 1993.
6. Interview with William McCormick Blair, June 18, 1992.
7. Interview with Arthur Schlesinger, Jr., Nov. 21, 1994.
8. Interview with Mike Peabody, Oct. 22, 1992.
9. Interview with Endicott Peabody, Oct. 17, 1992.
10. Interview with George Peabody, Oct. 22, 1992.

## Chapter 40

1. Interview with Henry P. Davison, Aug. 24, 1994.
2. Letter from Ward Just to Frances FitzGerald, August 16, 1991.

# Index

Abernathy, Ralph, 352
Abrams, Charles, 304, 309
Acheson, Dean G., 18
Acton, Harold, 331, 367
Adams, Charles F., 93, 96–97, 99, 106
Adams, Grantley, 191, 242
Adams, Sir Philip, 278
Aga Khan, 262, 268
Agnelli, Gianni, 178
Akers, Anthony, 218, 237
Albright, Alice, 258
Alexander, Archie, 212
Ali, Amjad, 390
Alice, Princess, 330
Alsop, Joseph, 99, 278, 318
Alsop, Susan Mary Jay Patten "Soozle," 52,
    55, 84, 86, 94, 98, 99, 153, 162, 174, 201,
    224, 278–79, 332, 352, 389–90, 400,
    405–6, 414, 415
  memoir of, 314
  MT's correspondence with, 146, 152, 175,
    181, 183, 193, 197, 203, 204, 212, 232, 235,
    240, 314, 407
  Ronald Tree's death and, 332
American Veterans Committee, 149, 178
Anderson, Clint, 235
Arcaro, Eddie, 228
*Architectural Digest,* 361, 372–73
Armstrong, Christa, 212, 325, 332, 337, 339,
    358, 400
Armstrong, Hamilton Fish, 61, 212
Armstrong, Joe, 385–86, 387, 398, 400, 405,
    406

Astor, Brooke, 280, 366, 370
Astor, Lady Nancy, 37, 141, 143, 144, 154,
    156, 174, 210, 329
Astor, Minnie, 110, 111, 113, 114
Astor, Vincent, 110, 111, 113, 114
Astor, William, 208
Attlee, Clement, 123, 202, 322
Attwood, William, 243
Atwood, Julius, 20, 29, 105
Auchincloss, Louis, 393
Avedon, Richard, 303
Avon, countess of, 330
Avon, earl of, 330 (*see* Anthony Eden)

Bacall, Lauren, 262, 278
Backer, George, 197
Baden-Powell, Lady, 37
Baden-Powell, Sir Robert, 37
Baguio School, 21
Bailey, David, 303–4, 320, 325, 350
Baker, Daniel C., 394
Ball, George, 243, 268, 278
Baltzell, Jean P. J., 197
Bamford, Sir Anthony, 336
Barnard College, 100, 101, 104, 383
Barondess, Jeremiah, 394, 395
Barrie, J. M., 306
Barton, Pat, 21
Baudouin I, king of Belgium, 237
Beale, Betty, 265
Beare, Robin, 346
Beaton, Cecil, 185, 248
Beatty, David (half brother-in-law), 141, 157

Beatty, Earl David, 140, 141, 142
Beatty, Ethel Field Tree, 139–40, 141
Beatty, Peter (half brother-in-law), 141–42, 157, 187
Beaverbrook, Lord, 114, 127
Benton, William, 219, 238, 276, 311
Berenson, Bernard, 25
Bergman, Ingrid, 270, 374
Berlin, Lady (Aline), 403, 407, 412
Berlin, Isaiah, 114, 121, 146, 172, 178, 193, 245, 264, 329, 345, 402, 403, 407, 408, 412
Berners, Lord, 182
Bernier, Rosamond, 361
Bernstein, Henri, 111, 112
Berry, Michael, 185, 207, 208
Berry, Pamela, 185, 207, 208, 248, 276, 281
Bingham, Barry, 198, 207, 225, 247
Bingham, Jonathan, 101, 257
Bingham (Birge), June, 101, 257, 383
Bingham, Mary, 198, 242, 264, 383
Birge, June Bingham, 101, 257, 383
Birge, Robert, 383
Black, Lesley, 130, 131
Blair, William McCormick, 197, 198, 202, 209, 212–13, 219, 220, 225, 226, 233, 234, 235, 262, 282, 291, 366, 393, 408
Blunt, Anthony, 306
Bolté, Charles, 178, 380, 390
Bonnett, Sara, 215, 217, 227, 271–72
Bor, Walter, 308
Borden (Stevenson), Ellen, 198, 199–200, 202, 237
Bowles, Chester, 219
Bracken, Brendan, 172, 204, 225
Bradlee, Ben, 395
Bradshaw, T. F., 337
Brando, Marlon, 226
Breck, Henry, 241, 248, 326, 377
Breese, William, 86
Bridges, Edith, 143
Britten, Benjamin, 208
Brooke, Edward W., 299
Brooke, Rupert, 159
Brooks, Joseph, 347
Brooks, Phillips, 17, 18
Brown, Earl, 119–20, 191, 197, 384
Brown, Preston, 302
Brown, Richard A., 196, 197, 228, 233, 235
Bruce, David, 277, 329
Bruce, Evangeline, 156, 277, 279, 319, 332, 337, 342, 347, 356, 357, 366, 367, 376, 385, 393, 394, 396, 397, 403, 408
Bryant, Ferris, 296
Buccleugh, duke of, 326
Buchman, Frank, 85
Buckley, Kevin, 352
Bull, Bartle, 304, 305, 387
Bullitt, William, 90
Bundy, Harvey, 28

Bundy, Harvey, Jr., 35, 41, 49, 54, 55, 69, 76–78
Bundy, Katherine Putnam, 27, 28, 29, 35
Bundy, McGeorge, 291, 416
Bundy, Mary, 351
Burgen, Barron, 334
Burgess, Guy, 306
Burgess, Mrs. John, 295–96
Butler, Alice, 175, 178, 180, 181, 185, 188, 223, 330, 333, 346
Byrne, Jimmy, 86, 90

Cahan, Anthony, 395, 399
Cahan, William, 354–55, 394–95
Cambridge University, 17, 21
Campbell, Joseph, 305
Campbell, Mrs. Donald, 295–96
Capa, Cornell, 120
Capa, Robert, 120
Capote, Truman, 303
Carstairs (Woollett), Charlotte, 190
Carter, Ernestine, 275
Carter, Jimmy, 376
Castle, William, 98
Cates, Jack, 315
Catlin, Ephron, 97
Cavendish, Lady Anne, see Tree, Lady Anne Cavendish
CBS, 110, 111, 314, 325, 361, 370–71, 388, 399
CCF (Congress for Cultural Freedom), 287
Cecil, Lord David, 178
Central Intelligence Agency (CIA), 211, 287, 302
Cerf, Bennett, 204, 205, 226
Chamberlain, Neville, 37, 144, 145
Cheston, George, 388
Cheston, Winifred Seyburn "Peggy," 60, 64, 388, 405
Chicago Council on Foreign Relations, 200
*Chicago Tribune,* 198, 301
Child, W. S., 85–86
Churchill, Lady (Clementine), 172, 188, 244–45, 258
Churchill (Hayward Harriman), Pamela, 13, 139, 192–93, 258, 384, 390
Churchill, Sarah, 172, 173
Churchill, Sir Winston, 11, 103, 123, 127, 145, 146, 153, 168, 172–73, 188, 204, 210, 242, 244–45, 258, 322, 325, 329, 382, 407
CIA (Central Intelligence Agency), 211, 287, 302
CIO (Congress of Industrial Organizations), 122, 178, 202
Citizens Committee for New York City, 364–65, 366, 386, 397, 407, 416, 418
civil rights, 110–11, 120, 149, 171, 191, 195, 237, 295–97
Clark, Blair, 267, 274
Clark, George, 258
Clark, Joe, 207, 212

Clark, Kenneth, 207, 245, 316
Clark, May, 258
Clark, Michael, 365–66, 378, 400, 407
Clark, William, 84
Cleveland, Grover, 199
Cleveland, Harlan, 271
Clift, Montgomery, 250
Cobb, Nina, 375
Colbert, Claudette, 339, 390, 398
Colefax, Sibyl, 328
Collingwood, Charles, 111
Collins, Edmund John, 144, 146, 162, 167,
    169, 176, 178, 180, 188, 190–91, 223, 251,
    315–16, 317, 330
Collins, Nellie, 315–16, 330
Columbia University, 304
Colville, Sir John, 172
Commager, Henry Steele, 366
Commission of Inter-Group Relations, 237
communism, 209, 219
   in United States, 121–22
Concord Academy, 286–87
Congress for Cultural Freedom (CCF), 287
Congress of Industrial Organizations
    (CIO), 122, 178, 202
Conway, Jack, 122
Cooper, Duff, 145, 172, 179, 210
Cooper, Lady Diana, 172, 179, 184
Cooper-Hewitt Museum, 343
Corning, Edwin, 98
Coward, Noël, 319
Cranborne, Bobbety, see Salisbury, Lord
Crile, George, 332
Crocker, Jack, 387
Crosland, Susan, 337
Cummings, Minnette Hunsiker, 53
Cummins, A. Holmes, 97
Cunard, Emerald, 179
Cunard, Sir Edward, 135–36, 189, 319
Cunard, Victor, 185
Cushing, Babe, see Paley, Barbara Cushing
    Mortimer "Babe"
Cushing, Harvey, 31

*Daily Telegraph* (London), 207, 290
Daley, Richard, 248, 278
Dali, Salvador, 157
Dalton School, 149, 160, 190, 211, 221, 242,
    287
Danielson, Patricia, 357, 358
Davidoff, Judy, 278
David-Weill, Pierre, 114
Davison, Daniel (cousin), 356, 386, 391, 414,
    416
Davison, Dorothy Peabody (aunt), 19, 43,
    49, 60, 180, 297
Davison, Harry, 386–87, 412, 416
Davison, Trubee (cousin), 356
Davison, Trubee (uncle), 43, 91, 297
"Day of Political Education, A," 207

Dear, Jack, 241, 242, 329, 330, 335, 336
de Forest, Robert Weeks, 23–24
Degas, Edgar, 30
de Gaulle, Charles, 179
de Havilland, Olivia, 130, 131
Democratic Advisory Council, 237, 243
Democratic National Convention, 227
Democratic Women's Workshop, 203, 207,
    218
Depardieu, Gérard, 266
Derby, Bootsie, see Morris, Mary Brewster
    Derby "Bootsie"
Derby (Williams), Edith, 14, 52, 54, 59, 65,
    67, 80, 91
Derby, Ethel Roosevelt, 54
D'Erlanger, Edwina, 136, 154, 317–18
de Rohan, Maurice, 340
de Sapio, Carmine, 196, 197, 218
Despont, Thierry, 357–58, 386, 407
Devereux, Antelo, 80, 83, 151, 258
Devonshire, duke of, 185, 208
Dewey, Thomas, 195
Dick, Edison, 205, 269
Dick, Jane, 201, 205, 227, 248, 251, 254, 269,
    276
Dietrich, Marlene, 319
Dilenschneider, Robert L., 371, 372
Dillon, Douglas, 18, 416
Dinkins, David, 414
Dockery, Marietta, 149, 297, 396, 401
Dorrance, Peggy, 53
Douglas, Norman, 331
Douglas, Paul, 195
Doxiadis, Constantinos, 307, 308–9
Drayton, John "Satan," 54
Dreyfus Corporation, 343, 388
Drogheda, earl of, 207
Drury, Edith, 354
Dulles, Allen, 160
Dulles, John Foster, 202, 219
du Maurier, Daphne, 173
Duncan, Douglas, 120
Dunnington (Peabody), Judith
    (sister-in-law), 216, 217, 324, 351, 355,
    393, 402, 410
du Pont (Roosevelt), Ethel, 89
Durante, Jimmy, 57
Dusseldorp, Dik, 340
Duvall, Bella, 188, 223
Duvall, Michael, 188, 223, 333
Duvall, Reginald, 177, 188, 214, 223, 333
Dwight, George H. P., 196, 199

Eberlein, Roxane, 278
ECOSOC (United Nations Economic and
    Social Council), 253, 257, 262, 267–68,
    270, 271, 275, 307
Eden, Anthony (earl of Avon), 144, 145, 152,
    188, 202, 209, 225, 285, 329, 330, 414
Edinburgh, duke of, 183, 184–85

Eisenhower, Dwight D., 199, 200–201, 202, 205, 209, 219, 229, 246, 252
elections:
　of 1932, 54–55
　of 1940, 102
　of 1944, 126
　of 1948, 195
　of 1952, 195, 197–206, 219, 232, 282
　of 1956, 219, 222, 224–30, 246
　of 1960, 203, 243–49
　of 1968, 305
Eliot, Charles, 24
Eliot, T. S., 263
Elizabeth, queen mother, 182, 189, 297, 331
Elizabeth II, queen of England, 208, 209
　coronation of, 206, 208
　as princess, 179, 184, 185, 189
Elliott, Osborn, 366
*Encyclopaedia Britannica*, 219, 237
Endicott, John, 17
Engelhard, Miss, 117
Eno, Amos, 97
Entenman, Edith, 158, 160, 163, 183, 217
Episcopal Theological School, 28, 29

Fairchild, John, 373
Farah Diba, 339
fascism, 61, 62–63, 77
Fataar, Paloma (granddaughter), 378–79, 415
Fataar, Ricky (son-in-law), 350–51, 378
Field (Tree Beatty), Ethel, 139–40, 141
Field, Fiona, 211
Field, Henry, 141
Field, Marshall, 139, 143
Field, Marshall, III, 80, 136, 141, 152, 153, 157, 165, 181, 200, 209, 219, 229, 388
Field, Nancy, *see* Lancaster, Nancy Perkins Field Tree
Field, Phyllis, 211
Field, Ruth Phipps, 136, 152–53, 157, 165, 181, 219, 229, 236, 243, 261, 278, 341
Finletter, Eileen, 200, 219, 229, 342
Finletter, Frances, 88–89
Finletter, Tom, 200, 214, 219, 227, 229, 243, 342
*Fire in the Lake* (FitzGerald), 322
Fish, Hamilton, 201–2
FitzGerald, Barbara Lawrence, 180, 181, 211, 302
FitzGerald, Desmond (husband), 112, 180–181, 211, 374, 384–85
　death of, 302
　early married life of, 98–101
　Frances's birth and, 101–3
　marital troubles of MT and, 133–38, 146, 149, 151, 152, 153
　in military, 105, 106, 108, 111, 114, 115–16, 117, 125, 127, 133, 134

MT's courtship and marriage with, 88, 89, 90, 92–97, 414
MT's divorce from, 151, 152, 154, 155–65, 391
FitzGerald (Francke), Eleanor (sister-in-law), 92, 99, 116, 150
FitzGerald, Frances "Frankie" (daughter), 105, 106, 108, 113–14, 115, 116, 117, 124, 125, 131, 132, 134, 146, 149, 151, 152, 153, 157, 160, 180, 183, 185, 208, 210, 211, 227, 234, 236, 239, 266, 277, 293, 302, 309–310, 352, 356, 373, 379, 415
　on Africa trip, 233
　in Barbados, 190, 191, 212
　birth of, 101–3
　boarding school for, 210–11, 221, 228–29, 234
　Desmond FitzGerald's death and, 302
　documentaries on, 349–50
　in England with MT and Ronald Tree, 167, 168, 170–71, 175, 179, 180, 182
　on European trip (1959), 239
　on European trip (1965), 275
　at Lazy K Bar Ranch, 217
　marriage of, 398
　menorrhagia of, 291, 292
　and MT's cancer and death, 395, 396, 399, 404, 405, 406, 408–9, 410, 411, 413, 414
　MT's distance from, 379–80
　MT's will and, 394
　parents' divorce and, 151, 157, 158, 159, 160, 161, 162, 163, 164
　at Radcliffe, 239, 258–59, 287
　Ronald Tree as stepfather to, 211–12
　Ronald Tree's death and, 331
　Ronald Tree's stroke and, 325
　Stevenson's death and, 277
　in Vietnam, 287, 290–91, 292, 322
FitzGerald, Harold (father-in-law), 92, 101, 116, 136, 149
FitzGerald, Helen Johnson "Bird" (stepmother-in-law), 92, 100, 136
FitzGerald, Marietta, *see* Tree, Mary Endicott Peabody FitzGerald "Marietta"
FitzGerald, Nora Fitzgerald, 92
FitzGerald, Steven, 92
Flanagan, Dennis, 120
Flitcroft, Henry, 168
Fontaine, Joan, 262
Ford, Henry, 178
Ford Foundation, 299
Forster, E. M., 264, 318, 413
Fosburgh, Jim, 225
Foulke, Louisa Wood, 77, 96
Foulke, William, 77
Fowler, Louisa, 49, 52, 53–54, 56
Foxcroft School, 221, 228–29, 234
Francke, Albert, 99, 116, 302

Francke, Albert, Jr. (nephew), 116, 150
Francke, Eleanor FitzGerald (sister-in-law),
    92, 99, 116, 150
Francke, Nora (niece), 116, 150
Frankel, Charles, 292
Frei, Eduardo, 271
Freud, Anna, 153, 158
Friendly, Fred, 375
Fritchey, Clayton, 199, 201, 214, 219, 235,
    256, 278, 353
Fritchey, Polly, 403
Frost, Winston, 89, 90
Fulbright, J. William, 209, 235, 252

Gabel, Hortense, 302, 383
Gabel, Sukreet, 383
Gable, Clark, 250–51
Galbraith, John Kenneth, 219, 246
Gannett, Mrs. Thomas Brattle, 80
Garaventa, Norma, 278
Garbo, Greta, 210
Gardiner, Anna, 27, 28
Gardner, Ava, 269
Gardner, Isabella Stewart, 24–25, 30
Garrison, Lloyd, 224
Getty, Anne, 355
Gibbons (Peabody), Barbara "Toni"
    (sister-in-law), 77, 125, 216, 351–52, 380
Gibbs, James, 143, 168
Giles, Frank, 239, 367, 407
Giles, Lady Kitty, 239, 407
Gillespie, Henry, 368, 385, 400, 402
Glass, Carter, 84
Godfrey, Lincoln, 80
Goheen, Robert, 373
Goldberg, Arthur, 278, 288, 289, 300
Goldman, Eric F., 225
Goldwyn, Sam, 204
Gonzalez, Rosario, 404
Goodman, George W., 384
Grace Church, 30, 34, 37
Graham, Katharine, 276, 277, 395, 415
Grant (Scull), Patricia "Trishy," 52, 82, 165,
    405
Greenfield, Meg, 228, 231
Grew, Joseph, 98
Griswold, Penelope (aunt), 44, 80, 179
Gromyko, Andrei, 238
Groton School, 18–20, 29, 32, 44, 48–49,
    54, 62, 71, 103, 223, 246, 333, 387, 388,
    393, 416
    FDR as viewed at, 54
    reunion at, 57, 60, 78, 254
    St. Timothy's and, 49–50, 54
Gruson, Marit, 319, 339, 367, 397, 398, 407
Guggenheim, Harry, 198, 219, 267
Gunther, Jane, 262, 278

Hadden (Kernan), Leslie "Coupie," 54, 80,
    81, 89, 193, 381, 413

Haggin, Louis, 340
Hahn, Kenneth, 310
Halaby, Lisa, 344–45
Halaby, Najeeb, 325, 343–45
Hallowell, Margaret "Marnie," 59, 80, 81,
    82, 91, 100
Hambro, Robin, 375
Hamilton, John, 93
Hardy, Robin, 350
Harriman, Averell, 18, 207, 212, 218, 219,
    225, 235, 247, 267, 275
Harriman, Pamela Churchill Hayward, 13,
    139, 192–93, 258, 384, 390
Harris, Kenneth, 322, 325
Harrison, Alfred, 93, 97, 99
Hart, Kitty Carlisle, 340–41, 343, 363, 366–
    367, 393, 397, 398, 408, 415
Hartington, Kathleen Kennedy "Kick," 145,
    160, 184
Harvard University, 20–21, 48, 62, 82, 88,
    93, 216, 217
Hawkins, Ashton, 366
Hawthorne, Nathaniel, 15, 163
Hawthorne, Sophia Peabody, 15
Hayward (Harriman), Pamela Churchill, 13,
    139, 192–93, 258, 384, 390
Hazzard, Shirley, 345
Head, Anthony, 208
Hearst, Dorothy, *see* Hirshon, Dorothy
    Hearst Paley
Hearst, John Randolph, 110, 136
Heimann, John, 335
Hellman, Lillian, 267
Hemenway, Russell, 218, 242–43, 404
Henderson, Sir Nicholas, 403, 414, 415
Hersey, John, 111, 149
Hewitt, William, 315, 390
Hickok, Mary Isabel Voorhees "Mezzy,"
    41, 45, 78, 79, 81, 82, 84, 108, 165, 167,
    193, 258, 415
Hill, Gladys, 390
Hill & Knowlton, 371–72
Hills, Patrick, 242
Hirshon, Dorothy Hearst Paley, 110–11, 112,
    114, 120, 134, 136, 182, 184, 187, 226,
    249, 278, 396, 398
    MT's divorce and, 149, 150, 154, 158, 160,
    161–62, 163
Hitler, Adolf, 67, 84, 96
Hofmannsthal, Raimund von, 114–15, 210
Holden, Doc, 113
Holmes, Nancy, 138
Hood School, 36
Hoover, Herbert, 54, 171
Horowitz, Vladimir, 65
Houston, Evelyn, 262
Hudson, Robert, 144
Huffington, Arianna Stassinopoulos, 355
Hughes, Fred, 368
Hulburd, David, 91

Human Rights Commission, 237
Humphrey, Hubert, 195, 235, 243, 244, 245, 248, 278, 281, 305
Hunsiker (Cummings), Minnette, 53
Hussein, king of Jordan, 345, 416
Huston, Danny, 391
Huston, John, 221, 227, 239–40, 293, 302, 341, 385, 390–92
    death of, 391
    Desmond FitzGerald's return and, 135
    Evelyn Keyes married by, 153–54
    MT in movies of, 250–51, 266, 374, 391
    MT's decision against marriage to, 138, 148, 151, 155, 156, 392
    MT's divorce and, 164
    MT's romantic relationship with, 128, 129–34, 137–38
Huston, Maricel, 391
Huston, Walter, 132, 148, 154, 164, 221, 391
Hyde, Henry, 133–34, 390

Inter-American Commercial Arbitration Association, 109, 112, 115
Isabel (nanny), 106, 113, 115, 116
Ives, Buffie, 227, 239, 262

Jackson, Sir Robert, 219
James, Charles, 214, 217
James, Henry, 13, 25, 172
Javits, Jacob, 364–65
Jay, Susan Mary, see Alsop, Susan Mary Jay Patten "Soozle"
Jellicoe, Sir Geoffrey, 189
Jenkins, Roy (Lord Jenkins of Hillhead), 325, 330, 335, 399–400, 403, 414
Jessup, John K., 120, 122, 149
Jevenois, Mademoiselle de, 60, 62, 63, 65, 75
Johnson (FitzGerald), Helen "Bird" (stepmother-in-law), 92, 100, 136
Johnson, Lyndon B., 203, 236, 245, 249, 255, 256, 268–69, 275, 278, 280, 281
Just, Ward, 291, 415

Kaiser, Philip, 277
Kaminer, Peter, 103, 160
Kauffmann, Henrik, 182
Kaye, Danny, 374
Kefauver, Estes, 226, 227
Kellor, Frances, 109, 115
Kennan, George, 12
Kennedy (Onassis), Jacqueline, 335, 368, 373, 402, 413
Kennedy, John F., 227, 244–49, 252, 255, 265, 268, 275
Kennedy, Joseph P., 144–45
Kennedy, Joseph P., Jr., 145
Kennedy (Hartington), Kathleen "Kick," 145, 160, 184

Kennedy, Ludovic, 208, 367
Kennedy, Robert F., 288, 300, 301, 304, 305, 310, 387
Kennedy, Studdert, 159
Kent, duchess of, 184
Kent, William, 168
Kernan, Leslie Hadden "Coupie," 54, 80, 81, 89, 193, 381, 413
Keyes, Evelyn, 153–54
Khan, Aly, 187
Khrushchev, Nikita, 246
Kidder, Peabody & Co., 16
Kindersley, Lord, 241
King, Patricia M., 375
Kingsley, Madge, 129
Kingsley, Sidney, 127, 129
Kissinger, Henry, 363, 370, 374, 397
Klotzer, Lillian, 346, 368–69, 395, 396
Knox, Frank, 200
Kollek, Teddy, 309
Kommer, Rudolph "Kaetchen," 114
Korean War, 202–3
Kübler-Ross, Elisabeth, 413

Ladd, Parker, 384, 385, 393–94, 397
Lambton, Lord, 172, 245
Lancaster, Claude G. "Jubie," 145–46, 147, 153, 154, 182, 318
Lancaster, Nancy Perkins Field Tree, 136, 141–47, 151, 153, 154, 155, 157, 168, 173–174, 183, 325, 346, 388
    death of, 329
    after divorce from Ronald Tree, 171, 172, 174–75, 182, 187–88, 243, 318, 328–329
Landers, Ann (Eppie Lederer), 332, 407
Lasker, Mary, 227, 233, 239, 243, 261–62
Lawrence (FitzGerald), Barbara, 180, 181, 211, 302
Lawrence (Train), Barbara, 185, 211
Lawrence, Mrs. James, 48–49
Lawrence, William, 34, 43, 81, 96
Lazar, Irving "Swifty," 341, 373, 376, 407
Lazy K Bar Ranch, 217
LDA (Llewelyn-Davies Associates), 310–14, 338, 339, 356–57
LDK (Llewelyn-Davies Kinhill), 311
Leacock, Jack, 326
Leander Club, 21
Lederer, Eppie (Ann Landers), 332, 407
Lee, John C., 17
Lee (Peabody), Marianne Cabot (great-grandmother), 17
Lee, Robert, 21
Leet, Millie Robbins, 231, 360, 415
Lend-Lease of Australia, 345, 358, 360–61, 363, 370
Lexington Democratic Club, 196, 212, 218, 233
Lieberson, Goddard, 226

*Life,* 243
  MT's work with, 117, 118–28, 148, 149,
    191, 197, 202, 214, 255, 297, 301, 374,
    384
Lilly, Doris, 131
Lincoln, Abraham, 199
Linlithgow, Lord, 191
Lippmann, Walter, 61, 64, 200
Litvak, Anatole "Tola," 150, 164
Llewelyn-Davies, Melissa, 308
Llewelyn-Davies, Patricia, 306, 308, 309,
    332, 338–39, 342, 357, 358, 414
Llewelyn-Davies, Richard, 306–14, 332, 338–
    343, 346, 353, 372, 386
  background of, 306
  business ventures of MT and, 310–14,
    326, 338, 339, 347, 348, 356–57, 383
  cancer and death of, 357–59, 360, 416
  LDA closed by, 356–57
  LDA founded by, 310–14
  with MT on Greek cruise, 308–10
  MT's first meeting with, 306, 307
  Ronald Tree's death and, 330
Llewelyn-Davies Associates (LDA), 310–14,
    338, 339, 356–57, 383
Llewelyn-Davies International, 338
Llewelyn-Davies Kinhill (LDK), 311
Llewelyn-Davies Sahni, 364
Lombard, Carole, 11
*Look,* 205, 218, 303
Lord, Mary Pillsbury, 252
Lovat, Lord Shimi, 127
Low, Robert, 304
Luce, Clare Boothe, 204
Luce, Henry R., 120–21, 122
Luers, Wendy, 382–83
Luers, William, 382
Lyman, Ronald, 80
Lynch, Rose Parsons (cousin), 44, 135,
    286
Lyons, Leonard, 248

McCarthy, Eugene, 247
McCarthy, Joseph, 209, 212, 219, 220
McCarthy, Mary, 171
McClatchy, C. K., 319
McCormick, Robert, 151
McCormick, Kenneth, 314
McCullough, George, 136
MacDonald, Jack, 20
MacFarlane, Michael (grandson), 378, 394,
    415
MacFarlane, Stuart, 378
McIlhenny, Louise, *see* Roberts, Louise
  McIlhenny "Weasel"
McKeever, Porter, 416
MacLaren, Lee, 307, 308, 332, 382, 387,
    407
MacLaren, Malcolm, 387
MacLaren, Roy, 307, 308, 336, 382, 387

MacLeish, Archibald, 268, 279
Mann, Horace, 16
Mann, Mary Peabody, 15–16
Marcos, Imelda, 291, 311, 312, 364, 374
Margaret, Princess, 179, 184, 185, 189, 218,
    220
Margolis, Jon, 301
Martin, John Bartlow, 198, 205, 227, 261,
    276, 293, 310, 341
Martindell, Anne, 375–76
Masaryk, Jan, 127
Masefield, John, 414
Maxwell, Elsa, 111
Melba, Nellie, 25
Merwin, Ruth, 199
Messel, Oliver, 235, 319
Mesta, Perle, 274
Meyer, Agnes, 219, 232, 233, 236, 243, 246,
    248, 276, 281
Meyer, Eugene, 219
Meyerson, Martin, 309, 332, 342, 343, 359,
    371, 372, 373, 394, 408, 412
Meyner, Helen Stevenson, 227, 228, 231
Meyner, Robert, 227, 231
Miller, Arthur, 250
Milliken, Minot, 60
Millington-Drake, Teddy, 400
Minow, Newton, 219
Mirabella, Grace, 354
*Misfits, The,* 250–51, 266, 374, 391
Mitford, Nancy, 179
Mohammad Reza Pahlavi, shah of Iran, 338,
    345, 356–57
Monroe, Marilyn, 11, 250, 251
Monroney, Mike, 235, 243
Montagu, Judy, 208
Montanari, James, 326
Montesquiou, Pierre de, 210
Moore, Anne, 395–96, 399, 401, 404,
    411
Moore, Grace, 73, 97
Moral Rearmament (MRA), 85–86
Morgan, Junius S., 17
Morris, DuBois S., 86
Morris, Mary Brewster Derby "Bootsie,"
    52, 54, 55, 60–61, 77, 81, 85, 86, 376, 381,
    415
Mortimer, Babe, *see* Paley, Barbara Cushing
  Mortimer "Babe"
Mortimer, Stanley, 99, 111, 113
Moulton, Arthur W., 30, 34
Mount Desert Island, 24
MRA (Moral Rearmament), 85–86
*Mr. North,* 391
Muir, Malcolm, 244
Munnings, Sir Alfred, 143
Murray, Philip, 122
Murrow, Edward R., 110, 111, 149
Mussolini, Benito, 62–64, 67, 68
Myerson, Bess, 383

Nabokov, Nicolas, 287
National Urban League, 110–11, 207, 212, 214, 224, 237
Newbold, Arthur, 80
Newman, Mildred, 356, 382
Newspaper Guild, 121
*Newsweek*, 244, 303, 350
New York Constitutional Convention (1967), 300, 301–4, 307, 383
New York *Daily News*, 104, 198
New York Democratic State Committee, 197, 198, 218, 237
*New Yorker*, 12, 16, 415
*New York Herald Tribune*, 64
*New York Post*, 197, 246
*New York Times, The*, 93, 112, 127, 165, 201, 256, 275, 333–34, 358, 400–401
Niarchos, Stavros, 224
Nicholas, prince of Yugoslavia, 208
Nicolson, Harold, 264, 318
Nicolson, Nigel, 11
Nietzsche, Friedrich, 263
Nitze, Paul, 219, 262
Niven, David, 172, 245, 293
Niven, Hjordis, 293
Nixon, Richard M., 229, 243, 246, 247, 249, 305

O'Dell, Mabel, 188, 192, 223, 245, 266, 286, 333, 346, 400
Office of Inter-American Affairs, 107–9
Ogilby, Remsen, 21
Onassis, Aristotle, 244–45, 258
Onassis, Jacqueline Kennedy, 335, 368, 373, 402, 413
O'Reilly, James T., 31
Oxford Group, 85

Pachachi, Adnan, 274
Paepcke, Elizabeth, 262
Paepcke, Walter, 262
Page, Thomas Nelson, 141
Pahlavi, Farah Diba, 339
Palewski, Gaston, 179
Paley, Barbara Cushing Mortimer "Babe," 62, 80, 99, 110, 111, 113, 150, 165, 192, 210, 214, 302, 327, 397, 398, 406
   death of, 346–47
Paley, Dorothy, *see* Hirshon, Dorothy Hearst Paley
Paley, Hilary, 163, 164
Paley, Jeffrey, 163, 164, 397
Paley, William, 110, 114, 136, 146, 149, 150, 160, 164, 192, 210, 302, 314, 327, 334–35, 371, 397–98
Paley, William, Jr., 397
Palmer, Gordon, 80, 151
Palmer, Pauline, 52–53, 80, 83
Palmer, Potter, II, 52

Palmer, Potter, III, 89, 96–97
Pan American World Airways, 325, 327, 343, 360, 371, 399
Paolozzi, Alice Spaulding, 50, 52, 54, 82, 400, 415
Parker, Cortlandt (great-grandfather), 23
Parker, Elisabeth Stites (great-grandmother), 23
Parker, Mary Frances, *see* Parkman, Mary Frances Parker
Parkman, Edith (aunt), 29
Parkman, Francis (cousin), 13, 22
Parkman, George (great-uncle), 27, 414
Parkman, Harry (grandfather), 23, 37
Parkman, Henry (uncle), 54, 60, 62
Parkman (Peabody), Mary Elizabeth, *see* Peabody, Mary Elizabeth Parkman
Parkman, Mary Frances Parker (grandmother), 12, 23–26, 60, 62, 66, 75, 80, 85, 99–100, 259, 326
   death of, 105
   Europe trip organized by, 84
   MT's first wedding and, 93, 97
   MT's stays with, 32, 34–35, 43, 44, 47, 48
Parkman, Samuel, I, 22
Parkman, Samuel, II "Naughty Sam," 22, 161
Parkman, Samuel, III (great-grandfather), 22–23
Parkman, "Torchie" (cousin), 380
Parsons (Lynch), Rose (cousin), 44, 135, 286
Parsons, Rose Peabody (aunt), 19, 43
Parsons, William (uncle), 43
Patten, Susan Mary, *see* Alsop, Susan Mary Jay Patten "Soozle"
Patten, William, 93, 94, 97, 98, 183, 201, 278
Patterson, Alicia, 198, 219, 233, 234, 235, 236, 246, 258, 265, 267
Patterson, Joseph M., 198
Peabody, Barbara (niece), 211
Peabody, Barbara Gibbons "Toni" (sister-in-law), 77, 125, 216, 351–52, 380
Peabody (Davison), Dorothy (aunt), 19, 43, 49, 60, 180, 297
Peabody, Elizabeth (ancestor), 16
Peabody, Elizabeth "Betsey" (aunt), 19, 80, 102, 183, 215, 327
Peabody, Endicott "Chub" (brother), 76, 77, 88, 97, 133, 211, 277–78, 293, 323, 352, 353, 354, 380
   childhood of, 34–35, 37, 41, 42, 44, 70, 71–72, 74
   marriage of, 125, 126
   MT's estrangement from, 180, 182, 216, 410
   MT's illness and, 410
   political career of, 216, 295, 296, 299, 324

Peabody, Endicott "Cotty" (grandfather),
    16–20, 21–22, 25, 26, 28, 29, 30, 32, 36,
    37, 42, 43, 48, 71, 96, 102, 105, 112, 115,
    163, 194, 318, 416
  death of, 125–26
  FDR as viewed by, 54–55
  grandchildren's view of, 44
  at MT's first wedding, 96
  sports encouraged by, 50
Peabody, Everett, 15, 16
Peabody, Fannie (grandmother), 12, 18, 19,
    25, 37, 43, 44, 48, 52, 53, 57, 60, 66, 102,
    115, 126, 151
Peabody, Francis (English settler), 15
Peabody, Francis (mill owner), 15
Peabody, George (ancestor), 16, 17, 308
Peabody, George (great-uncle), 30
Peabody, George Lee (brother), 88, 97, 148,
    152, 155, 163, 181, 182, 216, 296, 299, 323,
    352, 353–54, 380, 381, 413
  childhood of, 35, 37, 41, 44, 70, 71, 84–85
  and MT's illness and death, 410–11, 414
Peabody (Sedgwick), Helen (aunt), 19, 28,
    43
Peabody, Isaac, 15
Peabody, Joseph, 16, 17
Peabody, Judith Dunnington "Judy"
    (sister-in-law), 216, 217, 324, 351, 355,
    393, 402, 410
Peabody, Lizzie (great-aunt), 30
Peabody, Malcolm (father), 30–40, 42, 46,
    101, 280, 297–99, 316, 388
  bequests and will of, 241, 297, 323, 324
  childhood of, 19–20
  death of, 322–24, 353–54
  Desmond FitzGerald as viewed by, 97
  early career of, 30–37
  education of, 20–22
  and elections of 1952, 201
  Fowler's letter to, 53
  Mary's arrest and, 296
  Mary's courtship and marriage with, 28–
    30
  ministry chosen by, 21–22
  MT's correspondence with, 61–62, 67, 73,
    108, 112, 113, 133, 179, 180, 185, 215–16,
    374
  MT's divorce and, 156, 158–59, 160–61,
    162, 163, 165
  MT's schooling important to, 45
  and MT's second marriage, 165, 174, 179,
    182
  and MT's year in Italy, 61–62, 64, 67, 69,
    73
  promoted to Bishop, 74, 88
  religious studies of, 28–29
  retirement of, 295
  rules of behavior established by, 69
  St. Paul's post accepted by, 37–38
  social exclusion of, 47

sports encouraged by, 50
  as unemotional, 72, 77, 211
  in World War I, 31–34
Peabody, Malcolm, Jr. "Mike" (brother),
    165, 181, 217, 295, 297, 350, 352–53, 380,
    381
  childhood of, 34, 39–40, 41, 70, 71, 88,
    97, 133
  MT's illness and, 410
Peabody, Margery (aunt), 19, 183, 215, 380
Peabody, Marianne Cabot Lee
    (great-grandmother), 17
Peabody, Marietta, see Tree, Mary Endicott
    Peabody FitzGerald "Marietta"
Peabody, Martha Endicott, 17
Peabody (Mann), Mary, 15–16
Peabody, Mary Elizabeth Parkman
    (mother), 12, 22, 24, 25, 27, 30–39, 42,
    89, 99–100, 101, 259, 280, 316, 330
  activism and arrest of, 295–97, 349
  afterlife doubted by, 353–54
  death of, 351–53, 409
  debutante circuit and, 74, 76, 79–80
  Desmond FitzGerald and, 97, 98
  documentaries on, 349–50
  and elections of 1952, 201
  Fowler's letter to, 53
  Frances FitzGerald's birth and, 101–2
  Frances FitzGerald's relationship with,
    114
  Malcolm's courtship and marriage with,
    28–30
  Malcolm's death and, 322–23
  Mother's Record kept by, 32–33, 36, 38, 75
  MT's correspondence with, 61–62, 64,
    67, 73, 75, 108, 112, 113, 133, 179, 180, 185,
    215–16, 374
  MT's divorce and, 156, 157, 158–59, 160–
    161, 162, 163
  and MT's second marriage, 165, 176, 179,
    182, 350
  and MT's year in Italy, 60, 61–62, 64, 67,
    69–70, 73, 74–75
  nutritional views of, 42
  parsimoniousness of, 73–74
  St. Paul's move opposed by, 37–38
  social work of, 44, 47–48
  sports encouraged by, 50–51
  as unemotional, 72, 77, 211, 352–53
  world trip of, 27–28
  in World War I, 31–34
Peabody, Nathaniel, 15
Peabody, Pamela (sister-in-law), 350
Peabody (Parsons), Rose (aunt), 19, 43
Peabody, Samuel Endicott
    (great-grandfather), 17
Peabody, Samuel Parkman (brother), 19, 97,
    98, 155, 180, 181, 216, 277, 279, 297, 299,
    323, 330, 331, 350, 351, 352, 355, 380, 381,
    402, 404, 413

Peabody, Samuel Parkman (brother),
  *continued*
  childhood of, 37, 41, 44–45, 70–71, 88
  and MT's illness and death, 405, 409–10,
    412
Peabody (Hawthorne), Sophia, 15
Peabody Estates, 16
Peabody Trust, 16
Pell, Claiborne, 363
Pennsylvania, University of, 82–83, 85–86,
  88, 94, 100, 110, 343
Perkins, Nancy, *see* Lancaster, Nancy
  Perkins Field Tree
La Petite Ecole Florentine, 60, 62–70, 75,
  388
Philby, Kim, 306
Philip, Prince, 179
Phipps, Ogden, 153
Phipps (Field), Ruth, *see* Field, Ruth Phipps
Piel, Gerard, 120
Pierrepont, John, 387
Pius XI, Pope, 66–67
Pius XII, Pope, 224
Planned Parenthood, 189, 218
Plimpton, Calvin, 332, 343
Plimpton, Francis T. P., 267, 268, 343
Plimpton, Sarah, 267, 268, 269, 275
Pope-Hennessy, Sir John, 367, 415
Post, Marjorie Merriweather, 92
Power, Tyrone, 114
Prout, Curtis, 86, 87
Putnam (Bundy), Katherine, 27, 28, 29, 35
Pyne, Eben, 387–89, 391, 394, 402, 403,
  404–5, 408, 411

Radcliffe College, 24, 239, 258–59, 287, 375
Rauch, R. Stewart, 83–84, 258
Reagan, Ronald, 363
Reger, Bud, 241
Reischauer, Edwin O., 290–91
Reith, Lord, 145
Reston, James, 275
Reuther, Walter, 120, 122, 178
Rheinwald, Anne, 167
Rhodes, Zandra, 367
Richardson, Sir Gordon, 292, 293
Richardson, Lady (Peggy), 292
Rivkin, Donald, 384
Rizk, Khalil, 404
Robbins (Leet), Millie, 231, 360, 415
Roberts, Bayard, 86
Roberts, Louise McIlhenny "Weasel," 41,
  65, 67, 73, 81, 83, 86, 165, 211, 258, 415
Robertson, Jacquelin, 339, 345
Rockefeller, Nelson, 106–7, 108, 235
Roger, Odette Pol, 224
Roosevelt, Eleanor, 11, 78, 84, 122, 149, 201,
  237, 243, 246, 252–53, 254, 257, 279, 375
Roosevelt, Elliott, 165
Roosevelt (Derby), Ethel, 54

Roosevelt, Ethel du Pont, 89
Roosevelt, Franklin D., 18, 46, 54–55, 78,
  102, 122, 126, 171, 178, 199, 247, 254, 363
Roosevelt, Franklin D., Jr., 78, 80, 84, 89,
  183
Roosevelt, Theodore, 54
Roosevelt, Theodore, Jr., 71, 80, 83, 258
Ross, Arthur, 335, 343, 355, 360, 390
Ross, Steve, 397, 404
Rothschild, Jacob, 338
Rothschild, Lady, 339
Rothschild, Tess, 306
Rothschild, Victor, 153, 245, 306
Rusk, Dean, 249, 256
Russell, Aliki, 219
Russell, Bertrand, 306
Russell, John, 219
Russell, Sir John, 248

Sackville-West, Vita, 44
Sage, DeWitt, 93
Sahni, Randhir, 357, 364
St. Jude's Episcopal Church, 42, 81
St. Paul's Episcopal Church, 37–38, 39–40,
  54
St. Timothy's School, 47, 49–58, 83, 381
Salisbury, Lady, 182, 208, 209, 210, 233, 243,
  245
Salisbury, Lord (Bobbety Cranborne), 144,
  171, 182, 185, 208, 209, 210, 222, 225,
  233, 243, 245, 329
Samuels, John, 333–34
Sandy Lane Hotel, 241–42, 285, 329, 336–37
Sarah Lawrence College, 303
Sargent, John Singer, 25
Sartre, Jean-Paul, 154
Scaasi, Arnold, 385
Schary, Dore, 226
Schiff, Dorothy, 197, 265
Schlamm, William S., 315
Schlesinger, Arthur, Jr., 212, 238, 278, 288
  and elections of 1952, 201, 205
  and elections of 1956, 219, 244
  and elections of 1960, 244, 246, 247
  Kennedy administration and, 252
  Llewelyn-Davies's clothes given to, 358
  MT's correspondence with, 282, 299
  MT's death and, 408, 412, 414
  MT's first meeting with, 201, 315
  on MT's reliability, 383
  MT's speeches rewritten by, 360
  on Stevenson, 199, 264, 265, 282
Schmidt, Lars, 270, 374
Schrift, Bernice "Red," 118–19
Schuschnigg, Kurt von, 68
Schweitzer, Albert, 234
SCLC (Southern Christian Leadership
  Council), 295, 352
Scott, Edgar, 258
Scott, Hope, 317, 381

Scott, Sir Winston, 336
Scull (Warren), Anne, 80, 89–90, 176
Scull, Patricia Grant "Trishy," 52, 82, 165, 405
Seawell, William, 325
Sedgwick, Helen Peabody (aunt), 19, 28, 43
Sedgwick, May (cousin), 94
Sedgwick, Minturn (uncle), 43
Seligman, Arnold, 260
Selznick, David, 110, 114, 145, 303
Selznick, Irene, 110, 114, 145, 204, 221, 303
Senni, Countess, 66
Senni, Maria Giulia, 66, 75
Senni, Piero, 66, 67, 75
Sevareid, Eric, 277, 349–50
Seyburn (Cheston), Winifred "Peggy," 60, 64, 388, 405
S. G. Warburg, 343
Shady Hill Country Day School, 40–41, 45–46, 50, 78
Shaw, Irwin, 192
Shaw, Quincy A., 22
Shea, Jack, 227
Shearer, Moira, 208
Sherwood, Lydia, 50
Sherwood, Robert, 120, 207
Shoemaker, Sam, 159
Sicre, Ricardo, 269
Sinatra, Frank, 122
Sinclair, Andrew, 306–7
Singh, Natwar, 312, 390
Sitrick, James B., 332, 336, 363, 364, 378, 407
Smith, Adam, 384
Smith, Corinne, 28
Solomon, Anthony, 371
Sorenson, Theodore, 304
Southern Christian Leadership Council (SCLC), 295, 352
Sparkman, John, 199
Spaulding (Paolozzi), Alice, 50, 52, 54, 82, 400, 415
Spiegel, Sam, 351
Spry, Constance, 184
Stapleton, Hannah, 44–45
Stassinopoulos (Huffington), Arianna, 355
Steele, John, 244
Steinem, Gloria, 363–64
Sterba, James (son-in-law), 396, 398, 404, 405, 416
Stevens, Louise, 60, 64, 80
Stevenson, Adlai, 146, 152, 183, 195, 258, 259–260, 287, 299, 309–10, 332, 375, 385, 388, 406
    Africa trip of, 233–35
    background of, 199–200, 342
    biography of, 293
    death and funeral of, 276–79, 283–84, 288, 315, 337
    in elections of 1952, 195, 197–206, 219, 232, 282

    in elections of 1956, 224–30, 246
    in elections of 1960, 243–49
    MT's romantic relationship with, 231, 232–33, 235, 236, 237–38, 240, 244, 248, 260, 261–84
    between presidential campaigns, 207, 209, 212, 213, 218, 219–21
    at UN, 251–52, 256, 257, 261–62, 267–71, 274–76, 281, 282
Stevenson, Adlai, III, 200, 229, 233, 234, 235, 239, 278, 280, 341, 363
Stevenson, Borden, 200, 272, 280
Stevenson, Buffie, 199
Stevenson, Ellen Borden, 198, 199–200, 202, 237
Stevenson, Helen, 199
Stevenson (Meyner), Helen, 227, 228, 231
Stevenson, John Fell, 200
Stevenson, Lewis, 199
Stevenson, Nancy, 233, 234, 235, 239
Stites (Parker), Elisabeth (great-grandmother), 23
Stockton, Charles, 93, 97
Strasberg, Paula, 251
Streit, Clarence, 93
Strong, Sir Roy, 355
Sullivan, Ed, 227
*Sunday Times* (London), 112, 303, 325
Sydenham Hospital, 149, 152

Tammany Hall, 196, 203, 218
Taylor, Elizabeth, 262, 268
Taylor, Frank, 251, 266, 319
Taylor International, 372
Teague, Michael, 27, 286, 293, 296, 324, 331
Tempelsman, Maurice, 335, 360, 373, 402
Thant, U, 253, 275, 288–89, 301
Thayer, Charles, 90, 91
Thom, Huntington, 80
Thomson, Sir John, 373
Thorneycroft, Peter, 188
Tickell, Sir Crispin, 397
Tillett, Gladys, 251, 254
*Time*, 54, 67, 91, 111, 182, 303
*Times* (London), 239, 283, 329, 358
Tisch, Laurence, 371
Torlonia, Marina, 80
Toscanini, Arturo, 65
Toynbee, Philip, 160
Train, Barbara Lawrence, 185, 211
Travia, Anthony, 304
Tree, Arthur, 139, 140, 141
Tree (Beatty), Ethel Field, 139–40, 141
Tree, Jeremy (stepson), 142, 153, 171, 185, 187–88, 208, 223, 325, 327, 330, 331, 335–336, 350, 398
Tree, Lady Anne Cavendish (stepdaughter-in-law), 182, 185, 187, 208, 209, 224, 302, 325, 331, 336, 398
Tree, Lambert, 139, 140, 142

Tree, Mary Endicott Peabody FitzGerald
    "Marietta":
acting of, 46, 56
Africa trip of (1957), 233–35
ambassadorship sought by, 375–76
annual Tuscany visits of, 347, 366–67,
    386, 394
Asian fact-finding lecture tour of, 289–92
Australia trip of (1978), 345
Barbados trip of (1946), 135–37, 146
at Barnard, 100, 101, 104, 383
birth of, 11–12, 31
cancer suffered by, 354–56, 394–411
childhood of, 32–58
children of, see FitzGerald, Frances
    "Frankie"; Tree, Penelope
death and memorials for, 13, 411–15
debutante activities of, 72, 74, 76–82
Democratic party activities of, 196–206,
    212–13, 214, 218, 224–30, 235, 304–5
Ditchley first visited by, 167–69
education of, 36, 40–41, 45–46, 47, 49–
    53
England trip of (1924), 37
in England with Ronald Tree, 167–86
face-lifts of, 346, 377, 394
family background of, 15–32
financial problems of, after Ronald Tree's
    death, 333–36, 345
grandchildren of, 378–79, 394, 415
health problems of, 260, 346
at La Petite Ecole Florentine, 60, 62–70,
    75, 388
last will of, 394, 408
marriages of, see FitzGerald, Desmond;
    Tree, Ronald Lambert
memoir writing efforts of, 372–76
Middle East trip of (1978), 344–45
movie appearances of, 250–51, 266, 374,
    391
at New York Constitutional Convention,
    300, 301–4, 307
Northeast Harbor summers of, 32, 39, 42,
    52–53, 55–56, 60, 78, 81, 86, 125, 132, 153,
    200
at Penn, 82–83, 85–86, 88
physical appearance of, 56
psychotherapy of, 134, 151, 152, 158, 215,
    227, 260, 356, 382
religious views of, 413
at St. Timothy's, 47, 49–58, 83
scrapbook of, 415–17
at Shady Hill Country Day School, 40–
    41, 45–46, 50, 78
skin trouble of, 56, 67, 81, 346, 377
sports activities of, 50–52, 53, 56, 57
at UN, 251–57, 259–60, 267–71, 273–75,
    281, 288–89, 299–301, 350, 400
urban planning courses of, 304, 305
war relief work of, 103–4

Tree, Michael (stepson), 142, 147, 153, 165,
    171, 185, 187–88, 208, 223, 224, 302, 325,
    327, 330, 331, 332, 334, 335–36, 350, 398
Tree, Nancy, see Lancaster, Nancy Perkins
    Field Tree
Tree, Penelope (daughter), 308, 321, 328,
    333, 348, 379, 383
arrest of, 320–21
in Australia, 351, 368, 378
birth of, 187
childhood of, 190, 192, 208, 210, 212, 215,
    216, 217, 225, 236, 245, 259, 266, 268,
    269, 270, 273–74, 277, 285, 286–87, 288,
    292, 293, 297, 302
children of, 378–79, 394, 415
at Concord, 286–87
at Dalton, 221, 242, 287
marriage of, 350–51
as model, 303–4, 320
and MT's cancer and death, 409, 411, 414
and MT's Constitutional Convention
    work, 301, 303
rebelliousness of, 286, 320
Ronald Tree's death and, 331, 332, 334
Ronald Tree's stroke and, 324, 325, 331
at Sarah Lawrence, 303
at U.N. International School, 287
Tree, Ronald Lambert (husband), 124, 167–
    195, 206, 207, 208, 209–10, 217, 222,
    223–24, 228, 229, 238, 241, 251, 258, 265,
    270, 271–72, 274, 277, 280, 282–83, 285,
    299, 308, 353, 388
and adjustment to New York, 187–89
on Africa trip (1957), 233–35
in Barbados, 181, 183, 188, 189–92, 204–6,
    213, 217–18, 220, 221, 222, 223, 224–25,
    231, 232, 239, 241–42, 244–45, 248, 258,
    293, 322, 324–25, 329
Barbados book of, 322
Barbados legacy of, 329–30, 336–37
on Barbados trip (1946), 135–37, 146
bisexuality of, 317–20
Collins's departure difficult for, 316–17
death and funeral of, 327–37
Ditchley bought by, 143
Ditchley sold by, 183–86
and elections of 1952, 198, 199, 200
and elections of 1960, 247
Endicott Peabody's campaign and, 216
European tours of, 224–25, 227, 275, 279,
    285, 288, 292, 293–94, 297, 301, 302–3
family background and childhood of,
    139–41
health problems of, 308, 309, 324–27, 333
marital troubles of MT and, 218, 221, 225,
    285, 287–88, 303, 315, 316–17
MT's marriage plans with, 148, 150–65,
    384–85
MT's renewed interest in, 289, 291, 293–
    294, 315

MT's wedding with, 165–66, 350
Nancy's married life with, 141–47, 151, 153, 154, 155, 168, 173–74, 183, 325
New York Constitutional Convention and, 303, 304
Penelope's arrest and, 321
Penelope's rebelliousness and, 286, 287
Sandy Lane Hotel and, 241–42, 285, 329, 336–37
as stepfather to Frankie, 211–12
Teague's friendship with, 286
twentieth anniversary of MT and, 302–3
Trew, Robert, 312
Trilling, Lionel, 318
Trinity College, Cambridge University, 17, 21
Trollope, Frances, 47, 82–83
Trubin, John, 366
Truman, Harry, 183, 195
Tull, Osmondo, 191, 325, 331

United Automobile Workers, 178
United Nations (UN), 149, 188, 200, 401
MT at, 251–57, 259–60, 267–71, 273–75, 281, 288–89, 299–301, 350, 400
Stevenson at, 251–52, 256, 257, 261–62, 267–71, 274–76, 281, 282
United Nations Committee of Twenty-four, 257
United Nations Committee on Non-Self-Governing Territories, 268
United Nations Economic and Social Council (ECOSOC), 253, 257, 262, 267–68, 270, 271, 275, 307
United Nations Human Rights Commission, 251–56, 268
United Nations International School, 287, 293
United Nations Trusteeship Council, 256–257
Urquhart, Sir Brian, 253, 275, 283, 377, 378

Victor Emmanuel III, king of Italy, 68
Victoria, queen of England, 16
Vietnam War, 235, 268, 275, 287, 290–91, 305, 322
Viola (housekeeper), 261, 278
*Vogue*, 77, 91, 110, 171, 354, 390
Voorhees, Mezzy, *see* Hickok, Mary Isabel Voorhees "Mezzy"

Wagner, Robert, 212, 237, 308
Walker, Jimmy, 242
Walton, William (Bill), 139, 252, 317, 339, 373, 374, 398, 404, 407–8
Walton, William, 207–8
Warburg, Daphne, 187
Warburg, David, 131
Warburg, Eddie, 107, 108, 114, 131, 136, 137, 154, 165, 181

Warburg, Gerald F., 161–62
Warburg, Mary, 107, 108, 109, 112, 114, 129, 131, 132, 135, 136, 137, 154, 165, 181, 187, 192, 242, 280, 317–18, 332, 341, 358, 374, 415
MT's divorce and, 150–51, 159–60, 164
Ward, Barbara, 219, 233
Ward, Robertson "Happy," 242
Warhol, Andy, 368
Warnecke, Grace, 319, 339
Warnecke, Jack, 339
Warren, Anne Scull, 80, 89–90, 176
Warren, Chester, 89–90
*Washington Post,* 219, 276, 303, 375, 395
Watson, Thomas J., 107, 109
Weeks, John, 310, 313
Weidenfeld, Lord (George), 327, 367, 372
Weiss, Louis S., 152, 160
Weizmann Institute, 220
Welles, Orson, 114
Welles, Sumner, 18, 200
Wentz, Cecilia "Ceil," 260, 278, 285, 288, 376
Wharton, Edith, 76
*When the Moon Was High* (Tree), 183, 325
White, Patrick, 345
White, Theodore H., 120
Whiteside, Thomas, 97
Whitney, Robert, 80
Williams, Edith Derby, 14, 52, 54, 59, 65, 67, 80, 91
Willkie, Wendell, 102, 114
Wills, Sir David, 184, 328
Wilson, Harold, 276
Wilton, Lord, 184, 328
Wiltwyck School, 149, 152, 207
Windsor, duchess of, 124
Windsor, duke of, 122–24, 214
Wirtz, Willard, 219, 278
Wolfensohn, Elaine, 373, 378, 396
Wolfensohn, James, 335, 340, 357, 360, 364, 370, 372, 374
*Women's Wear Daily,* 303, 361, 373
Wood (Foulke), Louisa, 77, 96
Woolf, Harry, 357, 359
Woollett, Charlotte Carstairs, 190
World Affairs Council, 258
World War I, 31–34
World War II, 68, 96, 97, 103–4, 106, 121–122, 125, 130, 144, 145
Wrightsman, Charles, 239, 248
Wrightsman, Jayne, 239, 248, 356, 367, 370, 385, 393, 394, 399, 403, 408
Wyman, Thomas H., 371

Yost, Charles, 270
Young, Gavin, 358

Zipkin, Jerry, 390, 416
Zurcher, Susie, 238, 261